THE DOOMSDAY PEOPLE—
FIGHTING FOR POWER, LIFE, AND
LOVE ON THE TREACHEROUS SEAS!

JIMMY COLUMBUS
King of the Cuban Mafia, he defied
Castro—and declared war on the U.S.
government.

PHILIP MARTIN
His Vietnam experience and his hot
Spanish blood combined to make him a
deadly specialist in anti-terrorism.

LUCIA BARNES
The pretty little girl brought a special
abandon to the bedroom—and a murderous jinx.

HAROLD ULLMAN
He felt a keen guilt about his wife—and
rose to astonishing heights of heroism to
redeem himself.

ELIZABETH CAMERON
She rose from Iowa farm-girl to high-
grade Washington civil servant—before
her blistering baptism under fire.

SAIL ON A VOYAGE OF DEATH, DE-
FIANCE, AND DISCOVERY—TO THE
MONA INTERCEPT!

Fawcett Gold Medal Books
by Donald Hamilton:
The Matt Helm Series:

THE MONA INTERCEPT

Donald Hamilton

FAWCETT GOLD MEDAL • NEW YORK

THE MONA INTERCEPT

Copyright © 1980 Donald Hamilton

Published by Fawcett Gold Medal Books, a unit of CBS Publications, the Consumer Publishing Division of CBS Inc.

ISBN: 0-449-14374-0

Printed in the United States of America

First Fawcett Gold Medal printing: December 1980

10 9 8 7 6 5 4 3 2 1

AUTHOR'S NOTE

Experienced navigators like Captain Sergio Redivo of the Gulf tanker *Korea Galaxy* and Captain Tom Strøm of the Norwegian Caribbean Lines cruise ship *Skyward,* who were kind enough to let me make an inquisitive nuisance of myself on their respective vessels, will realize that I've taken some liberties with the geography involved in this novel. I hope they'll forgive me.

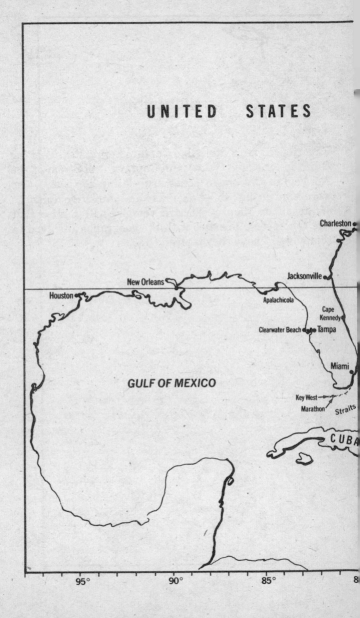

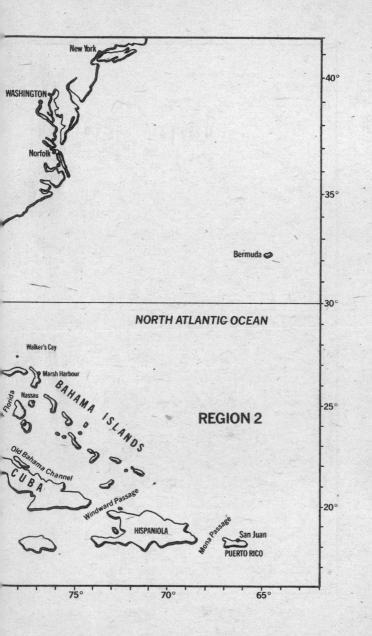

CHAPTER 1

October

Latitude 24°N; Longitude 81°W

Philip Martin braced himself in a corner of the bridge of the vibrating, plunging, rolling vessel that was built on the lean lines of a destroyer but was even more uncomfortable than its Navy counterpart since it was considerably smaller. Not that Martin knew a great deal about combat-type ships, Navy destroyers or Coast Guard cutters or any others; the only combat he had experienced, in a war he no longer recognized when he saw it in the movies or on TV—they seemed to be finding a lot of significance in it he hadn't noticed at the time—had been perpetrated on dry land. Well, more or less dry.

There were for the moment no lights visible in the Florida Straits, although he knew it was supposed to be a busy place for ships. The *Cape Alden* drove on through the night, destination Big Galleon Key, wherever that might be from here. When the name had first surfaced in the course of the investigation, Martin had looked it up; but the small, apparently deserted, blob on the map—probably just another glorified clump of mangroves—had meant very little to him since he was not familiar with the strung-out island area south of Miami, the Florida Keys, that had become a battleground in this endless conflict between the private boats bringing the stuff in, and the public boats, like the *Cape Alden,* trying to keep it out. Drugs were not Philip Martin's real concern anyway, or that of the government agency by which he was employed; and he wished they'd never got themselves involved in the stupid business, since whatever the moral aspects might be, it was obviously fast becoming another no-win situation like Vietnam.

9

It had been Richardson's bright idea. The wonder boy had come down from Washington to take over the Miami project full of bright ideas. He was obviously convinced that his mission was to teach the local agents of the ATD to straighten up and fly right for a change, and maybe it was. In that case it was a slap in the face for one Philip A. Martin, the previous incumbent (acting). Tony Richardson obviously thought it was; and the Old Man in Washington had given no indication that it wasn't—except that he had recognized ways of expressing displeasure, and public humiliation wasn't one of them.

If Mr. Meriwether had really been unhappy about the handling of the Miami accounts, it seemed likely that he'd have let Martin know about it in much more refined and subtle ways. He was very good at indicating when he thought you weren't performing well without making a major crisis of it. Therefore, Martin consoled himself, sticking a jerk like Richardson over him without warning, on the excuse that he'd been holding the post only in an acting capacity and the office really called for a higher bureaucratic rank, smelled of the kind of intrigue and trickery you could expect from Washington in general and the Old Man in particular. The optimistic explanation was that Meriwether had grabbed the chance to test one man he liked to see if that man was smart and disciplined enough to take what was handed him without brooding about the apparent blow to his pride, while at the same time setting up another he didn't like . . . for what? Well, that would undoubtedly become clear with time.

Getting busily to work at his new post, Richardson had exhumed and revived a couple of old accounts that Martin had, after careful study, buried as unproductive; and he'd tackled the one currently active operation with boyish enthusiasm, finally coming up with this flash of genius, to wit, that since the nefarious political plans of the subject in question were apparently being financed by the proceeds of drug smuggling, the best way to curtail his activities was to stop his smuggling.

They had already, by diligent surveillance and the providential assistance of a yachtsman who'd spotted and reported some mysterious activities involving the vessel in question, managed to get one boat intercepted and confiscated, with Coast Guard help, and the skipper jailed. If the current expedition was equally successful, and let them put out of action the second and last operating vessel of this little smuggling fleet—there were numerous others, of course; next to fishing and diving, smuggling was the most popular water sport along this coast—Richardson figured they'd have it made.

He was particularly eager for them to nab the big shrimper for which they were looking tonight, called the *Three Sisters*. It had been called to the attention of the Coast Guard by another angry yachtsman, who'd claimed to have been almost run down by a large commercial fishing vessel proceeding without lights in the general direction of Big Galleon Key. There was information that, if it was the right boat, it was skippered by Armando Colombo, the twenty-year-old son of the man in whom they were primarily interested, direct evidence of the parent's involvement in this dirty traffic according to Tony Richardson, who didn't seem to know much about incriminating evidence or about the Colombos, either. All the boy had to do to let his father, Don Jaime, off the hook was to testify, if arrested, that the fishing had been lousy so he'd decided to take the boat south and pick up a nice profitable load of grass instead, strictly without papa's knowledge or permission, of course. If Richardson thought there was the slightest possibility that young Armando would spill his guts if captured and implicate his parent, Richardson was dreaming. Kids with that background, with that kind of family pride, brought up in that dedicated patriotic way, didn't talk; in fact, they dared you to cut them to pieces so they could have the proud privilege of showing how good they were at not talking.

Martin hung on grimly as the *Cape Alden* rolled hard to starboard and staggered upright again. He wondered what a narrow splinter of a ship like this would be like in a real gale in the open ocean, instead of just a brisk night in the Florida Straits. He knew that he was under observation, of course. It was another popular water sport: watching landlubbers turn green. Unfortunately for the Coast Guard boys, eager for a little innocent entertainment at the expense of the tall, dark, slightly foreign-looking mystery man from a secret government agency, he'd taken the precaution of loading up with one of the latest developments in anti-motion medicine, a mixture of ephedrine and promethazine; and he was, happily, feeling no queasiness whatever. However, he'd been warned that, unlike Dramamine which put you to sleep, this newer preventive woke you up but good. He was aware that his mind was almost feverishly active.

11

Richardson was, he reflected, a horse's ass. A smooth horse's ass, but an identifiable equine posterior nevertheless. His beautiful plan totally ignored the nature of the man with whom they were dealing. There were other ways besides smuggling for a ruthless individual to finance a cause he believed in fanatically. A few loads of pot among the hundreds that were coming in did relatively little harm; would Richardson prefer to have Don Jaime Colombo take up kidnapping wealthy citizens for ransom, or holding up banks? And if a change to a different line of endeavor was not deemed desirable by Colombo, there were other smuggling vessels to be obtained by various means, not necessarily legal and harmless. So Don Jaime lost a couple of old commercial fishing craft he'd picked up for very little, so what? It was an annoyance, that was all; and did they really want to annoy their subject at this point in the operation and drive him to more drastic and dangerous action before they'd figured out how to deal with him permanently, and legally?

You did not kill a rattlesnake by cutting off its supply of mice. You caught it in the open doing its rattlesnake thing and stomped it into the ground or shot its head off. And in the meantime you were very careful *not* to tease it in its hole and make it mad, or people would get hurt. . . . A change in the ship's vibration brought Martin out of his thoughts. The sound of the engines, and the motion of the vessel, had diminished noticeably. There was shadowy land ahead in the darkness, and to starboard. He glanced at the *Cape Alden*'s youthful captain, whose name was Paul Jones—no relation to the legendary John Paul, just one of the other Jones boys, he'd said with a grin, when the introductions were being made.

"The water's pretty shallow ahead, Mr. Martin," Jones said. "A big shrimper like that, there's only the one channel she can use to get into the shelter of Galleon Key Bight. Of course that goes for us, too. Right now we'll just wait for him to go in and then, we hope, play cork-in-the-bottle. In the meantime we'll hide around that point to starboard, as close to the mangroves as the water will let us; there's a good big hole in there that most people don't know about. Thank God there's no moon tonight." The stocky young captain shrugged. "Of course we're gambling. We could be getting all uptight about a perfectly legitimate fishing vessel with a temporary electrical problem, safe at home by now. Well, it's a nice night for a boat ride." He turned away to give some orders.

Presently the cutter lay in still water with the shore looming as an impenetrable black shadow to starboard. Jones turned back to Martin. "Tell me something, just what the hell is ATD, or shouldn't I ask?"

"Theoretically you shouldn't ask," Martin said. "It's still rather experimental and a bit controversial; but to answer your question, in strict confidence, of course: the ATD is the Anti-Terrorist Division of . . . well, you can probably guess the department but you won't hear it from me. We've got to make a few gestures toward security to keep Washington happy. Of course, everybody's got special units set up nowadays to deal with terrorists and hijackers; but they all go into action after the fact. We've got a section like that, too; but the job of my particular bunch is more predictive and preventive. Kind of like the earthquake-warning boys. We're feeling our way, studying certain situations and certain individuals to see if we can spot the probability of terrorist behavior, defined in certain ways. And, of course, phase two, prevent it once we have it spotted."

The captain scanned the darkness outside the bridge before he spoke again, softly: "Defined in what ways, Mr. Martin?"

"We define terrorism as violence or the threat of violence directed at innocent and uninvolved victims in order to influence official action."

"That's pretty limited, isn't it?" Jones murmured. "You're leaving out hijacking for profit and political assassination and a lot of other crimes that are generally included."

"It really isn't as nit-picking as it sounds," Martin said. "There's a valid psychological distinction involved. Let's say, for instance, that a certain Frank and Fanny Smith are languishing in prison and their political brethren and sistren want them out. They form the Frank and Fanny Smith Liberation League. If all they do is raise money to hire lawyers and influence parole boards and public opinion, no sweat. If they buy themselves a war-surplus tank to crash the gates and stage a jailbreak, that's still no concern of ours—we don't call that terrorism—or if they try to promote a prison riot with the same goal in mind. They're dealing in direct action, not terror and intimidation. Naturally, if we learn about it, we'll tip off the authorities, but it's not our baby. But if we get the idea that the F.F.S.L.L. is toying with the notion of hijacking an airliner and threatening to kill all the passengers and crew if Frank and Fanny aren't released *pronto;* or if we come across indications that they're making arrangements to blow up a certain football stadium on a crowded Saturday afternoon if their demands aren't met—"

"I still think you're drawing some pretty fine lines."

It was black and still in the lee of the island. There was only a hushed rumble from the ship's auxiliary machinery. Martin could recall other quiet moments before action, also spent in desultory conversation about just about anything, to make the time pass faster. He shook his head.

"Not really, Captain," he said. "The point is that the man who'll stage an attack on a prison where his friends are being held has a totally different mental make-up from the one who'll try to achieve their release by trading on somebody's—everybody's—concern for the lives of innocent citizens. The first man is applying force directly to solve his problem. The second is using terror to achieve his goal indirectly. And the first man can't be spotted in advance, really. Push most men far enough and they'll resort to violence—against whatever or whoever is doing the pushing. There's nothing unique or distinctive about that reaction. But it takes a special kind of selfish arrogance to aim your violence at people who aren't really involved in your problem; a sick arrogance and a pathological callousness. It means that you think that your lousy little troubles—personal or political or racial or whatever—are so goddamn important that everybody ought to be concerned about them; and if they aren't you'll by God teach them concern if you have to kill them to do it. And the people who have this inflated notion of their own importance, which is what it really amounts to, and no regard for the importance of other people, they're the ones who can rationalize the planting of bombs in post offices and airliners, and the killing of people they never heard of, who never heard of them, all in the name of some sacred cause or other." Martin paused, and went on: "And the people capable of doing that *can* be spotted, Captain. There are certain psychological profiles. . . . But you can see why we don't like to talk too much about it, can't you?"

"Well—"

"We've got to observe the groups from which terrorism is most likely to develop—the Middle Kansas Bible Association isn't likely to produce much useful data. Many of the groups are political and very ready to scream harassment if they think somebody's paying too much attention to them. I think you can guess the people on whom we're concentrating in Miami. Their political aspirations are no concern of ours, and

14

if they break some local laws that's the business of the local law, or maybe the F.B.I., depending on how grandiose their plans are. In other words, if they merely want to fight their way back to where they came from, we aren't interested, as long as they keep it strictly between themselves and Fidel Castro. But when they try to involve others by engaging in terrorism and intimidation, and there has already been some of that as you know if you read the papers, that's where we come in. Our job is to try to prevent more of it, by identifying and, if possible, neutralizing, the individuals from whom it's likely to come."

Jones grinned. "And that's what we're doing here tonight, neutralizing?"

"That's the theory." The fact that he, Martin, didn't agree with the theory was none of Captain Jones' business; you didn't wash your dirty agency linen in public. Martin changed the subject. "Captain."

"Yes?"

"A warning. We rate these subjects on a scale of ten, for our own convenience. A rating of one-ten is a human doormat; a rating of ten-ten is a confirmed terrorist who's already proved himself by overt action. You should know that the young man we think is in command of this shrimper tonight is down for a tentative rating of nine-ten. We feel he's potentially just about as dangerous as he can get, he just hasn't had a chance to show it yet. And one thing about these people you've got to remember: they're very callous about human life but they're fair about it. In a real pinch they'll regard their own lives as lightly as anybody else's."

"You sound as if they're a new race of people you've discovered."

"On the contrary, they're a very old race, believing in the ancient virtue of dying gloriously for a cause, or just dying gloriously. Very unfashionable these anti-hero days when everybody's supposed to want to live forever, but that doesn't make them any less dangerous. So don't let your crew take any chances. They're probably used to ordinary drug-smugglers who, I gather, don't often resort to violence. Please pass the word that this one could be real trouble. . . ."

"Pssst."

The soft whistling sound came from the intercom nearby. Jones leaned over and said, "Bridge."

"Lookout," the speaker murmured. "I can hear somebody coming, but it's no damn slow old commercial diesel. . . .

Okay, I've got him spotted now. One of the Cigarettes is coming in, wide open. He's right off the point, can you see him?"

"Got him!"

Jones raised the big night glasses slung around his neck. After a moment's study he pulled the strap off over his head and passed the binoculars to Martin, pointing. The glasses made things much clearer, even in the dark; and Martin saw the white streak moving across the black water and, at the head of it, the speeding little craft itself, seemingly a very rakish shape, although he could not make it out clearly. He passed the binoculars back.

"Cigarette?"

"A guy named Don Aronow built some ocean-racing speedboats under that name. Later he started producing them for public consumption all fancied up, and we kind of wish he hadn't. Now there's a rash of seaworthy high-speed boats available, and they're faster than anything Congress will buy us. Lately we've managed to catch a few in the act and, after proper legal proceedings, turn them around to work for us. We sure could use one tonight if we had it, but we don't." He made a face. "Actually, we've got too much ship here for this particular job. It's like trying to kill a rat in a small closet with a long broom, but we'll have to do the best we can."

The speedboat had passed out of sight behind the point. "What do you think he's doing?" Martin asked.

"Well, the smugglers bring the stuff from Jamaica or Colombia or wherever in the slower, larger craft, and then transship it to the fast Cigarettes or Magnums for final delivery ashore. We may be lucky after all. It's blowing a little too hard tonight for them to pass the stuff across out in open water; they've got to have shelter to make the transfer. I think whoever's running the show sent this fellow in to take a look around before committing himself. . . ."

"Pssst."

"Bridge."

"Here he comes again, heading back out with the word. . . . Okay, there's Big Baby herself, way out there on the horizon, bearing: oh seven five relative. Coming right in, fat and sassy. I mean, target vessel in view, sir, heading for the channel at an estimated speed of five knots. . . . Come on, Baby!"

After a little, Martin could see the approaching shrimper

16

without optical assistance. She made a rather clumsy-looking shape in the dark, with a complicated arrangement of masts and booms showing black against the night sky, which was growing almost imperceptibly lighter now in the east.

"Okay, we've got her," Jones breathed at last, watching through the big 7 X 50s. "There's nothing we can do about the crew, they'll take off across the shallows in the speedboats when they see they're trapped, and those things can plane on a heavy dew. There's no way we could chase them even if the old *Alden* could do sixty knots; but we've got the big boat cold. We'll just let her get well in now, and start unloading, before we plug the rathole. . . ."

Even though he disapproved of the operation in principle, at least as far as the ATD was concerned, Martin could not help feeling a familiar expectant tightness in his throat as he waited. Apparently there wasn't much difference between participating in this kind of ambush on land, and doing it on the water. Then the captain spoke a soft command and the Coast Guard vessel began to move, nosing cautiously past the black point of mangroves to starboard and then leaping forward with a surge of power as, clear, she headed for the channel. The sudden glare of the searchlight and the amplified voice of the bullhorn were a double blow after all the dark and silent waiting. The powerful beam picked out the *Three Sisters* against the island background, with almost painful brightness. Her name showed clearly on the bow. Aft, men were already scrambling into the two speedboats that lay alongside. Ignoring the commands of the booming electronic voice, the sharp-nosed little craft roared away into the surrounding blackness, now graying with dawn.

Apparently, the *Three Sisters* lay too close to shore for the cutter to come alongside safely. It took some minutes for a boat to be launched and manned. Approaching the silent trawler—he'd invented a mysterious government reason for wanting to be among the first aboard; goddamn it, couldn't people understand a plain warning?—Martin ignored the lighthearted chatter of the Coastguardsmen around him. His vigilance was rewarded as the small boat bumped against the weatherbeaten wooden side of the *Three Sisters*.

A slight, dark figure stepped around the corner of the deckhouse. Martin saw the gleam of the submachine gun in the searchlight glare. He waited a bare instant to see if anyone else was prepared to deal with the situation—after all, it wasn't his unit or his patrol—but that was all the time

17

he could afford to waste. The automatic weapon was steadying to sweep the boat; and he fired three careful shots, remembering a friend who'd died in a distant jungle when a "dead" soldier with a machine pistol had suddenly come to life behind them. . . .

Later, Captain Jones came up to him as he stood by the blanket-covered form on the trawler's deck. The Coast Guard officer cleared his throat.

"I know how you feel, but the boys in the boat want to thank you for saving their lives."

Martin thought grimly that the younger man could not possibly know how he felt. There were emotions here that went far beyond the mere fact of killing, but they could not be explained to a man with the fine old Welsh name of Jones. This was no time for explanations, anyway. He remained silent.

"What the hell was the kid trying to do?" Jones asked, puzzled. "Fight the whole U.S. Coast Guard?"

Martin said carefully, "It was his first command. Papa had entrusted it to him and he'd lost it." He glanced toward the lean government vessel lying nearby in the pale morning light. "You ought to understand, Captain. Would you surrender the *Alden* to the enemy, any enemy, without firing a shot?"

Then he regretted the question because under similar circumstances, being a sensible and civilized man with a distaste for useless bloodshed, Jones probably would.

CHAPTER 2

November

Latitude 25°N; Longitude 76°W

He was never really comfortable, docking at Chub Cay in the Bahamas, Harold Ullman reflected, as he hung a fat white rubber fender over *Nancy Lou*'s side. He always felt a bit like a horseman visiting the ski slopes in boots and spurs, or a dedicated pool player wandering into a bowling alley, cue in hand. His graceful little cutter-rigged, twenty-seven-foot sailboat with her tall slim mast and delicate-looking rigging always seemed very much out of place among all the beamy, angular, brutal craft designed for big-game fishing. Just as he, slight, redheaded, freckled, and not very tall, always felt a little out of place among all the tanned and beefy and hearty fishermen.

He knew that, if they thought about him at all, the anglers frequenting Chub Cay considered his vessel a peculiar piece of seagoing machinery. Why work so hard to get somewhere at what was, by their standards, a very slow crawl? On the other hand, their specialized powerboats, although fast, always looked unseaworthy to Harold Ullman. Those high, canopied flying bridges and skyscraping tuna towers—all that top hamper above and no ballast below—just had to make a vessel vulnerable in a blow, not to mention all that glass. One big wave breaking across such a sea-going greenhouse would undoubtedly smash her open like one of the elaborate *piñatas* in the shapes of birds and animals the Mexicans made and hung from the ceilings so that the kids, blindfolded, could try to beat them apart with sticks to get the candy inside in celebration of some holiday. Christmas?

It had to be Christmas because that was when he'd been down there last with that screwball writer who'd insisted on supervising the taking of the proper, dreamy, misty photographs to go with his mood piece for *Traveler's World*, the very fancy, very glossy, very arty magazine that had since folded, but you had to admit it paid nicely while it lasted and really did a beautiful job of reproducing any halfway decent color shot. Unfortunately, class markets like that were scarce these days, making him sometimes wonder a bit about his chosen profession. Well, a man who knew both cameras and the sea ought to be able to make some kind of a living; and his New York agent, Bartholomew, had something lined up involving a tanker, which should be interesting as well as profitable.

Ullman yawned. He was having a hard time concentrating on cleaning up the boat before dinner. It had been a brisk forty-mile sail; and they'd stayed up late in Nassau the night before, in the pretentious Casino on the island that was no longer known as Hog Island, and how corny could you get? Paradise Island, for God's sake! But he really ought to stick to roulette or maybe just the slot machines and give up on blackjack; seldom as he gambled he could never keep those combinations clearly in mind. He certainly hadn't mastered the game last night, although it was always fun to try. But when you added his moderate losses to what they'd paid for a not very good dinner served by a not very good waiter in a not very good restaurant associated with the place—one of several, all of course described by the management with breathless superlatives—well, anyway, it was lucky the wind was free and he didn't have to provide a large and thirsty power plant with fuel enough to get them back to the U.S., since after almost a month in the Islands they were down to their last twenty-dollar Express check and a few bucks cash.

The sheltered harbor was becoming busy with sportfishermen returning in bunches with their little blue-and-white flags flying, the successful ones, to indicate what they'd caught today. Like Walker's Cay farther north, Chub Cay wasn't really the Bahamas. It was a convenient overnight stop coming and going, but it wasn't the picturesque foreign country you crossed the Straits of Florida to see. You might as well sail down to Key West and look at the sportfishing fleet there, except that they weren't so friendly to stray sailors in Key West.

After securing the protective fender at the proper height, and adjusting the docklines so *Nancy Lou* was riding to his satisfaction, Harold Ullman coiled the main sheet neatly and then got a sail bag out of the cockpit locker and went forward to bag the forestaysail. He heard Nancy, below, speak a sharp word of the kind that used to be called unprintable before everybody started printing them; and he knew she was trying to light the galley stove. The big Striker caught him by surprise. Intent on his task, and perhaps preoccupied with thinking about Nancy and her interminable feud with the perfectly docile and well-behaved Shipmate, he hadn't seen it enter the marina. Suddenly it was passing across *Nancy Lou*'s stern, bulky against the evening sky, a lot of boat to be maneuvering in the narrow space between the docks. He read the name and hailing port on the stern: *Stream Hunter*, Miami.

Ullman heard a woman's voice, distantly: "Stand by, darling. I'll put you close to that piling so you can drop the stern line over it as we go by; then just leave it to me and get the bow secured."

It made him look at the husky aluminum sportfisherman more closely. One of the forty-eights, he thought; but they've customized hell out of it, haven't they? They must have at least half a million bucks floating there. Well, it's their money.

Then he realized what had really caught his attention. Boats, even big expensive boats, handled by married couples—or unmarried ones, for that matter—were common enough; but almost invariably they came in for a landing with the man at the helm and the woman on the foredeck. Here, the husband, if he was a husband, was waiting forward with a coiled dockline ready, and the wife, if she was his wife, was up on the flying bridge managing the controls. Hastily, Ullman finished bagging the sail and jumped to the pier and hurried shorewards to help as marina etiquette required. The great gleaming powerboat came to a halt with her bow almost at the sea wall. She began to turn in place as the woman at the topside station played one of the big diesels expertly against the other. When the boat was lined up perfectly, the lady helmsman eased her forward and slid her into the inside berth along the concrete sea wall, with little more than a foot to spare on either side. There was something to be said for twin-screw boats, Harold Ullman reflected; there was almost something to be said for competent ladies who knew seamanship. This one must have grown up around the water. You didn't teach yourself to wring out a forty-eight-footer like that, making it look so easy, merely by taking a Power Squadrons course one evening a week.

He caught the bow line thrown by the man, who was a medium-sized, average-looking, brown-haired, tanned-young-businessman type in brief swimming trunks, who'd probably be bulky in a few more years if he didn't keep working hard at the handball. He hadn't grown up around boats; he didn't quite have the knack of heaving a line properly, although he had enough natural coordination to get the job done after a fashion. The woman—girl, rather—had dropped off the flying bridge in agile fashion and was now in the cockpit attending to the stern lines. She was a strong-looking girl, not tall, in neat khaki shorts and a yellow jersey. She'd be hard to photograph, Harold Ullman thought professionally; the camera always gave them a few extra pounds and she'd tend to look chunky, but she wasn't really. Her hair, cut quite short and boyish, was a pale blonde color, almost silvery, quite striking against the deep tan of her face. Harold Ullman had never seen her, or her husband, or their vessel before, which wasn't surprising. You got to know a certain number of the people and boats in these waters if you sailed here often enough; but the fishing circuit didn't intersect the sailing circuit in too many places, and sailboat people didn't pay too much attention to powerboat people anyway. Or vice versa.

"Thanks a lot, fella," said the man on the Striker's bow, after they had the other bow line secured.

"Sure thing," Ullman said.

He didn't particularly like to be called fella; but it didn't matter. They existed in different boating worlds. Already the girl in the cockpit was happily comparing big-fish stories with friends from a nearby powerboat who, like Ullman, had come over to help. The man moved aft to join the conversation.

Ullman returned to *Nancy Lou* to find the stove ablaze as usual, and Nancy frustrated and furious as usual. It always seemed a little unnecessary. She had a bachelor's degree from Smith and she was working on her master's in Coral Gables; and despite all that higher education she couldn't ever seem to comprehend that you merely filled the priming cup with alcohol, set it alight, let it burn down, and just when everything was good and hot and there was still a bit of flame remaining, not before and not after, you cracked the kerosene valve open and the well-vaporized fuel started burning nicely, hot and blue. But she always got impatient and tried to short-circuit the routine, or forgot to pay attention and let it burn out and cool down. Then she'd fire it anyway and get a lot of yellow flame and black smoke and complain that something was wrong with the crazy apparatus. . . .

"Just turn it off," he said, looking down through the hatch. "To hell with it. How about dinner ashore? The Club always serves a pretty good meal."

"We're flat broke."

It was a perfectly straightforward statement of fact. There was no sly reminder in her voice or words that his impulsive and inexpert attack on the blackjack table was at least partly responsible.

"Not that flat," he said. "I'll turn in our cruising permit here and we won't bother with stopping in Bimini; that'll save one dock fee. We'll just get an early start tomorrow and shoot for South Riding Rock and sail straight on through. If the wind cooperates we'll be in Marathon two nights from now; and there's enough gas in the car to get us home to Miami. It'll be better that way anyway; it'll give us an extra day to catch our breaths before we drive over to Sarasota to spend Thanksgiving with your folks."

She hesitated. "Well, all right." Abruptly, she laughed. "Sure, let's flip it. Our last foreign port, our last thin dime. Just let me get some clothes on."

She was wearing her skimpy black bikini with one of his old T-shirts over it. It never seemed quite fair to him that he, who loved sailing, should have to be careful to protect his freckled skin from the sun, while she, who still wasn't totally sold on it, could lie around the deck all day practically nude and take no harm; the shirt had only been put on for warmth when the evening breeze had come up to remind them that this was, after all, November, and the Bahamas weren't really the tropics, although they tried to kid you they were.

He watched her, turning away, pull the flimsy shirt off over her head, bending over to give herself room in the low cabin. Straightening up, she tossed the short, dark, tousled hair back into place with a shake of her head. Something about the familiar movement made him realize once more—it seemed to be easy to forget—that you did not love somebody because they could, or could not, light a Shipmate stove or play tunes on the throttles of a half-million-dollar sport-fisherman; and how did that rich-bitch blonde get into this anyway? He was aware of a rush of affection mixed with

23

unidentified guilt; and the scanty black scraps of bikini, to which he'd been exposed all day without significant reaction, were suddenly, he found, making her slim brown body look unbearably desirable.

"Nancy," he heard himself say, and he thought his voice sounded funny.

Apparently she thought so, too. Reaching around for the fastening of her brassiere, she stopped and looked at him with a surprised question in her eyes. Then she grinned.

"Hey, I thought you wanted to *eat.*"

She stood quite still while he descended the companionway ladder. Deliberately she turned then, presenting her back to him, inviting him to attend to the task she'd been about to perform. As the bikini top dropped at their feet, Harold Ullman found himself wondering absently, with the very small part of his mind that was not focused elsewhere, just how many hard-breathing gentlemen were now, at sunset, helping how many suntanned ladies out of their minuscule bathing suits all over these coral isles of romance. The second garment—if you could dignify the glorified G-string with that name—fell away, and she turned and came into his arms, her naked body making a disturbingly wanton contrast with his clothed one as they kissed. At length she freed herself and slipped into the port berth forward, more convenient than the starboard one tucked away behind the mast and a tiny dresser. He stripped hastily and joined her. They'd long ago worked out the proper routine for this. To insert two bodies into a space designed for single occupancy posed a bit of a problem, but of course it did not really arise as long as one remained on top of the other. . . .

Later, as they lay together wedged very close in the narrow bunk, he heard her giggle softly.

"What?" he asked.

"To hell with a new stove," she breathed. "First we've got to figure out how to squeeze a double berth into this crazy little ship."

◆

The following evening they came off the Great Bahama Bank at South Riding Rock just as the last light died. It was always an eerie ride across the Banks, Harold Ullman reflected, all those miles of shallow water with the bottom clearly visible under the keel—you couldn't help thinking that if somebody pulled the plug and let the water out, just a little of it, you'd find yourself helplessly stranded with your boat in the middle of an endless flat wet plain full of flopping fish, reaching from horizon to horizon. Now, as the Bahamas fell astern at last, the bottom dropped away into the depths of the Florida Straits and there was the adverse Gulf Stream current to contend with. However, the brisk easterly wind continued to do its stuff and they picked up the lights of the Florida Keys in the early-morning hours; by the time night fell once more they were closing in on Key Vaca and the town of Marathon. Negotiating the channel to the marina in the dark was a bit tricky—there were bad shoals on either side—but they'd done it before. With Nancy steering and Ullman, in the bow, calling off the reflecting markers as he picked them up with the spotlight, they made it without incident. An hour later, *Nancy Lou* was secure and more or less shipshape in her slip and they were on the road home.

"We'll have to come back next weekend to clean. . . ."

Ullman stopped. They had barely left the town behind, but his wife was already sound asleep beside him, curled up against the car door. She looked pretty and young and trusting like that, and he knew a warm sense of satisfaction and relief; things were starting to work at last. It had been a good cruise in every sense—they'd made all their landfalls on schedule, they hadn't run aground anywhere, the anchors hadn't dragged, and the weather had been good enough to let them swim and snorkel and explore at will. There had been none of the hairy sea-adventures that sounded good around a bar but actually meant that somebody'd goofed: the wild, desperate incidents that real sailors accepted and even kind of treasured in retrospect, but that people like Nancy considered perfectly dreadful wondering why any sane man would expose himself to *that* when he had a nice air-conditioned home to live in and good books to read and a TV set to watch if he absolutely had to scare himself silly. Not that the TV had much scare value these nonviolent days.

Nancy still didn't understand. The idea that you had to test yourself occasionally, just as you tested your cameras or the rigging of your boat, to find out if you were still all there, still ready, still competent to cope with it if it came— whatever *it* might be—seemed to be totally incomprehensible to her. She had only one word for it, that idiot term *macho*, the great cop-out word of the century. If it was tough or dangerous, or uncomfortable, or required skill, strength, or endurance, you dismissed it with a sneer as *macho* and saved yourself from having to do it. Like all her intellectual friends,

Nancy stubbornly refused to believe that it had nothing whatever to do with masculinity. It was an ancient survival mechanism totally divorced from sex.

There had been times when he'd come so close to hitting her it frightened him to think about it; but Jesus, how much *macho* could a man take? His pipe was *macho,* his boat was *macho,* his shotgun was super-*macho.* He'd given up the hunting when he saw that it actually horrified and hurt her; it wasn't all that important to him anyway. It had just been a pleasant autumn ritual he'd carried out yearly in memory of a favorite uncle, now dead; and he still occasionally wandered out to the club to shoot a couple of rounds of skeet. She could hardly get sentimentally upset about his smashing a few little discs of inanimate clay. Although, of course, she did get upset, now wanting the gun out of the house altogether; she could never be satisfied with one victory, she had to keep pushing for total capitulation, unconditional surrender. . . .

Don't start *that* again, he told himself sharply. You were thinking what a good cruise it had been and how it was all starting to work at last, remember? And if she wants a butane stove that lights at a touch, you'll get her a butane stove that lights at a touch, even if the damn explosive things scare you shitless. And a double berth, too, even though it's a hell of an unseamanlike arrangement, and we'll rattle around on that endless mattress like peas in a skillet any time we sail offshore. The message ought to be clear by now, stupid; she wants it to work, too. This time she made the effort, she gave it her best shot, and we had a great time together; and you can meet her halfway or better, okay?

It was always a long drive up from the Keys, particularly the first part involving the narrow, mostly obsolete Overseas Highway, as it was called, with all the narrow, mostly obsolete bridges joining one island with the next. It seemed even longer after a couple of days of hard sailing. Fortunately, the traffic was light, and it was not much after midnight when he pulled the little station wagon to the curb in front of the house. Nancy was still asleep. He leaned over to kiss her.

"Hey, Sleeping Beauty. We're here."

She blinked, yawned and reached for him and kissed him back. They weren't much for talking things out in detail, but something that had been getting pretty unsettled was, he knew, all settled now after their month afloat together. He'd probably lost an assignment or two on account of it, and she'd have to scramble to catch up with her education, but it had been worth it. She sat up, rubbing her nose.

"What time is it?"

He grinned. "What do you care? You've had your night's sleep while other people were sweating over a hot steering wheel. It's twelve-fifteen, if you must know. Go in and switch on the air conditioning; I'll get the seabags."

He heard her run up the walk as he opened the rear of the wagon and got out the two fancy new duffel bags they'd invested in for the cruise, one red and one blue, well broken in and salty-looking by this time. He was halfway to the front door she'd left open for him when he heard her make a startled sound inside, a little more than a gasp and not quite a scream. Then he saw her reappear in the doorway, backing away uncertainly from something inside. He dropped the bags and ran, pausing beside her, but only for a moment. There was, he knew instinctively, no time to take it all in: the ghastly, vandalized shambles of their home, and the strange inhuman figures, masked and gloved, looming in the living-dining area just beyond the arch of the short front hall. They were moving toward him.

He took one step forward and reached into the hall closet to the left and came out with the shotgun. Pump once, he reminded himself; there's no shell in the chamber. All the way back and all the way forward until it locks. And the safety, don't forget the damned safety. Take the big one first, the one in the ski mask, just blow his ugly faceless head right off his shoulders and it will at this range, with a full twelve-gauge load of double-ought buck it surely will; then you can swing on the shorter guy with the nylon stocking over his head. . . .

He heard the sweet, smooth clackety-clack of the shotgun action, and felt the push-button safety yield. He shifted his finger to the trigger, forcing himself not to anticipate the brutal recoil of the heavy load. . . .There was a sharp cry of protest and something shoved the weapon up and away. He saw Nancy's shocked and incredulous face as the firing pin fell and the shotgun discharged into the ceiling.

Improperly held, the weapon gave him a wicked rap on the cheek. A simple problem in marksmanship had turned into an incomprehensible nightmare. His ears were ringing from the blast and plaster dust was everywhere, brought down by the buckshot. He was struggling with Nancy for the gun—what was she trying to do to them; what the *hell* was she trying to do to them?—and a big fist came from nowhere and slammed him against the wall. He had never been hit so hard before in his life, and he knew that things were broken in his face. Dazedly, he tried to locate and reach the weapon that had slipped out of his grasp, but the whole world was spinning and he fell back dizzily against the wall. He heard the pump shotgun, in other hands, make its clackety noise again and braced himself to receive the charge, but there were only more mechanical noises of the same nature. Somebody was emptying the magazine, he realized, but why?

Then the weapon, reversed, swung like a scythe, smashing against his left thigh as he leaned there weakly against the wall, cutting both legs out from under him. Finding himself on the floor, he tried to crawl, but the legs refused to work. There was suddenly pain all through his body. He saw the shotgun, broken now, just barrel and action remaining, glint in the light above him as it swung again, glancing off his head. Dimly, he could hear Nancy screaming and the sound annoyed him. *Now* she was screaming; and what the hell for? What did she think would happen when she interfered like that and killed them both, because they were obviously dead. It was only a matter of time now.

And not much time.

CHAPTER 3

November

Latitude 24°N; Longitude 81°W

Thanksgiving was a big deal at the Boot Key Marina. Well, any holiday was a big deal at Boot Key, young Dr. Paul Williams Fenwick reflected sourly, as he prepared to head for the communal showers—installing a new waterpump impeller on a diesel was a dirty job and brought up the question of how the hell parts could manage to wear out on a motor that had hardly been used for a year. Picking up his kit, Fenwick grimaced at his face in the small mirror of *Haleakala*'s cramped toilet compartment, well buried down in the starboard hull of the big catamaran. The guy in the glass looked reasonably tanned and competent, he told himself bitterly, a reasonably athletic-looking gent of medium height, brown-haired and blue-eyed, not deformed or crippled in any way, so what was the chicken bastard still doing tied to this dock when he should have been off sailing the oceans of the world?

But Boot Key was a real togetherness marina, with the ladies holding exercise class on the dock in the morning and Happy Hour customary at the end of the main pier in the evening—the ostensible object here, aside from pleasant social contact, was to see the famous green flash in the sky as the sun set over the entrance channel, but the Fenwicks never had. There was also a farewell party whenever a resident boat left, and a welcome celebration whenever one arrived.

Thanksgiving was special because it really marked the beginning of the season in the Florida Keys. The boats of the sunbirds heading for the Caribbean had mostly come and gone; the first weeks in November, between the end of the summer hurricane season and the onset of the winter northers were recognized as the best time to depart, generally by way of the Bahamas, for the Virgin Islands and points south and east. The snowbirds fleeing ahead of the winter blizzards up north had practically all arrived and settled into their reserved Boot Key slips for the winter.

The marina held well over a hundred vessels. Some were merely passing through, some were year-round residents, but a very large percentage arrived each fall and headed back up the Intracoastal Waterway in the spring. Between those dates, Boot Key was a bustling floating community of friendly seagoing people, and Paul Fenwick had once enjoyed being a part of it but he was sick of it now.

He was particularly sick of Thanksgiving. He couldn't help remembering that it was the day after Thanksgiving the previous year—it seemed a century ago in another lifetime—that Deedee had had the first symptoms. Well, that wasn't quite correct. Actually it was the day when—perhaps because they'd overindulged a bit at the party the night before—the symptoms had become so painful that she couldn't conceal them any longer. She'd been forced to admit that she'd been having these odd little twinges from time to time and, well, yes, they'd really been going on since before they sailed from Chicago. Being Deedee, with her irrational fear of the medical profession still intact after five years of being married to a medical man, she'd figured she'd just get over them; besides, she'd said, she hadn't wanted to bother him with her small stupid bellyaches when they'd both been so busy getting *Haleakala* ready for the Great Adventure—the name, Hawaiian for "House of the Sun," had been Deedee's choice, remembered from their honeymoon on Maui where the great volcano was located.

Anyway, she'd said, it was probably just nervous tension and all she needed was a tranquilizer or something, everything was just so damned *exciting* now that all decisions were made and all ties cut and they were really on their way. She'd asked if he couldn't just feel her tummy and make sure it wasn't appendicitis and get her something at the Keys Pharmacy up the street—for a physician's wife, Mrs. Paul Fenwick retained some strange notions about the practice of medicine. There had been enough clues to give him an ugly hint of the truth, so he'd taken her straight up to Kleindienst at Miami's Jackson Memorial.

He'd known the answer when he'd seen the surgeon's careful poker face the day the results of all the tests were in and it was time for the great man to pass down the word from on high. No, that wasn't fair. It was the dirtiest job in the world, the one no doctor wanted, and Kleindienst did it as well as it could be done—much better than he, Paul Williams Fenwick, M.D., had managed the few times he'd had to face the same lousy situation in his own brief practice of medicine. There had been, as always, the final suggestion that if they wanted a second opinion Kleindienst would be more than happy to . . . blah, blah, blah.

"Dr. Kleindienst," Deedee had said from the hospital bed, in a small steady voice. "Dr. Kleindienst, please! We're all medical people here, aren't we, even if only by marriage in my case? Please don't make my husband have to look it up in his books, and don't make me have to pry it out of him afterwards. Just say it. Tell us what the chances are."

"I will be better able to answer that question after . . ." Then the big, clumsy-looking, red-faced man, who was one of the best in the world at his delicate surgical specialty, had stopped and looked at her hard as if recognizing something he'd missed earlier. "Ja. Of course. One gets into the habit, you understand." His voice had turned slightly guttural. "If we are optimistic, fifty percent considering the apparent extent of the involvement. If we are pessimistic, less. Is that what you wished to hear?"

"It's hardly something anybody'd want to hear, Dr. Kleindienst. But thank you for trusting us with the truth."

Actually, the fifty percent estimate had turned out to be wildly optimistic. There had been hardly any chance at all, and everyone had known it after the initial surgery, but of course they'd had to go through the routine motions anyway, even after all hope was gone. And she'd borne it all, brave and undemanding. All she'd really asked of him, toward the end, was the assurance that he was going to carry on as they'd planned, regardless.

"Do it," she'd whispered, pale and thin in the hospital bed. "Promise! I . . . I want to think of your doing it, wherever I am. You can manage alone, you know you can. Or . . . or get somebody else, I don't mind. But please don't let this spoil everything for you. Please!"

He'd promised, of course, and he thought she'd believed him—he'd been sincere enough at the time—but he was beginning to realize that it had been an empty promise. Gutless Fenwick, he thought; hell, the worst that can happen to you, sailing out there alone, is that you drown, and is that so bad? But the fact was that without Deedee's encouragement and support he didn't seem to have the initiative—okay, guts—to cast off the lines and point the big catamaran's twin bows at the empty horizons she'd been built to seek. Which was odd, in a way, because the whole idea had been his in the first place. . . .

"Ahoy, *Haleakala!*"

It was a woman's voice from the finger pier alongside. He made his way up into the cockpit and saw Mrs. Ellington standing there—well, Myra of the *Waterwitch*. At Boot Key, patronyms didn't count for much; you were known by your first name or the name of your boat. Myra Ellington, small and pretty and white-haired, lived with her husband, a stout, bald, retired Maryland contractor who'd cheerfully help you fix anything on your boat you couldn't manage yourself, on board a meticulously maintained wooden Matthews old enough to qualify as a classic. In it they made the yearly Waterway pilgrimage like clockwork. "I just wanted to make sure you're coming to the party," she said, when Paul Fenwick emerged in *Haleakala's* cockpit. "I didn't see your name on the list."

He said, "I'm sorry, but I don't feel much like parties these days, if you know what I mean."

The little woman looked at him shrewdly. "How long is it you've been working like a beaver on that boat and going nowhere and seeing nobody, honey? Four months? Six? 'Bout time you rejoined the human race, don't you think? Come on. It'll cost you all of two-fifty, but that won't break you. I'll take it down to the office and sign you up, if you like."

Paul Fenwick groped for a valid objection. "Isn't everybody supposed to bring a dish of something? My cooking isn't exactly gourmet quality."

"Honey, the ladies around these docks are cooking up enough victuals to feed General Sherman and his army of human locusts. You've got a bottle of wine or something on board, haven't you? That'll do fine." She hesitated. "Talking about human locusts, you know that homemade trimaran that flipped out in the Stream the other day in that little bitty squall with those hippie young folks on board? They've got themselves right side up and they're drying themselves out, but that crazy boat of theirs is pretty much a wreck. I don't figure they've managed to cook a hot meal since they got here, even if they had something left to cook, which I doubt. Well, Thanksgiving is Thanksgiving, if you know what I mean. If you could make that a five instead of two-fifty, kind of adopt one of them, well, *Pieces of Eight* is taking one, and *Gypsy Girl* is contributing for another, and Wally and I . . . Thanks, honey, and please do come. We know how you feel, but you can't hibernate forever on this boat like a bear."

She walked away briskly, her trim, youthful figure belied by the white hair. She was wearing the almost universal warm-weather marina-ladies uniform of jersey and denim shorts. The only real variation permitted seemed to be that the young ones wore them fashionably frayed around the thighs, while the older ones like Mrs. Ellington still clung to the dowdy, old-fashioned custom of terminating a garment neatly with a hem.

Paul Fenwick watched her out of sight rather grimly. He was annoyed by the pressure that had been exerted to make him conform socially, even though it had been well meant, as Deedee would have been quick to point out. Deedee had always been able to find the nicest motives for even the most unbearable busybodies. . . . But it was no time to be thinking of how she'd been—tall, slim, dark-haired Dorothy Dolores

Fenwick who wasn't any more. Deedee with her steady bright courage and her sudden dark little fears. Doctors. Dogs. Any boat that tipped more than, say, ten or fifteen degrees. . . .

That was how they'd come to multihull boats, because they didn't tip, and found themselves involved in a passionate dispute between the three-hull (trimaran) and two-hull (catamaran) aficionados, on the one hand, and the traditional defenders of ballasted monohulls, on the other, but to hell with that involved squabble. The important thing had been that while the orthopedic surgeon from Northwestern they'd tracked down through one of Paul Fenwick's boat-minded colleagues had been a real nut on the subject, his big Newick tri had been steady and stable as a football field even in a fresh breeze. It had been a wet ride but spray in the face was not one of Deedee's phobias; she'd loved every minute of it.

Back at the car, they'd thanked their enthusiastic skipper and agreed with him that it was pretty dumb to take something to sea that was supposed to float and then load it down with lead merely to keep it more or less right side up, when the old Polynesian seafarers had solved the stability problem so simply, centuries ago, with twin hulls or outriggers. After disengaging themselves, they'd paused by the car to mop themselves off and tidy themselves up a bit for the drive home.

"One condition," Deedee had said.

"What?"

"Well, two. We won't ever refer to an ordinary sailboat as a leadmine, the way they do. And we won't ever, ever say a *thing* about those damned old Polynesian nautical geniuses they're forever making obeisance to like sacred prophets. We're going to build a new boat, not join a new religion. Okay, Dr. Fenwick?"

"Okay, Mrs. Fenwick."

Well, they'd done it and, having had time to reconsider, they'd done it big. They'd wound up with two great unfinished thirty-eight-foot hulls in the back yard, properly joined by a deckhouse structure strong enough to support a freeway bridge. They'd learned to work with resin and fiber glass—itchy damned stuff—and real teak and teak-faced plywood. They'd bought stainless-steel fastenings in fantastic amounts at incredible prices; and gradually, they'd learned where to shop for good seagoing fittings at prices slightly less outlandish. They'd acquired enough tools to outfit a complete shop, and enough muscles to join the Longshoremen's Union. It had always seemed a bit unbelievable to John Fenwick, watching his wife entertaining guests at dinner, that the lovely lady at the other end of the table had, only a few hours before, been out back of the house squirming through one of *Haleakala*'s cramped and grimy bilges, greasy wrench in hand, in totally disreputable jeans, with a paint-smeared bandana over her hair.

But gradually there was less and less entertaining as the boat, and all the reading and studying and planning that went with it, took over their lives. However, there had been another reason for their dwindling social life: John Fenwick's growing disenchantment with his profession as, warned by the legal lightning that had begun to strike all around him, he found himself concentrating more and more on finding the approach to each serious case that would look best in a court of law, and to hell with whether or not it was best for the patient. The malpractice suit that finally hit him in spite of his precautions brought everything to a head.

"Okay, that does it, darling," he'd said on the day the court exonerated him on the grounds that his solution to the difficult medical problem had been the standard and conservative one, and a physician should not be penalized because he was unwilling to use his patients as guinea pigs for experimental and untested miracle cures. "If they want somebody who can keep everybody alive," he'd said bitterly, "let them go to church and talk to God—and sue hell out of Him when He loses a patient. I've had it. I'm taking my wife and my boat and sailing off to the beautiful islands of the South Seas. Start shopping for sarongs, Mrs. Fenwick."

It had sounded pretty good, pretty convincing, but he'd always wondered how much Deedee had guessed. Because, although he'd never had the courage to confide in her—let her keep a few illusions about the inadequate human specimen she'd married—he knew that he could probably have saved that poor damned little kid if he'd been willing to gamble; and the damned mother had known it, too. Well, she could blame all the lawyer-ridden patients who had preceded her, who'd taught the medical profession it didn't pay to take any chances at all these litigious days; and the strident bitch would probably have sued anyway if he'd taken the risk and failed—and then she might very well have won her case. To hell with her. Any parent who'd put a money price on a little

34

boy's life when a doctor had done his best . . . but, of course, he hadn't done his best. He'd had the price in mind, too.

It was funny in a way, he reflected; you could call it ironical if you preferred. He'd fled the life-and-death responsibilities and decisions involved in conducting a medical practice, only to assume the life-and-death responsibilities and decisions involved in skippering a small boat at sea, but there had been a difference: Deedee with her unwavering enthusiasm had been able to help him with those. But there had certainly been times when *Haleakala,* gigantic though she'd looked in the back yard, had seemed very tiny and vulnerable afloat.

In spite of the protests and warnings and even tears of people who thought they'd lost their minds—his parents had practically accused Deedee of dragging him away from a promising career to a watery grave—they'd managed to get off at last. At today's prices, the rental of the house had promised an adequate income, and there had been enough left in the bank to provide for emergencies. Learning as they went, they'd sailed out through the Great Lakes and down the St. Lawrence. There had been days when it had been unbearably awful and they'd been petrified with fear, not to mention being agonizingly seasick; but there had also been days—and nights—when it had been incredibly wonderful, the big cat hissing along steadily with a fair wind, the self-steering vane holding the course perfectly, while they had their drinks and dinner in the spacious cockpit and watched the seabirds fly and the coast go by—and perhaps, if the sea was empty enough, made love in the enormous double berth in the deckhouse and then argued laughingly about who had to pull on pants again and take the first evening watch.

Reaching the Chesapeake a little too late in the summer, they'd taken the Intracoastal Waterway south rather than risk meeting a hurricane off shore. They'd done it by easy stages, taking advantage of *Haleakala*'s shallow draft to explore where other cruising boats her size could not go, and using her tiny sailing dinghy for further sightseeing. It had been a beautiful, relaxed, happy, good-for-nothing time such as neither of them had ever known. Still happy, they'd wound up here at Boot Key giving the boat a complete overhaul while they waited for safe fall weather to set out for the Virgin Islands and the Panama Canal. . . .

Now, a year later, he was still sitting here, still making a

35

pretense of fiddling with the boat that had been ready for months, quite unable to make himself take the giant step of heading out once more, alone. It was, he knew, a well-recognized syndrome. Every marina had them: the would-be world cruisers who worked endlessly on their sturdy craft but never quite found the courage to shove off. He could even recall discussing the odd phenomenon with Deedee and laughing with confident superiority. Haha.

In the evening, drink in hand, Paul Fenwick wandered over to the main pier, pausing by a group that was watching round, bald Wally Ellington rearranging the fenders of a small cutter and adjusting the dock lines. Myra Ellington was there, wearing a neat light pantsuit in honor of the festivities. She turned and, seeing Fenwick, smiled in a distracted way.

"So glad you decided to make it, honey," she said. "Isn't it just awful?"

"What is?" he asked, puzzled.

"Didn't you hear about the poor Ullmans? It happened night before last. They're both in the hospital up in Coral Shores—that's where they live, you know. They couldn't find a place to keep their boat any closer. Anyway, he's not expected to make it. Wally's making sure their *Nancy Lou* is riding okay, for whatever good it will do them now."

"I knew the boat was just in from the Bahamas. What happened, did they have a car accident on the way home?"

The little woman shook her white head indignantly. "I don't know what things are coming to when people can get beat up and raped in their own homes! But I must say, she's the last person I expected *that* to happen to, a plain intellectual girl like that. The poor little thing. . . . Wally, you be careful on that ladder, there's a rung loose, hear?"

In spite of the serious nature of the tidings, Paul Fenwick couldn't help a brief grin as Mrs. Ellington turned away. He had a fairly clear picture in his mind of the girl who belonged to *Nancy Lou*—around Boot Key you got in the habit of thinking of people belonging to boats rather than vice versa—and Nancy Ullman was neither particularly small nor particularly plain, although she was rather aggressively intellectual, a slim, intense young woman with short dark hair who favored the oversized spectacles currently fashionable, and who had strong opinions about just about everything. She'd made herself fairly unpopular around the marina, he recalled, by hotly defending on ecological grounds the new

36

marine-toilet regulations that were blighting the lives, and pocketbooks, of all boat owners with vessels big enough for plumbing.

Playing the standard married-folks' game of speculating about the sex lives of other couples, Deedee and he had wondered how such a determined girl had ever let herself be won, let alone bedded—to use the old-fashioned term—by the rather slight and boyish and innocuous-looking young man with wavy red hair and freckles who was her husband. Well, it was too bad. The poor guy was apparently in a bad way now, and his strong-willed wife had got herself raped, but that was not really a safe subject for contemplation, not for a man who'd been celibate for the best part of a year. Fenwick dismissed a sudden, uninvited mental picture of the actually rather attractive Mrs. Ullman being . . . no, to hell with it. He was, he told himself firmly, a poor bereaved widower grieving chastely for his beloved spouse, deceased, and to hell with it; but he could use another drink.

At the end of the dock, the party was in full swing. He found himself stopping to chat with Jim Bennett of *Gypsy Girl* who was curious about *Haleakala*'s ingenious dual hydraulic drive that allowed her two propellers—one down in each hull—to be driven by a single auxiliary engine mounted, dry and accessible, up in the deckhouse structure. A couple of other men joined them, and various other technical boating matters were discussed; then the group broke up and Fenwick made his way toward the bar. As he started to fight his way through the crush, somebody plucked at his shirt sleeve.

He turned to see a small girl he did not know, with an odd gamin face framed by rather long, rather stringy dark hair. She wore slightly too-big blue jeans that were white with wear at the knees—probably the seat, too, if he could have seen it—and ragged around the ankles. Over this she had a short pink smock with puffy little sleeves that looked like one of the dresses his sister used to wear when quite young. Like the jeans, it wasn't very clean.

"You're from that big Harris cat, aren't you?" she said. "I'm supposed to thank you, I guess. So thanks."

It took him a moment to realize what she was talking about; then he grinned. "It was supposed to be an anonymous donation. I was supposed to feel warm all over doing good in secret, I thought."

"Secret, hell. That self-righteous fucking bitch never dropped

37

a buck into the collection plate unless it was a silver dollar so the whole congregation could hear it clang."

There was no reason, really, he warned himself, why that word should be more shocking than, for instance, "damned." It would obviously be better not to give the girl the stuffy disapproval she was working for. On the other hand, she was being cruelly unfair and ungrateful to Myra Ellington. He looked at her sharply, about to set her straight, and changed his mind. Hell, the grimy little tramp was of voting age and it wasn't his job to bring her up properly—undoubtedly a lost cause anyway at this late date.

"Where are your friends?" he asked.

"Over there. Already feeding their fat fucking faces," she said.

He looked where she indicated and saw, at one of the heavily loaded tables, two men with straggling beards and ragged jeans eating hungrily, although most other people were still on the booze phase of the operation. Human locusts, Myra had said. With them was a big pale girl with mouse-brown hair wearing a jeans-and-smock outfit like his companion; but with this one the smock made more sense since the girl was noticeably pregnant.

"What's your name?" Fenwick asked the girl in front of him.

"Lucia," she said. "Lucia Barnes. And you're Dr. Paul Fenwick who quit medicine to cruise the world, only your wife got cancer and died and now you can't seem to leave the dock. Well, single-handing is for nuts, anyway. What I'd like to know is, can you use a crew, Doc, at least as far as St. Thomas?"

The little girl really knew how to wake a man up, Fenwick thought grimly, resenting the blunt accuracy with which she'd summed up his situation. And her proposition was, of course, ridiculous. She couldn't really expect that he'd let a ragged gang of misfits like her and her friends aboard his and Deedee's beautiful *Haleakala*.

Lucia Barnes was watching him steadily. "That's on Charlotte Amalie," she murmured. "Down in the U.S. Virgin Islands. You were heading there anyway, weren't you?"

"I know where St. Thomas is," he heard himself say rather stiffly, instead of making the instant rejection he'd intended. He found himself trying to rephrase his refusal so it wouldn't hurt her feelings, although he couldn't really see why he should bother. He heard himself saying, with a glance toward the trio at the table, "If you mean them, they don't come with the highest recommendations, Miss Barnes. What makes you think I'd trust one of them to stand a watch on my boat, when they couldn't even keep their own right side up?"

"Hell, that thing isn't a boat, it's a floating fucking disaster area," Lucia Barnes said. "It wasn't designed, it just grew. They stuck it together from old orange crates and adhesive tape and put to sea to escape our lousy reactionary civilization without bothering to find out what the hell they were doing. But they can pull the strings if somebody gives them directions; and we can tell them what strings to pull, can't we? And you didn't build that handsome catamaran just to see Boot Key Marina, did you, Doc?"

It amazed him that they were still talking about it as if it were in the realm of possibility. It dawned on him, uneasily, that they weren't really discussing boats and crews at all. Already the alignment had shifted subtly: together the two of them, standing there, were telling the three of them, over by the table, what to do.

He looked down into the small dirty offbeat face for a moment, and the words he'd been about to speak didn't come. *Get somebody else, I don't mind,* Deedee had said, but of course she'd meant a nice, fastidious, lovely, seagoing girl like herself, who'd slip right into the space she was leaving vacant. Not a small, foul-mouthed refugee from a bathtub and laundry with odd, unspeakable promises in her greenish eyes. Because there was suddenly no doubt whatever that navigation and seamanship were only a small part of the deal that was under consideration here.

It wasn't fair, Fenwick thought resentfully. The little girl had all the weapons—well, she had the only one that counted—and at the moment he had no defenses at all and somehow she knew it. It had been a long time for a healthy man, even one consumed by grief. . . . And, dammit, it would feel good to get away at last, with any kind of a crew. He had to get away, somehow, or finally admit, to himself as well as to everybody else, his total ineffectual uselessness.

Of course there was no question of filling the empty space in his heart. A nice, fastidious, lovely girl would have struck out immediately; in fact, she'd never have got to bat. But this grubby but self-confident waif from a world remote from his, well, it wouldn't seem like such a betrayal of Deedee and everything they'd shared on *Haleakala,* above decks and below. . . .

39

CHAPTER 4

November

Latitude 24°N; Longitude 81°W

She disengaged herself cautiously and slipped out of the big double berth and stood up warily under the low deckhouse roof—the overhead, if you wanted to be nautical. One drawback to these damn cats, she thought idly, sleepily, fuzzily, there was generally plenty of head room down in the deep narrow hulls on either side, but up in the wide house built over the water like a covered bridge from hull to hull, there wasn't all that depth available so you had to watch your skull unless the fucking boat was enormous or designed very top-heavy indeed. Or unless you'd never grown above two-bit size like a certain unwashed little tramp called Lavinia Burnett. . . . Ooops, Lucia Barnes? Or was she Linda Brown today?

For a moment she really couldn't recall which name she'd been using here, and as always it scared her, although you'd think she'd be used to it by now. Lucia, she thought. It is Lucia here, isn't it? Such a dainty name for such a grimy character. And Linda, that's the clean, businesslike one in the neat sailor suit who sits primly behind a typewriter and you'd never, never guess from her prissy behavior that she sleeps with her boss. And Lavinia, now there's the real puzzle, who's Lavinia? Will the real Vinnie Burnett please stand up?

A certain lack of imagination there, Vinnie dear, she told herself. Us sneaky criminal-conspirator types ought to know better than to stick to the same lousy initials, oughtn't we? But ever since that time, that awful time she didn't like to think about, there had been that funny trouble about keeping her memories absolutely straight; and the simple, amateur trick did help when it came to remembering, and answering to, the name of the moment. . . . Now what the hell did the mark do with my clothes?

Mark? That's whore talk, honey, we don't use that kind of language in this house, we attract a very high class of gentlemen and they're not to be called marks, understand? The hypocritical old bag; but it had been kind of—but only kind of—interesting to learn what really went on in a place like that, that she'd only read about, and she hadn't been so goddamn bad at it, if she did say so herself. Of course, she reminded herself wryly, it wasn't as if she hadn't had lots of experience in the amateur division before turning pro. Anyway, it had been a great place to visit but you wouldn't want to live there; and that murderous little freak who sees himself as a fucking greaser Napoleon making a comeback from his fucking Elba, only he wants to go to an island instead of getting away from one—Don Jaime Colombo, but he'd never be anything but plain Jimmy Columbus to her. She couldn't let him think she was impressed by him or he'd walk all over her. Anyway, his proposition had made a good excuse for getting the hell out once she'd learned that what she was looking for, what she'd been looking for all her life, couldn't be found in that kind of a bed, either.

She suppressed a giggle, standing there in the dark. From cathouse to catamaran, the title of your memoirs, my deah? But you'd better watch yourself with that one. Those dedicated lousy burning patriots, they'll kill you for the fucking Cause as soon as look at you; and this one's really flipped since the death of the son and heir. And don't forget you're the only real link between him and all the tricky yacht stuff he's setting up now, well, half of it, anyway. You don't know much about the Florida end of the business, only that he's got somebody spotting for him here, too; but you can sure tie him up with Bucky and his crazy Texas operation. The Bosun, for God's sake! You can bet the little monster has it all worked out how to break that connection, meaning you, once it's served his purpose, and who's going to worry about what happens to a cruddy little beach-bum girl last seen working in a Miami whorehouse, for God's sake?

Clothes. Concentrate, sweetie. You know, like jeans and things. You can't slip out and use the pay phone on the dock stark naked, not even in the middle of the night, it rahly isn't done, you know. And the next time don't let the sucker pour so damn much booze into you; you know what it does to your head these days, ever since that time, and you really don't need any more useless gray mush in there, do you? But what is it my toes encounter? Can it be a blouse? And if blouse comes, can pants be far behind? Honey, you're drunk as a skunk, get the hell out in the fresh air and sober up.

Dressed, she paused to throw a parting look at the dim shape sprawled on the wide deckhouse berth in an attitude of total relaxation, a spectacular change even in sleep from the tense, taut attitude he'd shown when they met. She thought it must be nice to have something still mean so much, make so much difference, even just satisfying that ancient itch. The poor damn chicken bastard sitting here on his beautiful boat being faithful to his beautiful dead wife for damn near a year, scared to get himself any kind of a girl—or even admit he wanted one, needed one—because he'd forgotten all the moves of that game in the years of his marriage, and he was afraid of making a horrible embarrassing fool of himself in front of all these new nautical people he'd just got to know. Just like he's scared to make a fool of himself trying to take this bucket to sea alone, although the way he's got Ler rigged he could easily do it if he only tried.

On an impulse, she bent over and kissed the sleeping man very lightly, just to see if it did anything interesting to her, but it didn't. Well, at least he was a nice straight guy with nothing on his mind but nice straight sex, if you could call that nice; a pleasant change from that aristocratic little weirdo with his painful weirdo requirements, not that it made all that much difference. Dr. Paul Williams Fenwick stirred uneasily in his sleep but didn't wake. She gave him a light pat, a good-doggie sort of pat, and made her way out on deck, and up onto the finger pier—a scramble at this stage of the tide—and moved away along the dock.

The marina was quite beautiful in the night with the dock lights shining down on the sleeping boats and the stars bright in the black sky above. Well, she thought, if you liked marinas. All the fuss men made about boats and seamanship and the proper nautical language to go with them, as if it were a sacred fucking mystery or something. As if it took brains to memorize a few simple words, or even pull a few simple strings and work an elementary steering device, wheel or tiller. But be fair, she told herself, admit you had a head start on all the pretty dumb bitches who get invited to go Yachting with a capital *Y* and come tripping aboard so prettily on their high heels in their dainty fluttering dresses or spotless white pants only to find themselves, when the breeze comes up, all pale and bedraggled puking all over the goddamn boat. Like the Bosun's tall, gorgeous, Texas-belle, rich-bitch wife, who'd never forgiven him for her dreadful humiliation on what was supposed to be a lovely yachting honeymoon.

But all the nautical puking you did, you did as a kid in Bar Harbor when you had your own. . . . Fuck Bar Harbor. But it's funny that of all the fancy stuff they tried to teach you at all the fancy schools they kept sending you to, the only really useful stuff you learned was avast heaving my hearties and splice the mainbrace. Port. Starboard. Mainsail. Jib. A rope is a line a wall is a bulkhead a floor is a deck a door is a hatch a window is a port. Sheet. Halliard. Miss Burnett's Academy of Instant Nautical Knowledge. . . . Oh, Jesus! Wouldn't you think those hairy creeps would be sleeping after all the food and booze they put away for free?

They came up eagerly, yearning to hear all about it, preferably with Kodachrome slides in living color. The taller one, whose name was Kirby, asked: "Well, how did you make out?"

The shorter one, whose name was Mike, said sourly, "Stupid question number one zillion, man. With that simple casual unzipped look and the whisker burns on her chin, how the hell do you think she made out, or he did?"

That one was annoyed because he thought he had a prior claim, as if a bunk were a homestead and what he'd driven there was a corner stake entitling him to a quarter section or six hundred and forty acres. She glanced down and found that her trousers were, indeed, agape, such a terrible flaw in an otherwise shining example of perfect grooming, my deah. She zipped herself up in front and reached back to fasten her blouse behind.

"What the fuck are you doing here?" she asked, arms raised. "I told you I'd come to the boat. If he wakes up and sees us holding a council of war here on the docks at this time of night, if anybody does, they'll be suspicious as hell. Where's Billie?"

"Sleeping. If the lousy tub hasn't sunk and drowned her, it's still leaking like a sieve," said Kirby callously.

She regarded them bleakly. They weren't really human, of course, but then, who was?

"It's all set," she said. "But don't rush it, damn you. We've got to play it carefully, understand? You're reluctant to

43

impose, you're humble, you're grateful as hell for a free ride to the lovely islands of the Caribbean. Dig? Remember, it's his fucking boat, not yours."

"His boat, hell. As far as I'm concerned, it's in the common domain by this time. He isn't really using it, is he? He might as well have a room in a motel on shore." That was short Mike, the social theorist. "It's an obsolete establishment notion that a piece of legal paper can entitle a member of society who's not making good use of a certain item of property to withhold it from others who will employ it efficiently."

"Shit," said Vinnie Burnett. "That's what I'm trying to tell you: keep your obsolete establishment notions to yourselves."

Long Kirby said, "But dammit, Lucie, our *Freedom Machine* is all busted up, and after all the work we put in to build her and escape from this crummy land society of money-grubbing squares, we're entitled to *something,* aren't we? If we'd had insurance, that would be different, we wouldn't have to . . ."

"Who'd insure that instant derelict you guys built?" Vinnie asked. "Now get the hell aboard and pump her out so she'll float a little longer and keep out of sight until I tell you. We've got it made, I tell you, if you don't screw it by getting impatient."

"Well, you might comb that dishmop you use for hair," said Mike, still jealous. "Since you're so damned concerned about appearances."

"Remember," Vinnie said, "he's not to be hurt."

Mike was shocked enough to forget his resentment. "You don't have to say that, Lucie. What do you think we are? We have a very high respect for the sanctity of human life, as opposed to mere outmoded property rights. You know that."

Idly arranging her tangled hair with her fingers, she watched them go. Creeps. The sanctity of human life. Outmoded property rights. The *Freedom Machine,* for God's sake, that pitiful mess of half-cured fiber glass. She stepped into the phone booth at the side of the dock and found that she had to think hard to remember the number, but it came. . . . She heard the buzzing as the instrument rang over a thousand miles away in another time zone. Was it earlier back in Texas, or later? Earlier, of course, it was only about eleven there.

"Thank you for calling Buckmeister and Pond," the instrument said in her ear. "Mr. Buckmeister speaking."

44

Jeez, she thought, at eleven at night he gives me *that* routine. Hold everything! Don't make fun of him, don't kid him even a little, remember he's got no sense of humor at all. Treat him gently, always like the big handsome over-age baby he is.

"Darling," she said softly.

"Oh, it's you." The voice was peevish. "I thought you'd never call!"

"Did you have any trouble getting away to the office tonight?"

He allowed himself to laugh shortly. "I said my fool secretary had gone on vacation and left me stranded with a lot of paperwork that had to be ready for a customer at the crack of dawn. Christ, I was glad to get out of there. I declare, Thanksgiving dinner in Galveston with that stuck-up family of Madeleine's—what the hell have they got to be so proud of except a few holes in the ground that squirt oil? It's more than a man should be asked to bear, honey."

"Poor Bucky."

"I've been worrying myself sick about you. Are you all right?"

"Well, you wouldn't know your neat, crisp, clean, efficient little secretary right now, darling. I'm in disguise like we planned and the lady looks like a real tramp, but that was the idea, wasn't it, Mr. Bosun, suh?"

"That name should not be spoken over the telephone, Linda." His voice was suddenly stern and disapproving.

"Darling, I'm sorry. I forgot."

"Security is very important, honey. Do you have a report to make?"

"Yes, Bucky, dear. Those hippies managed to capsize and dismast that trimaran we picked for the first job, and it turns out it wasn't much of a boat anyway. I don't think my principal would have considered it acceptable. I sure as hell wouldn't have wanted to try sailing it to Colombia, or even Jamaica."

As she said it, she realized that this was also a terrible breach of security, but the man at the other end of the line didn't seem to notice.

"My God, Linda, you weren't hurt, were you?"

It gave her a funny feeling to realize that it mattered to the poor jerk. After that time, her fine loving New England family had finally washed its hands of her; but instead she had Elmer Putnam Buckmeister. For what he was worth, which wasn't much; but it was sweet of him anyway.

"Nice Bucky," she murmured. "Does he worry about his Linda? Actually, it worked out pretty well. Being shipwrecked with them like that, I've established a very satisfactory relationship with them as one dirty hippie to another. Well, three others. And, of course, nobody calls them hippies any more, but I can't keep track of all the jargon and you know what I mean. As I said, their boat won't do at all, certainly not beat up the way it is now, but I've got another one lined up, a sound one, and we've talked the owner into letting us crew for him south. . . ."

"We? Us? You're taking those misfits along?"

"They make an ideal cover, darling," she said. "Don't you see? If there's ever any backlash, if anything goes wrong, it's those three crummy freedom freaks who did the foul deed, not the innocent little newcomer girl who joined them just before their last U.S. port and came along for the ride without any idea what wicked plots they were hatching behind her back. As a matter of fact, the bearded crumbs are full of larcenous ideas of their own, and I think I can get them to do most of the dirty work for us."

"Linda, I wish you weren't involved. I don't know. I wish we'd never got ourselves mixed up in . . . This mysterious principal of yours is paying well and I need the money, but nothing is worth it if you . . ."

It took her several minutes more to reassure the poor patsy and make him brave once more. Then there were the arrangements to be discussed, and that took time, too. Finally, she promised to call him again when she had more definite information about their route, and hung up, having learned what she needed to know. It wasn't going to work, not as they'd planned. He just didn't have the guts to carry it out. She was going to have to hand it to him on a platter, somehow. . . .

Vinnie Burnett realized with a sense of shock that she was *interested,* something that hadn't really happened since that time. Nothing had been very important since that time, nothing had really touched her or intrigued her. But this was a risky, challenging problem, and she found herself truly absorbed in working it out, just as if she were a real person instead of a fucking zombie like that thing that wasn't her that they'd put away in that place—well, not like that screaming, jittering, bad-trip thing, but the human blank they'd made of it with their shocks and treatments, and turned loose at last saying what fine progress we're making dear and won't our family be happy to see us so sweet and well-adjusted. But of course our family hadn't been, not when we stopped all our fine, sweet, well-adjusted progress and got the hell out of there, for the last time, with the few tattered scraps of self that were left.

But enough about that time. If she couldn't count on Bucky accomplishing the actual takeover, she was going to have to do it herself. That meant a gun, not that she planned to shoot anybody, but she simply wasn't big enough to handle several large men and maybe a hysterical woman without one. Well, Jimmy would provide that; he'd damn well have to. And there was the point of delivery still to be determined; and if she'd known how *alive* she'd feel doing this. . . . Move over, Long John Silver. Make room for Vinnie, Mr. Blackbeard. Us pirates gotta stick together.

She picked up the phone and dialed the Miami number. There was the usual hassle about getting through to the great Mister Columbus, you'd think he was a Mafia don surrounded by bodyguards instead of the other kind of don—not that he didn't have the bodyguards, come to think of it, and a mean-looking pair they were, Jesus Cardenas and his gofer, the moron everybody called Bolo. It was Cardenas who took the call. Waiting, she reminded herself that respect was not in order. If she started deferring to Don Jaime like the rest of his hangers-on, he'd know it was because he frightened the piss out of her, and he'd be very quick to take advantage.

"Hi, Jimmy," she said breezily, when his voice came on the line at last. "Look, I'm down here in the Keys and I think I'm going to need a piece, you know, a gun. . . ."

Hanging up a few minutes later, she found herself shivering, although the night was not cold. It was not, after all, just a fun charade, an intriguing game. People could get killed. Don Jimmy wouldn't care; in fact, after what had happened to his son he was ready for some killing, but she knew that, for some reason, it was important to her that it shouldn't happen. It surprised her a little. She'd never considered herself particularly softhearted.

CHAPTER 5

December

Latitude 26°N; Longitude 80°W

It was, Philip Martin thought, like opening the cages in the boarding kennel and letting all the canines loose in the vet's expensively decorated office. They weren't quite squatting on the carpet or lifting their legs against the furniture, but you could feel even if you couldn't hear the soundless growls as they warned each other off: *Don't mess with me, Buster, I'm tough, I bite.* Even the one woman present, a lady who had something to do with PSCC—as far as they were concerned, everything to do with PSCC—had the same bristly attitude; and as a matter of fact, it was hard to tell her from the rest in her tailored pantsuit complete with vest and tie. Only the Coast Guard representatives in their snappy uniforms were at ease.

It was their party, in a conference room in their fancy regional headquarters high up in Miami's Federal Building. An urgent directive from Washington had caused this gathering, stating that things were in a bad way and therefore a new organization had been formed to deal with the crisis. The representative of this task force assigned to each designated operating area was to be given all possible cooperation by all local agencies involved, immediately. The directive went on to point out that there had been too much money wasted and too little accomplished. There had been too many people working at cross-purposes. There had been too many people failing to get the assistance to which they were entitled from other people. There had been too many people . . . The directive could have stopped right there, Philip Martin reflected sourly. There had, for a fact, been too damn many people trying to get a piece of the action; and although it was not really his concern, he found himself doubting that the addition of another, even a handsome lady in pants, would improve the situation greatly.

It would take more than a single female genius to get real cooperation out of this crew. There were the grim self-righteous crusaders of the Drug Enforcement Agency, who considered the administration's action a slap at them, as, of course, it was. There were the matter-of-fact Customs lads who looked on the problem as just another form of smuggling and would have preferred to be dealing with less controversial contraband like diamonds or Swiss watch movements. There were the prima donnas of the F.B.I., and the busy little boys of the Florida Marine Patrol, who had plenty of other things to keep them occupied but who figured that if it involved the law in state waters they were entitled to be represented. And, of course, the host organization, the U.S. Coast Guard.

A Coast Guard officer of impressive rank rose at the head of the table that occupied the center of the room. The chairs around it were not numerous enough to accommodate everybody, but they seemed to be considered positions of prestige, and there was a scuffle to grab the ones that still remained empty. Phil Martin settled down on an inconspicuous second-class chair along the wall.

"Seats, gentlemen, please," the Admiral said, rather belatedly. The conference room gradually became silent. "No smoking, *if* you please," he said, and the gray-haired Customs man at the table who'd been about to light up sighed in a resigned way and reinserted his cigarette into the pack and returned it to his pocket without haste—after all, his was the older Service. There had been Customs officials long before there had been Coast Guard officers. The Admiral cleared his throat and spoke: "We all know why we're here, but if there are any questions I'm sure the lady on my right will have answers to them. I'm privileged to present Miss Elizabeth Cameron of the Prohibited Substances Control Commission, who has been sent to coordinate, in this region, the worldwide offensive on which we're about to embark, to be known as Operation Extermination. Miss Cameron."

The woman rose deliberately and straightened the notes on the table in front of her. She was a tallish, slender woman with regular features and neat, dark brown hair cut short enough to expose her well-shaped ears. Her eyes were carefully made up, but her lips displayed only a discreet touch of lipstick. She had good cheekbones and a determined jaw. Martin waited to see if she'd pull self-consciously at her silly vest or straighten her ridiculous necktie—at just about the time the masculine half of society had decided that the traditional waistcoat and cravat were really getting pretty obsolete, the feminine half had pounced on these ancient tokens of male respectability with girlish glee. Miss Cameron left her natty costume alone. Point one for her. But it was inevitable that she would follow the Admiral into the steamy jungles of military terminology, and she did.

"We are losing this war," she said, looking up from her papers. "We win a few victories here and there, enough to look good in the press, but the fact is that the campaign as a whole is going against us everywhere. The newly organized commission I represent feels that if we are to turn the tide of battle we must mount a well-synchronized counterattack on all fronts. . . ."

She had a pleasant enough voice; and there was no real need to listen to her words. He, Philip Martin, was not a soldier in the glorious war against forbidden substances, thank God. He watched Miss Cameron standing there in her careful executive costume making her careful executive speech, and he amused himself by playing the old, old game of imagining what she'd be like without her careful executive trousers. What would it be like to lay a lady in a five-button vest and a four-in-hand tie? Come to that, what did a woman dressed like that wear underneath? No matter how mannish she looked exteriorly, it seemed unlikely she'd go for male attire interiorly, too. He visualized her in a man's undershirt and shorts. Not very sexually stimulating, Miss Cameron; I do hope you wear nice sheer pantyhose for the sake of those who love you. If anyone does; and always assuming those well-camouflaged limbs are worth displaying in nylon . . .

After finishing her speech, Miss Elizabeth Cameron answered, intelligently and knowledgeably, the questions addressed to her. Then the Admiral thanked her for her fine presentation that had made everything very clear, he was sure, to all of them. And he was sure they would all be happy to cooperate in the promising new unified operation she'd explained to them. After a few words about the importance of security, of which he was sure they were all aware, he adjourned the meeting. Martin waited by the door and joined the politely chattering group about Miss Cameron as she made her way out into the hall. There were still some men hanging on as they rode down the elevator; but the last kind of peeled off in the hall below, heading for the parking lot. Martin held the street door open for Elizabeth Cameron and waited while, wincing at the sun outside, she reached into her purse for dark glasses, placing them carefully on her nose. She ran a finger inside the crisp collar of her mannish shirt.

"You keep it warm down here," she said. "It's already fall up in Washington."

"Usually we have a norther or two to cool things off by this time, but they're late this year."

"You're Martin?"

"That's right."

"You pulled a lot of strings to attend that meeting, Mr. Martin."

"No. My Chief pulled the strings. He wanted me to see what we're up against."

She looked at him hard for a moment through the big dark glasses. "You sound as if we're on different sides."

Instinct told him this was not a woman you could afford to agree with or be pleasant to in the line of business; she'd walk all over you. Instinct, hell. He'd been given explicit instructions how to handle this. If the Old Man had thought diplomacy was needed he'd have used that diplomatic smoothie, Richardson, who, as a matter of fact, considered it a personal affront and a serious error in strategy that he had not been chosen to represent them here, if only because he was, after all, the project head.

"In a way," Martin said. "You see, my Chief is not concerned about the drug traffic, Miss Cameron. He says that, like Vietnam, it's something that would have been nice to win; but since time has demonstrated that it's unwinnable, why don't we just cut our losses and get the hell out while we've still got our shirts?" Before the woman could speak, he grinned and went on: "Save the indignation, Miss Cameron. You asked and I told you."

"It's a callous, inhuman attitude. Is that the way you feel, too?"

Martin grinned. "I'm not supposed to feel, Miss Cameron, I'm just supposed to take orders. In this case my instructions are to persuade you, since you seem to be in charge, to kind of overlook a certain local case we believe to be in the files that have been turned over to your commission. Restrain your attack on that particular objective, please. We're watching, we'll move when we're ready, we'll take care of the party involved; and we don't want any eager drug-sniffers lousing up our show."

She drew a sharp little breath. "You certainly have a strange way of making friends and influencing people, Mr. Martin."

"Bullshit," he said. "What's friendship got to do with it? Clearly, there's a conflict of interest here. Would you believe me if I told you there wasn't? Strictly speaking, as far as your particular operation is concerned, you ought to tell me to go to hell. Would you be impressed if I tried to sweet-talk you into making a favorable decision instead because I'm such a swell fellow and admire you so much and your noble work, too?" He thought he saw her lips move in a hint of a smile, and wondered if he should stop right there, but it was safer to press home the attack as instructed. "Of course I could be misjudging you, Miss Cameron," he said deliberately.

Her gray eyes were wary now behind the glasses. "In what way?"

"Well, some years ago it was pretty safe to figure that a lady holding a job like yours just had to have a lot on the ball to beat out all the men who undoubtedly wanted it. But nowadays—" he shrugged "—nowadays there's always a chance of running into a dumb, incompetent wench who got where she is just because somebody needed a token broad to put on display."

There was a little silence; then the woman facing him smiled slowly. "One could say roughly the same about you, couldn't one?"

"How?"

"Well," she said carefully, "well, it used to be that when one saw a man like you in a job like yours, one just knew he had to be good to have beat out all the Wasps. But now it could be just that he's somebody's token greaser, couldn't it, Mr. Felipe Aurelio Martinez?"

It was a bit of a shock, but it was beautiful, too. Mr. Meriwether had figured her just right; this was a tough fighting lady who'd never have responded to the kid-glove treatment.

"You've done your homework," he said flatly.

"Yes. I always do." She licked her lips. "I'm sorry. I shouldn't have used that word, but you made me mad. What is it you really want, Mr. Martin?"

"A chance to convince you that there are, in this specific

52

instance, considerations more important than the apprehension of one suspected malefactor who may just possibly be involved with drugs on the side." When she didn't respond, he went on: "There's a building called Omni, half shopping center, half hotel. They've got a restaurant called La Maison. Not the big, open, patio-type restaurant, but the little quiet expensive one behind closed doors just to the right of the hotel desk as you step off the elevator. Is seven-thirty convenient for you?"

She said, "I buy my own dinners, Mr. Martin."

"As you wish. I know a swell McDonald's, if that's more to your liking."

She was smiling once more. "You really work at being objectionable, don't you? La Maison is fine. Seven-thirty is fine. But you'd better tell me the name of this precious character you want to keep on ice, so I can check the files."

It was not information he liked to part with—the whole account might be jeopardized—but that decision had already been made elsewhere. "His real name is . . . well, some of his real names are Jaime Fernando Colombo y Menendez, but he calls himself Jimmy Columbus locally and he's probably filed that way."

"I'll look into it and let you know tonight whether or not it's feasible to grant your request, Mr. Martin; but I'll expect to hear some very good reasons why I should."

He watched her walk away, holding herself very straight. The contrast between her severe masculine pantsuit and her rather graceful, feminine, moderately high-heeled shoes was quite interesting but, he told himself firmly, quite irrelevant to the work at hand.

December

Latitude 30°N; Longitude 95°W

The sharp Texas wind fought to keep the glass door of the showroom open after Elmer Buckmeister released it; but the strong spring of the closing mechanism won the contest and shut out the noise and dust outside. He stood for a moment looking sourly at the boats on display in the great barn of a building: the flimsy little fiber glass sailboats with the ugly truncated keels that made them easier to load on a trailer, and the flashy little fiber-glass runabouts and bass boats with their bulky outboard motors or ugly stern drives. Junk, he thought, just plastic junk; and the big ones you deal in are no better. Tupperware boats, the British call them. It's all Tupperware these days. Well, masted or motorized Clorox bottles is what they really are.

He remembered the lovely little wooden Herreshoff sloop in which he'd learned to sail under the careful tutelage of his father, off Newport, Rhode Island; and the magnificent big wooden Rhodes cutter on which he'd later learned the fore-deck routines of an ocean racer, again with his father watching from the cockpit aft where he was serving, effectively, as sailing master although the title was, of course, never used. The day of the professional racing captain and sailing master had already come to an end, as far as ocean racing was concerned. They were all just friendly amateurs and good fellows out sailing together for fun—but it was odd how often the afterguards of the truly successful racers seemed to display the same shrewd, weathered, professional-looking faces, one of which invariably belonged to John Buckmeister.

It was a wonder, Elmer Buckmeister thought, how Pops ever got any boats sold, or bought, always off racing other people's boats like that. The brokerage office in Newport, and later in Annapolis, often seemed more like a Navy combat center than a place of business, with victories and defeats carefully analyzed with elaborate diagrams; and campaign strategies and battle tactics hotly debated into the night. But John Buckmeister must have known what he was doing in a business way; he'd done all right. Which, Elmer Buckmeister told himself bitterly, is more than *you* can say, exiled to this asshole of the universe called Houston, Texas, trying out your phony, folksy Texas accent on the few prospects who wander by. Hey, y'all, buy a boat from Buckmeister, he surely needs the business, hear? And y'all have a real nice day and come back real soon, goddamn your stingy ol' hides.

It had been the price of survival, this banishment from civilization. Madeleine's folks had been willing to bail him out, on certain conditions. Bring their darling daughter back from the effete and distant East, back to live in God's and Sam Houston's country within easy driving distance of the old family home in Galveston—well, somebody's old family home, but they'd paid plenty for it and fixed it up real nice, hadn't they?—and they'd be happy to underwrite his failing business and put it back on its feet again. If, of course, he took in a partner with good business sense selected by them. So Buckmeister and Son became Buckmeister and Pond; and where the hell *was* Dave Pond, anyway, that fat breezy extrovert bastard with his everlasting corny jokes? One of these days he was going to wisecrack himself right out of the partnership and to hell with Madeleine and her folks. . . .

"Hi, Dottie," Buckmeister said. "You seen Dave around?"

The thinly pretty, fluffily blonde girl at the switchboard in the main sales office had a way of looking at him that made him feel young again, a fine tall handsome figure of a yachtsman, tanned and strong, with the curly sandy hair and pale eyebrows that, for some reason, women seemed to find intriguing. Not this flabby sagging business character with alcohol and failure written plainly on his aging-boyish face. But while her eyes were pleasantly admiring, Dottie's voice was carefully proper and respectful as she addressed him in the way she apparently felt office help should address the folks for whom she worked.

"Mr. Pond asked me to inform you, Mr. Buckmeister, that he had to go to the Yacht Club to demonstrate a boat there to a certain Colonel Brennan who is just passing through on his way to Washington, Dee Cee. A T039, is that right?" Her proper earnestness failed her and she giggled. "I still can't keep track of all the silly things they call them, Mr. Buckmeister."

"You got it right, Dot," he said. "It stands for Trans Ocean 39, although anybody who'd cross an ocean in one would have to be drunk or crazy. But don't tell the client I said so."

The girl giggled again. "I won't, Mr. Buckmeister, I surely won't."

"Any other calls?"

"Not any, Mr. Buckmeister."

Buckmeister walked deliberately to the office door, hesitated briefly, and stepped inside. He could never help that faint sense of expectancy, the impossible hope that she'd returned in his absence and he'd step inside to see her sitting there, and wait for her to look up from her work in the quick, alert way she had, and give him her funny, secret, sexy little smile. . . . He stood looking at the neatly covered typewriter, the empty swivel chair, and the reception desk that held nothing but the plaque with the slip-in sign that currently read, as it had for months, *Miss Linda Brown.* Before that it had read *Mrs. Emily McNamara,* and what a dragon she'd been, and inefficient to boot. But she'd finally had the decency to get herself hit by a car in a rather damaging way, and he couldn't help loving her for that. If she hadn't, he'd never have met Linda.

For a moment he saw the chair occupied again by the rather small figure in the crisp white sailor-slacks she always wore to work and the striped seaman's jersey. Her office uniform, she called it. No sense wearing a dress and stockings and, God forbid, high heels, when she might have to climb all over some boat at a moment's notice. Why doesn't she call? he asked himself, what's happened way off there? There's been no word since Thanksgiving. Why did you let her go? How did we get mixed up in this crazy business, anyway? Just because you were so damned tired of taking handouts from those damned oilwells and she tried to help by finding you a way of making a little something on the side, of doing something profitable on your own, but it's mad, totally and criminally insane, and how could you ever have let her risk . . . And wherever she is, couldn't she at least have mailed an innocuous postcard to say she was all right? *Having wonderful time, folks, wish you were here.* But maybe she couldn't. . . .

He shook his head quickly with what was almost a shudder

56

and walked into the rear office to the left, the larger one, with its numerous photographs of fast yachts under sail inscribed mostly to Pops: to John "Bucky" Buckmeister, navigator supreme; to "Bucky" and his magic touch at the helm; to "The Buck," racing strategist extraordinary. And there were the books, of course: *Speed Under Canvas, Buckmeister's Yacht Racing Tactics, Buckmeister on Match Racing, The America's Cup—Near Miss at Newport.* You had to hand it to Pops, Elmer Buckmeister thought sourly, he even managed to cash in on *not* being selected to defend the old mug, although it broke his heart to fail after winning damn near everything else.

Down in one corner were a few similar pictures inscribed to Elmer, with thanks. Well, he'd been a pretty good foredeck hand, dammit; but the glory was all back aft, and they'd never given him his chance to prove himself back there, not really. Just because he wasn't an instant genius like Pops . . . but the word had got around: *Bucky's kid's a nice enough boy, but he really hasn't got it like his old man.* And if you didn't have money enough to campaign a fast boat of your own, you resigned yourself to spending your seagoing life as a foredeck ape—unless you could find a visiting Texas heiress all bug-eyed with the glamor of yachting and yachtsmen. The fact that she wasn't hard to look at hadn't hurt a bit. It had been a deliberate, cold-blooded campaign on his part and, he had to admit, it had been no more successful in the long run than his yacht-racing strategy on the few occasions he'd been allowed to practice it. Well, he had managed to marry the girl; but the rest had been total disaster. . . .

The phone on his desk rang, startling him out of his thoughts. He grabbed it quickly, hopefully; but it was only Dot. "I'm departing for home now, Mr. Buckmeister," she said in her stilted way. "I'll leave your phone plugged in. But don't you work too late, hear?"

He heard her shy giggle just before she hung up hastily, startled by her own temerity. It occurred to him that, the way the girl behaved around him, he might be able to promote something there if he wanted to; but of course he didn't want to. Not that he couldn't, now that Linda had proved to him that he wasn't the ridiculous enunch his wife had called him after that early, messy failure to which she'd contributed so largely. Hell, a man needed a little cooperation to penetrate fifteen million bucks, particularly when he was so tired he could hardly see. It had caught him totally by surprise. He'd never been a bedroom athlete; but he'd never had any trouble along those lines, either. But that dreadful night in Lauderdale when Madeleine had made it clear that she now expected a truly spectacular performance to make up for everything she'd suffered on their aborted honeymoon voyage. . . .

The phone rang again. He picked it up less hopefully this time, which was just as well, since it was just another letdown.

"Still there, *amigo?*" Dave Pond shouted in his ear. "That's right, keep the old proboscis to the old carborundum. I think we've got that clumsy ketch sold, the T039, but the soldier-boy has got to go home and count his pennies and consult his commanding officer, to wit, his wife. But he had that dream-boat look in his eyes. If he can scratch it up, we've got him. I told him eighty, okay? That'll leave us room to come down a few grand over the phone and make him feel he's getting a bargain he can't afford to pass up. Well, another day, another million. I'm off; see you in the morning."

Buckmeister had barely had time to return the phone to its cradle and let the grimace of distaste die from his face—the only good thing about talking to Dave Pond on the phone was that you weren't talking to him face to face so you didn't have to hide your feelings—when the instrument rang again. He picked it up mechanically, without any expectancy this time, and listened to the operator telling him that Barnes was calling, would he pay for the call? He frowned, trying to recall a client named Barnes; then he remembered the alias they'd picked for her, laughing because it seemed so melo-dramatic at the time. Lucia Barnes.

"Yes," he said quickly. "Yes, I'll pay."

"Darling." Her voice sounded quite distant.

"Where are you, Linda?"

"I'm in the Bahamas. To be specific, I'm in a phone booth on Green Turtle Cay, as far as I know the only phone booth on Green Turtle Cay. New Plymouth, I think is the name of the lousy little town. I mean, the cute, cunning, lovely little town."

"New Plymouth? But that's way up north in the Abacos! I thought you were heading over to Bimini and Nassau, and then heading south through the Exumas, on your way to St. Thomas."

"That's right, but nobody told the wind about it, darling. It blew like hell right out of the east. We couldn't lay Bimini at all. We finally made our landfall way up at West End, sixty

58

miles north, although some of the crew wanted to turn back to the U.S." He heard her laugh, prettily malicious. "You never saw such a seasick bunch of hippies in your life! But Paul and I managed to keep things going, only the diesel started acting up, and there didn't seem to be anybody who could fix it at West End. So after resting up a bit and cleaning up the mess, we headed for the big sportfishing marina up at Walker's Cay where they've got a good diesel mechanic. We had to have a part flown in from Fort Lauderdale, but he got us going eventually. But I didn't want to call you from there because they don't have a real phone, just a kind of ship-to-shore installation in the main office, a little on the public side, if you know what I mean. I hope you weren't too worried."

He said stiffly, "You could have written from West End."

"I'm all alone in the world, remember? Just an unwashed orphan of the storm, that's me. Writing loving postcards would have been out of character. Privacy isn't exactly rampant on a cruising boat, as you ought to know, Mr. Buckmeister."

"I'm sorry, Linda, I didn't mean . . ."

She went on, a bit coolly, "Now we're working our way south toward Marsh Harbour, spelled with a *u*, which seems to be the best place around to stock up on supplies and some gear we need, and top up the tanks. It's getting pretty late in the season, so Paul thinks we'd better head off shore as soon as we reasonably can and make the passage to St. Thomas direct instead of working our way down through the Islands by easy stages as planned. He's figuring on heading out through the North Bar Channel. Say a day to Marsh Harbour, a day in port, and another day—you'd better be ready for us in three days, although it could take longer."

"The North Bar Channel, just below Tilloo Cay?"

"You know it? Is it okay? Paul is a little worried about getting out through the reefs; he hasn't had much experience around coral. For that matter, neither have I."

"It's a good all-weather channel, and as I recall there's a shore range you can line up to keep you out of trouble."

"All right, darling. The North Bar Channel it is. Three days. Now I'd better hang up before one of them wanders by and gets curious about their penniless little shipmate making expensive long-distance calls to the States." There was a kissing sound. "Love you."

"Be careful, Linda. . . ."

Then the phone was silent and he laid it down slowly, trying to remember only the kiss and the final words—but who the hell was Paul? He was kidding himself, of course. Paul was the owner, Paul Fenwick, the poor sucker who was soon going to find himself boatless, but she hadn't made him sound like a sucker at all. Together, she'd indicated, the two of them had driven that big, bulky catamaran—a thirty-eight-foot cat was a lot of boat—to windward through those steep Gulf Stream seas with the three hippies vomiting helplessly when they weren't pleading to be restored to Terra Firma, U.S.A. A good stiff dose of Gulf Stream affected lots of people that way. Hell, Madeleine still turned green if you mentioned the name. . . .

So the Stream was still up to its old tricks, Buckmeister reflected grimly, remembering. Whatever Madeleine thought, the idea of humbling her, of putting her in her place, cutting her down to size, of establishing dominance immediately after placing the wedding ring on her finger, had never occurred to him. Sure he'd lied a little about how much he loved her and how little her money meant to him; what was a man supposed to say? But he'd truly been trying to make it nice for both of them: a gentle night sail across the Stream to Bimini under the twinkling stars (ha!) followed by a fairy-tale cruise through the Islands on the handsome sloop he'd borrowed for their honeymoon.

It was just his usual luck that a goddamn norther had come howling through ahead of schedule. He'd figured from the weather reports that they could beat it across easily and then wait out the blow in Bimini or Chub; but it had hit that night, catching them right out in the middle of the Florida Straits, and that was when the crap had hit the fan. Only it hadn't been exactly crap.

The thing was, when you sailed with people like Pops and his racing friends, you didn't meet many shore people like Madeleine. You didn't even know they existed, really, with all their fears and queasinesses. A few pleasant day sails in the sun weren't enough to warn you about the weird pampered attitudes they held. What was so terrible about a little rolling and pitching? Hell, the boat had plenty of stout handrails, didn't it? All you had to do was hang on. And what was so terrible about getting seasick? Everybody'd paid dues to that club. You simply whoopsed over the lee rail or spent a little time worshipping on your knees before the porcelain prayer bowl below; then you got your ass back on deck to see if you were needed. Admittedly, some got it worse than others, some were honestly incapacitated for a while, but Jesus, it wasn't terminal cancer after all, and everybody knew it.

To suddenly find yourself on a boat with somebody who expected to have her messes cleaned up and her head held and her chin wiped and sympathetic words crooned in her ear, for God's sake, while all hell was breaking loose topside and you had a forty-footer to handle alone right out in the middle of the Stream with tankers and freighters coming at you from all directions.... So maybe he had got a little impatient with her. It wasn't as if she'd been suffering from something serious like a broken leg.

And he had turned back when he understood she really meant it, hadn't he? Naturally the idea had startled him at first. It wasn't a hurricane after all, just another goddamn norther. He'd raced through so much worse, so many times, that it simply hadn't occurred to him not to keep going. He wasn't any great seagoing hero, far from it, but Jesus, nobody turned back for a little blow these days as long as the gear held up, particularly when they were almost halfway across already. He was simply taking them to the Bahamas like they'd planned together. Did she want to go or didn't she?

But he had turned back when she started getting hysterical about it, so what was the big complaint? It wasn't his fault she'd wound up kind of soiled and stringy and wrinkled after all the expensive trouble she'd gone to to present herself and her stylish yachting costume in perfect honeymoon condition. Hell, he'd told her that all she really needed was some old jeans and cutoffs and a handful of T-shirts and a bikini. And as for his making a ridiculous public spectacle of her, it was a borrowed boat and a sizable one, and the way the tide ran through those docks at Pier 66 he needed a little help with the lines and fenders if he was going to bring it in without damage. Maybe he had been a little fed up by that time, maybe he had used a little rough language to get her to haul her bedraggled Texas tail topside and lend a hand; a man could take only so much. What had she expected him to do, motor around in circles while she had herself a facial and permanent? She'd been the one who'd been so desperate to get ashore, hadn't she?

And what the hell, as he'd told her at the time, at that marina they'd seen so many pale and wilted ladies, and gentlemen too, coming in off the Straits during a blow, that another couldn't have interested them less. They hadn't known she was an immaculate Texas princess who wasn't ever supposed to be seen with a hair out of place.

So what was the great gripe? Where was the justification for the king-sized hate, the vicious bedroom revenge she'd taken that night at the hotel to which they'd moved, when he'd been much too weary to perform up to expectations; the vengeance she'd pursued so savagely afterwards—he'd never again managed to get it up in her presence—driving him to the bottle and, almost, to bankruptcy. Well, maybe that had been the idea, to pay him back for the dreadful humiliation and abuse to which she claimed he'd subjected her that night, by reducing him to the impotent and dependent and alcoholic condition in which Linda had found him. . . . Linda.

The familiar documentary movie—titled *Bitter Honeymoon?*—that had been played and replayed in his head for so many years with the same commentary, turned itself off abruptly. He drew a deep breath and crossed to the filing cabinet and got out the appropriate chart: *26320 Northeast and Northwest Providence Channels*. For being so close to the U.S., the Bahamas were very poorly charted and this number, covering all the northern islands on one large sheet, was, except for a few small harbor and channel charts, all that was available of an official nature. For more detail you had to consult the unofficial cruising guides.

The small-scale chart was enough to show him that the North Bar Channel just southeast of Marsh Harbour was, as he'd remembered, a good wide passage through the reefs; and there were several locations nearby where one could lie in wait for a boat coming down from the north and follow it out to sea without attracting attention. The area was generally, he recalled, full of cruising boats; it was, in fact, perhaps a little too well populated for what had to be done. However, there was the advantage that another cruising vessel, whether at anchor or underway, would never be noticed. They'd simply have to wait to go into their planned routine until they were safely out to sea. Linda, he was sure, would convince her Paul (damn Paul!) to head right out on the offshore tack.

His hands were a little damp as he folded the chart neatly. He found it hard to believe that they were really going to do it. He drew another long, shaky breath and picked up the phone and dialed a number in West Palm Beach, Florida. He could feel his heart beating heavily as he waited for somebody to pick up the distant instrument.

"Mrs. Lehman?" he said when a woman's voice answered. "Mrs. Lehman, this is Elmer Buckmeister in Houston. Could I speak with Mr. Lehman, please?"

"Oh, hello, Elmer," the woman said. "Just a minute. Morrie's right here. . . . It's young Buckmeister calling from Texas," he heard her say, and he heard a man's voice saying distantly, "It's about time."

Then Morris Lehman was on the phone. "Hi, Elmer, how's it going?"

"How are you feeling, sir?" Buckmeister asked.

"As good as can be expected. They won't let me do a goddamn thing, wait on me hand and foot. Won't even let me set foot on a boat, dammit, not for another couple of months, anyway. You going to find me somebody reliable to bring the *South Wind* back from the Bahamas or aren't you?"

"That's what I called about, sir. I have to go over there on business in a day or two, and I can bring her back from Nassau myself with some friends to help me, if that's reliable enough for you."

There was distant laughter. "I guess I can trust Bucky Buckmeister's boy to find Florida okay."

"There's just one thing. I'd like your permission to make a detour north through the Abacos, sir. It's not much out of the way and I'll be happy to pay for the extra fuel. There's a boat I'm supposed to check out for a client, presently lying in Marsh Harbour. Of course, if you have any objections, I can take an extra day or two and fly up and back from Nassau, but it would be more convenient. . . ."

"Oh, hell, give her a good run, she's a good little ship for a goddamn motorboat. Marsh Harbour? What's the name of that place we used to eat there, the Conch Inn? Sure, give her a bit of exercise; that way you'll have a chance to get to know her and see what needs fixing up, in case these damn doctors wind up telling me I have to put her on the market."

"I hope that won't be necessary, sir."

"That makes two of us. Okay, Elmer. You've got all the authorization you need to get her out of the Bahamas, I think. Have a good passage, and come see us when you get in. Wish I was going along. . . ."

Putting down the phone, Buckmeister grimaced wryly. Something about dealing with Pop's old friends made him feel as if he were still sailing toy boats in the bathtub. But they stuck, at least a lot of them did, you had to hand them that. Even after he'd moved from the East Coast they still kept calling; and if Morrie's heart gave out for good he was sure Mrs. Lehman would give him *South Wind* to handle, a nice piece of business considering the gold-plated way the old man had fixed up that Grand Banks 40 trawler when he was no longer permitted to race sailboats. A salable piece of merchandise.

He was stalling and he knew it. The next move was the one that counted, the one he couldn't take back, considering the kind of men Linda had apparently lined up to help him; Linda or the mysterious, nameless principal with whom he'd only spoken over the phone, just like a goddamn spy novel. Linda had said they were fairly rough people and he'd have to keep them in line and make them follow instructions. He drew another long breath, and picked up the telephone and dialed again. Another woman answered, this one with a harsh, nasal voice.

"I'd like to speak to Regan," he said.

"Who'd like to speak to Regan?"

"Tell him—" Buckmeister licked his lips "—tell him this is the Bosun calling."

CHAPTER 7

December

Latitude 26°N; Longitude 80°W

Sitting in the right front seat of the anonymous Ford sedan parked in one of the drab, cheap, older developments that had already made its contribution for better or worse—mostly for worse—to the booming growth of Miami, Philip Martin watched the faded pale green house down the block. Its neighbor on the near side was faded pale pink, and its neighbor on the far side, faded pale blue. Beside him, big blond Tommy Walsh was getting a little impatient and uneasy. He'd been here before, watching, and he was afraid of being recognized. Six-foot-two two-hundred-and-forty-pounders with straw-colored hair weren't common in this part of the city.

"Thank God, here they come at last," Walsh whispered as the front door opened. "That's Columbus in the doorway, of course. Our boy has a real handsome head on him, hasn't he? Too bad he was behind the door when the bodies were passed out. Jesus Cardenas is the little guy leaving; he's the *mayordomo*—well, ex-*mayordomo* since there's no real *domo* left for him to be *mayor* of, unless you count that exquisite example of cinderblock ticky-tacky over there."

"That's Bolo on his left?"

"That's right. Strong as a bull and good with a knife but absent between the ears. Bolo doesn't go in the morning until Jesus says shit. Okay, you've seen them and they look just like the photos I gave you, so let's split before we attract attention and blow the whole goddamn operation. . . ."

"Hold it."

About to lower the compact little twenty-power telescope he held, Martin put it firmly to his eye once more and, steadying his forearms against the car door, tried to capture in the limited field a slight figure with clipped dark hair that was running lightly up the walk.

"Who's that?"

"The daughter. Francesca Elena Maria de los Angeles Colombo y Aguilar, locally known as Frankie Columbus. There was a long-range snap of her in the bunch of shots you got."

They stamped them out of soft plastic, these days, all the little girls, and stuffed them all into the same bleached, frayed, grubby, shrunken jeans—rump-stretched and crotch-strained—and the same thin T-shirts or tank tops one size too small. Through the flimsy knit stuff the little tits challenged you with a boldness you'd better not believe, because if you did accept the obvious invitation and make the obvious moves you'd be a dreadful male chauvinist pig taking advantage of a poor innocent young thing and the fact that she'd waved it in your face wouldn't make a particle of difference; a woman should be safe from indecent advances even if she ran down the street stark naked. What she did to normal males along her nude-jogging route was just too goddamn bad. They shouldn't be that way even if they were. . . .

Martin caught his breath sharply. The face had suddenly come into focus in the one-eyed glass; and the tacky clothes

65

and the whacked-off hair had become instantly irrelevant. It was an unforgettable face, with the delicate heartbreaking beauty you saw in the old paintings. He wondered how he could have missed it even in a fuzzy telephoto shot. It was the kind of loveliness that made you doubt your adopted democratic principles and wonder if there wasn't something to aristocracy after all. Phil Martin swallowed the unfamiliar lump in his throat.

"Cute kid," he said. "Let's get the hell out of here. I've got a date."

Walsh put the car into gear. "You've got a date with our revered Leader, Mr. Secret Agent Richardson, account manager extraordinary and I do mean extraordinary, in fact, unique. We hope so, anyway. The outfit couldn't stand two like that. He wants to know what went on at that high-powered Coast Guard meeting to which, by a strange oversight, he was not invited; and why you haven't reported to His Highness yet. Why the hell do you think the Old Man pried him loose from that desk in Washington he decorated so beautifully and sent him out in the cruel field again to pester us working peons?"

"You're thinking, Tommy," Martin said reprovingly. "That's very unprofessional of you. Cogitation and cerebration are contraindicated at this juncture. If you must have thoughts, if they persist in intruding uninvited, please keep them to yourself."

Tommy glanced at him sharply, but spoke lightly: "Jeez, for a lousy *Cubano* you sure know a lot of fancy *Inglés* words."

"Who's a lousy *Cubano?* I'll have you know I'm a certified lousy *Americano* and I've got the papers to prove it. So let's have no more of this racial crap or I'll have you up before the S.P.C.A., or whatever the proper organization is to straighten out bigots like you."

They were just batting it back and forth lazily, relieved to be safely away from the critical area unobserved. It was always pleasant working with Tommy, with whom there was never any strain. Oddly enough, the real yahoos in the outfit weren't too hard to take because, after all, they weren't blade-proof or bulletproof, and they were uneasily aware of this. So they kept a pretty tight rein on their prejudices or at least their mouths, since it was well known that if one angered one of these unstable wop-spic-greaser types one might just get a shiv shoved into one all the way. But the goddamn liberal specimens who worked so hard to be toler-

66

ant could get on your nerves pretty badly, the way they prissy-footed around all mention of race, color, religion, or national origin. Tommy, with his relaxed kidding, was always a relief.

Martin said, "As for *Señor* Richardson, *amigo*, it is recommended that he should temporarily indulge in vigorous self-copulation just to pass the time pleasantly."

"Okay, I'm bright, I get it. He's to fuck himself hard, right?"

"Precisely. Until I return from my evening's engagement with an executive-type government lady who has all the answers we need and has promised to divulge them over dinner; and she even wants to pay for her own meal. In fact, she insists. But she has the subject under advisement, our subject, and will reveal her decision at the proper moment, after which I will promptly pass it on. In the meantime, tell our *Jefe Grande* that there's really nothing to report, which is why I didn't report it. When you've seen one of these intragovernmental dogfights—and I'm sure he has—you've seen them all."

"Yes, sir. I will so inform the Big Chief, although I may rephrase it slightly." Tommy paused. "Well, are you going to tell me or is it classified?"

"What?"

"Was it or wasn't it? I mean, was he or wasn't he? I mean, were they or weren't they?"

"Oh, Cardenas and Company. Yes, that's the little runt I saw heading out in a boat to confer with the Major out on Big Manatee Key, him and his dimwit shadow. So we've got our Miami Connection confirmed, for what it's worth; and I can tackle Miss Cameron with confidence. I'd have hated to first beg her to lay off and then have to come back and tell her, gee, thanks, but you can have him after all, ma'am, we had our eyes on the wrong fellow." After a moment, Martin went on: "How old is the kid?"

"Kid? Oh, the Columbus girl? Old enough for all practical purposes. A year older than her brother. Twenty-one."

"She looks younger."

Tommy threw him a shrewd glance. "She got to you, eh? At over a hundred yards, yet; Helen of Troy couldn't beat that range by much. But don't kid yourself, she's no dewy innocent in spite of that angel face. One of the floating generation. A year of college, a few jobs here and there, a lot of boyfriends; they come and go. We've checked them all out, at

67

least all the current crop, and found nothing on any of them. I think her daddy is keeping her out of everything as much as possible, unlike her brother. Whatever he's up to with the Major I'd say she's not involved, at least not yet, if that's what you're wondering. You want to be dropped at your hotel?"

"Just stop on Biscayne. I can stagger around the corner in spite of my love-struck heart. Tommy."

"What?"

"It's your turn to watch your step, *amigo*. This, today, was special and necessary. I had to know for sure, right now, and to hell with the shaky photo-identifications. But now we stay clear again, okay? Strictly long-range surveillance. Not just to avoid alerting the quarry, but because that's one of the most dangerous, unpredictable, overbred, predatory animals in the world, that little man with the fine big head. He was developed strictly for genteel homicide by a long and careful process of selection. Like a killer Doberman; the pups that won't go for the throat are stuck into a burlap bag with some rocks and dropped into the river. Well, that's just about the way this breed was developed, except that the ones that didn't have it wound up wiggling on somebody else's rapier."

Tommy gave him a narrow grin. "Well, you're the expert," he said.

Martin grinned back. "Sure, it takes one to know one, right? But *watch* it, damn you. And watch that jerk Richardson, too. That's one ambitious *hombre*, and they can turn rat-mean. We want to be ready for it if it happens, *comprendre?*"

Tommy nodded. " '*Sí, Señor,*' he said in his perfect Castilian Spanish." He hesitated. "I checked with the hospital this morning. That poor Ullman kid still isn't really with us, but they think he's going to make it. But the chances of his giving us anything new aren't very big. We already know from his young wife's description that the leader of the gang was big, blond, blue-eyed, and highly oversexed. How many big, blond, blue-eyed, randy gents do you think there are in Miami? On that description, I could be arrested any minute. Anyway, the connection is pretty fragile, isn't it? Just because the same gang of vandals happened to trash Montoya's place earlier in the week, and Montoya was once seen chatting with Jesus Cardenas in a slightly less than friendly fashion . . . that's pretty goddamn tenuous, Felipe. I think we're straining there."

"Just so we strain where they don't see us," Martin said. "You've still got a man on Montoya?"

"Simonds. He reports no further significant contacts observed, but he points out that doesn't mean there weren't any, since the orders state that inconspicuous has priority over observant."

"Well, let's continue to keep out of sight just the same. Columbus has cops and narcs and G-men to think about; let's not add to the little man's worries. Invisibility may get us something, although at the moment I couldn't say what. . . . You can drop me at the light."

"Be careful, yourself," Tommy said as Martin opened the car door to get out. "Watch out for this man-eating executive babe you're wining and dining. They're not too safe, either, I've heard."

Martin made an appropriately vulgar reply as he stepped out onto the curb.

CHAPTER 8

December

Latitude 26°N; Longitude 80°W

Dying wasn't so bad, Harold Ullman thought, but coming back to life was awful. He'd tried it several times and said to hell with it. It simply hadn't been worth the heroic effort and agonizing pain, particularly since there wasn't a great deal left to live for in this bleak Miami hospital room. He didn't know exactly what he'd lost, but something very important was gone, something especially fine he'd recently achieved that had suddenly been snatched away from him.

That was, of course, in addition to the direct physical damage which, he was aware, was considerable. Something was seriously wrong with his left leg, half his chest felt as if it were caved in, and there was another agony area around his face. By the time they got through patching him up he'd be another goddamn bionic man. And all because . . .

It faded there. He couldn't remember exactly what had happened; only that it had been the most shocking and disillusioning thing that had ever happened to him in his life. Well, sure, he'd stumbled on some hoodlums wrecking the house and a big masked guy had beat him brutally with his own shotgun and then kicked in a few ribs by way of farewell, okay. That much was clear, more or less, but the rest, the important part, simply wouldn't come. His mind, apparently, didn't think he was quite up to facing *that* memory yet.

Uncle Hal had warned him, of course. (Warned him of what?) Uncle Hal was dead now, had been dead for many years, but Harold Ullman still retained a clear memory of the stout, red-faced, balding old gentleman, his father's brother, the man for whom he'd been named. A childless widower, Uncle Hal had lived alone with his books and his pipe— Harold Ullman had started smoking one later in deliberate imitation of the uncle he'd admired—and the guns on the walls and the graying old pointer called Zachariah, Zack for short.

Uncle Hal made a regular Sunday pilgrimage to the local trap-and-skeet club; and Harold Ullman remembered distinctly the hassle that had resulted when his uncle had offered to take him along and teach him how to shoot. His mother had been very much against it—everyone knew that guns were dreadful, dangerous, immoral things—but his father had, uncharacteristically, overruled her decision, saying that it wouldn't hurt the boy to know a bit about firearms, he'd be less apt to shoot himself if he came across one accidentally.

Out at the range, the big shotgun had bumped him rather badly at first, Harold Ullman remembered; but he was damned if he was going to let on that it hurt, and after a while the flying clay targets started breaking—there was something almost scarily satisfying about seeing one explode into a puff of black smoke when the charge of shot hit it. After that, the recoil simply didn't matter any more.

They'd gone out regularly that summer, every Sunday, with old Zack pricking up his ears eagerly when he heard the guns and then curling up to sleep in the rear of the car when he realized it was a false alarm; there were no real feathered birds out there, just a bunch of pottery phonies. Then it had been autumn and the invitation had come that Harold Ullman hadn't really dared hope for but had dreamed about constantly.

During that time of waiting, he'd seen a TV show in which a sensitive young boy had been forced by a brutal relative to participate in a cruel hunt against his will; and he'd wondered where the scriptwriter who'd generated that piece of crap—he was picking up a few words like that by then, although he didn't yet dare use them aloud—where the man or woman who'd concocted that crock of shit had got his or her ideas about young boys. Jeez! Was there any normal kid alive who *didn't* want to get out there with a dog and a gun?

But the invitation had come and his mother's objections had, somehow, been overcome, and the first part of that hoped-for day had been a total nightmare. By that time he'd got pretty good at nailing clay targets if he did say so himself; but out there in the open Maryland countryside, tense and eager, he'd found himself totally unable to hit the side of a barn, let alone the crazily darting little feathered objects that burst out of cover explosively whenever he walked up, as instructed, past the magnificent, motionless piece of statuary that was old Zack on point. He was certain Uncle Hal was, any moment, going to call off the whole hunt in disgust. He knew that the dog, with even higher and less tolerant standards, had long since written him off as a total waste of his valuable canine time. Then Zack had gone rigid way off across a field, and Uncle Hal had said his legs were too old to hike that far and the fool mutt was probably just pointing a stump or something, but maybe somebody'd better go take a look. . . .

He'd always remember the lone bird getting up in that noisy, heart-stopping, buzz-bomb way they had; and the wonderful, terrible experience of feeling the big gun swing just right and the trigger yield at precisely the correct moment; and of seeing the flying game miraculously crumple in midair and fall. He knew he'd never forget the strange wild mixture of incredible triumph and unbearable grief he'd experienced as he took the dead quail from the dog's mouth and smoothed the feathers gently. Somebody touched his shoulder and he looked up at Uncle Hal.

"Now you know, boy," the old man said softly. "Always remember, the first thing the ape invented when he decided to become a man was a weapon; and he'd never have made it without. Only you can't tell them that, those folks back there in town. It's in us all, but they don't want to admit it. They'd rather live in a dream world peopled by basically gentle and peaceful human beings who never existed and probably never

71

will, at least, if they do, they won't exist very long. Some not-so-gentle-and-peaceful human beings will come along and wipe them out. But this they won't admit, ever, and you'll find they'll do strange and scary things whenever anybody threatens to expose that dim, nonviolent, never-never land of theirs. Don't ever let them catch you by surprise, boy. They'll stomp you into the ground like a snake, regardless of their peaceful protestations, rather than concede that they might possibly be wrong. Now let's get on with it; Zack's got a new covey pinned down over there, I do believe. . . ."

It had been a wonderful autumn followed by one more; then the pointer Zachariah, grizzled and rheumatic, had died one winter night in his sleep. To Harold Ullman it had been like losing a friend to whom he owed a great deal. Apparently it had been more than that to lonely Uncle Hal. He'd talked a bit about getting a new pup they could train together, but his heart had not been in it. Harold Ullman had come in after school one day to find him sitting motionless in the big chair in front of the dying fire, a battered old dog dish on his knees. Harold had put the dish back into the kitchen before calling the doctor, because he didn't want Uncle Hal to be remembered as a sentimental old fool.

Uncle Hal's will had left his nephew a sizeable sum of money, and the guns. Harold Ullman had stored the rifles he'd never been shown how to use, and the fine old double and over-under shotguns Uncle Hal had bought and hung on the walls to look at because they were so beautiful, although he'd admitted that he never could shoot one of those fancy, classy pieces worth a damn; he'd always been a country boy and a pumpgun man at heart. The familiar Winchester Model 12 had not been stored, of course, it wouldn't have felt right not to have one gun around; but now it was broken, smashed, and Harold Ullman could not for the life of him remember just how it had all come about; how he could possibly have goofed such an elementary marksmanship problem after Uncle Hal's careful training, not to mention a few pointers he'd received later, courtesy of the U.S. Army. . . .

"Mr. Ullman."

It was, he supposed, time to try again. He had to rejoin the living some time, although it was a lot more pleasant down in this dark and undemanding Demerol underworld in which he'd found himself after the early nightmare operating-room experiences he tried not to think about, when they were putting all the pieces back together again, not always under total anesthesia. He opened his eyes and fought back the panicky claustrophobia that always came when he was reminded of the cocoon of bandages and other stuff in which he was encased like one of those supposedly humorous cartoons of mummylike accident victims in hospital beds saying very funny things or having very funny things said to them.

"No, don't try to talk, Mr. Ullman."

A nurse was bending over him, middle-aged and plain. She held up a pad of cheap paper and a black felt-tipped pen.

"There's a police officer who'd like to ask you some questions," she said. "He's been waiting quite a while; do you feel up to seeing him now and getting it over with? The doctor thinks it's better if you write out your answers. We don't want to disturb anything, do we, now that our face is healing so well."

Then there was a uniformed figure at the side of the bed, and the questions began.

"What time did you come home that night, Mr. Ullman?"

It was so long ago that he could hardly remember. Since then, he'd had a long, leisurely tour of hell; it was hard to recall the details of what had gone before. After thinking hard, however, he came up with the answer and wrote it down, pleased to find that his fingers, at least, still worked properly, even if other parts of him were totally immobilized by wire and adhesive tape and plaster.

12:15.

"Did you see any suspicious vehicles in the neighborhood?"

NO

"What did you see when you entered your home?"

GODAWFUL MESS, he wrote, and then, MEN

"How many men?"

FOUR

"Did you recognize any of them?"

NO, MASKED

"You call them men, Mr. Ullman. Does that mean you're certain they were adults? Not just a bunch of hopped-up kids vandalizing people's houses for kicks?"

He thought for a moment, pulling the pictures out of the memory file, and examining them closely before writing down his answer.

NO KIDS

"Can you describe any of them, sir?"

73

He concentrated on the mental pictures for several seconds, and wrote carefully:

ONE 6+, 200+, FAIR, SKI MASK. ANOTHER 5 6-8, 130-150, DARK, NYLON STOCKING, MUSTACHE? OTHER TWO BEHIND NOT CLEAR

"That's very good, Mr. Ullman, very good indeed. You're very observant; you make an excellent witness. Do you always keep a loaded shotgun in the hall closet?"

The technique annoyed him: the fulsome praise followed by the swift, suspicious question. He wrote:

ONLY MAGAZINE LOADED NOT CHAMBER

"I understand; of course you wouldn't keep a fully loaded weapon standing around, sir. That wouldn't be very safe, would it? But did you have any particular reason for putting your gun where it would be handy? Had you made any recent enemies, received any threats, that sort of thing?"

He found himself getting angry. Why was the uniformed jerk wasting his time and strength by cross-examining him about a perfectly ordinary shotgun kept in a perfectly ordinary place? He wrote:

NO THREATS ORDINARY PRECAUTION GUN NO DAMN GOOD UNAVAILABLE

The policeman apparently sensed his irritation, and changed the subject quickly.

"I understand that you returned a day earlier than you'd planned, Mr. Ullman. Was there any particular reason for this?"

The question was strangely unsettling; the answer lay somewhere in the memory area he was forbidden to enter.

DON'T RECALL

"But it was thought locally that you wouldn't be home until Thanksgiving, isn't that correct? So the gang involved, if they'd done their homework, would have had reason to believe they could break into your house undisturbed."

Now the guy was simply showing off the careful police work he'd done around the neighborhood, and the brilliant deductions he'd made from the assembled data. What did he expect from a witness who could barely focus, applause? When no response came, the policeman changed the subject again.

"If the larger man was wearing a ski mask, how did you know he was fair, Mr. Ullman?"

HAIR ON WRISTS

74

"But you're not certain whether or not the smaller man, the dark one, had a mustache?"

IMPRESSION ONLY I

He tried hard to concentrate on the writing, but the letters were not forming themselves properly any longer, and the pain he'd been keeping at bay was starting to break through the outer defenses. He felt the pad and pen being taken from him.

"I'm sorry, Officer," said the nurse's voice. "We're getting tired now; we'd better rest."

"That's all right, I was just about finished. Thank you, Mr. Ullman. You've been a big help." The policeman rose and hesitated. "Perhaps I shouldn't say this, Mr. Ullman, but you should be aware that we really don't recommend resistance in situations like the one you encountered. But I guess that advice comes a little late, huh?"

Harold Ullman listened to the closing door and thought it was a weird attitude for an officer of the law to display: actually recommending publicly that citizens should permit criminals to go about their illegal business unmolested. Whose side was the guy on, anyway? He felt a stirring of the bedclothes and the familiar hypodermic sting in the right butt, the left being unavailable under multiple layers of medical armor. The pain was closing in now and he held on tightly, waiting for the drug to take hold. Presently he felt himself sliding down and down into that other world, the dark, gentle, painless one with which he was becoming very familiar. It was a bit frightening in a way. You could see how somebody who had it tough upstairs might get permanently hooked on this happy, lower spirit-land in which endless thoughts and memories drifted pleasantly through your mind; it was simply a matter of picking the mental film or tape you wanted to view and inserting it in the mental machinery and pushing the button. Okay, he thought, let's run through "The Boat" again, that's always nice.

The boat. It had been a hell of an expensive project, much more so than he'd anticipated, much more so than he could possibly have been able to afford if it hadn't been for Uncle Hal's legacy which, safely invested, had increased substantially in the intervening years—that was after the Vietnam mess, of course.

Harold Ullman had had no strong feelings about the conflict, except that it had seemed to be a pretty dumb mess for a sensible nation to get itself into. Why jump deliberately into the stinking sewer the French had just crawled out of? However, he couldn't see himself inventing some high moral principles he didn't have to avoid getting drafted and, perhaps, shot at. Or running off to hide somewhere. It was apparently considered perfectly respectable and even fashionable in some circles; but he knew that if he did it, he'd spend the rest of his life wondering if he hadn't cooked up a bunch of phony scruples simply because he was scared.

It was supposed to be, nowadays, a ridiculous reason for doing something—that it frightened you silly to think about it—but it had always seemed perfectly valid to him. What the hell, you couldn't go through life surrounded by gibbering fears when it was so easy to face them down. Well, as a rule. Some wouldn't face down. He'd always been afraid of heights, for instance, and after kicking himself up to a few high and terrifying spots he knew he always would be. Okay. Scratch mountaineering and flagpole sitting. But mostly, if you walked straight at your terrors, you discovered that they were shadow fears and you'd come right out the other side unharmed.

Well, he still didn't know about war and getting shot at, but at least he could tell himself that he'd faced it as far as seemed sensible and maybe a little farther. There had been no real need, for instance, to shoot such good scores in basic training when all the fumble-fingered city boys around him were endangering the whole rifle range with their wild, blind firing. A sensible guy would have carelessly thrown at least a few shots off target so as not to attract attention. Instead, he'd been surprised and pleased to discover that what he'd learned with a shotgun carried over pretty well to other weapons, although he'd heard it wasn't really supposed to work that way. Maybe the important thing was that it didn't bother him a bit when the piece reared up and belted him in the chops; he'd been there before. He'd really enjoyed mastering that ugly, clattering brute of a gun and his marksmanship, actually only mediocre but brilliant by comparison with that of the rest of that particular crop of draftees, had almost, he knew, earned him an assignment to a certain special unit where his life expectancy would have sent an insurance man staggering to the nearest bar for a couple of reviving double martinis.

But the PR boys had got to him first. Somebody had needed a photographer fast and, since his record showed some almost-professional camera experience in college, he'd been it. It had, of course, been a relief in a way, and he hadn't felt obliged to fight it any further. He'd put himself on the line, dammit. If they wanted to take him off, that was their business. But he knew he'd always wonder, a little, what it had really been like over there.

The rest of that undeclared war had been a long, dull stateside grind enlivened by an occasional photographic panic party; but he'd learned a lot about picture-taking under circumstances when it was very unwise to fail. The army had knocked a lot of fuzzy creative-art notions out of him and turned him into a reasonably effective working pro. So he had his career waiting; and what else was he going to do with his life besides working for a living? The answer came more or less by accident. During one of the endless standby periods when there were no more lenses to be cleaned or films to be developed, somebody had handed him a dog-eared copy of Captain Joshua Slocum's *Sailing Alone Around The World*.

He'd sometimes wondered how many lives had been changed by that book. Like most kids growing up near the water, he'd done some sailing; and now the more he read of the old sea captain's adventures, the more intriguing it seemed, just getting the hell out there in a little sailing ship of your own. He spent the remainder of his stint in uniform, whenever he had a moment free, doing research on boats. One day he found what he wanted in a small advertisement; after that it was merely a matter of writing for the literature and waiting for the creeps in Washington to pull their collective fingers out of their collective rectums and put an end to the murderous idiocy that, by this time, wasn't getting anybody anywhere except buried. . . .

"Mr. Ullman."

He wanted to protest angrily. Goddamn it, he still hadn't got to the interesting part of the videotape, the part that showed the boat being built in that funny little shop in Maine, and launched, and rigged—all the wonderful days and weeks and months of being under nobody's orders for a change. With his severance pay and the bonds he'd bought in the service and what had been in the bank already he could afford to loaf for a while, worrying about nothing but the boat—well, the boat and a girl he'd met, but she'd just damn well have to wait her turn and console herself with the fact that her name was prominently displayed on the little cutter's transom. And then there had been that first hairy, lonely, lovely cruise down the coast, when he'd had to scramble every wet, foggy inch of the way to keep ahead of his own abysmal nautical ignorance. . . .

"Mr. Ullman, there's somebody who'd like to see you, just for a moment."

"Harold."

Everything stopped at the sound of the voice. He opened his eyes abruptly, and it all came back with a rush, all the unbearable facts he'd wanted to forget a little longer. He was a married man and this was his wife, this slender handsome dark-haired girl now approaching the bed, whose name he'd proudly watched being painted on his new sailboat way back in those prehistoric days he'd just been dreaming about. They'd supposedly loved each other. There had been a few problems, it had taken a few years, but in the end they'd worked it out, and it was all going to be wonderful again. They'd crossed the last hurdle, they'd had it made, until . . .

He made some fumbling gestures, still watching her, and felt the pad and pen being put into his hands. He looked away from her and wrote rapidly; and showed what he'd written. He heard the nurse gasp. He saw Nancy go quite pale, her pallor emphasizing a dying discoloration around one eye. There was a healing cut on her lower lip. He saw that when she stepped forward she moved a little awkwardly, as if her whole body had recently been roughly handled, bruised, and more than bruised; well, that figured. One didn't have to be clairvoyant to guess what a man who'd viciously kick a barely conscious man would do to a woman in his power. Once, Ullman knew, the mere thought of such a thing happening to her would have broken his heart; it still hurt, a little. He saw that her face seemed suddenly to have become thin and ugly.

"But I couldn't let you *shoot*. . . ." he heard her protest. "You know I couldn't let you *kill*. . . ."

She was quite unbelievable, he thought grimly. She still couldn't see what she'd done to them. She still had to insist that she'd been right, as if her rightness had anything to do with it. For her goddamned self-righteous rightness she'd killed them both; because they'd never be alive that way again, together.

The nurse was pulling her away. "You must understand that we're under heavy sedation, Mrs. Ullman," she was saying soothingly as they left the room. "We're not thinking clearly yet. You mustn't take us too seriously, dear."

He lay there feeling the pain and ignoring it. It had been

such a simple thing, he thought. Just a simple test of loyalty. There were times when elaborate social theories no longer mattered, when fine humanitarian principles, no matter how correct, were totally irrelevant; times when if two people truly loved each other it was just a clear-cut choice between *us* and *them*. Faced with that choice, in a moment of common danger, she had, incredibly, chosen *them*. Harold Ullman looked at what he'd written:

GET THE TREACHEROUS BITCH OUT OF HERE

CHAPTER 9

December

Latitude 26°N; Longitude 80°W

La Maison, well up in Miami's conspicuous hotel-and-shopping-center complex called Omni, was small and refined—very, very refined. The maître d' checked your reservation with the chilly remoteness of an armed guard confirming a security clearance; but once your credentials were established he seated you with a grand flourish at the side of the tiny, quiet dining room and determined your drink preference; then, almost immediately, a respectful waiter glided up with your Scotch on the rocks with a dash of water—well, the water came in a small carafe on the side, and was added dropwise under your watchful eye so you could attain the exact degree of dilution desired.

Philip Martin sipped his drink and reflected that motherly waitresses were all very well in their place, and there was certainly a definite need for pretty serving wenches in scanty costumes and, for a preference, black mesh stockings; but for real classy dining nothing took the place of a truly professional male waiter in a black tailcoat and boiled shirt; and Francesca was a hell of a lovely name, wasn't it? And the Columbus girl is twenty-one years old, a little too young for you but plenty old enough to, probably, have put it out for every *pachuco* on the block. Anyway, you recently shot her brother to death and now your mission in life is to bury her daddy in jail or, perhaps, if somebody gets excited at the wrong moment, a more permanent location. So leave it, lover boy, leave it.

But there was always something special about *knowing* what you were looking at, outside and in, clear down to the genes and chromosomes. In a way it was like seeing a bitch from a registered kennel instead of the local animal shelter. With this one, all the data was available. Dirty jeans or no dirty jeans, the bloodlines were on record, and the record went back to long before the *conquistadores*. You knew what kind of pups she'd throw; they'd have this kind of aquiline nose and that kind of big dark eyes. You knew that in the end, if she lived that long, she'd be one of those small, sharp, bright-eyed Latin ladies who'd still be beautiful at eighty. And what an aristocratic snob you turned out to be after all, Mr. Philip Martin, and what an operative, dreaming about a pretty college dropout when you should be thinking serious thoughts about the Major and his phony sportfishing camp out on Big Manatee Key....

He got quickly to his feet as the maître d' approached, escorting Miss Elizabeth Cameron as if she were something rare and precious that he was presenting to the honored guest as a gift of the house. Martin had a moment to study her: very slender in a severely tailored black pantsuit relieved by a soft white shirt with ruffles at wrist and throat. She looked very handsome and very elegant, but she didn't look like anything you could possibly make love to. Tonight there wasn't even the impulse to visualize her in bedroom terms; any more than you'd entertain yourself, unless you were of that persuasion, by dreaming of fucking one of the Three Musketeers, who'd undoubtedly had the same lean, hard, swordsman look. It was just as well. A man-eating executive babe, Tommy had called her without even seeing her; and Tommy had been right. Just one pass, hell, any hint of desire, and this woman would have you exactly where she wanted you. This game would have to be played very cool indeed.

"I hope I'm not late," she said as she sat down at his side, with a quick smile of thanks for the maître d'.

"No, I was early. It was easy; I'm staying here. Besides, it's part of the secret-agent technique, to get to the secret rendezvous first."

"Is that when you are, Mr. Martin, a secret agent?"

He said, "You've done your homework, Miss Cameron; you said so yourself. You know what I am."

"Yes," she said, "I know. Up to a point. Of course, nobody ever comes right out and says what you people *do*."

"Do the people out at Langley tell you what they do?"

"No, but at least one can make some informed guesses. . . . I think I'll pass up the cocktails," she said as the waiter paused before them. "I'd like some wine with dinner, and it always tastes better if one doesn't put a lot of hard stuff before it, don't you think?"

"No," he said deliberately, tasting his Scotch, "as a matter of fact I don't think so, not really, although I know it's the traditional idea."

She gave him a quick, sharp glance. "I see. No polite agreement with the lady just to be polite, is that the policy?" She laughed softly. "Very well, Mr. Martin. Since we're being so forthright, I'll satisfy my nosy curiosity by asking you a very personal question. I've been wondering why . . . I mean you don't look like a man who'd be ashamed of his name or his ancestors."

He thought: now you know, *amigo*. She was bound to get around to it eventually and you wanted to see how she'd do it; and she came right out and did it straight instead of pussyfooting around it. *Gringos* one; greasers nothing.

He said, "Isn't that fairly irrelevant to our problem, Miss Cameron?"

She laughed again. "In other words, I should mind my own damn business?"

"You said it, I didn't." He grinned. "If you must know, my Papa was professor of history at the University of Havana, a very theoretical and opinionated sort of guy. For one thing, he thought Batista was a real stinker and expressed his opinion often enough that the feeling became mutual; that's why we left Cuba, actually, while that one was still in power. However, Papa had no more affection for Castro when he took over. That didn't leave us much of any place to go back to, so we stayed here—well, out on the West Coast, where Papa got a teaching position at a small private college first, and then at Berkeley. He liked it out West where most people, even those who speak Spanish, think of Cuba as just another funny little island up in the Bahamas or maybe down in the

81

Virgins. He was particularly concerned, after the general exodus, that we shouldn't get mixed up with the various noisy gangs of expatriates here in Miami." Martin paused. "Since you're not having a drink, maybe we ought to order, and see about that wine you wanted."

"If you like." When the decisions had been made, and the waiter and wine steward dismissed, she leaned back beside him comfortably and said, "All right, so your family settled in California."

"Uh huh, but are you sure you want to hear all this?"

"I asked, didn't I?"

He said, "Not really." When she looked at him quickly, he went on: "What you really asked is why a guy named Martinez is helping the U.S. government conduct operations against a guy named Colombo. Is blood thicker than water or isn't it?"

After a moment, she smiled. "Of course you're right."

"Why of course?" he demanded. "How would you feel if, in the course of a drug operation involving a gent named, say, McGregor, somebody started interrogating you closely because you have the good old name Cameron, also Scottish. A bit racist there, aren't you, implying that while you Scots can aspire to higher loyalties, us spics are incapable of surmounting our primitive tribal emotions."

She flushed; then she shook her head ruefully. "You play rough, Mr. Martin. I apologize very humbly—although, of course, us Camerons have been here a few generations longer, haven't we? But I won't pry any more if you really mind."

"Oh, I don't mind," he said. "I just wanted us to have it clear what we're really talking about. To proceed: Papa was a historian full of grand historical theories. He'd studied a large number of historical situations involving displaced people like us. He had nothing but scorn for the folks who, throughout history, had wasted their lives yearning for lost homelands. Flexibility and adaptability were needed to survive in this world, he said. Furthermore, he had very strong feelings about the duties and responsibilities of political refugees fleeing one country who were kindly afforded sanctuary by another; he thought there had been too many instances of such hospitality being abused. Maybe he overreacted a bit, maybe I wouldn't have done it quite the same way if I'd been old enough to cast a vote at the time; but anyway the Cuban Martinezes became the American Martins, and as you can hear we *habla inglés* pretty goddamn good, *sí?* And the male heir, after being thoroughly Americanized in various institutions of learning, even went off and fought a rather stupid little war because military service is, after all, one of the ancient historical duties of citizenship."

When he stopped, Elizabeth Cameron hesitated, and said carefully, "Your papa seems to be quite a person."

Martin shook his head sadly. "Tut-tut, always the double talk. What you really think is that he must have been a dreadful old tyrannical nut, deliberately rejecting for the whole family the ancient ethnic heritage, and then actually encouraging the only son to go out and get himself killed. The melting pot is strictly outmoded and patriotism is for the birds, right?"

"I wish you wouldn't put words into my mouth, Mr. Martin," said the slender woman beside him. "And do you really think patriotism is the right word for—"

"Just hold it right there!" He couldn't help the sharpness of his voice. "The court will entertain the lady's opinions on *that* subject after it has been established how many Purple Hearts she's entitled to wear." There was a brief silence. Martin went on, "I said it was a stupid little war, didn't I? You're welcome to criticize the political and moral aspects of it all you want. But unless you went out there and got shot at, Miss Cameron, you're not entitled to comment on the motives of those who did." He grimaced. "Sorry. I just get kind of fed up with the fashionable disapproval of people who were careful to stay safe at home. Let's just say it was a very interesting and educational experience; and it led directly to my present job with ATD, so I can hardly complain."

He threw out the initials deliberately to lead them away from the awkward subject, but she did not take the bait. Instead she frowned, obviously thinking back, and said, "You used the past tense."

"Referring to Papa? Yes, he's dead. They're both dead." He hesitated and went on: "The bulldozers were working in the rubble when I got back; there wasn't enough left to rebuild. I suppose somebody's got another little house on that lot now, in that tidy development just outside Berkeley; and everybody's saying how it just shows you shouldn't sell property to greasy foreigners who go around blowing each other up."

Elizabeth Martin licked her barely-colored lips. "They were killed? Murdered? Why?"

"Well, we had a hard time figuring that out," Martin said. "Why should some of the Miami Crazies, as they're called, suddenly get all upset about one old intellectual gent who'd been living unmolested on the other side of the continent for years, even if he had Anglicized his name and refused to contribute to any of the so-called patriotic movements? Then we learned that somebody in Castro's department of revolutionary education, or whatever he calls it, had very belatedly realized that there existed a fairly prominent Cuban professor of history with a fairly prominent Cuban name who'd been banished by Castro's predecessor and might therefore just possibly consider taking employment under Fidel. Perhaps there were internal political reasons why a sudden intellectual status symbol was needed. Emissaries were sent. Nobody knows what was said, but presumably Papa told them he didn't consider a leftist dictator much improvement over a rightist one; and that he was quite happy as an *Americano*. Well, the Castro emissaries were good Latins, and conspiracy is always in the blood. Maybe they were also angry; Papa wasn't always very polite. In any case, we have determined that a leak was arranged to one of the wilder little Miami groups, to the effect that the offer had been made and Papa was considering it, something like that." Martin made a wry face. "That poor naive old wop, Machiavelli, should have gone to Spain and learned something about real intrigue."

"But I don't see—"

"It was really very logical," Martin said. "The back-to-Cuba boys in Miami have been getting more and more hysterical as their ranks get thinner with the years and success moves farther and farther out of their reach. Currently, of course, with occasional gestures of friendship passing between the countries, they're practically rabid. But even back then, they were a pretty hair-trigger bunch; and the idea that an expatriate Cuban intellectual with an international reputation might actually be returning voluntarily to lend his prestige to the bearded devil . . . Fidel's flunkies had very little to lose. If there was no action, too bad, you can't win them all. If, on the other hand, the counterrevolutionary hotheads in Florida were crazy enough to chase clear across the continent and make an attempt on Papa's life, and were successful, again it was too bad, but the revolution wasn't out much; after all, he'd already said no. But if there was an attempt that failed, or if the crazies simply tried to threaten or intimidate Papa, he might just get frightened enough or angry enough to change his mind. Well, the

Fidelistos struck out. The attempt was made and it didn't fail."

"You were still overseas when it happened?" Elizabeth Cameron asked after a little pause.

"I got the word on my way home. It somewhat tarnished, shall we say, the pleasure of having survived. As soon as I could get to San Francisco after fighting my way out of the Army red-tape jungles, I went out and viewed the scene of the crime and paid my respects at the grave. When I got back to my hotel there was a note asking me to call a certain number in Washington, D.C. I did and found that somebody I'd never heard of had a job for a gent with my rather specialized, shall we say, Vietnam experience, who spoke Spanish fluently. The Old Man keeps his eyes open for suitable material, properly motivated."

"I see." After a moment. "That would be Mr. Meriwether, of the ATD."

"Correct. Section P, for preventive action. He also supervises Section R, for remedial action—they're the lads who go in after the fact and try to repair the damage. You know, place the snipers strategically, talk the hostages free, find and defuse the bombs, that sort of thing. Our job in P is to try to keep hostages from being taken in the first place. Or bombs from being placed, or whatever. Next question?"

She regarded him for a moment. "What should I be asking?"

"What you're thinking, of course. Was Don Jaime Colombo responsible for the death of my parents?"

She smiled faintly. "What you need is a ventriloquist's dummy, Mr. Martin, not a dinner companion. Well, was he?"

"The answer is no. There's absolutely no reason to think he was in any way involved. He's carefully kept himself clear of all those maniac groups; he probably despises them in his aristocratic way. We know the gang of nuts responsible, although we still haven't determined which one or two individuals actually traveled out there and did the job. We may never know. The police have pretty well stopped working on it; and I am under strict orders to do no investigating on my own. It was one of the conditions under which I was employed. Moonlighting for personal reasons is not encouraged. But it wasn't Columbo; so you can set your mind at rest. I am not conducting a personal vendetta on government time."

"Aren't you, Mr. Martin?"

He regarded her, frowning. After a moment, he grinned. "All right. I think I see what you mean. The experience has certainly given me a fairly strong prejudice against terrorists and terrorism in general. As far as I'm concerned, one of your drug peddlers is a noble and worthy fellow compared to these political freaks we deal with, of whatever nationality, who try to scare the world into correcting their particular grievances by murdering people at random. . . ."

He stopped, as the wine was presented, tasted, and pronounced fit for human consumption; then their dinners were being set before them. Elizabeth Cameron had a healthy appetite; and there wasn't much conversation for a while. She was a very slick article, Martin reflected wryly; she'd obviously determined to learn every last thing she could about him before making up her mind, but he had no idea whether her reaction, to date, was favorable or unfavorable. The lady would make a good poker player.

"I recommend a spot of Nassau Royale if you've never had any," he said later, after the plates had been removed, the tablecloth discreetly swept clear of crumbs, and the coffee poured. "It comes from the Bahamas. I believe they've got some here. Kind of a light and elegant Kahlua."

"Very well," she said. She waited until the liqueur arrived, and tasted it judiciously, and set down the glass. "Yes, very good," she said, "and now that we're well fed, Mr. Martin, I suppose we'd better get down to business. From the records I examined this afternoon at your request, I learned that as the result of a tip from a public-spirited yachtsman, a sizeable load of marijuana was seized recently off Big Galleon Key, wherever that may be. The vessel involved, the *Three Sisters,* seems to have been owned by this Mr. Columbus in whom you're interested, although another name appears on the public record. Columbus' son was actually in command and, I understand, tried to resist capture and was killed by one of the arresting officers. A certain Mr. Philip Martin." She looked at him thoughtfully. "No vendetta, you said, Mr. Martin?"

"The kid had a machine pistol and was about to wipe out the whole damned boarding party, including me."

"Yes, I'm sure your action was unavoidable and even, according to the Coast Guard report, quite commendable; but I find it curious just the same." After a moment, she went on: "There are indications that the same *Three Sisters* may have made other smuggling voyages in the past. Another fishing craft seized under somewhat similar circumstances some time ago—again, coincidentally, a private yacht was involved in the capture—may also have been financed by Mr. Columbus. There are suggestions that he has for years been making considerably more money than the records of his small Miami business can account for, money that is carefully not reflected in his way of life. He still lives in a rather shabby little house and drives a small and inexpensive four-year-old car. There are also hints that certain unsavory characters affiliated with organized crime here in Florida have been receiving substantial shipments of cocaine as well as steady supplies of marijuana. Various agencies have been trying hard to locate the source and now, with this latest capture, think they have it pinpointed: Mr. Columbus. This is the man you're asking us to forget about."

Martin shook his head ruefully. "You're loading the dice, Miss Cameron. You're making it sound as if little old Jimmy Columbus is the kingpin of the local drug-smuggling racket. Well, I have no doubt that if he's arrested you folks will build him up as a real mastermind of crime; but the fact is—and you know it as well as I do—that every jerk who can lay his hands on a boat and set a compass course south is heading down there to load up, knowing that he'll have no trouble finding a market when he gets back, syndicate or otherwise. If Columbus is doing it, he's just one of hundreds."

"If?"

Martin grinned. "Sorry, I was being defensive. There's not much doubt that he's doing it. That is, I don't know about the hard stuff you mentioned—hell, you don't need a boat for that, you can get rich on what you can carry in a suitcase—but the bulky merchandise, yes, he's been bringing it in all right; but he's got lots and lots of company. And if you do manage to get the ironclad goods on him, what happens?"

"What do you mean?"

"Read the newspapers," Martin said. "Take a look at the kind of sentences they're handing out for marijuana offenses these days; and pot is what you'll probably get him for, isn't it? The other stuff goes overboard in a weighted sack at the first sign of trouble. And just how hard do you think you'll be able to hit him? If you were the prosecutor, how would you like to tackle the case knowing that the handsome old exile, who'd lost everything when he was driven from his homeland, would testify that he was doing it all for his lovely daughter—now that his son has been murdered by the Drug Gestapo—so she could get an education and become a good American citizen? One slap on the wrist coming up."

"I see," Elizabeth Cameron said. "You want him to be punished more severely, is that it?"

He frowned. It seemed out of character and out of context. They were neither of them gods dispensing rewards and punishments.

"Punished, hell," he said. "I want to see him taken out of circulation, Miss Cameron. That's a dangerous man, a very dangerous man. He's typical terrorist material; the psychological profile is unmistakable. All the evidence we have indicates that nothing really matters to him but his sacred cause. He's been brooding about it for damn near twenty years, laying his plans carefully while everybody else, including the U.S. Government, was going off half-cocked. Now he's ready to move at last, and God help anybody who gets in his way."

"What *are* his plans?"

Martin hesitated; but the instructions were clear. Frankness and honesty were the watchwords of the day. He said, "We've established a connection between Columbus and a man calling himself Harry Ochs who recently took over an old fishing lodge on Big Manatee Key, which actually isn't very big. It's just bigger than Little Manatee Key, which you can spit across with a favorable wind. The funny thing is that Ochs doesn't seem to be much of an angler, and if you go out there and want to hire a professional bonefish or tarpon guide you'll find they're all busy that day and all the rooms and boats just happen to be booked, sorry."

"And Harry Ochs is what? Or should I say who?"

"Harry Ochs is Major Horst Ochsner, generally known simply as The Major. Well, he's entitled to the rank. He's held it officially once or twice; he's also been practically everything else from corporal to general, depending on the army he was serving in at the time. He's a professional soldier of fortune; and recently he's developed a profitable little specialty. It seems he's a genius at putting together a small, tough, strike or penetration force, just a handful of super-trained men who can drive through practically anything to reach and destroy their objective. In this case we've got every reason to believe the objective is Fidel Castro."

Elizabeth Cameron regarded him for a moment without expression; then she reached out deliberately for her liqueur glass and took a small sip of the contents. He noted that her hand, framed by white ruffles at the wrist, was slim and strong.

"But you should have no objection to that," she said calmly, "after what Castro's people did to your parents."

It was going wrong. He could sense it. The woman was coming out from behind the careful poker face at last; and she wasn't the woman he'd thought her, judging by the way she kept on repeatedly attributing to him petty personal motives, desire for punishment or revenge, that should have had no part in this discussion.

"I have no objection to anybody shooting down Fidel," he said. "Tyrants have been fair game since the dawn of history. Be my guest. I don't even call that terrorism; that's simply direct political action against a legitimate target. But it's kind of my job to see that it isn't done from American soil with American support—Washington doesn't want to be blamed for any more incidents of that kind—and it's particularly my job to see that it doesn't lead to anything more drastic and dangerous."

"More drastic and dangerous than assassination?" Elizabeth Cameron asked. "I don't follow you, Mr. Martin."

"The assassination of Castro is dangerous only to Castro," he said. "His safety is no concern of mine. Anyway, he can take care of himself. That's just the trouble; he damn well can. Columbus hasn't got a chance in hell of making his hit, or having it made for him. And aside from the international repercussions, that would be okay, too, and we'd just leave him to it, if we thought he'd take his licking like a little sportsman and pick up his marbles, what was left of them, and go home quietly. But he won't. I told you, he's typical terrorist material. Terrorists never take defeat quietly. They've always got to do as much damage as possible as they go down. And I might add that goes for Ochsner too, for slightly different reasons. He's another of the doomsday men, as my Chief likes to call them."

"Doomsday men?" Elizabeth Cameron smiled faintly. "Aren't you being just a bit melodramatic?"

"That's a very dangerous attitude for a lady in your responsible position," Martin said. "Because they exist all right: the individuals who totally reject the sissy modern notion that survival is always essential. History is full of them, men and women who went to the stake happily, certain they were bound for Paradise. Gents who charged into battle eagerly hoping that, by dying bravely, they could earn a first-class ticket to Heaven, or Nirvana, or Valhalla. Well, the life-hereafter bit doesn't seem all that persuasive these

89

days; but the doomsday folks are still with us. They're the people you've either got to let live on their own terms or you've got to kill them, and they never die easily. Hell, look at that kid I had to kill, for a few pounds of lousy grass, if you want to look at it that way; but he wasn't looking at it that way. As far as he was concerned, we could either let him through to do the job his daddy had given him, or we could shoot him; he wasn't coming back alive and unsuccessful. Ochsner is another case in point. If he's ever caught and brought to trial anywhere, for anything, he's finished, because there's some swastika stuff in his background that won't bear investigation. So the Major won't let himself be taken alive, and if anybody gives him half a chance—Castro or anybody else—he'll stage the damnedest instant *Götterdämmerung* you ever saw. And for different reasons, so will Don Jaime Colombo."

"I'm afraid you're being a little too psychological for me, Mr. Martin," Elizabeth Cameron said. "Let's get back to facts my simple mind can grasp. For instance, what is Mr. Columbus supposed to gain, besides personal satisfaction, if his plan does succeed and his Major Ochsner does manage to reach Castro and kill him?"

"Oh, that's just phase one," Martin said dryly. "Then he has a fine old *politico* named Esteban Ybarra—well, those are two of his names; like all of us he has a sizeable stockpile to draw on—ready to step forward and receive the instant homage of the liberated Cuban multitudes."

"I see. And you don't think that will happen?"

"Have you been over there recently, Miss Cameron?" When she shook her head, he said, "Well, I haven't, either. The easing of relations between the two countries hasn't yet got to the point where ex-Cubans are welcome back; and it didn't seem worth while to bleach my hair and go the disguise-and-phony-papers route. But I did get a colleague of mine, big, blond, and strictly Anglo, to take a trip over to Havana—well, Barlovento nearby—with a bunch of U.S. boats participating in a recent Cuban-sponsored fishing tournament in honor of Ernest Hemingway. I wanted to confirm my own theory that Columbus is indulging in the same wishful thinking as all the rest. The report I got back was that the fishing was great; and that the people, in spite of rationing and other restrictions, didn't look very much as if they were yearning for a return to Batista's rule. Oh, I don't say they're euphorically happy under Castro, and one day they may ditch him and get somebody else; but if they do it won't be a reactionary old aristocratic retread like Don Esteban. Columbus is dreaming just as much as the harebrained hotheads he scorns. He's just putting a little more thought and money behind his dreams."

"So you don't think he'll ever get as far as proposing this Ybarra for office, or however he plans to do it."

Martin shook his head emphatically. "Not a chance. That shoreline is so loaded with patrol craft and military installations these days that even the mosquitoes have to carry I.D.s. Columbus is thinking of the good old days when Castro himself made an easy landing on the Cuban coast from a yacht with the odd name *Granma*. Well, don't think for a moment Castro himself isn't keeping that old mini-invasion of his very clearly in mind and making sure it never happens again. Ochsner's strike group will probably never even make it ashore; and if it does, it'll be wiped out within sight of the beach. Castro will find it a hell of an expensive job—the Major is a pro, after all—and his boys will wish they were having it easy back in Angola, but they've got the equipment and manpower to do it, and no matter what it costs they'll get it done. And when they do, Columbus will inevitably figure that somebody betrayed him—these people never fail through any fault of their own, you know; they're always betrayed by somebody else, or so they claim—and he'll flip his everlasting lid. He'll grab the biggest weapon he can find and aim it at the most vulnerable and important target within range, terrorist-fashion, and he'll give us the choice of meeting his terms or else. And if that is allowed to happen it'll mean that our P-section has failed and it's time for our R-section to move in." Martin grimaced. "Miss Cameron, it's my job to see that the poor, brave, hard-working fellows in R are saved all that trouble and risk. All I ask is that you people stay clear and leave us room to function."

There was a little pause. "That's a very interesting presentation, Mr. Martin," said the handsome woman beside him, and he knew he had failed.

He watched her drain her liqueur glass and set it delicately on the table. Her profile was wonderful; it was a pleasure to see a lady with a real forehead, nose and chin, which made, so to speak, a definite artistic statement instead of just saying vaguely, gee-ain't-I-cute.

She went on evenly, "Yes, very interesting. But let's just analyze it, shall we? I suppose the personal background is technically irrelevant, but still, you've come forward as an important figure in this so-called anti-terrorist operation—a spokesman, even—and I find it very intriguing that you neglected to mention the qualifications that seem to have got you selected for this elite organization of yours, particularly the fact that you were once a member of the highly controversial JS-group in Vietnam. The Jungle Scouts. I don't think I need to belabor the point. The violent methods employed by the Scouts got a great deal of publicity at one time, even though the court-martials promised never materialized. But that was just par for that particular course, wasn't it, Mr. Martin?"

He said, "When somebody invents a nonviolent war, we'll all be happy to fight it, Miss Cameron."

She glanced at him briefly, and went on: "You're very quick to defend an indefensible war; you even seem to consider assassination a valid political technique. It makes one wonder just what violent solution you have in mind for this current problem of yours, presented by this unfortunate Mr. Columbus against whom, you're so careful to point out, you have no personal grievance whatever—although you found yourself, very conveniently, forced to shoot his son. Strictly speaking, you may be telling the truth, but I hope you'll forgive me for suggesting that you're being slightly ingenuous, to say the least, when you ask me to believe that you are motivated entirely by your high-principled opposition to terrorism in general."

"Go on," he said when she hesitated.

She licked her lips. "I hate to say it, Mr. Martin, but I find it very curious that your parents should have made such a point of moving so far away from their exiled fellow-Cubans and gone to such extremes to erase their Cuban identities—yes, yes, I know, your father held some peculiar theories on the subject, didn't he? But isn't it possible there was some guilt involved, also? Being anti-Batista sounds very noble and the man really wasn't very nice; but anti-Batista can be very close to pro-Castro, can't it? In any case I believe it's an established fact that your father held some fairly radical views. Could they possibly have led him to take some long-ago action on Castro's behalf, perhaps premature, that caused him to go into hiding in this country, concealing himself and his family from his own people? And could it be that, instead of that elaborate scenario of sinister Castro intrigue by which you tried to explain his death, some patriotic anti-Castro

Cubans he'd injured years ago simply found him out at last? And that now, trained to violence overseas, you're simply trying to strike back; and you've selected Columbus as your target because, although he may not have been directly involved in your parents' death, he's one of the more respected and conspicuous members of the local Cuban community upon which you want to take revenge?"

He looked at her for a moment when she paused. "Where are you from, Miss Cameron?" he asked.

The question took her by surprise. She had to study it from all angles, to determine if it was loaded, before she answered reluctantly: "Des Moines. Des Moines, Iowa. Why?"

"Nothing," he said. "Sorry to interrupt. Go ahead."

She frowned. "No protests or denials?"

He said, "Hell, I told you my story. Now you're telling me yours. One of us is wrong. What's the point in my saying it's you when I've already, in effect, said that at great length."

"But you don't even know it," she said quickly. "Maybe your parents never told you the truth. In any case, if there was a confrontation between your father and Castro's people, as you claim, you have absolutely no way of knowing what was said. You admit you were thousands of miles away at the time."

He grinned. "Oh, dear, now you're trying to shake my simple faith in my poor martyred parents. Aren't you ashamed of yourself, Miss Cameron?"

A little color came into her face, and she looked straight across the room. "In any case, this is all pretty much beside the point," she said firmly. "The important fact is that, as far as James Columbus is concerned, you've given me nothing to go on, nothing at all. Say that he is using the proceeds of his smuggling operations to finance a foray into Cuba. I'm sure the FBI and other agencies can deal with this lethal Major with the German name and whatever armaments he's been stockpiling; they've handled numerous such cases before. And if we in PSCC don't put Columbus away for a long enough prison term to suit you, for his drug-related activities, they'll undoubtedly make a case against him for his connection with this illegal invasion force; and if they should fail, the IRS will probably be waiting to charge him with not paying tax on large amounts of undeclared income. You say that you simply want the man out of circulation. I think it's safe to promise that you will get your wish."

"When?"

"When we have our case, we'll move," she said, impatiently now. "When they have their cases, they'll move. But I'm afraid I can't possibly agree to leave the field clear for you and your ATD simply because of some amateur psychological theories that lead you to think that this one small expatriate Cuban gentleman should be considered as a sort of human nuclear bomb threatening the whole U.S.A." She was reaching into her small black purse. She took out two bills and laid them on the tablecloth. "Please take my share of the check out of that, Mr. Martin, and leave the change for our nice waiter. Oh, and Mr. Martin . . ."

"Yes?"

They were rising now, and the waiter in question was hastening forward to move the table aside. Elizabeth Cameron ignored him, looking at Martin with a sudden hardness in her fine gray eyes.

"A word of advice," she said coldly. "Not for you, but for your superior on this assignment of yours. Please inform the remote Mr. Richardson that I really don't like dealing with underlings. The next time he wants a favor, please tell him he'd be wiser to take the trouble to appear in person."

He watched her leave the room, straight and slim in her black suit; then he shrugged fatalistically and sat down to finish his coffee and liqueur.

Ten minutes later he was calling Washington from a pay telephone in the lobby. When a girl's voice answered, he said, "Martin. Reference Columbus account. Can you put me through?"

There was a pause while she checked. "Sure, you've got priority, Phil. He was out for a while but I believe he's back home now; let me give him a try."

Then he was talking to Mr. Meriwether, relating what had happened. "I guess I flubbed it," he said at the end. "Sorry. The lady, among other things, objected to having an underling handling the negotiations. Next time, she said in effect, please send her Number One or forget it."

"Yes," said Mr. Meriwether, a thousand miles away, "yes, I rather thought that might be her reaction when I arranged for the information to reach her, when she was checking up on you."

It was, Martin told himself firmly, no time for a display of Latin temperament. The damn old intrigue-happy bastard, he told himself; but you should have guessed the truth when

94

you got those oddball instructions. Frankness and honesty, for God's sake!

Mr. Meriwether was speaking again: "You know, she's a fairly ordinary midwestern girl who made good in the big time on the strength of her rather spectacular handsomeness, some rudimentary cleverness, and a great deal of determination. From Des Moines, Iowa, to Washington, D.C., by way of New York, New York. And the big thing they learn along that route, my dear boy, is that the most important thing in the world—in their world, anyway—is to organize a telephone call in such a way that you get to pick up the instrument last and the other party gets to do the humble waiting. Naturally, in her new prestigious position with the PSCC, she'd consider it a slight to have to deal with a mere field agent like you. I was counting on that. I couldn't afford to use Richardson anyway. It's the only thing he's good at, but he is good at that; he could undoubtedly have twisted the lady around his little finger." There was a little pause. "I hope you're not offended, Philip. I thought you could put on a better and more convincingly abrasive performance this way."

"No hard feelings," Martin said stiffly. "Any time you need a straight man, Martinez is waiting, dumb, and happy. But what, may I ask, was the point?"

"Really, Philip! After the analysis you've made of Ochsner, isn't it obvious?" When Martin made no response, Mr. Meriwether went on: "Do we want to tackle a man like that unnecessarily, dear boy? When there are so many agencies hungry for the credit? Of course, we could have asked for help, but I'd much rather not. You see what I mean?"

"Well, more or less," Martin said.

"If we'd requested assistance—and I doubt that even with your combat experience you could have handled the situation out at the Manatee Keys with only the limited manpower at our disposal—if we'd asked for reinforcements, we would have been responsible for them, wouldn't we? But what happens now? I presume you followed instructions and gave the lady a complete summary of what we know. It seems inevitable that she'll pass it along. Since the Ochsner information is outside her field of drug control, she will undoubtedly make a present of it to one of the agencies dealing with that sort of thing, building up credit for the future—I scratch your back today and you scratch mine tomorrow. I hope you made the point that the man is terribly dangerous."

"Yes, of course."

"Good, that leaves our consciences clear. In the meantime, of course, I will be sending a strongly worded protest to the Prohibited Substances Control Commission, stating that their deputy in the Miami area has proved totally uncooperative even though we've voluntarily shared with her all the information we have; that she obviously intends to put her puny little anti-smuggling campaign above the interests of the nation as a whole in this grave and dangerous matter; and that unless she and the local agencies under her direction are instructed to stop meddling with our case and our subject immediately, we will not be responsible for what happens." Mr. Meriwether laughed briefly. "Of course the PSCC will ignore my communication, but it will be on the record, my boy, with copies widely distributed in the usual manner. And in the meantime, you may be sure, some eager-beaver agency will be acting on our information, the information given them by Miss Cameron, and flushing out Ochsner for us. I don't envy them the job, and I do hope they'll be very, very careful; but nobody asked them to charge in ahead of us. In fact, the record will show clearly that we asked quite the opposite, eh, Philip?" A throaty chuckle came over the wire.

"If something does go haywire down there in the Keys, it could be kind of tough on Miss Cameron," Martin said after a little pause.

"Yes, it will be her baby, certainly; but she had the opportunity to leave it in our charge. If something dribbles through the diapers onto her handsome costume—or her handsome career—that is her clean-up problem now, not ours. Objection?"

"No objection. Why should I have any, after getting kicked in the teeth?"

"Precisely. Did she accuse you of being a dangerous vigilante type of questionable parentage, politically speaking?"

"I didn't know the table was bugged."

"It wasn't, but those smart-looking career girls from the prairies are as predictable as sunrise. The sophistication seldom goes beyond the clothes and the make-up and the coiffure." There was a brief pause. "Philip."

"Yes?"

"Now we concentrate on Columbus. It's almost certain that he'll react violently when his plans are destroyed by the elimination of Ochsner; we must be ready for that."

Martin said dryly, "You seem to forget that I am no longer managing this account, Mr. Meriwether."

"I'll speak to Tony Richardson, of course. But I would like *you* to make a special effort to determine in what direction Columbus is likely to move, so we can be prepared. And I have left instructions that will enable you to get in touch with me directly at any time, as today, if there is something you feel I should know." Mr. Meriwether cleared his throat. "Naturally, except in a real emergency, you will operate through the proper channels of command. . . ."

Martin grimaced as he hung up; but it was never any use brooding about the devious strategies employed by your government superiors to consolidate their exalted positions, if that was what the Old Man was doing.

He thought instead about a slim woman with gray eyes who was not, unfortunately, quite as clever as she thought herself. It was too bad, and although she'd disappointed him and even, you might say, insulted him, he hoped she would not be too badly hurt. And you're building yourself quite a fine mental harem there, aren't you, lover-boy? Just how many pretty ladies does your dream world need?

CHAPTER 10

December

Latitude 27°N; Longitude 77°W

At anchor in Marsh Harbour, Great Abaco, Bahamas, Dr. Paul Williams Fenwick sipped canned beer in the spacious cockpit of his twin-hulled thirty-eight-foot sailing yacht *Haleakala,* and admired the handsome eye splice he'd just completed. Ever since launching, the inner end of the main sheet, where it was secured to one of the husky blocks that gave it power enough to control the catamaran's big main-sail, had been tied off with a knot; a perfectly good and immensely strong bowline, *the* knot that would always hold under all conditions and could nevertheless be released instantly. You weren't a real sailor, you hadn't even started to become a real sailor, until you could tie a bowline with your eyes closed.

Nevertheless, the knot, although quite adequate for strength, had recently begun to offend Paul Fenwick in that particular location. Knots were, after all, only temporary fastenings, and he'd decided that a permanent splice would look neater and more seamanlike—but the embarrassing fact was that he still didn't know how to splice such a braided rope. The old-fashioned, twisted, three-strand stuff was different. You simply separated the strands and then wove them back through the standing part of the rope a certain way. It took a little practice, but the principle was easy to grasp and easy to remember. Splicing braid, on the other hand, was kind of like putting together a Chinese puzzle involving the outer sheath and the inner core, counting and measuring and marking and tapering according to an intricate formula that was difficult to follow and impossible to memorize. He'd watched it being done a couple of times, but he'd never had the nerve to get out the tricky metal fids he'd bought for the purpose, and the little manual put out by the rope manufacturer, and tackle the job himself, until today. Now he regarded his handiwork with tremendous satisfaction, although he kept telling himself the feeling was childish. It was not, after all, as if he'd made a skillful medical diagnosis and saved a life. Or was it? Who could say that their lives, all five of them, might not depend on that splice some day soon, with the wind screaming and the reefs to leeward just waiting for something to carry away and permit the helpless vessel to drift out of control into the raging breakers?

Anyway, it was a good-looking splice for a first attempt, and it was a pleasure to have his boat almost to himself for a change. Even a thirty-eight-footer tended to get a bit crowded with five on board. He drank his beer very slowly to prolong the private moment and watched the activity in the anchorage around him. After Green Turtle Cay and its wonderfully picturesque little settlement of New Plymouth, where they'd spent several days, Marsh Harbour was kind of a letdown; just a big, bleak bay with some docks along the shore and, inland, a kind of ordinary-looking, supermarket sort of a town. That was where Lucia and a couple of the freaks—as she called them—were shopping, and he had no doubt they could spend his money without his help. He was, he had to admit, getting a little tired of the freaks. You could take only so much of people who felt they were entitled to a comfortable, indeed luxurious, living simply because they lived. You wanted to tell them that, in the absence of any useful contributions to the common good, their mere existence wasn't all that important in the great scheme of things; it wasn't as if there weren't plenty of warm bodies to go around.

That went only for the he-freaks, of course. The she-freak was slightly different. Come to think of it, she was a whole lot different. For one thing, she kept her mouth shut. She wasn't forever either whining or proclaiming; in fact, she seldom spoke at all. For another, she worked. You didn't even have to tell her—ask her. Nobody'd ever got around to deciding who was going to do the shipboard cooking; they'd never had the chance. She'd simply had breakfast on the table the first morning as they were preparing to leave Boot Key; and hefty sandwiches had come out the hatch at lunch time; and at anchor that evening there had been steak with all the trimmings. After which she'd silently gone ahead and washed the dishes and swept and swabbed out the galley.

With the growing burden she carried, she wasn't very useful on deck, and he had a hunch she wasn't much of a sailor even when she wasn't pregnant; but below she was worth her not inconsiderable weight—she'd be a big girl even when she wasn't carrying a baby—in pure gold. Even when, after reaching Miami by the sheltered route inside the Keys, they'd headed out across the hostile Gulf Stream with the wind almost on the nose; even then, pale and obviously queasy, with her scared friends trying to, for God's sake, stage a half-ass kind of let's-go-home-now mutiny when they weren't busy retching all over the boat, she'd been right on schedule with her neat, substantial sandwiches. She'd even, somehow, managed to keep snacks and hot coffee available all that howling miserable night, with the big cat going up and down and sideways like a kid's yo yo.

Well, it had been a good shakedown, literally as well as figuratively, for the long ocean passage that now lay ahead. They'd got the ailing diesel pretty thoroughly checked over at Walker's Cay—it was funny how a motor could suffer from *not* being used—and they'd just topped up all the tanks at the fuel dock at the head of the harbor here. He couldn't think of anything lacking except the last-minute groceries Lucia was now purchasing with her male-freak escort, the bearded members of which would undoubtedly indulge their private tastes in booze and smokes quite literally at his expense, and feel totally self-righteous about doing it. It wasn't that he minded buying the stuff for them so much, Paul Fenwick reflected; it was just that the creeps had never once in their lives, at least not in their *Haleakala* lives, employed the word "thanks."

It was very pleasant in the cockpit; it was too damn easy to be lazy on a boat. He reminded himself there was still a lot of work to be done, like checking the chart and the cruising-guide pages covering tomorrow's run past the island with the odd name Lubber's Quarter and out the North Bar Channel. He should also check the chronometer against the radio and bone up a bit more on celestial navigation; it was a long time since he'd used a sextant in earnest. It would be nice to get a weather report, too, but on this eastern edge of the Bahamas the VHF radio no longer picked up the short-range NOAA weather stations with their continuous broadcasts, and he'd probably have to wait until 0725 in the morning when station WAVS in Fort Lauderdale gave a regular Bahamas report, courtesy of a marine store called Charlie's Locker. After tomorrow, of course, it wouldn't really matter. They'd be out in the open Atlantic and they'd have to take whatever came along; but there was no sense heading out there in the teeth of a predicted gale.

When the she-freak appeared silently in the deckhouse doorway, he couldn't help glancing at her in quick annoyance. He'd forgotten that he wasn't really alone on board, and he wasn't pleased by the reminder.

"I . . . I'm sorry," she said, and went back inside.

He realized belatedly that he'd been hearing her working below all this time without quite recording the fact. Well, that wasn't quite right. Part of his mind had recorded it all right, but had actually accepted it as a comfortable and kind of companionable circumstance.

He couldn't help thinking that it was certainly different from having Lucia around. She wasn't what you'd call a comfortable and companionable person, with her steely courage that wasn't really courage at all but a total insensitivity to danger—when the male freaks had made their little demonstration, it was Lucia who'd picked up a heavy winch handle and told them to haul their fucking asses to hell below; the next head that stuck itself out the hatch would develop a large dent very fucking suddenly. There was also her rather frightening competence at everything from sailing to sex that contrasted so oddly with the kind of vague and spacy look she sometimes displayed; and of course her constant foul language. The small, tough, screwball girl was useful and reassuring to have around, but comfortable she wasn't.

Against his will he'd found himself forever trying to impress Lucia, whether on deck or in bed, even though he was aware that his efforts were doomed to failure. There was nothing he could possibly show her because she'd obviously seen it all. Well, almost all. He could feel that there was something for which she was still searching desperately, some meaningful experience that had escaped her so far; but she'd made it clear by now that she wasn't finding it with him.

Oh, they still shared the spacious deckhouse berth, and the second night out of Marathon, anchored in Angelfish Creek, she'd kidded him out of his self-consciousness about doing it so publicly, with the he-freaks sleeping just down the ladder in the starboard hull and, on the other side, the she-freak sleeping just down the ladder in the port hull. Lucia was always perfectly willing to oblige, he had no doubt she'd do it on deck in broad daylight in the middle of this busy anchorage if he suggested it; but he knew that while she might have been mildly intrigued by him—or maybe just by his relative innocence—at the start, it was by now merely a practical accommodation to his masculine requirements. Nevertheless, he had to admit that he owed her a great deal. At least she'd got him off top dead center, so to speak; the human machinery was operational again, as it had not been since Deedee's death.

He was aware of the she-freak making her way back down into the port hull, where she had her bunk just aft of the galley—either to rest her heavy body or go back to work. Her silent withdrawal gave him an uneasy sense of guilt.

"Hey, Billie," he called, "why don't you grab a beer and come up for air? You don't have to kill yourself working down there." He thought she hadn't heard him, but some moments later she appeared in the opening again, can in hand. She sat down silently on the other side of the wide cockpit and pulled the tab and laid it carefully on the cushion beside her for later retrieval—either of the he-freaks would have tossed it overboard for all their loudly expressed concern for the lousy condition of the world and all who lived in it. "Were you looking for something?" Paul Fenwick asked.

She glanced at the newly spliced mainsheet. "No, I just

wanted to see how you did. . . . But you've got it all finished."

"I'm sorry; if I'd known. . . ."

"It doesn't matter." She started to raise her beer, and grimaced, glancing down at herself. "I really shouldn't do this, I'm too big already and I've still got months to go."

He'd always thought it was an unfortunate way of perpetuating the human race; there had to be a better method. Not that the preliminaries weren't enjoyable, but the nine-months' execution of the project, once initiated, was pretty damn tough on the half of humanity that had to carry it out. Of course, the baggy jeans and the shapeless smock didn't really improve the view here; but the drawn features, the lifeless skin, and the dry hair were almost inevitable anywhere, as the body concentrated all its resources on the new life inside.

Watching idly, he saw that she was looking past him at a boat in the harbor. He saw her smile a bit at what she saw—and something very startling happened inside him as he realized that, smiling, she wasn't an ugly girl at all. There was an intriguing sweetness to the shape of her lips, and her blue eyes were direct and honest. He looked away and tried to forget what he'd seen; tried to will her to remain as she'd been, just a big, lumpy-looking she-freak—he'd accepted Lucia's cruel term uncritically because it was by far the most comfortable way to handle the situation. The crew of a small vessel was a very delicate fabric, and he sure as hell didn't need any jealousy from Lucia, not to mention from this girl's freaky friends. Not that the poor kid was anything to arouse a man's libido in her present condition, but even a pleasant word could be misconstrued; and he knew that his relationship with Lucia was already causing quite enough tension on board.

"They really shouldn't do that," Billie said quietly.

He looked around. Nearby, a rather handsome large sloop lay at anchor; and on the stern in gold was the name: $Q\text{-}T\text{-}\pi$.

"I mean," she said, "a beautiful boat like that should have a nice name, shouldn't it? And if they *had* to call it that, they could at least have spelled it out instead of getting, well, so cutiepie about it."

It wasn't fair, he thought. It was a totally unnecessary complication, having her go human on him now, with a demanding ocean passage ahead. He didn't want to think of her as a real girl—with a shy sense of humor, even—and he certainly didn't want to find himself speculating about where she'd come from; and who the hell cared that she'd recognized at a glance the mathematical symbol for *pi*, as in *Cutiepie?* It didn't make her any kind of a genius—but on the other hand it wasn't something you picked up smoking marijuana on a beach.

He heard himself saying, "Look, we've already sailed several hundred miles together, but I don't even know your real name."

"Wilhelmina," she said. "Isn't that awful? Wilhelmina Procter."

"Well, it's a mouthful," he agreed. "If you don't mind my asking, how long have you been with Mike and Kirby?"

"Ever since the night I died," she said calmly. Then, obviously realizing what he was thinking, she gave a little laugh and said quickly: "Oh, I'm not really crazy. Well, I don't think so. But I can't help feeling that I'm dead. I ought to be. I did my darndest to kill myself. I just, stupid me, overlooked the little fact that I swim like a fish." She looked at him directly. "You know, it's impossible to stop swimming when you know how. Really. You just can't do it. I tried very hard, but my arms and legs just kept right on working."

He licked his lips. "Why?" When she didn't answer right away, he said, "I'm sorry. It's none of my damn business."

"Oh, I don't mind." She touched her stomach. "Mostly this, I guess. I mean, after Peter went and OD'd . . . He's the one who, I mean, he's the daddy, and he was nice and very bright, maybe too bright for his own good, but he did keep trying all those crazy things for kicks; and afterwards there wasn't anybody or anything and I just couldn't crawl back home like that all ragged and dirty and pregnant. Not to daddy and his nice new wife and mommy and her nice new husband and hearing them all saying what *has* that big dumb cow of a girl gone and done to herself now, she's your child, darling, thank heavens she's not my child. So I just walked out from the beach with all my clothes on—it felt kind of improper, really—and started swimming out to sea, but I couldn't make myself stop and sink even though the clothes wanted to pull me down and make it easy for me. And then suddenly there was this crazy-looking boat right on top of me, like a great big water-spider gone wrong, and they were hauling me aboard and, well, I've been with them ever since. Lucia joined us later, of course." After a moment she went on gravely, "I know you don't like Mike and Kirby much, but they're really very nice. They even got a doctor from another boat to look at me and bought me pills and stuff. . . . Please make allowances for them. I know they're full of crazy ideas, but they don't mean to be unpleasant. It's just that, well, please don't take this wrong, but you do represent the square kind of life they disapprove of so terribly."

He realized that this was her main reason for joining him; she'd seized the opportunity to put in a word for her friends. He wanted to ask if they disapproved of him so terribly what the hell were they doing on board his boat having themselves a free ride to the Caribbean? But in fairness he had to admit that it worked both ways: if he disliked them so thoroughly, why did he keep them on board to help him sail his boat? Well, they could all presumably stand each other for the length of time it took them to get to St. Thomas, and after that. . . . After that, he wondered, what was this girl going to do, who'd already had experiences beyond his comprehension, living a kind of ragged-edge life he couldn't really visualize? He'd thought himself brave just because he'd given up a career he wasn't really enjoying in order to go sailing, with money in the bank to support his decision, not to mention a lovely wife who'd backed him all the way. This big lonely girl had apparently, after attending reasonable schools, run away from an intolerable broken-home situation, had a lover who killed himself with drugs, tried to commit suicide, and been taken aboard a homemade sailboat that soon capsized in the Gulf Stream. Now, several months pregnant, she was on another boat heading south, essentially alone in the world except for a couple of bearded freaks who seemed to have, for some quirky reasons of their own, adopted her as a pet; and who'd undoubtedly ditch her when they got bored with the idea, which would probably be, at the very latest, when the baby arrived. Well, dammit, it wasn't his problem.

"Sure," he said, "sure, but there's really no reason for you to do *all* the galley work and housekeeping. It won't kill Mike or Kirby to wash a dish occasionally. Or Lucia or even, God forbid, me."

"Oh, I don't mind," she said quietly.

"That's not the point. One person shouldn't get all the dirty jobs on board."

"But I don't *mind!*" There was a strange kind of desperation in her voice. "Really I don't! It's something I can do. I can't steer very straight and I don't know where all the ropes go or how to work those crazy winches but . . . I *want* to do it. Please." The blue eyes looked at him directly, and he saw the

104

shy little smile again and knew that he'd been waiting for it to reappear. "Don't you understand, it makes me feel important and indispensable, knowing you'd all starve to death in a floating pigsty without me? I'm just feeding my dumb ego. Please don't worry about it. I'm really enjoying myself very much."

He said reluctantly, "All right, but any time you want a relief—"

"I'll ask." She looked around quickly, and said, "There's a new sailboat coming in. It's really a lovely way to travel, isn't it?"

He grinned. "Halfway between Florida and the Bahamas you couldn't have mustered many votes for that point of view."

"Oh, I thought it was kind of fun. I just hope I won't feel so iggy next time it gets rough."

"There's Dramamine in the medicine chest if you want to try it, but you've got to start taking it an hour or so before. . . . Ah, there's our fearless forage party returning," he said, glancing shoreward. "I hope there's room on board to stow all that stuff; they seem to have bought out the town."

They watched *Haleakala*'s dinghy pull away from the city dock. There were largish male figures at bow and stern, and a small female figure amidships, rowing—obviously, Lucia had had enough of the freaks' awkward oarsmanship. The dinghy could be propelled by oars, sail, or a small outboard motor; but it had seemed unnecessary to rig for anything but manual power anchored a mere hundred yards off the dock—although Mike and Kirby had, of course, complained loudly about being turned into galley slaves.

Billie said, "I'd better get downstairs and make room; I've got some things to put away."

"Below," Fenwick said. "You never go downstairs on a boat, you go below."

She glanced at him searchingly, and seemed to find what she'd looked for. She smiled and said, "Aye, aye, Captain. I'd better go below and secure the loose gear before it goes adrift, sir. How's that, sir?"

"Very good, sailor. Carry on."

In the morning, the Bahamas forecast out of Lauderdale was for light easterly winds increasing somewhat and veering south toward evening; but the water was calm as *Haleakala* left the anchorage and headed out around the point under power. A few hours later and a dozen miles south, still under power, with Lucia perched on the starboard spreader some twenty feet up the mast, the big catamaran felt its way through the last sandy shoals toward the wide opening that led to the sea. So far today it had been a relatively slow run due to the tricky piloting involved; now Paul Fenwick reduced the speed still further. With the cat's shallow hulls drawing less than three feet of water, some corners could be cut; but there was no sense in blasting onto a coral head full throttle this late in the game, with the open ocean in sight ahead.

"Starboard a point," Lucia called. "Damn this glare, I can't see a fucking thing. You did get those centerboards up, I hope."

"Boards up."

"What does the crappy book say now?"

"Due east from that last buoy we should pick up a post or marker. . . ."

"Got it. Steady as you go."

"Steady."

Then the depthsounder started giving more reassuring readings, as they emerged into the darker blue water of the deep channel leading seawards. After a little, Lucia came running down the mast steps like an agile monkey. Fenwick, at the wheel, saw the smaller of the two freaks up forward, Mike, getting himself an eyeful while the looking was good, and it certainly was. Her grimy cutoffs were frayed and even deliberately ripped up the sides, far above the last possible level of decency, at least from this angle; and it was her boast that she'd long ago sworn off all that fucking underwear stuff entirely—well, except when she had to impress stuffy people in the secretarial jobs she'd told him she took occasionally when finances were low. Presumably, he reflected, she cleaned up her vocabulary at the same time as she pulled on panties or pantyhose; and he imagined she laughed like hell, silently, at all the squares she had to deal with who had no idea what kind of person the neatly and modestly dressed little girl behind the typewriter really was. Dr. Jekyll and Mr. Hyde move over, please.

But it was, Paul Fenwick had to admit, pretty tough on Mike, who'd made it fairly clear he'd been there first. It was an awkward situation, particularly in view of the fact that Lucia, he knew, wouldn't really object to satisfying both of them—hell, all three of them. Not that she was a nympho; she simply didn't consider this moderately pleasant biological activity all that important, and if shipboard morale required it, why not? Which made him, Paul Fenwick, the ogre of the piece, the fat capitalist villain hogging the best for himself simply because the ship happened to be his private capitalist property.

For a man who'd never, until very recently, slept with any woman other than the one he'd married—and they hadn't even anticipated the ceremony by very much—he'd certainly managed to get himself into some interesting company, he reflected wryly. He had a clear notion of how Deedee, quite sophisticated in many ways but very fastidious about sex, would have viewed *Haleakala*'s current ragged crew: the big girl who was carrying an illegitimate child, the little girl who was totally and unconcernedly promiscuous, and the three men who were walking stiff-legged around her and each other like hostile dogs. It wasn't, Fenwick thought ruefully, exactly what she'd had in mind for him when she'd told him he must carry on with the Great Adventure after she was gone.

No, what she'd really pictured lying in that hospital bed was undoubtedly something pretty conventional like the two of them had been, only with his newly recruited sailing partner's face carefully blanked out. Something nice and civilized, perhaps like the handsome young couple he'd just seen up at Walker's Cay where they'd had the diesel repaired; in the big, gold-plated sportfisherman, the man in his expensive shorts and the girl in her crisp white slacks, and for both of them, matching T-shirts displaying the boat's name: *Stream Hunter*. He'd noticed them because the big vessel had come in so smartly, rotating in the space between the docks as if by magic and sliding stern first into its narrow slip without touching the pilings on either side—and the girl, not the man, had been at the flybridge controls. Undoubtedly, loving him and knowing his weaknesses, Deedee had wished for him an attractive and competent shipmate like that. Instead he'd wound up with this grubby misfit crew. Well, at least he was no longer sitting in the Boot Key Marina contemplating his naval.

"Lemme take her, you're steering all over the fucking channel," Lucia said, coming aft to drop into the cockpit beside him. "We've got to leave that little rocky cay to *port*, you know; and why the shit are we still crawling like a fucking snail? There's plenty of water here. Move over."

107

"She's all yours," he said, and went below to pour himself a cup of coffee; but Billie, on her knees in front of one of the galley lockers, heaved herself up and poured it for him. "Why don't you ever take a break?" he asked her rather irritably, pitching his voice over the rumble of the diesel that had just been brought back up to cruising r.p.m, "Go topside and take a look; it's the last land you'll see for a couple of weeks. More like three weeks unless we're very lucky with the wind."

"I'll be up in a minute," she said. "I've just got to make sure this stuff doesn't go all over the place if things get rough."

They stood looking at each other for a moment, steadying themselves against a new, rhythmic, swooping motion as *Haleakala* began to feel the long Atlantic rollers at last.

"Well, I'd better go see if we can't get some sail up," he said abruptly. "To hell with all this powering; I think there's wind enough. Hang on down here; you don't want to get thrown across the boat."

"Yes," she said. "Of course."

In the evening there was no land in sight. There were no other boats, either. For a while there had been a couple of sails visible far down the Abaco coast and a white powerboat of some kind astern, but now they had the ocean to themselves, with the sun setting just a little to starboard of *Haleakala*'s wake as she made her way off shore, close-hauled under full working canvas, trying to get south as much as possible but forced by the wind to hold well to the east. There was no traffic on the VHF and Paul Fenwick switched it off.

After checking the precise time of sunset in the Nautical Almanac, he took his sextant and went on deck; he might as well grab a practice sight of Polaris while he still had a reasonably accurate dead-reckoning position to check himself against. The freaks were playing some kind of idiot card game on the deckhouse table, smoking up a storm and obviously hoping he would complain so they could feel downtrodden. Lucia was curled up in a corner of the big berth like a kitten, storing up sleep for her midnight watch. Down below to port, Billie was still busy in the galley; and Fenwick found himself wishing she'd lie down and rest occasionally. They had over a thousand miles of hard sailing ahead. The North Star turned out to be in the right place and so did *Haleakala*. Satisfied with his navigation, he stowed the sextant carefully, hit the switches for the compass light and the masthead running light, and went back out into the cockpit, away from the tobacco smog inside. As a doctor, he couldn't help disapproving; as a skipper he couldn't afford to make an issue of it; as a man he merely figured that the sooner the creeps killed themselves with emphysema the better off everybody would be.

The compass showed that the self-steering vane was holding the ship right on course. By now there was only a faint red glow astern to show where the sun had set, and the stars were out in force. He closed the deckhouse door to block off the light inside, and relaxed on the cushioned cockpit seat, listening to the soft rushing sound of his ship making her gentle way through the night in less than ten knots of wind. Not a single light showed anywhere around the dark horizon.

Chicago seemed very far away, and his parents; and Deedee was even farther now and forever unattainable. Even Boot Key seemed like another world, pleasant enough, but one he'd inhabited too long and was glad to be out of. He wondered whose life pretty, white-haired Mrs. Ellington was arranging now; and what had happened to the unfortunate Ullmans. The last he'd heard, the poor guy's condition had still been critical. He found that the thought of Mrs. Ullman's sexual ordeal no longer had power to arouse him, which was just as well; it had not been a nice reaction at all. It was no wonder priests were all slightly strange, fighting that celibacy battle all their lives.

The sudden light as the deckhouse door swung open was like a blow, and he said quickly: "Shut that thing, I can't see—"

Then one of them, the big one, Kirby, had him in a powerful embrace and as, astounded, he opened his mouth to ask what the hell, he caught a glint of light on something shiny chopping down: the same handy stainless-steel winch handle, always stowed in the cockpit, with which Lucia had threatened them a week or so earlier. He could smell the rank sweat-and-tobacco odor of Kirby as he tried to duck away, but the blow caught him glancingly alongside the head and the night seemed to explode in red fire. . . .

"Good, he's still breathing," he heard Mike say distantly after a little. "We don't want to kill anybody. Hold him, I'll get the dinghy overboard."

"We're already some fifty miles out; what good's that cockle shell going to do him?"

"Captain Bligh made it; let him give it a try. If he's not good enough, to hell with him, the arrogant bastard, think-
109

ing he can push everybody around just because he's got a piece of paper saying he owns a lousy yacht. . . ."

"What in the world are you doing?" This was a new voice, a girl's voice, not Lucia's, aghast. "Have you both gone crazy? What are you *doing* to him? *Stop* it . . . !"

There was a scuffle and the sound of a blow. Normally he would have been concerned, indignant; but he found himself unable to take it seriously. None of it was real, of course. Mutiny, piracy, hijacking. Those were only words. They didn't really happen.

Or did they. . . .?

CHAPTER 11

December

Latitude 27°N; Longitude 77°W

Lavinia Burnett lathered her small body liberally in *Haleakala*'s seldom-used shower. It was seldom used because fresh water was always in limited supply on a cruising sailboat, but also because the shower couldn't be used without pretty well saturating the toilet compartment—the head, if you wanted to be nautical—and also kind of steaming up the whole starboard hull. Anyway, aside from the Boy Scout owner of the catamaran and maybe that big sow of a Billie, there hadn't been any what you'd call real cleanliness freaks on board; and the one time Paul Fenwick had ventured to employ his own boat's bathroom for the purpose—well, one of the purposes—for which it had been designed, the bearded creeps had complained like hell about the resulting dampness of their private quarters just aft. Jeez, what a pair of griping jerks.

Anyway, they'd all wound up showering on shore when facilities were available, which hadn't been very often, or just taking a salty dip over the side at anchor. Not that it had mattered to her. The idea that everybody was supposed to forever smell like a rose was, as far as she was concerned, strictly advertising crap. But she had to admit that a shower did feel good occasionally, like now, and she had been getting pretty ripe, although it hadn't seemed to bother the boy scout much in spite of his soapy preferences. In fact, she thought he'd rather preferred it that way. It had put their crude, unwashed fucking on a different and, of course, much lower plane from the genteel copulation he'd performed with his dainty dead wife; and you just knew what kind of a sissy-prissy she'd been from looking at the glamor-picture he still kept over the nav-table in the deckhouse—she'd probably insisted on bathing and perfuming herself both before and after the sacred marital rites.

Anyway, it was time to switch gears again and become the immaculate lovable diminutive secretary of Buckmeister and Pond, Yacht Brokers Extraordinary; and what a mealy-mouthed little mouse *she* was, so watch your fucking language, my dear. Bracing herself against the motion of the boat, Lavinia Burnett reached for a towel; then a sudden uneasiness made her, still dripping, leave the cramped head compartment and run quickly up the ladder and through the empty deckhouse out into the breezy empty cockpit—but everything was fine, no ships were running them down, in fact there still wasn't a light in sight anywhere. The catamaran was comfortably hove to on the starboard tack with the big mainsail sheeted in hard, the little forestaysail backed to windward, and the roller-furling jib all wound up like a window blind—just lying there rocking gently, helm locked, heading a little south of east and drifting a little east of north. The masthead navigation light shone brightly overhead, coloring the surrounding water red, green, and white in the appropriate sectors; above it the stars were small and sharp in the black sky.

Lavinia rubbed herself down hard with the towel, standing there naked in the dark, and went into the deckhouse for her clothes and carried them out into the cockpit to put them on where she could keep an eye on things. The white slacks weren't too presentable, having been soaked in sea water with the rest of her belongings, when that crummy trimaran capsized off Marathon; but Bucky wouldn't expect to find his Linda in perfect Monday-morning office condition. A few creases and smudges would simply emphasize the hardships she'd endured in his behalf, their behalf, without confronting him with too much in the way of harsh reality. . . .

"Oh, shit!" she said.

Even in the darkness, the large bloodstain showed up clearly on the white pants leg. She switched on the cockpit light hastily and saw the other splashes on the cushion right where she'd dumped the clothes before putting them on. Those goddamn freaks, she thought; they couldn't even get off the fucking boat without bleeding all over it! All I did was shoot off his fucking ear, for God's sake, it's not as if I'd blown off his lousy head, although he'll never know how close he came. What the hell did the cowardly little bastard have to go and get suddenly brave for, anyway?

Grimly, she stripped off the pants again, examined the underpants for stains, none, and checked the jersey she hadn't yet put on, okay. She laid the jersey in a safe place on the deckhouse top, tucked firmly under one of the halliards so it wouldn't blow away; then, after dunking them over the side, she used the soaked and wadded slacks to scrub the cockpit carefully, not that it was all that important considering where the boat was going next, but some people did get all upset at the sight of blood. Bucky might take it into his head to come on board briefly with Regan and his take-over crew; and Bucky's fortitude was a very doubtful quantity. She dropped the stained garment overboard and watched it recede and sink quite slowly, the two white ghostly legs kicking lazily and eerily in the swirling black water. Too bad, those were the most respectable pants she had along, but bloodstains were always hell to get out, and whatever she put on now she'd probably have to wear ashore later in West Palm Beach—at least Bucky had been planning to use that Lehman delivery job as his excuse for the trip. Besides, she had to admit, the smears of human blood from a man she'd shot made her feel a little funny about wearing the garment again.

Suddenly chilly, she pulled the clean jersey on over her head and went to her seabag inside and got out a pair of new cast-iron jeans, still not properly broken in, and climbed into them. She put her feet into a pair of quite presentable blue boat shoes. All the clothes and cleanliness—particularly the shoes she hadn't worn for weeks—made her feel kind of unnatural, but that was all to the good because unnatural was the way she was going to have to be now for a while. Dear Bucky's sweet unnatural little Lucia—oops, Linda—forcing herself to soil her delicate typing-fingers with dirty profitable piracy for her employer-lover's sake.

"Now, my girl, you deserve a drink," she told herself aloud.

Below, she found the new bottle of fancy Matusalem rum the freaks had bought themselves in Marsh Harbour with the boy scout's money. No ice, of course. *Haleakala* had no refrigeration, just an icebox; and with a two-to-three-week passage ahead, there had been no point in loading up with ice that couldn't last more than a few days; the icebox had been used for safe storage of a million—well, more or less—eggs instead. Regan and his crew would have plenty to eat on their way to Colombia, or Jamaica, or wherever they were picking up their illegal cargo this time.

Back in the cockpit she found nothing changed. The wind held steady and light; and the long black seas rolling up from the south showed only an occasional luminous white crest. She switched out all the lights except the masthead light for better vision and leaned back comfortably on the cushions and sipped the darkish rum like brandy and felt its warmth go through her. It occurred to her that it would be easy to get really hooked on this sailing racket. It was kind of nice out here at sea; and that had been a hell of a fine ride across the Gulf Stream with the panicky freaks shitting their pants full, as well as spewing sporadically from all other available orifices. But the boy scout had stood up okay. He hadn't been a bad boy scout for a boy scout; and she could have had him for good, she knew, quite easily.

All she'd have had to do was go a little easy on him, let him think he was running things, and let him reform her a little. If he'd just been allowed to turn that grimy little foul-mouthed female tramp—very gradually of course and with lots of kindly masculine persuasion—into this clean, pretty, sweet-smelling and sweet-talking small angel of a girl who was sitting in his cockpit now, he'd have been so goddamn proud of her, and himself, that he'd have married her on the spot; and they could have sailed off into the sunset on his handsome yacht and lived happily ever after—except that she'd probably have cut his throat from boredom within a year. Or shot a great big bloody hole in him. . . .

Reminded, she dug the revolver out from under the cockpit cushion where she'd tucked it away for security afterwards; that was one damn thing you didn't want sliding around a boat and maybe going off accidentally. Jimmy Columbus had done her proud after first squawking like hell; and this was a stainless-steel job, which was a damn good thing; an ordinary gun, in these salty surroundings, would probably have been a mass of rust by now. Smith and Wesson, she thought, .38 Special, whatever that might mean. But that was what it said on the barrel, and on the box of cartridges she'd got with it. Cartridges. Good for you, Lavinia, dear, it isn't every girl who knows that what you stick into the gun is the cartridge, and the bullet is just that gray lead thing up front.

But you never realized, at any time, just what experiences would come in handy later. There was that weird, kind of scary, intense black guy she'd spent a couple of months with once, who'd called himself Ahmed, who'd got his kicks shooting cans and bottles on the beach—probably imagining they were white men, although he didn't seem to have a thing against white girls—with a little .22 pistol he had. He'd shown her how, and taught her a bit of the language, and it had turned out that shooting-people were just as finicky as boating-people about what you called their toys. But this .38 kicked a lot harder than his .22 and made a lot more noise, God, what noise!

She'd thought she'd blown up the whole fucking boat when she fired; and then watching that idiot freak put his hand to his head and discover he had only half an ear left on that side, and both of them thinking she had to be a hell of a shot to earmark one so neatly when all she'd really been trying to do—and it had been a struggle—was keep herself from putting it right between his eyes, the stupid jerk, what the hell made him think that just because she was a girl, and kind of a small girl at that, she couldn't possibly shoot beautiful virile wonderful him?

But it had really been worth the price of admission, earlier, to see their incredulous faces when they'd come inside from the cockpit to tell her proudly that the job was done and the poor damn boy scout was drifting off unconscious in the dinghy along with that simple lump of a girl who'd tried to interfere, and good riddance to both of them. But the freaks had thought their cute little accomplice in crime was kidding at first when she showed them the gun and told them now it was their turn to go overboard, so get the life raft out of the locker, fellows, unless you've got an irresistible desire to go swimming fifty miles off shore.

It had been kind of tricky for a while, getting them to believe she really meant it, but she'd got them herded into the cockpit and the Avon overboard, and Kirby had pulled the cord and the thing had inflated with a bang. That was when Mike had decided he wanted to be a one-eared hero. . . .

Screwballs all, but she'd handled it all pretty well, if she did say so herself. It had all worked out swell. The freaks had most certainly hijacked the boat from the boy scout, and if he survived he'd most certainly say so loudly to any fuzz that come along. And if they got caught when they drifted ashore in their rubber doughnut and blamed a wicked little girl named Lucia Barnes who'd masterminded the nefarious plot and then double-crossed them, well, first of all, who'd believe a couple of hairy freaks who'd spent their lives blaming other people for their troubles and those of the world, and second, who could find Lucia, a ghost girl who'd ceased to exist. . . .?

Starting to drain her glass, she checked herself, listening. There was a new sound in the darkness, audible above the splashings and creakings of the hove-to catamaran. She looked around quickly, trying to pinpoint the location of the big diesel she could hear closing in; and there was the boat, Mr. Lehman's big Grand Banks trawler, off the starboard quarter, a bulky black shadow against the black sea. She drained the last of her rum, hastily, and hurried into the cabin and hit all the light switches. Given half an excuse, that bloodthirsty little mick, Regan, was as likely as not to hose things down with an automatic something-or-other, even though he'd been been told that bullet holes were to be avoided as far as possible. As she stepped back out into the cockpit, with *Haleakala* lit up like a Christmas tree—spreader lights, deck lights, running lights, anchor light, cockpit lights—she knew a sick, drained, letdown feeling.

It was over. Now there was only to transfer crews and let Regan take over here. And then back to Houston and that fucking typewriter with dear chickenshit Bucky—the Bosun, for God's sake—whose strained fearful voice she could already hear asking anxiously if she was all right and everything was all right and what had happened and where was everybody. She could see him up on the flying bridge gauging the seas expertly as he brought the big trawler in close to yell his stupid, worried questions. Well, it was a damn good thing she hadn't counted on him to lead a boarding party across, cutlass in teeth, pistol in hand. He was obviously going to need a change of diapers after merely screwing up his courage this far.

Just the same, the gutless wonder did handle a boat nice, you had to give him that.

CHAPTER 12

December

Latitude 27°N; Longitude 77°W

Fenwick was lying in a puddle of water under a pale sky flecked with widely scattered clouds that swooped back and forth across his vision in a very disconcerting fashion. The ache in the side of his head made it hard for him to sort out his memories properly. Dinghy, he told himself at last, triumphantly; that's it! You're floating, rocking, in that goddam cranky little dinghy Deedee was always so crazy about sailing, like a kid with a new Christmas bicycle ... well, never mind *that*. Those data are obsolete, Dr. Fenwick. Let us concentrate on the current situation; let us bring our research up to date. He touched the side of his head cautiously.

Diagnosis? Laceration of the scalp, okay. You won't die from that, and the bandage seems to have checked the bleeding. Concussion? Fracture? He moved his head in a small experimental way. No vertigo, check. No nausea or vomiting, check. No double vision, check. Our considered opinion, Doctor, is that your life expectancy is just about the actuarial average for a man drifting in a nine-foot fiber-glass pisspot about fifty miles off shore. And just what got into those idiot freaks, anyway, and how do they expect to get away with ... But that doesn't concern you right now, Doctor. Retribution and restitution are not the immediate problem. Like the man said, Captain Bligh made it. All you've got to cover is fifty lousy Atlantic miles instead of a thousand lousy Pacific ones. Are you going to admit that a stuffy old British Navy officer with a mere umpty years of seagoing experience could possibly have been a better sailor than you?

Bandage, he thought suddenly. *Bandage?*

How the hell could you have bandaged yourself when you

just regained consciousness; and you know damn well that after laying your head open in the first place those creeps would never have . . . He raised his head very slowly. He was lying in the bottom of *Haleakala*'s dinghy, all right, his head toward the stern; and she was sitting on the middle thwart with the bailing scoop on her knees, braced against the boat's motion with a hand on either gunwale. He saw that her eyes were closed. Her rather long light brown hair was matted, and her loose, unbecoming clothes were splashed with water, and she had, he saw, a new dark ugly bruise on one cheekbone. She was the most beautiful thing in the world.

"Hi, Wilhelmina," he whispered.

"Oh!" She started, and her eyes flew open, and she caught the bailing scoop as it started to fall. "I guess I kind of fell asleep just sitting here," she said apologetically.

"What time is it?" he asked.

She shook her head minutely. "I haven't got a watch. It just got light a little while ago. How do you feel?"

"Fine, from the neck down," he said.

"I . . . I thought you were bleeding to death."

"Scalp wounds often hemorrhage extensively."

He saw her smile faintly. "Yes, Doctor."

"No ships in sight?"

"No. Just an awful lot of ocean."

She had a very shipwrecked look; and he realized that part of it came from the fact that the bottom of her smock was now ragged where a strip had been ripped off all the way around, presumably to tie around his head. Well, wet and bloody and bandaged, he was no shining specimen of sartorial yachting splendor himself.

He licked his lips. There seemed to be a lot that needed saying, but this was neither the time nor the place for it, and what he said was: "There should be a flashlight and a small kit of distress signals and half a gallon of water in that wedge-shaped little locker under the bow seat. Along with an anchor and line, but we won't be needing that out here. Maybe you'd better check and make sure the stuff's still there, so we'll know where we stand."

Billie swung herself around rather awkwardly and bent over, away from him. "It's still there," she reported. "Well, I see the flashlight and a red box and a plastic bottle. And some rope underneath."

He said, "There should be a little compass tucked away in the red box with the flares and signal mirror."

"It's there."

"We'd better have that. It's got a lanyard, doesn't it? Hang it around your neck so we don't lose it. Now taste the water, please. I can't remember when I changed it last."

After a moment she said, "It tastes a little stale, but I think it's all right."

"Better put everything back and secure the lid again, just in case we capsize or something. Now let's try something really difficult, like getting me out of the bottom of this boat. . . ."

"Don't bump your head on that steering thing," she said quickly, turning back to face him as he started to push himself up.

He looked up and saw that the tiller was there above him, secured amidships by a cord. The knots were clumsy, obviously made in the dark by somebody who didn't know a great deal about knots. But the startling fact was that the rudder, which was normally stowed alongside the centerboard trunk secured with shock cord, was now shipped in its working position on the little craft's transom.

"I didn't know what to do," Billie said, in answer to his questioning glance. "We were drifting kind of crosswise and it was all splashing aboard. I thought if I could just steer along with the waves, maybe I wouldn't have to bail so much. And then, after I got it working, I found that if I just tied it there like that, and moved up to the middle seat, the back end came up a little higher and the boat just seemed to go along straight with hardly any water coming in. I hope it was all right."

He drew a long breath, thinking of a pregnant girl with a bruised face set adrift in mid-ocean—well, for all practical purposes—with an unconscious man for company; a girl with hardly any previous experience with boats, in black darkness, working it all out in her head, without panic, and then executing and systematically refining her careful survival plan. . . .

"Yes," he said, "yes, it was all right. It was fine."

"Can I help you get up?"

"Better not have both of us thrashing around at the same time. Just try to keep the boat balanced."

Using the lashed-down oars, on one side, and the lashed-down spars on the other, he heaved himself to a sitting position and rested there for a moment, letting the pounding in his head subside. Then he looked around at last. The orange disk of the sun was just showing over the horizon to starboard. They were therefore, he reflected, drifting more or less north before the same southerly wind *Haleakala* had been bucking the evening before. North. Nothing there until you hit Cape Hatteras after five hundred miles or Cape Cod after about a thousand. He wished he could have another look at the small-scale chart, but he thought that was about right. He glanced at his watch.

"We'd better start sailing west as soon as possible," he said. "The last log entry I remember making put us fifty-three miles out. I don't think we can make that before dark, but we'd better give it a try. We're certainly not making any money drifting in this direction. Cast off those mast lashings up forward, will you?"

She hesitated. "Paul?"

Something in her voice made him glance at her quickly. "Yes?"

"Please don't . . . I mean, you're not trying to kid me, are you?" When he frowned, she went on quickly, "You really do think we can make it, in this tiny little boat?"

It shocked him to think that she'd been sitting there all this time prepared to do her best but fully expecting to drown nevertheless. He started to say something glib and reassuring, but he checked himself.

"I'm not the world's greatest sailor," he said carefully. "I've only been at it a couple of years. But I'd say it depends entirely on the weather. If it stays like this, we ought to have a pretty good chance. If it turns bad, we've probably had it. But the last weather reports didn't mention any disturbances on the way. Okay?"

"Yes. Thank you."

He checked her as she started to turn away to attend to the mast. "Have you ever sailed a dinghy?" he asked.

She shook her head, with a little laugh. "I'd never sailed anything before Kirby pulled me aboard that *Freedom Machine* of theirs."

Fenwick said, "We used this a lot for exploring, coming down the Waterway; and it was nicer under sail than with the outboard motor if we didn't have too far to go. My wife got to be really nuts about it. She was always sailing around any new harbor as soon as the anchor was down. That's mainly why we put that emergency gear aboard, just in case she ran into trouble, got swept out to sea, or something. She didn't know anything about it when she started, either, and at first she spent more time swimming than she did sailing." He had a sudden, swift, piercing memory of Deedee in her white bikini, surfacing beside the overturned dinghy and tossing back her streaming dark hair to laugh up at him—watching and worrying on *Haleakala*—after getting dumped into the harbor again. She'd said it was certainly curing her of her fear of tippy boats, but somehow it didn't seem to matter because it was such a *little* boat. He was aware that the big girl seated forward was watching him steadily; and maybe it was no time for reminiscing about his late wife, but on the other hand it wasn't any time for diplomatic discretion, either. He put his memories away. "What I'm trying to say is, if we do go over it's no big thing. There's plenty of flotation; we just turn it back rightside up and slosh some water out and crawl aboard and bail it dry. But out here let's not play *that* game unless we have to. It's kind of like riding a bicycle; it's all a matter of weight and balance."

Billie gave him a wry little grin and patted her stomach. "For weight, you've come to the right girl, Mister. Tell me what to do."

Stepping the mast in a sheltered anchorage wasn't much of a problem; stepping it at sea turned out to be considerably trickier because of the constant heaving motion; but eventually it was up and the centerboard was down and they were sailing. The same breeze that had seemed quite feeble on *Haleakala* was all the little dinghy needed to take off at a good clip; and in the puffs they both had to perch up on the weather rail to keep it more or less on an even keel. Some spray came aboard, and occasionally they shipped a little water over the lee gunwale. In the slack periods, Billie would slide down and bail until she was needed up to windward once more. It was in many ways a strange experience; and he saw that Billie felt it, too.

"Hey, this is kind of fun," she said after a while, leaning back for added leverage as the dinghy rushed across the face of an oncoming wave like a surfboard. "But kind of crazy, too," she said.

He thought that kind of crazy was a very accurate description. It was an unreal experience, as unreal as being attacked on his own boat by people he'd known for weeks and being cast adrift like a character in a melodramatic TV show. He hadn't quite believed in that, and he didn't believe in this: sailing briskly across the endless ocean in a tiny craft designed for a mill pond. It was like the kind of dream where the two of you pedaled shiny new ten-speed bikes across the African veldt among the lions and elephants; or calmly strolled up Mount Everest in dinner jacket and evening gown. It really shouldn't be working, not in real life; and there was always the knowledge that just a slight increase in the force of the wind would put them in deadly danger; but hour after hour went by and nothing happened. Toward the middle of the afternoon the wind actually dropped. By evening they were ghosting along at a bare knot or two over the long, glassy swells, watching the sun get low in the west, ahead, where there was still no sight of land.

The strangeness remained throughout the night. At times they drifted without any wind at all; at times they moved along quite well on the night breeze, checking course occasionally by the small luminous arrow of the compass around Billie's neck, but mostly by reference to Polaris. All night long he waited for it to happen; waited for the black storm cloud that would overwhelm them, the giant whale that would obliterate them with its flukes, the jagged rocks and crashing breakers that would capsize and smash and drown them, but absolutely nothing happened. In the morning the land was there.

It wasn't much land, just a scattering of low islands along the horizon ahead—technically cays, Paul Fenwick reminded himself, since this was presumably the Bahamas again, unless they'd managed to discover a new continent—but the gentle, friendly south wind kept them moving, and by midmorning they could see the occasional breakers where the outlying reefs disturbed the even progress of the long Atlantic swells, reminding him that they could still die out here, getting caught in one of those sudden explosions of white water—but again it didn't happen. They simply sailed onto the reef and saw the bottom rise up to meet them until they were sailing over rocks and coral and small darting fishes, all clearly visible through fifteen or twenty feet of crystal water.

"Paul, there's a mast sticking up behind that closest island. Judging by the size of it, there's got to be a big boat at anchor. . . ."

"There's a little boat coming out the pass to starboard, maybe their tender," he said. "Get the flares . . . no, they're heading right for us."

It was a small, blunt-nosed Boston Whaler with a sizeable outboard motor on the stern. It threw a fine wake as it raced toward them. A young boy in a wetsuit top was at the helm;

an even younger girl in a practically nonexistent bikini—
well, it didn't have much to restrain or conceal—was sitting
up forward with a diving mask pushed back on her wet
blonde hair. They came alongside with a flourish.

"What in the world are you folks doing out here in that
little bitty thing?" the girl called. "I mean, are you okay? If
you are, just pardon us for being nosy. . . ." The she stared at
them more intently, seeing the bloody bandage and the
ragged smock. She said breathlessly before they could answer: "Bobby, I told you they'd been shipwrecked; I told you!
That's fifty cents you owe me. Pay up or I'll tell Mommy."

CHAPTER 13

February

Latitude 30°N; Longitude 95°W

It was a hell of a time to be buying a boat, the Colonel
reflected, looking out the yacht broker's rain-spotted windows at the wet, gray, gale-whipped view. A hell of a time
and a hell of a place. You should buy boats in summer in
places with names like Gloucester and Marblehead, not in
winter in Houston, Texas—well, actually the little nearby
town of Seabrook just down the road from the big NASA
installation that he'd visited once on a technical mission that
hadn't made much sense, unless somebody'd been planning to
carry a Marine landing force on a future space shot to blast
a beachhead on Alpha Centauri or whatever.

Wipe that grin off, Brennan. They sent you a lot of funny
places during your thirty years; places that didn't seem any
more sensible, at the time, than outer space. North Korea, for
instance. What the hell were we supposed to be doing up by
that foul-ball reservoir, anyway? We had the damn war won;
we'd secured the friendly territory we'd been treaty-bound to
defend, hadn't we? The gooks were on the run and the south

was safe. So who'd had the bright idea of crossing the line and starting a strategically idiotic new war up north, anyway, pulling the Chinks into the action as everybody knew would happen? Stupid question. That glamor-bastard with the floppy cap and the corncob pipe, that's who. With the help of God and a few Marines, the S.O.B. took the Philippines, too, remember? And the glory, don't forget the goddamn glory. If there was any of that around for the taking, any time, anywhere, you knew who'd grab it. Only this last time that tough little *politico* from Missouri had the final word and you've got to give him full credit; but a lot of good men would still be alive if he'd pulled up his socks and said that word sooner. Never mind, Brennan. You're supposed to be buying a boat, remember?

The receptionist-secretary, a slight, smallish girl with soft brown hair gently framing a rather pert, piquant little face came into the inner office silently and placed a sheaf of papers on the broker's desk. She was wearing very crisp white slacks and a striped, short-sleeved jersey with a sailor collar.

"Here are the contracts, Mr. Buckmeister."

"Thank you, Linda."

It was all very businesslike; but Brennan saw his wife's eyebrows rise slightly. Marge was very good at spotting any funny business and, tipped off by her expression, Brennan saw it too: the yearning way the man behind the desk watched his small secretary leave the room. Not that the little ass in the innocent, immaculate white slacks wasn't quite interesting; but Buckmeister's look went beyond simple, objective male appreciation. And that, too, was kind of beside the point.

"Right there, Colonel," the broker said, pointing. "Three copies, please. Well, I guess in the Army you're used to doing things in triplicate, haha."

He was going to let it pass, but Marge said gently: "My husband was in the Marines, Mr. Buckmeister, not the Army. It's all the Armed Forces, but we do make the distinction, you know."

"Sorry, ma'am."

He signed his name carefully: Hobart Massey Brennan, Col., USMC, Ret. It still gave him an odd, ambivalent feeling to see that *Ret.* at the end. Bittersweet was the word you might use, Colonel Brennan reflected; that is, if you were the kind of person who went in for fancy words which of course he wasn't. Anybody, including his own three kids, now grown, would tell you that Hobie Brennan was a tough, unimaginative, no-nonsense military character, nothing fancy about him. Anybody, that is, except his wife, who wouldn't tell you anything. She'd kept the Colonel's secrets for years, and before that she'd kept the Lieutenant-Colonel's, and the Major's, and the First Lieutenant's, and the Second Lieutenant's, and the Midshipman's—that was in Annapolis before they were married, of course, but she'd kept them anyway. She wasn't going to start giving anything away now. However, he knew she hadn't been a bit surprised when he'd told her, at last, the crazy thing he hoped to do after retirement—if she was willing of course.

It had been a lot to ask of her. He knew she'd been hoping for a real home after all the gypsy years of following wherever the orders led. Even the shabby house they'd rented in Annapolis while they caught their first breaths as civilians and got Melissa married, and scoured the coasts—or he did—for the proper vessel; even that temporary and run-down dwelling place had undoubtedly seemed wonderful to her, and he'd often been tempted to call the whole thing off and, instead, see if they couldn't find a nice place on the water where, if he simply had to get his feet wet, he could keep a little sailboat at the dock. And then after she'd had the pleasure of living in her own house for a while, maybe in time they could work up gradually to . . .

But that was the point. There might not be that much time. When you'd passed the half-century mark and your body had started giving you occasional uneasy reminders of the abuse it had received in the line of duty, and the hardware that had been dug out of it on various occasions, you began to realize that this blood-and-muscle machine wasn't going to last forever; and that if you had any odd wild dreams you wanted to fulfill, you'd better get after them while the old biological apparatus was still more or less functional. He'd done the soldier bit, as his offspring might put it. He'd proved he could be damn good at it, if he did say so himself. He'd also, he figured, with thirty years' service, fully repaid the debt that he owed—that any citizen owed—to the land that had given him birth; and if you considered that a corny notion, as many seemed to these days, to hell with you.

He was square with everybody and obliged to nobody. The kids were making it on their own. Financially, things would be in good shape even if this screwball venture turned out to be a complete fiasco. Over the years Marge had handled everything very sensibly, his pay and the modest inheritance from her mother, so he could afford to flip it a little now. He thought grimly: a *little?* Seventy-eight thousand seven hundred and eighty dollars and thirty-three cents isn't exactly *little,* Brennan. Rocks in the head you've got, as the kids would say and are probably saying right now. Daddy's flipped it but good.

As he handed the pen back to Buckmeister after signing, he knew that he was as apprehensive as he'd ever been in his life; in a way more scared than that first time in the Pacific so many wars ago—he'd been lucky enough to catch the action before it was over; many of his classmates hadn't—before they hit that treacherous strip of sand on one of those last stepping-stone islands that somebody had named, very appropriately as it turned out, Beach Red. But all he'd had to fear then was death and the possibility that he might let down the Corps and his own unit under fire. Nothing, really, compared to what he faced now: the possibility that the bright dream that had sustained him over thirty years might turn out to be only a delusion.

The broker had to lift the front of his sporty white turtleneck sweater to replace the ball-point pen in his shirt pocket. He was also wearing white duck trousers and the kind of boat shoes, also white, that were supposed to let you cling like a barnacle to a reeling deck with hurricane seas washing over you. He was deeply freckle-tanned, with a kind of faded, sandy, boyish handsomeness; but something about the nose indicated that, between hurricanes, he'd paid a few visits to the Yacht Club bar.

He said, "Well, that does it, Colonel. Mrs. Brennan. We surely do thank you-all very much. We're having the Coast Guard documentation transferred to you; we'll have it to you before you shove off, for sure. She's a real fine little ship. I know you-all will be real happy with her. We've made arrangements with the Club; you're welcome to use the slip she's in as long as you need it. If there's anything we can do to help you in fitting her out—not that she needs much fitting out—just holler loud and clear and we'll come running."

There were handshakes all around, and the little girl in the sailor-suit gave them all the relevant papers neatly tucked away in an envelope; then they were leaving the office and walking through the large, hangar-like display room between the boats for sale, but not by the firm of Buckmeister and Pond who didn't deal in little stuff like this. These were stock, mass-produced craft, mostly power craft, all very bright and shiny. And small and handy-looking compared to what he'd let himself in for, Colonel Hobie Brennan reflected wryly. If he wasn't willing to settle for a day sailer at the dock, something like this, something of conservative size but capable of cruising in sheltered waters, with twin motors for easy maneuverability in tight places, maybe something that could be towed around to suitable cruising grounds on a trailer, would have made a very reasonable first boat for a middle-aged military gent who hadn't really sailed, to amount to anything, since he was a Firstclassman at the Naval Academy.

He could see the two of them reflected in the glass of the big doors, fondly shepherded by the reflection of Buckmeister—well, for damn near eighty grand, the superannuated beach boy ought to be fond of them, by God. It no longer bothered Brennan that his wife was a bit taller, quite a bit taller; he could grin at the memory of what they'd been called at one base. What was it now? T-and-P. There had been a World's Fair on at the time and the symbol had been a pylon and a sphere, for some public relations reason dubbed Trylon and Perisphere. T-and-P. Well, so maybe he was a little on the round and chunky side; he'd come back from plenty of places where taller, rangier, handsomer men had stayed for good. . . .

The Arctic blast of the Texas norther hit them as Buckmeister opened the door for them. They gave him a final, hasty good-bye and hurried to the rental car. As he started the motor and turned the heater to high, the Colonel heard his wife make a choked little sound, almost a girlish giggle. He looked at her quickly. She was watching Elmer Buckmeister—call me Buck, he'd told them in typical salesman fashion, but they hadn't—disappearing inside, behind the array of gleaming boats for sale.

"I'm sorry, dear," she said, "but his accent always does something to me, it's so very phony. But coming to Texas for a bargain boat is rather like going to Scandinavia for a bargain camel, isn't it?"

He felt a little annoyed. It was a serious moment, not an occasion for levity. He said rather stiffly, "You know it wasn't so much the price, Marge. There just wasn't anything suitable on the East Coast; we checked everything between Maine and Florida, remember? And what the hell, Houston isn't such a bad place to start cruising; by the time we've followed the Intracoastal Waterway east a few hundred miles we should know her pretty well and be ready for a little offshore work."

She patted his arm. "I know, I was just joking. Hobart, where is Apalachicola?"

"What?"

"Apalachicola?"

"Oh, that's way east. About seven hundred miles from here. That's where this east-west section of the Waterway ends, and we'll have to sail about a hundred and fifty miles kitty-corner across the Gulf of Mexico to pick up the north-south stretch down Florida's Gulf coast, which starts just above Tampa. Why?"

"Well, I was reading about a boat that disappeared around there. Several boats. Apparently they were hijacked; at least that's one theory."

The Colonel grinned. "Anybody who tries to hijack the *Spindrift* is in for a big surprise, like a couple of fast rounds of .45-caliber hardball. . . ." He stopped awkwardly, remembering. The faithful old service pistol that had accompanied him for most of his military career had recently been lost when he'd left it for repairs with a gunsmith whose premises had promptly been burglarized. Brennan grimaced and said, "Well, we can't take time for it now, but I'm glad you reminded me. It's probably all bullshit, but maybe I'd better pick up some kind of a sidearm when I get a chance, just in case."

The memory had spoiled the day just a little; he'd been quite fond of that old .45; but the sour feeling evaporated as he guided the station wagon into the local Yacht Club grounds and followed the drive past the clubhouse and down to the docks. Parking, he stepped out into the icy Texas wind and walked forward to look. There was always an immense pleasure in that first look, no matter how short a time he'd been away.

There were all kinds of vessels lined up before him, from powerful sportfishermen with flying bridges and outriggers and sky-high tuna towers to sleek ocean-racing sailing craft with slim, tall masts but he could see only one. It had taken so many years, he thought, but it was worth it. He was a little ashamed of himself for deceiving his wife, if she was really deceived, which he doubted. It had never been a question of finding a merely suitable boat; it had been a question of finding *this* boat. Well, this design. When it had first come out he'd spotted the architect's drawings in one of the yachting magazines to which he subscribed—as an antidote, he'd always said, to the dry military literature he had to plow through in the line of duty. He'd known his long search was at an end: *this* was the boat. It had merely been a question, when the time finally came, of finding a secondhand one for sale at a halfway reasonable price. New they were out of sight nowadays, in spite of being built in the Orient.

With her jaunty bowsprit and sturdy masts she looked businesslike and seaworthy among all the frothy fun-boats. The Colonel thought the graceful clipper bow and the broad stern with its carved, old-fashioned nameboard added up to a special kind of seagoing beauty. He thought: If only we can handle her properly, just the two of us, big as she is. If only Marge enjoys it. . . .

"Hobart."

The Colonel looked at his wife, who'd joined him. "Yes?"

"Now that it's ours, do you mind if I do something about those awful curtains? I really don't think I'll be able to sleep in that stern cabin with that pattern screaming at me."

Colonel Hobart Brennan drew a long breath of relief. The first thing Marge did at any new station was hang new curtains. No matter what kind of quarters they'd been assigned, that made it home.

CHAPTER 14

February

Latitude 26°N; Longitude 80°W

That winter the northers had been very late hitting Miami. Generally they started in the fall before Thanksgiving and came whistling through at fairly regular intervals until spring, to the consternation of the tourists who'd thought they were coming to a tropical climate. The usual cycle consisted of about three days of cold weather with high winds that gradually veered from northwest to northeast; then those would die away and come in more gently from the south bringing several warm and pleasant days; and then they would swing to the west and north once more, and the cycle would be repeated. On the newspaper weather maps one could see the fronts marching in steady succession across Texas, Louisiana, Mississippi, and Alabama, before they hit the Florida panhandle and finally came roaring down on Miami and the Keys.

But that year the weather had been warm, even hot, clear through December; and it had continued pleasant with only an occasional weak false alarm into the last days of January, an almost unheard-of situation, which the Chamber of Commerce fervently hoped would set a pattern for many years to come. However, when the first real front came through it was a true screaming norther that dropped the temperature fifty degrees in an hour, littered the streets with palm fronds and coconuts, and imprisoned all the expensive shiny fishing and sailing boats in their expensive harbors for the duration—all except those whose skippers hadn't listened to the forecasts and had been deceived by the bright morning sunshine into venturing out into the Stream. The U.S. Coast Guard had to go out after many of those. Because when the cold winds howl out of the north, one does not fool with the Gulf Stream, that great warm river in the ocean that runs right by Miami's front door. The strong northbound currents fighting an opposing gale can generate seas that no boat can survive—the so-called Bermuda Triangle had probably derived most of its sinister reputation from this simple natural phenomenon, reflected Jaime Fernando Colombo y Menendez sourly.

Here in the *Estados Unidos* he called himself, of course, simply Jimmy Columbus, that being a name they could pronounce in their crude fashion. He did not want to attract unfavorable attention—not that he truly cared what the perfidious *Americanos* thought of him; it was simply his goal to remain inconspicuous until his work was accomplished; and here they did not like wops or spics or greasers who put on airs and employed old aristocratic Latin names, at least not if there was no longer the old aristocratic Latin money to go with those names.

There were, of course, interesting ways of repairing that deficiency, Columbus thought grimly, as there were ways of avenging the Yankee treachery that had caused the deficiency or had at least prevented it from being rectified early when it would have been easy, at the *Bahia de Cochinos,* the place where a dream had died at the whim of a boy-faced American president who'd withheld the support that had been promised. Had *El Barbado* truly been involved in the later removal of that cowardly Yankee politician? If so . . . well, to be fair, it was something in his favor, to be put on one side of the scale to counterbalance, a little, the great weight of evil on the other. Not much, but something. There were probably a few things to be said in favor of the devil, also. A very few.

But that was of no importance now. What mattered was this infernal storm. After weeks of fine weather, to have it break just now was infuriating. Of course there were some advantages; the meddling Coast Guard, for instance, would be so busy nursemaiding helpless Yankee yachtsmen that it could not watch the Straits properly for other traffic. Perhaps it would be assumed that no boatman with any sense would try to come up the slot in this weather. Which was quite true, of course, but who had ever claimed that Olson had sense? A great deal had been said, and said scornfully, about the *machismo* cult of the Spanish; but he, Columbus, could supply detailed information about the ritual insanity of the Norse, forever compelled to prove their mad ability to totally disregard all dangers of the sea. Well, one *Sueco* at least. If the stubborn Swede had managed to lose his boat and the profits of the latest transaction, he, Jimmy Columbus, would give the blond maniac some real danger to ignore. If he had survived.

But when he turned the car into the marina, the *Ellida* was there—named after a legendary Viking ship, Olson had once explained, as if anyone cared. He had also explained, in his slow deliberate way, that the name was pronounced *El-eeda,* not *El-eyeda,* as if anyone but a Yankee, or a Britisher who shared the same barbaric language, could mispronounce so simple a word.

Columbus drew a long breath and, without approaching the sea wall where Olson kept his vessel with the other charter fishing boats, drove on through the almost-empty parking lots. In this weather, the well-to-do boat-owning Yankees would all be sitting at home in front of their TV sets in their usual mesmerized fashion. The city-run Miamarina was a relatively austere installation that did not seem to attract so many of the elaborately clipped poodles, lifebeltsmothered children, noisy cockpit cocktail parties, and sooty charcoal grills on the piers, that infested some of the more relaxed private harbors; it was more a simple boat-parking facility than a fashionable vacation community and social center. Columbus cruised through in the shabby little four-year-old Ford Pinto that always reminded him painfully, by contrast, of the big Mercedes. . . . Well, never mind that. There would be more fine cars and horses and sportfishing boats when the family regained what had been stolen from it by the bearded usurper whose days were now numbered; but this was no time for dreaming of the bright future. He turned back along the park toward Biscayne Boulevard. He had seen enough at a distance.

The mad Scandinavian had lost half his windshield and covered the hole with raw plywood. One of his outriggers was gone and both radio antennas, explaining why he'd sent no further messages since the code sentence announcing a successful delivery. Part of his bow rail had been driven inboard, perhaps by the same monstrous wave that had smashed the glass. It was twisted out of shape as if a giant hand had attempted to tie knots in the one-inch stainless tubing. He must have come roaring up the straits into the teeth of the norther, like a crazy submarine half awash, taking it green clear over the flying bridge, helping his Negro mate nail a board over the hole when the windshield collapsed, and belting down a stiff drink of *brännvin* as he liked to call it—otherwise known as aquavit—and clawing his way up to the topside controls once more to continue his insane progress, all the while no doubt whistling one of those irritating tunes in a minor key from the cold dark land from which his family, very sensibly, had emigrated. Lunatic. The instructions had provided for reasonable delays; but if he'd waited for calmer seas somebody might have thought that Hans Rurik Olson, the latter-day Norseman, was afraid of a little weather. . . .

If only, Columbus thought grimly, if only he could afford to employ only sensible, comprehensible Cubans for the work; but he had realized early that it would be most unwise to give the impression of a wholly Spanish-speaking organization if somebody came to realize that the organization existed. He had even gone to considerable trouble to find an obedient and easily controllable Anglo to manage the less important but more vulnerable and therefore more potentially dangerous new arm of the operation in Texas; the expendable arm that could be sacrificed if necessary, as the stone crab could sacrifice one claw in the interest of survival.

Of course there were so many movements, organizations, and operations; still so many groups of dedicated, aging, politically minded peasants here and in Key West still holding their small impotent meetings and bickering with each other about the exact methods to be used in forcing a return to the island home that, as the impoverished exile years and decades passed, became in their foolish minds a place of wealth and happiness that they had never actually known there. But he and his family had known it, Columbus thought grimly; he and his young daughter and son—the son recently murdered, and payment would certainly be exacted for that—and the wife who had faded away, shamed and heartbroken, in the initial unaccustomed poverty they'd suffered, before he'd discovered the simple and obvious remedy, in this bleak land that had received them so reluctantly. . . .

But the peons were useful, one had to admit. They attracted much attention with their simple-minded plots, their dull little forays in their shabby little boats, and their everlasting clumsy smuggling and stockpiling of guns and other weapons. They made highly useful diversions for the true work of the counterrevolution that was not designed for the happiness of grubby *campesinos* and those turncoat members of his own class who had allowed themselves to be infected by subversive egalitarian notions that were hardly any better, Columbus felt, than the imported Russian theories of the enemy.

But anyway, the Swede had made it. And there was no hint of suspicion yet. Mr. James Columbus was still considered a highly respectable and conservative member of the assimilated Spanish-speaking community, not one of those wild-eyed expatriate crackpots who dreamed endless, hopeless dreams of reversing the inevitable course of history. In a way, he reflected wryly, it was rather frustrating to have to move among these Yankee sheep unrecognized, regarded as just another exile who had made a sensible adjustment and settled down to a nice little neighborhood business; cheerful, friendly, down-to-earth Jimmy Columbus who talked English as good as anybody, almost; you wouldn't know he'd been a millionaire under Batista. . . .

"*Buenas tardes*, Don Jaime," said the attendant as he left his car in the parking lot across the narrow street from the Restaurant Miranda.

"Buenas tardes, Miguel. I will not need it for about two hours."

"Sí, señor."

Very respectful. It was pleasant in a way, it was what should be, but here there was always the suspicion of hypocrisy or the simple hunger for a tip. It was not the truly natural thing it should be between classes, and would be again one day, not here perhaps but over there. He could see himself approaching in the restaurant window, a neatly dressed figure with that terrible disproportion between the fine, large, handsome, aristocratic head and the rather small and unimpressive body. It was not a real deformity like a hunched back or a shriveled limb, although in a way it had probably saved his life, preventing him from training and fighting with the other patriots who had been so cruelly betrayed. *(This is a paramilitary force, Buster, not a freak show,* was the way the secret recruiter had put it when he had offered his services in the company of some friends, no longer alive.)

But on the whole it was simply a sly little joke of nature that made him seem like an imposing figure seated behind a desk or table, until he stood up. It was a thing one could cram down people's throats with wealth and position behind one; one could flaunt it like a challenge and dare them all to laugh at their peril; but as a poor *émigré* in a hostile land one necessarily became a clown of sorts. But it had its advantages, too. The funny little man with the big noble head who could laugh at his own ridiculous handicap could hardly be suspected of being involved in dangerous schemes and intrigues. Not cute, harmless little Jimmy Columbus, ya gotta be kidding!

Juan Miranda nodded at him as he entered, and jerked his head toward the back room. Columbus reflected that he was never quite sure about Miranda, so comfortably settled in his role as restaurant-keeper. Another sensible adjustment, but perhaps a little too sensible? Could a man really forget what he had been once; what he had lost? But of course a man could, many had. They'd been willing to settle for a second-rate security in a foreign land that despised them. Miranda would bear watching; he looked too satisfied with what he had here. Like some others, he might require a small lesson in loyalty.

As Columbus made his way between the tables, the restaurant door opened abruptly behind him.

133

"Daddy. Hey, Daddy, can I talk to you a minute?"

It always set his teeth on edge: the disrespectful form of address, the fluent *Americano* language totally without accent. . . . And the way she looked. He knew what he would see when he turned, her mother's face, her mother's eyes, her mother's slender figure—and the indecently tight denim trousers, faded and worn and not very clean. The indecently thin T-shirt that bore the idiotic legend "I'd Rather Be Sailing." And, as a gesture toward the gale outside, a quilted blue ski parka ragged at the cuffs. The lovely dark hair cut off short like a boy's; except that nowadays it was the boys who wore it long. Like the young hooligan waiting for her in the battered little sports car at the curb outside, visible through the glass of the door.

He made the effort, and he felt himself smile at her as a father should, and he heard himself say playfully: "Talk, *querida?* You want to talk to your old papa, how nice. Come, we go have a nice little talk."

She laughed at his teasing. "Oh, Daddy!"

He sighed in an exaggerated way. "How much today?"

She smiled at him fondly and shrugged her slim shoulders under the shapeless, ragged jacket. As if he could not nowadays afford to buy her pretty clothes—or at least decent, clean, whole clothes! As if he had not worked hard and risked much to be able to do so! He took out his wallet and produced a bill and then, as if as an afterthought, another. He put them into her hand and she kissed him quickly.

"You're an old sweetie," she said, and darted off.

The sports car rattled away. There was not much time left, Columbus thought darkly; she was almost lost. The name was already lost with Armando, the family was dying, but the blood could still be saved, but it would have to be done soon. The small female child in the beautiful white baptismal garment who should have become the gracious Doña Francesca Elena Maria de los Angeles Colombo y Aguilar had almost been transmuted by circumstances into a typically sloppy and ill-mannered little tight-pants Yankee tramp—he forced himself to think the ugly word—calling herself Frankie Columbus. He could not fight it here in this coarse and vulgar country; and if she married here, what kind of peasant stock would she select?

No, in order to have even a small chance of redeeming her, and the ancient line from which they came, he must return her to the gentle aristocratic environment in which she belonged; and it would have to be done soon. Well, it would be soon, now, very soon. Only a few months more and the thing would be done. Belatedly, perhaps, in the opinion of many who had long since given up the struggle; but one hoped not too late—and, in truth, the longer the usurper was permitted to generate hatred and disillusionment among his once naive and gullible followers, the easier the return to sanity and reason should become. The recent exodus was a hopeful sign. . . .

Columbus was aware of the people at the surrounding tables regarding him with affectionate amusement, all except those occupying the large round table in the corner, dominated by a heavy man with a great, black, drooping mustache who ignored him completely, even pointedly. Somebody would have to speak to Ramiro about behaving more naturally. But elsewhere in the big room, he was aware, there was amused sympathy mixed with some reluctant criticism at the sight of the odd-looking little man smiling dotingly after the pretty daughter long after she was gone from sight. Nice little Jimmy Columbus; but he really shouldn't let that motherless young girl run wild like she does. . . . He turned abruptly and entered the back room and let the forced smile go as the door closed behind him.

It was a small dining room for private parties, with a long central table surrounded by straight wooden chairs. There was light from the discreetly curtained windows facing the alley. Two seated men had risen politely as Columbus entered; the third took more time getting to his feet. He was the most Americanized of the three, Pete Orosco, slim, mustached, and darkly handsome, a rather confused young man, Columbus reflected, who had the proper hatred for the enemy as well as for the overbearing Yankees among whom he'd been thrown as a boy when his parents found refuge here, but who nevertheless seemed to have absorbed some of their disrespect for rank and quality.

Beside Orosco was the large man known only as Bolo. The word could refer to a certain type of knife, or to a very stupid person, and Columbus thought it was very appropriate here in both meanings. Bolo was swarthy and muscular, with an odd, cropped bullet head set on a very short neck. Seeing Columbus' eye on him, he jerked forward in a convulsive semblance of a bow; but it was the lean, leathery little jockey of a man on his right who spoke the greeting, Jesus Cardenas, whose family had served the Colombo family for generations. After responding properly, Columbus seated himself and made a small gesture of permission. He waited until Jesus and his companions had resumed their chairs.

"I saw Ramiro outside," Columbus said then, carefully ignoring the question of why young Orosco, not normally included in their deliberations, had been invited today. Jesus would have his reasons, and they would be presented in due time. He went on: "Is that wise? He cannot help looking like the pirate and conspirator he is."

"I thought he might be needed, *Señor*," Jesus said. "His boat is available and he knows the waters. If the Scandinavian crazy has run into difficulties in this storm, a search . . ."

"The *Sueco* crazy has damaged his vessel again, but he is now safely in the harbor. We hope he will condescend to join us soon. What has the *Cubano* crazy to report?"

Jesus grinned at the affectionate insult. "Don Esteban and his people are ready," he said.

"Don Esteban and his hangers-on have been ready for almost twenty years," Columbus said. "Ready for anything as long as it involves no personal risk or expense or labor. Don Esteban Ybarra still thinks all that is required is for him to show his handsome face and the Cuban people will overthrow the Marxist impostor and elect him *Presidente* by acclaim. But he will still make a fine figurehead when the time comes, he improves with age like good cheese, so we must keep him happy, eh, Jesus? What about the others?"

"Elsewhere preparations are proceeding in a satisfactory manner, I am asked to inform you."

Orosco was listening, trying intelligently to guess what was not being said from what was. Perhaps, indeed, it was time for him to admit some younger men into his counsels, Columbus thought; some who had demonstrated the proper quality of enduring hatred, like this one.

He spoke to Jesus. "They are providing themselves with the necessary weapons, as agreed? I will not get involved with firearms in those quantities. That is too closely watched these days, and too much of a clue to our intentions if discovered. The drugs, that is a different matter; everyone smuggles those."

"These are professionals; they will acquire what they need from their own sources," Jesus said. "But the Major wishes me to remind you that the second installment is soon due."

"It will be paid on schedule. What have you discovered on that other matter?"

"It was not done by the Coast Guard personnel. There was

a government man along from an agency that was never identified. He shot very fast and very straight. His name was Martin, born Martinez."

Columbus was silent for a moment. "Martinez? You are quite certain? Of course you are, old friend. Well, if it is that Cuban family, no more could be expected; there was never any class loyalty there. I want to know all about this turncoat Martinez, his business associates, and the agency for which he works."

"I know the hotel at which he stays, *patron*. It would not be difficult—"

Columbus shook his head quickly. "If he dies violently, who will be suspect? We cannot afford to attract that kind of attention; we have business more important than private vengeance. Get me the information. Perhaps we can leave Mr. Martin something to remember us by, when the time comes."

"Sí, señor."

"And now, Montoya."

That was where the problem lay, apparently. Jesus' quick glance toward Orosco said they were coming to the reason for the younger man's presence now.

"Montoya has seen the light, Don Jaime," the little man said. "He does not wish the kind of attentions given his house extended to his wife and children. He will cooperate and he will not talk. He has already suggested a suitable boat in his harbor, forty-eight feet, twin diesels, thirty knots; a reasonably new sportfisherman with all the equipment to make it look very genuine, a true rich man's toy, no apparent threat to anyone. The owners have been heard discussing a voyage to Cozumel early in the spring. It is a lengthy passage of over four hundred miles and a discreet interception should not be too difficult. Montoya will arrange his work at the Yacht Club to watch and listen; he will give us the necessary route information as soon as it is available. The Bosun should have time to make his arrangements. Here is what we have on the vessel and its owners so far."

Columbus took the slip of paper and glanced at it, committing the information to memory. He struck a match and watched the paper go into flame, and ashes, in the cheap glass tray before him.

He said, *"Muy bien.* But let him communicate any further information directly to the Bosun; we want no more to do with it here."

"Sí, patrón."

There was a little silence. Now was the time. Columbus waited patiently for Jesus to speak once more.

"There is a problem," the little man said at last.

"Yes?"

"It is a pity Montoya was so difficult and had to be convinced that we truly meant the warning we gave him. Leaving a message at his house that he would comprehend worked well enough; but that unfortunate business at the other house. . . ."

"It was necessary to strike elsewhere as well," Columbus said. "As I explained to Olson at the time, we could not afford to draw attention to Montoya by having it happen to him alone. It was essential that several residences in the neighborhood should suffer so it would seem a local wave of crime and vandalism directed at Spanish and Anglos indiscriminately."

"Sí, patrón. But the news from the hospital is not good. It is now definite that the man will live."

Columbus frowned. "So? That merely leaves the police investigating a simple break-in instead of a murder, does it not?"

Jesus glanced toward Orosco. "Tell the *patrón,* Pedro."

"The Swede took off his damn mask, sir," the younger man said.

When Columbus did not speak, Jesus said, "And one hears that there is now talk in official circles of the young couple making the identification. And you forget—pardon, Don Jaime—that it is not only a break-in but a rape that is being investigated."

Columbus was annoyed with himself for forgetting. He looked at Orosco. "Tell what happened, exactly."

"The woman hit him while he was beating on the man. He seemed to go nuts. Not wild, exactly, but his eyes got funny and he looked at her for a moment, you know, sir, like the gears were shifting in that slow Scandihoovian brain. The stupid bitch swung on him again, yelling at him to leave the man alone, and he simply wrapped her up in his arms like King Kong and marched into the bedroom, tossed her on the bed, peeled her like a banana from the waist down, and gave it to her good. You've got to hand it to the guy, sir, he's got the equipment to do it with. Only she was fighting him the whole time, and she kind of pulled his ski-mask around so he couldn't see right. He had trouble straightening it after he

138

got up; and finally he just yanked it off as he came back into the other room where the man was lying.. . ."

"Why did you not report this before?"

Orosco spread his hands. "I'm sorry, Mr. Columbus. I didn't think . . . I mean, I thought the guy was dead. Olson had pounded him into a pulp with that busted shotgun, damn near."

Columbus frowned. "So. Well, there are only two choices, are there not, Jesus? We remove the Swedish who can lead them to us. Or we remove the man who can lead them to the Swedish." He sighed regretfully. "The first alternative is most attractive. I am weary of this Olson. Unfortunately, we need him so the other must go. But I still do not want us involved directly, you particularly; there is more important work for you, *viejo*. Let the Swede solve the problem he has created. I will tell him so when he comes." He turned back to Orosco and said flatly, "You should have stopped it."

"No, Mr. Columbus." The young man was a little pale under his dark, Latin skin, but his voice held no hesitation. "The instructions were specific, sir. I was to get a couple of tough young guys, Anglos preferably, and give him a hand in entering two-three houses. Give him a hand, Mr. Columbus, not stop him."

Columbus smiled slowly. The boy had promise; he did not allow himself to be intimidated. Columbus said, "And after what you had witnessed, with the woman still lying on the bed with no trousers on, you were not tempted. . . .?"

Orosco said, "Mr. Columbus, I'm as horny as the next guy, but with a dead man on the floor—what I thought was a dead man—all I wanted was to get the hell out of the joint before somebody else wandered in on us. Anyway, I'm not sure I'm interested in anything that blond ape leaves behind. One of the *gringos* I'd brought had some ideas in that direction, but I told him I'd kick his balls right up between his ears if he wasn't out the door in five seconds flat."

Jesus said, "We most also consider the problem of the woman herself." When Columbus glanced at him sharply, he went on: "Pedro says he could not see how much of Olson's face she had managed to uncover; but she might have seen enough before he turned away from her. There have been official hints that she did."

"The stupid Norse bull! Merely because the wench struck him. . . .!" Columbus made a sharp little gesture of disgust. "To indulge himself thus by way of retaliation was unforgivable, but to leave them both alive afterward, that borders on insanity!" He sighed. "Almost, I am tempted. If Olson were not the only one available who can get the boat through those waters when the time comes; the only one who can be counted on not to succumb to a fatal attack of caution at the wrong moment. . . Ramiro has too little skill and too much regard for his own safety. He can only be trusted to land the other party after the serious work has been done. So, the *Escandinavo* must be preserved until we have no further use for him. Very well, I will inform him that he must attend to the woman, also, in order to protect him, and us, from the results of his carelessness."

The big, silent, dark man beside Jesus cocked his head in a curious, animal-like way. He nudged Jesus with his elbow and made a small sound under his breath.

Jesus said, "Bolo says he comes now."

Columbus nodded, wondering as always just how much the hulking moron comprehended and how much he managed to communicate; but Jesus alone knew how to understand and utilize the man. Columbus said quickly, "Two things, Jesus. If Ramiro must come here, he should at least learn how to act naturally. If I were a policeman I would arrest him on sight, the way he behaves."

"I will instruct him, Don Jaime."

"Also, Miranda will bear watching."

"*Sí.* It shall be done."

Then Olson was entering the room by the door that led directly to the alley. With him was his blonde. She looked almost slight beside the *Sueco's* rawboned figure; but she was actually a well-formed and moderately tall woman with pale fine hair pulled back sleekly from her face and made into a knot behind. She wore a smart blue trousers-suit with a fragile scarf of the same color knotted loosely at the throat. Over it was a long blue coat. With the long wide coats and the long wide trousers, the emancipated modern woman managed to wrap herself in almost as much hampering cloth as the fettered Victorian ancestress she scorned, Columbus reflected sourly; but actually he was looking for the bruises.

It was something he could never help. Olson's handsome blonde, like his handsome boat, was often somewhat battered; and Columbus could never keep himself from trying to visualize the bedroom scenes; these two strong blonde creatures battling fiercely like great mating carnivores until the woman was subdued, not entirely against her will, but beaten and naked with her long fair hair in wild disorder. . . . No. It was no time for such distracting thoughts. Besides, today there was no visible damage to stimulate such thoughts; there had not been time. She must have joined him at the dock just now, and they must have come straight here. But she would have a difficult time tonight, that was a certainty. After a successful mission and a stormy boat ride, Olson would be ready for a little brutal diversion.

One resented the breach of security, of course; but it was something one had to tolerate, employing Hans Rurik Olson. And Columbus had checked on the woman discreetly and learned that she had a history of associating with unsavory male characters and of keeping her mouth shut about their affairs. Now she had Olson, or he had her. Obviously a vulgar woman despite her elegant good looks, possessed by a violent and vulgar man, so why was there always that small sense of envy. . . .

"Sit over there," Olson was saying to the blonde. "As always, like the monkeys, you hear not, you see not, you speak not, understand?"

"Monkey yourself," the woman said calmly, removing the long coat deliberately before she seated herself. "I don't talk; I never have. You know that. Don't flex your muscles at me, you big squarehead."

"Squarehead, is it?" Olson was smiling at her fondly. "That, I will remember."

The woman laughed. "I'm trembling, see me? Now get your damn business over with so we can get on to something important."

"She was once a Chicago gangster's moll," Olson said with a grin, speaking to nobody in particular. "She is a wicked and immoral person. But she has a point. Ja. Here it is. Count and pay. As the lady says, there wait for us matters of more importance than money."

A small, zippered canvas bag hung from his shoulder by a strap of webbing. He tossed it onto the table in front of Columbus and stepped back, a tall, wide man who gave the impression of almost bursting out of his shabby work clothes, as if the half-unbuttoned blue shirt and the snug denim trousers were too flimsy to contain, if it came to a test, the power inside. He was fairly grimy and he smelled of old sweat and engine oil. Unlike the woman with her very fine, very pale, very straight hair, he was the curly, wavy species of *Escandinavo*. The rebellious yellow hair was not worn long by modern standards; it looked more as if he had simply neglected to visit a barber recently than as if, like so many nowadays, he was making a statement or following a style. On the back of his head perched a shapeless yachting cap.

Normally clean-shaven, Olson had not had time for a razor for several days. The blond stubble made his strong, long, bony face look even tougher than usual. Out of that face, beneath the sun-bleached eyebrows, looked a pair of pale blue eyes. Columbus always found those eyes disconcerting. They mirrored an ancient Viking confidence in the total superiority of Hans Rurik Olson and the primitive race to which he belonged over all other men and races—mere playthings created for the amusement of the savage blond warriors from the north. It was, Columbus knew, a distorted reflection of his own Latin arrogance. That was what made it so disturbing, to recognize the same contemptuous, superior attitude in this deluded barbarian throwback. There would never be any proper respect or deference from this one. He reached abruptly for the bag and opened it.

"That catamaran, it was very good after all." Olson spoke idly as he watched Columbus count the money. "I was not certain at first because it didn't resemble a real boat; but the boys report that it sailed well and the shoal draft made loading as easy as we'd hoped. No rowing back and forth with an overburdened dinghy or leaky rowboat. They merely pulled up the centerboards and beached her. The truck backed across the sand right up to her and they simply tossed the stuff aboard."

"I will keep it in mind," Columbus said. "Maybe later we will use the technique again. But we cannot afford to show a consistent pattern; we must always change."

"To be sure, she handled like a pig with the full load on board; multihulls like that aren't made to carry much weight. But there was a favorable wind and they made pretty good time anyway, ja? Regan is a good man and a good sailor. . . . Satisfactory?"

"Of course," Columbus said. It was, perhaps, the only consolation, dealing with the Swede. The count was always correct. Olson never tried to slip a little into his pocket on his way from the contact point as Ramiro, for example, undoubtedly would have done. "No problem with the delivery?" Columbus asked.

"Ha, on the day I have trouble with little men like that, I give up *brännvin*," Olson said with a grin. "It was a simple

142

covering operation. My big black Ernesto was up on the bridge with me; between his shotgun and my .357 Magnum we had it all under control. The boys unloaded the cat into the speedboats in record time. Our friends are businessmen, at least when the other party to the transaction knows the score. They say any amount, any time, they'll be happy to handle it for us at the price."

"And the catamaran?"

"When she was empty, we took her out and scuttled her in three hundred fathoms. I did not like that, she had served us well in spite of her odd appearance, but . . ." He shrugged resignedly, and took the sheaf of bills Columbus extended, riffled it casually, and thrust it into the pocket of his dirty jeans. "However, for the work you want done in the spring, we must have something entirely different. For all that crowd and its equipment, at least forty-five feet; anything less will become logy with that much weight on board, and we cannot afford to yield up too much speed. I would like power enough for at least thirty knots so we can cruise at twenty-five without strain. . . ."

"I know. I have the figures you gave me," Columbus said. "We have some prospects; the Bosun is investigating. We will let you know."

"Ja. Well, it is a pleasure to do business with you, Mr. Columbus. . . ."

"A minute before you go," Columbus said. He glanced toward the seated woman, and beckoned Olson closer, lowering his voice. "There is some cleaning up to do," he said. "Or to put it another way, you left some loose ends dangling out in Coral Shores; they must be neatly tied for your sake as well as ours. Two loose ends. Jesus will give you the information."

There was a small moment of silence. Olson's pale blue eyes were narrow. "And what if I should tell you that business was not to my liking and I undertook it only as a favor to a valued customer. . . ."

"It was not the favor you did me that has brought trouble, *Señor* Olson. It was the favor you did yourself in the course of it."

Abruptly the Swede threw back his head and laughed uproariously. "Ja, of course! One must pay for one's baser impulses, true? I will check with your *mayordomo* in the morning. Right now . . . Come, my angel." The blonde rose gracefully and joined him at the door. Making the gesture seem quite gallant, the big man urged her out ahead of him by cupping a large hand over the rear of her slacks where the blue material was stretched most intriguingly smooth and taut. Columbus could hear his voice before the door closed. "Squarehead, is it? That, I think, we should discuss further. . . ."

After the door had closed, some time after, Jesus pursed his lips and turned his head to spit deliberately on the rug. He made an elaborate thing of wiping his mouth with the back of his hand.

"Precisely, *amigo*," Columbus said. "It will be a pleasure when the time comes. But not yet."

Driving the ugly, noisy, cheap little American car homeward in the dark, later, after attending to the money—it was a pleasure to know that he was actually a rich man once more, although he could not, of course, afford to show it here—he stopped at a gas station he had never patronized before. While the tank was being filled, he made a telephone call from the booth at the side of the lot. He counted five rings before the instrument was picked up at the other end.

"I have a collect call for anyone from Mr. James," the operator said. "Will you pay for the call?"

Formerly she would have asked if the charges would be accepted, Columbus thought; but apparently the stupid *Americanos*, who never bothered to learn anybody else's language, could not even comprehend their own, so this simple-minded question had been substituted.

A female voice, a rather young female voice, said, "Yes, Operator, we'll pay. . . . Jimmy?"

There had never been any respect from this one, either, he reflected wryly; no Don Jaime here or even Mr. Columbus. She had no respect for anything. It had angered him at first. She had not been at all the type he'd requested; there had been a misunderstanding and it had angered him at first. It was not what one paid, and paid high for, at a place like that. Not to be insulted, and even playfully ridiculed for one's appearance; but as it had turned out, the taunting little girl had known exactly what she was doing, using his rage to accomplish a very satisfactory . . . But never mind that. It had been an interesting variation, but one of which he had soon tired. However, he had found much better employment for her undeniable talents.

"Is the Bosun there?" he asked.

"Fuck you," the girl said pleasantly a thousand miles

144

away. "Don't play games with me, Jimmy. Did they make the run okay? Did they get rid of that fucking cat so it can't be traced?"

"Everything is very okay," Columbus said, reminding himself that it was useless to be angry with the foul-mouthed little bitch. "It would be even more okay if you did not have such tender principles about . . ."

"It's my lousy risk more than anybody's, isn't it? And stealing rich people's fancy seagoing playthings is one thing, but killing them. . . . Well, that would take all the fun out of it, don't you see? Anybody can shoot holes in people, what's so smart about that? Anyway, the idea makes me sick to my fucking stomach. You want to talk to him?"

"One thing first," Columbus said. "That Hatteras he suggested, the one being chartered for the Caribbean cruise, is much too slow for the job this spring. Can't the man read the simple numbers we gave him? We've located a vessel here that I think will serve the purpose. Write this down. . . ." He gave the data from memory and went on: "It is not for sale as far as I know, but there could be a mistake in his listings, could there not? Anyway, see that he makes inquiries about it and reports it to me in triumph, so I can put him in touch with one of the employees of the Yacht Club where it is berthed, who will supply more information as it becomes available."

There was a little pause; then the girl said, "You want him to stick his neck out. You're setting him up, aren't you, Jimmy?"

"Of course. That is what he is for, what else? You knew that from the start, when you found him for us and went to work for him."

"Went to work *on* him, you mean." Columbus heard her sigh at the other end of the line. "Oh, shit. I mean, he's actually a kind of sweet and helpless sort of guy. . . ."

"To you they're all sweet and helpless guys."

"Yeah, sure. I'm just a sentimental little slob. Okay, but in the meantime be nice to him, Jimmy. Don't tear him down now after I've gone to all the trouble of building him up. His fucking—I mean his non-fucking—wife has done enough of that, the frigid bitch. You tell him what a great operation he's running here, and what a hell of guy he is. Tell him the North Bar Intercept was a tremendous success due entirely to his administrative genius, terrific seamanship, and fantastic courage. Lay it on thick, damn you."

"The what?"

"Oh, he's getting it all organized; he's even inventing names for them now; very systematic. Like that name he's got for himself, the Bosun, for God's sake! Intercept this and intercept that like a fucking spy novel. But you'll play along with him, understand, unless you want him back on the bottle again and no damn use to anybody. Oh, and he's just sold a local sailboat to some easterners who've promised to send us postcards, lots of postcards, to let us know how they're getting along. Part of the friendly spirit of Buckmeister and Pond, concerned about their customers; and you'd be surprised at how often the folks do write and tell us how much they like the boats we sold them. So we should be able to put a finger on this one if we want it, and it ought to be a good candidate for another long run when you're ready; a TO 39—"

"Translate, please."

"That's a Trans-Ocean thirty-nine-foot ketch. Built by the Lam boatyard in Taiwan. Diesel auxiliary, plenty of fuel capacity. . . .Well, he'll tell you all about it. He's dying to, and even if you don't need it, you'll damn well say what a clever guy he is to spot it and keep track of it. Understand? I have a hard enough time keeping him brave and sober without you spoiling everything with your lousy *hidalgo* arrogance, so cool it, Jimmy, cool it. Okay, I'll put him on. . . ."

Hanging up the telephone a few minutes later, Columbus saw that his car was ready and the attendant waiting; but he could not bring himself to drive home to be met, he was quite sure, by the housekeeper's querulous complaint that the Señorita Francesca had not yet returned and it was not good for the Señor to permit a well-bred young lady to be out unchaperoned all hours of the night. Permit? He knew exactly what would happen if he tried to forbid it. It would merely cost him the few precious contacts he now had with his daughter and it would accomplish nothing, not here in this land of disrespect and rebellion. For her own salvation, later, he would reluctantly sacrifice her affection, but not for nothing. . . . Would he sacrifice her, if his duty demanded it? The question sneaked into his mind unbidden: how much was a man required to pay for his country and his class and his beliefs? But there was no question of sacrifice now, he told himself. The sacrifices had all been made. His wife, his son, was not that enough? Now it was all arranged and well

146

arranged, if only that wild barbarian Olson did not destroy everything with his crazy undisciplined impulses.

It had been a mistake to think of Olson. The thought led to a sharp mental image of Olson's elegant blonde, with Olson's grimy hand bestowing an inelegant caress upon the seat of her elegant trousers; which led to a further mental image of what might be transpiring between them now that they'd had time to become throughly intoxicated. Columbus sighed and put more coins into the telephone. A cigarette-hoarse contralto voice answered. He identified himself as was the custom there.

"Tonight," he said. "I need—"

"I know what you need, honey. I know what all my clients need. Come right along; I have just the young lady. We aim to please." The hoarse voice laughed. "Even if you did steal one of my girls away from me. Well, that little bitch had too big and dirty a mouth on her, anyway."

CHAPTER 15

April

Latitude 41°N; Longitude 74°W
Latitude 24°N; Longitude 81°W

In addition to keeping the weight off his damaged leg, the cane was a very useful costume accessory while traveling, Harold Ullman decided—the cane, reinforced by a certain picturesque haggardness. Of course the crutches he'd recently discarded would have been even more effective psychologically, but they'd have been a lot more awkward to handle and the cane did just fine. To hell with paying first-class air fare. All that got you was a few free drinks he could do without and a slightly wider seat he had absolutely no use for after spending months in the hospital taking nourishment through a straw. He'd never been a big man, and in his present emaci-

147

ated condition he found the tourist-class seats plenty wide enough for comfort.

But with the cane and the limp and his obvious weakness he got the kind of service you used to get in first class and didn't any longer. All the pretty stewardesses kept hovering around to make sure he wasn't going to die on them and sue the airline. No, that wasn't fair. They were nice conscientious girls and they really wanted to help. He found himself studying them carefully and trying to estimate, since this was a carefully selected and trained group of girls, how each one would have reacted. . . . No, that was over. To hell with it. But what had happened to the fine upstanding cavegirl in her fashionable sabertooth necklace and smart leopard-skin gown who grabbed a club and fought savagely beside her man in defense of the old family cavern?

But he hadn't even asked that of Nancy, he thought grimly, unable to keep the old gnawing bitterness at bay. He hadn't at all expected her, for instance, to jump the smaller guy and scratch his eyes out while he was dealing with the big one; or even to snatch the pictures from the walls, say, and start heaving them at the enemy as a useful battle distraction. If she'd wanted to cower in a corner like a useless movie ingenue he wouldn't have held it against her for a moment. It was accepted between them that she was a strictly nonviolent girl; and he respected her for her fine humanitarian principles even though he didn't really think much of the principles. He hadn't expected, or asked for, her help.

All he'd asked, all he'd ever asked, was that she would permit him to follow *his* principles, one of which said that any sonofabitch who broke into his home in the middle of the night—forget the mindless vandalism—had better be prepared to either dive headfirst through the nearest window or cope with a twelve-gauge load of double-ought buck. It was not, dammit, a decision he'd made lightly. When you owned a firearm you were morally obliged to consider the circumstances under which you'd use it, if at all, against a human target. He'd given the matter a great deal of careful thought and he'd laid out careful guidelines for himself: if the guy is going away from you, don't shoot; if he keeps coming, shoot. There were, of course, amendments and variations that took into account, for instance, the physical size of the burglar and whether or not he was armed—you didn't want to massacre some unarmed kid you could manage barehanded—but he'd worked it all out long ago to arrive at what seemed to be the safest and most sensible compromise for these days of crime and violence. Yet she'd had the arrogance to treat him like an irresponsible kid who didn't know what the hell he was doing with that big gun, whom she with her superior wisdom had the God-given right to keep from making a terrible mistake. . . .

Cut it out, he told himself sharply. It's settled. It's finished. It's *over*. Just because you saw her again yesterday, maybe for the last time ever, doesn't mean you have to fight the whole thing through once more when you should be thinking of what you're going to say to these New York editorial characters you'll be meeting tomorrow. You are now a free man, a divorced man, or you will be as soon as the final red tape is tied into a pretty bow by the legal experts. You own a boat; you don't own a house. You own a lot of camera gear; you don't own a car. And you don't have a wife. The lady is once again Miss Winters; she's no longer Mrs. Ullman.

It had all been done in a very civilized fashion, he reminded himself; and it had been very gentlemanly of him to let her bring the suit to keep too many curious questions from being asked, even though after what had happened it meant that everybody would think—and undoubtedly did think—that she'd shed him in disgust because he'd failed to protect her from a fate worse than death, as a dutiful husband should. And he'd hardly been able to bear the subtly beaten look she'd displayed yesterday, even though the obvious marks of her ordeal had long since healed. It was clear that the fine self-confidence and proud self-respect that had attracted him from the start had been terribly shaken by what had happened to her that night.

And he certainly hadn't helped by demanding a divorce. But goddamn it, some things were unforgivable; *had* to be forever unforgivable. Otherwise what were matrimony and loyalty all about? He might never again have to face four thugs single-handed—he certainly hoped he wouldn't—but the least he could do was make sure, as a simple matter of survival, that if it should incredibly happen again there'd be no loving intellectual wife to jump him from behind with the highest intellectual motives. Only a suicidal fool would give that shocking, ghastly betrayal a chance to happen twice.

The La Guardia hassle was worse than he remembered it; or maybe his ATQ—his airport-tolerance-quotient—was lower than it had been, which, under the circumstances, wasn't unlikely. He blew himself to a taxi even though the fare was outrageous and, upon reaching his hotel room at last, lay down on top of the bed to recover from the day's experiences. After a while he sat up and called the agency. The rapidity with which the secretary got Bartholomew on the line showed that the potential assignment might actually be a fairly important one. Maybe the magazine involved was pulling up its socks at last under its new management.

"Hey, boy, what are you doing at the Algonquin; I didn't know they'd let a lousy camera bum into that artsy hotel." Bartholomew didn't wait for a response, but went on: "How are you feeling, boy? How's the leg?"

"All stuck back together in one piece, more or less."

"It was that bad, huh? They got you on crutches or something?"

"I was allowed to throw them away last week. Just a cane."

"Well, if you can do without the damn stick, just for a couple of hours tomorrow morning, it would be a good idea. They want to put you on a ship and you don't want to look too damn crippled to get around, if you know what I mean."

"I think I can hobble around without it safely for a little while if you think it's important. What ship?"

"I'll let them tell you that. I'll just give you a hint: remember Mostert's *Supership* book about the big tankers? Well, it hasn't been explicitly stated and probably won't be, but I think that's what they want, but on a smaller scale of course, a magazine scale rather than a book scale, and as far as possible in pictures rather than words."

"Oh, a photographic hatchet job."

"Hush, boy, the word is exposay. And I want you to give them lots of starboards and ports and fore-and-afts and yohoho-me-hearties, you know what I mean. I've sold you as a salty nautical expert; don't let me down. I have a strong hunch from something that was said that none of the other candidates they're considering, terrific photographers all, of course, really knows the pointy end from the blunt one. What's needed, obviously, is somebody who can go up on the ship's bridge and *know* what the stumblebums are doing wrong and, of course, record all the dreadful incompetence in living Kodachrome. And you must bring a lot of fine idealism to the interview, boy. Save the world from the whales. Up with porpoises, down with tuna. Lay it on thick. You know the situation over there. Any old crusade, just so it builds circulation, but right at the moment it looks as if they've decided to save our oceans from the demon oil. Your appointment is

150

at ten; you see Soligson, the photo editor. Eleventh floor. Give me a ring when you get out of there."

As he replaced the phone in its cradle, Harold Ullman couldn't help grinning wryly. It was always like entering a different world, which was what people like Bartholomew were for, to save people with cameras like Harold Ullman from having to live in New York and scrounge up their own assigments, assuming they could learn the ropes or even wanted to. And for this the Bartholomews took a cut of the proceeds that would make an innocent writer paying his innocent ten or fifteen percent faint dead away—but half of something was, after all, better than all of nothing.

But it had been a mistake to come to the Algonquin. The Algonquin was Nancy's hotel. The building was old, the rooms were small, and the elevators were slow; but the restaurant was tops and she'd loved the beautifully old-fashioned, luxuriously shabby lobby where drinks were served in the evening and you could watch all the important and interesting New York intellectuals wandering in and out. And it was a good thing, he reflected, that Nancy hadn't been listening to Bartholomew's cynical briefing, or he'd have to spend all night being set straight about the dying oceans and about the whales and porpoises and other endangered denizens of the sea—and the hell of it was, at the moment he wouldn't really have minded. Being divorced, he was discovering, was a damned lonely business. . . .

The following afternoon early he took the plane back to Miami. Relaxing in his reclining seat he tried to feel triumphant but found it difficult. He thought: I don't mind ordinary jerks so much, but Jesus, I hate noble jerks who're trying to save the world without knowing a thing about it, trying to save the seas without knowing a thing about them. Jeez, what a bunch of landlubbers. And if there's anything worse than a bunch of noble landlubber jerks, it's a bunch of noble landlubber jerks with high shining principles who make it quite clear that if you care to fake a few shots to get them what they want they're certainly not going to embarrass you, or themselves, by scrutinizing the pix too closely—as long as they're *good* fakes, of course, and nobody else can spot them. But who are you to talk, Mr. Ullman, the guy who marched right in there without a cane, acting as if he'd never had a broken bone in his life? Let's belay that talk about jerks, hey, jerk? But anyway you got the job, and nobody can

151

say you don't need it, considering the bills you've still got to pay.

Disembarking in Miami, he found himself creating a bottleneck in the jetway, so-called, with his slow pace and his cane. As soon as there was room he stepped aside to catch his breath and let the other passengers hurry past; one man was pushed against him by the crowd and murmured a soft apology as he went on. Something about the man made Harold Ullman look after him, frowning, although there was nothing particularly noticeable about the middle-aged, medium-sized individual with the thinning brown hair. *Yesterday,* he thought, *aisle seat, other side of the plane, three or four rows back.* He frowned thoughtfully. So the same man had ridden up to New York with him, so what? He, Harold Ullman, wasn't the only person in the world with overnight business in that sprawling metropolis on the Hudson.

Nevertheless, a small alarm bell was ringing somewhere, and a little red warning light was flashing on the control board. Cut it out, he told himself firmly, just because a large gent once made hamburger of us with our own gun let us not have paranoia on top of all our other problems. Security circuits: off.

He realized that there was nothing in the world he wanted, at the moment, as much as a place to lie down and rest; but his watch told him that the DC-3 would be taking off for Key West, with one stop at Marathon, in twenty minutes. The thought of limping clear through the giant Miami airport to the proper terminal was intimidating; the thought of spending yet another hour in a plane seat was sickening; the thought of, upon arrival, trying to find one of the elusive Marathon taxis to haul him to the marina was appalling. There was a hotel right here; and to hell with pajamas and toothbrush. On the other hand, he did have the reservation, and he had called the dockmaster at Boot Key to say he'd be moving aboard the boat tonight. Anyway, he wanted very badly to get home at last after all these months, such as home was these days. . . .

There was the usual magnificent view of the Keys as, with the sun low in the west, the twin-engine prop job finally circled for the landing with the blue-green water below and the white beaches and the scattered little mangrove keys—and of course the main islands with their resorts and developments, but even those didn't look too bad from the air. Then the plane was down and taxiing back along the strip to the small terminal building; and he was making his clumsy, painful way down the steps to the ground and in through the gate. A familiar-looking, stocky, elderly man wearing a fishing cap was coming forward to greet him. For a dreadful moment his weariness kept him from remembering the name, then it came to him: Walter Ellington, of that ancient Matthews on A-dock, the *Waterwitch*.

"Myra thought you might have trouble getting a cab," Wally said. "You got a bag or anything?"

Harold Ullman said awkwardly, "I certainly appreciate—"

"Bag," Wally said. "You know, like in suitcase?"

"A little brown overnighter, but I can—"

"You can go park your tail in the station wagon before you fall on your face. You know our old wreck. I'll be along in a minute." Later, as they drove west along the crowded Overseas Highway, Wally said, "Jerry says you've been to New York about a picture-taking job."

Jerry was Jerry Olds, the Boot Key dockmaster whom he'd called that morning. Harold Ullman was too tired to want to talk about New York, or anything else for that matter, but if Wally was interested, it was the least he could do, considering. He mustered a grin.

"That's right, I'm going to be cruising the beautiful Caribbean and getting paid for it, real hardship duty," he said. "Well, I've got a ride on a kind of middle-sized tanker, one of those flag-of-convenience ships you read about, and I guess we'll actually head straight south through the Mona Passage to Puerto la Cruz in Venezuela, where we'll load up with oil. Nobody seems to know exactly what happens after that, maybe we come directly back to the States, maybe not. They seem to kind of play it by ear. Anyway, it'll be a few weeks before the ship gets back from her present voyage. They'll let me know where and when. That'll give me a little time to catch my breath."

Wally glanced at him. "Looks like breath isn't all you need to catch. Good thing you're not racing sailing dinghies; you wouldn't be worth a damn as ballast. Well, Myra's got dinner waiting, for a start. Some women take up knitting or needlepoint; Myra's hobby is feeding people."

"I know." Ullman said. "Look, I can't say how much I—"

"You got a new neighbor, you know. *Seabreeze,* thirty-foot sloop," Wally said. "Fellow named Simonds, just in from the Bahamas. The Huddlestons, who had that berth, headed north in their *Georgy Girl* a little early this year; wanted to stop in Jacksonville a few weeks to see their married daughter. Well, here we are. Old place hasn't changed much, has it?"

Harold Ullman got out stiffly and looked around. The familiar marina did, as Wally suggested, look much the same as always. There was a sailboat up on the marine railway in front of the boatyard office; the bottom had been scraped clean and would undoubtedly be painted in the morning, weather permitting. There were many boats he recognized and some he didn't. He reached for his suitcase, but Wally beat him to it, and they walked out onto the dock.

He'd already searched out the familiar mast with, at the top, the fantastically expensive new navigation light he'd bought to comply with the latest change in the regulations—the Coast Guard seemed to have the idea that all yachtsmen were millionaires and all chandleries and supply stores were on the verge of bankruptcy and could only be saved by being allowed to sell you priceless, mandatory new safety or navigation gear at least once a year and twice on leap years. The rigging seemed to be in good shape, as far as he could tell at a distance. As they approached, he saw that somebody had run a couple of extra docklines and put out a fender he was sure he hadn't hung there, leaving the boat that night last fall when, a few hours later, his life had been changed forever. He remembered that he'd planned to come back the following weekend to make things shipshape.

"The northers were late this year, but we had a couple of dillies in February," Wally said. "But she rode pretty good in here, no problem."

It was a hard thing to explain, Harold Ullman thought, how you felt about your own boat. There were some bureaucrats out on the West Coast who'd come up with a brilliant idea: the way to get more marina space these crowded days was to get people to *share* boats. Sure. And the way to get more housing space was to get people to share wives, or husbands, or kids, or homes. Sometimes you wondered just how obtuse people could get if they really tried, since they managed to be pretty damn dumb without trying. Even at the moment, grateful as he was, he couldn't help a faint little sense of jealousy: somebody else had got to look after his *Nancy Lou*'s needs this past winter and he'd missed out on the pleasure of doing it himself. He stood for a moment looking down at the graceful little cutter lying motionless in her slip. He noticed that the decks were damp.

"Looks like you had some rain. . . ."

He checked himself, glancing at the older man beside him, who was carefully looking elsewhere. There hadn't been any rain of course. Somebody in the marina, probably Wally himself, had spent a couple of hours this afternoon scrubbing months of grime off the non-skid fiber glass in preparation for his arrival. He saw that the ports and hatches had been opened to air out the cabin for him, and he had a hunch there had probably been some tidying done below. And there was not one damned thing he could do about it, he knew; he wasn't even supposed to say thanks, at least not more than once. All he could do was pass it along. Cruising folks looked after their own. Some day, somewhere, he'd come across another boatman in a bind and that was when he'd be expected to pay back the debt he'd incurred here.

"I'll just put your bag in the cockpit unless you want something out of it," Wally said.

Shortly, they were having drinks in the comfortable deckhouse of the *Waterwitch*, farther out the dock. She was a handsome classic powerboat built back in the days before mass-produced fiber glass, back when real craftsmen took real pride in what they could do with wood. Mrs. Ellington—Myra—was bringing him up to date on recent marina events while she moved briskly between the galley and the deckhouse table.

"You're forgetting the *big* happening of the year," Wally said at last. "You remember that big cat over on B-dock, Harold? I think it was one of Newick's designs—no, Bob Harris'. Owned by that young doctor from Chicago with the pretty wife."

"Fenwick," Ullman said. "I remember. She got cancer, didn't she?"

"That's right. It was a real tragedy. She passed away but he stayed on. Well, you know Myra, always feeding people like I said. . . . Where's that clipping? Here, you can read it for yourself."

It was pleasant in the cabin, and Harold Ullman found that he was no longer on the point of exhaustion. The Mount Gay rum helped, of course, but there was also the triumphant fact that he'd actually made it clear up to New York and clear down here, something he had not been at all certain he could accomplish in his present condition. He was no longer an invalid; he was functioning again. Now he could relax. He was home. He took the newspaper page and spread it and read the item circled in red crayon.

PIRACY AT SEA

Hijacked Couple Makes
Heroic Voyage To Safety

It was quite a story, and it did not really fit Harold Ullman's mental picture of the owner of the catamaran—what had they called it, *Mauna Loa,* no, *Haleakala*—a slightly stuffy and fairly ineffectual-seeming young guy who was forever hosing things down and polishing things up, but who never took his boat away from the dock. One of the non-sailing sailors. The idea that this rather conventional-seeming character had invited a bunch of long-haired hippies aboard to help him sail his boat to the Caribbean was surprising enough; that he then, after being overpowered and set adrift well out at sea, had managed to bring himself and a female companion safely ashore in a small open dinghy was even more startling, considering that he'd never given the impression of being that much of a seaman.

Well, it was easy to be wrong about people and boats. If you saw a real timid-looking gent sitting on a real shaky-looking tub you wouldn't sail across the Stream to Bimini on a bet, chances were he'd just come around the Horn and was heading for the Cape of Good Hope on his way around the world.

"Reporters!" Wally said. " 'Piracy at Sea'! If it's piracy it's got to be at sea, doesn't it?"

"Where does Myra come into it?" Ullman asked.

"Well, she's the one who got those people invited over here for Thanksgiving dinner, where the Doc met them," Wally said. "Shows what happens when you insist on shoveling food into people."

"You stop it now, Wally," Myra said. "But there's one funny thing nobody seems to have noticed."

"What's that?" Ullman asked.

"Well, when Paul left here he seemed real interested in that little smart-alecky hippie girl, but he seems to have come back with the big stupid one."

"How do you know she was stupid?" Wally asked. "She never said anything."

"That's what I mean," Myra Ellington said. "Anyway, we

had policemen and Coast Guard and reporters and everybody else hanging around asking questions for a while, but thank heavens it's got quiet again. It just shows you that Marathon's the yachting crossroads of the southeast; the hub of the Keys as somebody once said. Everything and everybody come through here, good or bad. Now you sit over here to port, Harold, and tell Wally if you want light meat or dark. . . ."

It wasn't late when Harold Ullman walked back toward the *Nancy Lou,* but it was night of course, with the docklights shining on the calm water and the still boats, some dark, some with cabin windows glowing yellow and radios or TVs murmuring inside. He paused to look briefly at the white sloop in the slip next to his. Not much of a boat—the judgment came automatically—and not much of a sailor, either. One of the bulky, clumsy craft sold to folks who were impressed because somebody'd managed to cram, maybe, eight berths inside when the competition could only boast of seven. The fact was, of course, that more than four people trying to exist on board a thirty-footer for any length of time was a clear invitation to mutiny and murder—hell, four was stretching it right to the limit. He had only two good bunks on board twenty-eight-foot *Nancy Lou;* occasional guests could sleep on the settee or the cabin sole.

And whoever the guy was, he didn't know how to make up a halliard or cleat a dockline. The way he had those tired old clotheslines, or whatever they were, wound around those flimsy mooring cleats, he'd have to use a knife if he ever had to cast one off under strain.

"Hi, there."

Ullman had started to turn away, not realizing that the owner of the boat—presumably—had just put his head out the main hatch. He found himself hoping his expression had not been too critical, as he turned back, watching the man scramble up to the finger pier and approach him. The stranger was young, under thirty, and fairly husky in his jeans and T-shirt, with a mop of unruly blond hair and a rather good-looking pale face but unfortunate skin, the kind in which the pores showed prominently. For a moment, Harold Ullman felt a faint, tingling sensation of hostility, and he realized that he would always have that reaction now to large blond male humans; but this was a smaller man, not the kind of semigiant who could cave in your face with one blow of his fist. The stranger held out his hand.

"Bill Simonds," he said. "I guess we're neighbors. I've been admiring that boat of yours. She's a real little seagoing ship."

They shook hands and Ullman said, "Harold Ullman. Well, you seem to get around all right; Wally Ellington says you're just back from the Bahamas."

"That's right. I spent a couple of weeks up north in the Abacos, just loafing around."

"We . . . I was there last fall," Harold Ullman said. "Made the clockwise circuit, West End, Walker's Cay, Great Sale Cay, Allans-Pensacola, and on down."

"Allans-Pensacola, that's the one with the radio tower," Simonds said. "I stopped there, too, just the other day, coming the other way. Nice little harbor. Well, I just wanted to say—" He glanced at the cane. "—just wanted to say I've got to drive into town in the morning to get some groceries; if you need to do some shopping there's plenty of room."

"Thanks a lot," Ullman said. "I'll take you up on that if I don't oversleep."

A moment later he was making his way carefully down the wooden ladder to *Nancy Lou*'s deck, feeling the little cutter yield to his weight. He was aware that Bill Simonds was returning to his own boat, but he did not look that way. Getting down the steep, narrow companionway ladder was a bit of a problem with the uncooperative leg; but seagoing boats were built with plenty of handholds, and he found that he could lower himself by his arms without incurring any dangerous strains in the doubtful area. He made a bet with himself that he'd find that the batteries had been fully charged; and the dial of the battery-condition indicator proved him right. What the hell *could* you do to repay people like that?

He turned on the main switch, and the light over the galley, and made his way forward. As he switched on a light in the sleeping cabin, he caught a glimpse of his face in the bulkhead mirror. It looked thinner and older and tougher, he thought. It was not quite the same shape he'd grown up with; there was a slight lack of symmetry and, of course, a few hairline scars that he'd been assured would soon fade, particularly if he got out into the sun a bit. It was a pale face, like the face of the man in the neighboring boat, who'd just spent several weeks sailing in the sunny Bahamas, he said; the man who couldn't cleat a dockline or coil a halliard.

Harold Ullman grimaced at himself in the mirror, and turned away, and limped forward to get *Nancy Lou*'s log book, stored with the big navigation volumes on the shelf above the foot of his bunk. He searched for the proper page, remembering. Nancy had been navigating, he'd got her interested in that, and she'd been very much disturbed about the island they were approaching which failed to correspond with the chart, and the guidebook they were using, in a certain important respect. But they'd made it into the sheltered bay all right, and anchored, and rowed the rubber dinghy ashore, and explored a half-overgrown road through the mangrove jungle. . . . He found the right page, and read his emphatic reminder to himself at the bottom:

NAV NOTE! ALLANS-PENSACOLA TRACKING STATION ABANDONED
RADIO TOWER REMOVED CORRECT CHART 26320 ACCORDINGLY

He sat there for a while staring at his own handwriting, remembering the man on the plane who'd accompanied him to New York and back. And here was this phony yachtsman who hadn't sailed where he'd claimed to, conveniently established in the adjoining berth presumably to keep an eye on him, Ullman, but why? Goddamn it, he thought bitterly, hadn't they done enough to him already, couldn't they leave him alone now? He found unwanted memories returning: a girl in a lighted doorway backing fearfully from something inside, a group of masked inhuman faces closing in on him, the same girl's distant screams, fading. . . . Nancy. If it wasn't over, if somebody was keeping track of him for some purpose connected with that night last fall, were they watching Nancy, too; and why should that concern him now? She was no longer any responsibility of his. Let that handsome lawyer who'd hovered over her so solicitously during the divorce proceedings protect her now with his legal tomes; she'd made it quite clear that she desired no other protection, hadn't she?

Harold Ullman drew a long breath and checked in his pocket that he had the proper change. He made his way up into the cockpit, scrambled onto the finger pier, and limped off to the pay phone at the end of the dock, angry at himself and at the discovery that you could not erase six years of marriage with a few angry words and a small court action.

CHAPTER 16

April

Latitude 26°N; Longitude 80°W

It was a Howard Johnson room that looked like any Howard Johnson room that looked like any Holiday Inn room . . . in other words, it was the standard plastic cubicle available in any standard plastic motel/hotel in any big city like Miami, where this one was located. Entering, Phil Martin tossed his raincoat on the nearest bed and took out a pack of cigarettes.

"Better not," Tommy Walsh said. He was sprawled by the window in one of the two round upholstered chairs on either side of the low round cocktail table. Beyond the window was a gray, drizzly Miami view that was undoubtedly breaking the heart of the Chamber of Commerce; but at this time of year the condition was temporary. A fierce spring thunderstorm had just passed through, and was still muttering to itself in the distance. Tommy laid aside the copy of *Time* he'd been reading. He said, "Our *Jefe Grande* has decided to save us all from lung cancer if it kills us. If you smoke up this place, if you leave a butt lying around, you'll get us all court-martialed on capital charges. The new idea is, you protect a man from tobacco by sending him to the gas chamber; that's *so* much better for his lungs."

"Where is he?"

"As a matter of fact, Washington called him back north to attend a conference, God bless them. He left strict instructions to maintain close surveillance on those ridiculous *Hermanos de Septiembre* and that social club he's convinced is a terrorist hangout; and, oh yes, if we had any men left over and they were thataway inclined, they could be used for checking up on Mr. Columbus if it made us feel better, although he's convinced it's a waste of time. An aristocratic gentleman like

Don Jaime would not, he feels, soil his hands with any real dirty business. You know, Felipe, if I wasn't such an easygoing slob I might actually get a little tired of that stupid son of a bitch."

"Join the club," Martin said. "What's the immediate problem here?"

"The boys are on their way in from the Keys, where they've been keeping an eye on our freckled friend Ullman. They have requested guidance; they wouldn't explain over the phone. I gather things are going to hell as usual, but we'll have to wait for the details. How are things progressing at your end?"

Martin shook his head ruefully. "Merely speaking fluent Spanish doesn't seem to qualify one to work miracles, dammit. I can't seem to break through the wall of silence in this town. Nobody's talking, nobody's cooperating. Montoya is still too scared to help in any way. After the shambles they made of his house last fall, he obviously sees his wife and kids lying dead in the street if he steps out of line. So we're going to have to figure out just what the second assistant dockmaster and general handyman of a yacht club is supposed to do for Columbus, without his assistance. Hell, *I* don't want to see his wife and kids lying dead in the street, either."

"And that restaurant guy, Miranda?"

"That's a different bird entirely," Martin said sourly, "like a hawk is different from a pigeon. But the trouble is, Columbus knows it just as well as I do. He knows you don't lean on Mirandas like that, because Mirandas get mad and shoot back, even if they have to die for it. But on the other hand, while Miranda isn't going to play Columbus' game any more than he absolutely has to, like letting him use the back room occasionally, he doesn't want to play my game at all. The old, old loyalties are operating there, *amigo*. He's got nothing but aristocratic scorn for the loud-mouthed expatriate crackpots, sure, but that doesn't mean he'll go so far as to betray them to a renegade turncoat with a badge, like me." Martin grimaced. "Well, all we can do is wait, and in the meantime try the other angles I suggested. Have you got anything for me there?"

"Just one recent incident," Tommy said, "besides the tired old standbys: the classic disappearing-yacht phenomena like the *Pirate's Lady* and the *Flying Dutchman*, that get revived every time the subject of yacht-hijacking comes up. But aren't you straining a bit, Phil?"

"You're always saying that," Martin said with a grin. "Well, maybe I am. But it may also be an angle that's being overlooked. After all, Columbus had a two-bit army of mercenaries to pay, out there on the Manatee Keys; and the Major doesn't come cheap and he doesn't work on credit, even in training. . . . Any signs of action in that quarter?"

"Not yet," Tommy said. "Not really. More like reaction, if you know what I mean. They're not moving yet, but somebody else is. My intragovernmental seismograph indicates a few curious rumblings in one of the small, special agencies."

"Miss Cameron's made a deal with them, is that it?" Ullman said.

Tommy nodded. "So it seems. She may be getting a bit desperate by this time, trying to make a real impression on the U.S.C.G., which is like trying to melt the South Polar ice cap by breathing hard. They'll damn well run their drug war their own way and to hell with pretty ladies in pants. So she's unearthed this kind of orphan organization with a little navy all its own; and I figure she's giving them Ochsner, and in return they're to help her out on special assignments involving her Operation X or Operation Extermination or whatever the hell she calls it. Her own little private anti-drug battle fleet, and fuck the U.S. Coast Guard. The only question is, this outfit she's picked, what's taking it so long to get moving?"

"We don't know what date Columbus has set," Martin pointed out. "Presumably they don't, either. And Ochsner will undoubtedly try to keep Manatee Key clean and pure until the last possible moment, just in case somebody comes snooping. They've got to wait until they can catch him with an island full of machine guns and grenades and bazookas. It would be embarrassing to stage a dramatic raid on a fishing lodge and find nothing but fishing tackle. Well, I hope the boys are careful when they move in."

"Yeah, those old ex-Nazis don't have a hell of a lot to lose." Tommy shrugged. "But back to the subject, what makes you think Columbus is going to act the way you think?"

"Because if he acts any other way there's not much we can do about it," Martin said wryly. "The important thing is that Columbus has a payroll to meet and armaments to buy and those paramilitary operations always get fantastically more expensive than anticipated. Well, he knows a place or two where money, or its equivalent, grows right out of the ground, but in order to get there he needs a boat and they took his away from him, twice. Now, you can bet Elizabeth Cameron has her people out hopefully checking every legitimate boat purchase within a thousand miles; anything that's big enough to get down there under sail or power and carry a load back. She'd do that even if she wasn't interested in Columbus, trying to spot other potential smugglers. There's no sense in us even looking for those records. We haven't got the manpower, and she's not going to let any suspicious transactions get by her. So we just forget about that. If Don Jaime gets his next boat legit we're out of luck. But what if he gets it illegit?"

"Wouldn't a smart girl like Cameron think of that?"

Martin shook his head. "She's a real handsome lady, *muy bonita;* but if she's smart at all, which the old man seems to doubt, she's bureaucracy-smart, not people-smart. And the current bureaucratic dogma says that despite all the furor in the press, boat-hijackings don't really happen, and particularly they don't happen in connection with drug smuggling. You ask Customs, DEA, the Marine Patrol, the F.B.I., anybody, even the Coast Guard, and they'll all tell you firmly that in spite of the recent hijack-hysteria there actually haven't been more than a handful of documented cases in recent years. They'll also tell you it stands to reason a big-time smuggler, like Columbus, who's got plenty of money to buy himself a boat—through a dummy if necessary— would hardly be fool enough to turn a simple marijuana bust, if it comes to that, into a case of piracy and maybe even murder by taking one by force on the high seas. That's the official government line, *amigo*, and they'll rattle it off for you any time you stick your dime in the slot. They'd like you to believe, and I think they've actually got themselves convinced, that with a very, very few exceptions all these talked-about yacht-hijackings are simply a press-inflated myth like UFOs and the Bermuda Triangle."

"But you think they're wrong?"

"About UFOs and the fatal Triangle I venture no opinion," Martin said. "And they may even be right about hijackings in general. But they're dead wrong if they try to apply their pretty theory to Jimmy Columbus, as Cameron is probably doing. What does he care about murder raps? He's not planning to stay around long enough to face one; he's going to be the power behind the next president of Cuba where he can laugh at any mention of extradition. And there's another thing about him Elizabeth Cameron is very apt to overlook, and even if she doesn't she won't understand the significance of it

163

because her midwestern brain just doesn't work that way. So she'll calmly ignore the fact that this is one very arrogant little man."

"Meaning what?"

"Figure it out," Martin said. "You're Don Jaime Fernando Colombo y Menendez, and you've lost two boats—not to mention your only son—because crude Yankee yachtsmen wouldn't keep their long snoopy noses where they belonged. How are you going to feel; what are you going to do? Why, you're damn well going to get compensation, aren't you? You're going to take it out of their lousy busybody hides. *Madre de Dios,* one must teach these *gringo cochinos* in their fancy yachting caps not to interfere with a *hidalgo's* little affairs of business, *si?"*

After a moment, Tommy said dubiously, "That's a lot of long-range mind reading, Phil."

"Hell, I *know* the man's mind," Martin said grimly. "What do you think I'm here for, anyway; why do you think I was assigned to this particular account? Largely because the Old Man knows I've got a fine Spanish mind just like it, dammit." After a moment, he grinned abruptly. "Now tell me about this one incident you've dug up that fits the specifications."

"Yeah, sure." Tommy slipped a sheet of paper from a manila envelope. "Read that Xeroxed newspaper item first; then I'll give you the rest, as far as I've got it to date."

Martin drew the slick paper toward him and made a face at it. " 'Piracy At Sea.' How redundant can you get?" He read the newspaper account rapidly, and glanced at the date. "Last December, damn it. It takes some people a long time to generate a half-ass idea. If I'd just thought of checking sooner. . . ."

"There's more recent information," Tommy said. "A half-inflated rubber life raft was washed up on one of the Carolina banks in a storm early in March. It took them a while to get around to tracing the serial number, through the warranty card originally returned to the manufacturer. That six-man raft was purchased by a certain Paul Fenwick, M.D., of Chicago, Illinois, for use on his thirty-eight-foot sailing catamaran *Haleakala,* the one that story was all about." Tommy slid a glossy photograph across the table. "There was something inside the raft," he said.

Martin looked at the photograph and winced. "Thanks, old buddy. You've just saved me the price of lunch. Any I.D.?"

"Not really, but the general measurements and what's left

of the clothing check with the description of one of the hippie gents involved in the hijacking. I'd say it looks very much as if that catamaran ran into bad trouble not too long after they took it over, and they had to bail out in the raft. The record shows they weren't the greatest sailors in the world. They'd already managed to capsize their own boat and half-wreck it; that's how they happened to be crewing on this Dr. Fenwick's."

"I don't suppose the *Haleakala* has turned up anywhere."

"Not a trace. Not under that name or any other, according to all agencies concerned."

"Has this picture been tried on the Fenwick, male, or the Proctor, female?"

"Not yet. On that, we're cooperating with the authorities up north, saving them from having to send a man down. The Fenwicks have a new boat, a forty-foot sloop, and they're living on it in Palm Harbor, a big marina up in West Palm Beach. I thought you might want to tackle the job yourself, so I kind of neglected to mention it to *El Jefe* before he departed."

Martin grinned. "The morale in this joint is lousy," he said. "Whatever happened to *esprit de corps?*" He frowned. "The Fenwicks, plural?"

"That's right, he married the girl. Nothing like a nice sea voyage to inspire romance, apparently, particularly in a cozy little nine-foot dinghy. They've even got a baby, born last month."

Martin raised his eyebrows. "Even for a baby doctor who presumably knows some short cuts, that's pretty damn quick work. How do you do it in a dinghy? I know, I know, don't tell me. Like the porcupines, very, very carefully." He grimaced. "Joking aside, I guess we can assume that the lady was previously pregnant even though the newspaper reporter discreetly made no mention of her condition, and if his story is correct, young Dr. Fenwick only met her a few days before they shoved off from the Keys. Which makes him either a hell of a sweet guy or an awful patsy, and it'll be interesting to find out which. . . . Well, here come the troops."

Masterman entered first, looking like a middle-aged businessman in his neat brown suit complete with tie. Looking at him, it was hard to believe that he'd killed several men and was highly competent with any firearm short or long, particularly short. Behind him was young Simonds in jeans, denim jacket, and Navy-type watch cap. Inexperienced and liable to go off half-cocked, and a little too fond of the ladies, but bright and trainable. They both looked slightly uncomfortable as they stopped inside the door.

Masterman, as the senior, did the initial talking. "Hell, we didn't mean to make a formal delegation of it, Phil. That is, we thought we'd have to tackle *him* so we figured we'd better come together."

"What's the problem?" Martin asked. "Try the bed. Us executives have got all the chairs."

Simonds sat down at the end of one of the beds. Masterman remained standing. He said with sudden harshness, "I'll be damned if I'm going to be responsible for a man's life under these conditions, and Bill here feels the same way. It was okay as long as we had him lying in a safe hospital bed, but now that he's up and moving around, to hell with it. With half a dozen men we might just be able to get away with it; with only two, and Bill mostly stuck on that cottonpicking boat, it's no damn good."

"Has he made you?"

"I think so. Anyway, he knows I flew up to New York with him and came back down. Jesus, I can't stay close enough to do him any good if I'm needed and not get spotted. Even if he doesn't know it yet, if he only suspects, he'll be sure the next time he sees me anywhere around."

Simonds said, "I think he's sure now; because he damn well made me the first time he looked, and that would confirm his suspicions of Sam, wouldn't it?"

"What went wrong?"

"Man, I'm no sailor, I told *him* that from the start," Simonds said. "It was a joke from the beginning. I've got a nice seventeen-foot Hewes Bonefisher on a trailer I keep at my folks' place in Clearwater for when I go on leave. I can take that little outboard anywhere and back at thirty knots, but that doesn't make me a big-boat sailor, a sailboat sailor."

"You were the best seagoing talent we had available," Martin said.

"Well, your best is not good enough. Ullman just strolled along the dock and took one look at that tub you got me and got a bad-smell look on his face. I don't know what he saw, something about the way the ropes were tied, but he knew right away that I was probably a nautical phony. And then we started chatting about the Bahamas—you remember, that was how I was supposed to get cozy with him, comparing cruising notes—and I hadn't said three words before I put my big foot right into it. Who'd expect a chart and a guidebook both to be wrong? But they were, I checked afterward, and he'd been there and he knew damn well I was lying when I claimed to have anchored there too. And what I want to know is why the hell can't we *tell* the poor damned beat-up sonofabitch what we're doing to him, using him for bait?"

"You know why. Security."

"Fuck security. Jeez, the way this thing is set up, nervous as he's likely to be after what happened to him last fall, and now knowing he's being shadowed, if there is some action and we come barging in to help he'll probably tee off on us with a marlinespike or belaying pin or whatever's handy. And I wouldn't blame him one little bit, but that doesn't mean I want to get clobbered by the guy whose life I'm trying to save, even if Richardson, the cold-blooded bastard, doesn't feel it's too damn important to keep him alive as long as we learn who comes to silence him. But dammit, after spreading it around everywhere that these people can identify the jerks who trashed their house that night, we owe them *something,* don't we? Like protection?"

It was, Martin reflected, interesting to know that Simonds wasn't as tough as he looked, and sometimes acted. The young man had a conscience, not necessarily an advantage in this line of work, but pleasantly humanizing.

"Well, you can switch over and protect the woman for a while," Martin said. "But first you'd better get that damn boat out of there and back up to Biscayne Bay, whatever that marina is just south of here. . . ."

"Dinner Key."

"Dinner Key. I'll notify the owner, or do you want him to give you a hand bringing it up?"

"I can make it all right under power."

"When you get rid of it, work out a schedule with Sam for keeping an eye on the wife. Ex-wife. The boys who're watching her now can take over down there in the Keys. . . ."

When they had left, Martin rose and walked to the dresser and poured himself a drink, offering the bottle to Tommy Walsh, who shook his head.

"The hell of it is," Martin said, "it was my idea."

"I know," Tommy said.

"I thought it would be clever to recruit the poor bastard, figuring he might be willing to stick his neck out a bit to help catch the guys who put him into the hospital, not to mention the divorce court. Just drop a word here and there that he'd got a good look. . . . Hell, even a greenhorn like Simonds can

167

see it: with Ullman's cooperation the thing was perfectly feasible. Without it, it's a bust, and a risky bust. But Richardson came down with that dread Washington disease, security fever, and now we're supposed to do it this impossible way without Ullman's knowing it, and we've even put the girl in jeopardy without *her* knowledge. Shit!"

"Well, looking on the bright side, if you want to call it that, it doesn't seem to be working." Tommy pointed out. "It's been several months since we started leaking it around, hasn't it?"

"Almost. And not one attempt to silence them that anybody's been able to spot. But as you say, under the circumstances it's just as well." Martin shook his head. "I don't like this whole business, *amigo*. We can't seem to get a grip on it from any angle. It's moving somewhere, I can feel it, but it's totally out of control."

He stepped to the window with his glass and stood looking out. The rain had passed, leaving everything wet and pretty and shiny in the tender new sunshine.

CHAPTER 17

April

Latitude 27°N; Longitude 80°W

The Palm Harbor Marina, about sixty miles north of Miami, was located between two of the bridges crossing Lake Worth and the Intracoastal Waterway from West Palm Beach on the mainland to Palm Beach out on the sandy strip of offshore land that, starting at Miami Beach, parallels that coast of Florida like a slightly misprinted line on a small-scale chart. It was a big, well-kept marina with excellent facilities and they'd been lucky to get space there, Paul Fenwick reflected, since it was also close to all required medical services.

Finding a place where they'd let you live on board wasn't easy these days, particularly near big cities. It was an odd thing. Eyesore trailer courts proliferated endlessly; if you wanted to live in a tin box on wheels you'd have hardly any trouble finding space for it. But if your choice of domicile was a graceful sailing yacht, God help you. Fortunately, the marina slip had kind of come with the boat when he bought it, although some finagling had been necessary to keep it. The fact that Billie and he had, after the newspaper stories, been minor celebrities for a while, hadn't really hurt.

The boat was a stock Valiant 40, cutter rigged, three years old, and Paul Fenwick was working hard at bringing back the teak trim around the cockpit. The work involved some sanding and a lot of bleaching and oiling. Many people, including *Faraway*'s previous owners, didn't believe in it, claiming they really *liked* that nice weathered gray color; and why use durable expensive teak if you were going to go to all the trouble of treating it like more vulnerable wood? But Fenwick enjoyed working on his new boat—his new second-hand boat. Before they'd moved aboard, he'd refinished all the woodwork below decks with Billie's help. He'd also had the diesel worked over by a competent mechanic and had then given the engine room a thorough cleaning himself. He'd checked the standing and running rigging—he was getting quite good at splicing, if he did say so himself—and sent the old sails out for inspection and repair and bought several new ones. Now he was starting on the topside trim and thinking, a bit surprised, that he was, goddamn it, in many ways happier than he'd ever been in his life.

He found himself fighting the idea, a little. It seemed disloyal to his lost *Haleakala,* the boat Deedee and he had, largely, built with their own hands, but that was just the point: *Haleakala* had had too many painful memories attached. *Faraway* as yet had none. It also seemed disloyal to his lost Deedee—but Deedee had been a very independent and self-sufficient person. He'd loved her deeply and there had never been any doubt in his mind that she'd loved him, but he'd also known that she'd never really *needed* him, although the reverse had been far from true. Even toward the end she'd never required or asked for his help. Alone she'd faced the terrible present pain and menacing future blackness unflinchingly—strange considering her funny little everyday fears.

Something very important had come to Paul Fenwick fifty miles out in the Atlantic with the knowledge that, for all her undoubted courage, the girl who was with him—not to mention her unborn child—was totally dependent on him for survival. Good as the weather had been, she could never have made it without him; she simply lacked the necessary knowledge. Of course there had been no real heroism involved in spite of that embarrassing stuff in the papers, but still he *had* brought them safely to land; and now he was still very important, even essential, to her and her child. It gave him a satisfying sense of responsibility such as he'd never known.

Of course it was more than just an ego trip, as the freaks would have put it; there was also the fact that, already, he could hardly imagine life without this big, calm, quiet, gentle girl he'd found in such a strange way. It made him happy just to hear her humming softly to herself as she performed one of her innumerable self-imposed tasks below while the baby slept in the tiny stateroom just to port of the companionway, which had been converted into a nursery. Not that things were perfect; one couldn't expect that so soon. That it wasn't his child didn't bother him a bit; it was hers, and she loved it, and they'd have one together, maybe even two, as soon as they got around to it, and to hell with that. But he was going to have to do something drastic about that goddamn gratitude of hers. He'd tried to tell her how he felt, but he could never quite seem to get through her stubborn sense of obligation, of a debt to be paid, that hung between them like a thin, impenetrable nylon curtain. . . .

"*Faraway,* ahoy!"

He looked up to see a moderately tall, lean man in a seersucker suit and sports shirt standing above him on the finger pier holding an attaché case. The black hair, the olive skin, and the aquiline features hinted at Spanish ancestry, but the voice was unaccented.

"Dr. Fenwick?"

"That's right, although I'm not working at it right now."

"My name is Martin, may I come aboard?"

"Sure, but if you've got leather soles I'd appreciate your taking off your shoes."

"Rubber all the way, Doctor. I know that much about boats, but it's about all I know." The stranger made a long step from the pier, clearing *Faraway*'s lifelines, and reached inside his coat. "Just to make it official," he said. "No sweat, Doctor. Just a few questions."

Fenwick glanced at the leather folder with the gold badge. He couldn't read the inscription on the badge; he had a hunch he wasn't really supposed to. He grinned wryly.

"Well, we're hardened to it," he said. "Question away, but first, how about a beer?"

"If you're having one."

Fenwick capped the bottle of teak oil on the cockpit seat. "I was just about to take a break here, anyway. I suppose you want my wife present."

"If Mrs. Fenwick doesn't mind."

It still pleased him to hear her called that, although you'd think a man would soon be cured of such juvenile bridegroom reactions the second time around.

"I'll get her. Excuse me a moment. I don't want to yell and wake the baby." He let himself down the companionway ladder and moved through the big main saloon, still unaccustomed to the generous headroom, so different from *Haleakala*. He found her in the forward cabin where they slept, putting away some clothes fresh from the marina laundromat, from which she'd just returned. She turned to look at him questioningly and he said, "The Man is here again, as the freaks would say. Some kind of a Federal agent. I offered him beer; I hope we've still got some cold. Where are the potato chips?"

She said quickly, as he turned back toward the galley, "You don't have to bother, Paul. I'll get it."

There it was again, he thought, that goddamn eagerness to serve, to be allowed to pay another small installment on the debt she'd got it into her stubborn lovely head that she owed him because he had, for God's sake, made the tremendous sacrifice of marrying her. He turned back quickly, but checked what he'd been about to say because this was obviously no time for it—but dammit, it never was.

She said, "I suppose he wants me, too."

"Who doesn't?" Fenwick asked, looking at his wife, quite tall and no longer shapeless with pregnancy, in her neat black slacks and a crisp boy's shirt worn with the tails out. Lovely was perhaps overstating it slightly; but her face had lost its haggard look and her hair was soft and bright in the light from the hatch overhead. He reached out and tucked back a wisp of it that had fallen across her forehead. "But he can't have you," he said.

She smiled. "Silly. Run along and entertain the company. I'll be up in a minute."

"Sure."

Returning through the main cabin he opened the door just aft very cautiously. Inside, asleep on the double berth that

171

took up practically all the tiny stateroom was an unmistakable human, unmistakably healthy, very small male child. It didn't do anything particular for him, except in a professional way—he felt very responsible for its well-being since he was supposed to be the resident expert on the subject—but he didn't have anything particular against it, either. The father had shot himself full of happyjuice and died; somebody had to take over the papa spot; why not Paul Williams Fenwick, M.D.? If he hadn't kind of liked children, dammit, he'd have taken up surgery or dermatology or podiatry or something. He closed the door gently and returned to the cockpit.

"She'll be right up," he said.

The Federal man was sitting behind the wheel, obviously trying to imagine what it would be like, steering this boat under way. "Big boat," he said. He looked aloft. "That's a *tall* rig. Can you and your wife really handle her by yourselves?"

"A sistership won a couple of single-handed races to Bermuda," Fenwick said. "One man all by himself. The couple who had *Faraway* before us brought her all the way from the West Coast by themselves, by way of the Panama Canal. They had to sell, they thought, because the girl was having a baby." He grinned. "Of course they didn't have a built-in pediatrician as we do."

Martin glanced at him curiously. "If you don't mind my asking, Doctor, do you really *like* this . . . well, this bumming around in a boat?"

Fenwick laughed. "You mean it's such a terrible waste of my education and training?"

"Something like that."

"My first wife and I went through all that, Mr. Martin," Fenwick said. "We decided that now was the time. For various reasons I was a bit disenchanted with my profession at the moment; I needed to take a break and think things over. And there was money in the bank and a good-sized house all paid up—as a matter of fact, that's what made it possible to buy this boat just now after losing *Haleakala*. We thought, why wait until we're old and sick and retired and can't enjoy it any longer?"

"I see. But you're not really planning to make boating your lifetime career?"

"Not at all. We'll get the big South Seas cruise out of our systems—Billie enjoys it, too—and then we'll move back ashore and I'll swing that pick and tote that bale some more, medically speaking. I think I'll come back to it with a considerably different attitude; I hope so. I rather expect we'll always have some kind of a boat, but it probably won't be as big as this one since we won't be using it for a home." He got up to take the tray Billie handed out the hatch, and moved aside to let her emerge. "Billie, this is Mr. Martin."

Martin took the can that was offered him and helped himself to a pinch of potato chips. "Thanks, Mrs. Fenwick. I'm very sorry to be bothering you both, but there are some new developments. To get to the point: a life raft that was bought by you, Doctor, a couple of years ago, washed up last month on a beach way north of here, actually clear up toward Cape Hatteras."

"*Haleakala*'s raft, that six-man Avon?" Fenwick frowned thoughtfully. "It doesn't really make sense. She was a very seaworthy boat and there wasn't any general bad weather in the area for several weeks after we were set adrift. Of course there are always local squalls, but with any kind of handling she should have managed those without difficulty."

Billie asked, "Was . . . was anybody on board the raft, Mr. Martin?"

He nodded. "There was a body. I'm afraid it wasn't in very good condition. I have some photographs here, but if you'd rather not look at them . . . Dr. Fenwick, with his medical experience, is probably more hardened to this sort of thing. Maybe he can tell me all I need to know."

That was polite bullshit, of course, Fenwick thought irritably; the man wouldn't have requested Billie's presence if he hadn't hoped she'd look at his damned pictures. Fenwick held out his hand and took the sheaf of eight-by-ten glossy prints Martin produced from the attaché case he'd opened on his lap. The subject was hardly recognizable as human.

Billie asked, "May I?" When Fenwick hesitated, she said, "Please. It's all right. I'm a grown-up girl now. I've had a baby and everything, remember?"

Fenwick passed her the prints reluctantly. He saw her pale as she looked at the first one; but she went through them all conscientiously.

"What do you think?" he asked when she was through.

"Kirby often wore those bib overalls; as a matter of fact he had them on that last evening, didn't he?" Her voice was quite steady. She turned to the Federal man. "That shiny thing on its . . . on his ankle. I can't quite make it out in any of the pictures. Kirby wore an ankle bracelet, silver or

173

stainless steel, I never looked at it all that closely. But he told me once the inscription read Peace."

Martin nodded. "That's fine, Mrs. Fenwick. That checks. Thank you very much." He studied some notes. "Kirby, that would be Kirby McPherson, right? And the other man involved in the hijacking was named Michael Breen. And of course the woman, Lucia Barnes."

Billie said quickly, "We don't know that Lucia was involved. She was in the cabin when . . . when the other two attacked Paul; she may not have known anything about it."

It was very nice of her, very fair of her; but Fenwick had to repress a grin. Any woman, even gentle Billie, always got a certain note in her voice when she was trying to be fair to another woman, particularly one she detested.

Martin said, "That's quite right, Mrs. Fenwick. She may have been just another victim of the hijackers, not quite as lucky as the two of you, who survived their attentions. Or she may have played along with them after the fact to save her skin, until something happened to make them all take to the life raft. I get the impression from what you told the authorities earlier that you don't, either of you, feel that Miss Barnes was the kind of a girl who'd place her virtue above her life, if it came to a crunch."

Fenwick glanced at his wife, and said rather awkwardly: "Look, Mr. Martin, I'm not running the girl down, she was a good sailor and a bright kid, but to use her own terminology she'd fuck anything in pants; it didn't really mean a thing to her. And she wasn't so fond of me, or Billie, that she'd let any kind of grief or anger stand in the way of making the best of the situation afterwards."

Billie said dryly, "Yes, Lucia was a very *practical* person."

"In other words, if we find she came to terms with the hijackers it doesn't necessarily mean she had guilty prior knowledge of what they planned to do."

"That's right," Fenwick said.

"Of course, under the circumstances it's possible we'll never learn what happened out there."

Billie asked, "Have any . . . other bodies been found?"

"No," Martin said. "Apparently it took a long easterly gale to blow this ashore. A floating body, even in a lifejacket, wouldn't have drifted the same way. The raft still held enough air for reasonable buoyancy. The question is still what made them take to it in the first place."

"What was the cause of death?" Fenwick asked.

"As far as we can make out, the man simply died of dehydration. Thirst. The company says that raft's survival pack normally carried a pint of water per person—two pints per person if there were only three people on board, but even that wouldn't last very long. They'd have to depend on the rain-catching equipment; and apparently they just didn't get enough rain to do the job. It looks as if the other two died first—assuming they hadn't knocked the girl over the head earlier—while Kirby McPherson still had the strength to give them hasty burial at sea. But again: what occurred to make them abandon ship?"

Fenwick said, "There's always a chance of being run down by a freighter or tanker. A sailing vessel's supposed to have the right of way out there; but big ships don't always maintain the best watch in the world, and some of them don't even take the law too seriously. Another possibility is . . . well, speak no ill of the dead and all that stuff, but Mike and Kirby were kind of seagoing slobs and after all, *Haleakala* was a catamaran, if you know what I mean."

Martin shook his head. "That's why I'm here. I don't know. I was hoping you'd tell me."

Fenwick sighed. "It's the old multihull lecture, Mr. Martin. I don't know if you're aware of it, but it's a very controversial subject in yachting circles. Here on *Faraway,* a normal one-hull boat, we're sitting over roughly eight thousand pounds of lead. No matter how hard the wind blows, even if you lay the mast in the water, all the weight way down there in the keel will bring her back upright like a pop-up doll, assuming you didn't leave any ports or hatches open so she'd fill and sink. But a catamaran like *Haleakala* is kept upright simply by the wide spread of her twin hulls. There's no ballast to bring her back if she goes over. This makes for a lighter boat, a faster boat, a steadier boat—which was why we got one—but it does mean that, although it would take a hell of a gust of wind to flip her, she can be flipped. In any kind of uncertain weather somebody should be right there in the cockpit to ease the sails fast if a squall hits. But those two were always goofing off. They'd put her on self-steering and wander away for a snack or a smoke and forget to come back. It looks very much as if one of them just went to sleep on watch and a squall caught them by surprise. At least it's a definite possibility; it's the way they capsized their own boat a couple months earlier."

Martin nodded. "I guess unless something else turns up,

it'll have to go down as one of the mysteries of the sea." He put the photographs back into his attaché case, and snapped the case shut, rising. "Well, I won't take up any more of your time. You certainly have a handsome boat here, and I wish you the best of luck with your cruise. Thanks for the beer."

They watched him climb ashore, and walk off the finger pier onto the main dock, and shorewards out of sight.

"Seemed pleasant enough," Fenwick said idly. "But he was wearing a gun under his coat, did you notice? And he never did say exactly what government agency he represented."

"I hate him!" Billie whispered.

Startled, he looked at her and saw that her eyes were wet. She rose abruptly and, avoiding the hand with which he reached for her, scrambled through the main hatch and down into the cabin. Fenwick hesitated, and quickly gathered up the empty beer cans, placed them on the tray with the potato chips and carried them below and set them aside. Billie was standing by the mast where it ran through the cabin, clinging to it, her forehead pressed against the hard cold aluminum of the big spar. She shrugged off his hand when he touched her.

"I hate him hate him hate him," she gasped. "What *right* does he have to come here with his nasty Latin *machismo* and look at you like that?"

"At me?" Fenwick asked, baffled. "I didn't notice him looking at me any particular way."

"He knew!" she breathed. "He knew all those things I told you, about my being picked up that time with all those other crazy kids . . . well, I told you. And the way Peter died and the baby and being with those men on that trimaran, he probably thinks I slept with them on alternate nights. And he was wondering the whole time what kind of a spineless worm you are to let yourself be trapped like this by a big ugly tramp of a girl with a police record, who didn't even have brains enough to use the pill properly. . . . What are you doing?"

Standing behind her, he put his hands on her hips and drew her back against him, away from the mast. "I was worried about you," he said. "Before. I asked Dr. Finebaum. He said not to worry, it was going to be an easy delivery, because you had very good pelvic development. He was perfectly right. You do."

"Stop it," she whispered, quite still in his hands.

"I think you're being very tactless," he said, speaking to the back of her head. "Here I pick a girl to marry and you

176

keep running her down. Even if you think I made a lousy choice, you might keep your damned opinions to yourself. Why hurt my feelings by pointing out what terrible taste I've got in women?" After a little, he said, "The medical textbooks say that the changes in the endocrine balance after parturition are apt to lead to temporary emotional disturbances."

"Paul, please," she breathed. "You're just talking nonsense. I haven't got a temporary emotional disturbance and my endocrine balance is simply wonderful. I should never have let you persuade me. . . ."

"Let me?" he said. "Lady, you couldn't have run fast enough to get away from me. Certainly not in that condition." There was a little silence and he went on, still holding her, feeling the good warmth of her through the sturdy material of her slacks: "If Deedee and I had had a child, and I'd later asked you to marry me, you'd have had to make the dreadful decision whether or not to take me with that impossible motherless brat tagging along. Wouldn't you? What's so different here?" She didn't speak and he plunged ahead desperately, "It was the best deal of the month. When I woke up in that dinghy and saw you sitting there. For just the price of one lousy catamaran and a crack on the head, I'd got myself a fine, large, healthy wench of surpassing beauty."

"You mean a pregnant scarecrow with stringy hair," she whispered; then, after the longest moment of his life he heard her laugh softly, and he knew they were saved. She turned and came into his arms.

CHAPTER 18

April

Latitude 30°N; Longitude 90°W

It was one of the long, low, dark, old-fashioned sporting goods stores that catered only to fishermen and hunters. The tennis players, golfers, and handball players, the backpackers, the mountain climbers, the bird watchers, the bicyclists, could go elsewhere; and if you wanted a smart, bright anorak or a stylish jogging outfit they'd be happy to refer you to the department store down the street—a picturesque, narrow, dark, one-way New Orleans street that gave you a hint of what the city under the levees might have been like before the horseless carriage came along and spoiled it.

Emerging from the store, Colonel Hobart Brennan shook his head slightly, like a man trying to recover from a serious shock. It had never occurred to him, sheltered in the Armed Forces, that a qualified American citizen with an unblemished record who required a firearm—say, because he was cruising a lonely coast where yachts had been known to disappear—could not simply step into a sporting goods store and obtain one, if he had the money. Yet he had just been informed that except in his home state this was not the case; the law now condemned the out-of-state traveler without a gun to remain unarmed and defenseless regardless of need.

The Louisiana spring sunshine was bright and warm, but the Colonel was not really aware of it as he walked mechanically toward the parking lot where he'd left the rental car, wondering what had happened to the country he'd spent thirty years serving to the best of his ability. Maybe it was nearsighted to judge a society by its attitude toward weapons, but he couldn't help that; weapons had been his lifelong business. He remembered his first .22 rifle and the pride Sergeant Donaldson had taken in teaching the Captain's boy to shoot—that had been in military surroundings, of course, but he'd never had the impression, back in those days, that civilian attitudes were greatly different, except perhaps in the largest cities. Elsewhere, however, kids ran around with .22s, or single-barreled .410 shotguns, as a matter of course. It was considered an essential part of growing up. But now, apparently . . .

He never finished the thought. He was suddenly aware that he was hearing the sound again. It had been a long time, but he remembered it very clearly. Like the last time, it started distant and you might easily mistake it for the rumble of a high, passing jet. Perhaps that was why nobody else on the street seemed disturbed; but he knew it for what it was. He remembered the last time he had heard the great black horses of doom thundering across the sky, and had known exactly what they portended, and had made his arrangements accordingly—but that time a miracle had occurred, making a hash of all omens and predictions. There would, he knew, be no second miracle. The sound swept over him, menacing and overwhelming, and then receded in the distance and was gone. Okay, he thought, thanks, it's been a good run after all, a damned good run, maybe I'd hoped for still a little more, but okay and thanks for letting me know.

He'd stopped walking. Passing people were glancing at him curiously; obviously they'd heard nothing at all. Well, that figured; the message was for him alone. And if he told anybody, the doctors, say, they'd make all kinds of tests and maybe even wire him for sound and run him on that treadmill machine until his ass was dragging and at the end tell him his heart was still in fine shape and they didn't really know what kind of attack he'd had, but if there was a recurrence don't hesitate to call. Marge would know, of course. As a soldier's wife, a Marine's wife, she'd understand all too well. But he had no intention of telling Marge, this time. There was no need for her to know.

The marina was at the north end of New Orleans where the city came to a sudden stop against Lake Ponchartrain. It was a large marina in two sections; and *Spindrift* lay in the outer basin at a dock near the New Orleans Yacht Club, not to be confused with the larger Southern Yacht Club across the way. Well, the bigger club might be slightly more prestigious, Brennan reflected, as he parked his car under the trees outside, but it could hardly be kinder or more hospitable.

Of course he'd been lucky in running into old Curly Williston, now also retired, whom he hadn't seen since they met on leave in Japan during the Korea hassle. Curly had had them up to the Club bar for a beer and that had been the start of it. Advice and help had been instantly forthcoming. They'd been steered to the best boatyard for repairs to the rigging that had been damaged while maneuvering outside that infuriatingly dilatory Industrial Lock on the Mississippi, which had been a hell of a lousy welcome to an otherwise very pleasant city. An electrician had been located to straighten out the recurrent alternator problem; and most important perhaps, dock space had been found for them even though the big marina was crowded to overflowing. After the endless lonely canals and bayous through which they'd come, learning along the way, their instant acceptance—you might even call it adoption—by other, more experienced boating people had been heartwarming to say the least.

Emerging on the dock Hobart Brennan paused, as always, to enjoy the sight of his sturdy white boat with her slim masts and jaunty bowsprit. The folding Bimini top was raised to shade the cockpit, amidships. Back in Texas, that top, with its associated plastic windshield and all-around weather curtains, had practically saved their lives, giving them a sheltered steering station almost as comfortable as that of a powerboat—and it had been needed, Brennan reflected, goddamn right it had been needed. For being as far south as it was, that was one *cold* damn state in winter. But now in Louisiana in the spring the curtains had been removed and stowed and the top served only as an awning against the sun. He saw that Marge was entertaining guests in the cockpit—well, one guest, female, juvenile; no doubt one of the local kids who were always sailing around the harbor in their little dinghies or self-propelled surfboards.

However, as he came closer, Brennan realized that the girl wasn't juvenile; she was merely small. She looked vaguely familiar: a neatly proportioned little figure in a striped jersey and clean but somewhat crumpled white slacks that looked as if they'd spent some time tucked away in a seabag. The costume triggered his memory, although the slacks—if they were the same slacks—had been more presentable when last seen. In fact they'd been quite crisp and immaculate when quiet, businesslike little Miss Brown had brought the contracts into the yacht broker's office for him to sign. Buckmeister and Pond, he reminded himself; and Buckmeister had gone in for white slacks too, and a white sweater, and boat shoes, and, at a guess, a drink or two or four every evening at the local Yacht Club bar, or maybe even six if it had been a rough day. But maybe he was doing the man an injustice, Brennan told himself; actually, he'd had that dried-out look so it was possible he had it licked and more power to him.

"Look who's here, dear," Marge said as he stepped aboard. "You remember Miss Brown, Miss Linda Brown. She recognized our boat and came over to see how we were getting along."

Brennan bowed over the small hand the girl offered him. At close range he found her oddly disturbing, although he'd been aware of no such reaction at their last, brief meeting. The pants weren't particularly tight and the breasts under the knitted jersey were actually, it seemed, confined by a discreet brassiere, very unusual these days when peekaboo nipples were all the rage; and come to that, even for her size she wasn't very spectacular in either the rump or the boob department. The firm little mouth made no attempt at pouty sensuality. At a glance she was simply an almost-plain small girl with nondescript brown hair; yet he'd never received a clearer message: yes, sir, Colonel, sir, shall I remove my nice white trousers myself or would the Colonel prefer to do the honors? The damned little wench was teasing him and laughing at him without ever moving a hip or cracking a smile.

"I was just telling Mrs. Brennan," she said after retrieving her hand, "I got a ride here on that big Trojan across the way, and then I saw your boat lying here and came over to say hello. I gather you also had some trouble in that crazy bottleneck humorously known as the Industrial Lock. They may be a lock, but industrious they certainly aren't."

Brennan laughed ruefully. "I know, we almost lost our mast tangling with a big commercial fishing boat; I wanted the skipper to call the lockmaster for me and find out when the hell they were going to let us through. We'd been waiting all afternoon, motoring around in circles. I didn't dare use our radio because we'd been having some electrical problems and I didn't know how long our batteries were going to last."

"Oh, I'm sorry about that," the girl said. "You mean there was something wrong with the boat? I'm sure Bucky, I mean Mr. Buckmeister, wasn't aware of it when he sold it to you."

"No, apparently it was just something that vibrated loose and started shorting out with all the running we did under

181

power; we hardly had the sails up at all." He changed the subject. "Are you taking kind of a postman's holiday, Miss Brown?"

She hesitated. "No, as a matter of fact I'm slightly unemployed at the moment. I—" She glanced toward Marge. "I was just weeping on Mrs. Brennan's shoulder; she'll tell you all about it. It's the old, old office-wife story, Colonel, and I was an awful little fool, but you don't want to be bothered with my troubles." She smiled brightly at Marge. "Thanks lots for the tea, Mrs. Brennan, and I'll be running along. They tell me there's a motorsailer in the inner basin that's looking for a crew—somebody had to go home in a hurry—and maybe I can convince them that you don't have to be Hercules to be handy around a boat."

"Wait a minute." Brennan glanced at his wife, and back to the girl. "Are you a pretty good sailor, Miss Brown?"

She grinned at him perkily. "What am I supposed to say to that? I've been doing it most of my life, if that's an answer."

"Off shore?"

"Just about everywhere."

Brennan said deliberately, "Well, I haven't done much sailing since I left the Naval Academy, and Mrs. Brennan has had even less experience. And we certainly didn't get much sailing practice in those muddy canals between Houston and here. As I said, we've hardly had the sails up. We're starting east in a day or two, we've got a forward cabin we aren't using, complete with head, and I don't think Mrs. Brennan—Marge—will mind cooking for three if you'll lend a hand with the dishes. We can only take you as far as Tampa; our younger daughter and her husband are meeting us there for a cruise down to the Florida Keys, but if that fits with your plans, we'd appreciate a little help, particularly on that open-water jaunt beyond Apalachicola. I gather a lot of boats run into trouble there, and I'd rather not tackle it short-handed."

There was a brief silence. He was aware that Marge was looking at him curiously, but he did not want to meet her eyes. There was no need to tell her, but it would be stupid to ignore the warning he'd just received. As he'd told the girl, Marge had had relatively little boating experience. If it should come unexpectedly, perhaps off shore, she'd be in a bad spot without somebody else on board to help.

"Well, gee—" The girl looked quickly at Marge. "If you're sure I won't be in the way, Mrs. Brennan."

"We'll love having you, my dear."

"Well . . . well, you don't have to twist my arm. I'll go get my gear; I'll be right back."

They watched her jump lightly to the dock and run off. Brennan saw his wife regarding him quizzically.

"What was *that* all about, Hobart? I thought you were looking forward to meeting the challenge of the open sea all by yourself, with just a little help from me."

He grinned. "She's a sexy little thing, isn't she? I'll expect you to take a good long walk in every port we come to, old girl."

She was still watching him; and he knew he wasn't fooling her very much, if at all. "Of course, dear. Just hang a handkerchief out the porthole when it's safe for me to come back."

No, she wasn't fooled, any more than she'd been fooled by his bright chatter that other time. She'd simply waited him out then, talking casually about what they would do afterwards, until he'd been forced to say it: *I wouldn't make too many plans, Marge, this looks like a bad one.*

Everybody had known it, of course. After Tarawa and Eniwetok and Kwajalein, nobody'd had any illusions about what kind of resistance they'd meet when they hit the main islands, the home islands. He hadn't really needed the warning he'd been given back then. A look at the maps and estimates had been enough. But the brains in Los Alamos had produced, and the tough little man in Washington had had the guts to use, the scientific miracle of the century, confounding the harbingers of doom; and they'd all torn up the last-minute wills they'd made and the final letters they'd written their loved ones, and gone back home to the lives they'd really had no right to resume. Thirty-some years of borrowed atomic time, Brennan reflected. Not a bad deal at that.

He watched Linda Brown come running back along the dock. She was carrying a small red nylon pack. It was too bad, he thought idly; under other circumstances it would have made an intriguing project. Absolute marital fidelity was, of course, not expected in the Corps except by a few starry-eyed brides; but reasonable discretion was. Like a good military wife Marge trusted him in good military fashion—in other words, she trusted him not to fuck around within a mile of the flagpole.

CHAPTER 19

April

Latitude 26°N; Longitude 80°W

For his release they took him from the Stockade where he'd served his sentence—a cluster of dreary shops and barracks down near the airport—back up to the Dade County Jail near Miami's Civic Center at Northwest Fourteenth. The delays and red tape there almost wrecked it. He had to keep telling himself firmly that he'd made it through all these endless days and weeks; he could fake it a few more hours, the model prisoner, *ja*, Hans Rurik Olson, the dull, stolid squarehead like a bullock in a pen—but he had the faces memorized. One day they would meet elsewhere; one day there would be an accounting. A man was not an animal to be put in a cage.

Then he was out and he had killed nobody, struck nobody, but it had been too close; there had been too many thick necks asking to be broken, too many fat overbearing faces pleading to be smashed into bloody pulp. If only the dying had been involved he could never have restrained himself. He would have gone out happily if he could only have taken with him two or three of the jailpigs—he'd had the suitable ones marked. But the fear was that they would not kill him. Instead they would use the excuse to lock him up away from the sea and the sky forever, and that could not be borne. He walked quickly away from the ugly, ten-story lump of concrete, breathing deeply of the warm, free Miami spring air.

"Hans. Over here."

He wheeled heavily, blindly, in the direction of the voice. He was still half-dazed with the liberty he did not quite dare trust lest it turn out to be another of their malicious tricks, in which case somebody would die and never mind what they did to him afterwards. But the little gray car was there and

184

the woman was there. As he stopped and bent over to speak
to her, she took his face in her hands and drew him down
farther and kissed him on the lips, reminding him of what
else had been lacking, besides freedom, in that unnatural
place in which they'd had him trapped. Did not that Consti-
tution they talked so much about prohibit cruel and unusual
punishment? To execute a man for his misdeeds, that was
perfectly reasonable; but to deliberately keep him alive and
drive him insane by locking him up away from women and
wind and sunshine. . . .

"Poor baby," Gloria murmured. "Pretty rough, huh? You
want to drive?"

He shook his head. "No. Take me—"

"I know, baby. This is Gloria. Remember Gloria? You don't
have to tell me."

Getting in beside her, he could smell good soap, and a hint
of cologne, and woman; she was not a whore to soak herself in
cheap perfume. Greta Fägelkvist was her original name, but
her parents had changed the spelling to Fogelquist because
even in Wisconsin the Swedish alphabet and Swedish spell-
ings were not well understood. A bird on a branch was what
it meant, or a twig with a bird on it; something like that. And
as Greta Fogelquist the attractive blonde Wisconsin farm
girl had gone to nearby Chicago to seek her fortune and had
found it—at least there was money every month, no large
sum but adequate—but whatever she had done to earn it she
did not speak about. It had, however, involved leaving Chicago
and changing her name to the one she was using now: Gloria
Farnsworth. He was not supposed to remember the earlier
name that had been given to him in confidence.

She could look like an angel, drink like a man, and make
love like a tigress; and she was the only woman who'd ever
made him afraid—afraid that when the liquor was in him
and the mood was on him he would hurt her badly without
being able to help himself. With none of the others had it
mattered enough to worry him. Her hair was smooth and
beautiful, like polished fine gold drawn back from her handsome face; and she had on a light tan costume with trousers
that he had not seen before, a replacement perhaps for the
pale blue trousers-suit that had somehow got so badly damaged that accursed night after the first winter storm, when
they'd celebrated his latest successful mission for the little
greaser a bit too noisily and the *förbannade* neighbors had
called the police and the first intruding pig, seeing her like

that, in only the torn jacket she'd snatched up when the pounding came on the door, and the laddered tights they had not yet got around to stripping off her, being distracted by some interesting drunken preliminaries that did not require her total nudity . . . the first pig inside had stared with his little pig eyes at her long fine legs gleaming through the ruined stockings and had licked his ugly pig lips salaciously and made some dirty comment to Pig Two and had got his ugly pig nose flattened for it as he deserved. But the magistrate or judge or whatever His Fucking Honor was called had not considered it adequate justification for striking an officer, particularly since there had been complaints and warnings before. . . .

"Okay, Baby," Gloria said. "I'll wait in the car."

They'd arrived without his realizing it—or perhaps he had deliberately refrained from looking ahead so he could see it all at once, all in one piece: the water, the marina, the tall masts and white hulls; and his own *Ellida* riding buoyantly between the stern pilings and the sea wall. He got out of the car and walked down there slowly and stepped aboard near the bow and stood for a moment checking on the repairs that had been made while he was gone, but it was all fine. Ernesto was a good mate and a good nigger, although he'd cut your throat if he heard you use the word. The missing antennas and outrigger had been replaced; and somebody had done a good job on the windshield, probably Ernesto himself; that big black man could do just about anything on a boat. The bow rail had been straightened and refastened. It was hard to get heavy stainless-steel tubing looking exactly right again after it had been violently bent, but it was as good as could be expected. Some day he'd have to give the little lady a whole new shiny bow pulpit to dress her up and make her happy. He ran his hand regretfully over the place where the sweeping curve of steel was no longer quite fair. What makes you do these things, Hans Rurik? he asked himself, but there was no answer.

He moved aft into the cockpit and used a key to open the locker to starboard of the lower steering station, used mainly to manage the boat when fighting a big fish. He took out a smallish bottle of clear white liquid; the Americans were more practical perhaps with their flat pints that fit so neatly into a pocket, but he'd found a place that would supply *Skåne Akvavit* in the right, round, medicinal-looking half-liter bottles that, somehow, seemed to make it taste better. A full liter was too much glass to handle on a boat under way and, of course, there was always the fact that once a man opened a bottle he felt morally obliged to drink it dry.

With the bottle in his pocket he climbed the ladder to the topside controls. Seated behind the wheel up there, he took a moderate, ritual drink and patted the wheel before him lightly.

"Ja, min lilla flicka," he said softly, *"nu har du din Hans Rurik tillbaka igen."*

Yes, my little girl, he thought, now you have your Hans Rurik back again. He was never quite certain how much Swedish she understood, being American-built; but after all, a man could get along very well with a boat, or a woman, even without any common language between them. And the fool who considered a boat an inanimate speechless object had never conned a good vessel of his own through the long dark watches of the night. And so much for the sentimental pilgrimage; Ernesto had done a good job, and now a quick check below and then back to the apartment and, Hans Rurik, you will keep your *förbannade* big hands under control, *förstor du?* She is a fine woman, a lovely woman, and she must not be hurt like that little curly-haired tramp in . . . He shut that memory away. After all, he had not *intended* any harm. But that was just the trouble, he never did. Well, almost never.

He capped and pocketed the bottle and made his way back down the flying-bridge ladder and started to unlock the cabin door, and found it unlocked. He stood there a moment, frowning; then he pulled it open.

"Welcome aboard, Captain," said the slim, dark young man reclining on the starboard deckhouse settee, a bottle of beer in his hand. "Pete Orosco, in case you don't remember."

"I remember. What do you on my boat?"

"I wait for you, *mi capitán.* The *patrón* sends his greetings."

"Who gave you the key?"

"Key? For that lock? You've got to be kidding." Orosco grinned as Olson looked quickly toward the door. "No, *amigo,* I didn't scratch or break anything on your precious boat. What do you think I am, clumsy? Don Jaime congratulates you on your release and hopes you will now stay out of trouble because he has work for you soon. Okay?"

"Don Jaime was not so much help when they took me to jail that I need to consider his wishes now."

"You're being unreasonable, Captain," Orosco said lazily.

187

"Even back then he couldn't afford to do anything that would lead them from him to you, or vice versa, could he? And now they are watching him closely, and he says you are not to show yourself at Miranda's, they have the restaurant under surveillance, too. In a way it was well that you got yourself put away. You were not around for them to find when they started looking for a man who could run a boat, who might have run boats for the *patron;* so they watch Ramiro instead with his pirate mustache and that makes them happy and satisfied. But you must be very careful. You're not to contact the *patron;* he will get in touch with you, through me. As for the job, it's another run, and there will be a load arriving soon, on the other side of Florida this time. Do you know Black River, over near the Everglades?"

"*Ja,* I know Black River."

"The first little cove to the north off Bonefish Bay. Regan will rendezvous with you there after picking up his load; he's getting the boat now. A blue thirty-nine-foot ketch—well, she'll be blue by the time you see her—named *Pretty Baby.* Ugh. We'll give you the time as soon as we know it; you can notify the buyer to have the speedboats ready. You'll cover the transshipment as before and pay off Regan. We'll let you know where to drop off the money. Okay?"

Olson frowned. "I like my orders from the top, Orosco. Or at least from Number Two."

The young Cuban grinned, unruffled. "Jesus has a tag on him. Even Bolo. I'm still in the clear; I guess they figure Don Jaime would never entrust important matters to a snot-nosed little *pachuco* like me, who just hangs around and makes eyes at the pretty *Señorita* Columbus. So I do the legwork. Captain?"

"Yes?"

"The *patrón* says to keep the cork in the bottle and the cock in the pants. I don't know why you need to fool around anyway, with that tall beautiful blonde willing to haul your ashes for you. She looks like woman enough to . . . All right, all right, don't hit me, Skipper, I'll wash out my mouth and be good. But, hell, you haven't even cleaned up the last mess you made yet. He says you'd better attend to that while you're waiting for Regan to do his stuff."

Olson frowned again. "It is still important after this time? The man did not die, and what did I do to the woman that her husband had not been doing every previous night—or maybe just once a week, judging by the spindly look of him? Why so big a fuss?"

"The Lady Libbers have discovered rape, *amigo*. They say it is not sex but violence, whatever that means. They are pushing the police to make the streets of Miami safe for liberated womanhood. Leave no stone unturned, no violated female unavenged, no rapist at liberty to forcibly fuck again. And the word is still that these people can identify you. They must be taken care of. You don't want to go back to that place you were just in, do you, or to a larger institution with stronger bars on the windows? And Don Jaime doesn't want you there, either. So he's had me do a little research for you: the girl was living in Sarasota with her parents for a while—I guess you made her dissatisfied with hubby, one way or another, because she divorced him right afterwards—but now she's back in graduate school, living in a one-room-and-kitchenette deal down near the University. 3220 College Way, second floor rear. She's got a new boyfriend, the lawyer who helped her with the divorce. His name is Leonard, J. Barton Leonard."

"What about the ex-husband, Ullman?"

"It's good and bad. He was living on a sailboat down in the Keys—still is, for the moment—but he's got himself an assignment to take pictures for a New York magazine, on a tanker heading for the Caribbean, first stop Puerto La Cruz in Venezuela. He'll be leaving in a few days—he picks up the ship in Wilmington, North Carolina—which doesn't give you much time to take care of him here; but it might be better if it happens out of the country, anyway. Nobody's going to ask too many questions about a nosy cameraman who gets himself mugged, permanently, in some stinking Latin American alley. Hell, some places down there they'll kill you for a roll of film."

"Yes, but I cannot very well be in Venezuela and Black River at the same time."

Orosco hesitated. "Your lady friend says she has some interesting contacts who might be persuaded to help, if you can spare her for a week or two."

"You've talked to Gloria?"

"Don Jaime said she was an interesting person with a fascinating background who, in your absence, might have some valuable suggestions. She has indicated that, with your approval of course, she'd be willing to make a few phone calls to some old Chicago friends, friends of influence, and even take a quick South American tour, for a price."

Olson was scowling. "I do not like that. I don't like your

damned Don Jaime checking up on my woman; and I don't like you bothering her about things when I'm not around; and this is man's business anyway."

"That redheaded punk and his wife have got to go. That's the word. How you do it is your affair, sure." Orosco shrugged elaborately. "But the lady seemed interested and the *patrón* is willing to finance her expedition up to a reasonable amount in order to keep you available to arrange things here. Talk it over with her at least."

Olson stared at him, feeling baffled and angry. "Well, she waits for me in the car," he said. "Don't leave that beer bottle where it can roll off and break if a big wake comes through; this marina is a goddamn wave trap."

"Hasta la vista. I'll give you a few minutes to get clear before I leave."

Back at the car, Olson got in beside Gloria without speaking and, as she sent them away, took the half-liter from his pocket, uncapped it, and let several burning swallows go down his throat. He felt trapped and harassed, and the good sense of returning freedom he'd had, seeing his boat again, was gone.

"Please?"

He became aware that she was holding out her hand for the *brännvin* as they rolled through the extensive parking lot surrounded by grass and trees. He gave it to her, and watched her drink, and took it back and had another swallow while she gasped and laughed.

"You're sure you didn't get the varnish remover by mistake, Baby? Or the stuff to bleach the teak?" He said nothing and she went on: "I suppose he was waiting for you, the time you spent inside. I told him you'd want to come here first. The parlor snake. That was what my grandmother used to call Rudolph Valentino." After a while she asked, "Well?"

"Well, what?"

"Are you going to let me go?"

"I do not *let* you do anything. And you do not *let* me do anything. No strings, was not that what you said at the start?"

She touched his knee lightly. "I'd like to do it, Hans. I'm pretty sure I know some people with good South American connections. If it means your safety, I want to do it."

"You want a nice trip to the Caribbean, that is what you want."

"Sure. Waving palms, sunny beaches, gorgeous sharks,
190

delightful hurricanes. What girl could resist? Besides, he wants to pay me five grand. You wouldn't want to stand in the way of my getting rich, would you? Don't drink it all, damn you, leave a little for Glory." After a while, handing back the bottle, she said, "Anyway, they've got a job for you, don't they? You'll be busy. I'll probably be back before you even miss me."

"Who misses anybody? For two months I have thought of you not at all." His voice was thick. His hand, which had been resting on her thigh as she drove, found its way between her legs. "It's barely I recognized you outside the jail. Who is that strange, forward, ugly woman, I asked myself, who makes advances toward Hans Rurik Olson?"

He heard her laugh softly, and he felt his hand gently removed and placed in less intimate surroundings. "Easy, Baby. I know it's been a long time, but there's no place to park and this damn Honda isn't big enough, anyway. We'll be home in a minute. . . ."

CHAPTER 20

April

Latitude 29°N; Longitude 90°W

There were only a few people stirring on the other boats when, after an early breakfast, Colonel Hobart Brennan steered *Spindrift*, under power, cautiously out the Apalachicola boat basin. It was a simple little refuge that couldn't really be called a marina; just a small, dredged, rectangular harbor off wide Apalachicola Bay, without any fancy docks or piers. You tied up to the massive bulkheads—several boats abreast if the place was crowded—and if you were tired of eating on board you could picnic under the scanty trees or patronize the café in town, perhaps after a small libation at one of the bars, one quite respectable, the other pretty much a waterfront dive except that it wasn't quite on the water.

They'd been told that the picturesque large wooden hotel in the center of town had until recently offered a very pleasant drinking place, but the aging building was condemned now and empty. If you were fancy and insisted on lying in a real slip, and maybe even sleeping in a real bed in a room on shore for a change, you could tie up at the Rainbow Motel just around the point, inside the swing bridge at the mouth of the Apalachicola River down which they'd come the day before, following the Intracoastal Waterway, which emerged here after ducking inland for thirty-odd miles.

"Steady as you go," the girl on the bowsprit called. "Okay, you've got the channel, Skip; just follow the buoys. You want me to yank the stops off the main and mizzen? I think we'll have a sailing breeze by the time we get out in the Bay."

Hobart Brennan reflected that he was a fortunate man. Miraculously, he'd been allowed all the fine years after the first warning; and now he'd had two beautiful weeks after the second, a cruising experience very different from their earlier rather grim and determined and amateurish winter grind along the muddy canals between Houston and New Orleans. And he knew that a large part of the difference was due to the small girl now running barefoot along the deck in her demure little red halter and neat little white shorts. She would, he thought, have made a damn good Marine, willing, obedient, and totally fearless; when he'd accidentally let the jib halliard go aloft in that squall in Mississippi Sound she was out of her foul-weather gear and up the mast instantly in spite of the rain and lightning and *Spindrift* rolling like a pig in the choppy sea. He could still visualize her clinging to the gyrating masthead like a monkey, a very wet monkey, as she untangled the wind-whipped mess up there, and then came sliding down to hand him the line that had got away from him.

"Butterfingers!" she'd chided him, tossing the drenched hair out of her eyes to grin at him in cheerful, disrespectful, tomboy fashion.

When, with hardly any experience to guide you, you found yourself responsible for eighty grand worth of boat and several lives, it made a tremendous difference to have somebody on board who knew exactly what should be done and did it, or showed you how to do it, without being pushy about it; somebody young and agile and quite unconcerned about her appearance or dignity who'd wrestle a muddy anchor aboard or scrub out the head or go over the side without hesitation when, in harbor, an expensive winch handle—those things cost over fifty bucks—got kicked overboard in ten feet of water. And whatever emanation or force field it was he'd felt the first day, that had caused that uneasy stirring inside him, it was gone as if she'd pulled a switch and turned herself off. He wouldn't try to deceive anybody into thinking he looked upon her as a boy, or even as a daughter; he was still quite aware that she was an attractive, unrelated young female; but the thing he'd feared, that he'd somehow find himself spoiling everything by making a totally unintended, compulsive, inexcusable pass at the kid, was no longer a danger.

Of course, having dealt with troops all his adult life, he was quite aware that she was a phony. She had to be. Brown-nosing they called it in the Corps; or simply sucking up the Old Man. There simply did not exist in real life a nice-looking young girl who was eager to please, so willing to get her hands and even herself dirty, so ready to work like a coolie at any task that was suggested, so constantly cheerful and friendly and tactful in the enforced company of two dull, middle-aged characters like Marge and him. Whoever Linda Brown really was, she wasn't this small paragon of all the seamanlike and social virtues. Somewhere inside, there was a real girl who griped when she was tired, whimpered when she was hurt, hated disposing of stinking garbage and cleaning greasy frying pans, and was scared to death of heights, perhaps, or of lightning; a girl who couldn't help yawning undiplomatically when she got bored with older folks' tedious conversations.

He was very curious about the real Linda Brown; but he knew his curiosity would probably never be satisfied. But the fact that she could grit her teeth—as he was sure she sometimes did in private—and maintain this fictional character convincingly, had earned her his deep respect. Clearly she had told herself that she was going to pay her fare to Tampa by being the best one-hundred-pound crew member possible, no matter what it took; and it was a damn pleasant change after long years of dealing with spoiled male brats who forever felt obliged, and entitled, to express their lousy little pipsqueak personalities whatever the cost of their units and the Marine Corps as a whole.

"Go ahead and get the main ready for hoisting," Brennan called when the girl paused by the mast and glanced aft for instructions. "Marge and I will get the mizzen. We'll run them up just before we turn that last buoy out there and swing east."

"Coffee, anybody?" This was Marge, finished with the dishes, sticking her head out the main hatch.

"Let's wait until we get sail up," Brennan said.

"All clear with the main," Linda called. "Are you going to want the working jib or the big jenny, Skip?"

If she had a flaw, it was calling him Skip, short for Skipper; but he'd be an unappreciative bastard to complain about a detail like that. He told her, with the light winds they'd been having, they could probably carry the big overlapping genoa jib; and he watched her drop down the forward hatch to get it. It occurred to him that his daughter, Melissa, and her Navy husband, Lieutenant (jg) Roger McCulloch, were going to have a hard act to follow; and that he was going to be damn careful, after the kid was gone and they were on board, to keep his big mouth shut about Linda-said and Linda-did. Come to think of it, talking about spoiled brats, their youngest might be said by some prejudiced folks to fall into that category, and whose fault was that?

"It'll be nice to see Melissa again."

Marge had left the hatch to come aft and work along the mizzen boom, removing the ties that secured the rolled-up Dacron sail. She looked, he thought, quite attractive in her tailored dark-brown slacks and a tan shirt—beige she'd probably call it—worn tidily tucked into the pants. She said when she was a girl only Russians wore their shirt tails out, and she'd never liked the Russians even when they were our noble allies, certainly not enough to imitate their quaint sartorial customs. She also said that jeans might be cheaper and more practical, but she didn't have the right kind of bottom for jeans. After years of marriage, it no longer surprised him even a little to discover that they'd been thinking about the same subject.

He nodded. "I wonder how those two kids are really getting along. Melissa certainly isn't much of a letter-writer. It's been about a year, hasn't it?"

"Yes. A year next month. It was such a lovely spring wedding, wasn't it?" Marge said reminiscently. "All right, this sail is ready to go. . . . And they'll get along just fine, if he only slaps her down hard occasionally to make up for the fact that her daddy was too tender-hearted to turn her over his knee when she was a child."

He grinned. "Says who? You know damn well you couldn't

194

bear to see our pretty little doll-baby cry, either. I'm afraid we left young Roger a tough row to hoe. Well, you'd better take the wheel while I get on the halliard." He raised his voice. "Mizzen going up!"

Wrestling with impressive areas of sail, the small figure on the bowsprit didn't turn its head; but the voice came back: "Aye, aye, Skip. Yell if you need me. I'll be ready here in a minute. . . ."

The gentle southwesterly wind gave them an easy full-sail reach eastward along Apalachicola Bay. There were a few moments of uneasiness at the highway bridge leading out to St. George Island offshore—like all bridges it looked lower than its charted height—but they passed under the span without incident thanks to *Spindrift's* relatively low ketch rig and the fact that the VHF antenna was mounted on the shorter mizzenmast—if it had added its several feet to the mainmast, it would have got itself wiped out long ago along this bridge-plagued route. The ICW channel, defined by buoys and tall posts with numbered reflective signs, wandered up the wide bay in apparently aimless fashion, actually avoiding invisible shoals shown clearly on the chart. At last it ran reasonably straight for a while, closing with the long, sandy barrier island to starboard; and they could see the opening to the Gulf ahead. East Pass. Linda had reported having heard from various yachtsmen that it was generally easier and safer than the narrow dredged exit to the Gulf opposite Apalachicola and, being further east, it would keep them a little closer to the Florida coast and shelter in case of emergencies during the hundred-and-fifty-five mile offshore run to Anclote Key, just a day's sail from Tampa.

To port was the mainland and the town of Carrabelle, another possible jumping-off place, but they'd fueled up and laid in all necessary provisions in Apalachicola, so there was no need to make the detour to that small fishing village, actually several miles off their route. Ahead, the Intracoastal Waterway, which they'd now followed for some seven hundred miles from Texas, came to an end for a while. They'd pick up the next leg of it tomorrow at Anclote Key.

Hobart Brennan, who'd landed on fiercely defended beaches under heavy fire, nevertheless felt his heart beating a little faster as, with Marge and Linda winching in the big genoa to compensate for the change in course, he aimed his little two-masted ship at the pass and the open Gulf of Mexico. Two hours later, having seen only a few small fishing boats, they were alone on an endless expanse of water with, for the first time since he'd signed the final check for *Spindrift,* no land in sight anywhere. It was a moment for which he'd been waiting for a long time, Brennan knew. He'd finally made it offshore.

"Course one three five," he told Linda, letting her take the wheel. "I've got to go do some more figuring."

She probably thought him a Nervous Nellie, he reflected wryly as he bent over the chart table below; she'd undoubtedly sailed with experienced navigators who considered a lousy little one-hundred-fifty-five-mile offshore passage no more than a step across the street; but as usual she was too tactful, or kind, to show it. Nice kid. The navigational problem was actually quite simple. They were leaving the panhandle of Florida, which ran east and west, and heading for the main body of the state, which ran more or less north and south, just cutting across the upper right-hand corner of the Gulf of Mexico. There should be nothing to it. All that was needed was to use the old cross-country orientation trick: don't head straight for your objective but well to one side or the other, so you'll know which way to turn when you hit the road or stream or fence that'll guide you in—in this case the west coast of Florida proper. He'd already set a course a few degrees north so that when he picked up the other shore tomorrow he could safely turn to starboard, south, looking for his landmark: the big power plant near Tarpon Springs, just opposite Anclote Key. One of these days he'd have to get himself a sextant and tackle celestial navigation. . . . He killed that thought. Never mind one of these days. Today was good enough. He was offshore in his own boat at last, living the dream that had entertained and sustained him since his Academy days.

Spindrift drove on to the southeast, making pretty good time as the wind strengthened. Toward evening, while Marge worked in the galley, the other two members of the ship's company brought down the genoa and replaced it with the working jib and the forestaysail; two smaller sails that would be easier to manage in the dark if the wind continued to rise, but it didn't. It steadied at a fine reaching breeze good for five knots with this somewhat reduced sail area. Relaxed and happy at the wheel, where he'd spend most of the day, Hobart Brennan found himself almost resenting the appearance of Linda, wiping her mouth with the back of her hand.

"Chow," she said. "Your turn, Skip. Don't keep the cook waiting. . . . Oh, what kind of watches are you going to want us to stand?"

"I'll take her until midnight after I've eaten," he said. "Then you and Marge can flip a coin to see who spells me until four. Hell, it's only one night."

She glanced at him shrewdly. "I know. Your first night offshore. You want to put the sun to bed and make sure it gets up again in the morning."

He grinned. "Don't be so damn superior and blasé about it, small fry."

Her face changed. "I didn't mean . . . I just think it's, well, kind of sweet. And you, too."

There was nothing to say to that, and he turned away, embarrassed, wanting to look back to see if her eyes were really wet, and wondering what the hell had got into the kid. He hadn't meant to hurt her feelings; and dammit, he certainly wasn't sweet. Below, Marge had the table set in the main saloon. With this wind, neither the motion nor the angle of heel was enough to force them to eat off their laps. After dinner, he checked the continuous weather reports on the VHF; ten to fifteen knots southwest with no significant frontal activity in sight. He returned to the cockpit to relieve the wheel, happy to find Linda no longer showing any sentimental or emotional symptoms—he might have imagined the whole thing. A large commercial fishing boat or shrimper was passing in the distance, otherwise the sea was still empty.

Later, as the sun set spectacularly to starboard, he heard Marge in the aft cabin, and then he didn't hear her any more; apparently she'd lain down to nap until she was needed. A slight murmur of sound forward told him that Linda was listening to her small transistor radio; another flaw, perhaps—he really couldn't understand modern kids who had to keep that kind of noise going constantly—but at least the girl was considerate about it and always kept the volume down. The last vestige of sunset faded from the horizon, and *Spindrift* swung along through the darkness under a black sky displaying a million stars. When the red flare rose off the port bow, he found himself watching it idly for a moment as if it were just another celestial manifestation. Then, quickly, he leaned forward to take a rough bearing over the steering compass.

"All hands on deck! Linda, grab that handbearing compass as you go by, will you?"

By the time they reached the cockpit, the flare had burned itself out.

"What is it, dear?" Marge asked.

"I thought I saw a distress signal, just about due east. Linda, do you know how to use that thing?"

The girl glanced down at the instrument she'd brought. "Sorry, Skip, I just pull the strings to make the boat go. Where it goes is somebody else's business."

"Well, I've used them on land and taken a few practice sights. . . . Take over here. Same course, until we see what's going on, if anything."

"Skip."

He glanced at her, seeing her small face grave in the red glow of the binnacle. "What is it?"

"We just left Apalachicola, remember? A few boats coming out of that place never showed up again. This is an empty damn corner of the Gulf of Mexico. It could be a trick; it's been used before. Have you got a gun on board?"

"No gun." He glanced at Marge and saw that the girl had put into words what his wife had also been thinking. "Okay. We'll be careful."

"There's a flare!" Marge said quickly, pointing.

He managed to catch the arching red comet over the sighting vane, and read the figure on the lighted dial of the HB compass.

"Zero eight six," he said. "Give or take a bit. Let's ease sheets and bear off. If they're really in trouble, I guess we'll have to get the sails down and make the approach under power for better maneuverability, but let's see what we're up against, first."

Moments later, *Spindrift* was surging along with the wind on the quarter while, in the cockpit, they strained to spot a light, or the shadowy shape of a boat, in the darkness ahead.

"Skip."

"What?"

"How about giving the Coast Guard a call?"

He felt rebuked; the kid was keeping her head while he was acting like a raw recruit—which was exactly what he was, out here.

Marge said, "I'll do it. Do I make it Mayday?"

"Not yet," Brennan said. "Right, Linda. It could just be some panicky jerk out of gas or something. Just get through to them and tell them . . ."

"It doesn't work," Marge said from below.

"What do you mean it doesn't work?" Brennan demanded,

startled. "The weather was coming in loud and clear right after dinner."

Marge stepped back to give him room as he leaned through the hatch to check the set, which was placed so it could also be operated from the cockpit, although not as conveniently as he'd have liked. Marge was right. The VHF didn't seem to be quite dead, but even the weather channels gave out only feeble squawking sounds, quite incomprehensible. He had a quick premonition of doom. The thing to do, he knew, was get the hell out of here, fast. Suddenly the omens were wrong, the signs unfavorable. The sense of ambush that had often kept him alive in the past was screaming for a retreat.

Behind him Linda's voice said urgently, "Another flare, Skip. Dead ahead. I think I see a light. . . . No, they're on fire!"

They were closer than he'd expected. Straightening up, he could see the distressed vessel clearly: a small powerboat with a cabin. The cockpit area was ablaze, and some dark figures were huddled on the forward deck as far from the flames as possible.

He drew a deep breath and said, "Judging by the size, that thing is probably gasoline-powered; they don't put many diesels in those little ones. That means it can blow any minute. We haven't got time to get the sails off; we'll have to shoot right up there and hope they can all scramble aboard over the bowsprit. But you'd better start up the mill anyway, Linda, to make sure we'll swing the right way when we pull away. If she falls off to starboard into those damn blowing flames . . . Anybody know how fireproof Dacron sails are?"

But it was wrong and he knew it was wrong. He knew that he would never, in a military situation over which he had control, have given the order to advance feeling as he did—or would he? Was there ever a commander who didn't have premonitions of total disaster before an operation; who didn't see warnings in the sky and hear portentous sounds—and laugh at himself a few days later? And could he leave people to burn to death and drown because Colonel Hobart Brennan, USMC, Ret., had some queasy fears about his ability to manage a rescue at sea in his pretty new sailboat? Maybe that was all it was, just a kind of nautical buck fever.

"Okay, I'll take her, Linda," he said. It was quite possible the kid could do a better job, but he couldn't put the responsibility on her small shoulders, and the grief and guilt if something went wrong and people died. It was his ship. He said, "You and Marge stand by the sheets. Cast off everything when I give the word, let it all flap, to hell with it."

They could smell the thick stench of burning as they came downwind on the smaller boat. Somebody shouted at them, but they could not make out the words. Brennan reminded himself not to gauge his turn by the wind on his face; that was apparent wind, affected by *Spindrift*'s speed. He could only go by the direction of the blowing flames and the dark waves, but he told himself: Remember, she takes some time to turn, you've got to put the wheel over a little short of . . .

"Helm's down," he said softly. "Cast it all off and cross your fingers."

Forward, the jib and staysail broke into noisy flapping; then the main boom started to dance as the big sail swung out and lost its steadying breeze, and the mizzen began to rattle and flap above him. He checked the boat's swing. She was shooting into the wind very nicely, he thought, watching the burning boat approach, but a little slow, a little short, but better so than crashing up there with a full head of steam. . . . Okay, a touch of power now, just a nudge to put her up there. Neutral. Not bad for a goddamn amateur.

The blunt high bowsprit, actually a long heavy plank guarded by stainless-steel railings, was thrusting over the much lower bow of the powerboat; and people were scrambling up onto it. He felt the jolt as the bobstay hit. The smaller vessel started to pivot with the blow, bringing the flaming stern dangerously close—and he saw at last what he would have seen sooner if he had not been wholly intent on making a good approach: the cockpit quite intact over there and, in the middle of it, a large container of burning rags presumably soaked in oil. Marge, seeing it at the same time, grabbed his arm quickly, warningly, but it was much too late.

They were already on board, and there were guns in the hands of the men who were now charging aft along *Spindrift*'s deck. Even then, sheltered in the cockpit, he'd have had it all his own way if he'd only had a weapon. The way the light on the fire revealed them clearly up there on the open deck and bowsprit, it would have been simple target practice; but the country that had been happy enough to let him defend it for thirty years, gun in hand, couldn't bear to let him have a firearm to defend himself. There was obviously no point in going up against guns with a winch handle or his bare hands; being a dead hero was work that was always available. You didn't have to grab the first opportunity that came along. He raised his hands submissively, therefore, as the leader reached the cockpit.

On the smaller boat a figure had stepped out of the cabin to aim the nozzle of a large fire extinguisher at the decoy flames. And any dumb officer who'd lost his command falling for a trick like that would have been court-martialed and kicked out of the Corps so fast he wouldn't have stopped bouncing for a week. The rage and self-contempt inside him were so great that for a little while he wasn't really conscious of what was happening, although his disciplined mind made certain notes about the enemy. Number: four plus the one still on the decoy boat. Leader: a small tough runt of an Irishman. Arms: handguns only, no shotguns, rifles, or automatic weapons, at least not in sight, but no telling what the character on the other boat had available, so keep him in mind.

Then they were being herded into *Spindrift*'s cabin. Their guard was a heavyset man in grimy work clothes who hadn't shaved for a week, but the revolver in his hand looked reasonably well cared for and would probably fire on command. Brennan held back politely to let the girls go first, Linda and then Marge. One of them switched on a light below in response to an order from the guard. Meanwhile, the little Irishman was taking a man forward to help him get the flapping headsails down, while the remaining pirate or hijacker or whatever the technical term might be was holding the painter of the little powerboat to keep it from drifting away. The bewhiskered buccaneer nudged Brennan with the muzzle of the gun; and as he moved in his turn toward the hatch, Brennan felt all the violent, self-accusing emotions drain away abruptly. You can kick yourself later, Colonel Dumbo, sir, but right now just remember that a guy who goes poking people with guns doesn't really know a hell of a lot about guns.

The moment came at the foot of the companionway as he stepped forward and felt their guard reach the bottom behind him. He waited, and there came that nudge again, to the right of center, and he pivoted left, chopping down and back with his left arm, knocking the weapon aside, while his right hand drove a savage edge-of-the-hand blow to the throat. Above, the sails were still slapping and rattling noisily, and the whiskered man made no sound at all. The only sound was that of his revolver hitting the teak cabin sole with a dull thump; but there was no time for that at the moment.

Whiskers, screaming soundlessly, mouth agape, was clutching at his crushed windpipe with both hands. He went to his knees, and Brennan brought his own knees up under the hairy chin with all the force he could muster, seeing the head snapped back viciously by the impact. He stepped away to give the body room to fall, and looked for the gun, but it was right there.

Marge held it, cocked; she'd obviously been prepared to use it if he should need assistance. They looked at each other for a moment. "All right, old girl," he said softly.

"Be careful, dear," she said, lowering the hammer expertly and reversing the weapon so he could take it.

Brennan glanced down. "I think I broke the neck," he said, "but if it moves a muscle, cut its ugly throat with the butcher knife."

He had a glimpse of Linda, back against the bulkhead looking very pale; well, there were folks who could sail and folks who could fight, and fighting was his business. He turned and, wishing he could afford to turn the cabin light out, crouched on the ladder, listening. By the sound, they had the jib down and were lowering the forestaysail, but the main and mizzen were still making plenty of noise. He heard the man in the small cruiser shouting to the man holding the bow line.

". . . fisherman in Carrabelle is going to be kind of puzzled at how his cockpit got all scorched; maybe he'll figure his boat was hit by a meteor. Well, Regan knows your rendezvous; I'd better be heading back, it's a long ride in a stinking little tub like this."

The voice was vaguely familiar but Brennan couldn't see the face in the darkness; and he couldn't be bothered with solving the problem now. He waited. The man on *Spindrift*'s stern tossed the line onto the bow of the smaller boat, turning it loose. Brennan heard the motor fire. He cocked the revolver and took careful aim; and something struck him an unbearable blow in the back. He heard the crash of a gun below. One of them must have come down the forward hatch and sneaked up behind him. It wasn't the greatest military operation of his career, he thought bitterly; and he knew he had only an instant left, since they were bound to shoot again. He took care with his own shot and made it good, seeing the man aft collapse over the stern rail and hang there like a piece of laundry on a line. At least he'd made sure of one, for whatever good it would do now; two, if the one below really had a broken neck. They hadn't got him free; they'd had to pay their dues in the get-Brennan club along with all the small, tough, Oriental characters who'd applied for membership in the past. The gun behind him crashed again, and a second bullet drove into his back. He lost the revolver and felt himself sliding down the ladder, making himself turn as he fell so he could see his murderer, and catching himself at the bottom with a terrible effort.

Grief hit him hard as he saw Marge lying there with blood in her gray hair, where she'd been struck down from behind. Just beyond her, unbelievably, crouched a small girl in white shorts with a shiny weapon in her hand and an ugly, unfamiliar face—the killer-face he'd seen too many times on men but never before on a woman. He understood now the strong reaction he'd had to her in New Orleans. It hadn't been sexual desire at all, but the instinctive warning that one predator often received in the presence of another. He was struck by the irony of it: taking precautions against the possibility of his own death, for Marge's sake, he'd invited his death to sail with him. Another lousy appointment in Samarra.

Strangely, there was no hatred. The kid had done a good job, he thought; a very competent job indeed. She'd fooled him all the way—well, almost all the way. He'd known she wasn't what she seemed; but it had never occurred to him to look on her as an enemy. The thing was very beautiful when you came to think of it. The way she'd gently persuaded him that East Pass was the way to go, near Carrabelle where her accomplices waited in a stolen boat. The way she'd calmly warned him of danger to learn if he had a gun. The way she'd disabled the radio, as she undoubtedly had, and then dispelled suspicion by being the one to suggest using it to call the Coast Guard. As a professional, he could admire a skillful ambush; but why was the kid crying in the moment of her victory?

He saw her tear-streaked little face, and the shiny gun steadying for another shot, and he wanted to tell her not to waste the cartridge because they were coming for him now. He could hear the hammering of the great steel hooves and the rumbling of the giant wheels as the immense black carriage thundered past, bearing him away....

CHAPTER 21

April

Latitude 30°N; Longitude 95°W

Elmer Buckmeister passed the empty receptionist's desk in the outer office that no longer had a name plate on it because she was gone for good, of course. After what had happened she could hardly come back here, if only because he couldn't have endured her presence reminding him of what she had done and what he had seen that terrible night offshore. They had not yet hired anybody to replace her.

He wondered where she was now but it didn't matter, really. That was over. You might say, Mr. Buckmeister, he told himself formally, that everything is over. You've finally done it after years of trying. This time you've finished yourself but good, you and your Bosuns and your idiot intercepts. A little boy playing at piracy. Blackbeard Junior. Sir Henry Morgan Returns. The Son of Long John Silver. Why didn't you get yourself a black eye patch and a wooden leg while you were at it? Yo ho ho and a bottle of Scotch. And speaking of Scotch . . .

The phone rang, startling him. He hesitated. Since his return he could never pick up the instrument without expecting a cold official voice at the other end saying Mr. Buckmeister we would appreciate your coming down to the police station—actually he didn't even know where it was or if they called it that around here—to answer a few questions. Would they do it like that? It seemed unlikely they'd be that considerate. Probably they'd come roaring up in a car with a flashing light on top, two big men in uniform—Texas Rangers no doubt—and hold a pistol on him and make him put his hands against the wall while they searched him in the humiliating way he'd seen it done on TV; and then they'd put handcuffs on him and march him out past fat gloating Dave Pond and shocked little fluffy blonde Dot at the switchboard in the main office. How the hell, he asked himself, did I get myself into this anyway? And how many men had allowed the cry of the wild testicle, and a little money, to lead them into mad situations where they found themselves feebly asking themselves just that question?

Warily, he picked up the jangling instrument. "I'm departing now, Mr. Buckmeister," Dot's voice said in its stilted way; and then more informally: "Don't you work too hard, hear?"

"Thanks, Dot," he said, proud that his voice sounded fairly normal. "I'll lock up when I leave."

"You have a real nice evening, Mr. Buckmeister."

He had a momentary surge of . . . well, not real desire but mechanical masculine interest as, looking out through the glass door of the outer office, he caught a glimpse of her thin young figure with its dandelion-head of tortured hair making its way between the boats in the showroom, swinging its narrow hips in pitiful mimicry of Hollywood seductiveness. He knew, because she'd made it perfectly clear—now that Linda was gone—that the scanty body in the too-tight sweater and the too-snug slacks was available to him on demand. Well, he'd have to fancy it up with a few words about love, of course, but even now he was sure, if he hurried to catch her before she disappeared, that he could coax her back and up into a bunk in one of the display cruisers with hardly any effort at all.

For a moment he was tempted. It would drive the ugly memories away at least temporarily: the intriguing problem of getting her shoes and pants off gracefully, and whatever a kid like that wore underneath, and himself inside her, while reassuring her gently all the while with soothing words to the effect that he was doing it all with the greatest respect and affection in the world and only because he could no longer struggle against the irresistible passionate force, like super-gravity, that was inexorably bringing their two helpless bodies into intimate conjunction. But he knew that he was only teasing himself a little, testing himself to check that the male machinery, which had been inoperative so long, until Linda had skillfully put it back into service, was still functional after what had happened. But it was all right. He could feel the stirring that assured him he could do it all right, even though the girl wasn't really very attractive, but to hell with it. He'd found troubles enough that way without buying any more.

The Apalachicola Intercept, he thought with self-contempt; how Linda must have laughed when he took it all so goddamn seriously and organized it so goddamn systematically, like a small boy assigned a cookie cutter all his own just to keep him busy in a corner of the kitchen and out of mama's hair. He could see it all with sudden clarity: all they'd ever wanted was access to his boat records, and maybe a straw man to hand over to the authorities if things went wrong. How they must all have laughed, Regan and his thugs and the mysterious principal with the Spanish accent who was still only a voice over the phone. The North Bar Intercept. And that new one, the Yucatan Intercept; he wondered if they'd go ahead with that after what had happened. But they'd probably change the target now—you do sound like a real pirate chieftain, Mr. Bosun, with your intercepts and your targets—not trusting him to keep his mouth shut; and should he? Would it help if he marched right down before they could betray him, as they undoubtedly planned to, and made a full confession, and volunteered the little information they'd permitted him to have?

Sure. They'd only give him ninety-nine years instead of life, to paraphrase the old song. It was still murder, and although he'd pulled no triggers he was still deeply involved, even though she'd promised him faithfully there would be no killings, haha. Only four dead so far! Well, six counting those men she'd set adrift in that rubber raft earlier—he'd seen the small piece in the Miami paper they took in the office to check the ads—who'd apparently perished of thirst and wound up washed up on a beach somewhere near Hatteras, at least one of them had. But we were talking about Scotch, weren't we?

He got the sealed bottle, the testing bottle, the self-control bottle, out of the file drawer and set it on his desk. He got the glass from the small adjacent bathroom and put that beside it. Then he sat down to consider the situation carefully. It was poison, of course. For him it was suicide, a slow, undignified, self-inflicted death that could drag on for years but was just as inevitable for all that. He'd debated it every evening since he'd got back and decided against it and he might hold out tonight; but he knew that an evening would come when the decision would make itself the other way, and why not? What was left to stay sober for, anyway? It was simply a question of, when they came, whether he would be hauled away clearly aware of what he'd done and what was in store for him, or whether he'd be dragged off mercifully anesthetized; and when you put it like that, logic was all in favor of anesthesia, wasn't it? He'd dry out well enough in jail waiting for them to bring on the rope or the electrodes or the gas, whatever they used here in Texas.

Abruptly he buried his face in his hands, seeing it all again: the soft spring night and the stars and the pretty two-masted sailboat rocking on the dark empty sea with running lights and cabin lights aglow as he pulled away in the boat they'd stolen in Carrabelle—and then the repeated crashes of the shots, clearly audible over the sound of the motor. He'd turned back after some hesitation that was, he'd told himself, perfectly natural. He'd seen Regan and a companion running along the deck with dully gleaming guns. Regan had bent over something near the cockpit and moved toward the main hatch very cautiously. He, Buckmeister, was coming alongside by that time; and the other man had caught the line he heaved and secured it hastily and left him to scramble aboard unaided—leaving to cover the forward hatch at Regan's signal.

"Oh, Jesus Fucking Christ!" Regan had said softly. "Oh, my sainted dear mother, will you look at the lousy fucking massacre the fools have made here, God save us all!"

There had been a man Buckmeister should have recognized but didn't, hanging over the stern rail with black blood dripping from his nose and mouth and the bullet hole in his head. Swallowing hard, Buckmeister had turned away from that and joined Regan at the hatch and looked down into the bright hell that was the comfortable and cheerfully lighted cabin, with the three dead bodies and the spreading pools of blood and the small girl looking like an innocent lost child, barefoot, in her neat little halter-and-shorts outfit, sitting against the bulkhead with the gleaming pistol resting on her bare knees and endless silent tears streaming down her face. And then the ugly business of cleaning it all up, and the sharks, and the everlasting pumping.

"Keep at it, goddamn it!" Regan had said. "Keep sluicing it down and pumping it out, it's still running pink, goddamn it. It's never we'll get rid of it if we give it time to congeal in the fucking bilge. . . ."

"Bucky."

Despite his often-expressed preference, there was only one person in the world, besides Linda, who regularly called him that; not so much because he desired it, he knew, but because

207

her sense of suitability was offended by the yokel name—
Elmer, for God's sake!—that her husband had been given at
birth. He lifted his head and looked up unbelievably. Madeleine
hardly ever came to the office; and then only to voice a
grievance—but tonight her expression was quite gentle as
she looked at him sitting there with the goddamn bottle on
the desk before him.

Seeing her, he could never help thinking how beautiful it
could all have been with a little luck. Sure, he'd married her
at least partly on account of her daddy's oilwells, and she
knew it perfectly well, but they could have overcome that
handicap if everything had not gone so terribly wrong from
the start; if that ill-fated honeymoon cruise hadn't led her to
the mistaken belief that his object, besides the damn money,
was total domination and humiliation, causing her to fight
back desperately with all the destructive, feminine weapons
at her command. Quite unfamiliar with boats and boatmen,
she'd simply failed to understand the basic principle that out
there the ship always comes first, and that the captain's job is
to keep the goddamn bucket afloat and moving in the right
direction no matter whose lousy little feelings get hurt in the
process. But this immutable law of the sea, which he'd taken
for granted after years of sailing, had been totally unfamiliar
to her; and she'd taken his attitude personally, as a deliberate assault on her integrity and self-respect—the basic misunderstanding from which the marriage had never recovered.
He'd often wondered why she'd bothered to stick around so
long when divorces were so easy to get.

She must have been heading for a cocktail party when
some impulse had caused her to come here instead—she'd
had her own social life for years. She was wearing a black
velvet skirt in that intermediate length the designers seemed
to try every few years, not clear down to the ankles but well
below the knees; and a thin satin blouse that wasn't quite
white, one of those loose, rather shapeless, but on her quite
graceful, garments that seemed to be in fashion currently;
this one with flowing satin sleeves and a low peasant neck-
line and a kind of drawstring at the bottom pulling it together around her hips. He still found it rather shocking that
his wife would dress for a festive public occasion with no
brassiere on, with her nipples showing clearly through the
thin satin, and with her loose upper garment so obviously
unstable that any small accident of movement, any casual
breeze, would expose her breasts completely—but he realized

that this was an old-fashioned attitude and they were still very nice breasts. She was wearing sheer black stockings and strap sandals with high, slim heels.

Slender and blonde, she was so lovely still, after all the years, that he could never quite remember to hate her when he was in her presence. The hatred, the violent frustrated dreams of vengeful ravishment and scornful retribution that left her lying tattered and spent as he walked away contemptuously to begin a fine new life without her—these wild imaginings always evaporated the instant she entered the room. The idiotic fact, he knew, was that somewhere along the line he'd fallen in love with her; the mongrel dog cringing in adoration before the cruel master or, in this case, mistress. It had nothing to do, of course, with the hatred he bore her; the two emotions were quite capable of coexistence. Nor did it have anything to do with the feeling he'd had for Linda; there had been nothing idealized about *that*. It had been quite easy for him to love them both in different ways, since they did not, in his mind, exist on the same plane.

"She's gone, isn't she, darling?" Madeleine said.

He frowned, hearing the words but finding no meaning in them. He asked stupidly, "What?"

"The little receptionist." Madeleine's voice was quite calm. "For a while I thought it was the blonde switchboard girl, the one who just left—I was waiting for her to leave, as a matter of fact. That really hurt, a cheap, obvious little bitch like that. But the other one . . . well, she was also a little animal, of course, but at least she was a strong and intelligent and rather attractive little animal. But she's not coming back, is she?" When he did not speak, she reached out and picked up the bottle and looked at the unbroken seal. "I hate her, you understand," she murmured." I would, quite literally, love to scratch her eyes out. But I think I may owe her a great deal. Where does this go?"

Still uncomprehending, he jerked his head toward the filing cabinet. "Bottom drawer," he heard himself say. "Madeleine—"

She disposed of the bottle and closed the drawer and turned back to him, touching him lightly on the cheek. "Let's go home now . . . oh, I almost forgot. Does that phone work?"

"Yes, it should be plugged in."

He watched the slim finger with the carefully lacquered nail pushing the buttons; then he listened to the one-sided conversation: "Oh, Louellen, darling, I'm really sorry . . . no

209

honey, I'm perfectly all right, but something terribly important has come up. . . ." She laid the instrument down and looked at him. "We'll take my car; yours will be all right here, won't it? I'll drive you to work in the morning."

He found the sudden strength to say, "Madeleine, what the hell?"

She looked down at him for a moment. "What the hell is right, darling. Let's just say that your wife has been waiting for months for your pint-sized mistress to split the scene, or however the kids put it nowadays. Now that I'm sure she's left for good, I'm taking my husband home. If he doesn't mind. Shall we go?"

He remembered to turn out certain lights, and to lock the doors behind him. Then they were riding homeward in the silent Mercedes that, like so many things, was largely a present from daddy; and she was speaking softly.

"Damn you, Bucky," she murmured, "why did you have to make it so hard? Just because I got everything wrong and acted like a stupid bitch once, for a little while so long ago. . . . And don't forget why you married me in the first place. Didn't it ever occur to you to ask yourself why I married you? Did you really think I was so dumb I didn't know? Didn't it occur to you that I might, dumb me, actually . . . actually be kind of fond of you in spite of . . . You made such an unconvincing fortune hunter, my dear." She drew a long unsteady breath. "I thought we could still . . . I thought it would work out all right. . . . And it would have, too, if it hadn't been for that damned boat!"

He licked his lips. "I don't understand. If you knew about Linda . . ."

"Was that her name? I ought to have guessed. When they look like that they're always Lindas." Driving, she took a hand from the wheel and touched his knee apologetically. "I'm sorry. Remember that I can't help hating her; how can I? How do you think it makes a wife feel, forced to stand by while another woman repairs the dreadful damage she's done in her stupid defensive anger? But I couldn't do it myself. You wouldn't trust me enough to let me do it, even when I realized at last . . . even when I tried. And you were destroying yourself so horribly. I had to . . . to humble myself and let her do it for me. If that makes me a cold-blooded, calculating bitch without any self-respect whatever, it's just too goddamn bad. It was the only chance we had left."

It was always a fairly long drive; and the sun was low in

the sky by the time they reached the big handsome house that, like the car, owed a lot to Daddy. He got out when she stopped in the driveway and went around to help her out and saw an odd kind of uncertainty, for her, in the quick, almost shy smile with which she thanked him. Inside the house, she went a little distance into the large, luxurious front room and turned and waited there while he closed and locked the front door.

"Our timing has always been lousy, hasn't it, darling?" she said when he reached her. "Look, it's still broad daylight. Why, over at Louellen's they're just starting on their cocktails."

He knew that the words did not mean at all what they said. She was asking him a question and he tried to frame a suitable answer.

"To hell with Louellen," he said, hearing his voice unexpectedly harsh.

"Yes. That's what I hoped you'd say, dear. To hell with Louellen."

She turned and walked quickly down the hall to her bedroom, large and light and not particularly feminine, at least not in a fussy or frilly way. He stood inside the door while she released the Venetian blinds and returned to him, standing before him; and they'd still hardly touched each other and didn't now.

"We're not very good at this, are we?" she murmured after a moment. "I guess we just haven't had much practice. The theory is, Mr. Buckmeister, you grab the lady lovingly and stop her interminable chatter in the manner that seems most appropriate. . . ." She stopped and looked at him searchingly. "Look, darling, if you really don't *like* me after all these years, and I wouldn't exactly blame you, please say so now before I make a complete goddamn jackass of myself."

It was a crazy thing for her to say, he thought. It should have been perfectly obvious, he thought, that he loved her so much and wanted her so badly that he couldn't speak for the constriction in his throat. Then, somehow, she was in his arms, her mouth fiercely returning his kiss, her body willingly accepting and responding to the growing boldness of his hands through the soft warm velvet and smooth cool satin; and he knew suddenly that she had guessed all his old, ugly, impotent, savage dreams and was deliberately offering herself to him like this, in her pretty, vulnerable party clothes. He sensed from her unreserved yielding that tonight she was

211

prepared to disregard any damage to her fragile cocktail costume, to allow it to be hopelessly crumpled and crushed without protest, even violently torn if that was his pleasure. It was an atonement she obviously felt obliged to make for the destructive campaign she'd waged so long ago to consolidate her initial bedroom victory, when there had always, whenever he felt a hint of returning desire, been a new hairdo that couldn't be mussed, fresh make-up that shouldn't be smudged, a fabulous new dress that mustn't get rumpled under any circumstances. . . . But this was not a night for vengeance and violence; and he couldn't accept her sacrifice. He stepped back, breathing deeply, fighting for restraint. Looking down in the striped half-light of the shaded room, he found a satin bow at the hip and gently pulled it untied, letting the gathered blouse fall loose; then he located the tab of the skirt fastener under it and drew this down just as carefully, and patted her lightly on the rear.

"Can you manage the rest all by yourself?" he asked, trying to control his unsteady voice. "If not I'll be happy to assist."

She laughed softly and he knew that, whatever indignities her conscience had ordered her to endure and pretend to enjoy at his hands, by doing it like this he had passed some kind of test and made her happy. Moments later he was joining her in the enormous bed. Her arms went around him as he entered her strongly, as he'd dreamed of doing, and felt her welcome him home. . . .

Later, after their breathing had returned more or less to normal, and they'd become perspiringly aware of the artificial chill of the room and, laughing, had sought the shelter of the bedclothes together, she moved in his arms, turning away from him. It was not rejection or a withdrawal, he knew; it was simply a question of human engineering, the outer curve of her body now fitting smoothly into the inner curve of his as she curled up against him in a trusting manner that broke his heart—because it was all coming back to him. The wonder of having it happen at all was being lost in the terror of having it happen too late.

Tomorrow he would have to tell her, of course. He should have told her tonight before . . . he should never have let her commit herself like this without knowing. Good old Blundering Buckmeister, reliable as a clock when it came to doing the wrong thing. He would tell her and tonight's happiness would all go out of her, lost forever, and she would take charge at once, very brisk and businesslike to hide her hurt. She'd call Daddy and consult the lawyers about the very best manner in which to handle this new predicament from which her idiot husband must be saved as he'd been saved before. And there would be trials and appeals and glaring publicity and Daddy's smart lawyers would maneuver skillfully in the courtroom, while Daddy's tall oil rigs did close-order drill on the courthouse lawn.

It would drag on and on and in the end they might even save him, but there would be nothing left to save him for, and probably nothing left to save. By that time they would no longer be people. They would only be newspaper figures: the stupid philandering husband who'd been a sucker for a murderous seductress, and the loyal wife who'd stuck by him nevertheless. . . . It could not be allowed to happen, he knew. He'd done enough damage here already.

She was breathing softly and regularly, sound asleep in his arms. It was quite dark by now. When he disengaged himself she made a small sound of protest. He bent over and kissed her and whispered that he'd be right back, and the lie seemed to satisfy her. Soon her breathing was even once more. He drew the light blanket over her shoulder against the standard, frosty Texas air conditioning, and waited still another minute or two, standing by the bed, until he was satisfied she was sleeping heavily. Then he reached into the drawer of the bedside table for the object that was as much standard equipment for the bedside table of a Texas ranch girl as a box of Kleenex. He carried it into the bathroom, and locked the door securely before turning on the light.

It was, he thought, a hell of an ugly thing. It had a history, of course; they always did. Great-great-uncle Jason had carried it at the Alamo, or great-grandfather Ames had employed it well at Gettysburg. No, it wasn't as old as all that, of course, but somebody in the family had worn it somewhere, and used it ruthlessly no doubt, while helping put together the endless acres on a corner of which had later been found a certain dome-shaped formation that was now geological and financial history. Instant population control, he thought, looking down at it. The Surgeon General has determined that living is dangerous to your health; we recommend Dr. Colt's infallible single-action cure for longevity.

He cocked it and raised it experimentally and knew at once that it wouldn't work. For one thing, he couldn't do that to her, arousing her from a sound sleep with the shattering

213

crash and letting her come stumbling in here only half awake
after groping around for the simple key, if she could find it,
that worked the push-button lock from the outside. . . . But
also he simply didn't have the courage. He was bound to
flinch at the last moment; it was quite inevitable. With his
luck he'd only manage to ridiculously blow off an ear or
horribly blow off a jaw or carefully place the shot so that it
did not kill but left her with a mindless human vegetable to
care for for the rest of her life. He lowered the big hammer
awkwardly and laid the big weapon on the dressing table
among the pretty containers of feminine beauty preparations. He opened the medicine cabinet above and found the
little plastic container of the yellow capsules she sometimes
used to make her sleep. It was almost full. She must have had
the prescription renewed quite recently.

It was still, he knew, a terrible thing to do to her, but of the
choices available to him it seemed the least terrible. He
filled a glass with water and, drawing a long breath, began to
wash the capsules down his throat until they were all gone.
Then he looked around for a suitable place, a place where he
would not fall over noisily and bring her in here before it was
finished, before the chemical had completed its work. At last
he got into the bathtub and settled himself there.

It was not, he decided, a very dignified death, naked in a
tub, but why should he change his style now? It hadn't been
such a hell of a dignified life, either.

CHAPTER 22

April

Latitude 26°N; Longitude 82°W

Lavinia Burnett woke up with a throbbing headache and the
uneasy knowledge that she was in the wrong cabin of the
boat. Up in *Spindrift*'s little wedge-shaped forepeak was
where she belonged, but now she was back in the big aft

stateroom and what the hell was she doing there? The Brennans would be totally disgusted and disillusioned with her for getting stinking drunk like this and sleeping it off in her clothes, sprawled untidily on one of their bunks. It would spoil everything, all the comfortable friendly shipboard feeling that had made the past weeks such a revelation, setting the clock back to well before that time she did not like to think about when, in that place she did not like to think about, they did weird electrical things to her to snap her out of the bad-trip nightmare she'd have come out of all right by herself if they'd just left her alone. But her folks, finding her like that, had insisted on something being *done*. Well, it had been done, all right; and nothing had ever been the same again.

The fact was, she'd never known anything like the beautiful, peaceful time just past. Her nagging, bickering, pretentious family had never been like that. It had been like being born again all shiny and new and *nice,* sailing with two great people who really liked each other and liked her too. . . . *Oh, Jesus, no!*

No, she thought as memory returned, *no, no, no, NO!*

Then she was crying again helplessly, Burnett the human drip, as if tears would help. I hate you, she told herself, hate you hate you hate you I don't want to live with you any more all you're good for is hurting people. And sometimes fuck fuck fuck if you want to call that good. But why did that wonderful little round guy who loved his nice tall gray-eyed wife and his handsome boat and was so cute about wanting to learn everything nautical, why did he have to suddenly turn into a scary human killing-machine that had to be stopped before it ruined everything? And then there wasn't anything left to do but . . . *She* couldn't be allowed to wake up and see him lying there like that, could she? It had really been much *kinder* to. . . .

Monster, she thought. It's a monster, that's what it is, that thing they put inside you with their fucking shocking machine. *This* is what it's been looking for all along, all the long years of looking; and now it's licking its fucking bloody chops way back there in the dark, inside that ugly half-rotten mess you call a mind, licking and licking and looking and looking . . . and why the hell isn't this boat rocking the way it should? What's going on here, anyway? She sat up abruptly, her head pounding with agony, and scrubbed away the tears with her knuckles and pulled down the limp halter that was grossly neglecting its duty, as somebody came down the companionway ladder and aft through the narrow passage into the cabin.

"Such a dainty little thing it is," Regan said, eyeing her sourly. "Why don't you comb your pretty hair, my lovely, just a little, and drag your sweet ass topside? It's wanted elsewhere you are, although as an object of desire you leave something to be desired at the moment, my darling."

"Why don't you go fuck yourself, Regan?" she said.

"Why should I, when you're available, my sweet?"

"That will be the day!"

Then she looked at the small, wiry, dark man with the slightly oversized shoulders with sudden uneasy concern, wondering just what the hell had happened in here during the days—she thought it was three but it could have been more—that she'd kind of lost track of. Not that it mattered all that much, but a girl did like to know exactly what her relationship was, and had been, to the men around her. But looking at him she saw that he was merely talking big and sexy, man-fashion; there was an odd flicker of wariness in his eyes that told her he'd made no pass and did not intend to make one. Fear? In Regan? Well, he was a sensible man in his way; and if she were a sensible man would she have anything to do with an unbalanced, bedraggled, drunken little female with ever-streaming eyes who went around shooting people she loved?

She said abruptly, "I'll be along in a minute. I don't need help to powder my nose."

"It's surely glad I am to hear that; it's hard to tell by looking."

"Regan," she said as he started to turn away.

"What, love?"

"If there's anything worse than a professional thug, it's a fucking professional Irishman."

"So?" he said, and something ugly moved across his tough monkey face. "And if there's anything worse than an amateur hoor, it's a fucking amateur gunman. Or gunwoman."

They stared at each other for a moment; then Vinnie laughed shortly. "What are you so mad about, Regan?" she demanded. "I'll tell you what. You flubbed it, that's what. You blew it. You left an experienced professional soldier to be watched by a clumsy amateur goon, and that little military gent got loose in a breeze and wiped out half your crew and would have got the rest, including you, if I hadn't saved you.

216

So let's not have any more crap about amateur gunmen. You were about as amateurish as it can get."

To her surprise, he didn't flare back at her. Instead he nodded soberly. "It's right you are, my sweet. I did not expect that from an officer, even a Marine officer. Usually they sit in their plushy quarters in their shiny shoes and let the grunts do the dirty hand-to-hand work. And he was not a dangerous-looking little man, you'll admit. But if it pleases you, I'll confess I blew it and you saved the day. So, with Regan's everlasting gratitude established, will you come now, or as soon as you can make yourself presentable or at least tolerable?"

"I'll be right up."

"Bring your gear. They're sending somebody for you. We'll have to struggle along without you here, hard and lonely though it will be. Oh, and you can wash your face a little but don't shower or pump the head. You'll see why when you get on deck."

She watched him go and then got up, wishing her head would split and get it over with. How anybody could get hooked on that lousy stuff was beyond her. There were so many other things you could take that had the same pleasant, pain-killing, memory-eradicating effect without the punishment that came afterwards; but since that time she hadn't dared use any of them even when they were available. Even alcohol wasn't exactly safe for her, witness the way she seemed to have misplaced several days; but at least it had seen her over the worst of it and now, after her exchange with Regan, she was beginning to feel halfway human again even though she didn't look it. The small, happy, suntanned person in the mirror she'd almost come to take for granted during the past weeks had been replaced by a pinched, haggard, greasy-looking little red-eyed creature that looked as if it had crawled out from under a decaying log.

She made some kind of a pass at her face and hair and decided not to worry about a change of clothes until she could have a shower. It was not, after all, as if there was anybody left she cared to impress with what a clean sweet pure little thing she was; and she didn't have an unlimited supply of clean clothes available. She reclaimed her little pack from the forepeak and went on deck and recoiled in surprise; they were, for God's sake, indoors, explaining why Regan hadn't wanted a lot of stuff pumped overboard. Warily, she stepped clear of the companionway ladder, aware of the little Irishman

217

grinning at her expression as she looked around. It was a great big ancient boatshed in which even *Spindrift*'s thirty-nine feet—more if you counted the bowsprit—had plenty of room. The masts were down and lying on sawhorses at the side of the building with the slack rigging trailing from them. The building was open to the water astern, and rusty iron rails ran down there, presumably for the marine railway by means of which the boat had been hauled. The limited view she could see was swampy and desolate.

She glanced at Regan. "I thought it was supposed to be kind of a hurry-up job."

"Change of plans, sweet," he said. "Another property he's had his eye on for another purpose—you probably know about it—has become available a little sooner than expected. This one stays hidden here on the edge of the Everglades until we've taken care of that. It's just as well. No profit in hurrying-up right into the arms of the Coast Guard. You reported that a daughter would be waiting for them in Tampa complete with husband, remember? Presumably the girl will have started a search when her parents' ship did not reach harbor on schedule; so it's just as happy I am to let this one cool off a bit before I sail it south. Besides, there's the renaming and painting to be done."

"If he hadn't scuttled that catamaran he'd have a real little fleet," Vinnie said sourly. "Boats all over the fucking place. Where do I go?"

"You put that little pack on your back and you walk up the dirt road behind the boatyard to the main highway and you turn right. You continue to walk, and you do not let yourself be picked up by any men although some will doubtless offer their gallant services, of one kind or another. But it's a woman you want. She'll ask where you're going and you'll say Miami and she'll say it's a lucky, lucky girl you are, she's heading down into the Keys herself, but she'll drop you at the right intersection as she goes by and from there it's not very far." He glanced at his watch. "So be off with you now." He hesitated. "Lavinia."

"Yes?"

"Once more, an apology. I was out of line. Regan is not ungrateful."

"Sure."

He was wrong, no men offered to pick her up as, after stumbling painfully along the endless dirt track through the marshy Florida coastal jungle, she found the paved highway at last and trudged along the edge of it feeling utterly miserable again. The spring sunshine was too bright and hot, and the fucking cars roared by unheeding while sweat soaked her halter and the waistband of her shorts and her boat shoes hurt her feet, which had seldom worn any shoes at all for several weeks. The aching of her head made everything just a little hazy and unreal. Maybe she looked like jailbait to the drivers who might have been interested, or maybe she just looked too sick and dirty to be worth anybody's trouble; and wasn't that a comforting thought?

Then a car stopped at last and Regan had said a woman but this was a kid, but the sex was right, and the jackass conversation was right, and she tossed her pack into the rear of the battered little vehicle and got in wearily beside the driver, who sent them away with as much acceleration as the car was capable of, which would hardly have bugged any eyes at the local dragstrip. The girl was pretty enough if you were a man and liked chili; and Vinnie Burnett wondered in what cathouse the creepy little big-headed bastard had picked up this tender Latin morsel and then she saw the resemblance: the fine aristocratic features that looked so different in a young girl's face. That scared her a little. She knew enough about Columbus by now to know that he wouldn't have risked using another member of his family—not after losing the boy—unless things were getting tough; she also knew enough to know that now that she, Lavinia Burnett, could involve the daughter by speaking out of turn, her life, Lavinia Burnett's, wasn't worth much if it ever had been. And what the hell did the little Cuban tart in her skintight jeans with her little tits bouncing around inside her stenciled T-shirt—something from *Star Wars,* for God's sake, how corny could you get—what did she have to feel so superior about anyway? Her goddamn clothes weren't so fucking immaculate either.

It was a long hot ride without conversation. At last she went to sleep against the car door but her dreams weren't good, and she woke with a start to see that the juvenile little Latin lovely was skillfully guiding the sedan along one of Miami's freeways. The younger girl spoke at last.

"Now you're supposed to get in the rear and hide on the floor. Don't show your head until somebody tells you."

Vinnie glanced over her shoulder and started to say it would have been nice if they'd picked a fucking car that wasn't built for midgets; but something in the girl's face silenced her. It made her feel suddenly very old and rather sad, because the pretty Spanish kid beside her was obviously feeling very serious and very proud. She was just beginning to realize, it seemed, that she'd been entrusted with an important and dangerous mission of great significance to the patriotic work of the counterrevolution that would soon overthrow the bearded tyrant at last—and, of course, install the Columbus family once more in a beautiful hacienda like the one in which this girl had been born or, since she was probably too young for that, *should* have been born, *would* have been born, if it had not been for the evil machinations of the Marxist usurper. Sitting there at the wheel of the crummy little beat-up Pinto in her grubby jeans and stupidly labeled T-shirt, the young Señorita Something Something Columbo Something was obviously dreaming of herself as a serene aristocratic beauty in hoop skirts and crinolines like she'd seen in TV reruns of *Gone With The Wind*. With, perhaps, her arm in a sling due to a small—but of course adequately painful—wound incurred fighting bravely at her daddy's side in the glorious battle of the restoration.

Anyway, it was clear that she, Lavinia Burnett, was, in this girl's mind, no longer just a small female tramp in grimy white shorts, but a dangerous secret agent of enormous value to the Cause, being smuggled into Miami past the forces of repression at tremendous risk. Well, okay. Who was she to shatter anybody's fucking illusions, who had none left of her own, having recently killed the last one with her own hands?

"Good thinking," she said, and the Spanish girl beamed. "Yes, ma'am, in this business you can't be too careful."

She climbed into the rear. Even for her it was a tight fit between the seats, and as she tried to make herself comfortable with her pack as a pillow she couldn't help wondering what they did when they had a full-sized human to transport unseen. All the melodrama had made her tired; and she let herself drift off to sleep again—hell, anybody who'd ever slept in the forepeak of a yacht under sail wasn't going to have any trouble dozing off wedged into a crack in a junior-grade Ford. When she woke up again, there was a roof over them, and she heard the girl's voice outside the car, and another voice, male, that she recognized.

"You really ought to do something about that crummy old car, Daddy, any time it hits a rough place in the road it skitters around like crazy."

"Did you have a nice visit with your aunt in Sarasota, *querida?*"

"Oh, she's awful stuffy, but Tio Miguel is a doll."

They were obviously talking for the benefit of anybody who might be listening. Somebody closed the garage door, shutting off their voices and part of the light. There was a gentle tapping on the roof of the car, and a different man's voice spoke.

"You can get out now, *Señorita,* but stay away from the window, *por favor.*"

She crawled out stiffly and brushed away the loose dirt that clung to her clothes and her damp skin—you'd think they'd have the decency to vacuum the heap occasionally if they were going to carry passengers back there, she thought irritably. The wiry little *mayordomo,* Jesus Cardenas, was watching her with no more than polite interest. It seemed as if she couldn't raise a spark in anybody today. She must look even worse than she felt; but actually the nap had helped and the headache was subsiding. The garage had one window, not clean, and the big lifting door that was now closed, and a smaller door that apparently led into the house. There was the usual array of rusty tools and old tires that always accumulated in a place like that. Abruptly, she started at the realization that there was somebody behind her. She turned to see the muscle-bound, neckless, swarthy gofer looking down at her with vague, shiny, dumb brown eyes.

Cardenas said, "Do not mind Bolo, *Señorita.*"

"I don't mind him. I just wish you'd put a bell on him, like a cow."

"He means no harm. Would you care for a Coca-Cola while we wait?"

"Mr. Cardenas, you're an angel. If you can produce two cokes you'll be two angels."

Cardenas spoke in Spanish to the larger man, who shuffled off into the house and returned with two bottles and an opener. She hadn't realized how thirsty she was until she found herself chug-a-lugging one whole coke without stopping; then she took time to enjoy the sweet lovely wetness of the second. Just as she finished, the small door opened, and Jimmy Columbus entered, as odd-looking as ever in a dapper light suit, with his small unimpressive body and his big noble head.

"*Señorita* Burnett." He took one of her dirty hands and kissed it, bowing. "We are in your debt, very much in your debt. Regan has explained over the telephone how you saved a very bad situation."

221

She found herself wanting to giggle but knew it wasn't a good idea; but really, the gentleman ought to hold off on the gracious hand-kissing until the beat-up lady had a chance to take a bath and put on a long satin gown.

"Yes," she said, "and it's the last one, too. The deal was no killing. . . ."

She never saw the signal given. One moment she was standing there; the next she was on the garage floor with a stinging ear and, once again, an aching head—Bolo had knocked her down from behind.

"Yes," Columbus said softly, "Regan also said there were some sentimental afterthoughts, which is why I had you brought here, *Señorita,* in order to persuade you to reconsider. . . ."

She'd met them before. There were always guys around like that. They thought a fat lip or a black eye or a kick in the ribs would make you their groveling slave for life. They didn't realize that, for a few people, the treatment worked the other way, canceling all debts and obligations. . . . Suddenly she found herself loving the hurt of her ear and glorying in the new ache in her head; the sadistic little bastard had just solved everything. She was aware of relief and immense gratitude. Now there was nothing left to tie her to these jerks, if there ever had been anything but a little money, a little fear, and a common interest in a dangerous and exciting project.

But she had a new and better project now. The monster lurking back there in the darkness inside her head had found what he was looking for; and the blow allowed her to turn him loose with a perfectly clear conscience. Come on little monster, nice little monster, there's your meat, that funny-looking gent with the big pretty head. Just a whiff to get the scent so you'll know him when feeding time comes, and then back into the black cave for you. For now.

She rubbed her ear childishly and made her voice shrill and indignant. "Jeez, Mr. Columbus, you don't have to knock a girl's head off. I didn't mean—"

"I'm terribly sorry, my dear," he said smoothly. "I thought you did. Please?"

He reached down to help her rise and waited while she brushed herself off again, reflecting it was a damn good thing she hadn't wasted the effort of changing into clean clothes the way she kept winding up on everybody's dirty floors. Then she looked at the misproportioned figure before her and

222

thought, okay, Skip, I'm going to stuff and mount this freaky specimen for you and Marge, and I'm so damned sorry for everything. And if that was ridiculously inadequate under the circumstances she couldn't help it; it was the best she had to offer. But at least she could think about it at last without bursting into tears. The funny thing was, being clouted on the ear didn't make her want to cry the least little bit.

She licked her lips fearfully, and threw a wary glance at hulking Bolo. "What . . . what do you want me to do, Mister Columbus?"

"The same as before, of course. Just as we planned."

"That big Striker at the Yacht Club?" She frowned. "But how can we be sure . . . I mean, the way our poor old patsy, Buckmeister, bugged out of there that night in a blue funk after washing his hands of me forever, well, he could have panicked completely by now and spilled everything to the cops. And he knew about that boat; we had him checking on it, remember?"

"I think there is very little danger of that."

Columbus reached into the pocket of his shirt and brought out a newspaper clipping. She took it and unfolded it. It was from a very recent Houston paper and the heading of the item read: YACHT BROKER SUICIDE. Mr. Elmer Buckmeister, partner in the well-known firm of Buckmeister and Pond, had been found by his wife dead of an overdose of barbiturates, apparently self-administered. Mrs. Buckmeister was quoted as saying that her husband had been in good health and had had no business problems she was aware of; she had no idea what had caused him to do such a terrible thing.

"Oh, the poor guy!" Vinnie heard herself say softly.

"A very becoming sentiment," Columbus said, "but the fact is this removes one danger, although it also prevents us from utilizing the man as a scapegoat and distraction as fully as I'd hoped. But there is no indication that he approached the police before taking his life—I had somebody watching him, on Regan's advice—so I think we can safely go ahead with the next operation as planned. They want to hire a crew for a fishing voyage to Cozumel with some friends; actually, they require chiefly somebody who can function as cook and steward since the owners, a wealthy young couple from New Jersey, usually manage the boat by themselves. They had a young black man engaged, but unfortunately he got careless on his motorcycle and is now in the hospital with some broken bones, very sad. In the morning you will see the

223

assistant dockmaster at the Club, a certain Mr. Reuben Montoya, who will take you to the boat. He has already recommended you highly. You will be Laura Briggs—you like those initials, don't you? Jesus has your papers, including a passport and a couple of references from other yachtsmen who have sampled your superlative seagoing cooking and have found your behavior and semanship beyond reproach. Any questions?"

Even though her spirit was now broken, she had to show some respect for her own skin. "Yes, Mr. Columbus. One. How do I get away with it afterwards?"

"You will be shot, my dear."

"Gee, thanks lots!"

"Before the others are set adrift, they will hear a struggle and the report of a firearm. Regan will come strolling aft casually blowing smoke from the barrel of his pistol and saying that the crazy little bitch went for him with a kitchen knife so what could he do?"

"Just so Regan knows where he's supposed to put that fucking bullet. I mean, where he's *not* supposed . . ."

Again there was no visible signal. Suddenly she was simply on her knees with her left arm twisted up between her shoulder blades. Columbus was looking down at her coldly.

"Your comments are not required, *Señorita,* only your obedience. Please remember that you are personally responsible for at least four deaths, the two men off the catamaran whom you set adrift, and the couple on the ketch whom you shot. You have been involved in two other deaths; and the law reads that if someone is killed in the commission of a crime, those committing the crime are responsible no matter who pulled the trigger. A word to the police and you will spend the remainder of your life in prison, assuming that the tenderhearted authorities do not manage to overcome, in your flagrant case, their delicate objections to capital punishment. . . . All right, Bolo."

She picked herself up again, flexing her arm experimentally. "You might have told the big clown to take it easy!" she blurted. "A one-armed girl isn't going to do much cooking."

Columbus ignored her outburst. "Just do as you are told and you will be all right. And while we hope there will be no flagrant errors made this time, you will be expected to support Regan's operation in all ways necessary, including the use of the firearm I provided if that seems indicated. I am happy to know you can do so well with it; it makes you much more useful. With your new papers, you will find adequate compensation to date. Later, after you return, I will probably have more work for you, also remunerative." The little man stared at her for a moment. "Just one thing."

"Yes, Mr. Columbus."

"Curb those sentimental impulses, *Señorita*. Remember that your own life is at stake."

"Sure, Mr. Columbus. You don't have to tell me."

"I hope not."

He regarded her bleakly for a moment longer, and turned on his heel and walked out, which was just as well since she was having a hard time refraining from laughing in his handsome face. Or spitting in it. But it was kind of fucking scary when you came to think of it. Were there really people around who fell for this head-batting, arm-twisting routine? What the hell kind of fucking human sheep did he find out there to practice on, anyway? Were there actually flesh-and-blood men and women around who'd take that kind of bullying crap and not promise themselves the pleasure of retaliation? Down, little monster, down. I'll tell you when it's time.

Docilely obeying the instructions of Jesus Cardenas, she got back into the car after tucking away in her pack the bundle of money and documents he gave her. After she was well hidden once more she heard the garage door go up. Then Columbus' voice reached her, pitched loudly enough to be heard by anyone who might be interested.

"Please do not stay out too late tonight, Francesca."

"Oh, Daddy! You're always telling me not to be too late; if you had your way I'd be in bed at some crazy hour like nine o'clock!"

Then the girl was behind the wheel and the motor was running and they were driving away. It was getting dark now; and all lights were on by the time Francesca Columbus dropped her off near a small motel not too far from the waterfront. The proprietress was dubious about her appearance until she apologized cheerfully for her perfectly *filthy* condition but she'd been on a yacht and they'd been sailing offshore for *weeks* and she'd hardly had her clothes off the whole time and she was certainly looking forward to a nice hot shower and night in a real *bed*. That magic word, yacht, always won them over even though in reality the boat in question might be only fifteen feet long with a tent for a cabin and a bucket for a head.

In the morning, clean and suitably costumed in a neat

jersey and her almost-new jeans, she found her way to the nearby Yacht Club and located Mr. Reuben Montoya at the fuel dock. He was a plump dark man with a thin black pencil-moustache, whose brown eyes seemed to be contemplating a secret sorrow, but then Latins always loved to be sad about something. He was dressed in an official-looking cap and neat white coveralls; and he led her along the docks between the expensive boats to an impressive sportfisherman equipped with one of those tall spindly Tinkertoy lookout towers, known as tuna towers, from the top of which one could spot the fish and even control the boat. With a sense of shock she realized that she'd seen the vessel before while sailing with the boy scout and the freaks, when *Haleakala* had stopped for engine repairs in Walker's Cay in the Bahamas. This was a complication she hadn't expected and it obviously hadn't occurred to Columbus, either. But it was too late to back off now.

"Here's Miss Briggs, the young lady I told you about, Mr. McHugh," Montoya said. "Excuse me, miss, I got to get back to the office."

There were three people on the big boat's high foredeck. The woman was an obvious prick, with long dark hair and a thin brown body she was exposing with the tiniest scraps of white bikini as a public service, obviously convinced that the sight of her bare epidermis was turning this particular dock into erection alley and a little stimulation was *so* good for the boys. She had a dissatisfied, pretty little rodent face; and if the large porky gent beside her was her husband, as his proprietary air seemed to indicate, she had every right to be dissatisfied. Lavinia Burnett knew that oversized baby-faced salesman-type all too well; and it was obviously going to be a lovely voyage with Big Boy planting himself strategically in every narrow passage so she'd have to squeeze past him and then, of course, chivalrously "steadying" her against the motion of the boat with his enormous flabby hands that, oops, inevitably managed to make accidental contact with breast or rump depending on what this particular creep's feely-preference happened to be. And the skinny witch screaming that she was leading her husband on, as if he needed leading, although a ring through the nose might be a hell of a good idea at that. With the other end of the chain anchored in concrete.

So far so good. Whatever happened to those two couldn't happen too soon. Then there was the guy Montoya had addressed as Mr. McHugh. Not quite so good for her purpose, he seemed to be a reasonably nice guy, at a glance, but square. My God, practically cubical. It was kind of too bad about him, but she had to keep playing the game until the right cards turned up, even if a few innocent people got hurt along the way. This neat young-businessman type in his neat blue shorts wasn't somebody she'd burst out crying over no matter what she had to do to him. Still okay. So far she hadn't seen anybody on board she'd really feel terrible about.

"Permission to come aboard, sir," she asked McHugh with a tomboy grin to let him know she was kidding—but still, it showed she did know the proper etiquette.

"Sure, hop aboard." He moved aft to meet her in the cockpit. "Montoya says you're a pretty good cook and don't get seasick."

"Well, I haven't poisoned anybody yet," she said. "On the other hand, I'm not much good at tricky soufflés and hummingbird tongues sautéed with wine sauce."

He grinned. "We're pretty much meat-and-potatoes on *Stream Hunter*. Do you know anything about big-game fishing? Can you rig a bait?"

"Sure," she said, "but I'm a little light to manage the gaff on big stuff like marlin. . . ."

"Haven't I seen you somewhere before?"

This was a different voice. Lavinia Burnett was surprised at her own calm as she turned to see a sturdy girl with short pale hair emerging from the deckhouse wiping her hands on a greasy rag. She was wearing dungarees—shirt and pants—and there was a black smudge on her cheek.

Vinnie heard herself say readily enough, "I thought this boat looked familiar. Weren't you up at West End—no, Walker's Cay—last fall?"

The girl nodded. "We had to leave the boat there and fly home, an emergency at the plant, remember, darling?" She glanced briefly at McHugh, obviously her husband, and back to Vinnie. "You were on a sailboat, some kind of multihull thing, weren't you?"

"That's right."

Vinnie checked the impulse to continue talking and make up a good sailing story, any good sailing story, just to keep the conversation moving in a casual way. But either the McHughs had left the Bahamas before the account of *Haleakala*'s hijacking broke in the papers or they hadn't. Either

227

they'd read about it up north or they hadn't. In any case the less said about the damn cat the better.

But it was too bad. This strong-looking girl with the odd violet eyes was not the rich-bitch doll she'd hoped to find here—expendable. This was, for all the skillful and expensive styling of the silver-blonde hair that contrasted so sharply and intriguingly with the greasy hands and smudged face, a tough, competent young woman who'd made it the hard way and knew where it was at; and it was just too goddamn bad. She hadn't wanted to have anybody like that involved, Vinnie thought sadly; she hadn't wanted to have to hurt anybody like that. Just the goddamn mass-production victims that were no loss to anybody; they were bred and raised and trained to be victims, by the millions. Why the hell couldn't she have found a full boatload of those?

But three out of four wasn't too bad, and she simply had to keep going through all the motions required of her by Columbus until she saw the right way to bring him crashing down; and okay, she was expiating her own black guilt at the expense of Don Jaime Colombo and what the hell was wrong with that, it couldn't happen to a nicer guy, could it? Anyway, she encouraged herself, the girl looked like a real survivor and might make it no matter what happened, unlike those two bearded freaks who'd probably died of fright in their life raft the minute they realized there wasn't a supermarket or beer hall handy.

Nobody seemed to be remembering any embarrassing history or calling any cops. The critical moment was past, and she was still in the clear, but the blonde girl was regarding her steadily, in a funny, appraising way.

"Is this what you do?" she asked. "Just bum around on boats?"

Lavinia Burnett sensed that the question was not as hostile as it sounded; and considerably more important. Instinct made her answer boldly: "Is there a better place to bum around?"

Instinct had been right. The girl grinned approvingly. "I know, it's exactly what I did and loved it until I met my husband. . . ." She glanced at McHugh. ". . . and sometimes I still act like a boat bum, right, darling?"

"Well, you don't have to do it with a dirty face. Hold still."

Lavinia Burnett watched the young man take the rag from his wife's hands, find a clean area, and use it to gently remove the grease from her cheek, and then kiss her without

228

embarrassment before stepping back to view the result of his labors. The fucking world was knee-deep in loving couples, Vinnie reflected grimly; but why the hell couldn't these two be obliging and hate each other like the other two so she didn't have to like them? But the man had told her to curb those sentimental impulses. *Señorita,* and the man had been perfectly right, although for reasons he didn't suspect, she hoped.

The blonde girl said, "You can stow your gear up forward, starboard side. Then I'd appreciate it if you'd give me a hand in the engine room. I think the guy who crammed those giant diesels aboard must have had somebody just about your size in mind for doing the maintenance."

Vinnie sighed lugubriously. "It never fails. Every boat I come to they stuff me down the bilge because nobody else will fit."

The girl laughed. "I'm Jan and this is Chuck," she said. "Don't worry about the two up forward. You'll meet them soon enough, lucky you."

CHAPTER 23

May

Latitude 28°N; Longitude 82°W

The Tampa-Clearwater area was not Philip Martin's favorite part of Florida, partly because more than any other part it seemed to be Senile City, an elephant-graveyard sort of place where, it seemed, every elderly person in the country with a bit of money came to die; but also because it was way over on the west coast of the state and difficult to reach by car from Miami since the freeways and turnpikes all seemed to run north and south. Still, he managed to arrive early enough in the afternoon to make arrangements to meet the people in whom he was interested and then check with the

Coast Guard for information, with time left over to clean up in his hotel room and repair to the cocktail lounge and stake a claim on a quiet corner booth where they could talk with some degree of privacy.

He'd barely tasted his drink when he saw his people coming. There was always something about a career Navy officer out of uniform that was unmistakable. This one was wearing a bright plaid madras sports coat and red summer slacks and very white shoes. Well, if you wore nothing but the same damned sailor suit every day of the working week, there was undoubtedly a psychological need to blossom into gaudy rags on vacation. These days of flowing male locks, the short service haircut was also conspicuous; it gave the guy a tough, aggressively masculine look that was probably unintended. They just came off the assembly line that way, and it felt perfectly natural to them, and they saw no reason to change. Lieutenant (jg) Roger McCulloch, USN. Actually, he appeared to be a pretty nice boy in spite of the bright clothes and cropped hair, tall and quite good-looking without making a production of it.

The girl, Melissa McCulloch née Brennan, was breathtakingly pretty, although she had no real right to be. Actually, technically, she was a bit on the plump side, a smallish bouncing blonde butterball of a girl with, rather shockingly, very fine brown eyes. There was always something arresting about a real brown-eyed blonde. Her features in themselves were not remarkable, but she had a lovely smooth gleaming cascade of soft bright Alice-in-Wonderland hair and a truly wonderful complexion, clear and rosy and delicate. . . . Suddenly Martin realized that he was being a damned fool. The kids weren't all that handsome. It was just the fact that they were madly and hopelessly in love that made them seem that way. They'd undoubtedly just been to bed together and now they were wondering how quickly they could get this dull interview finished and get back to their room and do that beautiful thing again, the thing that they alone had invented and only they knew about and would never, never tell to anybody else in the world—except that of course the whole world knew about it just seeing them walking together in that golden glow.

The girl was wearing a loose blue-and-white-checked sundress, kind of a little-girl dress prettily trimmed with white, tied with a little bow at each shoulder. Very convenient, Martin thought sourly, no trouble for Roger at all, just a

230

gentle pull on each ribbon and it would all drop away and there would be his Melissa all ready for him again except for the little panties, if she was wearing panties, which should pose no problem for a determined military man trained to overcome grim obstacles in the service of his country. Hell, the way she was looking at the guy she'd probably have the panties off before the dress hit the floor. It was really rather indecent, and very unfair to all unattached, unsenile males within range.

But their happiness wasn't perfect. As they came closer he could see the shadows in the clear brown eyes of the girl and the concerned way the boy watched her when she wasn't looking. They both showed a little surprise, quickly concealed, when he rose to attract their attention and he knew why, of course; he had not given his name as Martinez and he had not sounded, over the phone, like Frito Bandido.

"Mr. Martin? I'm Roger McCulloch." The boy shook hands and turned. "Melissa, Mr. Philip Martin. Right, sir? You did say Philip over the phone, didn't you?"

"Right the first time," Martin said. He bowed to the girl, who smiled back. He said, "And now I do my best parlor trick, the hand is quicker than the eye, Mrs. McCulloch." He passed his I.D. before them and made it vanish, and grinned: "Of course, if you really want to examine it, you've a perfect right to."

"Never mind." The trick had not been a success; Melissa McCulloch's voice was cold and her smile had vanished. "I'm afraid we've seen too many of those, Mr. Martin, and not one of them has done us a bit of good. . . ."

"Lissa!" The boy's voice was a soft warning.

She glanced at him. "All right, darling. I know, I promised."

"What can I get you to drink?" Martin asked quickly, pulling out the round table so the girl could get behind it, letting the men find places on either side of her. While they waited for the drinks, he asked, "How long have you been married?"

The girl gave him a searching look. "Are we so damned obvious? Actually, we're old married folks, we've been married almost a year. And the next question is, why do we look like honeymooners? Answer: because we are. Roger was suddenly offered a crack at very important sea duty right after . . . well, anyway, we didn't have much of a honeymoon then so we're taking it now. Or we were, until this . . . this

231

thing happened." A wry little smile touched her lips. "Well, all right. I guess we're not spending *all* our time brooding about it, or can you tell?"

It was a nice girl and a bright girl and, he thought, a rather tough little girl in many ways. There was a lot of determination in that little chin; and the big brown eyes were used to having their own way, but they hadn't always been getting it recently. Martin could fill in the story, the bones of which she'd tossed him so casually: the tears and recriminations when the boy had put his career ahead of their honeymoon, the long cold lonely months of waiting, the rather cool reception she'd managed nevertheless on his return, and the final betrayal of her dignified, wounded reserve by the violent yearnings of her healthy young body and the very real love she bore the guy and her own sensible mind telling her that she'd been acting like a spoiled and silly child—and then, of course, the wonderful and beautiful reconciliation and rediscovery still going on. All this, and the other thing, was in the air as they all tasted their drinks and talked for a bit, politely, about the fine weather this coast had been having recently and the beautiful beaches and the sad encroachment of developments and pollution.

"Mr. Martin," Melissa McCulloch said at last, "Mr. Martin, I don't know what you're really here for, but I'd like to tell you two things that are, as they say, not negotiable. If you don't want me to walk out on you, please don't tell me again how drug smugglers make an awful lot of money and can afford to buy their boats so why should they take the risk of stealing them and anyway there have been only a very few confirmed yacht hijackings in spite of all the fuss in the papers. I've heard that song so many times in the past few days I can play it without the music. And the other thing I don't want to hear from you is the little idiot verse about how stupid, inexperienced boatmen are forever shoving off on great voyages and getting themselves into terrible predicaments and causing everybody a lot of trouble. I—"

"Melissa."

She glanced aside. "Yes, darling, I know I promised, but I get so damned *tired* of hearing these damned everlasting bureaucratic routines over and over everywhere we—"

"Melissa, why don't we at least hear what the man has to say before we jump down his throat?"

There was a little pause. Then her hand went out and closed tightly over her husband's for a moment. "Okay, I

232

know, don't say it, I'm being an unreasonable little brat again. Consider me spanked. All right, Mr. Martin, you have the floor. Can you help us find my mother and father?"

He looked at her for a moment and remembered another girl, more handsome really but not so young, to whom he'd thought he could talk directly and honestly, but he'd been wrong. But that incurable optimist, *Señor* Felipe Martinez, wasn't to be deterred by one little kick in the teeth.

He shook his head. "No."

Her eyes narrowed sharply. "What do you mean?"

"I'm sorry if there's been a misunderstanding," he said evenly. "I'm not here to help you, Mrs. McCulloch. I'm here hoping you can help me."

He knew a sudden pang of very sincere jealousy when, after just a moment's hesitation, Melissa McCulloch, instead of getting either reproachful or indignant, gave him a funny crooked little smile. The boy really had himself something here.

The girl said gently, without malice, "Oh, my God. An honest bureaucrat at last?"

Martin spoke carefully: "Some months ago over in the Atlantic off the Bahamas there was another boat disappearance. The details don't really matter, just that we think it *might* just possibly be connected with a case we're working on. If we're right, there's no reason why the disappearances should stop with one. Therefore we have been watching for additional cases, to see if we can establish some kind of pattern that may, in the end, lead us to the man responsible. We think he's a man we'd very much like to see in jail for, I must admit, totally different reasons—but any good reason will do."

Melissa McCulloch nodded slowly. "May I . . . may I ask what happened to the people on board the boat that disappeared?"

"There were five of them. Two were set adrift in a sailing dinghy and made it ashore; they are now married and, we hope, living happily ever after. We think at least two others were either set adrift in a rubber raft or found it necessary to abandon ship for some reason; we know that one of these died of thirst and presume the other did also. There was a fifth who may or may not have died with them."

"I see." The girl's voice was thoughtful. "It sounds . . . rather complicated."

"Yes," Martin said. "We haven't really figured out what

233

happened; we may never figure it out. The boat hasn't been seen since, at least not to our knowledge."

"But . . ." She licked her lips. "But what you're saying is that most of the crew wound up in the small boats, one way or another. They weren't murdered on the spot."

"No, they weren't murdered on the spot."

"Then there's a possibility, I mean, there's some indication that these hijackers, whoever they are, have a policy of not k-killing . . ."

The steady voice faltered. Melissa McCulloch turned quickly away and started groping blindly in her purse. Her husband put a large clean handkerchief into her hand. The men then sat in silence while the girl did certain things to her eyes and nose, drew a long breath, and sat up straight once more.

"Well! Let's hope *that's* over. Sorry, Mr. Martin, I know it's a hell of an unfashionable attitude these days, but I . . . but I just kind of happen to l-love those . . . those c-crazy d-damn p-p-parents of mine. . . . Oh, God, there she goes again!" She sniffed vigorously and dabbed at her tearstained cheeks. "Oh, damn, I'd better go into drydock for repairs. Let me out, darling." Standing up, she looked around when her husband touched her arm lightly, and smiled at him with wet, brilliant eyes. "Don't worry, it just springs a leak now and then, but it never, never sinks."

Martin waited until, having watched her out of sight, Roger McCulloch sat down once more. Then he said, "I hope you don't mind belated congratulations, Lieutenant. That's quite a girl you've got there."

"Well, I think so, sir." A little smile came to the boy's face. "She was the apple of her daddy's eye, as you can probably see. Fortunately, I had very good basic training, five sisters. I don't know if I'd have made it if I'd been an only child."

He gave Martin a quick, inquiring little glance as if to see if the other man suspected him of running down his wife behind his back. That had not been his intention at all. He was very proud of her the way she was and simply wanted everybody to know it.

Then the small blonde girl was coming back, all tear signs erased, and sliding into the booth. "All right, Mr. Martin," she said briskly, "let's see what we can do for you. What do you want to know?"

"I'd like the whole story of this cruise your parents were on, as far as you know it. If you can bear to go through it all again."

234

She sighed. "Well, if my husband will let me have just one more martini—he's a dreadful bully, Mr. Martin—I guess I can manage to tell you what I know from their letters and phone calls. . . ."

It took a while. When she had finished, Martin said, "That's a nice, clear presentation, and I thank you very much. So they cruised from Houston, where they bought the boat, to New Orleans, where they spent a couple of months making repairs and waiting for warmer weather. Then they headed for Pensacola, and finally Apalachicola. From there your mother called you last week to say they were shoving off in the morning and you should be prepared to meet them in a couple of days here in Clearwater Beach." He hesitated. "Just one thing. Linda. You mentioned the name a couple of times. Is Linda your sister, Mrs. McCulloch?"

The girl shook her head. "No, I have no sisters, just a couple of older brothers. Linda's the crew, a kid they picked up in New Orleans to help out temporarily, particularly on this long offshore run. *Spindrift* is a pretty big boat for two older people to handle. Thirty-nine feet. The girl is supposed to have had quite a bit of seagoing experience, and Father apparently decided he could use some help this first time out of sight of land. Besides, having three on board makes the watchstanding problem simpler, sailing all night. Linda Brown. They seemed to be . . . quite taken with her."

"It wasn't quite as casual as Melissa makes it sound, sir," Roger McCulloch interrupted. "I mean, they didn't just pick up a stray girl on the dock; they'd met her before. She'd been secretary or something to the yacht broker from whom they bought the boat."

Melissa McCulloch made a little grimace. "Yes, very romantic, really. A great office love affair, we were given to understand; but finally the man came to his senses or his wife caught them or something, and the girl was fired and decided to hitch a boat ride east. She wound up in the New Orleans marina where my parents recognized her. I guess they all fell into each other's arms." She grinned tomboyishly. "You'll gather I wasn't really expecting to love dear little Linda Brown, Mr. Martin. Roger says I was jealous and he's probably right. Who wants to compete with nautical perfection? Or any other kind?"

"Was she going to continue on the cruise with you?"

"No, thank God. She was getting off here in Clearwater

Beach. I gather the boat's not really comfortable for five; there are just two good staterooms."

"Can you give me any kind of a description of the girl?"

"Not really." Melissa McCulloch shrugged her bare shoulders. "Just that she was rather small and quite wonderful; she even cooked pretty well. You're interested in Linda, Mr. Martin?"

Martin hesitated, but she deserved honesty and he said, "Yes, this is strictly confidential, but the fifth person on the other boat that disappeared, one of the two still unaccounted for, was also a rather small young lady, named Lucia Barnes. Same initials, you'll note."

There was a little silence. "What does it mean?"

"I don't know and I don't want to guess at this stage," Martin said. "You can do that as well as I can. Do you have the name of the yacht broker in Houston for whom she worked, the office-lover type?"

"Well, actually it wasn't Houston proper, but a suburb or something called Seabrook, but I don't think I can recall the name. . . ."

"Of course you can, Melissa," Roger McCulloch said. "Hell, they had an office in Annapolis for years. Buckmeister and Son, but Bucky Buckmeister died some years ago. He was quite a famous yachting character who wrote several books on sailboat racing. This has to be the son."

Melissa McCulloch said quickly, "Of course, I remember now, and he married a wealthy Texas beauty and a bottle of booze at the same time. . . . Ugh, aren't I the small-town gossip? Anyway, the firm kind of went downhill, didn't it? Then he closed the office in Annapolis, and I guess I just didn't make the connection when Father mentioned whom he was buying his boat from way off there in Texas. Buckmeister's rich wife must have set him up in business again back home, her home. Is there anything else we can tell you, Mr. Martin?"

"No, you've been very kind and I won't take up any more of your time. You may as well stay right here and finish your drinks if you like; I've got to get back up to my room and make a few phone calls." Martin hesitated. "What are you planning to do now?"

"Well, we've kind of exhausted all the official possibilities and I understand the intensive search has been called off. . . ." Melissa McCulloch glanced at her husband. "You'll probably think this is crazy, but Roger and I are going to go looking for them."

Martin frowned, glancing at the husband. "That could get dangerous, Lieutenant. These people aren't playing for marbles."

The girl said quickly, "Oh, we're not going to look for the *boat*. That's probably hundreds of miles away by now."

Roger McCulloch said, "We've been studying the charts, Mr. Martin. As far as the boat is concerned assuming that she was taken by force, the hijackers probably got her out of this area, the area the Coast Guard was likely to search, as fast as possible; so the chances of our bumping into a bunch of armed pirates aren't very great."

"But I'm sure the Coast Guard has already—"

"To hell with the Coast Guard!" Melissa McCulloch drew a quick breath. "I'm sorry, but I'm just sick of the everlasting You Ess Coast Guard, and that goes for the Florida Marine Patrol, and the smug, smug F.B.I., and the Drug Enforcement people who won't even listen. . . . All right, the Coast Guard has probably done a good job of looking in all the obvious places north of here. We can take it that my parents are not floating around out in the Gulf of Mexico between here and Apalachicola, either in their own boat or in a life raft. But I . . . I get a nightmare, Mr. Martin, about being notified next year, or the year after that, that a couple or three bodies have been found half-hidden in the mangroves on some deserted key along that Godforsaken swampy coast up there, where they managed to crawl ashore with the last of their strength, and if we'd only looked, really *looked,* we might have found them in time."

Martin glanced at the husband, who nodded. "We've chartered a little shoaldraft cabin cruiser and as soon as we've checked with a few more official sources, and provisioned the boat, we're going to start working our way north up along the coast and around to Apalachicola. The winds were westerly when they disappeared and stayed that way for several days; we've been studying the currents and figuring the probable drift. There's always a chance, and anyway in a little boat like that—" He grinned at his pretty wife, who blushed. "—well, sir, I won't have to chase her so far when I want to catch her."

Saying good-bye, Martin had a pleasant feeling that he was leaving two young people who had things pretty well under control. They were going to be all right. The boy, he thought, was fairly certain they wouldn't find anything, and the girl probably knew it, too, but it was something she had to do for her own peace of mind, and her husband was happy to go along with her wishes—after all, as he'd indicated, you could make love to your bride of a year, newly regained, just as well or maybe a little better along a deserted coast as at a crowded beach resort. They'd have learned a lot about each other by the time they got back and he had a strong hunch they would both like what they learned; and that her missing parents would have been pleased to know how well they were working things out together. Nice kids.

Nevertheless, they had disturbed him deeply and left him with an uneasy sense of his own loneliness. He'd tried a couple of times to find what they had found, and failed. There had been, for instance, slim, dark Teresa who'd wanted to make a militant Cuban patriot of him complete with pineapples and Tommy guns; and there had been healthy blonde Barbie who'd wanted quite the opposite, a tame nine-to-five all-American robot. . . . When he reached his room, the phone was ringing. It was Tommy Walsh calling from Miami.

"I've been trying to get you; I've got news for you," Tommy said. "First, they've come up with the boat-hijacking mastermind we've been looking for, or they think they have, and his name is not Columbus."

Martin fumbled for a cigarette one-handed, sitting on the bed. "Tell me."

"You've heard of Texas Rangers, no doubt."

"Uhhuh, they chase rustlers and Indians."

"Actually, they're the Texas State Police nowadays, but that term is not popular in the Lone Star State because it's associated with a law organization they don't like to remember from the old carpetbagger days right after the Civil War, or do you prefer to call it The War Between the States?"

"Stop showing off your erudition, *amigo,* and break my heart with your bad news."

"Well, there was a suicide in Houston recently and word has just come in that the local cops found certain ramifications and called in the State boys, the Rangers, who have now determined that the gent who killed himself, a man named Buckmeister, Elmer Buckmeister, was actually the head of a rather extensive gang of hijackers. He even called himself by a code name: The Bosun. Fancy, huh? The guy ran a yacht brokerage business, very handy for spotting suitable victims; and it's thought he simply went out and picked up vessels on order. I want a fifty-foot yacht that sleeps twelve beautiful blondes, complete with blondes, Mr. Bosun, when can you make delivery?" After a pause, Tommy went on: "It's a hell of a scandal, apparently, Buckmeister himself was pretty well known in the yachting world or at least his daddy used to be; and he was married to all the oil wells in Texas. Why the hell would a guy like that turn pirate on the high seas, for God's sake?"

Martin drew a long breath. "Maybe because a pretty, sexy little girl asked him to."

There was a brief silence. "What do you know that I don't?" Tommy asked at last.

"What have you found out about Lucia Barnes to date?"

"Not very much. Seems like that young lady didn't exist much until she turned up with those hairy freaks on that homemade trimaran, the *Freedom Machine*. Why?"

"By coincidence, or something, I've just been getting the word on Buckmeister from another angle. He doesn't sound like very high-powered material. Alcoholism and business failure. The general feeling is that his wife put him back on his feet in a business way; but somehow he wound up with a secretary or receptionist named Linda Brown, a small clever girl who wasn't too particular with whom she slept. Does that ring any bells?"

After a little, Tommy said, "Assuming it's the same girl, is your theory that this Lucia/Linda is working for herself or somebody else?"

Martin said wryly, "If she's working for herself, we're all wet, and that can't happen, can it? Not to us smart people. So she's got to be working for somebody else, somebody named Columbus, right?"

Tommy Walsh laughed softly on the other side of the state. "*Señor*, I surely do love your strict adherence to the scientific method. Absolute objectivity at all times, just follow where the evidence leads. As long as it leads to the right place, of course." After a moment, he went on: "I'll work on establishing a connection. In the meantime, there's a development on the Ullman front. No sign of danger to husband and wife so far, it's still a water haul and Richardson is getting antsy about the waste of manpower; but the red-haired guy is taking off with his cameras shortly—well, in a week or two or three. He's got an assignment to do a ship story; that's what his trip to New York was all about. We've checked with the company, the Petrox Corporation, and he's scheduled to go out on a 20,000-ton job called the *Petrox Prince* whenever she gets back from her present run, but she's been sidetracked temporarily to make a delivery somewhere; apparently those tankers don't know from one minute to the next where they're going. It depends on who needs what, where. But at the moment they think he'll pick up the *Prince* in Wilmington, North Carolina, whenever she gets back, and then ride her down to Puerto la Cruz to pick up a load of oil, and from there it's anybody's guess, maybe straight back to the States, maybe not."

"Puerto la Cruz. Where the hell is that?"

"Venezuela."

"What arrangements are being made to cover him?"

Tommy hesitated. "That's the problem. Mister Richardson feels he'll be perfectly safe on shipboard, and anyway there's no easy way we can put a man on board to cover him. Mister Richardson also considers that he'll obviously be safe in South America, since nobody's going to send anybody all that way after him when they haven't shown any interest in him here, and anyway we can't have our people running all over the world, Washington will raise hell about the expenses. Besides, Mister Richardson feels we're neglecting that dangerous organization, the *Hermanos de Septiembre*. . . ."

"That bunch of senile winos!" Martin grimaced. "Tony's probably right about his being safe on shipboard; but Puerto la Cruz. . . . It could be what they're waiting for, to hit him outside the country. Anyway, we set him up, we're obliged to keep an eye on him, and his wife, until we're absolutely sure. . . . Okay, I'll see what I can do to convince Mister Richardson that we still owe those people a reasonable amount of protection. Anyway, I'm finished here; I guess I might as well climb in the car and head back. See you in the morning."

Hanging up, he looked sadly at the bed for which he had paid, or the government had; but he was gripped by an uneasy sense of urgency. He knew that he would not have slept well anyway, leaving the city of Miami—and those poor Ullman patsies who'd had it tough enough already—at the tender mercies of a jerk like Richardson.

CHAPTER 24

June

Latitude 28°N; Longitude 69°W

That spring the weather was unusually fine in the Gulf of Mexico above the Yucatan Straits and the western tip of Cuba. There was almost a total lack of the rainy squalls that generally cruise those waters. On the canopied six-man life raft, with four on board, the rain-catching equipment remained dry except for the inevitable salt spray that pervaded everything. Well, it had been a no-luck cruise from start to finish, Janet McHugh thought grimly. The company had been awful. The winds had been adverse. Even the sailfish that usually besieged the boat in great numbers around Cozumel, just begging to be hooked, had been conspicuous by their near-absence. The generator had broken down. They'd picked up a load of fuel that was even dirtier than you expected Mexican fuel to be, so she'd had to spend more time in the engine room changing filters than she had navigating. It should really have come as no surprise that they'd wound up this wonderful voyage by drifting helplessly in a rubber raft; the only surprising thing was that it hadn't sprung a leak, at least not yet.

Big, blond Babe Gregertsen, nicknamed for his resemblance to an enormous happy child—a resemblance that had led a lot of people to trust him financially to his and the company's considerable profit—had been least affected by the shortage of drinking water. With a pistol bullet in the abdomen he wasn't drinking anyway; and he died on their second day adrift. Pretty, dark Sue Gregertsen, unwounded, suffered loudly for five days more. You'd have thought she was the only one in that dim, dank, rocking rubber cave who had something to complain about. She blamed everybody for everything, particularly Chuck McHugh. If Chuck—the captain, for God's sake!—hadn't left her husband to fight those beasts and bullies alone, Babe wouldn't have got hurt, not to mention what had happened to that nice little girl who'd done the shipboard cooking and cleaning. (That was of course, the same nice little girl whose face Sue had slapped, earlier, in a fit of drunken and, as it happened, unjustified, jealousy; not that Babe would have passed it up if it had been offered, but it hadn't been.)

The marathon recriminations went on and on. If Chuck had been any kind of a captain, any kind of a *man* even, Babe wouldn't have died and she, Sue Gregertsen, wouldn't be reclining in a puddle of nasty water in a gyrating overgrown innertube with her hair a sticky mess and her complexion ruined and nothing on but a frayed and soiled bikini and, no, she was damn well *not* going to eat any of that disgusting raw fish, what did they think she was, a cannibal or something?

Gradually her complaints diminished in volume if not in duration. When the accusing whispers finally stopped for good, they rolled her weakly out the raft's door after a brief policy discussion; however, Chuck was sure he could continue to catch enough fish to keep them alive, and it was a fairly unappetizing notion even though, these tolerant days, it no longer seemed to meet with quite the degree of social disapproval, judging by current literature, that had greeted the Donner party the previous century when its camp menu had become known. But Sue shouldn't have mentioned cannibalism and put ideas into hungry people's heads.

With the Gregertsens gone—and little Laura Briggs by this time almost forgotten as part of their long-ago life B.R., before the raft—the McHughs regarded each other with an odd sense of rediscovery. It had been hard to relax and compare notes as man and wife in the presence of, first, a wounded man dying in agony and, second, that nonstop female whine. Janet McHugh thought: I suppose I should feel sorry or guilty or something. If we'd been true Christians, whatever that is, we'd have sympathized with her and given her a little more than her share of the canned emergency water and forced her to eat, and maybe she'd have lasted a little longer, God forbid.

She studied her husband appraisingly as he slouched against the raft's flotation chamber. In his filthy once-blue shorts, with new sores on his bare legs and a week's dark beard failing to conceal the growing emaciation of his sun-blackened face, peeling pinkly in some places, he was hardly recognizable as the wealthy young sportsman who'd recently been trying for a trophy sailfish out of the fashionable Mexican gamefishing capital of Cozumel. Not that she was in a position to criticize, she reflected with a wry glance at her own noticeably shrunken body more or less covered, to the extent that buttons and zippers still functioned, by some damply wrinkled and rather revoltingly stained and grimy thin material that had originated as a pair of crisp white linen slacks and an immaculate tailored silk—well, nylon—blouse in a delicate shade of violet that, the saleslady had said, just matched her eyes, modom. That so-refeened Miami saleslady should see modom now, Janet McHugh thought ruefully, scratching herself.

"Darling," she whispered. "Alone at last."

Maybe it wasn't very funny, and maybe this wasn't the time for humor with Sue Gregertsen so recently dead; but she was startled to see no trace of response in her husband's face. Always before he'd been the first to manage a grin when they got themselves into a tough spot afloat.

She tried again, shaping the words painfully with her cracked and swollen lips: "Next time, please consult me before you bring people to dinner, dear. I could have told you there wasn't a thing on board to eat. Or drink." There was no reaction, and she went on desperately, saying anything that occurred to her in an attempt to re-establish communication: "I hate to criticize your business associates, dear, but my God, weren't they awful? How is it that people who're more or less endurable on shore can be so totally unbearable afloat?"

But Chuck just kept staring at her uneasily with those haggard eyes. It hadn't occurred to her, as long as Sue was there, that her husband might not be thinking the same kind of ruthless and determined and grimly optimistic thoughts she was, just keeping quiet, as she was, so as not to encourage the whiny recriminations unnecessarily. But suddenly she understood that he'd been taking Sue's accusing foolishness seriously, allowing her to undermine his self-confidence and his self-respect. Furthermore, she realized that he'd merely been humoring her a moment ago. He'd actually been shocked by the ugly suggestion she'd made. He'd talked her out of it diplomatically, but he was still regarding her uncertainly, wondering if she'd lost her mind to even consider such a horrible thing. And now her flippant words, far from reassuring him, were confirming his suspicions that she'd slipped over the edge. Obviously, he had not pulled the big red SURVIVAL switch that she'd thrown instinctively the minute the raft had hit the water and she'd realized what lay ahead. He was still thinking along polite, sissy, prissy, conventional lines.

"Jesus, Jan, they're *dead!*" he protested now. "You really ought to show a little respect for ... I mean, maybe they weren't the greatest for the long haul but, hell, it wasn't supposed to be an endurance contest. Just a few days of sailfishing off Yucatan and a quick run back to Key West where they'd catch a plane home so Babe could be back in the office Monday. Anyway, Babe did all right; it wasn't his fault—"

"Wasn't it?" she interrupted. "Telling a bunch of armed pirates what they couldn't get away with, in his usual loud-mouthed way? Flexing his big flabby muscles at them, just asking one of them to pull a trigger? Not to mention the fool stunt he pulled earlier, up on the bridge, that really put us into the soup! Between him and that idiot girl we hired to help out in the galley—and what got into her I have no idea—we stood a good chance of all getting killed. In fact, I still don't understand why those hijackers didn't finish the job once those two got them started shooting."

"Well, yeah, okay." Chuck's tired agreement didn't carry conviction. "Yeah," he said heavily, "not that it makes a hell of a lot of difference now, huh?"

Janet stared at him, aghast. It was dawning on her at last that her husband had given up and was on his way out with the others. She thought incredulously: my God, that Robertson family lasted thirty-seven days after their sailboat was sunk by whales off the Galapagos Islands; that Bailey couple, for Pete's sake, went a hundred and seventeen after theirs went down in the same area. Damn near four months on a raft smaller than this; and here we're just winding up our first week with two down already and one ...

"Stop it!" she said sharply. "We're alive and the current is carrying us east toward the Straits of Florida. All the shipping in this part of the world goes through that slot; we're bound to be picked up eventually. If that stupid bitch hadn't fired off our few lousy flares the second day before we could stop her—at a ship barely over the horizon!—we'd be rescued now."

"Sure," Chuck said. "Sure."

But he obviously no longer believed in her, nor did he have

any faith left in himself, or in rescue. While he managed to keep them in fish for another three days, he talked less and less. The morning after another ship passed in the distance without seeing them, she woke from an uneasy cat nap—all she ever managed these days—to find him dead beside her.

It frightened her a little, not because she was particularly afraid of death or of being left alone, but because she couldn't quite understand what had killed Chuck McHugh or, for that matter, Sue Gregertsen. Healthy people didn't just curl up and die from being a little hungry and thirsty—or did they?

She tried to feel some kind of grief but it didn't come. She knew that if she'd been home with a tall, cool drink handy, if she'd been clean and well fed and expensively dressed, the rich and smart and attractive just-made Widow McHugh, she'd have cried for Chuck, bitterly and quite sincerely. Right now she didn't have that much emotion, not to mention that much moisture, available. What she really felt, she forced herself to admit—it was a time for brutal honesty—was relief; the same sense of liberation she'd known each fall on Kennequid Island off the coast of Maine where she'd been born and raised. It was the feeling that always came to her when the rich summer people were gone at last, back to wherever rich summer people went; and the island belonged to its winter people once more.

It was the time of year when she could start being herself again after all the months of putting on her country-girl act—her elfin sea-sprite routine—for the summer visitors. On Kennequid they all made a good seasonal thing of the local-Yankee-yokel performances that were expected of them. But now she could forget about that silly summer nonsense and concentrate on the grim, wild, wonderful game of winter survival as it was played along that rugged coast. And if any yo-yo with a gun thought he could get rid of Captain Jaspers' little girl Janet by setting her adrift in a *boat,* for God's sake, any kind of a boat in any kind of weather, he had large rocks in his little pointy head.

But first of course there was Chuck, and what about that? She shrugged and set herself to the herculean struggle, in her dehydrated and half-starved condition, of getting the inert body out the raft's opening. Afterwards, she checked the horizon instinctively as she rested from the effort in the canopy opening. Nothing. She had, of course, lied to Chuck about their position, to keep his spirits up. If they'd actually been in the main Gulf Stream, drifting steadily eastwards off the Cuban coast at up to a couple of knots, they'd certainly have sighted something by now or been sighted by somebody. Ten days was two hundred and fifty to five hundred miles at that rate of drift; and there wasn't all that far to go. The trouble was, as navigator, she'd taken them well north after clearing the Yucatan Channel, in order to keep away from Cuba. Too many yachts in the past had encountered Cuban patrols with overgenerous ideas about their own territorial waters and had wound up in Cuban ports and a lot of trouble. It had seemed better to take no chances. *Stream Hunter,* cruising at twenty-two knots with her big twin diesels, didn't really need the small boost she could have achieved by staying in the best of the favorable current.

When it happened, they'd been well above the regular shipping lanes; and it was becoming fairly obvious that instead of being carried east toward Florida and the Atlantic, the raft had been caught by one of the many eddies of the Gulf Stream feeding north into the Gulf of Mexico and was now drifting up into that large expanse of empty water; next stop Texas, a thousand miles away, or maybe even Mexico off to the west, depending on the winds and currents. Janet McHugh shook her head irritably. It was the goddamned *helplessness* that made you mad. What dodo had come up with the notion of building totally unmaneuverable life rafts in which you could do absolutely nothing but sit and wait to be rescued? All it would take would be a rudimentary, hollow rubber keel that automatically filled with sea water, say, and a small mast and sail, and an oar for steering. . . .

She saw the scimitar fins moving in. She knew what they were after, of course, and she didn't particularly want to see what happened next, so she turned away and made herself comfortable, if the word was applicable, on the raft's yielding floor. Poor Chuck. Then she scolded herself: That's pretty damn inadequate, Mrs. McHugh, poor Chuck indeed!

But the fact was, she was realizing, that her husband had always been summer people to her, a different breed. She'd always had to be very careful not to shock him and his funny, sheltered, artificial city notions of what life was all about. The fact was, of course, that summer people didn't really *know* what life was all about because they had such weirdo notions about death, never having faced it themselves and trying to avoid ever having to face it by passing protective laws right and left, as if you could legislate the old man with the scythe right out of existence. They didn't realize that the only way to deal with that skull-faced gent was to meet him head on and fight him to a standstill as long as possible. . . . Well, never mind that. Summer people. Chuck McHugh.

Actually she'd met him in Florida in the middle of winter. That was the year, having perfected her technique farther north, that she'd brought it down to Florida to see if it would work in the land of year-around boating. The problem was quite simple. An experienced man could ask for a real, professional boat position; a woman, regardless of experience, couldn't. The only work ordinarily available to girls with seagoing ambitions involved either stoves or beds; and she had no intention of winding up as either ship's cook or ship's concubine.

The Janet Jaspers job-hunting technique had involved simply hanging around the charter fleet with cute, wide-eyed, sexless, tomboy fascination, nobody's girl and everybody's kid sister, always happy to run an errand or lend a hand, particularly if it allowed her to demonstrate that she was capable of getting around a boat's deck without falling overboard, and that when the time came to cast off the stern line or spring line or bow line she'd get the right rope every time. When she cleated a line it stayed cleated; when she tied a knot it stayed knotted. When, after a long successful day offshore, a client wanted his catch cleaned and filetted, there was little Janet with a nice sharp knife, glad to help out and let the charter boat's captain and mate get at the necessary clean-up work on board; and she hoped it didn't pass unnoticed that the boat-crazy kid could really whip out those filets like an expert and didn't seem to mind a bit getting her hands slimy.

The theory was that you made yourself a useful, cheerful fixture around the docks, knowing that sooner or later one of them would get into a bind and, already accustomed to having you around, he'd have this brilliant idea and it would be *his* idea, and he'd defend it against all comers, even you when you looked eager but uncertain and asked humbly if he really thought you were up to it. . . .

"Sure, kid, you can handle it," Captain Jim Easley had said heartily the morning after his regular mate Broderick Kotoski, having tied one on the night before, had wound up in the clink for busting somebody's jaw with a fish-killing priest shaped a bit like a policeman's billy and employable for similar purposes. "Now hurry up and get the bait aboard," Captain Jim had said, "while I check out the engine. I've got this rich sport coming over from the Lodge who wants to learn all about big-game fishing in one easy lesson, or maybe two or three depending on how it goes. He'll do everything bassackwards, of course; but I'd rather have one of those than a know-it-all telling me how to run my boat. If you don't know how to rig a mullet or ballyhoo we've got time to . . . Oh, you do? Great." There had been an awkward little pause. "Look, kid . . . what's your name again? I forget."

"Jan. Jan Jaspers."

"Well, Jan, what I mean is, being nice to the clients is part of the job, but fish is what the man is paying for and fish is what he gets, if you know what I mean. Oh, if he wants you to fetch him his hat or sunglasses or a cold beer, all right, some of them like to order folks around and we aim to please. Within limits. But you don't have to put up with any bullshit, if you know what I mean. If he starts giving you a hard time, let me know right away."

A great old guy, Captain Jim; but there had been no problems of that kind. Young Mr. Charles Cotton McHugh, of the New Jersey firm of McHugh Enterprises, Inc. (sales offices New York, New York), advised by his doctor to stick his nose outdoors occasionally, for a change, had suddenly discovered saltwater angling for big fish, and had thrown himself into learning the sport with the intense concentration that, presumably, had made him a successful businessman. He'd totally ignored all distractions like sunburn and seasickness and aching muscles and reasonably attractive—well, some people thought so—girl mates. Janet McHugh reflected grimly that if Chuck had applied the same dedication to surviving, just now, nothing could have killed him; but that was the trouble with summer people, they took survival for granted. By the time they realized it was something you had to be ready to work at hard, any time, even fight like hell for, it was already too late for most of them.

It had been a modest white marlin, Chuck's first billfish, that had finally changed things—that and the mildly alcoholic victory celebration in the cockpit on the way back in. Insisting on her joining him in a drink, he'd suddenly looked at her sharply, as if realizing, for the first time, that she was intriguingly white-blonde, even with her hair deliberately whacked off short and boyish. She saw him become aware that she was nicely golden-tanned and pleasantly shaped, if perhaps a bit on the short and sturdy and durable side of feminine perfection. Even though she made a professional point of never, on board or on the docks, flaunting the fact with a bikini, or even too-tight shorts and too-skimpy halters, she saw him discover that she was a girl, not just a competent ally in his learn-to-fish campaign.

"I guess you think this is really kind of ridiculous," he'd said with sudden diffidence. "A hundred-and-eighty-pound man getting all excited about outwitting a sixty-pound fish, with lots of expert help. Only, well, I was brought up in the city, Jan, and all this . . . well, hell, it's for *real*. When that magnificent thing came out of the water like a crazy missile. . . . I wonder what it's like to be hooked to a really big blue. Look, I'm not trying to get out of line or anything, but if you're not doing anything for dinner tonight . . ."

Of course he had got out of line eventually, or maybe by that time the line had simply got erased. Anyway, they'd been married in the spring. She'd soon discovered what she'd more or less expected, that a man on shore making money wasn't quite the same person as a man on a boat having fun. She'd also learned that there were more summer people in the world than you'd ever dream, living on Kennequid; and that all of them were convinced that the natural state of the human being was to be born protected in an air-conditioned obstetric ward, live protected in an air-conditioned condominium, and die protected in an air-conditioned geriatric ward; and that any experience—unless deliberately and courageously incurred in the name of sport—that involved exposure to perfectly normal fluctuations of weather and temperature, and perfectly ordinary risks and dangers, was to them an obscene perversion of the natural, sheltered, and controlled order of things. A totally bassackwards race of people, as old Captain Jim would have said; hothouse folks who considered their artificial glass conservatory to be the real world, and the real world an uncomfortable threat that must be outlawed. . . .

Cut it out, Mrs. McHugh, she told herself sharply in the rocking raft; your job right now is to catch the fish, never mind the philosophy. But she sat there a little longer in the irritating saltwater puddle that, no matter how carefully the raft was sponged out, inevitably collected in the depression made by her posterior in the yielding floor—soon she would no longer be able to remember what her dry-ass life had been like.

Well, it had quite often been a lot of fun. There had been

plenty of money and they'd got along pretty well even after the initial raptures of exploration and discovery had subsided. There had been people and parties and she'd found her quaint island-girl act very useful: she could keep a dinner table in stitches describing how as a kid she'd helped her old daddy pull lobster pots off Kennequid with ice forming on her junior-sized oilskins. But they weren't real people, and the longer she lived among them the less real they became with their strange hothouse notions, but she'd learned to keep her unfashionable opinions to herself. Chuck McHugh's brand-new bride was considered oddball enough already. (My dears, did you *hear*, he found her working on a *boat*, cutting up *fish* and things!) She'd concentrated on learning this strange newfangled life as she would have concentrated on learning the halliards, sheets, and braces of an old-fashioned square-rigger on which she'd found herself, and she thought she'd done a pretty good job.

The thing she really wanted she had not, of course, asked for. She had not married Chuck for that, she truly hadn't. The money and what it might buy hadn't influenced her, honest; and her upbringing had conditioned her never to ask. A present wasn't worth anything if you had to ask for it. But Chuck wasn't stupid, and he'd undoubtedly seen that the month they'd spent back in the Keys the following winter, fishing with Captain Jim, had been a very happy time for her, even though playing tug-of-war with a big fish meant very little to her except that it was something you could do from a boat. Her pleasure had undoubtedly influenced his decision to stop fishing off other people's boats and get a real sportfishing vessel of his own—their own.

It was another thing that had set her apart as that oddball young Mrs. McHugh. The wife was supposed to fight the husband's boat-ambitions every step of the way, and yield ungraciously only when she was promised on-board TV, stereo, wall-to-wall carpeting, microwave oven and, of course, absolutely arctic air-conditioning—that is, if she didn't state firmly that Big Stupid could go right ahead and waste their money on a silly boat if he liked, but he'd better not expect her to put foot on the nasty thing ever. For the pretty blonde bride-of-a-year to join eagerly and knowledgeably in the endless discussions concerning the auxiliary machinery for the big five-hundred-and-seventy-horsepower Detroit Diesels and the various brands of radar, loran, and depth-recording equipment, was thought highly unfeminine and practically subversive except among the few weathered sportfishing ladies around; and even they, like Chuck, considered a boat as just an accessory to their priceless rods and reels, a subsidiary piece of fishing tackle.

That was the wonderful thing about it all; in everything that really mattered, *Stream Hunter* was hers. As soon as Chuck realized that she knew more about boats than he did, instead of being offended as many men might have been, he simply turned the purely nautical aspects of the operation over to her with a sigh of relief, and concentrated on things important to him, like the outriggers and the fighting chair and making the cockpit a completely efficient area for angling purposes. After *Stream Hunter* was launched, they'd simply continued this division of responsibility. Chuck had learned how to handle the boat after a fashion, of course, just as she had mastered the fundamental principles of pumping up a big fish, but most of the time he left the flying bridge to her; the fighting cockpit was his kingdom.

He had, in fact, been quite proud of her seamanship; of the skillful way she could back down on a fish in heavy seas without taking half the ocean over the transom, or drop the *Hunter* into her narrow slip like a coin into a pay telephone. They made a hell of a team, Chuck would say with his arm around her after they started doing well in the tournaments; boys, you can hire some pretty good sportfishing captains, sure, but if you really want the best you've got to marry one, and this one's taken.

A nice guy, Chuck McHugh. She would cry for him when she had some tears available, she really would. But she didn't think he'd ever realized how much *Stream Hunter* had meant to her, and how the mere existence of the boat had made tolerable those long, shorebound stretches of totally artificial glasshouse living. It was like a hidden door to which she had the key. She wasn't really trapped any longer in this unreal existence, it was merely the small penance she endured—and endured gladly for the sake of her husband and her New England conscience—for having a childhood dream come true, although even in her wildest daydreams as a kid she'd never dared imagine herself owning, even in part, a vessel as big and beautiful and powerful as the *Hunter*.

The psychiatrists and psychologists would dirty it all up, of course. They'd make Chuck's compulsive big-game fishing into a symptom of sexual inadequacy expressed as exaggerated *machismo*, the way they dismissed all hunters as virility

251

freaks, although what those outdoors sports that were so obviously derived from the ancient need to put food on the table had to do with sex was never clearly explained. As for her, since she didn't have the proper little round gadgets between the legs for *machismo,* they'd have to find some other lousy sex-explanation for what the boat did for her, like some young girls were supposed to be mad about horses at a certain age because . . . well, she'd forgotten just what foul theory the experts had dreamed up to account for that. Couldn't people just like fishing or hunting or boating or riding because they *liked* it?

Anyway, Chuck had certainly had no noticeable sexual inadequacies and neither had she, as they'd demonstrated often enough on the big double berth in the *Hunter*'s master stateroom and sometimes elsewhere on board if the impulse hit them suddenly, or on a quiet beach or . . . Beach. Suddenly she remember, surprised at herself for forgetting, that they had, after all, had a few early problems with her inhibitions until that day in the Bahamas when, just the two of them, they'd conned the *Hunter* through the coral heads up to the leeward side of the sandy little cay without a name and dropped the anchor and run the dinghy ashore. They'd spent the morning swimming and fishing, and had settled down to a belated picnic lunch on the incredibly white beach at the edge of the incredibly blue, incredibly clear water, with the *Hunter* watching over them offshore. Well, Chuck would have laughed at the notion, but she'd always felt the boat as a living presence, a silent but strong and reassuring member of the party.

There had been some reason to celebrate—that successful tuna tournament out of Bimini—and on impulse she'd stuck a couple of bottles of champagne into the picnic cooler instead of the single bottle of wine she usually provided. She couldn't remember just how the playful rough-housing had started, after they were well into the second bottle, but she remembered running and dodging, laughing, along the lonely beach, and allowing herself at last to be caught and dragged down and stripped of her scanty scraps of bikini, although previously she'd always insisted—and Chuck had humored her in this—on sex being performed as a kind of secret and respectful ritual, in complete darkness. She could recall very clearly how in the breathless moment before all intellectual activity ceased in favor of pure sensation, the stern, ever-present New England guardian of her morals had shown her, as in a mirror, how

252

they must look, two perspiring hairless animals grappling indecently on the sand under the revealing, disapproving sun. She'd heard herself laugh happily in her sudden understanding that it wasn't like that at all, and if some misguided folks thought it was, who cared? It was one subject, she had to admit, that the summer people approached more sensibly. . . . Oh, dear. She found that she was, after all, crying weakly for her lost husband and her brief, lost marriage, or trying to, although nothing much came.

Behind the grief was the anger. The grief was for Chuck; but the anger was for her lovely dream boat and the way it had been stolen from her by a bunch of yo-yos taking advantage of the oldest law of the sea, the one that obliges you to rush to the aid of any vessel in distress. And even then they might have got clear if Babe Gregertsen had kept his big mouth shut and his hamlike hands to himself. . . .

She hadn't liked the looks of the supposedly distressed little powerboat from the start. One of those rakish express cruisers built on an offshore-racing hull, it didn't belong way out there in open water. To be sure, a crazy man named Magoon had tried to cross the whole Atlantic in a somewhat similar hull so he could take home one of the few offshore records he hadn't already put on his mantelpiece (actually, on the first try, starting from the far end, he hadn't made it past the Azores), but still this was basically a fast commuter, not a deep-sea craft, so what was it doing out there, not even on the direct course to Key West? But the voice on the short-range VHF had said both sterndrives were out, please help. She'd liked it even less when the *Hunter*'s normally reliable long-range SSB radio had acted up as she was trying to reach the U.S. Coast Guard and report, as recommended these hijack days, that their position was such-and-such, that they had encountered an emergency situation and were closing in to investigate; and that they'd keep in touch. But there was no response from Key West. It was time for Captain Jaspers' little girl to play it very cagy until she saw just what was on board that broken-down thunderboat.

She'd suggested to Chuck, down in the cockpit, that if he streamed the life-ring at the end of its floating polypropylene line she could cut around and tow the buoy within reach of a boathook on the drifting craft; in the meantime somebody could be breaking out that new coil of five-eights nylon. . . .

"You're going to tow them?" That was Babe, beside her on the flying bridge. He'd been telling her all about how he'd

253

discovered America for Columbus (or was it Leif Ericson?), or won the America's Cup for Ted Turner, or something. She'd long since learned to tune the big blowhard out when he tried to impress her with his famous yachting friends and his own fantastic seamanship. "You'll never haul that bucket clear to Key West against this head wind," he pointed out. "You'll pull that one flimsy cleat right out of its foredeck; besides, it'll take a week."

"I thought we'd take her back to Cozumel," Janet had said. "You and Sue can fly home from there. Unless maybe your boss will give you an extra couple of days off."

It wasn't quite fair, of course; but there were times when Babe had to be reminded who was sales manager and who owned the company. Babe let it go by him, or pretended to, studying the vessel ahead through the bridge binoculars that were supposed to be strictly reserved for the person on watch up there; if deadheads on the flying bridge wanted to glass something they could damn well supply their own optical equipment. But you couldn't expect the world's greatest seaman, self-elected, to observe such little niceties of nautical protocol.

"She's lower in the water; the pumps must have stopped," Babe reported. "I say let the insurance company worry about the damn boat; we're not in the salvage business. All we're obliged to do is . . ."

"*Stream Hunter,* this is *Misguided Missile,* do you read me?"

They always had cutie-pie names for those fast, streamlined ones, Janet reflected sourly as she picked up the VHF mike.

"We read you, *Missile.*"

"One of our pumps just quit; it's gaining on us fast. We're going to have to abandon. Can you take us aboard?"

"Let me check with the skipper, *Missile.* Back to you in a minute."

"Look, ma'am, this damn boat is *sinking. . . .*"

"Just a minute." She was aware that Babe was staring at her as, turning, she beckoned Chuck to the bridge ladder. "I don't like it, darling," she said softly. "That boat was floating high and dry when we first spotted her, and nobody said anything about a leak, just the sterndrives. All of a sudden she's going down like a rock. And I can't get through to the Coast Guard."

"Does it matter? If they're sinking, we've got to pick them up."

Summer people. One moment they acted as if everybody and everything was conspiring to murder them; the next moment they took for granted nobody and nothing could possibly dare harm them.

"We don't have to pick them up from that boat," she pointed out carefully. "Let's tell them to get their life raft over and we'll take them off that. We can say we don't want to risk banging up the boats at close quarters in this swell. It'll give us a chance to see how many there are and what they're carrying in their hot little hands."

"Bossman, I don't like to argue with the lady." This was Babe Gregertsen getting back at her for the way she'd reminded him of his lowly position in the local pecking order. "It's your boat, Chief, but seems to me if somebody drowns or gets taken by a shark while we're futzing around with life rafts and thing, we're not going to be in too good a spot, legally speaking. . . ."

The VHF was squawking again. "*Stream Hunter, Stream Hunter,* this is a Mayday, for Christ's sake, I repeat, this is a Mayday. We can't keep her afloat much longer. Will you pretty please get your goddamn finger out . . ."

"Anybody'd think this was the age of the buccaneers!"

That was Sue down in the cockpit making her contribution as she hitched at the bikini bottom she was forever about to lose off her skinny rump. Summer people. Always running around practically naked at the slightest excuse, instead of recognizing the sun for the dangerous enemy it was, afloat. As far as Janet was concerned, bathing suits were for bathing, jeans and such were for working, but when you were simply cruising pleasantly in a wonderful boat like the *Hunter* you could show her your appreciation by looking reasonably nice.

"What are you afraid of, Jan?" Sue demanded scornfully. "That they'll come swarming aboard with their cutlasses between their teeth, all two of them? Don't be afraid, Babe will protect you, won't you, honey?"

Babe had protected them, all right, all right. But first, Janet had looked at her husband and seen the answer in his face. Summer people stuck together. And they'd had the unwritten, unspoken rule between them, she and Chuck, that the immediate nautical tactics might be hers and usually were, but she allowed him the last word in matters of overall strategy and to hell with Women's Lib. After all, who'd made the boat possible in the first place? To save him from having to say it, she shrugged her shoulders minutely.

255

"Well, if that's the vote, I'll lay us alongside. But make them toss you their lines, and hand-hold them, will you, darling? Be ready to let go if we have to pull clear in a hurry."

"Sure, Jan."

She brought them in slowly, keeping the *Hunter*'s bow well clear and swinging the stern in with a touch of reverse so the two boats lay facing in opposite directions, cockpit to cockpit, rolling in the swell. She heard Chuck call for a line and saw one of the two men visible in the smaller boat spread his hands helplessly. That was the moment dear Sue, who normally wouldn't dream of dirtying her hands on a crummy rope, decided to demonstrate just what she thought of the boss's wife's ridiculous precautions and picked up one of the *Hunter*'s ready docklines and threw it and, of course, missed. The girl was a total menace on a boat. Sue gathered up the line in a lubberly bundle and leaned far out, as the vessels swung together, to hand it to the nearest stranger, a small wiry man with a monkey face.

He grabbed her wrist instead of the rope and flipped out a pistol from somewhere. Suddenly, the smaller craft's cockpit was full of men and weapons.

"You up there on the bridge! Kill those engines or I'll blow the little lady's head off!"

There was, of course, no choice. Between the loss of one not very valuable female human being, and the loss of the *Hunter* and the whole remainder of her crew, there was no choice at all. Janet's hand was resting on the twin shift levers. There was nothing to do but slam the mills into gear and ram the twin throttles right up to the stops, summoning the full thousand-odd horsepower of the two big Detroit Diesels. The wheel was already hard over. The rush of power would throw the *Hunter*'s stern right into the drifting boat. The man might get off one accurate shot before the jolt, not more; and then the *Hunter*'s prop wash would hit, probably swamping the rakish little pirate vessel, low as she was getting in the water.

The brain had given the signal, the muscles had started to respond, when there was a bearlike roar behind her—a bellow of shocked and incredulous rage—and she was yanked right out of her seat by Babe Gregertsen's enormous hands. She should have remembered that summer people could never stand to let anybody die even if it cost a thousand lives to save that one. Here it had cost them the ship's hired cook and Babe himself—although admittedly he'd helped that along by another of his bonehead plays—and it had cost Sue's life in the end, so his great gesture had gone for nothing. It had also cost *Stream Hunter* and Chuck McHugh. . . . Damn, she was crying again, only this time there were real unbelievable tears on her cheeks. But they weren't salty and they weren't tears.

A sudden rain was driving in the open canopy door and she heard the crash of thunder as, shocked at her negligence in letting the squall sneak up unnoticed, she scrambled for the water containers to collect as much as possible while it lasted. But it kept on and on, beautiful beyond belief, until she'd filled everything on board including herself with the glorious wet stuff; she'd even stripped and washed herself off and rinsed out her salt-encrusted rags, not that one little soapless rinse could achieve the miracle of restoration the woebegone garments required by this time. But the improvement, such as it was, was good for the morale while it lasted. However, a successful angling session soon destroyed her brief pretense to cleanliness; there was no dainty way of killing and butchering a sizeable fish like a dolphin. But she had water. She had food. If only Chuck had hung on a few hours longer. . . .

A week later she was picked up by a shrimper out of Tampa, with a big black mate who lifted her gently aboard saying, when she tried to speak:

"Not to fret yourself about anything, Missy. We'll soon have you smelling and looking purty again, in some nice clean clothes, with some meat on those poor little bones."

Which was, she reflected wryly, as good a way as any of telling her what a stinking, scrawny, bedraggled object she'd become, but that was all right. She'd made it. They couldn't kill Captain George Jaspers' little girl Janet by setting her adrift at sea, for God's sake. She knew more about the sea than any bunch of yo-yos with guns would ever learn; and now it was her turn.

Not vengeance. That was pointless. Nothing could bring Chuck back. But *Stream Hunter* could be found and recovered; and the people who'd taken her could be taught that it was very, *very* bad manners to go around stealing other people's beautiful boats. . . .

CHAPTER 25

June

Latitude 10°N; Longitude 65°W

They jumped Harold Ullman outside the best whorehouse in Puerto la Cruz. It was really a pretty nice whorehouse as such places go; you could almost call it a family whorehouse. It was clean, and it was air conditioned—almost essential this close to the equator these pampered days, although presumably previous generations had managed to entertain themselves in such establishments, although a trifle sweatily, without refrigeration.

The Tropicana girls were young and, in many instances, quite appealing in their sheer, frilly, summer-looking dresses or sharply creased super-tight pants; there seemed to be no middle ground between those extremes. The drinks weren't too generous, but they weren't too overpriced, either. The beer was okay, too, a brew called Cerveza Zulia bottled right there in Venezuela. Harold Ullman didn't really think much of it, but he would have been the first to concede that he was no true connoisseur of beer; for a choice, he only drank the stuff when he was sailing in very hot weather. Here he drank it because it seemed the safest thing available.

He didn't sample the other merchandise available, although there was of course no longer any reason not to. Strangely, the thought did not please him very much. You'd think a man who'd finally achieved freedom from a somewhat less than totally successful marriage would be eager to stretch his new-found bachelor wings, so to speak, and sample all the experiences now available to him, sexual and otherwise; but the disturbing fact was that he found himself missing the secure, warm feeling of knowing there was somebody waiting for him at home, somebody familiar and attractive and often, if not always, very nice, for whose sake he could damn well make the not-very-great sacrifice of rejecting such not-very-tempting extramarital opportunities for exercising his masculinity. He wondered how, if Nancy had known the number of times he'd passed it up on distant assignments—and they hadn't all been whores by any means—she would have reconciled the information with her idiot *macho* theories about him that, he was surprised to discover, infuriating though they'd been to live with, were beginning to seem merely kind of cute and perverse and feminine in retrospect.

And goddamn it, he wished she hadn't looked so damned *downtrodden* the last few times he'd seen her during the divorce proceedings, or sounded so uncertain and unsure of herself when he'd called to let her know that something strange was going on and it might be well for her to take a few precautions. She'd been such a bright and proud and gutsy girl, even though there had been times when he could hardly stand her. Maybe he had been pretty hard on her, regardless of justification, doing it the way he had. Preoccupied with his own injuries and grievances, he certainly hadn't given her much help with her problems, as her lawyer hadn't been backward in pointing out. The big handsome jerk had acted more protective than the business relationship really justified; Ullman had got the impression they'd been seeing quite a bit of each other—not that it was any of his concern, now. But Mr. J. Barton Leonard had better be nice to her. He had something very good, very important, but at the moment very fragile, right there in his hands, and Harold Ullman hoped he knew it.

But tonight, of course, there was no reason whatever for the recently unmarried Mr. Ullman not to spend his money on any lady who pleased him without thought of unfaithfulness; and he knew it was simple cowardice that kept him from it. With his recent scars and his awkward leg, he'd been reluctant to try free-lancing anew—after the years of doing it under contract—with a girl he didn't know, whose language he didn't speak very well, who'd seen hundreds of men with their pants off. Anyway, he'd visited the place more or less in the line of duty; but he'd realized very quickly that he'd made a mistake. Although the joint was peaceful and friendly for what it was, it was still a dumb place to bring a camera; and it turned out that he didn't know enough Spanish to kid them into cooperating with the project he'd had in mind: getting a few shots of one of the young Italian engineers from the ship relaxing with one of the girls, as part of his picture story on tanker life.

He'd been aware of no *gringo*-go-home attitude in the town, earlier, but even as he made his first clumsy attempt to explain what he wanted to the pretty, busty, black-haired young woman in flowing, flowery pink who'd attached herself to Salvatore—nothing really suggestive or embarrassing; she could keep all her clothes on and her face didn't even have to be recognizable—he could feel it enter the place like a hostile presence. As a professional photojournalist he was fairly sensitive to hostile presences; you had to be, to survive. There were times when the job demanded that you ignore them and stick around stubbornly to be shot at by guerrillas or have your cameras smashed by cops; but you soon learned to distinguish carefully between what was that important and what wasn't, and this wasn't. The crusading magazine that had hired him was concerned with immaculate concepts relating to nautical safety and marine ecology. Shots of a South American sex-drive in operation were not on the high-priority list.

Again, there were times when you made two stories of an assignment, the one the client had ordered and the one you thought he should have, and covered both, hoping to be able to sell him the truer version later. Sometimes it worked, and always it gave you a certain artistic satisfaction; but there really wasn't much chance of its working here. They'd made it pretty clear what they wanted; and artistic satisfaction alone wasn't worth getting beat up for. Harold Ullman had therefore grinned apologetically and spread his hands helplessly to indicate that he'd made an error in judgment and was sorry. He'd left money for his beer with plenty to spare and got the hell out of there, hoping he hadn't spoiled anything for Salvatore and the rest of the boys from the ship. Puerto la Cruz was one of their favorite ports.

It was a reasonably clean and prosperous little city, not the kind of grimy tropical poverty-hole often found in that part of the world. The third mate of the ship had told Harold Ullman that it had been a hell of a rowdy, wide-open town back in the old, bold, oil-boom days; but now things had settled down and the oil industry had been taken over by the Venezuelan government. Puerto la Cruz had cleaned up its act and turned itself into a pleasant community where well-dressed Spanish-speaking citizens strolled of an evening along the wide street by the harbor, or had a drink or two in one of the attractive, open-air places along the beach. There was an enormous new resort hotel, too, and at least one very good air-conditioned restaurant nearby, where they'd all had dinner before setting out to show Harold Ullman the seamier side of Puerto la Cruz, which had turned out to be a fairly mild sort of sin street for a seaport town. It had been enough to demonstrate, however, that you could still get laid in this corner of Venezuela if you worked at it hard enough. Apparently you could still get mugged here, too.

He knew at once that he was being followed away from the place; they hardly gave him time to feel relief at being safely out of there. They simply fell in behind him as he started up the sidewalk of the wide street that gave no indication of the nature of the establishments on both sides. Well, hardly any indication. There were no neon signs, or red lights, or importunate *porteros* grabbing you by the arm and pleading with you to enter and meet the girl of your dreams, but there were a couple of dozen empty cars nosed in toward the curb, mysteriously awaiting the return of their owners in an otherwise empty part of town. There was also the canned music from the place next door where you had your drinks and preliminary get-acquainted conversation on the patio under the stars until it was time to go indoors for more robust and athletic activities. But the fellows from the ship had explained, in their clumsy English, that though the surroundings were more picturesque in the Estrella, the girls weren't as nice as those in the Tropicana. . . .

Harold Ullman knew he was stalling; and there was really nothing to stall about. The choice was very simple: keep walking until they jumped him, or dodge quickly back into the now-hostile Tropicana and beg his dinner companions to escort him safely back to the ship, completely ruining their evening ashore and making himself look pretty foolish in the bargain, because of course there would be no lurking men visible when he came out with reinforcements. He slowed his pace uncertainly. His first thought was that it was unlikely that murder was intended. A couple of the local lads had simply taken it upon themselves to teach the offensive photographic *gringo* a little respect for Venezuelan womanhood. But had they?

Instinct told him that he hadn't aroused *that* much hostility inside, not enough to take those virile preoccupied gents away from the seductive dark ladies for whose services they were paying. He'd merely been a small irritant, not an active annoyance; his apologetic withdrawal should have satisfied them. After all, they had more urgent and important things on their minds. That left two possibilities, he thought, working it out in his head as he kept moving slowly. One: it was actually a simple mugging planned by a pair of urban *bandidos* tempted by the sight of a rich *Americano* stupid enough to walk the streets at night displaying an expensive camera. Well, that could be; but considering everything else that had happened to him it would be a howling coincidence. Possibility number two: somebody had followed him clear from the U.S., and having come a couple of thousand miles to do a job, and hired local talent to perform it, it wasn't likely they'd limit the job to minor mayhem. It was a wild notion, but so was being followed anywhere, or coming home to find a bunch of masked thugs wrecking your house. And if it was that kind of a world, okay, he'd see if he couldn't cope with it a little better now that he'd had some painful practice.

He drew a long breath and started walking once more as briskly as his leg allowed. Nancy would call it stupid *macho* pride and stubbornness, he reflected wryly; to hear her tell it, testicles were the ruin of the world. But he knew with sudden clarity that what had happened to him that night last fall when their world had ended would never happen again. Nobody would ever again haul him off to a hospital in that condition, at least not without calling the morgue wagon for the other guy. And maybe for him, too, but that was a risk that had to be run—something Nancy would never understand, living in that soft dream-society of hers that had so little basis in reality, where risk was a dirty word. And Nancy would no doubt spin some more of her lovely amateur psychiatric theories about irrational masculine behavior if she learned that her silly ex-husband had got himself carved up outside a Venezuelan cathouse by stupidly stopping to fight instead of sensibly diving for shelter. Somehow he found the idea rather touching.

He heard a car coming and glanced around, aware that his pursuers had faded into the shadows. It was not a taxi, just a medium-sized white sedan a couple of years old from which, after it was parked, two men emerged. They disappeared into the Tropicana. Well, he didn't really want a taxi. To hell with it. All he wished was that he hadn't been so proud of his rapidly improving leg that he'd left the cane on the ship; a man could do a lot of damage with a cane. He kept on walking toward the corner ahead, letting the camera slip from his shoulder, and wrapping the strap firmly around his right hand. It was an old box anyway. You didn't carry your best cameras around a foreign town at night any more than you brought along your whole bankroll.

He'd guessed that they would come in fast as soon as he turned the corner into the deserted street beyond, and they did, almost too fast. He'd stopped and stepped aside, back against the wall, and he barely had time to make a slashing swing at the nearest as he appeared, wielding the camera like a mace at the head of the big burly dark man leading the attack. He saw the gleam of a knife and somewhere inside him, he was aware, there was panic struggling to get out, but he fought it back. Then the camera connected with a solid and expensive sound. The husky knifeman reeled aside, almost knocking down his smaller companion. He clapped both hands to his head and sat down hard.

Something was happening to him, Ullman realized; something he'd almost found once but somebody had interfered. The night had turned a funny red hazy color and he stepped forward and deliberately kicked the seated man in the face, and the man almost turned a complete back somersault, his head hitting the concrete, his legs flopping high, ridiculously, before dropping limply back to the sidewalk. One down, Ullman heard somebody speaking in an odd whisper.

"Now *you*, little man!" the voice said. "Come, come, *amigo*. Here's where it's at. Come and get it!"

He realized that it was his own voice, although not quite his own. He moved forward swinging the camera deliberately by its shortened strap. Something gleamed on the pavement, the knife, and he scooped it up smoothly, without taking his eyes from the smaller man. That one had recovered from the impact of his partner's body, but he'd lost his brave momentum and now he was backing away: a thin individual in ragged work clothes. Watching him closely, Harold Ullman got the knife into his right hand, transferring the camera strap to his left.

There were, he knew, all kinds of theories about knife-fighting, and at one time he'd been under the impression that a slight acquaintance with fencing foils might give him an edge of sorts if he ever, unlikely though it might seem, had to use a blade in anger. This notion had been laughed to scorn by a drunken ex-Marine mercenary who'd kind of adopted him during a small African war he'd once attended for photographic purposes. Sonny, the man had said, if you stick your knife hand way out there, fencing style, and if the other guy has a knife and knows what he's doing, you'll never get it back in one piece. If you've got to let him carve something, give him the left to whittle on while you gut him with the right. But mostly the left is to get his knife aside and make way for yours, Sonny, so put it out front there where it can do some good, and if you've got a briefcase to wave at him or even just a bag of groceries, use that, every little bit helps. The ex-Marine's name had been O'Brien, what else; and he'd died in an ambush a few days later.

The little man made a clumsy lunge. Harold Ullman swung the camera left-handed at the oncoming knife hand, knocking it aside, and drove in with the borrowed blade but missed contact as his opponent scuttled back fearfully. Angry with himself, he knew that he'd lost a very good opportunity to end the fight by not going in all the way with complete determination. Back to square one, goddamn it. Next time *kill* the sonofabitch.

He moved in with the battered remnant of the camera swinging out front and the knife ready behind it; and the little man turned and ran. The red fighting-haze faded, and suddenly Harold Ullman felt quite sick, but he was goddamned if he was going to puke on the field of victory. A movement made him turn sharply, but it was just the larger man crawling away brokenly on hands and knees. There was a shockingly powerful impulse to use the knife on the broad helpless back, and it wasn't any sense of humanitarianism or fair play that restrained him, just the practical fact that a dead body would cause a hell of a lot of trouble. And he'd probably never come back to Puerto la Cruz, so it was okay, perhaps, to let the sonofabitch live since there was hardly any chance of their meeting again. But goddamn it, he was getting tired of violent people who wouldn't leave him alone.

The security guards let him through the gate without question. The big hoses were still connected and the *Petrox Prince,* lying at the dock, was still absorbing Venezuelan oil in inconceivable quantities. She was several feet lower in the water now than when he'd left. A few crew members were keeping an eye on things under the lights. He felt awkward with the recently acquired knife cold under his shirt and the broken camera concealed under his arm, but they greeted him cheerfully in Italian and broken English as he made his way up the gangway and aft to the tall superstructure and inside. He climbed the stairs to his cabin on the third deck up, just below the cabins and offices of the captain and chief engineer. It was a big cheerful stateroom looking out on the tanker's deck with its catwalk and hatches and pipes and manifolds. He drew the curtains and got his pipe and stuffed it full of tobacco and lit it; he never carried it here for fear he'd absent-mindedly walk out on deck smoking, which was of course strictly forbidden.

He took out the knife and looked at it: a crude implement with a riveted wooden handle, but sharp enough for all practical purposes. The camera was beyond repair; he dropped it out of sight in his gadget bag. Now, at a distance, the whole encounter seemed like a dream, but he knew it had changed him in some significant way or, at least, made official a change that had been in the making for a good many months. There had once been a nice young red-haired guy named Harold Ullman. There was still a young red-haired guy named Harold Ullman, but he wasn't quite so nice any longer. Being nice didn't seem to have a hell of a lot of survival value these days.

There was still something to be done and, having got the pipe well alight, he moved to the desk in the corner and rolled a sheet of paper into the portable typewriter he used for writing up his notes and photo-captions. He started by using her address but crossed it out. The lawyer-boyfriend's address was better; that way it would come to his attention as well, and he might take some sensible action if she didn't. To Miss Nancy Winters, c/o Mr. J. Barton Leonard, of Holloman, Pearson, Grimes, and Leonard, Attorneys at Law:

DIAGNOSIS CONFIRMED PROTECTION INDICATED
BE CAREFUL HAROLD

It didn't satisfy him. It didn't say quite what he wanted to say. He tore up the page and went through the whole thing again on a clean sheet with one word added to the message he'd give to the radio operator in the morning:

DIAGNOSIS CONFIRMED PROTECTION INDICATED PLEASE
BE CAREFUL HAROLD

CHAPTER 26

June

Latitude 10°N; Longitude 65°W

"And where the hell were you, Phil?" Wendell Anthony Richardson demanded.

He stood by the window of his room in the Melia de Puerto la Cruz, the town's newest and finest resort hotel, associated with a similarly fancy establishment in Madrid, Spain, according to the literature on the dresser. For forty-seven-fifty a day you got a balcony and a bidet and an elegantly appointed cubbyhole the size of his wife's dressing room back in Georgetown, Virginia, Richardson reflected sourly. What had happened to the *real* luxury hotels, the ones that gave you high ceilings and a little room to stretch?

Turning, he could see himself reflected in the full-length mirror on the closet door: a tall, blond, lean—well, almost lean; he had to keep working on that—handsome man nearing fifty, wearing a short-sleeved white sports shirt and immaculate cord slacks; but he didn't feel as good as he looked. It had been a long haul down from Washington to Caracas, and there had been no plane immediately available to Barcelona, the field closest to Puerto la Cruz. He'd had to hire a taxi; and a four-hour Venezuelan taxi ride was something to experience, particularly after a day spent above thirty thousand feet. Even a bath and a change of clothes hadn't quite revived him. He found himself wondering if he wasn't getting too old for this I-Spy business, but dismissed the thought irritably. He was just getting too old to be running two-thousand-mile errands to the equator for other people without half his intelligence or competence. Well, if things worked out, he wouldn't have to put up with *that* much longer.

He wasn't wearing a gun, of course. He didn't even have

one in his luggage. Those days, at least, were long gone and good riddance. He had graduated from the mandatory-firearms category; he was no longer classed as action personnel; and while, of course, he made the expected noises in public about how office work gave him claustrophobia and how he yearned to get out into the field again where a man could *breathe,* privately he'd found it a great relief.

It had therefore come as a shock when that senile old goat Meriwether, who should have been retired for incompetence years ago and soon would be—he'd soon have enough evidence to present to the Internal Affairs people—overhearing one of those careless, meaningless remarks that were made by everyone stationed in Washington as a matter of ancient custom, had beckoned him into the Inner Sanctum and said that, if he really felt that way, there was a job that needed doing in the Miami area. Several accounts down there did not seem to be producing results. If Tony really wanted a break from the dull Washington routine he, Meriwether, would be greatly obliged if he'd take a run down that way and straighten things out. Of course it was not an order, but apparently young Martin—while very effective as an agent, of course, he was saying nothing against Martin—was a little out of his depth as yet handling that much administrative responsibility. It might be well for a senior man to be on the spot to keep things from getting too badly fouled up. But it was, of course, entirely up to him.

But of course it wasn't, really. He couldn't afford, with the situation close to critical, to let anyone get the idea that he wasn't nearly as eager as he'd pretended to get out and manage a field account again, or even a whole field office. Even though it was no time to be away from Washington with everything coming to a head, he'd mousetrapped himself very neatly with his big mouth, he reflected bitterly. Now he'd had to waste a whole winter in that land of everlasting goddamn sunshine and ratty palm trees and fat women in skinny bikinis, with frequent frantic dashes north to keep track of the situation, quite essential, of course, even though it gave that disloyal crew in Miami too many opportunities to conspire against him. As now.

"So where were you?" he repeated.

Phil Martin said with a grin, "Well, for one thing I was in Puerto la Cruz, Venezuela, Tony, which was more than anybody else in the outfit could say last night."

That was rank insubordination, of course, grin or no grin. "Meaning just what?" Richardson asked dangerously.

"I know we decided he'd probably be safe down here, or you did, but things were kind of slack in the office for the moment, so I decided I'd take a quick run down to check up on him at his first port of call and see if he'd picked up any sinister company. As it turned out, he had."

"Just a spur-of-the-moment decision?" Richardson said sarcastically. "A hunch out of the blue."

Martin's dark face showed annoyance. "Damn it, Tony, it was my baby in a way; at least the original idea was mine, remember? And having had a hand in setting the poor guy up, I felt, with due respect and all that, that I couldn't in good conscience let him go roaming around the Caribbean totally unprotected, even though there'd been no sign of interest all this time. I know we discussed it earlier and you weren't convinced; but as I said, there wasn't much doing in Miami, and if you want me to call it leave and pay for it out of my pocket, I'll be happy to do so."

"You are, of course, prepared to justify taking leave at a time when your superior was absent and the office had been left in your charge."

It was an error in tactics; and Martin smiled thinly. "Now I am. What happened last night is my justification, isn't it? It's what we've been waiting for, isn't it? Somebody *has* been listening to the rumors we've spread around, about the Ullmans being able to identify their attackers, or at least the leader of the gang. Somebody who has other uses for the guy and doesn't want him embarrassed by a lot of official interest."

It was senseless to fight over unfavorable terrain. Richardson changed the subject smoothly: "Very well, say you're right, you still haven't answered my original question. After charging off without permission to protect this poor little red-haired fellow for whom you feel so responsible, you didn't. Where were you?"

"Hell, I was right there, right up the street. I just saw no reason to interfere. He was doing all right. In order to stop it I'd have had to shoot, and they don't like guns down here, not other people's guns. One shot would have brought out all kinds of *policia* loaded down with submachine guns; they wear them like our cops wear thirty-eights. I figured I'd give him a chance to work it out for himself and he did." Martin grinned reminiscently. "Damn right he did. You should have seen our carrot-top clean up on those cheap *bandidos*. Hell, at one point I thought I was going to have to shoot *him,* just a little, to keep him from killing one and causing everybody a lot of grief. He had a spot all picked out to plant that liberated blade he was holding; he was seeing red and breathing fire like a goddamn Berserker." Martin drew a long breath and said softly, "It's always something to see if you've got a strong stomach. I saw it a few times in the service. Not many; most of them come through hopelessly brainwashed these days; but a few. It's ... very interesting when they wake up at last and realize that maybe the world is not the sweet peaceful place they've been told all their lives, but dammit they can handle it anyway." Martin grimaced. "I think we'd better tell him the whole story, Tony, and tell him quick, or we're going to have more trouble than we need, more trouble than anybody needs."

This was romantic nonsense. "We've been over all that; and I want no more of your unilateral decisions, Phil. The man has no proper clearance. We can't possibly take him into our confidence."

"He's not cleared for knowing, but he is cleared for dying, is that what you're saying?"

"According to you, having come of age or attained his manhood or however you put it so dramatically, he is now competent to tackle the whole world barehanded." Richardson made a sharp little gesture. "That decision has been made. It stands."

"You're making a mistake, Tony," Martin said softly. "That's not just a harmless little picture-snapping citizen any longer, if he ever was. He's been beaten to a pulp and spent long painful weeks in the hospital. He's got a limp he didn't have before and a face that isn't quite his any longer. He's lost his wife one way or another; I think there's something we don't know abut that divorce. I think something happened that night they're not telling the world about. But remember, his instinct even back then was to go for a gun, even if he somehow didn't manage to use it very successfully. Now that freckled, nice-looking, boyish-looking young fellow is finally starting to get mad deep down inside. He's had it up to here with people pushing him around—and you say we should keep right on shoving? You wouldn't rather just play catch with a couple of grenades instead and see how long it takes for one of the pins to fall out?"

This was just vague psychological theorizing, and Richardson put an end to it briskly: "Let the record show that I have been warned, very melodramatically. Now tell me what you've been doing since it happened."

There was a moment of silence and he thought Martin was going to be stubborn and continue the ridiculous argument, but the younger man drew a long breath and said, "Well, the first thing I did as soon as I could get through to Miami was to tell Tommy Walsh, who's holding down the fort, to yank Bill Simonds off whatever he was doing and put him back to guarding the wife. He knows her habits, he had time to study them after he was brought up from the Keys, so he's the best man for the job. Just in case action down here might be paralleled by action up there."

Richardson clenched his teeth, hardly able to contain his sudden rage. He said thickly, "You do seem to take advantage of my absence to get your own way, don't you, Phil? You disapproved very loudly of my putting Simonds on that September business, as I recall."

"Goddamn it, *amigo,* the woman obviously has to be protected until we see what's cooking; and we don't have all the manpower in the world, as you so often point out. I simply picked the most qualified agent with the least important project on his hands—"

"In *your* opinion the least important. You know I disagree with you very strongly on that."

Martin grimaced. "Jesus, Tony, the *Hermanos de Septiembre* are just a bunch of ineffectual old soaks talking big about blowing up the world—hell, for all the hot air they put out, they couldn't blow up a toy balloon far enough to make it pop. And while we're on that subject, that goes for the gang of clowns we're wasting time on down in Key West, too, just another goddamn encounter group of friendly alcoholic conversationalists chatting happily about wreaking death and destruction in the name of the counterrevolution as they swill their cheap Muscatel. There's only one outfit currently active in the Miami region that we really need to worry about and that's the one belonging to our friend Columbus. He's about ready to move, I figure; he must have his preparations just about made by now, and if that handsome Cameron woman doesn't get her neat little trousered ass into gear we're going to have to go in after Major Horst Ochsner all by ourselves and break it up, and I'm not looking forward to it one little bit. That's another hair-trigger lad I'd prefer to play no games with at all."

Richardson drew a long breath, fighting for self-control.

"Are you quite through?" he asked gently, and went on without waiting for a response: "You know, Phil, I seem to be operating under a misapprehension. I thought I was the general account manager for the Miami region, at least for the moment. As a matter of fact I seem to recall that I was sent to take over temporarily because you weren't doing very well. Please correct me if I'm wrong."

There was a moment of silence; and Richardson was uneasily aware that a strange predatory expression had moved across the other man's dark face for a moment; and the dark eyes had, for a moment, had a hooded look just like that of a bird of prey. He could not help remembering that Martin had come to the Anti-Terrorist Division from Vietnam, where he'd been a member of a combat group whose methods of warfare had come in for a certain amount of criticism. And of course these field men with their guns did often tend to think of killing as a simple solution for just about everything; but if this one thought he could intimidate Wendell Anthony Richardson . . .

Martin grinned abruptly. "Sorry, Tony. No offense intended. It's just that because of my racial origins I'm supposed to be an expert on these Latin groups and keep you advised as to the relative dangers they represent. I'm just doing my duty, as it says here in the fine print."

Richardson had no intention of letting him off so easily. "And of course I'm under no obligation to follow your advice, right?"

"Not any."

"Very well. Now that we have *that* clear, please be so kind as to let me know what else has been done."

"I got the little guy," Martin said. "He still had his knife, but he wasn't very good with it; nobody ever seems to sell one of those things with a simple manual of instructions. Then we rounded up his friend, who was in pretty bad shape. His face was pretty badly bent from Ullman's kick; and he also had something of a concussion from being slugged with the camera. He was puking all over everything including himself. But he was lucid enough between pukes, and he sure as hell didn't want any more *Yanquis* to go to work on him; Ullman had softened him up but good. I might have had trouble cracking the other one, but with the big guy babbling like a brook I guess the little one figured he might as well grab a little conversational credit, too."

"Well, what did you learn?" Richardson demanded.

"It was a pretty lady," Martin said. "A pretty blonde lady. *Una rubia muy hermosa.* And the price, in case you're interested, was two hundred *bolivars,* one hundred apiece. That's twice what it costs to get banged in the local bordellos, outrageous. Inflation is getting a foothold everywhere. I believe the current rate of exchange is about four *bolivars* to the buck."

Richardson was frowning. "A *woman?* You're certain?"

Martin grinned. "They may not know much in these backward Latin countries, Tony, but one thing they do know is how to tell the hes from the shes. Either the big guy we're after, the one Ullman's described, with the ski mask, has an army of Amazons available for detached duty, or just one very helpful and decorative girlfriend with interesting connections. She wore a tailored pantsuit outfit, carried a Norwegian passport, and called herself Mrs. Einar Johanssen. She stayed right here at this hotel, but she checked out the day before yesterday, heading for Caracas. I had Tommy take Masterman out of Key West and send him straight down there to see what he could find out about her—I thought you wouldn't mind neglecting that account for a little now that we've got a live clue here."

Richardson started to speak and checked himself. It was, of course, a deliberate program of sabotage; naturally this transplanted foreigner who should never have been employed by the division—he'd see that all such subversive elements were cleared out, very soon—resented having been replaced by a senior operative and was doing his best to make said senior look bad by carefully undermining all projects favored by him, while doing everything in his power to bring his own pet account to a triumphant conclusion.

"Go on," Richardson said coldly.

"I haven't heard from Caracas yet," Martin said. "I thought I'd better stay here and make sure the subject got off safely. They were disconnecting the last hoses and hauling up the gangplank, and he was photographing up a storm, when I left to meet you here. We should be seeing the ship heading out pretty soon." He gestured toward the window. "The tugs were just moving in to pull her clear of the dock. He should be safe enough at sea. We'll have to find out where they're delivering their cargo up in the States and make arrangements to cover him there. Meanwhile, we can be tracing the dame and, we hope, getting a line on her boyfriend. Let's hope he'll lead us to some interesting new information about Mister Columbus. It's about time we got a little leverage there."

Looking out the window at the harbor, Richardson said, "What did you do with the prisoners?"

"Turned them loose."

"It didn't occur to you that I might want to question them further when I arrived?"

"Hell, Tony, you don't speak Spanish; and where would I have kept them, in my hotel room? We had a pretty long conversation. I'll write it out in my report, but if there's anything special you want to know, maybe I've already got the answer."

"I presume the lady didn't make full payment in advance. How were they to get the balance, if she was leaving town?"

"Through the local *jefe,* Mr. Big in Puerto la Cruz. A gent named Lupe Dominguez who runs everything here as long as it's shady. They were actually just obliging the lady as a favor to Lupe, who was obliging her as a favor to somebody they both knew in the States. I told you the blonde had connections. But I couldn't get any names or even any cities. They said they didn't know and I believed them; who'd trust a pair of punks like that?"

"Well, there's only one thing wrong with the scenario you just laid out for us, Phil," Richardson said evenly. "The ship isn't going back to the States, at least not yet."

"Oh, shit. Where are we going to have to chase him next?"

"They've changed the routing on us," Richardson said. "I just got the word before I left Washington. The *Petrox Prince* is picking up 140,000 barrels here, part Marine Diesel and part Bunker C, whatever that may be. They'll deliver all but 11,000 barrels in Balboa, at the Pacific end of the Panama Canal. Then they'll sail up the coast a little ways to a banana port called Puerto Armuelles, where they'll drop off 7,000 barrels. The last 4,000 barrels get dumped in a hole called Golfito, just over the border in Costa Rica. After that they'll probably come back here by way of the Canal, load up again, and head for the States. Probably. There are, I'm told, forty-two gallons to the barrel, in case it matters. I don't know why anybody thought that information would interest us, but it was submitted with the rest so I pass it along." Richardson looked sharply at the younger man, who was frowning. "Well?"

"I can't cover him in the Canal, if they really want him," Martin said. "For a guy with a game leg, he gets around that

ship like a monkey; I watched him. He's going to want al
kinds of camera angles of those famous locks, isn't he? An
all it takes is one guy with a scope-sighted rifle within a
couple of hundred yards of the ditch—make that three hun
dred if the sniper's good, four if he's tremendous. It woul
take the whole damned U.S. Army—or whatever army's in
charge there these days—making a clean sweep of every
thing within a quarter of a mile of the Big Ditch to protec
him."

"Then we'll just have to hope that his recent close escap
will make him keep his head down," Richardson said. "Any
way, it's not your problem, Phil, not any longer. I'll wait her
to make contact with Masterman, and between us we'll mak
whatever further arrangements are necessary along the ship'
route. We can hope that, having failed here, the lady wil
expose herself by trying again; and that if we catch her she'
be willing to talk. In the meantime, somebody has to run th
Miami office."

He was aware of that dark, hooded stare once more; the
Martin grinned cheerfully. "Sure, Tony, whatever you say.'

After the junior man had left, Richardson moved swiftly t
the telephone wondering how long it took to get a Miam
connection from this benighted country. And how could any
one expect him to run an operation effectively in the face o
open hostility and obstructionism from his subordinates'
Maybe he did spend considerable time in Washington, bu
that was no excuse for the way his orders were foreve
disregarded the instant his back was turned.

As he waited for his connection Richardson saw, lookin
out the window, a black tanker with a tall white superstruc
ture aft appear from behind an island to the east and hea
out to sea, riding low in the water with the cargo she carried
The distance was too great for him to make out the name, bu
the Petrox logo on the stack was unmistakable. The tele
phone rang; and a moment later he had Walsh on the line—
Martin's bosom pal, he reminded himself, and a very importan
part of the conspiracy against him, Richardson.

"But we had definite instructions—" Walsh began whe
he'd finished speaking.

"I am countermanding those instructions," Richardson said
"Can't you understand plain English? I thought I'd made i
plain before and I'm repeating it now: the September accoun
has clear priority. You'll have to arrange things accordingly
That's an order."

"Yes, sir," Walsh said. "I'll get hold of Simonds and let him know."

Hanging up, Richardson found that his hand was shaking. It was unfuriating to meet this pretense of dumb innocence when it was perfectly clear that they were all laughing at their ringleader, Martin's, clever efforts to make the unwanted new account manager foisted on them by Washington look helpless and incompetent. Well, he'd see about Mr. Martin and his gun and his greasy greaser arrogance when the time came. In the meantime, the capture of this blonde mystery woman, this *rubia muy hermosa,* ought to confound all those who sneered at his, Richardson's, abilities in the field. It would be another step toward his ambitious goal.

CHAPTER 27

June

Latitude 26°N; Longitude 80°W

It felt strange to Nancy Winters to be taken to the movies again; it made her feel young and girlish as if she were back in high school. Harold hadn't been much for movies although he had, she remembered, insisted on seeing *Star Wars* when it came through; and now Bart wanted to catch a rerun of *Close Encounters of the Third Kind*—a pretentiously mystifying mouthful of a title, she'd always thought—since he'd missed it the first time around. She wondered what there was about those galactic epics that was so fascinating to men. Well, she didn't know about *Close Encounters* because she hadn't seen it yet; but actually the answer was easy enough as far as *Star Wars* was concerned. Deprived of his bang-bang Westerns and his kick-punch-gouge adventure and cop shows by the recent very sensible and satisfying trend toward TV nonviolence, Harold had been happy to settle for those crazy ray guns and weird electronic swords; and the darting rocket ships with their idiot murder beams, zap-zap-zap. She hoped *Close Encounters* would be less childish. Bart had assured her it was supposed to be quite a subtle and significant cinematic effort, but she had her doubts.

At least she was going to get a good dinner out of it; and it was really very nice of Bart to take her to the moderately expensive second-floor restaurant at Miami's city marina, known as Miamarina, even though he knew the associations it had for her—he was really very sweet about helping her with these things she had to do to exorcise the past. She saw the two of them reflected in the inner glass doors ahead as they entered the building. They made a good-looking couple, she decided: the slim brown-haired girl with the big fashionable glasses and a nicely fitting pair of fawn slacks that made her waist look very small and a soft white silk shirt with long sleeves—she noted with pleasure that the dumb broad seemed to be standing up straight again and actually looking people in the eyes—and the husky, handsome dark-haired young man with sports coat and open-necked sports shirt and neat summer slacks. It was a minor detail, of course, but it was kind of nice to go around for a change with a man who kept his shoes polished; Harold could never be bothered.

But in this familiar place she couldn't help wanting to call to the girl in the glass: hey, lady, haven't you got the wrong guy, what happened to the young fellow who used to bring you here? Well, Harold was down in the Caribbean by this time, he'd told her about his new assignment over the phone; and whatever he thought of her she hoped he knew she wished him well in spite of everything. Somehow, the fact that he'd been concerned enough to call and warn her about possible danger, melodramatic though the idea might seem, had killed the bitter resentment she'd been nourishing for so many months. She hoped he felt the same way. These endless feuds between people who'd once been married were often pretty ugly. Regardless of rights and wrongs one could try to be civilized.

Upstairs, a handsome lady in a long dress came to greet them. She checked the list on her little desk when Bart said, "Reservation for Mr. Leonard."

"This way, please."

He'd got them a table by the windows—actually the whole wall was glass—looking out over the harbor and the boats; he was very good about things like that without being pompous about it. Well, not very; lawyers always tended to be a little

276

bit pompous, it was part of the professional act and she made allowances for it. She ordered a daiquiri and he asked for a dry martini up with a twist. It was a pleasant restaurant, and although there were many customers in fairly basic and durable clothes—boat people from the marina, probably—there were also some who'd dressed up a bit to dine here.

She found herself wishing she'd put on something a bit more festive and sexy, but she hadn't quite had the nerve. You got locked into these damned roles. Once you were established as a tailored sort of pants and pantsuit person you could no longer casually put on a pretty dress and heels and nylons, not just for going to the movies for God's sake, without seeming to make a dramatic statement. At least if she did, she would feel as if she were waving her arms and yelling: looky, I'm a *girl*, why doesn't somebody *do* something about it?

It was as hard a role to get out of as the poor-little-untouchable-invalid routine she also seemed to be stuck with these days. He was a nice guy, a very nice and gentle guy, but there were times when she wished fervently that he'd stop being so goddamned noble and protective; she was getting a little tired of being treated like a bruised flower. . . . She was suddenly aware that Bart had taken something from his inside jacket pocket and slid it across the table to her, and she started rather guiltily, hoping that her wanton and unseemly thoughts hadn't shown on her face.

"It's for you," he said. "They called it into the office first so I know what's in it; I had them send a copy over afterwards. I . . . I was tempted not to give it to you. It's just more of the same. But it is addressed to you so I'm kind of obliged to pass it along, regardless."

He wasn't quite making sense; but he was certainly making her uneasy. She picked up the envelope and tore it open and drew out the flimsy sheet of paper inside, with its pasted-on strips of words printed in capital letters:

DIAGNOSIS CONFIRMED PROTECTION INDICATED PLEASE
BE CAREFUL HAROLD

For a moment all she felt was annoyance at this jarring intrusion on their pleasant evening by something and someone she wanted to forget. She was angry with Bart; he could have waited until morning, couldn't he? But of course he couldn't. The message was urgent or Harold wouldn't have sent it; but what exactly did it mean? Bart reached for the paper.

"Okay, you've seen it and I've done my legal duty. Now let's tear it up and forget it."

"No." She extracted the telegram from his grasp. "You're being silly and prejudiced, darling. Something's happened and he's trying to warn me."

"Frighten you, you mean. It's just part of his campaign of psychological warfare, like forcing you into a divorce at the worst time possible for you, and warning you about little green men hiding in the bushes. The man's on a boat, goddamn it! What could happen on a tanker down in the Caribbean that can affect you up here in the slightest?"

"They call them ships, darling. And ships go into ports; he was supposed to land somewhere in Venezuela, remember?"

"A place called Puerto la Cruz that isn't even on the ordinary maps. I looked it up out of curiosity. I had to use a big atlas to find it." Bart's voice was impatient. "So what could possibly occur in a distant little tropical seaport that would justify a cryptic scare-message like . . ."

His voice seemed to fade away. She had just reread the telegram while he was talking and found the *real* message it contained. It gave her a strange breathless feeling like an astronomer suddenly receiving a decipherable signal from a distant star. The warning itself, that was nothing. Well, that was not quite true, of course. It meant that Harold had found real evidence of danger, more than just the mysterious surveillance he'd warned her about; and there had been that Honda that she had, she thought, seen behind her several times the last few days, but she'd told herself she was just jittery and the Japanese had probably made a million little cars that silver-gray color. When she'd once actually stopped to make sure, one way or another, the gray car that had come past had been the larger Accord and not the tiny Civic she'd been certain she'd seen earlier, so it had obviously all been imagination and coincidence, or so she'd decided at the time, but maybe she should reconsider that decision now.

Anyway, Harold's new warning was thoughtful and the fact that he'd asked her to be careful was also nice since that had not been necessary except for emphasis. But there was that one totally superfluous, intimate, almost pleading little word that made the whole message quite different from a mere dutiful warning from a former husband to an ex-wife toward whom he felt a slight obligation for old times' sake.

There had been absolutely no need for him to say please.

She was angrily aware that tears had come to her eyes. I wasn't *fair*, she thought desperately. From thousands of miles away, however far it was down there, he was telling her he still cared and he had no right to care, he'd thrown away his right to care. *Please* be careful, indeed! Why hadn't he just put a darling on the end and made his lousy mushy long-range sentimental worrying about her obvious to everybody who read his lousy wireless. *Please be careful darling* was, she knew, the complete message she was supposed to read regardless of what was on the paper, and what *right* did he have to send it to her now? Who the hell cared if he cared *now?* It was too late for him to care, dammit. It was too late for him to tear her up like this with his goddamn caring; she was doing all right without it, she was doing just fine, thanks, and he could damn well just leave her alone. If he'd *really* cared, he wouldn't have rejected her so brutally when she needed him so badly, no matter how terribly he'd been hurt and whose fault it had been.

She started to crumple the paper and hurl it away from her, and checked herself. She wasn't even going to give him, wherever he was, the satisfaction of having her make a conspicuous fool of herself. She smoothed it out and folded it carefully and put it into her purse, blinking to clear her eyes before she looked at Bart, hoping that her glasses prevented him from seeing the moist shiny evidence of her stupid tears.

"You're right, darling," she said firmly. "He's just being silly and paranoid. Is it permitted for the lady to have another drink?"

Surprisingly, it turned out to be a very happy dinner after such a bad start. He was really a very enjoyable companion and, with two daiquiris inside her, she was quite bright and witty, too. Afterwards they came out into the cool night under the lights still laughing at something that had been said, and when she started to turn toward the parking lot he took her arm gently.

"Let's go take a look at the boats," he said. When she hesitated, suddenly uneasy, he said quickly, reading her mind: "Even if there's something to it, which I don't believe for a moment, nobody's going to bother you here with all these lights and people." He grinned boyishly. "Anyway, I won't let them."

"All right, let's look at boats," she said, knowing that they weren't talking about boats at all.

She wanted to remind him that they didn't have all the time in the world if they were going to catch the movie; then she realized that this, too, was quite irrelevant. Don't be stupid, Nancy dear, she told herself severely. She walked beside him along the water, past the boats moored stern to the sea wall, their bows secured to pilings out in the water; and she let him draw her behind one of the concrete supports of the roof that covered this section of the dock. Actually, she remembered, there was a kind of scenic observation deck and walk up there. Then she was being kissed the way a girl should be kissed, no more of those restrained little gentlemanly good-night pecks she'd been getting; and he was doing something to her blouse but he stopped when she made an involuntary sound he took for a protest. She wondered if they could be seen from the restaurant windows above, but she didn't really care as she captured his retreating hand and led it back along the path it had already cleared to where it wanted to go, pleased that she'd had sense enough not to wear a brassiere. Their lips met eagerly once more and she found herself responding the way a girl should respond, all trauma forgotten.

"Would you . . . mind very much missing the movie?" he whispered.

His hand was warm on her breast inside her immodestly unbuttoned blouse, much bolder and more explicit than his hesitant words. It was no time to laugh, she warned herself; but for a sophisticated legal genius he was really a very funny boy.

"No," she answered gravely, "no, darling, I wouldn't mind a bit."

He stepped back, withdrawing his hand, and looked down and, rather clumsily, fastened up her shirt once more. Then he looked up with a question in his eyes; and suddenly they were laughing and running hand in hand across the parking lot to where they'd left his car; and as they came around the end of the last row they saw that it was blocked. Parked squarely across the rear of it so it could not be backed from the curb was a small gray Honda. Bart started forward.

"What the hell . . . ?"

"Bart, no!"

Suddenly ice cold, she clutched his fingers, still linked with hers, and tried to hold him back, but he pulled free and marched angrily toward his immobilized vehicle, while she stood where he had left her looking around fearfully for the trap she knew was here.

"Bart, please come back!" she called. "Please! We've got to . . ."

There was only one refuge: the restaurant a hundred yards away. There was only one sensible thing to do: run like hell in that direction hoping to meet people, cars, anything. Then she realized that it was all right for her to run. It was all right to leave him; nobody wanted to harm J. Barton Leonard. If she fled she would not be betraying him as she'd once betrayed somebody else, or he'd thought she had. In fact, she'd probably be leading danger away from him. She turned to run and stopped, going sick and weak inside. Her retreat was cut off. A large dark form, actually quite black against the lights of the restaurant building, had come out from between two of the parked cars they'd just passed and was moving deliberately toward her.

She did not have to see it clearly, of course. She knew it too well. In some ways she knew more about this blond giant of a man—tonight there was no ski-mask to hide the hair—than she did about the man who'd just kissed her passionately; and in some ways this stranger, if he could still be called that after what he'd done to her, knew more about her than Bart did, too. He knew, for instance, that she was, or had been, a normal healthy girl with normal healthy reactions over which she did not always have complete control. She remembered what she'd spent seven months trying to forget, how he had laughed triumphantly when, his great weight crushing her, he had wrung that obscene bit of information from her disobedient body. . . .

She started to cry out to Bart for help but checked herself; she'd once got another man cruelly beaten, and big as Bart was, she did not think he was a match for the huge individual who was now stalking her. It seemed crazy that people should still be having dinner in the restaurant so close, and chatting on board the boats in the marina; and that cars could still be driving peacefully, lights on, along distant Biscayne Boulevard. Scream, you stupid wench, she told herself, yell your silly head off, help, help, help. But her throat seemed to be blocked and no sounds came, as she slipped between two of the parked cars and fled accross the sidewalk and the grass beyond, hearing her pursuer crash heavily against one of the cars as he forced his bulk through the narrow space behind her.

"Hey, you!" That was Bart's voice. "Leave her alone, damn you!"

She had time for a premonition of total disaster before she heard the sound of the blow, like an axe chopping wood. She knew that her only salvation was to keep running but she couldn't. She stopped and turned to look; and she'd seen this movie before, one man down and the other moving in purposefully, only this time there was a smaller gun in the murderous hand, aimed down, and killing was obviously intended. She found herself racing back there breathlessly and hurling herself against the massive figure, reaching for the gun barrel to wrench it aside as the shot crashed. Then, startled by her own success, she had the weapon in her grasp and she was pulling and twisting with both hands and one of the big man's fingers was caught in the trigger guard and he was roaring with pain like an animal.

Something snapped and the revolver, or was it a pistol or automatic, she had no idea what the different nasty things were called, came clear, and she backed away with it and reversed it, holding it two-handed as she'd seen it done on TV, finding the trigger and seeing the man she'd hated for over half a year over the shiny blue barrel—and dear God she couldn't do it. Everything she'd ever read, everything she'd ever heard, everything she'd ever been taught to believe, told her it was a criminal immoral action she *must* not take. . . .

The first furious blow knocked the weapon flying from her hands. The second snapped her head back viciously and sent her staggering backwards. She caught herself but kept retreating blindly, stunned and shocked and helpless before the savage onslaught, struck again and again, until something caught her heel and a final blow whipped her around as she started to fall, so that, in spite of scrambling instinctively to catch herself, she found herself sprawling headlong, feeling the pavement of a park walk rip her hands and knees as she went down. She lay there for a little while quite dazed, only half conscious really, trying feebly to push herself off the ground, distantly aware that she was choking and coughing and gasping and retching in a very unattractive manner—it seemed to be happening to somebody else. She got it stopped. Strangely disoriented and seriously concerned about the damage she must have done to her nice clothes sliding along the ground on her stomach in a totally undignified fashion like a kid missing a football tackle, for God's sake, she managed to sit up at last.

Her purse was gone, of course; she'd dropped that when she ran to Bart's assistance. Now her glasses were also gone and the park lights had turned all fuzzy and something was seriously wrong, she knew that something incredibly rude and wicked had been done to her, but all she could see at first, sitting stupidly in the middle of a walk in a public park, was her skinned knees ridiculously protruding from gaping rents in what had a moment before been a very handsome and expensive pair of slacks. She was dismayed to find herself rubbing her hurt hands on her expensive white silk shirt, again like a heedless scrimmaging kid instead of a responsible woman. Looking down worriedly, she was startled to discover that the shirt, badly disordered by her fall of course, wasn't even white any longer. The front was redly soaked with blood in quantities that couldn't possibly have come from a pair of mildly lacerated palms.

Then the strange dead numbness that she'd been trying to ignore faded, and the pain came, forcing her to confront at last the truth she did not want and had been trying very hard to reject. Uncertainly, fearfully, she raised her hands to her face and, aghast, took them down again and stared with disbelief at her dripping fingers because they'd found nothing familiar to touch. A wild scream of incredulous protest formed in her mind. She'd known that she'd been hit of course, even rather badly beaten; she'd simply done her best, helped by shock, to erase the unacceptable memory. She'd been vaguely prepared to accept the fact that, as once before, she'd have to live with some ugly, embarrassing disfigurement for a while if she lived at all—why was a black eye always good for a laugh?—but she'd never conceived of the possibility that she might have been destroyed.

But she had no time to give voice to the terrified scream inside her. The man had paused briefly to examine a hand with a finger that stuck out at a sickening angle. It was the pain of hitting her repeatedly, heedlessly, with such a hand that had stopped him at last and turned him, she sensed, a little crazy. But now he was coming again and she found herself crawling from him weakly, and scuttling on hands and knees, and finally running, if you could call her stumbling progress running; and blood from her face was splashing everywhere, getting all over everything. She saw the prize of the ghoulish race and hurled herself upon it, heedless of the further damage to her spattered clothes, grasping it and rolling to avoid the kicks she knew were seeking her and finally, clear for a moment, bringing up half-sitting against a neatly painted trash container, thrusting out the gun.

Everything was sharp and clear despite the lost glasses and the throbbing, steadily growing, pain. She could see the monstrous figure confronting her, its great thighs bulging in greasy jeans, its great chest heaving under a blue work shirt; and the really frightening thing was the way, stopped by the gun's threat, the man had turned to examining his broken finger again with childlike concentration, trying to straighten it and whimpering when it hurt, like a great bear with a wounded paw.

As she pushed herself to her feet cautiously, still aiming the gun, she tried not to look down, not really wanting to see—not that it mattered now—all the awful things that had happened to the rather becoming costume on which, a lifetime ago, she'd expended considerable thought and care, but she caught a horrifying glimpse of herself anyway, suddenly all rags and dirt and blood. She had a ridiculous impulse to apologize to Bart because his date was making such a disgusting spectacle of herself. . . . Bart. She looked for him and knew a tremendous relief when she saw him sitting up, back there where he'd been left, clutching a wounded leg with both hands. Only his leg, thank God; apparently she'd been in time to deflect the murderous bullet a little, perhaps enough.

She was, she told herself, glad, glad, glad that he was alive and would probably be all right and that was one life she was not responsible for damaging permanently—well, if she could keep death away from him now. Suddenly she knew what the gun was for. She realized why she'd reclaimed it after losing it once. It was not for her; she'd already proved that she was incapable of using it merely to save herself; but Bart could still be saved. Not that she loved him so much, she wasn't even sure at this moment that she loved him at all, but she had to preserve him now, she knew, to make up a little for what she'd once in her arrogant self-righteousness done, or allowed to be done, to somebody else. . . .

She found her thoughts coming with surprising clarity. She told herself firmly that she did not scorn Bart for just sitting there; after all he *had* tried and he *was* wounded. But she could not help remembering someone who, she knew with absolute certainty, would have come to her now if he'd had to drag himself with a broken back because that, she understood at last, was what *macho* was for and what love was for.

284

A cry of hopeless grief sounded inside her: *Oh, my darling, how could we do everything so wrong?*

But now the big man was coming on again, enraged, like a great beast bound to finish destroying what had hurt it. She knew that the gun could not save her now and that she didn't really want it to. The pain was becoming too much to endure. Why were hurt noses supposed to be funny? This shocking, brutal injury wasn't funny at all, it was agonizing; and she could hardly breathe without choking on her blood. She could hardly see for the quick swelling of the fearfully battered flesh around her eyes, and she was becoming horribly aware of her shattered mouth: the torn lips, the broken teeth, and the ghastly, unbelievable gaps where there were no longer any teeth. She tried not to think of how she must look, unrecognizable, a revolting blood-soaked scarecrow with a nightmare face; she hoped Bart was too far away to realize what a dreadful human wreck had so quickly been made of the attractive girl he'd kissed. It was unbearable to think of him seeing her like this, remembering her like this. . . .

But the terrified scream of protest had died within her. Now there was only the strange lost feeling of knowing that she was damaged beyond repair; that this time they could never really put Nancy Winters back together again no matter how hard they tried; and that she couldn't even bear to have them try. She wanted to cry for the waste of it. Of her. It isn't fair, she thought, I had it made, I was almost well after that awful business last fall, and now this! I can't go through it all again, I *can't!*

She couldn't endure that agony of healing and rehabilitation again. She couldn't learn to live all over again for the second time, this time with a face ruined by those massive fists and a mind ruined by this pain and horror and ugly, bloody degradation. And this evil had to be stopped, and not only for Bart's sake; it simply couldn't be permitted to go on and on defiling and destroying. . . .

He was coming and, knowing that she had no marksmanship at all, she waited to make quite certain; waited for the great hands—this time ignoring the gun as she'd known they would; the man was quite mad with his own pain and fury—to close fondly about her throat, their strength seemingly unimpaired by the injured finger. Then she pushed the weapon lovingly against the great body and began to fire, changing the angle a little for each shot until, just as the final welcome blackness came, the last cartridge discharged well to her right, his left, tearing through his great ugly heart.

CHAPTER 28

June

Latitude 12°N; Longitude 60°W

It was crowded and tricky around Aruba, and Harold Ullman stayed on the bridge of the *Petrox Prince* watching the young third mate, Amadeo Fiorenzo, set up the traffic problems on the elaborate collision-avoidance computer that was, at the moment, working off the big S-band radar—the equally big X-band instrument gave a better picture in bad weather conditions but today was bright and clear.

"You see this one," the third mate said, pointing to a circled bright dot on the computer screen that represented an approaching ship. "There he is, look, out there to starboard. That one we must avoid so I will turn a bit to port, so, but not enough to disturb this one passing off the port quarter. The computer tells me how far I can turn without coming onto a collision course. . . ."

The *Prince* was a very international ship. Fairly new, she'd been built somewhere in the Orient, she was registered in Liberia, she sailed for an American company, and she was crewed wholly by Italians—fortunately for Harold Ullman, who didn't know the language, the officers and some of the men spoke pretty good English. The fact that he knew a little about the sea had led them to accept him and demonstrate for him all the elaborate nautical gadgetry of which they were very proud. It made him feel guilty, knowing that the magazine that had sent him here wasn't interested in their gadgets. Well, that was not quite true. Strictly speaking, the magazine people weren't interested in the stuff as long as it worked, but they hoped it would stop working dramatically and that he could get some spectacular pictures of it not working.

Well, he could give the *Prince* a clean bill of health in the navigation department even if it did make the bloodthirsty New York landlubbers weep bitterly into their dry martinis—they'd been quite certain that all flag-of-convenience ships were broken-down rust-buckets with inadequate or inoperative navigation gear, sailed by drunken or lazy incompetents. They'd hoped they were putting him aboard another *Argo Merchant* that simply hadn't managed to run aground yet; and he knew they'd be overjoyed if, somehow, he could manage to put the tanker on the rocks for the benefit of his camera and their crusading publication. Well, the way an editor expected things to be was very seldom the way things actually were. Of course the photographer who got rich was the one who could make them look that way, one way or another. After spending months in and around hospitals, Ullman reflected grimly, the way to resume an interrupted photojournalistic career and pay his bills was *not* to shatter the preconceived notions of people who were willing to shell out good money to implement their noble campaign against the ogre petroleum and all who trafficked in the nasty, slippery stuff. . . .

"So," said Fiorenzo, setting the new course with a fractional turn of the autopilot knob. "Now you will see that we will pass well clear."

"I could use that thing on my boat," Harold Ullman said, glancing at the massive computer. "The only trouble is, it must weigh a ton, it would sink her like a rock. . . . Good morning, Captain."

Captain Giuseppe Martino was tall and dark and youthful, wearing comfortable slacks and a faded sports shirt—there were no uniforms on this ship, and there appeared to be not much discipline either; but Harold Ullman had noticed that things seemed to get done and that the captain seldom found it necessary to repeat an order, although he never raised his voice. Everything was always accomplished in a very friendly fashion, but there was never any doubt who was in charge. Now Captain Martino, after replying to their greetings, wandered out onto the open wing of the bridge briefly, and then came back to glance at the screens of the computer and the operating radar. He paused beside Harold Ullman.

"Tomorrow, Panama," he said. "You have been through the Canal, Mr. Ullman?"

"As a matter of fact I haven't, Captain."

Martino grinned boyishly. "Well, as a matter of fact, neither have I. This is a new run for the ship. We will learn together, no?"

He asked Fiorenzo a question in Italian, nodded at the answer, and left the bridge. It had been nicely done. On the much smaller private vessels with which he was acquainted, Harold Ullman had known many skippers—and he had to admit that he was probably one—who couldn't bear to delegate authority in a tough situation; but Martino had simply demonstrated his availability and at the same time his complete faith in the ability of the young third mate to take the ship safely through these busy waters.

Then they were past the Dutch island with its gleaming tanks and refineries, past the anchored tankers waiting for orders and cargoes; and they had the Caribbean Sea to themselves once more. The collision-avoidance system was switched off, but the radar stayed on, its screen showing the shape of the South American continent to port, invisible over the horizon.

"What time tomorrow are we supposed to hit Cristobal?" Harold Ullman asked.

"We should be in the harbor well before noon," Fiorenzo said. "But when they will send us the Canal pilot, who knows? It depends on how many ships are ahead of us. If we don't have to wait too long, we should be able to make the transit in daylight, but I'm told there are sometimes big delays."

Harold Ullman said, "Well, I guess I'll take a little hike up forward before lunch. Now that we're heading west, I want to get some shots of those windlasses in the bow with the light on them."

"Soon you will have this whole ship on film, Mr. Ullman."

"That's the general idea."

A long catwalk connected the poop deck, as it was called—the second story, so to speak, of the superstructure aft—with the elevated bow deck. It let you go forward easily without running the obstacle course of pipes and hatches, valves and manifolds, cranes and winches, on the main deck below. In addition to the substantial railings there were a couple of stout metal shelters along the raised steel footpath, where you could take refuge from boarding seas in that kind of weather—low as she rode when fully loaded, Ullman reflected, the *Prince* undoubtedly took a lot of solid green stuff aboard in a storm—but today everything was dry and pleasant.

In fact, when he reached the bow, Harold Ullman found himself listening for something and hearing hardly anything at all. At this distance, the better part of two hundred yards, the sound and vibration of the great Fiat diesel in the stern did not reach him. There wasn't even any wind. They were running along at fourteen knots before a fourteen-knot trade wind; the resultant breeze along the deck was zero. It was eerily warm and still there, way up forward, with twenty thousand dead-weight tons of tanker going downwind as if on rails, totally silent except for the muted rumble of the bulbous stem splitting the water far below.

He concentrated on photographing, carefully and thoroughly, the big steam winches that handled the anchor chains and could also be used for warping the ship into a dock. A little complicated technical stuff often looked good on the page, making a nice contrast to ocean views with blue skies and puffy trade-wind clouds. Besides, the machinery looked a little rusty—inevitable when you combined hot steam with a corrosive seawater environment—but the magazine would take it for a sign of neglect and think it was great.

Actually, he was wrestling with his conscience and getting nowhere. Don't be a goddamned sentimentalist, he told himself severely; you're here to do a job, a hatchet job, and even though they're pretty good, pretty careful, you can find enough stuff to crucify them if you really try. Like a rusty winch. And that Butterworth machine they use to clean the tanks overboard. And the Loran A that isn't working—never mind that that navigational system is practically obsolete and the new Loran C is doing fine, and the ADF is lovely, and the first mate is a genius with a sextant and could bring us home with all the electronics out. It isn't as if you'd come aboard under false pretenses, remember? They know whom you work for; they didn't have to let you on the ship. But why did they have to be such a nice bunch of guys and good seamen to boot?

Irritably, he rewound the exposed film and reloaded. Then he climbed down the ladder to the main deck and made his way aft, picking up a few shots down there. He stopped outside the pump room, located under the poop deck, to say hello to one of the motormen named Lorenzo, who'd just come up for air, he said; he'd been down in the bowels of the ship overhauling one of the big oil-transfer pumps.

"Trouble, always trouble," Lorenzo said lugubriously, wiping his hands on some greasy waste. "Always some pump all wrong, no?"

Again, Ullman reflected sourly, evidence he could use to convince the goddamn editorial landlubbers what a falling-apart tub the *Prince* really was; where a seaman would know that there was always something all wrong on any ship, even the newest, even the smallest. Hell, he could think of a handful of unsolved problems on his own twenty-eight-foot sailboat, and when he got those taken care of, there would undoubtedly be something else to worry about. Ships were like that, and griping sailors were like that, too; and with the number of pumps a tanker carried, it would be a real miracle if they all worked at the same time, but of course you didn't have to go out of your way to tell the dear magazine reader that. . . .

Back in his cabin he laid the camera aside and took care of the exposed roll of film, stowing it with the others in the protective container in his suitcase. He made suitable entries in his notebook; and then found his pipe and loaded and lit it—his goddamn virility symbol according to Nancy, and in a way he had to admit that it was. At least it was a protest, but not only against her. He was damned if he was going to be browbeaten into quitting smoking by a lot of idealistic jerks bent on saving everybody from everything. Whose goddamned emphysema was it, anyway? He was getting sick and tired of people trying to preserve his life against his will. Seatbelt lights and safety bumpers and maybe airbags soon and certainly all that expensive and bulky crap the Coast Guard made him lug around on his boat that might just possibly save him some day but never had yet; and pretty soon you wouldn't be able to go out a door without signing an affidavit to the effect that you'd been informed that the sunlight outside was a deadly carcinogen and dangerous to your health, as of course it was. And what the hell's the matter with you today, Mr. Ullman?

But he knew what the matter was. He was goddamned lonely, that was what the matter was; and the fact that it was a basic and fundamental loneliness he'd inflicted on himself in his haste and hurt and anger didn't help a bit. But it was something that did not bear thinking of here, cruising off another continent, so he thought instead about the broken camera he'd jettisoned over the side when nobody was looking and the crude knife stowed away in his suitcase with the films, clear evidence that somebody wanted him dead, but who? In any case, he'd damned well better watch himself if he went ashore in Panama City, but what about the Canal? To think of somebody laying for him along the bank with a long-range rifle seemed melodramatic as hell—he didn't even know if it was geographically and politically possible—and to stay under cover and pass up all those spectacular canal shots he'd been looking forward to taking, which the client would expect to see, although he might not use them, seemed utterly ridiculous; but still there had been one attempt and it had to be presumed that if somebody was prepared to kill him with a knife they wouldn't hesitate to use a firearm if necessary. And it would be nice to live at least long enough to attain that cancer ward Nancy'd always been predicting for him, and why the hell couldn't he keep her out of his mind today. . . .?

The knock on the door startled him. He got up from the couch on which he'd been reclining, smoking, and thinking, and went over to open.

"Hi, Cesare," he said. "Come on in. What have you got for me there?"

But the chunky, dark little radio operator did not immediately hand over the flimsy he was holding. His face was troubled.

"*Notizia grava,* Mr. Ullman," he said warningly. "Very serious, sir."

Harold Ullman felt a black premonition go through him like a wave of nausea; and he knew almost exactly what he was going to read as he took the wireless message from Cesare Pasquale's reluctant fingers and unfolded and read it.

REGRET INFORM YOU NANCY WINTERS MURDERED BARTON LEONARD INJURED REQUEST YOU RETURN MIAMI SOONEST GRIMES

Who the hell was Grimes, was his first clear thought, but Grimes was just one of the lawyer-boys and who cared? He was merely stalling. He was trying not to face the knowledge with which he would have to spend the rest of his life: they had done such terrible things to each other and now it was forever too late to make amends.

CHAPTER 29

June

Latitude 9°N; Longitude 80°W

Studying herself critically in the mirror, in her room in Panama City's Holiday Inn, Mrs. Emma Bessemer (U.S. Passport #323474) wondered if it was time, yet, for the major transformation she had in mind. All the materials were in her luggage, including the long brunette wig and the brown-eyed contact lenses and the cheap, fluffy, girlish stuff to wear, but she didn't want to make the switch prematurely. After all, there had been no indication yet that anybody was looking for a tall, tailored-pantsuit blonde, whether that fair lady with the smoothly drawn-back golden hair was a willowy Yankee dame called Gloria Farnsworth or a cold Norwegian *fru* named Frieda (Mrs. Einar) Johanssen—or the gracious, glamorous, wealthy Mrs. Bessemer. You had to hand it to them though, she reflected, for a bunch of creepy patriots, spelled kooks, they were quick with the phony passports. She still had one in reserve, the one that went with the wig, but if she never saw that little big-headed freak again, with the beautiful dark devil-face, it would be too damned soon.

In fact, if she never saw any of them again it would be too soon, and that went for Mr. Hans Rurik Olson and his big fists and that other part of him that was also sizeable. She'd finally made up her mind. Now she regarded herself in the mirror and touched her cheek with a gentle finger and thought: you're a pretty thing and I like you just the way you are and you've played that dangerous game *quite* long enough, sweetheart. Not that it hasn't been a great game, an exciting game, and worth every risk now that you're out of it with a whole skin—and he *did* help back when you were feeling really down and needed help badly—but the guy is nuts, you know he's nuts, and so goddamn strong, and he's going to kill somebody one of these days—in fact, I think he already has, some whore somewhere, from what he said once when he was drunk, at least he busted her up very badly, I think.

So far he's controlled himself with you—well, within the very lenient rules of that crazy wild sexy game the two of you played together—but one day the leash will slip and the beast will be loose and that will be the end of your pretty face and maybe even your pretty you. It was fun, like a bullfight kind of, a long lovely sexy bullfight, but now it's time for you to leave and stay left. Just do this one last thing for him in payment for what he did for you that time when you were ready to cut your throat, and everybody will be square with everybody. Always leave them smiling; and where the hell is that funny jakey Crown guy, anyway? He said he'd be back soon. She smoothed her tailored white linen jacket over her sharply creased white linen pants—a nice crisp tropical-looking costume, she thought with satisfaction—and readjusted once more the fragile blue scarf at her throat.

It had been strange being in touch with Chicago once more after all the years, kind of like old home week. Varsi had still been there, of course, guarding the phone—and everything else—for Boss; and she remembered that it had taken her a ridiculously long time, all those years ago, to realize that was a name and not a title. Herman Boss. She'd really been a pretty dumb kid. And Varsi had not forgotten the time that rather husky dumb hayseed girl from Wisconsin named Greta Fogelquist, who'd been hired in the office, one of their offices, as secretary and kind of assistant accountant—she'd had some business-school training that way—had floored him with a strong right to the eye when he thought he'd do her a great big masculine favor out of the simple kindness of his heart. He hadn't forgotten, either, how Boss had come in just then to find that breathless scared blonde kid all braced to swing again and his Number Two nursing a fast-blooming shiner; and Boss had laughed like hell at both of them, his great rumbling laugh. But then he'd looked again and seen something promising under the tight ugly slacks and the cheap frilly blouse and the frizzy hairdo—and she'd had sense enough to keep her fists to herself when that invitation came.

No, Varsi hadn't forgotten; but the feud had been dormant a long time. Ever since Boss had discovered that she was really very useful in the office where he'd found her, as well as elsewhere—she'd had that knack with numbers; she wondered if she still had it—and had put her in charge of certain books and ledgers; and finally the day had come when he'd told her, with honest regret, that she had to vanish now because of what she'd learned and because of what the Feds were up to, and Varsi had, of course, had his own idea of how her disappearance should be arranged. But he, Boss, was willing to gamble on her loyalty, so if she'd simply change her name and drop out of sight according to certain instructions, and forget, he'd see that she was always taken care of. They'd both kept the bargain; and nowadays Varsi was willing to admit that maybe he'd made a mistake, but he'd never forgotten completely, not Varsi.

He'd been very suspicious, of course, when she called a few days back; maybe he'd even hoped, a little, that she was going to prove him right after all by trying to cash in on what she knew, even though it was pretty obsolete knowledge by now. But she'd given him the straight proposition: a little good-bye help with something she had to do and they could, in Chicago, forget altogether about that girl who'd once been called Greta Fogelquist who'd come to know a little too much, and save themselves all that tricky bookkeeping—she'd always wondered how those regular secret disbursements had been entered in the account. It had been the smart move anyway, she reflected. Boss couldn't be expected to live forever or even remember forever if he did live, not when she was no longer a real threat; and this way she wiped out a couple of debts at the same time, Boss's to her and hers to Olson, and walked away free and clear.

Varsi had taken her proposition to Boss and Boss had said okay; but the Venezuelan clown to whom they'd sent her in Puerto la Cruz had tried to get by with supplying bargain-basement manpower that let itself be run off, for Christ's sake, by a redheaded punk swinging a lousy camera. _Señor_ Goddamned Dominguez had been very apologetic over the phone when she'd called from Caracas to check on how it had gone; and he damn well should have been. So she'd had to call Chicago again and this time, to get rid of her probably, they'd offered her the best, Crown, explaining that he'd been down in Mexico cooling off after some rather tricky employment, and had then been sent to Colombia to take care of a little matter there involving a local _jefe_ who'd got a bit greedy with respect to the merchandise passing through his territory. He'd had to be shown, and others of his breed, that no matter how much *mordida* you managed to collect you could never, never take it with you and it was always better to keep your demands on the modest, or at least reasonable, side.

Crown was apparently in business for himself these days, an independent contractor so to speak—and the pun was damn well intentional—and he wasn't working out of Chicago any more, but he was still always available to Boss, Varsi had indicated, and they'd pass him the word. And they had, and he'd come, faster than she'd hoped. It had been strange seeing him again after what had been between them. He was no longer the shy gangling country kid awed by the glamorous blonde lady she'd become by the time he'd turned up in Chicago, who was well known to be Herman Boss's private property. She supposed she could be said to have seduced him, intrigued by the contrast between his diffident cowboy manner that seemed to have been patterned directly on Gary Cooper, and the reputation for skillful violence he'd already acquired; and Boss had had a little infidelity coming, goddamn it, the way he played around. But she did not think either Boss or Varsi had known about it or they would have used it against her long ago, or against Cowboy Johnny Crown.

But he hadn't changed all that much, she reflected, giving some final touches to her hair. He was still a tall lean figure with very bright blue eyes—maybe a little too pale and bright for comfort—and sandy hair and eyebrows and even eyelashes, who walked with a rolling gait as if he'd just stepped off a horse after a long ride. He didn't wear high-heeled boots and a big hat these days, but his pants still fit low on his narrow hips like jeans even though they weren't jeans. She could see him clearly, stopping inside the hotel room door this morning, right over there, frowning as if he thought somebody was playing a trick on him and he didn't like it.

"They didn't tell me Mrs. Bessemer was you, ma'am," he'd said rather stiffly.

"Would you have come if they had?"

He'd looked surprised by the question. "I told you once, when you had to leave like that, all you ever had to do was call if you needed me. But you never did."

She hadn't expected him to remember that after the time that had passed. Promises like that tended to get conveniently forgotten. People like that, people who remembered their promises over the years, didn't really exist—but perhaps they did. After all, she'd kept her word to Boss and Boss had kept his to her, and you could sneer all you wanted at honor among thieves, but maybe it wasn't quite such a lousy world after all.

"Thanks, Crown," she'd said. "That was nice. I liked that."

But he hadn't been ready for it, not for sentiment, not yet, and he'd said brusquely: "Tell me about it. Varsi says you've already botched it once and spooked the game. That should make it worth more to somebody."

"I don't have your kind of money, Crown. You're dealing with them. Put it to them."

He'd grinned abruptly. "Forgive me, ma'am. It's a habit. A man's got to keep trying it out. If he doesn't, they'll think he's going soft and they can get him cheap. You're looking real good these days, if you don't mind my saying so."

"No woman minds hearing that. You're looking pretty good yourself. Well, there's a ship passing through the Canal, probably tomorrow, a tanker, twenty thousand tons, called the *Petrox Prince*. The man you want is youngish, has red hair, and will probably be hung all over with cameras like Christmas tree ornaments. They'll be tying up at the Balboa docks down by the highway bridge to unload some oil; and there's a good chance he'll come into town with the ship's officers in the evening, he did in Puerto la Cruz. I'm told those sailor guys generally wind up in one of the casinos, probably the one in the Hotel Panama, whenever they have a free night here. Of course, where you want to do it is up to you."

He'd asked some questions, which she'd answered to the best of her ability, and he'd left saying he would probably be gone all day. Now in the evening she was waiting for him to return and, she realized, fussing with her goddamn hair and her goddamn scarf and her handsome new goddamn ice cream suit like a jittery young girl waiting to be taken to her first high-school prom. She wanted a drink very badly but he was kind of a funny innocent guy about women, or had been, and although she had a bottle in her luggage she didn't want to greet him half-sloshed with a glass in her hand, although there were lots of men who preferred their girls well-wined and wispy and willing.

But when he came at last, after dark, he wasn't just a gangly cowboy type with a cute lock of sandy hair falling over his forehead, all ready to respond shyly as he once had to the experienced charms of an older woman—and she wasn't really all that much older, not enough to make any difference now. But tonight he was a cold and preoccupied professional considering tomorrow's professional operation and she could have been standing there naked and it would have meant nothing to him. So they had dinner together, which wasn't very smart perhaps, but she had her brunette identity in reserve and he undoubtedly had some inconspicuous cover to fall back on, and who was seen with whom in Panama wasn't likely to make much difference elsewhere, if elsewhere was far enough away as she intended it to be very soon.

She answered his further questions as well as she could, and had her drink now that it would not label her as an unladylike hotel room lush, and watched him working it out in his head across the table. Arizona, she remembered, born in Flagstaff, wherever that might be. A real honest-to-God cowboy and then rodeo stuff. Then a stint as a trickshot artist with a carnival, knocking the ashes out of a cigarette in a pretty assistant's mouth, breaking a handful of glass balls she tossed before they hit the ground, that kind of fancy stuff. One of the naturals, she'd been told when she asked, and it seemed a funny thing to be natural at, as if all the endless centuries of human development had been aimed only at producing a creature that could instinctively master that fairly modern invention, the firearm. But anything that went bang, apparently, he could shoot it and shoot it well. And then volunteering for Vietnam, for Christ's sake, totally sincere about fighting for his country in that dumb, pointless hassle.

That was what had done it to Johnny Crown, of course; not the killing over there, although they gave him every medal they had, being so goddamned happy to have at least one soldier who shot straight and loved it and thought they were great guys for providing him with all those fine guns and lovely targets. But when he came back, instead of a ticker-tape parade, he got a lot of crap about being a uniformed murderer sneaking home from a dirty war with bloody hands. There was also the fact that nobody'd give him a decent job, medals or no medals.

So, disillusioned, Johnny Crown got his trickshot guns out of hock and went to Chicago because that was where the gangsters were and he thought they might have work for a man with his talents. The story was that somebody laughed at the cowboy kid from Arizona with the high-heeled boots; and strange and loud things happened very fast, and nobody laughed any more. Boss had seen his possibilities and bailed him out of that; and now he was here, Johnny Crown, and he did have that lock of sandy hair still falling into his face. He also still had that faint aura of controlled violence—that pale thing you could see in his eyes—and it was stronger now. In his way he was a hell of a lot more dangerous than Hans Rurik Olson, she reflected. For all his brutal strength, Hans wouldn't last two seconds against Crown, who'd made killing his career. The thought made her feel kind of funny way down inside; and what *was* it about her that needed that smell of danger to really . . .?

"All right," Crown said abruptly. "I think I've got it. My apologies, ma'am. I'm afraid I haven't been a very entertaining dinner companion."

"Ma'am?" she said, liking the funny polite way he talked to her. The time for sentiment had come and she reached out and touched his hand on the table. "You didn't use to call me ma'am, Johnny. . . ."

In the morning she awoke and knew at once who was beside her or, rather, who wasn't. It certainly wasn't Hans. She didn't hurt anywhere for a change; and she hadn't had any of her good clothes ruined, either. In fact, Crown had arranged them very neatly on a chair as he undressed her, and while he wasn't as funny and shy about it as he had once been, he still acted as if he considered it a real privilege. It had really been a very gentle and gentlemanly performance— well, up to a point, nobody was a gentleman beyond that point—and she wondered that a man in his profession could be so, well, tender; but of course that was what had made it good, the fact that gentle though he'd been with her—again up to those final moments when no real gentleness could exist—she'd been aware all along that this was also a man capable of killing on demand. She thought wryly: Well, I guess you don't really need a punch in the jaw to turn you on, precious, all you need is the knowledge that danger is there.

The phone rang abruptly, causing her to start. She reached over and picked it up. Varsi's voice reached her over a kind of singing connection.

"Blondie?"

"Hey, do you know what time it is here?"

"Never mind the time," Varsi said. "The word is abort. Tell the Cowboy and get him to hell out of there."

"Why?"

"You're both sticking your necks out for a guy who's dead.

Your boy in Miami tried to strangle some broad and got careless; she got his gun and put the whole damn cylinder minus one into his chest. And Dominguez says the bloodhounds are only a day or two behind you. So abort, right?"

"Right, Varsi."

"We did our part, okay?"

"Okay," she said. "Tell the man it was nice knowing him and I won't bother him again."

"I'll tell him. Blondie?"

"Yeah, Varsi."

"Take care. You're not a bad chick, for a chick."

"Sure, Varsi. You're not a bad creep, for a creep."

She heard him chuckle in that windy city all those thousands of miles to the north; then the connection was broken and she replaced the phone. She had a moment of thought, of regret, for Hans Rurik Olson, but there was really no time for that. Crown was sitting up beside her and she knew that, jolted awake by the phone, he was holding some kind of a gun under the bedclothes.

"It's leaving time," she said. "It's all off. They're baying up the trail behind me, Varsi says, or whatever bloodhounds do on a trail; and the guy I was doing it for just went and got himself dead. I've got to check out of here quick and find a place where I can switch personalities. . . ."

"I've got a place," he said. "No problem. I always set up the escape route first." After a little pause, he looked at her directly and said, "It will take two."

"Sure, Johnny," she said.

As she dressed rapidly she knew it had been, as they said, preordained; and the rest of it was also preordained clear to the end that was bound to come, considering the line of work he was in. She had a clear view of it for an instant, the smashed and machine-gunned car or maybe the bullet-riddled hide-out shack, and the two torn bodies sprawled indecently in the spreading pools of blood and other stuff, because violent death wasn't, she knew, as clean and neat as Hollywood always made it look but what the hell, they'd have some good times first, like last night, and who the hell wanted to live to be old and ugly, anyway?

CHAPTER 30

June

Latitude 26° N; Longitude 80°W

The Pan Am morning flight from Panama City brought Harold Ullman into Miami International in time for a somewhat belated lunch, which he ate right there at the airport. He hadn't informed anybody what plane he was taking or even that he was coming, to hell with them all. Nobody'd shot at him in the Canal, even though he'd deliberately given them every chance for reasons that weren't exactly clear to him; and nobody'd jumped him in Panama City when he'd gone ashore with the ship's officers as usual, unable to face spending a whole evening alone in his cabin waiting to take that morning plane. Well, alone would have been all right, but he'd known he would not be alone. The memories would have been right there with him, telling him everything he hadn't done that he should have done, everything he had done that he should have done differently or not at all, and that one particular unforgivable thing he should not have done, which, he knew, would never leave him now; and there was no way he could atone for it, ever.

And then the cruel irony of winning thirty bucks at blackjack, for God's sake, in the little casino in the big hotel, the only time in his life he'd ever come out ahead at that idiot game; and remembering the big casino in Nassau where he'd lost most of their going-home money and how nice she'd been about it and the way she'd looked, slim and brown in her little black bikini. . . . Cut it out, he warned himself sharply, now you're just milking it for tears, leave it!

After the usual tasteless airport lunch, or maybe it had been totally delicious and he'd simply been unable to taste it, he found a booth and called Bartholomew in New York and told him the decision that had kind of made itself some time during the past grim day or two. Bartholomew didn't like it at all, of course.

"You took the job, didn't you?" Bartholomew said.

"Look," Ullman said, "tell them about my wife and how I'm just too damn shook up to finish—"

"Your ex-wife," Bartholomew said coldly, "and from what you told me earlier you're the one who shed her and not the other way around, so don't overdramatize it now." When Ullman didn't speak the agent went on: "What's the matter with you, anyway? This is a big break for you; they like to use the same people and this is your *entrée*, dammit, you can't just go and kick everything overboard like this. I'm sure even if you did have to come back prematurely you covered yourself with enough shots to make a story, you always did use film like toilet paper. Get the stuff processed and take care of your business down there—I'm truly sorry about that, my boy, and I hope I wasn't out of line but somebody had to bring you to your senses—and then bring it all here and let's see what you've got. If absolutely necessary, we'll tell them you'll make another trip at your own expense to pick up what's missing. This is *important* to you, Harold, believe me."

"It's still no," Ullman said harshly. "Okay, so let's *not* be polite if you don't like it that way. Just tell them to take their lousy job and shove it. I've hurt enough people for the year; I'm right up to my annual sadist quota. I'm damned if I'm going to crucify a bunch of nice Italian boys who sail a ship real good just to make circulation for somebody's crummy magazine."

He hung up and it was very damned noble of him no doubt, and it didn't make him feel a bit better. His bad leg was aching by the time he got his suitcase and the heavy camera bag transported to the taxi stand, not to mention the awkward cane he couldn't use with both hands full and had to hang over his arm where it threatened to get between his legs and trip him. He gave the address of the parking garage where he'd stored his vehicle; and pretty soon he was trying to find curb space for the little truck he'd bought after the divorce, near the offices of Holloman, Pearson, Grimes, and Leonard, Attorneys at Law.

It was a big building and, riding the elevator to the seventh floor, he leaned against the side wishing he'd dared to have a second drink with his lunch but it had been too damned risky. He didn't feel as if he was properly in control as it was.

301

Another shot of booze and he'd probably break his cane over the head of the next clumsy oaf who jostled him on the street.

Mr. Grimes was in and the highly refined receptionist, a pale blonde in a sleek, close-fitting, matte-black dress, graciously consented to determine if Mr. Grimes would see Mr. Ullman. He would; and he came out and did the lawyer-glad-hand bit and ushered Ullman solicitously back into a very fancy paneled office with a big desk and leather-upholstered furniture—well, Naugahyde—and asked what kind of a flight Mr. Ullman had had and said it was really a terrible thing, simply terrible. He was a tall, smooth, pink-faced man who looked as if he ought to spend a little more time on the squash court and a little less time in the barber's chair.

"Well?" Ullman said at last, when the flow of soothing verbiage had dwindled to a trickle. Grimes frowned. Ullman said, "Your wireless requested me to return to Miami soonest. Here I am. What am I here for?"

"Well," Grimes said, "the police found Miss Winters' purse with that message you sent her through us and asked me to—"

"The police?" Ullman stared at him. "Your radio message didn't say anything about cops. I thought I was needed here to take care of . . . I mean, I thought there was something important . . . something I could still do for *her*."

"Oh, no, Miss Winters' parents came over from Sarasota and claimed the . . . the deceased. Under the circumstances they will, of course, make all the arrangements for proper interment."

She was slipping away from him. They'd already taken her away; soon it would be as if she'd never been.

"What you're saying, Mr. Grimes," Ullman said softly, "is that you hauled me back from the middle of an important assignment, a thousand miles and more, just to do a favor for a bunch of cops. And you couldn't even be bothered to use the word 'police' in your message so I'd know what I was coming for."

"I thought you'd be happy to do your duty as a citizen—"

"Fuck my duty as a citizen, Mr. Grimes. It's their duty as cops to keep people from being murdered and they didn't, so I don't owe them a goddamned thing. Who did it?"

"What?"

"Who killed her?"

"I gather he's been identified as a man named Olson. Hans Olson."

"A good Scandihoovián name. Was he big and blond?"

"Yes, it was apparently the same man—"

"And they've had seven months to catch him and he's still running around free and they think I can help at this late date—"

"No, not exactly, Mr. Ullman. Miss Winters managed to get the man's pistol and . . . and shoot him fatally, but too late to save herself. He was apparently a very powerful man."

It shocked him and turned him sick inside, wondering to what unimaginable depths of terror and despair she'd been brought, to be able to pull the trigger of a firearm, that dreadful homicidal device she'd so feared and hated.

"How did it happen?"

"I don't have all the details. My young associate Barton Leonard—"

"Where is Leonard?"

"He's in St. Luke's."

"Can I see him?"

"Yes, but the police particularly wanted me to make sure you got in touch with them immediately—"

"Fuck the police. What the hell do they need me for if the man's already dead?"

"They want to know how you happened to send such a timely warning—"

"It didn't do much good, apparently. Where did it happen?"

"Down in the park by the marina. Miss Winters and Leonard had been to the marina restaurant for dinner."

"Did Leonard see my message?"

"Yes, of course. That is, it was phoned in here. He had them send over a copy for him to deliver to Miss Winters."

"And after receiving my warning he let her wander around a goddamn park in the middle of the night?"

Grimes looked away. "You'll have to discuss that with Leonard."

Ullman laughed. "Sure. He probably told her to pay no attention, it's just Ullman being his usual obnoxious ex-husbandly self. Great legal advice as usual." From Grimes' expression he knew he was right. "How badly is he hurt?"

"Leonard? He has a bullet through his right thigh, a little above the knee. Fortunately, no bones were broken and no major blood vessels were involved."

___"He's a lucky little fellow, isn't he? What policeman do I see and where?"

"Captain Rader, at Headquarters."

"Captain what?"

"Spelled with an 'e'."

Ullman looked bleakly at the man behind the desk. He said, "Since you're so great on cooperating with the police, you'll undoubtedly be calling him when I leave. Tell him I'll be in as soon as I've had a talk with Leonard. He doesn't have to put out a dragnet or APB or whatever they call it; I'll be in. I hope he pats you on the head for being such a good little stoolie and making such a nice prompt report."

He rose and turned toward the door, picking up the cane. After a couple of hard days it was still useful for assisting his weak leg; and there might be other employment for it also.

"Ullman." Grimes' voice was harsh, and closer.

He didn't look back, but he stopped. "Yes?"

"I'm trying to make allowances, Ullman, but I must say I don't care for your attitude."

He turned slowly, feeling a wicked hope go through him. Grimes had come around the desk and had reached out as if intending to grab him by the shoulder if he wouldn't turn around. . . . Come on, Ullman thought happily, six inches more is all it takes, Lawyer Grimes, take a good hold, and it's just a little red-haired runt with a game leg so you can't possibly be afraid. . . . And low, he told himself, very low with the cane and the knee in the face when he doubles up and the cane again until he goes down, and then you kick the living shit out of him right there on his pretty wall-to-wall carpet; and remember that little creep in Puerto la Cruz who could have got you dead because you didn't go in hard right away *all* the way.

Something uncertain showed in Grimes' eyes, and the hand dropped. The lawyer took a careful step backwards and then walked hastily around to his chair behind the desk.

"As I say, under the circumstances I'm willing to make allowances," he said.

Ullman drew a long breath. "I'll give Barton Leonard your regards," he said.

Walking out he wondered if he would really have done it. It would have been pretty goddamn stupid and caused all kinds of trouble, certainly. But the bastards had better start keeping their goddamn hands to themselves, he thought, I've had enough of their shit, I'm not taking any more. Beat-on-Ullman week is all over, boys.

Barton Leonard didn't look very bad, which was in a way too bad. It was hard to feel sympathy for a guy who'd come out of it all with just a bandage hidden under the bedclothes. They regarded each other in silence while the nurse went out and the door closed behind her. Ullman sat down on the chair beside the bed without being invited. He told himself that recriminations were pointless. It was useless to ask the bastard why, having been warned, he hadn't been carrying a gun or something to protect the lady for whom he'd made himself responsible, if he simply had to drag her to waterfront restaurants surrounded by lonely parks and parking lots.

But obviously he hadn't believed the warning, and he probably didn't believe in guns, even though his position and contacts might have made it possible for him to procure and carry one legally under the circumstances.

"How'd you happen to go to the Green Dolphin?" Ullman asked.

"She wanted to," Leonard said. "She was trying to . . . to prove something to herself, I think. Something about you." He shrugged minutely. "I had to let her go about it her own way, Ullman. I had to let her find her own way back from . . . from where you'd sent her."

There was a challenge in that, of course, as well as a bitter truth; but Ullman disregarded it. He hadn't come here for a fight.

"Tell me what happened," he said, "if you don't mind."

"I suppose you're entitled to know," said the man in the bed, and he spoke for a while in a dull monotone, finishing with: "She died to save my life, you know. If she'd kept on running, if she hadn't turned back for my sake, she'd have been safe, he'd never have caught her. I think . . . I think she even shot him in the end so he couldn't come back and finish me off." His voice broke. "Oh, God, it was horrible, all torn and bloody like that and her face, her poor lovely face. . ."

Ullman swallowed hard and got up quickly and walked to the window and looked out at sunny Miami, which didn't look a hell of a lot different from sunny Panama except that it was bigger. He thought: He's doing it too, we're all milking it for tears to show ourselves how bad we feel; and by his own account he just sat there watching it happen with a lousy

305

little bullethole in his leg, but who are you to criticize, you weren't even there, and why weren't you there?

He said, "Thanks. I won't bother you any more. Hope it heals up okay."

Leonard's voice stopped him at the door. "You don't think much of me, do you, Ullman?"

He turned sharply and, since he'd been asked, opened his mouth to describe exactly what he thought of a stupid cowardly irresponsible sonofabitch who'd let a girl be killed after a clear warning. . . . He stopped himself sharply. Once before, badly hurt, he'd lashed out vengefully with what had seemed to be ample justification at the time; and had wound up smashing something priceless and beautiful that couldn't be replaced. Not that this jerk couldn't be replaced, they stamped them out by the millions all alike; still it was about time he, Harold Ullman, stopped going around breaking things thoughtlessly—now that it was too late.

"Hell, you did your best," he said.

The man in the bed licked his lips. "I . . . I think she loved us both," he said, apparently determined to make soap opera of it. "We just didn't deserve her," he said.

"That's right, we didn't deserve her." Ullman managed to keep his voice even. "Take care."

Captain George Rader—the full name was on the desk plaque—was a rugged-looking man of medium height with a square, lined face and crisp gray hair cut in a kind of flat-topped bush that emphasized the rugged squareness. He was in uniform with a gold badge on his chest and a revolver at his hip and handcuffs on his belt, which seemed like a lot of hardware for a man who probably spent most of his days in the office, with that rank. The desk was gray metal like the bank of filing cabinets along one wall. There was a window that looked out upon another part of the building.

"I'm very sorry you've been bothered, Mr. Ullman," Captain Rader said after shaking hands. "In fact I feel very badly about it. I hope you'll accept my apologies."

It wasn't quite the greeting he'd expected, and Ullman looked at the older man more sharply. "Apologies for what, Captain?" he asked.

"Well, I'm afraid Mr. Grimes must have misunderstood completely. It was certainly not our intention to have you make a special flight; we simply wanted to talk with you at your convenience, whenever you got back. Just to clear up the record, you know."

Incredulous anger stirred at the back of Ullman's mind. My God, he thought, hasn't he looked me up at all, doesn't he know he's talking to a *journalist,* for God's sake? Does he think I've never met a cover-up before? But what the hell can there be to cover up?

But Grimes would never have made a mistake like that. They'd wanted to question Harold Ullman at first, if only because of his obvious connection with a murder victim, but then, apparently, after investigation, they'd found some information that had led them to decide they didn't want to question him any longer, and perhaps answer his questions in return. His instinct told him that all they wanted now was to sweep the whole thing under the rug and forget it—instinct, hell. Experience. He'd met the routine too many times before in the course of his career. When they started turning away witnesses they should have welcomed eagerly, dismissing them in that polite and greasy way, it was always a definite indication that something embarrassing had turned up and the lid had been clapped on to keep it from being exposed to public view. But why did they have to make it even uglier than it already was?

"I see," he said. "So you're not interested in questioning me after all."

"Well, I wouldn't say that, Mr. Ullman. . . . Oh, please sit down. I see you're still having a little trouble from that business last fall."

Ullman hung the cane over the arm of the chair and grinned. "Hell, I just carry it so the pretty stewardesses will feel sorry for me, Captain. Nothing like a sympathetic stewardess on a long flight."

"I see what you mean, haha." The gray-haired man sat down behind the gray desk. "Well, there was a wireless message, wasn't there? A sort of warning to your wife—your ex-wife. I suppose we'd better dispose of that."

Ullman said, "I was jumped in a little Venezuelan seaport by a couple of thugs with knives. Considering everything else that had happened, I thought I'd better make sure she was being careful. Just in case somebody was after both of us."

"Yes, Mr. Leonard told us how you'd probably reasoned it out. Pretty melodramatic, really, don't you think, Mr. Ullman?"

"Maybe," Ullman said. "Having my house vandalized, my wife raped, and myself put into the hospital is also pretty

307

melodramatic, Captain. Not to mention little things like strange men following me around. When things like that happen, and when a couple of toughs then come for me with obvious homicidal intentions—"

"You don't seem to have taken much harm."

"They weren't very good. I cracked one's head with a camera and the other decided he had important business elsewhere."

"In other words," Captain Rader said judiciously, "not exactly professional talent, not the kind of people who'd normally be hired for a hit, to use the jargon." He cleared his throat. "Have you considered the possibility that what you encountered down there was merely some clumsy thieves, perhaps attracted by the camera you say you were carrying?"

"A coincidence, you mean? I'm followed up here and I'm attacked down there and the two things have absolutely nothing to do with each other or with what happened last fall?"

Captain Rader made a tent of his fingers and regarded it thoughtfully as if to determine how the design could be improved.

"You say you were followed here. Exactly what do you mean by that?"

"Shortly after I was released from the hospital, as soon as I was capable of getting around pretty well under my own power, I flew to New York on business. A man who rode up with me on the plane also rode back with me the following day. When I came to the marina to move aboard my boat—my wife got the house when we were divorced—there was a new boat in the next slip and the guy on board hadn't been cruising where he claimed to have been cruising and didn't know a boathook from a spinnaker pole. . . ."

"That would be Mr. Simonds, no doubt. Mr. William Simonds." Captain Rader laughed heartily. "Mr. Ullman, were you never a clumsy beginner on a boat, and did you never try to impress your more experienced fellow-yachtsmen with what a terribly salty fellow you really were, maybe even stretching the truth a little about the magnificent cruises you made?"

"I see," Ullman said slowly. "You've checked on Simonds?"

"Yes. You mentioned the name over the phone to Miss Winters, remember, and she repeated the conversation to Mr. Leonard. He passed it on to us and we had no trouble whatso-ever tracking Simonds down; he'd given his correct address at the marina when he checked in with his boat. I'm afraid Mr. Simonds is hardly the sinister conspirator you imagine, Mr. Ullman. In fact, he's given quite a satisfactory account of himself; and I'll add that he was very red-faced indeed when he heard what wild theories you'd built on his rather innocent sea stories that just didn't happen to be quite true."

Ullman drew a long breath. It was the old stone wall and there was never any use in beating your head against it. There was absolutely nothing to be gained by asking this gold-badge cop if he, Harold Ullman, was really supposed to believe all this bullshit—nothing to be gained and something to be lost, perhaps, by warning these clever pros that he was kind of a pro himself in his innocent photographic way, and that he was quite capable of recognizing a snow job when he saw it. He gave the man his best boyish grin.

"I see. And you think the guy on the plane was just a guy on a plane who happened to be traveling from Miami to New York and back at the same time." He shrugged casually. "Well, I'm not quite convinced, Captain, but I guess the evidence is on your side, so there's no more to be said, right?"

The rugged face across the desk looked relieved. "As I said, we're very sorry that you've come all this way for nothing, and, of course, if there's anything we can do . . ."

"Yes," Ullman said. "There is. You can let me look at the pictures."

There was a moment of silence. Captain Rader cleared his throat. "The pictures?"

"Two people were killed in a city park. Another was wounded. Are you going to tell me, Captain, that no police photographs were taken?"

The policeman shook his head. "No, I wouldn't tell you that, Mr. Ullman. I'll only tell you that you don't want to see them."

"Don't tell me what I don't want!" It came out a lot stronger and harsher than he'd intended, and he saw the automatic resentment on the cop-face across the desk and that wasn't good. Let the bastard think he had everything under control. "I'm sorry, Captain. It's been a tough couple of days. But you seem to forget what I do for a living. I've seen some pretty grim photographs and taken a few. I don't think a few more are going to kill me. I've heard enough hints from Leonard, and now you, to know it wasn't pretty. Don't let me spend the rest of my life imagining it, because I've been around a bit and I've got a very rough imagination. Let me see it the way it really was so I can put it to rest."

The policeman was studying him closely. "I hope you don't mind my saying this, Mr. Ullman, but you did divorce the girl; at least Leonard kind of implied it wasn't really her idea, although it was done from her end."

"For a lawyer, that guy runs off at the mouth, doesn't he? Okay, I made a mistake, Captain. I was sick and angry and I made a bad mistake. Given time, maybe it could have been retrieved. . . ." He shrugged. After a moment, Rader reached for the uppermost manila envelope in the filing basket on his desk. He sent it sliding toward Ullman.

"Remember, you asked, Mr. Ullman."

He had a moment to prepare himself. He told himself that he knew exactly what he was going to see. As a photographer, he'd seen it a hundred times before; he'd even taken it and developed it and printed it himself a few times, as he'd told the cop. They never died nice when they died violently; and it was going to be the same old lousy bundle-of-rags shot. . . .

Well, you asked for it, he told himself grimly, looking. Like the man said, you asked for it and now you damn well sit there and take it. You don't make one single goddamn sound for the satisfaction of Tough Copper across the desk. No moans or groans or Oh-nos or Oh-Jesuses or Oh-God-Nancys. Just keep your mouth tightly shut and *look,* goddamn you, and remember they just *think* it was a guy named Olson who did this to her a few nights ago but you know better. You know when she really died and it wasn't this week, and you know the name of the real killer and it isn't Olson.

As he looked, a picture formed in his mind even more unbearable than the pictures he was viewing—and it always looked worse in black-and-white with all that black, black blood—because this other picture could so easily have happened instead. He saw her beside the hospital bed a few months ago with the fading bruises on her face and the strange new uncertainty in her bearing and the unhappy question in her eyes to which she'd needed an answer so badly. He saw himself, not because he was noble or forgiving or any of that crap, but just because she was his wife who'd been hurt—never mind how or why—he saw himself reach out a hand to her from the bed and he saw her take it and, perhaps, press it to her cheek momentarily, her eyes wet with tears, although she wasn't really a crying girl; and she'd have known perfectly well that it didn't mean he thought her any less of a

310

dumb opinionated interfering broad for what she'd done, but she was *his* dumb opinionated interfering broad and they could fight it all out later as they'd fought out other things before; and in the meantime no matter what had happened to him he was sorry as hell about what had happened to her, sick about it, but he hoped she knew it didn't make a particle of difference to how he felt about her and never would.

But he hadn't done it like that, not he. He'd sacrificed her brutally to his rigid notions of loyal wifely behavior, just as she'd sacrificed him earlier to her rigid humanitarian ideals. . . .

Just the one little gesture so easy to make that he hadn't made, preferring instead the incredibly cruel rejection that had wrecked their last hope of saving anything at all from the disaster that had struck them, even, as it had turned out, her life. Because as her husband he wouldn't have let her die like this. He'd have respected the danger he sensed and taken some precautions. At least he wouldn't have been an ocean away when she'd needed him.

He spoke without looking up. "I'd like a copy of this one, Captain."

"Listen, you don't want." Captain Rader checked himself. "All right. Take that. We've got the negative."

Ullman slipped the other prints back into the manila envelope. Then he picked up the one he'd selected. There were still things in it he could not bear to look at directly, but he could see the slender arm in the torn white sleeve streaked with dirt—one of her good silk shirts—with the darkly blood-soaked cuff that must have got that way in the dreadful moment of discovery when, her hands to her face, she'd learned the full extent of what had been done to her while the blood ran through her fingers and down her wrists. . . . And you're as bad as that soap-opera jerk in the hospital, he told himself angrily, will you stop tormenting it now? Deliberately, although he usually had great respect for photographic prints and required it of others, he folded this one across the middle, image in, so it would slip into the side pocket of his jacket, and to hell with the crack in the nice glossy emulsion.

"Thank you, Captain," he said.

"There does seem to have been a bit of coincidence involved," the policeman said. "If they'd picked any other restaurant . . . You see, Olson kept his charter boat at that marina. He was aboard that night, apparently, having a drink in the cockpit. He had a girl but she's out of town somewhere—we haven't traced her yet—and he'd been driving her car. Anyway, we figure he must have seen this familiar-looking young lady strolling along the sea wall toward him and then stopping quickly in the shadows to consult with her escort. He must have thought she'd recognized him. Actually . . ." Rader looked embarrassed. "Actually, I believe they were necking a little, although Leonard's kind of evasive on that point. But they were late for the movie they'd planned to see, Leonard says, so in a moment they went running toward his car, and Olson must have thought they were hurrying to get out of there because they'd seen him and were scared, and he had to stop them before they could get away and call us. There's some reason to believe he'd been making a study of her habits, planning to silence her eventually, but you'd have expected him to wait until he could get her alone in a less public place. But his hand was forced or he thought it was—"

"So you think somebody *had* been following at least one of us around with hostile intentions, Captain!" Ullman interrupted. When the policeman didn't speak, he went on: "But why the hell should he feel obliged to silence her after all these months? Hell, he was wearing a mask when we saw him last fall. I don't think either of us could add much to the descriptions we gave right afterwards. Certainly there was no danger of us picking him out of a line-up or whatever you call it."

He stopped, sensing that he was on dangerous ground again; he was close to that stone wall again. Obviously, Rader had said a little more than he'd intended and was regretting it. And what the hell kind of games were they playing here, anyway?

"Yes, of course," Captain Rader said. "Well, if there's nothing else . . ."

"What about the others?" Ullman asked.

Rader frowned quickly. "I told you, we've just checked out Simonds carefully—"

"I wasn't talking about that. There were four in the gang that trashed our house that night, Captain, the big guy you call Olson, a black-haired guy with a mustache, kind of slim—well, you have my description—and two others I never saw clearly. Now that you know the leader, can't you trace his probable associates—"

They were both standing now, and Rader was coming around the desk. "Mr. Ullman, please. I'm sure you mean well, but it's not necessary for you to tell us how to conduct our business. We don't try to tell you how to take your pictures, do we?"

Ullman heard his own totally unintended hoot of incredulous laughter. "Captain, you've got to be kidding! If there's one thing we have to get hardened to in my racket it's officers of the so-called law telling us how to, or how not to, or where not to take our pictures, and busting our cameras or our heads if we don't obey instantly and to hell with freedom of the press. Hell, a newsman friend of mine still gets headaches from the baton some crazy cop bounced off him in that old Chicago convention hassle."

They were no longer the polite civil servant and the cooperative citizen; the hostility was out in the open now. He saw the narrowing of the cold cop eyes—they always seemed to be issued special eyes to go with the special guns and the special handcuffs—but Rader cleared his throat and spoke evenly.

"I'm sorry you feel that way, Mr. Ullman. Now, if you please—"

Ullman said harshly, "You know I'll find out, don't you, Rader?" It wasn't smart; it would have been smarter to go out as he'd intended, to all appearances duped and docile, but there was suddenly too much rage inside him to permit it. He said, "My agent's mad at me right now, but he'll get over it when I bring him this story with pictures. Shall we call it Gold Coast Cover-up, Captain? Or Snow Job In Miami? What are you hiding? A rapist runs loose for seven months while the cops sit on their hands, and then he commits murder and, by God, they aren't even around to nail him for that, the poor damned victim's got to do it for them! And why did Olson feel he had to kill her anyway? And don't give me that crap about his thinking she'd recognized him a hundred yards off across a marina at night, a man she'd only seen with a mask on months before!"

Rader cleared his throat. "I think you'd better leave it alone, Mr. Ullman. You're letting your imagination run away with you again."

Ullman stared at him and said, deliberately goading: "That's a nice gold badge, Captain. I'm going to have it before I'm through. I know just the place to mount it on my boat. It will dress up the cabin very nicely, thank you."

It was lovely, it was all there, exactly what he'd been working for: the suddenly red cop face, the narrow furious cop eyes, the hand on the gun, and the harsh cop voice saying: "Now, listen, you little red-haired punk . . ."

He was ready again, gripping the cane and planning how to use it, seeing how it might be done—and knowing this was no pudgy lawyer with an overbarbered face. This was someone who lived in the real world, not Mr. Grimes' peaceful dreamland, the same nonviolent never-never land in which she'd had such faith, which had betrayed her so cruelly in the end. It might be done, he knew, but he wouldn't survive doing it; not against a street-wise and experienced man like this; and it wasn't time to make that trip yet. He let himself show a slow, reluctant grin.

"So now we know, Captain," he said softly.

He watched the policeman's taut body relax; and he knew a sudden respect for the older man as the thin mouth twitched slightly with involuntary wry humor—both men knowing exactly what had almost happened here and why it hadn't.

"Get the hell out of here, Ullman," Rader said without heat. "You're not writing any stories or getting any badges. You're just poking around the zoo and teasing the animals."

"That's right, I'm not writing any stories. But I am finding out why you felt it necessary to hand me all that bilgewater." After a moment, Ullman said, "Why the hell not just tell me, Captain? Freedom of information and all that jazz. Why make me do it the hard way?"

He saw the other man start to say, instinctively, that there was nothing to tell, and check himself. They'd gone beyond all the facile public-relations lies. Rader merely shook his head minutely. After a moment, Ullman turned and walked out of there; and when he got to the parking lot outside, a vaguely familiar masculine figure was heading for a car across the way. It was almost too good to be true. He couldn't, for a moment, believe it wasn't a trick or a trap, but they weren't that clever—and then he couldn't believe what he was going to do about it, but he did it anyway.

"Hey, Simonds," he called. "Bill Simonds!"

The blond man turned, today a natty shape in city clothes; but the face was the same as Ullman remembered it, youthful and rather handsome in a heavy way but with that pale coarse skin. There was a trained wariness in the way he stood that reminded Ullman of Captain Rader and hinted that some kind of ugly professional collusion was involved here—so watch yourself, brother, he warned himself, this one is dangerous, too, whoever he really is. And they've got something to hide, they've all got something to hide, so, no matter who the guy is, maybe you can just possibly get away with it if you

314

work it right and find out what the secret is and use it to protect yourself, and if you don't it doesn't matter too much anyway, now.

"Hey, Bill," Ullman said cheerfully as he approached, putting onto his face once more the nice boyish grin that in the past had earned him a lot of pictures people hadn't wanted him to take at first. He held out his hand. "I was just talking to the Captain in there, Bill, and I'm afraid I've caused you a lot of trouble, getting you dragged down here, me and my crazy imagination—"

Then he had Simonds' proffered hand, and he was yanking on it hard and slamming the knee up with all the force he could muster. Simonds was doubling up right on cue and it was time for the cane across the back of the head, and it was all pretty unreal, all pretty mad, but *somebody* was damn well going to tell him how Nancy had come to die and what kind of lousy games they were playing with her death. If they thought he had any scruples whatever about how he got the information out of them, there was a folded photographic print in his pocket that might persuade them otherwise—if *that* could be done to her, who the hell cared what was done to them?

To his surprise, he had no trouble at all backing up the little truck to the unconscious man concealed between the parked cars, loading him aboard, tying and gagging him securely, and driving off with him.

CHAPTER 31

June

Latitude 26°N; Longitude 80°W

Phil Martin nursed his Scotch on the rocks to make it last in case he had to wait, but he did not really think he'd have to wait. Elizabeth Cameron had given the impression of being a very punctual lady; and she'd been right on schedule the only other time they'd arranged to meet, for dinner so many months ago. He wondered now at his own sense of anticipation. Aside from her striking appearance she hadn't proved to be much of a prize—a typically petty and conventional female bureaucrat, in fact—and he'd never quite understood, he told himself, why being a liberated female involved dressing like that; you'd think they'd want to emphasize their new free womanhood now that they had it, instead of pretending to be little men with funny chests. Nevertheless, he hadn't been able to put her out of his mind; and when she'd called this afternoon to suggest a brief meeting that might be to their mutual advantage he'd recognized her voice immediately. He'd found himself rather disturbingly glad to hear it.

The same disconcerting sense of pleasure struck him again when he saw her enter the little cocktail lounge right on time, straight and slender as he remembered, and very businesslike, of course, in one of her severe trousers-outfits complete with mannish vest. This suit was powder-blue and beautifully fitted as before—and again there was the small, contrasting, feminine frivolity of the graceful shoes with the moderately high heels. Deciding that his objection to the costume was really pretty theoretical, he rose from the booth as she approached and stepped forward to greet her. When she offered her hand, instead of shaking it as she presumably expected, he bowed deeply and raised his lips with a flourish.

"*Señorita*. You bring sunshine on a dreary day."

She laughed at his nonsense, removing her dark glasses. "Dreary? It's ninety in the shade out there and bright enough to blind you."

"You no like my *hidalgo* act, hey? So hokay, Mr. Martin at your service, ma'am."

"You must have fun trying to keep your different personalities apart," she said lightly.

He said, although he had not intended to say anything of the sort: "Sometimes it is not so much fun, *Señorita*."

She glanced at him sharply, and there was a little silence. "Yes, I know," she said softly. "Sometimes I have trouble separating the naive Iowa farm girl from the ever-so-sophisticated government lady from Washington, D.C." Then she said quickly, "I think I'll have a vodka martini, if you don't mind." While they were waiting for it, seated now, she said, "It's nice of you to meet me like this on the spur of the moment. I'm afraid the last time we talked I wasn't very cooperative. . . ."

316

A long-legged cocktail waitress in a very abbreviated costume put a glass before her. Elizabeth Cameron picked it up, and responded to his salute, and drank sparingly.

"What is it you say, *salud?*"

He grinned. *"Salud y pesetas y amor....* Anyway, there's a long rigamarole that means health and money and love and the time in which to enjoy them. Pretty well covers the field, doesn't it?"

"Yes."

"It's been a while," he said, studying her face and deciding that she looked tired and wondering why that should concern him. He asked, "How's the great operation going? Have you got them all exterminated yet? Wasn't that the code name, Operation Extermination?"

She shook her head minutely. "Please don't. If you read the papers you know it's still coming in by the shipload. We can't seem to make any impression on . . . Damn it, Martin, it isn't just a game to joke about! Sometimes I feel so goddamn frustrated I could cry." Before he could speak, she went on in a different tone of voice, more briskly: "That Major Ochsner of yours—Harry Ochs as he calls himself currently—will be picked up very shortly. I thought you'd like to know. Nobody's supposed to have an inkling, of course, so I'd rather you wouldn't say where you heard it. Isn't that a hell of a way to run a government?"

"Yes, but there's no evidence anybody's ever figured out a better." After a moment, he asked, "Why are you telling me?"

She looked surprised. "Well, you're kind of entitled to know since the original information came from you. And you did say it was a dangerous situation, didn't you? You said that if that man Columbus' Cuban plans were frustrated he might do something terrible. Well, they're going to be frustrated very soon. Even though I feel you're exaggerating the danger, I thought you'd better know so you'd be prepared. We've learned that Ochsner is receiving a shipment of arms at last. The raid will be made before he has a chance to either hide the weapons or move south with them in accordance with Mr. Columbus' grandiose Cuban invasion plans."

"I hope the raiding party's been warned to be careful."

Elizabeth Cameron hesitated. "I told them what you said. I'm afraid they weren't . . . tremendously impressed."

"I know," he said. "The old Fetterman syndrome."

"Fetterman?"

"Lieutenant Fetterman—if I remember the rank correctly—

was a very confident army officer without much respect for Indians. That was back in the eighteen hundreds. He'd been heard to say that he could ride right through the whole Sioux nation with a single troop of U.S. Cavalry. Well, one day he tried it. I may have some of the details wrong, maybe it was the Crows or Blackfeet or Shoshones, but one thing I do remember for sure: Fetterman and his whole command were found dead and scalped—just like a gent named Custer who had somewhat similar ideas and got exactly the same treatment a little later. Folks around here have been dealing with nice docile marijuana smugglers so long they've forgotten there are people in the world who shoot back." He regarded her for a moment. "A word of advice, Miss Cameron. It's not your problem. It has nothing to do with drugs. Wash your hands of it now. Stay clear."

She said, "Thank you for the warning. . . . Mr. Martin?"

"Yes."

She hesitated oddly; she was not a hesitating girl. "I . . . I didn't come merely to tell you that. I've been thinking about our dinner conversation last fall. I wanted to make an apology and ask a question. It occurs to me that I acted like a fairly obnoxious bitch; I had no right to question your motives like that, or those of your parents. All I can say is . . . well, in this racket everybody plays pretty dirty. You find yourself using any weapons you can lay your hands on, and saying and doing things automatically after a while that would have shocked you terribly a few years earlier, just to keep your feet on your particular rung of the ladder and maybe get a toehold on the one above. You . . . forget that you're dealing with real people with real feelings that can be hurt, if you know what I mean. If I hurt yours, I'm sorry."

For a moment he hated her. With a few words she'd destroyed all the defenses he'd raised against her. As long as she was merely an ordinary, determinedly ambitious, bureaucratic dame in pants, no matter how handsome, he was safe; but no ordinary bureaucrat, male or female, had ever apologized for anything since the dawn of bureaucratic history. They might try to justify their behavior, or they might demonstrate conclusively how they hadn't really said what they'd seemed to say, or how it wasn't significant anyway; but they'd never come right out with the straight-from-the-shoulder apology: *I was wrong, I'm sorry.* Except that this one just had.

He cleared his throat. "And the question?"

She turned to look at him directly, and her gray eyes were steady and searching. "It occurred to me that I might have an apology coming, too. Do I?" When he didn't answer immediately, she said, "Maybe not an apology. But when somebody plays a rather stupid and arrogant female for a goddamn fool, it's . . . well, it's nice if he says he's sorry. It doesn't help much, but it's nice."

He said, "All right. I'm sorry."

He heard the quick intake of her breath; apparently she hadn't been quite sure. "Well, that's a lot of sorries, isn't it?" she said. "I . . . started wondering why you made such a point of being abrasive; and why your elusive Mr. Richardson had sent his rather undiplomatic second-in-command to conduct the delicate negotiations. It occurred to me, much later of course, that maybe I was supposed to be small-minded enough and annoyed enough to do exactly what I did do." She was silent for a moment, still regarding him steadily; then she went on; "I guess I misjudged you. I really didn't have the impression you were . . . that devious."

There was a question in her voice. He had no business answering it, of course. It was totally unprofessional, but goddamn it, it wasn't as if she were a KGB agent to whom he was betraying his country, and to hell with all this interagency feuding anyway.

He spoke carefully: "This was handled straight from Washington. My chief is a very careful and skillful manipulator who doesn't always tell the manipulatees what he's up to. You can color us both stupid together, Miss Cameron." Then he went on quickly: "Not that I wouldn't have done it knowingly if I'd been ordered."

"Of course not," she said softly, "but then you wouldn't have done it so convincingly and I flatter myself I would have known you were doing it." She studied the glass she was holding. "May I ask what the purpose was, besides making a jackass of the cocky career lady?"

"You're taking care of Ochsner for us, aren't you? Or seeing that he's taken care of."

"I see. So it was anticipated that I would use what you told me. . . . Yes, of course."

Martin said evenly, "Columbus we've got to deal with, that's our job; but our manpower is limited and Ochsner is peripheral, so to speak. All we need there is for him to be removed by somebody, and it's a tricky job, and my chief in

319

Washington has very strong feeling about us going up against one of the doomsday men, as he calls them, when we don't have to. In other words, why should we get our tails shot off by the dangerous Major, who's not our primary target, when there are eager-beaver agencies around that'll happily hijack the job if it's left out in the open kind of casually where they can grab it—and that way we have no responsibility since we didn't request their assistance. Quite the contrary. The record will show clearly that they butted in where we'd specifically requested noninterference. We're covered all the way." He paused. "Which is why I warn you again to please stay clear. It could get nasty out there."

There was a little silence; then she said, "So you really do take this soldier-of-fortune seriously. But what makes you think I won't pass on what you've just told me to the people who are planning the raid on the Manatee Keys. . . .?"

"You're not being quite fair, Miss Cameron," he protested. "Do you think I *want* them to get hurt? I hope you will pass it on. Definitely. But I'm afraid they won't listen. They'll figure I'm just trying to con them out of a great opportunity for valiant and glorious service so I can grab all the credit for myself and my gang. That's the way they think, all of them, and I doubt that you're going to change . . ."

He stopped, as the leggy cocktail waitress paused at the table. "Mr. Martin, Mr. Philip Martin? There's a phone call for you. You can take it at the end of the bar."

"Excuse me." He was very much aware of Elizabeth Cameron still sitting there as he walked away between the tables to pick up the phone lying on the bar. "Martin here," he said.

"You'd better get your arse over here on the double, Felipe," Tommy Walsh's voice said. "Richardson's coming in with Masterman, I just got the signal. Ullman's flown home for some reason connected with the lousy Winters murder; and they lost their blonde in Panama and decided she wasn't so important after all, or Richardson did. And we've mislaid Simonds."

"Meaning what?"

"Bill was supposed to relieve Larry Hallenbeck on that idiot September surveillance job—what the hell's supposed to happen in that crummy clubhouse shack *El Jefe* has us watching so carefully I wish somebody'd tell me—but he never relieved the watch. Larry gave him half an hour and called in, just now. The last we saw of Bill here he was heading for the main Miami cop shop earlier this afternoon to give them an official deposition to nail down what he'd told them earlier. But they say he left there several hours ago. I've sent Linkowski over to check their parking lot. I figured you wouldn't want me to arouse too much police interest yet. But you'd better get the hell over here. I'm sitting here all alone and things are getting too confusing for my simple boyish mind, not to mention my simple boyish authority."

"Don't cry. I'll be right over to hold your hand."

"Sorry about busting up your date with the pretty executive lady. How were you making out there?"

"Silencio! You speak of the woman I love, *Señor.*"

Returning the phone to its cradle, he found himself wishing he hadn't said that. It was just the ordinary crude kind of kidding he always carried on with Tommy Walsh; but somehow as he turned back to the booth he felt oddly disloyal to the slim woman awaiting him for speaking of her, and their relationship, in that flippant manner—and why he should suddenly owe her loyalty, little as he still knew her, was a subject that would not bear careful scrutiny. She looked up when he stopped beside her.

"Sorry," he said. "Without Felipe Aurelio Martinez in attendance, the whole U.S. Government has ground to a shuddering halt as usual. I must go and get it functioning again." He stood looking down at her for a moment, liking the delicate shape of the ear partially revealed by the short, dark brown hair. She wasn't wearing a tie today and the soft open collar of her blue silk shirt exposed the graceful line of her throat; for some reason it made him think of a certain operatic theme that always brought tears to his eyes, being the sentimental Latin type he was. And when you, Señor Martinez, start thinking of a dame, not in terms of tits and cunt, but in terms of music, then it's time for you to beat a hasty retreat, goddamn it. But he knew it was already too late for that. He ventured to place his hand lightly on her shoulder. "Thanks for keeping me informed."

She reached up and covered his hand briefly with hers. "What is it you say, *de nada?*"

"Yes. I'll be in touch."

"Please."

As he walked out, he decided he owed it to the cocktail waitress with the long, handsome legs to give her face a little attention, but it was just an ordinary female face. Outside, the sunlight was as blinding as Elizabeth Cameron had said, even this late in the afternoon; and as he put on his dark glasses against the glare he thought: now just how the hell did *that* happen, anyway?

Tommy had new information for him when he entered the hotel room they were still using for an office. "Not good," Tommy said. "Car still there, keys hanging in the door lock. At a guess, he was interrupted by somebody just as he was about to get in and drive away—but why would anybody want Bill? He's not even working on the Columbus account currently; and the *Hermanos de Septiembre* are too damn ineffectual to even think about a kidnaping, let alone carry it out. Besides, he knows most of them by sight; he wouldn't let them catch him by surprise."

"No blood or scraps of cloth or what we laughingly call clues, empty cartridge cases for instance?"

"Hell, nobody's going to get away with firing off a gun behind Police Headquarters. Not without one of those perfect Hollywood silencers I wish they'd make available to us working stiffs. No, Linkowski couldn't find anything at all. No signs of violence. Just the car, the keys, and no Bill. . . ." The phone interrupted him. He picked it up and listened and held it out to Martin. "For you. Captain Rader."

Martin took the phone and carried it to one of the armchairs nearby. "How are you, Captain?" he asked, sitting down.

"I'm okay, but I almost wasn't this afternoon. I thought I'd better warn you."

"About what, Captain?"

"Well . . ." The voice on the phone sounded a little self-conscious, which didn't go with the picture Martin carried in his mind of the tough, gray-haired policeman. "This is kind of theoretical, Martin, but do you know what *lobo* means?"

"Lobo? That's a wolf, isn't it?"

"A special kind of wolf, in one sense of the word, one that hunts alone, outside the pack, and maybe doesn't follow all the normal kindly social rules of wolf behavior, if you know what I mean." At the other end of the line, Captain Rader cleared his throat. "Well, it happens to people sometimes. I thought I'd better let you know that a subject in whom we're both interested has gone kind of *lobo* on us. He was in here this afternoon, that young fellow named Ullman, Harold Ullman. He asked to see the pictures in the Winters murder—his ex-wife, remember? Apparently there was still something there, some affection, despite the divorce, and you saw those photos, they weren't pleasant. I don't know what you have in mind, but I don't think you'd better tackle that boy carelessly, Martin. He's all ready to go for somebody's throat. He almost went for mine, and I'll tell you something, I wasn't a damn bit sure that if he decided to come, this lousy little .38 they have us carry was going to stop him. Just a tip from one public servant to another."

Martin frowned. "You mean he's cracking up over his former wife's death?"

"Not exactly. A shrink probably wouldn't find a thing wrong with him; he's got it under control—until he decides to turn it loose. What I mean is, he's plenty sane enough to know we're handing him a lot of crap. He's been around; he knows a cover-up when he sees it, he knows we've got something to hide, both of us—well, maybe he doesn't know about you yet, but don't count on his not finding out, Martin. That boy is going to learn every last little detail about his ex-wife's death or die trying, and if he does die it won't bother him too much the way he's feeling. And if you or I die while he's trying, it'll bother him even less. Like I said, *lobo*."

Martin frowned. "What time did you see him, Captain?"

"Well, he just flew in from Panama this morning; he got around to us around three o'clock, I guess, prepared to answer questions like a good citizen. Only after he saw those photos and listened to the line of bull I was handing out . . . well, all I can say is, watch that boy. He's not safe."

"Thank you, Captain. I appreciate the warning."

Martin sat for a moment after putting the phone aside, thinking hard. You got these odd flights of fancy from unlikely people, Meriwether and his doomsday men, Rader and his *lobos*. Yet the phenomenon did exist and you'd damn well better not forget it.

"What time did Bill Simonds take off for police headquarters?" he asked.

"About two-thirty from here."

"Well," said Martin deliberately, "it looks like Ullman's got him. At least they were both there at the same time, just about."

"Ullman?" Tommy Walsh looked incredulous. "You mean that nice young photographic guy? But that's crazy—"

Richardson said the same thing at greater length when he turned up several hours later. He'd apparently had to fly all around Latin America and the Caribbean to make his connections after being unable to get on the direct morning plane from Panama; and he looked it, and Richardson without a crease in his pants was as self-conscious and irritable as a woman with a run in her stocking.

"That old cop must be punch-drunk or something," he said. "Forget that crazy *lobo* business, Phil; let's talk sense. Simonds is a trained man. If he's let himself be taken by somebody twenty pounds lighter with a game leg, then a review of his competence is very much in order; but frankly I don't believe it. And why would Ullman kidnap him anyway?"

Martin said, "I can think of a reason. And so can you, Tony, if you bear down on it."

But Richardson looked honestly puzzled; the man was really incredible. He had no sense of guilt at all, even after going behind his, Martin's, back to withdraw protection from a girl who had then been murdered. And now he could see no reason whatever for that girl's husband—well, ex-husband—to resent the officials who were obviously and clumsily trying to conceal the circumstances of her death. To Tony Richardson there were no real people out there, only pieces to be moved advantageously in the careful, ambitious, bureaucratic chess game he was playing. The idea that one of those pieces might get mad and strike back was beyond his comprehension. After all, he was the United States Government, wasn't he? How could a little red-haired punk with a limp presume to challenge him and all the power behind him when all he'd been doing, really, was his job. . . .?

Richardson's puzzled frown cleared. "Oh, you mean the Winters girl, his former wife? But he doesn't know that we—"

"But he's sure as hell finding out, Tony," Martin said. "You can bet your last Panama centavo that he's finding out, right now. I called the place down there in the Keys where he keeps his boat. The Boot Key Marina in Marathon. Yes, Mr. Ullman's little truck is in the parking lot. No, Mr. Ullman's boat is not in its slip. Yes, the dockmaster had the impression Mr. Ullman went on board with a companion, although said crew member wasn't on deck when they pulled out—but Ullman's been handling that boat without help for years; the crew was probably below cooking dinner, it was about that time. Anyway, they're somewhere out in the Gulf Stream by now."

"I suppose you *have* notified the Coast Guard."

Martin drew a long breath. "Think hard, Tony, and maybe you'll come up with a good reason why it might be highly

324

inadvisable for us to involve any other agencies, and possibly the newspapers, in our little problem. Rader, okay. He's one man, he was in it anyway because of the murder, and he's got his own reason for keeping quiet. But do you want a lot of innocent Coast Guard lads hearing what Ullman has to say by way of explanation if we have him snatched off that boat of his with whatever's left of Bill Simonds, assuming that he doesn't just toss the gory debris to the sharks when he's finished making it talk?"

Richardson said irritably, "You're making a big melodrama of this, Phil, and I don't believe a word of it. I mean, he's just a goddamn civilian, a photographer, practically a kid, and here you have him committing kidnaping and torture. . . ."

"We call it interrogation when we do it," Martin said sourly. "Damn it, Tony, what does it take to wake you up? I told you down there in Venezuela that this redhead was nobody to fool with any longer; now he's backfired on us just the way I predicted. What the hell did he grab Bill for if he *wasn't* going to make him talk? Of course there's still a possibility that Simonds just went home with a sexy blonde policewoman who happened along, but we've got to assume the worst, don't we? Say our red-haired boy's got him, why did he haul him off to sea if he didn't want to have him out where nobody could hear him yell? As far as I'm concerned, Ullman's sore at the run-around he got from Rader, he's determined to find out what really happened to his wife, or rather, why it happened, and if he has to use the big pliers out of the toolbox or the long carving knife out of the galley he'll use them. Or whatever suitable hunk of metal he can heat up on the galley stove. Or maybe he'll just lash the patient to the mast and drop a noose over his neck and start cranking with one of those fancy winches all those boats carry and see just how far Simonds lets his neck get stretched before he talks. I mean, goddamn it, Tony, the guy's got red hair and he's *mad!* I told you he came damn close to knifing one of those punks who jumped him in Puerto la Cruz, just to see the nice blood run. And that was *before* his wife got murdered. Now I figure—and Rader confirms—that it's killing season on the Ullman calendar. He's fucking sick and tired of being on the receiving end and he's dishing it out for a change. And let's just hope Bill Simonds has sense enough to give in while he's still got a full complement of fingers and toes and eyes and testicles, not to mention lives."

"Simonds won't talk," Richardson said. "He's had better training than that."

"Bullshit, Tony," Martin said. "Under the proper circumstances anybody'll talk, you know that." But of course, he reflected grimly, Richardson didn't know it. Basically a desk man, he had all the fine stoical ideas about what other people's behavior should be that seemed to float around those government offices; the same shiny hero-theories that, in the military, had you telling the enemy nothing but your name, rank, and serial number, no matter what. Great patriotic stuff, if your work never took you closer to an interrogation cell or POW camp than Washington, D.C. Martin remembered his own thoughts earlier in the day, and went on: "It's not as if he were in the hands of the KGB, remember? He might let himself be maimed and crippled if the safety of the nation were at stake, but let's hope he's got more sense than to hold out on a simple matter of administrative security. I doubt he'll be that stubborn. He's probably got a pretty bad conscience about the whole lousy business like the rest of us."

Richardson said stiffly, "If that's intended as a criticism . . ."

Martin grimaced. "All I'm saying is that I don't feel very pleased about setting up a bright and attractive young woman to be strangled to death after first having her pretty face brutally demolished. I don't know your reaction, Tony, but it doesn't make me feel good at all. I don't think it makes Bill Simonds feel very great, either, not so great that he's going to play iron man when the poor girl's former husband starts asking perfectly legitimate questions about why she had to die like that."

"Nevertheless, he'll answer for any breaches of security. . . ."

The phone rang. It was on the table between the twin beds; and the room was silent as Tommy Walsh, nearest, reached for it. It was pretty crowded in there by now, with Walsh and Masterman and Linkowski and Hallenbeck perched or sprawled on the beds, while the senior personnel occupied the room's two chairs, at the little cocktail table by the window. Tommy listened briefly and glanced at Richardson.

"It's the marine operator. Do we accept a collect call from the sailing vessel *Nancy Lou*. . . . Yes, Operator, we'll pay for the call." There was more silence while he listened; then he looked up again and said, "It's Ullman, all right. He wants to speak to a *Doctor* Martin. Dr. Philip Martin."

"I'll take it," Richardson said. He reached for the instrument, and spoke into it. "Yes . . . no, this is Anthony Rich. . . ." His face reddened and he lowered the phone and, after a moment, handed it back to Tommy Walsh and rose and walked quickly into the bathroom, closing the door behind him. Tommy put the phone to his ear and shook his head.

"Sonofabitch hung up," he reported. Nobody smiled or spoke, but the general attitude to be sensed in the room wasn't quite as disapproving of the man who'd phoned, Martin thought, as it had been. "I guess we just wait for him to call back," Tommy said.

But twenty minutes passed before the telephone rang again. Richardson had come out of the bathroom and poured himself a drink and sat down in his former chair to drink it. He did not stir when Tommy again picked up the instrument and said yes the charges would be accepted and handed the phone to Martin. The voice that spoke in Martin's ear had a faint flavor of New England.

"Dr. Martin? Sorry for the delay but the marine operator's very busy and we've got to await our turns out here on the water. I hope we won't have to waste our time with any more misunderstandings. Just for the record, please tell me your middle name. Over."

"Aurelio," Martin said.

"Good enough, Doctor. Well, I suppose you know how this ship-to-shore works. I mean, I can't hear you until I release the transmit button here, so you have to wait for me to finish talking before you talk. Over."

"I know."

"Dr. Martin, my name is Harold Ullman and I'm calling from my boat the *Nancy Lou*. We're about five miles off the Keys, riding the Gulf Stream north, heading for Miami. I've got one of your patients crewing for me, William Simonds. Bill says you know about his problem, kind of an occupational malady. Over."

"Yes, I'm familiar with the case, Mr. Ullman. Has he had a recurrence?"

"That's right, but it doesn't seem to be too serious. He's resting quietly at the moment. However, he wanted me to ask if you could possibly manage to meet us at the Dinner Key Marina down in Coconut Grove tomorrow. Our ETA, if the wind holds, is about noon."

"Yes, I can make that."

"I'd appreciate it if you'd see about a slip for us. The boat's been there before; they should have a record of all the information they need. Over."

"I'm quite willing to arrange for a slip and meet you there, Mr. Ullman. However, if the medical situation is uncertain perhaps we should arrange an earlier rendezvous."

"Oh, no, Bill is getting along okay; and considering sea conditions out here, and other conditions, he feels that a transfer to another boat would be inadvisable. There's always an element of danger in an operation like that, and it's a lot of trouble for everybody. Bill doesn't even think an ambulance is required; he'd rather not have a big fuss made over him. Incidentally, he's given me a complete record of his medical history in writing, everything leading up to this condition, just a precaution in case I couldn't get hold of you and had to explain the case to somebody else. But of course that won't be required now, will it? I'm sure everything will be fine. See you tomorrow at Dinner Key. Good-bye, Dr. Martin. *Nancy Lou,* WYH 7799, clear."

There was a brief silence after Martin returned the phone to Tommy Walsh, who replaced it in its cradle. Then Richardson spoke without looking up from the glass he was studying thoughtfully.

"Replay, Walsh."

Tommy fiddled with the recorder until he found the beginning of the conversation, and started it running. Nobody spoke until the tape was finished; then Richardson stood up abruptly and moved quickly between the beds to reach for the telephone. Martin thought grimly: Now comes the speech about how we can't let the little squirt get away with it.

"That arrogant little punk!" Richardson said harshly. "Who the hell does he think he is? If he thinks he's going to get away with *that.* . . ."

Martin sighed. "Obviously, he's got the whole story of how we tried to use them, Tony, clear down to your name and mine. And he's still got Bill."

"Simonds is going to have some explaining to do, letting himself be taken like that and then spilling his guts. . . . I've got a good mind to call the Coast Guard and have them both yanked off that boat."

"Aren't you kind of curious about what he wants?"

"Whatever it is, he's not going to get it!" But Richardson had withdrawn his hand from the telephone. "However, maybe it's better to give him plenty of rope before . . . Very well, although I hate to do it, we'll play it his way." He looked around bleakly, as if seeing them all for the first time. "In the meantime, who's covering the September Club?"

Hallenbeck shifted position on the nearer bed. "Nobody at the moment. I was told to come in."

Richardson's face showed a tired patience. "I suppose by now I should be resigned to the fact that nobody can follow a simple directive around here. Didn't I make it clear that I wanted round-the-clock surveillance of that place? Phil, if you're not too proud to do a little legwork for a change . . . Hallenbeck will grab a few hours' sleep and relieve you in time for your rendezvous at Dinner Key." He paused. "I hope our people in Key West at least are on the job."

Tommy Walsh said, "The last report from Donny Brent was right on schedule. No significant activity. But here in Miami, Jernegan is going to want relief soon over on Antoine Street. He's been stuck out there since noon."

"Well, you might as well get some fresh air for a change, Walsh; you've been here most of the day, haven't you?"

Martin said quickly, "I thought we'd agreed that Tommy was overexposed on the Columbus account, Tony. There's a good chance they have him made by this time; why take the risk? Suppose I head over there, and Tommy takes my—"

"Really, Philip." Richardson's voice was wearily tolerant. "It does seem to me I should be allowed to make a simple administrative decision without an argument."

Tommy said quickly, "Never mind, *amigo*. I'll stay out of sight like a good little spook."

"No argument intended, Tony," Martin said, "but there's another factor I think you ought to consider. I just had a drink with Cameron of the PSCC and she let me know . . ." He reported the gist of the conversation. "When they raid the Major, we've got to be prepared for a violent reaction from Columbus. I really feel that from now on we should have double surveillance on that account at all times. If action has to be taken fast, one operative's not going to be able to handle Columbus and his two regular henchmen, even assuming that's all there is to handle."

Richardson nodded slowly and spoke in a kindly voice: "Ideally, of course, you're quite right, Phil, but unfortunately this is not an ideal world. I won't even ask where you think I should obtain the extra personnel. I know that in your obsession with Columbus you'd like me to neglect all the other important accounts for which this office is responsible, but I can't in good conscience do that, particularly since I'm not at all convinced you're right about Columbus' reaction; and without Ochsner what can he really do? When Cameron's people move, we'll take some preventive measures; in the meantime, if you don't mind, let's just carry out the arrangements I've suggested. Please."

Leaving, Phil Martin told himself it was no use being mad at the stupid *mozo*, but that did not prevent him from considering various remedies for what ailed Mr. Anthony Richardson, including direct and painful, and preferably permanent, physical violence. This made for a long night, particularly since there was nothing about the low cinderblock building he was supposed to keep under observation—colored a faded arsenic green, if it mattered—to distract him from his angry thoughts.

In a way it was too bad. There were much more pleasant things, and people, he could have been thinking about; but there was also the trouble, he discovered, that he'd begun to *like* the damn woman, quite apart from being suddenly and surprisingly in love with her—you could fall in love with all kinds of people for all kinds of reasons. Unfortunately, it wasn't possible to use somebody you really liked as a subject for the kind of casual and sometimes, to be perfectly honest, rather disrespectful and even somewhat degrading, to the woman, erotic fantasies that helped pass the time on a long watch like this.

CHAPTER 32

June

Latitude 26°N; Longitude 80°W

At dawn the north end of Key Largo became visible off to port, and against the emerging green of the familiar, long, low island—as the name implied, it was the largest of the Keys—Harold Ullman could make out through the binoculars the distant entrance to the marina of the fancy and exclusive Ocean Reef Club, which he'd never seen up close since they did not welcome uninvited visitors and he didn't know anybody rich enough to invite him. Beyond, the chain of islands continued on to the northeast into the hazy, early-morning distance. Miami was a far-off misty dome of vaguely defined big-city pollution off the port bow.

He always preferred to make this overnight run up from the Keys well out in the Florida Straits, taking advantage of the favorable current of the Gulf Stream, and accepting the dangers of the fairly heavy ship traffic in order to avoid the risk of being set onto the outlying reefs in the dark. Now that daylight had arrived, however, he was allowing *Nancy Lou* to close with the coast. She was running on autopilot carrying all working sail, jib, forestaysail, and full mainsail; heeled well over on the starboard tack and making a good five knots through the water, with the Gulf Stream adding another two and a fraction according to his latest navigational calculation.

As he stood there checking his position, a trio of porpoises surfaced under the bow, playing their usual I-dare-you-to-hit-me game with the oncoming sailboat. Instinctively, Ullman found himself turning toward the main hatch to call Nancy on deck—porpoises had always delighted her no matter how often she saw them—and he knew again the desperate sickness of remembering, of seeing again in his mind the dreadful broken bloody thing in the photograph that reposed in the pocket of his shore-going jacket. He wondered again how two reasonably intelligent people who'd loved each other pretty well, although obviously not as strongly and unquestioningly as they'd needed to, could have managed to louse up their lives so terribly, even with help.

But of course they'd been given all kinds of help in destroying themselves. All kinds of people, it seemed, concerned with their own projects legal and illegal, had casually used the Ullman household to further their own damned interests, public and private, and to hell with who got hurt and killed. In spite of the hint of collusion that had come to him, seeing Simonds in the police parking lot, Harold Ullman had been considerably shocked to discover that he'd actually abducted an agent of the U.S. government. He'd been even more shocked to learn that, if what he wanted was a man with guilty knowledge of the reasons for Nancy's death, he could hardly have done better. In spite of what you heard and read these days about the CIA and the FBI, he reflected, you found it hard to believe that people hired with the taxpayers' money, your money, actually played these secret ugly games with your life. He checked the compass course, made a small adjustment to the autopilot knob, and went below.

"You bastard," Simonds said from up forward, "let me have that milk bottle again, you bastard."

"You ought to do something about those overactive kidneys," Ullman said, finding the plastic quart container and moving up cautiously to place it into the bound hands.

"Fuck you," Simonds said.

"Need any help?"

"I'm a big boy now; I can open my pants and pee all by myself."

"Well, don't spill it. I don't want to have to pump it out of the bilge."

It was one of the many little problems of kidnaping that were never faced on TV, he reflected, where the super-continent hero and heroine could remain bound hand and foot for days with never a fear of disgracing their pants or pantyhose. Braced in the doorway separating the cabins, automatically compensating for the vigorous motion of the boat, he watched Simonds, wrists and ankles lashed with tough, tarred marline, awkwardly elbow himself to a sitting position on the narrow cabin sole between the two forward berths.

The only sign of injury was to the right foot, which was shoeless and neatly wrapped in bandages from *Nancy Lou*'s first-aid kit. Ullman noted that a small spot of blood had worked itself through the white gauze but it was dark and dry; apparently the bleeding had checked itself some time ago. He felt a small sense of wonder at himself, but no particular remorse; but it certainly wasn't something he'd remember with pride. Nancy would undoubtedly have been shocked and horrified by his brutal behavior—or would she, now? After all, in the end she'd been driven to go much further and kill a man. It was, he thought, a crazy world full of crazy people; and if being nuts was what it took to make it around here, he could be as nutty as anybody. As he had proved last night.

Topside again, he emptied and rinsed out the plastic bottle in the racing water along the lee rail, reflecting that the life of a kidnaper wasn't all it was cracked up to be; he might as well be a male nurse. He washed off his hands and dried them on his slacks, the same brown slacks he'd put on in Panama almost too long ago to remember, he realized. They were looking rather baggy and bedraggled by now, but he hadn't taken time to change into seagoing clothes except to make the necessary switch to rubber-soled boat shoes and, later, to pull on an orange foul-weather jacket against the spray. Straightening up, he made a practiced three-hundred-and-sixty-degree survey of the horizon, lookout fashion. *Nancy Lou* was still moving well; and after the slight chill of the night it was obviously going to be a warm, clear Florida spring day. There were no Coast Guard patrol craft in sight—at the moment he could see only one other vessel, a small freighter off to starboard, heading south—and no planes or helicopters in the sky. Maybe the government creeps were going to play it straight, but considering their record to date it wasn't something he could rely on, and there was at least one obvious precaution he could take.

He had the same wary feeling he'd had the first time he'd taken *Nancy Lou* offshore knowing that all kinds of unknown dangers lurked ahead and he'd have to avoid them by the exercise of extreme caution and lots of plain common sense, since he had absolutely no experience to guide him. The difference was that learning to cope with the open sea from scratch, so to speak, had been fun, whereas this, except perhaps for a certain savage satisfaction at meeting the callous manipulating bastards on their own ground, was no pleasure at all. He went below and stood looking down at Simonds for a moment. The prisoner glared up at him with a hatred that was perfectly natural under the circumstances: a trained young man who'd considered himself competent, he'd been tricked and captured and forced to talk by a smaller and weaker individual who wasn't even in the business, as he liked to refer to it.

"Just so you know what's coming, Simonds," Ullman said, "I'm taking us through the Keys by way of Angelfish Creek just ahead, and then along the inside route up Biscayne Bay to our rendezvous with your friends at Dinner Key. We'll miss the boost of the Gulf Stream going that way, but there are usually several cruising boats spending the night at anchor in Angelfish and I should be able to find somebody willing to take a letter ashore and mail it for me. You know the document I mean, the one you were kind enough to write out for me last night. I'm going to close the ports and hatches so you can't hear, and blindfold you so you can't see. I don't know if you boys play as rough as the CIA is supposed to, but you've given me no reason to think otherwise, and I don't want to get some poor yachtsman into trouble just for being obliging and running an errand for a fellow-boatman. That's why I'm making sure you can't tell anybody which boat I hailed. If I come back down here and find that you've moved, or disturbed the blindfold in any way, I'll work you over with a ball-peen hammer—it's right over there in my boatswain's bag—until you'll never want to see a mirror again. That's a promise. For reasons that should be obvious, Mr. Simonds, it would give me a hell of a lot of simple vindictive pleasure, so don't tempt me. Okay?"

"Fuck you," Simonds said.

But his eyes shifted in an uneasy way and Ullman knew he would make no trouble; he'd already conceded this game and to hell with it. But it wasn't a nice thing to do to any man, even one who, by his own account, was as much as anybody responsible for what had happened to Nancy, since he'd admitted he'd at first been assigned to protect her, and had even learned she was being followed by somebody; and still he'd blindly obeyed the arbitrary orders sending him elsewhere, with only a token protest. . . .

Angelfish was a tricky little passage, but with a favorable tide *Nancy Lou* cleared everything nicely today, although there were a couple of shoal spots that had caused her trouble in the past. A few hours later, gliding up wide, shallow Biscayne Bay with a dying wind, Harold Ullman was pleased to glance at his watch, with his destination in sight, and know he was going to make his 1200 ETA with a little to spare. At the outer buoy of the entrance channel he rounded up into the wind and doused the sails and took time to furl and cover the mainsail neatly and bag the staysail—the roller-furling jib took care of itself like a window blind—wondering how long it would be before he could go sailing again. Unreal though it seemed, he was now a dangerous criminal, if anybody wanted to get technical about it; and if he'd miscalculated it could well be years. In his present reckless, heedless mood the thought didn't bother him a bit. Join the bughouse gang, he thought, let's all be bats together.

The little one-cylinder diesel took them down the long lane of channel markers in its usual rough and noisy and reliable fashion, and into the final passage between the islands sheltering the marina. Inside, the sprawling complex of docks—at least as big as Miamarina a few miles north—was a forest of masts and outriggers and tuna towers. At the end of the outjutting dock nearest the entrance, a well-dressed man was sitting on one of the boxes in which the marina inhabitants stowed the dockside gear they preferred not to carry on their boats. Rising, this man studied *Nancy Lou* for a moment as she approached and then waved Ullman closer.

"Slip C39," he shouted.

"C39, aye-aye."

"I'll be right over to help you with the dock lines."

He was a tall man in a dark business suit, with a dark hawklike face; and Ullman was a little surprised. There had been nothing about the voice, over the radiotelephone or here, to indicate Spanish descent, although the middle name, Aurelio, should have been a tip-off—and if there's anything less important at the moment than the guy's racial antecedents, Mr. Ullman, you'd have to dig hard to find it. But he seemed to be trapped in a vague mist of unreality, and it was hard to keep clearly in mind the painful fact that this time he would not, in a few minutes, be heading for the nearest phone booth on shore as he'd always done before after bringing the boat up from the Keys alone—they avoided incurring the additional radiotelephone charges unnecessarily—and making his call and hearing her voice and seeing after a little the beat-up old Datsun wagon pull up near the dockmaster's office to take him home. . . .

The docking was the usual busy scramble during which no one spoke except on the matter at hand; then *Nancy Lou* lay still at last alongside the finger pier with all lines and fenders properly secured. Ullman stepped ashore.

"Mr. Martin?"

"That's me," the tall, dark man said. He jerked his head toward the boat. "How's the patient?"

"Mad. Damage minor." Ullman studied the man for a moment and decided that he'd been lucky to have Simonds to deal with; this one wouldn't have been so easy, either to take or to persuade to talk. He glanced ashore, where a large car had just driven up. The three men it contained were all staring intently at C Dock. "Looks like you've got reinforcements moving in, Mr. Martin."

"You didn't say anything about my coming alone. They're supposed to wait for my signal."

"Is that Richardson?"

"The smooth, blond, handsome one, yes."

"I gather he kind of owes me a wife."

335

"We all do, but apologies won't help much, will they?"

"But you wanted to do it reasonably with our knowledge and consent; it was Richardson who—"

"Never mind that," Martin said sharply. "We haven't got time for that, Mr. Ullman. If you have anything important to say to me, let's hear it."

Ullman glanced ashore and grinned faintly. "I see. You're not sure he's going to wait for your signal, is that it?"

"He's in charge," Martin said. "He agreed to give me a little time, since you indicated, so clearly and undiplomatically, that you preferred to deal with me; but the exact amount of time was never established."

"I see, I hurt his poor little feelings. Well, he wasn't exactly tender with mine." Ullman drew a long breath. "I'm returning your boy only slightly the worse for wear, Mr. Martin. The question is, what are you going to do about this terrible case of kidnaping and assault? Before you answer I'd better tell you that there's a statement from Simonds in the mail right now—" he glanced at his watch, "—yes, it should be mailed by now; the guy I left it with had a fast powerboat and was in a hurry to get home, never mind where. It's addressed to somebody who'll know how to use it if anything happens to me, real melodrama stuff."

Martin looked darkly amused. "And what would you expect to happen to you, Mr. Ullman?"

Ullman shrugged. "Hell, I saw *Three Days of the Condor* and a few other movies, and I've read a few thrilling books purporting to show how you guys operate. I could disappear or get shot or something. Or I could just wind up in court to answer serious charges. But please remember, I know a lot of media people as they're called; I'm in that line of work. The person to whom I sent that statement will know what to do with it. And then you people can have lots and lots of fun explaining to the press how, without warning or permission, you set up the poor innocent Ullman family as bait for some lousy undercover project of yours and carelessly let the wife get killed and then either assassinated the husband illegally or persecuted him legally when he had the gall to object. People just love to read nasty stuff like that about arrogant government agencies nowadays, Mr. Martin."

Martin said dryly, "That's quite a speech, Mr. Ullman."

Ullman allowed himself a brief grin. "I've had all night to rehearse it."

The taller man threw a glance shorewards, where the

occupants of the big car were now getting out in a purposeful manner.

"Two things," he said quickly, "before they descend on us. First, how bad is Simonds, really?"

Ullman told himself once more that it was really nothing to be ashamed of, under the circumstances. Much worse things had been allowed to happen to much more important people—more important to him, anyway.

He said stiffly, "Mr. Simonds is missing a little toe. I snipped it off with a bolt-cutter."

Martin's eyes widened slightly; then the tall man nodded. "I told Richardson you'd be getting hard to handle. That did the job?"

Ullman said defensively, "Hell, I could have beat on that tough boy all night and nothing would have happened, you know that. I had to do something to let him know I *really* meant business. Afterwards, I showed him a nice post-mortem photo of my wife, my ex-wife, which helped convince him that no part of Mr. Simonds was likely to be sacred to me, no matter what he might feel about it. I put on a good crazy act—and I guess it wasn't all an act—and I indicated that I was happy to keep snipping away and tossing pieces of Simonds out the hatch, laughing fiendishly all the while, until I got what I wanted. And a bolt-cutter is really quite an impressive instrument with powerful levers and sharp jaws and long red handles. We keep one on board in case the mast goes and we have to clear away all that stainless-steel rigging in a hurry. And Simonds had a bad conscience anyway about what he'd let happen to Nancy so, when he realized I was actually serious in my psychopathic way, and wasn't the least bit bothered by the sight of blood, he decided to cooperate before I did some really important damage."

"A bolt-cutter, eh?" Martin said. "That's a new one. I was thinking in simple terms of knives and pliers. I guess I'm behind the times." He glanced over his shoulder at the men who were now crossing the grass toward the sea wall. "Well, the little toe is supposed to be practically a vestigial digit, like a puppy's dewclaws. I guess we can overlook one little toe if we really want to. But blackmail aside, why should we want to? Or to put it differently, what is it *you* want, coming here, Ullman? You could have dumped him somewhere, alive or dead, and tried to disappear. We'd have caught you eventually, but you could have tried."

"Who the hell wants to disappear?" Ullman asked harshly.

337

"All I want is to do what I should obviously have been asked to do months ago if you bastards hadn't been all bogged down in your lousy security. I'm a photographer; faces are my business. I got a good look at two men last fall when we walked in on them all unsuspecting. Masks or no masks, I might have been able to make some kind of identification if I'd been shown some relevant photos, but the cops had no idea where to start. All they showed me, when I got well enough to look, was a bunch of habitual criminals. But you've got a certain specific gang of crazies in mind, according to Simonds. If you've been on the job since last fall, you should have some kind of dossiers by this time, including photographs; so let me see them. I may not be able to make an identification that'll stand up in court, but I can probably pick out the most likely candidate. The big fair-haired number-one man is dead—well, number one on that particular house-wrecking job, at least—but maybe I can spot number two for you, and maybe he'll lead you where you want to go, or we can rig it so he does."

Martin hesitated, frowning. "You want to help us?"

"Hell, no, I don't *want* to help you. I hope you all strangle on your veddy dry martinis," Ullman said bitterly. "But I haven't got much choice, do I? I can't reform the whole lousy U.S. government, but I can damn well . . . do you realize, Martin, that the people who hit our house that night didn't even *know* us?"

"What are you trying to say?"

He'd had the whole night to work it out after learning what had really happened; but it was still hard for him to put his feelings into words.

"Look," he said, "if I get myself involved with a bunch of fanatics, as Mr. Montoya up the street apparently did, and they decide to take action against me to keep me in line, okay. It makes sense. It may not be legal or moral but at least it's comprehensible; I know who's doing it to me and why. And if somebody decides to steal my boat or my camera gear, that's still kind of reasonable, if you know what I mean. They shouldn't do it, but I can understand it. But to know that Nancy . . . that our lives have been all messed up, and hers lost, because some crazy jerk went eeny-meeny-miny-moe, let's trash the third house from the corner tonight, we want it to look like a general crime wave not just a specific intimidation job. . . . It's time the bastards learned to confine their lousy games to the professional players and leave the spectators

338

out of it. I don't give a damn what their glorious cause is, right or wrong; they can damn well refrain from blowing up or beating up or raping or strangling or vandalizing us innocent bystanders. This innocent bystander has had it up to here with being a patsy for every jerk around with a marvelous mission or a shiny badge. Well, I've had a crack at the shiny badges; now let's do something about these bastards who think they've got a right to involve everybody in their lousy little private wars."

Martin nodded slowly. "As a matter of fact, that's exactly what this unit is for. What do you propose to do?"

"Just what you did before, use me for bait, if I can spot a likely candidate in your files. It's late, but it may not be too late; Simonds says this Columbus man has got important business pending and he's probably going to need every man he's got. They were apparently worried enough about protecting that blond gorilla to send somebody clear down to Venezuela after me; let's see how they feel about the dark one with the mustache. I'll pick out the most likely guy and you put some pressure on him and let them know who fingered him somehow—apparently you've got ways, you did it before. Let's see who comes to shut my mouth this time. If somebody does, we'll know I selected the right man, won't we?"

Martin said slowly, "It's a reasonable proposition; it may even work. But after what's already happened I don't have to point out to you that if it does work there's considerable risk involved."

Ullman looked at him for a moment, and said grimly, "Mr. Martin, I have recently made a shocking discovery. In spite of all the propaganda to the contrary put out by the manufacturers of life preservers and seat belts, not to mention the insurance companies, there's really no law saying we're all obliged to live forever. You worry about setting it up the way you did last time. I'll worry about me."

"All right, I'll try to sell it for you." Martin glanced shorewards. "But you'll have to eat a lot of shit first, if you know what I mean. Just between us, that *hombre* who's marching this way likes to hear himself talk. Keep it under control now, *amigo*. I can't help you if you don't."

Ullman nodded. "Just one question, if you don't mind. Simonds told me what you people were covering up, but he didn't seem to know what Captain Rader had to hide. But that cop was certainly feeling embarrassed about something. Professionally embarrassed."

Martin hesitated, came to a decision, and grinned. "The Captain is sensitive about the fact that a large part of the time his men were out scouring the town for that terrible vandal-rapist-since-turned-murderer, Mr. Hans Rurik Olson, he was right under their noses doing time in the local *calabozo* for being drunk and disorderly and punching a policeman in the nose."

Ullman drew a long breath, and looked at the three men striding briskly up the dock with the smooth-looking blond one half a step in the lead. "Well, I suppose it's funny," he said. "But not very."

CHAPTER 33

June

Latitude 26°N; Longitude 80°W

Getting out of the taxi outside the gate, Elizabeth Cameron was a bit self-conscious about her clothes, as if she were arriving at an important party without having learned whether the ladies would be in short dresses or long. She felt more awkward and insecure than she had in years, as she gave her name to the guard.

"Yes, Miss. Just go around the end of the building there and you'll see them at the dock," the man said.

It was eerie down there at the waterfront so late at night in a part of Miami she'd never visited before. She hadn't had a chance to do much sightseeing in the busy months she'd been here. She walked quickly—a little fearfully—along the lighted street or driveway running between the tall chain-link fence on her left with the menacing barbed wire on top, and the bulky corrugated-metal building on her right, which looked like a warehouse or perhaps a boat shed. Ahead, she could see the water of the harbor and the massive, resting shapes of ships tied up at other docks in the distance.

Her rubber-soled shoes made small scuffing sounds clearly audible over the distant murmur of city traffic, and she knew that she was very apprehensive and that it was a very dumb thing she was doing, but you couldn't be smart all the time. The decision was made, right or wrong, so there was really nothing to worry about besides clothes. The trouble was, of course, that boats were totally outside her field of experience. She was aware that the white flannels and the blue blazer were no longer a mandatory part of the yachting scene, and what she was doing tonight could hardly be called yachting anyway; but she hated to turn up in jeans if everybody else was going to be wearing some kind of special boating costume or expecting to see her in one—like the tricky ski clothes or jogging suits or tennis dresses or other specialized uniforms that seemed to go with the sports she'd never had any chance to learn, being too busy learning how to survive, and a little more, in a hostile business environment.

Actually, she hated jeans, associating them since childhood with barns and manure and hard grubby chores around the farm they'd lived on until they'd moved to the shining metropolis of Des Moines, where her dad had joined his brother in the struggling family feed business. Current fashions notwithstanding, she still considered denim a totally unsuitable material for civilized wear and even an insult to other folks around who'd taken the trouble to dress properly. But on the other hand, jeans were generally a safe and practical choice outdoors. You could get wet and dirty in jeans without looking ridiculous, whereas if you had on smart, sharply pressed slacks, say, and maybe a neat, crisp little blouse, just one big wave—and she supposed boats did take waves aboard occasionally—could turn you into a bedraggled joke. And isn't that a hell of a petty consideration, Miss Cameron, when you are embarking on an expedition on which men will be risking their lives, and maybe even yours?

Well, she retorted, would it be better to brood about what it might be like to be killed?

Coming around the end of the building, she saw two boats lying along the dock under the lights. They had apparently just been put into the water after being moved out of the big metal boathouse—there was a tractor and a crane for the purpose—and they seemed like very big boats to be handled like that. She'd thought only canoes and rowboats were stored on shore. These looked, to her landlubber eyes, big enough to cross oceans, large rakish motorboats with roomy deckhouses and high control bridges on which men were running mysterious tests on the instruments and the idling motors. Other men were milling around in what seemed to be a very disorganized fashion, and most of them were armed, some with holstered pistols and others with ugly-looking two-handed weapons—submachine guns?—which they seemed to brandish in a very casual manner. She told herself that the funny dizzy breathless feeling she was experiencing was due to the Dramamine she'd taken before coming here; and then she told herself to stop kidding herself, she was just plain scared. But at least her choice of costume was correct. The men were all wearing sloppy work clothes with jeans and dungarees predominating.

In fact, the plump cheerful young man who came to greet her gave her quite an approving glance; apparently he had nothing whatever against dames in denim. He did regard her thin, short-sleeved blue gingham shirt rather critically, but relaxed when he saw the sweater in her hand.

"Good, good," he said. "You'll find it hard to believe at this time of year, but as I told you over the phone it still gets chilly out there at night, particularly at twenty knots. We'll be shoving off in a few minutes. That's our flagship over there, the *Gooney Bird.* Why don't you go aboard and make yourself comfortable? There's coffee in the galley; help yourself."

She walked past the first boat, named *Frivolous Falcon*—somebody seemed to have ornithology on the brain—to the *Gooney Bird,* which lay rumbling softly to itself with water spitting out of its twin exhausts. She stepped cautiously down into the cockpit area, half expecting the boat to tip dangerously with her weight, but it was reassuringly solid. She made her way into the deckhouse, which was a big empty cabin with benches down each side and a steering wheel forward; apparently, the boat could be run from down here as well as from up top. She could hear men moving above her, and from time to time one motor or the other would give a sudden roar, startling her badly. Coffee seemed like a good idea, and she found the kitchen—oops, galley—down a small stairway or ladder beside the wheel; and then it seemed smarter not to drink a lot of stuff until she'd determined what kind of facilities were available for disposing of it afterwards, since it was going to be a long night. There was also, Dramamine or no Dramamine, the potential problem of sea-sickness to be considered and where to go if it should hit her.

The idea of hanging over the side of the boat vomiting helplessly in front of all those men didn't appeal to her at all; and you certainly are a great girl for worrying about appearances, aren't you, Miss Cameron?

But the little toilet compartment she found seemed quite adequate, although the essential plumbing had an unfamiliar look and above it was posted a large sign: EXCEPT FOR TOILET PAPER DEPOSIT NOTHING IN THE HEAD YOU HAVE NOT EATEN FIRST. Head? All right, head. She determined how it worked, apparently by electricity; and with that important information stored away for future use she emerged and filled a plastic cup with coffee and returned to the deckhouse and sat down to sip it slowly while she waited.

It made her feel a little guilty to remember that the plump, cheerful young commander of the expedition, named Jerry Rawls, was operating under a slight misapprehension. He thought she was coming along on this raid, which really had nothing to do with her work involving drugs, just to get acquainted, since they'd be cooperating in the future on problems more directly connected with her duties as the local representative of PSCC, and it would be wonderful not to be totally dependent on the Coast Guard whenever a boat was needed to pursue a plan or inquiry that seemed promising. But Rawls would not have liked it if he'd known that her presence here tonight was a conscience matter, not a career matter—which was as close as she could come to explaining it to herself without getting into a lot of high-minded nonsense about principles and obligations, and if her male colleagues ever dreamed that she entertained such naive thoughts they'd consider her dangerously unsound but what could you expect of a mere woman, anyway?

The boat was filling with armed men, and Jerry Rawls was standing before her. "Maybe you'd like to ride up on the flybridge; it'll be kind of crowded down here. More coffee?"

"No, thank you."

Rawls disposed of her empty cup while she pulled on her navy blue turtleneck, which his blue eyes approved, although she was sure that a little more protuberance would have elicited even greater approbation—she was wryly aware that she wasn't really constructed to proper sweater-girl dimensions. One of the men now filling the deckhouse benches asked a question and Rawls said:

"Boys, this is Betsy. Look but don't touch."

"Look who's talking," somebody said. "Watch yourself, Betsy, we call him Octopus for short."

"Silence in the ranks!"

Even though she didn't particularly approve of the nickname or any nickname—if you were christened Elizabeth, not a bad name, why couldn't you be *called* Elizabeth?—the cheerful exchange gave her a nice feeling of acceptance and participation; and she gave them all a smile as she went out. A metal ladder brought her up to the flying bridge, where she was placed at the left—port?—end of a comfortably upholstered bench seat facing an impressive control panel and a low windshield. Rawls took the other end, while the steersman, introduced as Jack, sat between them. Rawls spoke softly into some kind of a radio and somebody answered.

"Falcon ready, yo."

"All lines," Rawls called to somebody on the deck below, and men ran around down there casting off the ropes holding the vessel to the dock, somewhat hampered by the two large inflated rubber boats, one on top of the other, lashed up forward. "Take her away, Jack," Rawls said.

As they cruised slowly through the harbor Elizabeth Cameron took a scarf from her pocket and tied it over her hair. A few minutes later she was glad she had done so as, with the lights of the city falling behind them, they seemed to rise out of the water and start rushing through the darkness at tremendous speed, accompanied by a great rumbling roar from the motors below. It was a thoroughly frightening experience at first and she expected it to end any moment with a dreadful crash, but as it went on and on she found her tense muscles relaxing and she began to half-enjoy the crazy charge through the night, even though she no longer had the slightest idea where they were or what direction they were heading.

Occasionally, a lighted buoy would appear blinking at them ahead, and draw abreast and fall behind; sometimes she'd catch a glimpse of a dark one rushing by, or a post carrying a reflective number that was just a brief gleam of light and color in the night; or the dim shape of a low island would slide by on one side or the other, sometimes both. She lost all sense of time and distance; but as the night wore on she found herself pleasantly relieved by the discovery that she didn't have the slightest feeling of nausea, perhaps because of the preventive medicine she'd taken, or perhaps just because the motion, although harsh and jolting, wasn't really as wild and swooping and rolly as she'd expected. It was more like riding in a car driven much too fast along a very bumpy road.

"Easy now," Rawls said at last, reaching out to touch Jack's arm.

Gooney Bird slowed and settled. Rawls reached for a switch and all lights went out except for the dim red instrument panel. Looking around, Elizabeth Cameron saw that the other lights, red, green, and white, which had followed them so faithfully, had also disappeared; it took a moment before she could distinguish the dark outlines of *Frivolous Falcon* still holding position back there. Their progress now seemed painfully slow after the long high-speed hours. They seemed to be getting nowhere at all, but gradually she became aware of the dark shape of land ahead, a promontory or island, she couldn't tell which.

"There's Manatee," Jack murmured. "Right on the nose."

"Pretty fair navigating for an amateur," Rawls said, and he spoke softly into his radio: "Far enough. Launch and load."

"Launch, yo," the radio answered.

"When you've got your boys away, move around the point and block the entrance channel. Remember, there's supposed to be a fast little runabout at the dock up the inlet there, probably well over thirty knots, so don't let it get out; you'll never catch it."

There was activity on the *Gooney Bird*'s bow deck now; the rubber boats were being eased overboard and men were scrambling into them. One dark figure came to stand below the bridge.

"Wait for daylight if you can," Rawls said. "If not, if they spot you, you'll have to play it by ear. But remember they've now got enough firepower in there to fight the Battle of the Bulge, but it was just delivered so it's probably not ready for action yet. The idea is not to give them time to get at it. And secure that damn boat first thing so nobody slips away."

"Yo."

The artificial-sounding voice of the radio said, "Boats launched. *Falcon* moving into assigned position."

Elizabeth Cameron watched the other boat gliding away, a darker shape in the darkness. Belatedly she was aware that her name had been spoken—well, that nickname she didn't really like. She looked quickly toward Rawls.

"Down into the cabin with you, Betsy," he said. "If there's

345

any shooting, I don't want to have to explain to the PSCC why I let their prize lady administrator stop a stray bullet."

She said quickly, "But the boat isn't armor-plated, is it? I can just as easily get hurt down there. . . ."

"Betsy." His voice was very soft. "This is a ship. I am the captain. You do not argue with ship captains, Betsy. Nautical Lesson Number One."

She controlled her annoyance and made her voice light. "I'm sorry, sir. No mutiny intended, sir."

"Good girl. To show your forgiving nature, how about handing us up some coffee? If you can manage without lights."

As she climbed down the steep ladder, she was aware of the rubber boats paddling silently away to be lost against the vague loom of the shore. She made her way through the blackness of the deckhouse and down into the galley and managed to fill two cups more or less by feel without spilling too much or burning herself too badly. She passed them up to the flying bridge. Then she paid a visit to the toilet—oops, head—and checked her hand just in time, as it was fumbling for the flush button in the dark. As she recalled, the mechanism made quite a bit of noise and obviously this was a time when silence had priority over sanitation. She poured some coffee for herself and drank it in the deckhouse, sitting by the open cockpit door where she could hear what went on outside, but for a very long time nothing at all happened.

Suddenly there was light at the deckhouse windows and she was aware that she'd fallen asleep and she was shocked at herself but also a little proud of herself; if she could sleep at a time like this she couldn't be too much of a coward, could she? But it was probably just the Dramamine working, she reminded herself.

Then she realized that she'd been awakened by a sound and she could still hear it: a hoarse, distant voice, actually a loud-speaker or bullhorn on shore, shouting some kind of orders or instructions. She stepped out into the cockpit in the gray morning light, but she still couldn't make out the words. A long time passed; then the radio up on the flying bridge spoke clearly:

"*Bird* this is Shore. Camp secured. Boat secured."

"Anybody hurt?"

"No casualties. But Swastika Boy is missing; they say he went off somewhere overnight."

"Search the island."

"Already under way."

"You can start bringing out the prisoners. . . . What the hell is *that*?"

Elizabeth Cameron heard it, too, a sudden wild snarling roar that seemed to come from well inside the point beyond which *Frivolous Falcon*—what a silly name—waited to cut off all escape by water. The radio squawked breathlessly:

"Shit, they had another boat way back in the mangroves, one of those goddamn big souped-up thunderboats Ochsner is breaking out. . . . OPEN FIRE OPEN FIRE. . . . Watch it, *Falcon,* here he comes!"

There were sharp little popping sounds ashore and it made her feel weak and strange to realize that she was hearing real gunfire, not recorded on videotape or film. Rawls gave a quick order above her and she caught at the doorjamb just in time to keep from being thrown the length of the cockpit as the big motors roared under her feet and *Gooney Bird* lunged forward; but she could still hear the rising banshee scream of enormous engines over there sounding like the unbearable climbing howl of a jet plane at takeoff. They were approaching *Falcon* now, and she could see armed men in the cockpit and on the foredeck and up on the bridge all waiting, staring shorewards. Suddenly, they all began to shoot at something not yet visible to Elizabeth Cameron, adding to the crazy ripping crackling sounds from the shore.

"There he is. . . . Oh, Christ, he must be doing fifty already and he's still got his foot down!" That was Jack's voice. "Jerry, goddamn it, the bastard's just not going to stop!"

Rawls was shouting into the radio: *"Falcon,* get clear, get clear! Bobby haul your ass the hell out of there the goddamn kraut's gone *kamikaze.* . . ."

She heard him groan, and she saw at last what they'd seen earlier from their higher position on the bridge: the long, low, sharp-pointed, wicked-looking hull, a great aquatic projectile, hurtling out of the mangroves straight toward the larger vessel blocking the channel. *Falcon* was starting to move, white water boiling out from under her stern, opening a gap behind her, but the onrushing speedboat scorned the escape offered. Still accelerating, the pitch of its screaming exhausts climbing steadily, it was tracking *Falcon* like a homing missile. Elizabeth Cameron was close enough now, and it was light enough, that she could see that the lone man in the cockpit had short gray hair and seemed to be grinning; at least she could see the flash of teeth, somehow evil, in a weathered middle-aged face. She remembered the wildly melodramatic terms used by Philip Martin: doomsday men, instant *Götter-dämmerung*. Then the two boats came together and the world came to an end. ...

Later, much later, it was evening again and she was leaving the hospital in Miami, some hospital in Miami, without quite remembering how she'd got there, but that was of course not true, she remembered, all right. She remembered exactly how she'd got there and why; she just wished she wouldn't. She had a Band-Aid on her forehead and a bandage on her hand and terrible pictures in her head.

She told herself that she felt so funny because of the ringing in her ears, diminishing now, but she knew that was not true, either. She felt so funny because she was going to break into little pieces any minute now, just as soon as she could afford to let go at last, but she had to find a suitable place to do it. Not in front of all those grim men whose comrades had died, who must not be bothered with a woman's stupid hysterics; not in front of the businesslike Coast-guardsmen who'd come to help; not in front of that white-coated doctor who'd wanted to stuff her full of something nasty and tranquilizing and would have done so if she'd given him half an excuse; but somewhere warm and friendly and safe. She found herself turning back and she heard herself ask a question of the girl at the information desk, and she was walking down a hall to a telephone booth and putting coins in the slot and praying there would be an answer, and there was.

She heard herself say quite steadily, "Philip, I need help. Can you come and get me?"

"Where?"

She told him and hung up and sat for a long time wondering at herself, calling to a man she'd only met three times in her life—that was actually, she realized, the first time she'd used his given name—instead of somebody she really knew and trusted, but who? She forced herself to leave the shelter of the booth and walk slowly toward the street again, knowing that the girl at the desk was regarding her with concern, which annoyed her. It was a hospital, wasn't it? So what was so strange, in a hospital, about a bandaged lady zombie, they must get them every day of the week, and why couldn't people mind their own business? Then she told herself she wasn't being fair, the girl meant well, why take it out on her?

Outside, the evening air was warm after the refrigerated atmosphere inside and she leaned in the doorway and then, minutes later or maybe hours, Philip Martin was there, tall and lean and reassuring, coming around the car that had just pulled up to the curb, taking from her hand the sweater she'd forgotten she was carrying, and leading her across the sidewalk and helping her in and closing the door. She leaned back against the headrest and shut her eyes, but that was no good. She could see too many ugly things with her eyes shut. She was aware that, as they drove away, Philip spoke briefly into a mobile phone unit under the dash.

"Did . . . did you get my message?" she whispered after they'd driven a while. "I thought you'd want to know about Ochsner as soon as possible."

"Yes. Thanks. We're . . . the information is being acted on."

"It . . . blew up," she whispered. "They said afterwards that it was all loaded with . . . with . . ." She rubbed her forehead with both hands, carefully avoiding the Band-Aid. "I can't remember. Some kind of explosive. Just a floating bomb. Why would he do something like that?"

"I told you. Some people like company when they go. Probably his only regret was that he couldn't get a nice big Coast Guard cutter instead." Then he turned to her angrily, driving. "Goddamn it, I told you to wash your hands of it. I told you to keep clear. I told you it could get nasty. What the hell were you doing there anyway, taking a boat ride just for kicks?" After a moment he reached out and touched her bandaged hand lightly. "Sorry. But you could have been killed. How bad is that?"

She looked down at her hand. "Nothing. I just cut myself a little. Broken glass, I think. . . . I had to go, Philip. I tried to warn them, I kept telling them what you'd said, but they just laughed and wouldn't listen. And I'd started it, hadn't I? So, if they wouldn't listen to me, I just had to go with them, didn't I?"

After a moment, looking at her again, he said softly, "Yes. Of course you did."

The look in his eyes made her angry. She hadn't been talking for his respect or admiration; what was there to respect or admire? A girl couldn't help being born that kind of stupid, could she?

"Where are we going?" she asked.

"Where do you want to go?"

"Where I can . . . throw a wingding in private. I hope you

don't object to hysterical women because you've got one. The lady's about to blow her stack."

"I suggest my hotel room," he said in an expressionless voice. "I'd like to stay close to the phone tonight. If you don't mind."

She glanced at him and knew he was wondering if she would be corny and misconstrue the suggestion. It was a kind of test, but going with him would be a kind of test also, telling her something she needed very much to know, she realized, but perhaps at a price.

"Yes," she said. "That will do."

The rest of the ride was just a haze of movement; and the ringing in her ears, although steadily fading, still made everything seem very far away. Then he was closing the room door behind them and leading her to a chair and excusing himself to make a quick telephone call and coming back to put a drink in her hand.

"You didn't get knocked out or anything, did you?"

"No."

"Then I guess a little Scotch won't hurt you." He pulled a chair around and sat down facing her and said, "Now tell me. If you want to."

She nodded. "His name was Rawls, Jerry Rawls," she said. "A nice boy. He'd made me go down from the boat's bridge, earlier. I guess he saved my life. When I climbed back up there after it . . . after the explosion he had a . . . a thing right through his neck. Aluminum. A piece of molding or something. Like a spear. He held my hand and tried to tell me something but he died. And Jack the steersman—helmsman?—wasn't even there, he must have got blown right off the boat, I never saw him again. And the boat was all broken along one side, at least the deckhouse was, but it didn't sink, but the other ones, Ochsner's and the one they called *Frivolous Falcon*—isn't that a dumb name?—were all gone. Just pieces and stuff all over the water." She took a big gulp of her drink and discovered to her surprise that made the glass empty. "I . . . I didn't know things like that really happened. But the *really* bad thing, I mean the really *bad* thing . . ."

He said, "Easy. Take your time."

"When it happened," she said steadily, "when it happened it was like the end of the world and I threw myself down in the cockpit and buried my face in my arms and things kept falling all around and it . . . it went thump right beside me, I heard it. Or felt it, I wasn't hearing very well, I wasn't hearing at all, I thought I'd gone deaf, and when I looked it was right there. . . ." Her voice was rising but she couldn't do anything about it and she was on her feet for no particular reason and she felt him take the empty glass from her hand and set it aside. "It was a piece . . . just a piece of . . . it was an arm and the fingers were still moving but how could they when it wasn't even . . . wasn't even *attached* . . . ?"

Suddenly she was making crazy gasping sobbing choking sounds and clinging to him helplessly and being led to the bed, where she lay face down stuffing part of the pillow into her mouth to stop the idiotic noises but it didn't help very much. And all the time, the small remaining sane part of her mind kept wondering how, with her everlasting stupid concern for appearances, she could be making such a fool of herself before a man she didn't know and feeling no embarrassment at all. After a while the moronic racket did stop and she sat up and swallowed hard and rubbed her nose with the back of her unbandaged hand, looking up at him.

"I guess," she said unsteadily, "I guess that's it. The show's over for tonight. Every evening at eight-thirty. Parental guidance only."

He grinned. "Go wash your face. I'll make you another drink."

"Philip?"

"Yes?"

She was aware that her hair was a mess and one of her shirt tails was out and to hell with it. If he wanted glamor he could turn on the TV.

"Why did I call you?" she asked, honestly puzzled.

"So I could see how you looked with a red nose before I made up my mind," he said. "Except, of course, that I'd made it up already."

She licked her lips childishly. "Have I?"

"Of course or you wouldn't have called." He helped her rise and urged her toward the bathroom door. "Go on, *querida*."

She looked back at him over her shoulder. "I think . . . I think this is a perfectly ridiculous thing," she said. "Shouldn't you kiss me, or something?"

"When you ask for help around here, Elizabeth," he said, "help is what you get. Let us not confuse the issue with a lot of irrelevant osculation."

His voice was oddly strained and she looked at him more closely and realized with a shock that, although she'd never felt less seductive in her life, this dark and rather dangerous-looking man wanted her badly. He wanted her so badly, she saw, that he didn't trust himself at all; and he was asking her not to make it harder for him because it would damage something that was valuable and important to them both if he allowed himself—even with her permission—to take advantage of her on this rather ugly day, in her present shaken and vulnerable condition. Which was, of course, exactly what she'd come here to find out without ever having thought it out clearly.

She smiled. "Irrelevant osculation," she murmured. "That's nice. I like that, Philip. But don't make that drink too strong if we're going to be so strong-minded."

In the bathroom mirror, she didn't look like anything to kindle burning desire in a man; but she hadn't made it all the way from Des Moines, Iowa, the hard way, without learning a little about it. She knew it wasn't always, or even often, a simple matter of tight sweaters and black lace lingerie. They were very complicated people really, men were, and this one was more complicated than most; but the important thing was that he did want her and that, wanting her, he was nevertheless willing to wait, and capable of waiting until things were right and good, which they most certainly weren't tonight.

As she fixed her face and struggled with her hair, she decided that the plain, tired female in the glass really didn't look so bad in her beat-up way. At least she had an honest look, which was more than you could say for the sleek, phony executive lady who usually confronted her. Honest—and happy? It was, she reflected, a peculiar day to be happy and even disregarding the terrible sights she'd witnessed only a few hours earlier, what did she have to be happy about, anyway? That she'd somehow managed to get herself irrevocably involved with a man from a totally different background, who'd been born to a language she didn't know and a religion she didn't really approve of, whose family, if he had any in this country, would probably disapprove of her? She felt as if she were again on that boat rushing through the black night toward an unknown destination; and she knew that the destination could again be total disaster; but she was smiling as she turned from the mirror.

But the smile died when, emerging, she saw him at the telephone with the cold grim face of a total stranger.

"I see," he was saying. "So the desk hero loused it up and got himself shot and Tommy . . . Where'd they take Tommy?

Okay, I'll check there. What about Richardson, as if anybody cares? Same place? Well, hold the fort, I'll be right over. For whatever good it will do now."

It wasn't fair, Elizabeth Cameron thought. There had been enough for one day. They didn't need this, whatever it was.

"Trouble?" she asked when he looked her way.

He wasn't really seeing her. He nodded absently. "Excuse me," he said and punched a number on the phone and talked to somebody and asked a question. Then he said flatly, "I see. DOA. Thank you very much. . . . Oh, what about the other one, Anthony Richardson? Critical? When will the doctor be able to . . . all right, I'll call back then. Thank you." He drew a long breath and looked up at her and said, "I'm sorry, I didn't get you that drink."

She said, "I know what DOA means, Philip. A friend?"

He nodded. "A very good guy named Tommy Walsh. And the stupid sonofabitch who thought he could run the bastard show in the field all by himself after parking his ass behind a desk for over a decade, this ambitious executive hero took Tommy out and got him killed for goddamn nothing. And maybe himself too, but we wouldn't be that lucky. Those pompous jerks never get what's coming to them." His voice was savage. He ran a hand over his face and said more quietly, "Please delete that, Elizabeth. We do not wish for the death of anyone in the outfit; and we do not speak harshly of our superiors, ever. Well, hardly ever. But we knew that Columbus would react violently if anything happened to Ochsner; yet after your warning came in, Richardson wouldn't let me handle it although that's what I'm for, that's what my military experience is for, that's what my field experience is for. He insisted on going out there himself, bravely sharing the danger with the troops, running it all himself. When I tried to argue about the idiot way he was setting it up he grounded me. Insubordination. One man less to help out and the team was short-handed already, the way that office genius had spread everybody from hell to breakfast. But he was bound it was going on his record as a great personal triumph. . . ." He shook his head abruptly and rose and came to her. "Feeling better?"

"Don't worry about me. I'm all right now."

"I'm going to have to get down there and go through the motions of trying to find a missing guy named Columbus before all hell breaks loose."

"I can take a taxi."

"Thanks. I've got a few more calls to make here first." He looked at her for a moment; it was a moment of complete understanding as if they were man and wife and had been for years. "We're not doing well today, Elizabeth," he murmured. "Just a couple of losers."

She put her hands on his shoulders and rose to kiss him lightly on the mouth because there was no question of temptation now.

"Call me when you can, my dear," she said.

As she went out, remembering to take her sweater from the back of the chair where he'd hung it, she was ashamed of herself for the very selfish thought that the way it had worked out was terrible, of course; but under any other circumstances he would not have been there when she telephoned in distress.

CHAPTER 34

July

Latitude 24°N; Longitude 82°W

It was a good-sized hospital some distance outside Key West up the hundred-and-fifty-mile patchwork of elderly bridges and narrow causeways and ancient pavement—modernization was under way but it still had a long way to go—that linked the Florida Keys, like beads on a string, with the mainland and Miami. Having been brought there in an ambulance, Janet McHugh couldn't visualize the geography quite clearly and it worried her. She knew that, although they were discharging her as recovered from her ordeal, her body still wasn't functioning quite normally after all the time she'd spent in the life raft after *Stream Hunter*'s hijacking; but she'd always been very good about directions and locations and it frightened her to think that a little hardship might have dulled her mind.

354

Outside the front door, the brash, good-looking young PR man the company had sent down to help her deal with the press and keep her happy—she'd have loved to know just how far he was expected to go in carrying out those instructions—ushered her solicitously, a little too solicitously, into the rear of the enormous hired car that looked as if it belonged, if not at the very head of the funeral procession, at least not too far back; there was even a uniformed black chauffeur. It seemed to Janet McHugh that McHugh Enterprises, Inc. was entertaining delusions of grandeur both for themselves and for her; they were acting as if she were the new-made widow of General Motors. A drive-yourself Chevy would have done the job perfectly well.

It was supposed to be flattering, of course. It was supposed to show how concerned they all were about her well-being. Actually, it was a pretty deadly insult, she reflected, demonstrating what a trashy and impressionable female creep they considered her, a sucker for elongated Cadillacs. They were obviously taking no chances—or thought they weren't—of antagonizing the fortune-hunting little blonde tramp who'd been rigging fishy baits on a charter boat when Chuck McHugh found her and fell for her cheap and obvious charms; and who now by the terms of the will pretty well held the destiny of the company in her greedy little hands. They were going to bow and scrape to her, and keep her in handsome escorts and glossy limousines, until they knew exactly what kind of a dumb and self-important bitch they had to deal with.

In a way it was a challenge. It was almost enough to persuade her to head for New Jersey right away and hire some good lawyers working for *her* and determine just how much clout she really had up there and how big a scare Captain Jaspers' little girl Janet could throw into those mushy summer people who'd always considered her one of Chuck's few serious errors of judgment. She'd never bothered her head much about the business, but it obviously wasn't something that required genius considering the people who were involved in running it—aside from Chuck, who'd been a little special—and if she could survive three weeks on a raft she could damn well survive a few offices and boardrooms. But that would have to wait. At the moment she had other things to do. Well, one other thing.

She'd been brought down to the hospital's front door in a wheelchair, but she'd had to walk out to the car, and it disturbed her how shaky she still was, even though she'd been marching up and down the hospital corridors in a weakly determined fashion for several days. She shifted position uncomfortably on the luxurious seat and was tempted to shock her companion by mentioning that, after spending several weeks with her glamorous derrière parked in a puddle of saltwater, the glamorous heiress beside him still had a very tender ass.

But they were turning onto the main road now, heading north and east, and she was recognizing the landmarks and everything was falling into place in a reassuring way.

It was a lovely place to be. Well, any place was a lovely place to be, alive, when you'd come so close to being dead; but the Keys always pleased her: the fantastically blue water and the fantastically green islands and the fantastically blue sky and the bright sunshine. To be sure, the developers and exploiters had done their best to spoil the area, but they hadn't quite managed it yet. A clear picture formed in her mind of the road—they called it the Overseas Highway—running back to Key West and forward to Marathon and Islamorada and Key Largo and the old lift bridge across Jewfish Creek leading to the mainland and Miami; or you could drive a bit farther and use the new, high Card Sound bridge and pay the toll. So the head was still working all right, and all she had to worry about was the legs. And the stomach which, poor shrunken thing, never seemed to get enough to eat these days.

"There's a resort up ahead in Marathon called Faro Blanco," she said after they'd driven a while. "It's got a pretty good café and grill on the highway. About ten miles now, left side, after we come off that endless bridge they call Seven Mile Bridge. I'd like to stop there and get a hamburger, if you don't mind."

The breezy young PR man, whose name was Jonathan (call me Johnny) Bradshaw, put a hand on her arm and a look of concern on his face. "Are you sure you should, Jan, baby? I thought the doctor-man said—"

He was quite a specimen, she reflected coldly; and they'd probably had a hard time deciding between him and some polite young gentleman who'd treat her with the utmost respect and address her as Mrs. McHugh, ma'am. The consensus of the board, or committee, or whoever made those decisions, had obviously been that this flip, phony character was more her type. Well, there was nothing like seeing yourself

356

the way other people saw you for keeping your ego in check.

Actually, he wasn't bad-looking if you liked the modern crop of hard, pretty boys with carefully girlish hairdos that made them look very sweet indeed—sweet and, she'd always thought, a little sinister like pearl-handled pistols, dainty but deadly, since they had no scruples or principles and would allow themselves to be used for any purpose whatever as long as it paid. Johnny Bradshaw had big hornrimmed glasses that were probably calculated to make him look intellectual and trustworthy, with clip-on shades, and he was wearing the usual Florida uniform of light slacks and a colorful short-sleeved shirt, but he hadn't been down here long enough to acquire the tan that was supposed to go with the uniform, so he looked a little pale and unhealthy. Well, she wasn't exactly bursting with health herself; but she wasn't so feeble she couldn't do something about that overconcerned and oversolicitous hand of his if it became a real problem. However, there was no sense in starting a feud unnecessarily.

She said, "I'm absolutely starving to death and the doctor said I should build myself up; so let's start building." She changed position slightly to get rid of his touch and smiled to show there were no hard feelings and went on with a childish eagerness that wasn't altogether feigned: "I want it just the way I dreamed about it on that damned raft. I guess you think that's pretty lower-class dreaming, Johnny; a real lady would have filet mignon dreams, wouldn't she? But I just dreamed hamburgers, great big juicy rare hamburgers—oh, damn, he said I mustn't, didn't he? All right, have them grill hell out of it just to make the medical profession happy. A little mustard. No relish. To go. You and the driver get yourselves some coffee or whatever you like, and we'll drive down to their marina and look at some boats while we're eating."

It was obvious that he thought he was dealing with a female nut and wondering how he could turn it to his, or the company's, advantage—hamburger at ten in the morning, for heaven's sake—but it tasted wonderful. It was the first real, nonhospital food she'd eaten since she'd come ashore; but she found herself having to remind herself sternly not to wipe her messy fingers on her nice clean dress, life-raft fashion. You're back in the world of the napkin and the Kleenex, honey, she told herself, and don't you forget it. Bradshaw was having coffee and the driver, whose name was Markham Johnson, was having coffee and a doughnut. She must have wolfed down her hamburger in a most unladylike fashion because they still had a long way to go.

"Don't hurry, I'm going to stretch my legs a bit," she said.

Getting out of the ridiculous hearse of a car she stood for a moment, uncertain in her high heels, looking around. She would have preferred to wear slacks but none of the clothes in the suitcase Bradshaw had brought her from up north had really fit even though they were her own; all the pants had been so big she'd have had to tie a clothesline around her waist to keep them up. Only this loose white sleeveless dress had looked halfway reasonable on her new skinny figure; and there had been no footgear to go with it except the damned white pumps.

The marina was laid out in two sections separated by the fuel dock; and on previous occasions, bringing *Stream Hunter* here, they'd always wound up in the large basin to the west. She'd already had Johnson take them past that so she could check all the boats but the one she was looking for wasn't there, of course—it wasn't going to be that easy. They'd driven on to park by the smaller eastern basin where the waterfront road was wider; and now she had a view of the little boats lined up along the outer breakwater with the wide expanse of Florida Bay beyond. Closer was a row of larger vessels, mostly power but a few sail, tied up stern-to in slips along the inner sea wall. None of those looked familiar, either.

On the transom of one of the powerboats was a black sign with luminous red printing. Curious, she teetered across the road, annoyed by her own weakness and the goddamn heels, and walked slowly and carefully along the water in that direction and stood looking at the taped-on cardboard placard: FOR SALE. The boat was named *Searcher*. It seemed like an omen of sorts since a search was exactly what she was planning and something stirred in her mind that was half mischief—it was time she learned just what this heiress racket was worth—and half yearning for something that had recently gone out of her life.

The boat before her was about forty feet long with a shippy, sturdy look very different from *Stream Hunter*'s sleek and powerful and racy appearance. It was one of the slow pseudo-trawler designs that were becoming quite popular now that fuel prices had risen to the point where big fast boats like *Hunter* would bankrupt the average citizen who tried to keep the enormous tanks full. This one, she thought, would probably cruise at eight to ten knots, running all day on a teacup of diesel. It was not a real trawler, of course; those were tough, deep, crude, chunky commercial craft designed to carry heavy loads of fish. This was a lighter and yachtier vessel but it did have the square roomy deckhouse and walk-around decks and high bulwarks and total lack of streamlining characteristic of the type—who needed streamlining at eight knots—and it probably also had considerable cruising range. It had a short mast and boom for setting a small steadying sail perhaps, and for swinging the dinghy aboard. Built somewhere in the Orient for economy, she guessed, but that was nothing against it; they could do very good work over there, and nowadays many American companies had excellent stock boats constructed over there for sale here. A survey would determine how well it was put together; she didn't have to concern herself with that.

A young man in swimming trunks, very brown, was polishing something up on the flying bridge. He paid her no attention which wasn't very good for the ego; she wasn't all *that* scrawny, dammit, and did he want to sell his boat or didn't he? Then a woman—girl—inside the deckhouse caught sight of her through the glass and stepped quickly out on the side deck.

"Is there . . . can we do something for you?"

The voice was hopeful. The girl wore a scanty red polka-dot bikini; and she was half-pretty with a mop of light brown hair curled all over her head and a nice little brown body and big brown eyes, but the designer had goofed when he got to the mouth, which was petulant and pouty.

"Yes, I'd like to come aboard if you don't mind," Janet McHugh said. She glanced at the sign. "This boat *is* for sale, isn't it?"

"Oh, yes!" the girl said eagerly. "Yes, it certainly is! George, this lady wants to look at the boat."

"All right, I'm coming, just a minute."

It was all there, Janet McHugh thought grimly, in the girl's eagerness and the man's reluctance. It was all too clear who wanted to sell and who didn't; and it was the same old corny story she'd encountered around the marinas a hundred times before. It always made her ashamed of the female half of the human race; but in this case she could hardly knock it since, as it turned out, it enabled her to arrange to buy a nice, sound boat at a very reasonable price—and render Mr.

Jonathan Bradshaw quite speechless in the bargain. Unfortunately, he recovered quickly.

"Well, I've got to hand it to you, Mrs. Mac," he said as they were driving away. "When you see something you want you don't mess around. But—"

"But what?"

"I don't want to butt in, I don't know a damn thing about boats, but those folks are taking you, you know that, don't you? You're not supposed to jump at the first figure mentioned, particularly when the girl obviously wants to unload that tub the worst way. I tell you what, this marine surveyor we're getting in before we finalize the deal—he's kind of an appraiser, isn't he?—he's going to find something wrong, he's bound to. Okay, leave it to Johnny-boy. With just a little leverage like that I can get that price down to fifty-five for you easy, or at least an even sixty. Those people are *hungry*, baby, they want *out*."

She shook her head. "Leave it alone, Johnny," she said. "The price is fair and the poor guy's taking a beating at home; I don't have to screw him, too."

After a moment, Bradshaw squeezed her arm lightly and let it go. "Sure. You're nice people, Mrs. Mac. I guess I just haven't had too much practice dealing with those."

She was too tired to sort out all the implications of that; she merely said, "If you really want to be helpful, you can get out a notebook or something and let me give you a list of what's got to be done. We're going to visit a nice old guy I used to work for here named Captain Jim Easley. I was going to stop by and see him and his wife anyway for old times' sake; I called from the hospital last night to let them know I was coming. But he knows all the local boatyards and people and he can tell you whom to see. . . . Mark, please take the first right after the next bridge."

"Yes, ma'am."

She glanced at Bradshaw and saw that he had a small note pad ready. It was getting hard for her to concentrate, but she said, "First we need a good mechanic to look over the power plant so he can run it while the boat's still in the water; he should check the generator at the same time, of course. Then she's got to be hauled so the surveyor can go over her carefully, top to bottom. Incidentally, it's always the buyer's responsibility to pay for that, sale or no sale, so don't argue about it. If the surveyor is satisfied, and I think he will be, get a lawyer to nail down the deal and switch the documentation to my name; but before she goes back into the water I want the bottom scraped and given a good coat of anti-fouling paint; she's grown a real weed garden sitting in that slip." Janet McHugh drew a long breath and grinned. "Well, that's about it; and while you're running around in the heat, getting it all under way for me, I'll be eating a big slab of Mrs. Easley's homemade pie and taking a nap in their guest room. . . ."

You could always count on boat people, she thought half an hour later sitting in the kitchen with Captain Jim's wife who had, as she'd confidently expected, baked one of her pies— French apple, as it happened—in honor of the visit. They were, of course, talking over the old days when she'd crewed for Captain Jim and become for a short time almost part of the family, her own parents being dead and the two Easley children having married and moved away from the Keys. But there was always something special about boat people. Now Mrs. Easley, a small, round, red-faced, gray-haired woman, rose briskly and said without hints or prompting:

"But it's your first day out of the hospital, child, and now we're going to take that pretty dress off you and tuck you in bed for a little while the men make their arrangements. I wish you'd change your mind and stay overnight. You don't look fit to make the drive to Miami."

"I'll make it," Janet said. "I've got to; there are a lot of people I've arranged to see tomorrow."

"Who are these people who can't wait?"

"Wait? All they do is wait! It's weeks now since I reported the hijacking and, from what I can find out over the phone, nobody's done a thing about it. They've just put *Stream Hunter* on a list along with *Pirate's Lady* and *Flying Dutchman* and all the other famous missing yachts that keep staying missing. They feel that takes care of their responsibilities. I've got to see if I can't shake them up a bit, Aunt Martha. If I can't, I guess I'll just have to get out and do it all myself."

"That's foolish talk," Mrs. Easley said. "Now you lie down and take a nap."

"All right, but first let me talk to Captain Jim. . . . Or maybe you know if Brodie Kotoski's still around."

"That Brodie!" Mrs. Easley said. "You want nothing to do with that man, Janet! Why, you certainly must remember that Captain Jim had to fire him and hire you on as mate because the big ox was always in trouble! Rum trouble,

361

woman trouble, fight trouble, even jail trouble! What do you want with Brodie?"

"I need a captain for my new boat."

"Brodie? You should be back in that hospital seeing a head doctor, child!"

"He's a good man with a boat."

"Sometimes. When he is sober. But he is not a good man with a young girl."

"I'm not a young girl, I'm an old married woman, a widow even; and Brodie and I came to an understanding long ago. He won't get out of line. And I think I'm going to need a man like that, Aunt Martha. Tell me where I can reach him and let me use your phone."

Mrs. Easley looked at her for a moment, and moved her plump shoulders briefly. "You come into the back room and lie down now before you fall on your face. If you must have Mr. Broderick Kotoski, I will have Captain Jim call him for you, and impress on him how he will find himself chopped into very small pieces and fed to very large sharks if he takes advantage of our girl in any way. . . ."

CHAPTER 35

July

Latitude 26°N; Longitude 80°W

Visiting the Yacht Club docks was always, Philip Martin reflected, like landing on a different planet. Of course the same was true when you entered a country club or ski resort or hunting or fishing lodge. There was always the special atmosphere of the sport with its mystique accepted and understood by everyone around, and the special language and equipment that went with it, and the way they all looked at you and determined at a glance, somehow, that you were not a proper Martian or Venusian or Jupiterian and therefore didn't really count. But here the equipment was particularly impressive and, unlike ski poles or golf clubs or guns, rather beautiful even to the uninitiated.

It was a bright morning with the heat of the oncoming Florida summer clearly implied in the burning sunshine. He was too warm with his coat on but in order to leave it in the car he'd have had to shed the gun harness as well and it wasn't worth the effort; he didn't really mind a little heat. After checking at the dockmaster's office for the man he wanted, temporarily absent, he walked slowly along the dock between the handsome boats and stood at the end looking out toward the islands, the same islands that sheltered the large Dinner Key Marina only a few blocks south where Harold Ullman's little cutter *Nancy Lou* still lay with the owner still living on board, human bait for a human predator that didn't seem interested.

The photograph Ullman had selected as most closely corresponding to his memory of the late Hans Rurik Olson's slender, mustached, nylon-masked accomplice had been that of a young man—one of several young men—who hung around pretty Francesca Columbus and sometimes ran unimportant errands for her father. Even if the identification was correct, it seemed doubtful that Pedro Orosco could be important enough to Columbus' plans to cause Don Jaime, in hiding, to make a long-distance effort to save him from arrest and conviction on a relatively minor charge. Doubtful but not quite certain, Martin reflected; and he was doing a little extra work on Orosco to determine if, perhaps, he had not underestimated that young man, whose role as love-struck swain might well be cover for more important activities related to the Columbus household.

Anyway, it was a lead of sorts in a situation that offered very few leads, now that Columbus had gone underground. Furthermore, it gave Ullman a role to play that kept him out of mischief. Martin grimaced wryly at the thought. Although he'd sensed a definite potential for violence there, he'd certainly underestimated how far that green-eyed young man would go if sufficiently provoked. *Lobo,* indeed.

A three-man team had been given the job of surveillance and protection. Linkowski, assisted by Donny Brent—recalled from the useless Key West operation, which had been scrubbed—had the duty of covering Ullman when he went ashore; while on board his boat he was watched over, strangely enough, by Bill Simonds, who'd requested the job since it involved simply living on the neighboring boat—the same sloop as before, lent by the same cooperative owner—and keeping an eye on *Nancy Lou* and alerting the shore agent on duty whenever Ullman headed for town. This could all be managed easily enough by a man with a damaged foot, now healing well; the strange thing was that Simonds would be willing to help protect the man who'd humiliated and maimed him.

"Look," Martin had said to him, "I don't know what kind of revenge you have in mind, Bill, but—"

Simonds had shaken his head quickly. "No revenge. I was mad as hell at first, naturally. Nobody likes to be made to look that bad, not to mention what he did to me. But god-damn it, Phil, I had it coming; we all did after the way we tried to use those people without their knowledge; and the red-haired bastard didn't get any rougher than he had to. I'm never going to love him like a brother; but after going off and letting the wife get killed like that I'd appreciate a crack at preserving what's left of the goddamn Ullman family. Until I can get around a little better, it's all I'm good for anyway."

Actually, Simonds had been lucky all the way around, Martin reflected wryly. With Richardson disabled, nobody was interested in investigating the competence or security angles of the crazy, embarrassing incident; but almost as important was the fact that he had in a sense been granted absolution. They were all responsible for what had happened to Ullman's attractive young ex-wife, but Simonds alone had been allowed to atone for his part of it with a little blood and suffering. It wasn't something Martin would have expected the younger man to feel, but obviously he did feel it; which indicated that he was brighter and more sensitive than Martin had thought him; a young agent worth watching.

There was still no sign of the man Martin had come to see; and he stood looking out over the anchored boats in the harbor thinking that it was a pleasant place and a pleasant view. He was going to miss Florida when and if orders took him elsewhere. There were too many people, of course, and they weren't all attractive; but the clear water and the endless islands were always intriguing. You could see that a little boat might be very enjoyable in these surroundings, with the right company. . . . Cut it out, *amigo,* he told himself sharply, you haven't got time for that, and you don't know a damn thing about boats, and a girl brought up in corn country is always bound to get miserably seasick afloat anyway.

But then he reminded himself that, come to think of it, Elizabeth Cameron had apparently survived her wild night boat ride with that crazy commando outfit, whatever the hell they'd called themselves, without much discomfort until the stupid bastards had let themselves get blown sky-high despite all warnings; and damn her for risking her life like that for her stiff-necked sense of responsibility—but would you desire her so much if she were otherwise, *Señor* Martinez? And *Dios*, how lovely she'd looked sitting on the bed that night in her rough boat clothes with her hair tousled like a child's and her face shiny with tears and no defenses left; a real girl, no, a real woman, no longer just a carefully costumed executive-type manikin. . . .

"You wished to see me, *Señor* Martin?"

He turned to look into Reuben Montoya's dark, plump, sad face with its narrow black mustache. The Yacht Club's assistant dockmaster was wearing his customary cap and coveralls and at first glance he appeared neat and competent, but a second glance showed the uneasy fear inside him—and what the devil did Montoya have to be so afraid of now that Columbus had gone into hiding taking with him, among others, his two bully-boys?

Martin smiled reassuringly. "Don't worry, *amigo,* I have no more questions about your friend Columbus."

"*Señor* Colombo is no friend of Montoya," the assistant dockmaster said stiffly. "I have told you that. I do not know this man you ask about. Only by reputation."

It was beside the point, and it had been said before, but Martin could not help repeating: "You've been seen more than once in conversation with this man's associates, Jesus Cardenas and the one known as Bolo."

Montoya made a sharp gesture of irritation. "I tell you again I talk with many people here. It is my job. I do not remember them all. What is it you wish, *Señor* Martin?"

"Just a little information about a boat that used to dock here," Martin said. "We're interested in a sportfisherman called *Stream Hunter*. It was hijacked recently returning from Cozumel, Mexico. The crew was set adrift. Only one person, the wife of the owner, survived. I thought you might be able to tell me something about them, since you looked after their boat here, I gather, when they weren't using it."

"We look after many boats here," Montoya said, "but of

course I remember that one. I read the terrible thing that happened. What can I tell you? She's a modified forty-eight-foot Striker sportfisherman, very handsome, very fast for her size, very expensive. Not quite a Rybovitch, perhaps, but a very fine fishing machine and beautifully equipped. Come, I will show you where she was docked. Right over here, A14. It's strange that you should ask about her today, Mr. Martin. The lady just called yesterday. Mrs. McHugh. She has a new forty-foot trawler yacht she's bringing up from the Keys— well, her captain is; she's at a hotel here in town waiting to go aboard—and she wanted to make sure her slip would be available. Poor lady, it must have been a terrible experience for her, *muy malo,* but I am not surprised she was the one who survived, she was always the sailor of that family. The husband was interested only in fish. . . . Here we are." He stopped at a finger pier alongside which rested a large single-masted sailboat. "We use the space for transients when the regular boats are not cruising; this one I will have to move to another dock before Mrs. McHugh's new boat arrives."

Martin wondered what an ordinary boat slip lacking the boat under discussion was supposed to show him, but it was just part of the razzle-dazzle, he realized; of Montoya's sudden transformation from a sullen, reluctant witness from whom the words had to be dragged by force, to a helpful and cooperative chatterbox frantically volunteering information, mostly worthless, right and left. Well, one way of avoiding questions you did not want to answer was to talk so fast they could not be asked; but what was it Montoya was afraid to be asked?

Martin said, "I've only read some rather sketchy newspaper accounts so far. How many were aboard when they left for Cozumel?"

"I did not see them go, *Señor,*" Montoya said. "However, I do recall that Mr. and Mrs. McHugh had invited another couple from New Jersey, I believe a business associate and his wife, not good people. They were here for a couple of days while the boat was being prepared for the cruise. Gregertsen, that was the name. He thought he was a seaman, that one, a large pig of a man with a loud voice; and the wife, a real *puta* except who wants to do business with an alcoholic whore? A glass or two beforehand for pleasure, perhaps; but this *Señora* finished the whole bottle each night she was here and usually wound up screaming drunkenly at her husband.

366

I was really very unhappy for the McHughs, *Señor;* they were fine people and they had been looking forward to this trip very much. They would have done better to sail by themselves. You know the old saying, *Mas vale estar solo que mal acompañado.* Better to be alone than in bad company."

The translation was a deliberate insult, of course, a sneer by one expatriate at another who had rejected the old country and the old ways; it implied scornfully that Martin probably needed help, by now, to understand the language to which he had been born, but what could one expect of a turncoat who even carried a *gringo* badge and a *gringo* gun? Yet the fact was that Montoya himself had apparently tried to break free of the past to some degree; he'd moved his family to the nonethnic neighborhood of Coral Shores. But he had been followed there with threats and intimidation—and what had he been forced to do that now filled him with guilt and fear, and how could he be made to talk? Well, it could not be done here and now, that was clear. More information was needed; more leverage.

"Do you know where Mrs. McHugh is staying?" Martin asked.

"She has a suite at the Four Seasons. She is quite a wealthy lady now—and only a few years ago she was just another ragged-ass beach-bum girl helping out on a charter boat down in the Keys."

"A real little Cinderella, eh?" Martin said. "But just the same she must be quite a girl. You'd think she'd be ready to stay on dry land for a while; it isn't everybody who'd have the guts to turn right around and buy a new boat after losing the old one like that and spending weeks on a rubber raft."

Montoya said sourly, "It isn't everybody who could afford it, *Señor.*"

The assistant dockmaster's warm and sympathetic feelings toward those fine people, the McHughs, seemed to have cooled abruptly at the thought of the money the young widow had inherited—or was Montoya grasping at any excuse to disapprove of her, to justify to himself some hurt he had done her? Since the subject made him so nervous and voluble, it seemed more than likely that the *Stream Hunter* hijacking was another Columbus job like *Haleakala* and *Spindrift* and Montoya knew more about it than he should; but as a line of investigation it seemed hardly more promising than the Ullman gambit.

The fact was that Columbus' hijacking sideline was of

367

minor importance now, like his drug smuggling, and even his involvement in armed conspiracy. None of this was needed for his apprehension although it might be useful at his eventual trial. He'd gone too far at last, he was directly responsible for the murder of a government agent; and that made his other criminal activities almost irrelevant as far as the immediate situation was concerned. All that was necessary was to find him. The trouble was that he had managed his disappearance so effectively that there was really nothing to do for the moment but pick at the tangle he'd left behind and hope that at least one of the unraveled threads would lead somewhere.

Leaving the Yacht Club, Martin found a pay telephone and called the Four Seasons Hotel. It annoyed him how little he knew about the woman he was calling. The boat-hijacking angle had been Tommy Walsh's baby and somehow in the confusion that had followed that disastrous night a month ago nobody'd picked up on it. It wasn't until they'd belatedly started sorting through the information that had still been accumulating from the sources Tommy had lined up that this latest yacht-disappearance had surfaced, so to speak; and even then it had been shelved while more important-seeming clues were being examined—fruitlessly as it turned out.

Tommy would have had a complete dossier on the lady ready for him by this time, Martin reflected grimly; but it was no use thinking about that, or about hatred or revenge or retribution. They'd got big Tommy from behind, of course; they'd obviously had him marked for a long time and they'd taken him out ruthlessly when they made their run, to give themselves a clear head start perhaps, but also no doubt in payment for the death of Armando Colombo so many months ago. Sŏ in a way he was at least partly responsible for Tommy's death, Martin reflected grimly; since it was his action that had brought this vengeance down on the organization. But the man more directly responsible for making a target of Tommy Walsh was still in the hospital with a bullet hole that should have given him a nice, painful, terminal case of peritonitis but somebody'd been dumb enough to shoot him full of antibiotics so now it looked as if he would, unfortunately, make it after all. And Meriwether, the cold-blooded old cobra, had been on the whole quite shockingly and complacently satisfied with the way things had turned out.

"Yes, we'll have to scramble now to repair the damage and

I'm very sorry about Walsh," he'd said smoothly over the phone. "You're in charge down there, of course."

"For how long?"

"My dear boy, I am not clairvoyant. After this is over, I may need you elsewhere; but in the meantime I hope you'll do your best to anticipate Columbus' next move because I'm certain and I think you'll agree—the psychological profile is unmistakable—that he will now retaliate for the ruin of his Cuban hopes by making a violent countermove of some kind." There had been a pause. "Oh, you were referring to Richardson?"

"Uh-huh. Richardson. The hospital says he's out of danger."

"I'm happy to hear it; it is the one bright spot in *that* situation. But it is a very sad thing, my boy. It is unfortunate when an agent of such seniority demands a field assignment and then makes a serious error that jeopardizes the whole operation and even costs the life of a valuable government employee. It makes it so difficult for us to make use of him elsewhere, in any important capacity. After all, field personnel have the right to receive their instructions from headquarters people whose judgment they can trust. I am very much afraid that Mr. Richardson's usefulness to us is at an end. It is too bad. He was a very promising administrator, very promising indeed."

The regret in Meriwether's voice had not been overwhelming and the picture was clear. As desk men often did, Richardson had made the mistake of shooting off his mouth bravely about his desperate yearning to see *real* action once more. He'd quickly been taken at his word and, as expected, as hoped, he'd messed up the tricky situation he'd taken over—and Meriwether couldn't have been happier at having thus eliminated a smooth and dangerous claimant to his administrative throne. Of course there had been a little incidental breakage but that could not be helped. And getting high-principled and angry about the way things were was a waste of time. Either the job was worth doing or it wasn't; and if it was you'd damn well better just get at it and stop brooding about the ambitions and competitive vagaries of human nature, in Washington or anywhere else.

Mrs. Janet McHugh's voice sounded clear and pleasant over the phone, although rather tired. When Martin identified himself she immediately assumed, and he did not correct her, that he'd been steered to her by some government official with whom she'd already talked. He gathered that, just out of the hospital, she'd been grimly making the rounds of the law-enforcement agencies to determine what was being done about the crime that had cost her her husband, not to mention her boat and considerable hardship. She seemed quite cooperative; she regretted that she was tied up today and most of tomorrow; but if Mr. Martin cared to drop by for a drink tomorrow evening, by which time she'd have had a chance to move out of the hotel and get settled on board the new boat she'd just acquired, she'd be happy to answer his questions to the best of her ability. *Searcher.* Slip A14 at the Yacht Club. Yes, of course he could bring an associate, that would be perfectly all right.

After hanging up, Martin hesitated briefly; then he lifted the receiver once more and dropped more coins into the slot.

"Miss Cameron, please," he said when a receptionist answered.

After a moment she came on: "This is Elizabeth Cameron."

"Phil Martin here," he said.

"Oh." There was a little silence; and when she spoke he knew she'd had to work hard to keep any hint of reproach from her voice. "How are you, Philip?"

"Apologetic," he said. "It's been a busy month. Busy and damned unprofitable. Does the name McHugh mean anything to you?"

She was silent for a moment and he could imagine her little frown of concentration, but her response was cautious: "Why do you ask?"

"A Mrs. Janet McHugh just bought, somewhere down in the Keys I believe, a forty-foot trawler yacht. I think that's the seaworthy, roomy, long-range kind of boat the smugglers love. I thought you might just possibly have your people keeping track of sales like that."

"Well, it's supposed to be a fearful secret, but as a matter of fact we have been trying to cover that angle. Just a minute. Yes, here it is. *Searcher.* Forty-foot Marine Trader trawler, aft cabin model, Taiwan built, hundred-and-twenty-horsepower diesel, cruising range well over a thousand miles." He heard her laugh ruefully. "I keep learning more about boats than I really want to know."

"Any reason why this *Searcher* sale caught your eye particularly?"

"As a matter of fact there is, Philip," she said after a momentary pause. "It's a very contradictory situation. On the one hand the woman who bought the boat seems to have hired herself a very rough crew. The captain, a local character named Broderick Kotoski, has quite a violent reputation and we think he's been involved in a few drug runs—of course that's not unusual among the more unsavory waterfront types. And he's picked one of his cronies for mate and cook and general handyman, a nasty little weasel of a black man named Billy France, who does have a record in our files."

"You said contradictory. If that's the bad news, what's the good?"

"Well, Mrs. Janet McHugh herself—Janet Jaspers before her marriage—has never been in any police trouble anywhere that we can find, which is damned unusual for wandering young girls these days; they generally manage to get themselves picked up somewhere. There's no indication that she's ever been hooked on anything except boats, and she's worked on boats as everything from cook to deckhand to, if you'll believe it, engineer. Her last job before her marriage was mate on a charter fisherman docked in Marathon and the captain and his wife practically adopted her into the family, they thought so much of her. As you may know, on that boat is where she met her rather wealthy young husband and now, with him dead, she's got a controlling interest in a profitable small corporation up North which puts her in a position where she can write a check for a forty-foot yacht—sixty-five thousand was the price—and hardly feel it at all. So she certainly doesn't need the money; and she doesn't seem the type to go into smuggling just for kicks. Still, she has hired this very tough crew and Kotoski picked up a couple of firearms for the boat just the other day. Of course, as a farm girl, I don't consider that particularly incriminating; we always had a few guns around the house and felt safer for them, but still what does a rich young widow want with a shotgun and a .30–30?"

"You've really done some work on this," Martin said.

"We're trying to check out any sales involving suitable boats that seem the slightest bit unusual. And now that I've compromised departmental security completely, are you going to tell me why you're interested in the lady?"

"Because I'm having drinks with her tomorrow evening and you're invited."

"I see." Elizabeth Cameron paused. "Or, rather, I don't see."

Martin said, "Frankly, I don't think Mrs. McHugh belongs on your list. I think she bought that boat with something other than marijuana in mind and I want to find out just what it is. I'd like to know what impression she makes on you; and I thought you might like the excitement of meeting a real life suspect face to face. Afterwards, still in the line of duty, I suggest dinner at a Cuban restaurant I know. The owner's a distant relative of mine; he's also a very close-mouthed gent who may have a little information I can use. I've been trying to pry it out of him for months; I have a hunch he's just about ready to open up. And you're supposed to smile at him prettily and soften him up for me. Like all us Latins he's a sucker for beautiful ladies."

He heard her laugh softly. "Yes, I've noticed. We can hardly get any business done around here the way the phone's been ringing steadily and flowers arriving every hour on the hour."

He drew a sigh of relief. If she could joke about it, it was going to be all right. "I'm truly sorry, Elizabeth," he said. "I've wanted to call but things have been going badly and I figured you probably had troubles enough of your own without having mine inflicted on you."

This was only partly true, of course. The fact was that he'd come down with a serious case of buck fever. It had never happened to him before, but knowing he was so close to achieving something very important and desirable, he'd been so afraid of making a false move, while distracted by Tommy's death and Columbus' disappearance, that he'd made no move at all beyond a single call to make sure she had recovered from her harrowing experience at Manatee Key.

"Apology accepted," her voice said. "What time tomorrow?"

He told her.

CHAPTER 36

July

Latitude 26°N; Longitude 80°W

Janet McHugh stood at the end of the Yacht Club dock and watched her ship come in. For a stock boat, a slow boat, just an instrument with which to get her real boat back, *Searcher* didn't look too bad, she decided. There was a nice flare to the high bow, and a businesslike look to the high bulwarks that protected the decks and made it easy and safe to get forward even in bad weather. She liked the shippy appearance of the mast and cargo boom and, goddamn it, at least she wasn't trapped on the beach any longer. She had a way of getting out on the water again, even if not in the dashing, glorious, high-speed style to which *Stream Hunter* had accustomed her. Of course there was still something missing; now she'd have to do it, for all practical purposes, alone.

There had been a time when, single, she hadn't minded being alone. Now it disturbed and annoyed her to find that, after only a few years of marriage, she felt kind of incomplete without a man around; somebody with whom, for instance, she could now have shared her pleasure in her new boat. She even found herself, ridiculously, missing Johnny Bradshaw, he of the loud mouth and the wandering hands; but she'd sent him back where he'd come from with thanks—and he had been a help—since there wasn't really room for him on the boat and he'd been a little too curious about her motives for buying it and her plans for using it.

He'd have made a bad combination with Brodie Kotoski anyway; Brodie who was now coming in practically full throttle, goddamn his showoff hide. He was obviously going to demonstrate to the lady owner what a hell of a shiphandler she'd hired, and God help everybody if reverse didn't grab when he needed it. Well, he'd better be a shiphandler since he couldn't navigate for shucks offshore and barely knew how to read an inshore chart.

She turned and walked back along the dock toward the empty slip, resisting the temptation to make frantic, soft-pedal, slow-down gestures as the husky white trawler came charging between the docks with barely diminished bow wave. Either you handled your boat yourself or you let somebody else handle her; and if the latter, you didn't interfere with the way that person chose to go about it, particularly when he was deliberately trying you out. She saw the stocky figure on the flying bridge reach for the gear lever at the last possible moment and slam it aft. The diesel roared, *Searcher* squatted and, turning very smartly for a single-crew boat, came to a shuddering halt and shot backwards into her slip. A touch of forward gear to check her, and she lay there rocking. Okay. Hooray. Ain't we the salty go-to-hell character, though?

Walking past the boat to the end of the finger pier, Janet caught the bow line thrown her by the small man who'd come out of the deckhouse. That would be Billy France, the cook hired for them by Brodie; and from the shifty look of him she'd do well to keep a close check on the galley accounts. It had rather surprised her that Brodie Kotoski would be willing to share the forecastle with a black man, but as a New England girl she still wasn't sure how all those odd southern prejudices worked; and was Florida really the South, anyway? She turned to get the stern line from Brodie, who'd dropped down into the cockpit to throw it, but the assistant dockmaster, Montoya, in his official-looking cap and white coveralls, had come over to help. He made the catch and secured the line to the big cleat on the dock.

"Thanks, Reuben," she said when he straightened up to face her.

"You're welcome, Mrs. McHugh. It's good to have you back. Please let me know if there's anything you need. Well, I must get back to the fuel dock."

She frowned, looking after him as he hurried away, wondering what had got into him. No words of condolence about Chuck, no words of admiration for her new boat; that wasn't Reuben Montoya at all. He used to be quite sociable and chatty, even coming aboard for a beer occasionally. She felt a little hurt; then she dismissed the incident and turned to face Brodie Kotoski, in clean khakis, with a black-billed khaki cap. He was squarely and solidly built with a look of immense stability; you had the impression that fists, clubs, and heaving decks had done their worst but Broderick Kotoski was still standing on his goddamned feet ready for the next assault—although she could remember once when he'd gone down and she saw that he was remembering it, too.

His nose had been broken long ago and carelessly set if he'd bothered to have it set at all. His small black eyes, under bushy black eyebrows, were looking her over boldly as was their habit—but she'd settled *that* problem once and she hoped for all time, with his own damn billy-club, the short fish-killing priest he liked to carry that had once got him put in jail and so left his job with Captain Jim Easley open for her. But Captain Jim had been sick that other day, some months later, and Brodie and she had taken the clients out; it was when they were alone together, cleaning up the boat afterwards, that he'd made his try. Expecting it—he hadn't been exactly subtle—she'd been ready with the club. It had taken her fifteen minutes to bring him around afterwards, and she thought they had a certain understanding now. These big men and their big muscles and the hurt, hurt look each one invariably got when you didn't give him the ladylike, pushy-pully, oh-please-let-me-go, wrestling match he expected that generally left you with bruised arms and damaged clothes even if in the end he did condescend to abort his amorous project out of the pure kindness of his gentle masculine heart. But oh so sad and misunderstood-looking when you used a knee or a fist or a wrench as if you really meant it. What the hell did they think a girl learned growing up around the waterfront, anyway? She became aware that Brodie was giving her a report on her boat's performance.

". . . not too much speed of course, she seems to cruise best between eight and nine, but she tracks nice and doesn't seem to be bothered much by a chop. No problems with either the mechanics or the electronics, but Billy says that alcohol stove is a pain in the ass; takes all day to boil coffee." He cleared his throat. "I'd like to say I appreciate your taking me on like this, ma'am."

She grinned at him. "Well, I didn't hire you for your pretty face, Brodie. We're going to be poking our noses into some tough places and I wanted somebody who didn't care whose brains he beat out so naturally I thought of you. But that's kind of a lightweight cook you got us."

"Don't worry about Billy. He can take care of himself."

"To hell with taking care of him," Janet said. "It's me and the boat he's supposed to take care of. But first he'd better get us provisioned for a long cruise. Here's the key to the car, over by the bushes to the right; and a list of what I think we'll need. Anything else that occurs to him, tell him to buy it. I've got a seabag and a garment bag in the trunk, and some liquor and charts up front; have him bring it all aboard, please, before he goes shopping."

"We're a little short of ground tackle, ma'am. I'd like at least one good big anchor instead of these measly little lunch hooks, and some hefty chain and line. Assuming these tough places we'll be going to don't all have fancy marinas where we can tie up."

She nodded. "Get what you think we'll need, I'll leave it to your judgment. Now I'm going to find myself something to eat and take a nap. Doctor's orders. If I'm not up by seventeen hundred, beat on the hatch, will you?"

When she woke, she didn't know where she was at first; then she lay for a while in the big double berth in the aft cabin savoring the pleasure of being at home on a boat of her own once more, to hell with hospitals and hotels. Getting up, she caught a glimpse of herself in the mirror of the built-in vanity where the previous lady occupant had undoubtedly spent considerable time making up her pouty little mouth. It was strange taking over somebody else's boat like this. She had a feeling *Searcher*'s former crew hadn't quite left yet.

The glass wasn't kind to the scrawny blonde in brassiere and panties; and she couldn't help thinking it would be damn nice just to lie on a beach somewhere and eat and rest and eat some more and get herself reasonably healthy-looking again, but the clock was running against her. The more time that passed, the harder would be the task she had set herself. She pulled on a pair of new black linen slacks that fit after a fashion—what there was of her to fit these days—and a man's white broadcloth shirt worn loose outside the pants, and stuck her feet into a pair of new white leather boat shoes, and ran a comb through her hair.

Emerging in the deckhouse, she found it empty of people; but there were cartons of canned goods covering the deck at the forward end and she could hear Billy rattling more cans below. Through the windshield she could see Brodie, on the foredeck, overhauling endless amounts of brand-new three-strand nylon anchor line. Apparently things were getting done; and she knew a familiar feeling of excitement. There was always a pleasurable thrill in getting a boat ready for sea.

The deckhouse, with big windows all around, was half kitchen and half dining room, to use the landlubber terms. The stove, sink, and icebox were to starboard facing an L-shaped settee and a teak table to port, next to the sliding door that let you out on deck. She found bread and cheese in the galley and made herself a sandwich and got a beer out of the icebox. Munching the sandwich as she worked, with occasional sips of beer, she found the liquor and some plastic glasses and a tin of mixed nuts and tried not to think of how much nicer everything had been on *Stream Hunter*. This was a good plain sturdy little ship; she shouldn't be disloyal to it.

"Billy."

"What?" He stuck his head out the forward cabin hatch. He had a frizzy crop of graying hair and big white teeth in a black skull-face. His eyes were insolent but lacked the appraising boldness of Brodie's; Billy France was fighting the black-white battle, not the male-female battle. "You want something?"

"Could you make a little room here? We're having guests."

"Hell, I'm getting it cleared away as fast as I can." His voice was aggressive. "I gotta figure where to stow it all first, don't I?"

There was something to be said, she reflected, for the old bucko-mate, belaying-pin days.

"At least shove it over to the side so we can use the settee and table," she said. "How are you at mixing drinks?"

"The best," he said, losing some of his antagonism. "Used to work in a bar when I got tired of cooking on the water. The best."

"Well, here comes your chance to prove it, I think."

Janet slid the door back and stepped out on deck. The afternoon was bright and hot and still and all the boats in the harbor lay motionless under the blue Florida sky. Two people, overdressed for boating, were coming out the main dock

377

toward *Searcher*'s slip. They were not quite what she'd expected from yesterday's brief telephone conversation—one was dark and Spanish-looking and the other was a woman—but they came out the finger pier and stopped before her.

"Mrs. McHugh?" the man said. "I'm Philip Martin. This is Elizabeth Cameron of the PSCC."

"Please come aboard."

She wasn't usually envious of other women, even when they were good-looking; but she couldn't help thinking, as Elizabeth Cameron made her way through the gate in *Searcher*'s rail, that this slender, handsome, dark-haired lady wasn't really fair to organized castaways: *On her, skinny looks good, dammit!* And the crisp, well-tailored white pantsuit worn with a very-pink blouse that somehow seemed to work although it shouldn't have—it wasn't all that becoming a color. She saw the quick thank-you smile Elizabeth Cameron threw over her shoulder at the man as he steadied her briefly, and she understood that the two of them weren't just business associates or if they were now they wouldn't remain that way for very long. Somehow the knowledge increased her feeling of resentful inadequacy although she could see no reason why it should. At the man's polite gesture, she followed the woman into the deckhouse; and heard Martin follow her inside and slide the door closed behind them. She told herself she was damn well not going to apologize for all the grocery cartons, like a young bride terribly embarrassed because her house was in *such* a mess.

"PSCC?" she asked, raising her eyebrows.

It was the man who answered. "Prohibited Substances Control Commission." He grinned. "That's governmentalese for drugs, Mrs. McHugh."

Looking at him, she knew a small sense of fear—fear that he would guess what she was thinking, because this man was definitely not summer people. It was strange, she thought, he probably called a deck a floor and a bulkhead a wall and tied a square knot backwards, but if you cast him adrift in the middle of the ocean you knew he'd last as long as guts and brains and determination could possibly keep him alive, and maybe even a little longer.

Not that she liked him. This wasn't one of the short, round, soft Latins like Montoya; this was one of the tall, sharp, hard ones, and sexy besides. She had a deep distrust of sexy-looking men, although, to give him his due, you'd never have to fight this one off. He'd never force himself upon an unwill-

378

ing woman; but he'd have considerable faith in his ability to make her willing, and it was quite possible that faith would not be misplaced. She saw that he was carrying a small revolver under the jacket of his light summer suit.

"I see," she said. "And are you Prohibited Substances too, Mr. Martin?"

He shook his head. "No, but we're working together. I'm actually investigating a criminal conspiracy for another agency, but the illegal activities involved seem to have been financed by marijuana and other drugs smuggled, at least in part, in hijacked boats. I thought, considering your recent experiences, you might possibly have some information that would help us track these people down."

"I see," she said again. "Please sit down. What would you like to drink?" She raised her voice. "Billy, it's grog time."

When the drinks had been served, Elizabeth Cameron said, "I'm not sure I'd have the courage to go boating again after . . . It must have been quite an ordeal, on that life raft."

Janet said, "Yes, particularly since it didn't happen, Miss Cameron." She smiled thinly at the older woman's surprised look, and went on: "You are aware, of course, that there is no such thing as yacht hijacking. It's just a figment of some cheap journalists' overactive imaginations, like the Bermuda Triangle and UFOs. And even if someone should go haywire and actually hijack a boat, outlandish as the thought might seem, he'd never, never steal it for the purposes of smuggling drugs—I'm shocked at you for even suggesting such a thing, Mr. Martin. Drug smugglers are all wealthy and sensible businessmen who're not going to escalate a simple, safe, drug operation into risky piracy and murder when they've got plenty of money with which to acquire boats legally. So, since there's no possible motive, and since it never happens anyway, it follows logically that *Stream Hunter* was never taken by half a dozen men with guns, and we were never set adrift in the Gulf of Mexico, and my husband and the Gregertsens didn't die on that lousy rubber raft. I simply imagined the whole thing."

Martin was grinning. "I see you've encountered the bullshit curtain."

She hadn't meant to blow off steam like that; and she made an apologetic gesture. "I'm not being fair. They're not really that bad; I guess I'm just tired from chasing around all those offices and hearing the same silly routine in each one. But did you hear the one about the FBI? Obviously the FBI can't

379

do anything about boat hijacking because they don't know anything about boats. . . . Now you're supposed to ask why they don't know anything about boats."

Martin said obligingly, "Why doesn't the FBI know anything about boats, Mrs. McHugh?"

"Because they don't need to know anything about boats in that exalted bureau, because they're all qualified to walk on water." Their laughter made her feel better, and she gave them a grin and went on more seriously: *"Stream Hunter* is forty-eight feet long. The tuna tower sticks up thirty-some feet from the deck. Her diesels produce almost twelve hundred horsepower. She displaces over twenty-eight thousand pounds. Fourteen goddamned tons of boat and nobody can find her! Could it possibly be that nobody's looking, Mr. Martin?"

He was watching her closely. He glanced at the cartons of canned goods and said, "But that's not true, is it? You're looking."

"Well, that's right," she conceded. "I'm looking. Or I will be as soon as we can get ready for sea."

"What are your plans?"

Obviously he wanted to know for some purpose of his own, but instinct told her he wasn't going to be stuffy and try to stop her; and it would help to talk it all out with somebody.

She said, "I'm assuming they won't bring the *Hunter* anywhere she's too likely to be recognized. That eliminates all the popular marinas and anchorages Chuck and I used to visit here in southern Florida and over in the northern Bahamas. I think I'll gamble that they'll take her south where she's never been, handy to the smuggling routes from Jamaica and South America. At least it's worth a look. My immediate problem is whether to take the slow and easy route down through the Bahamas or just charge straight south—well, southeast actually—to the Caribbean by way of the Old Bahama Channel."

Martin was shaking his head ruefully, and Elizabeth Cameron was also looking puzzled. Martin spoke for both of them.

"I'm afraid we're geographical morons, Mrs. McHugh. Could you show us on the map?"

Janet laughed. "We call them charts, Mr. Martin." She saw the thick roll of paper where Billy had left it after bringing it in from the car, on the galley counter; and she got it and selected one sheet and peeled it off and spread it on the dinette table after their glasses had been moved to make room. She pointed. "Here's Florida. We've got the Bahama Islands over here to the east of us. South of us, running off to the southeast, here, are the Antilles, Greater and Lesser, the whole long chain of them. Cuba and the Windward Passage here. Then Hispaniola—that's Haiti and the Dominican Republic—and the Mona Passage. Then Puerto Rico and the Virgins and the Anegada Passage; and finally a whole string of little islands curving on down to South America." She was gaining confidence now and feeling less inadequate; charts were something she knew and was good at. She went on: "There are three ways to get down there by boat. You can cut pretty straight east from here through the Bahamas and out into the open Atlantic and then turn south, if you have a good seaworthy boat and like deepwater sailing. A lot of sailboats go that way. Or you can just head over to the Bahamas the same way, but turn south at Nassau, say, and island-hop your way down, a reasonably sheltered trip, finally making a short open-water jump over to Haiti. Or you can slip down this channel here, separating the Bahamas from Cuba: the Old Bahama Channel. It's the most direct route from here but it generally involves bucking adverse winds and currents; I wouldn't want to try it in that direction in a sailboat and it could be pretty rough even in a boat like *Searcher*. Some of the big cruise ships out of Miami use it."

Martin frowned at the chart. "Do you really think there's a good chance that your stolen boat is down there?"

Janet hesitated. "It's not so much a question of what I think, Mr. Martin; it's a question of what I can do. The *Hunter* could be stashed away in some little hurricane hole right here in Florida—hell, almost anywhere in tidewater U.S.A. by this time—or she could be stored on shore in somebody's boatyard with a hundred other laid-up boats, but if she is I'll never find her by myself. As a matter of fact, I've engaged a firm of private investigators to check on all that, as far as possible. What *I* can do is work my way down through the Antilles and then, if necessary, west along the coast of South America from Venezuela as far as Pot Heaven, otherwise known as Colombia. I can snoop around all the likely harbors and anchorages and ask silly questions and wave dirty Yankee money under people's noses, and if *Stream Hunter's* there, if she's even passed through, I'll find out. Since that's about the only thing I can do, it's what I will do. Why not? I haven't anything else on my engagement calendar at the moment." She paused, and went on: "It isn't that I really *like* going at it blindly like that, Mr. Martin. I would much prefer to have something definite to go on. You haven't got a clue that might help?"

"Not at the moment," he said, "but I haven't heard your whole story yet. Maybe if you give it to us in detail—if it's not too painful—something useful will turn up."

Janet laughed. "If I could stand living it, I guess I can stand talking it. I'll have another beer, Billy, if you don't mind. . . ." When it was brought to her, she leaned back with it, tasted it, and began to speak. It took the best part of half an hour, and even after all her previous tellings of the story she found that it hurt more than there was any sense in; after all, it should be ancient history by now. "Well, that's about it," she said at last. "The *Lady Maude* rushed me to Key West; I was afraid they'd blow that ancient diesel the way they had it pounding away. I guess they figured they'd caught me pretty close to the point of no return, and the doctors tell me they weren't far wrong. And there's not a damn thing I can do for them without hurting their feelings; they made it perfectly clear they weren't doing it for a reward. An ambulance rushed me to the hospital and here I am." She glanced at Martin. "Any gleams of light?"

Martin said carefully: "A while back a good-sized ketch disappeared off the west coast of Florida. Later we found a fast little twenty-foot fishing boat that had been stolen farther north washed up on a mangrove key off that coast in semiwaterlogged condition; somebody'd pulled the plug hoping it would sink but boats that size are required by law to have built-in flotation. The odd thing was that the cockpit showed signs of fire but the gas tank was intact and still held some fuel, so what had burned? We're theorizing—but of course it's only a theory so far—that the little boat was used by hijackers and they built a decoy fire in the cockpit and then called the ketch in to save them because, help, help, their boat was going up in flames. Just about the same technique that was used on you."

Janet said harshly, "Too bad the gas tank didn't catch and blow them up. Anybody who'd abuse a distress signal at sea. . . . Anything else?"

"What was Mrs. Gregertsen's first name?"

She frowned. "Susan. Sue. Why?"

"Then who was Laura?" He went on quickly: "I thought there were just two couples on that raft, you and your husband, and the Gregertsens; but you mentioned a Laura just now. Several times, in fact."

"Oh, I'm sorry." She was annoyed that she hadn't made it clear. "We hired a girl named Laura Briggs to help out; I was damned if I was going to spend my time cleaning up after Sloppy Suzie. . . ." She checked herself, and grimaced. "Well, I guess you've already gathered it wasn't exactly a happy ship. Anyway, we got this girl aboard to help; but Laura never got as far as the raft. They shot her in the galley when she tried to get brave with a kitchen knife. Poor kid. She was the first casualty of the Battle of the Yucatan Straits."

"Was she?"

Janet looked at the dark, hawklike face with puzzlement. "What are you trying to say, Mr. Martin?"

"Did it happen in front of you? Did you see her . . . did you see the body?"

"Well, no, but we heard the shot, and the man came out with his gun and said . . ." She stopped, aghast. "You mean you think *Laura* . . ."

"Did anything, well, strange happen on board before the hijacking; anything out of the ordinary?"

"Strange? Well, there was the radio of course. . . ."

"What about the radio?"

"The big SSB had never given us any trouble before, but when I tried to call Key West to give our position and advise them that we were closing in on a vessel in distress it was quite dead." She found herself hugging herself as if it had suddenly turned cold; somehow it was hard to face this vision of betrayal. "Are you suggesting that Laura Briggs could have . . . It's hard to believe, Mr. Martin. She was a nice kid, willing and cheerful, and she knew her way around boats. She even knew how to fight off that amorous ape, Babe Gregertsen, without making a Federal case of it, if you'll excuse the phrase."

Martin said, "A sailboat, a catamaran named *Haleakala*, was hijacked in the Atlantic off the Bahamas. The crew is all accounted for except for two people, one a smallish girl named Lucia Barnes. I told you about the *Spindrift*, the ketch that vanished in the Gulf of Mexico. A diminutive female named Linda Brown was helping out as crew. And now we have your *Stream Hunter* and Laura Briggs. What did she look like?"

Janet McHugh drew a long breath and tried to visualize the girl in question. "She was small and tanned and nicely put together, brown hair, pleasant face but not strikingly pretty. I wouldn't have called her a sexpot, she certainly didn't seem to work at it, but Babe couldn't keep his fat hands off her and Chuck admitted he found her attractive, so she must have had something I couldn't see, being a woman. Even so I . . . I liked her. I really liked her quite a lot. I guess that's why it never occurred to me to suspect . . . to doubt that she was killed just the way we were told."

"How did you come to hire her?"

Janet shrugged. "Well, we had a young black man lined up who'd had experience as a steward on a larger yacht, but he cracked up his motorcycle and wound up in the hospital, so we asked . . ." She stopped abruptly, remembering whom they had asked; remembering also Montoya's odd behavior earlier in the day. She was aware of the sharp eyes of the government man watching her; and she laughed casually. "Well, we asked around, and I guess the word got around; anyway, this kid in jeans came wandering up while we were stowing the last supplies aboard. I guess I was actually doing a final check on the engines, grease up to my ears as usual. Poor Chuck, I think he'd really have liked to be married to an immaculate princess he could stick up on a pedestal. I remember the way he mopped off my dirty face to make me respectable while we were . . . were talking to . . ." Janet's voice broke unexpectedly. She'd been talking mainly for distraction, but obviously she shouldn't have started on *that*. She cleared her throat firmly and forced herself to go on: "Anyway, the girl said she'd heard we were short a cook, and she looked clean and intelligent and talked as if she knew port from starboard and bow from stern so, well, we just took her on with a sigh of relief, one problem solved, and took off like a rocket for Cozumel."

"I see."

He knew she was concealing something, that was obvious; but he made no further effort to question her, which was interesting. Also very interesting was the fact that he had carefully not asked what she was going to do if she found *Stream Hunter*. As a government agent he probably didn't want the responsibility of knowing. Correction: he knew all right. He'd seen the kind of crew she'd recruited; he might even know about the firearms Brodie had got her. But as long as he wasn't told officially he could ignore it. She wanted to laugh. The lovely, sinister, sexy, calculating sonofabitch was using her and, since she was quite willing to be used for this

384

purpose, she could simply enjoy the knowledge that there were a few nice ruthless men left in this icky sentimental world. And she hoped that good-looking clotheshorse of a woman appreciated what she had there and planned to take good care of it; she'd have to go a long way to find another.

Elizabeth Cameron stirred. "Is that boat really so important to you, Mrs. McHugh?"

"No landsman ever understands what a boat can mean to someone who grew up on the water," Janet said quietly. "But that's not exactly the point. The point is that it was *my* boat—mine and Chuck's—and they took it, and Chuck died as a result. Let's just say that I don't want to live in a world where a bunch of armed yo-yos can march aboard my boat and calmly order me over the side. And since nobody else seems to be doing anything about it besides spouting double talk and making silly lists in quintuplicate, *I'm* doing something about it." She grinned abruptly. "It's too damned bad, isn't it, Mr. Martin?"

"What is?"

"If I were a man you could sneer at my virile attitude and call it *machismo*. But how can there be the *machismo* without the *cojones?*"

"With all due respect, Mrs. McHugh, I think you have plenty *cojones* or you wouldn't be here, alive." He rose, and the woman rose with him. He said, "I thank you for your time, *Señora,* and I wish you the best of luck with your search."

She watched them leave, a handsome couple, and she had a sudden disturbing image of them in bed together, but she didn't really know why she'd had it or why it had disturbed her, and what did it have to do with anything, anyway? There was work to be done.

"Billy!"

He took his time about coming. "What now?"

"Get up on the bridge with a can of polish and polish something, I don't give a damn what. Keep an eye on the dockmaster's office. When you see Montoya locking up for the night, you wait until he's heading for the parking lot and run after him. Say Miz McHugh wants to see him for just a minute, it's urgent, it can't wait till morning because there's been a change of plans and we're shoving off tonight. Got that?"

"Yes, ma'am."

She turned to Brodie, who'd come aft. "Get that deck clear.

Just dump the stuff below. We'll be heading out as soon as he comes. I hope you got some shells for that shotgun. . . . What's the matter now?"

The two of them were still standing there. Brodie said uneasily, "What's the scattergun for? We didn't hire on to kill anybody, Mrs. Mac."

"The hell you didn't," she said. "You can't have been kidding yourselves I picked you for your super-seamanship or gourmet cooking, a couple of hardcases like you! Anyway, we're not going to kill anybody tonight." She felt herself grin in an unpleasant way. "Not quite."

CHAPTER 37

July

Latitude 26°N; Longitude 80°W

Miranda's Restaurant wasn't very crowded on a weekday evening and they had no trouble getting one of the rather stark wooden booths along the wall.

"No cocktails here," Philip Martin said. "Just beer and wine; and I don't recommend the wine."

Elizabeth Cameron was looking with interest around the big, well-lighted room with its plain wooden furnishings. A murmur of Spanish reached them from a table nearby. Martin saw her glance at the middle-aged couple there, and at him. She smiled a little and he knew—and was pleased to know—that she understood why she'd been brought to this foreign enclave surrounded by the plastic glitter of Miami; and it wasn't just to interview Juan Miranda. The lady was entitled to learn something about the antecedents of the gentleman with whom she was becoming involved, even though he had largely rejected them for a different language and a different citizenship. Under other circumstances he would, of course, have taken her to meet his parents but that was no longer possible. He reflected wryly that distant cousin Juan would be surprised to know that he and his restaurant were officiating *in loco parentis* tonight.

He was relieved that his companion made no glib, conventional, appreciative comments; she wasn't here to approve, only to observe. He wondered if she was aware of the powerful effect her profile had on him when she turned her head in that graceful manner, alert and intrigued. Well, no attractive woman was ever wholly unconscious of the men around her, and she must know she was beautiful from that angle, but he did not think the pose was deliberate. Then a waiter in black trousers and white apron was placing the menus before them, breaking the spell. She turned back to face Martin, and shook her head in answer to his question.

"Nothing to drink for me right now, thanks. I had enough on that boat to hold me for a while." She waited until the man had moved away. "Philip."

"Yes?"

"I'm worried about that girl."

The brief private moment was ended, and they were once more public servants of sorts.

He asked, "Because she's probably going up against some tough people, if she can find them; or because she's obviously prepared to stretch the law a bit if she has to?"

Elizabeth shook her head. "No, it's not that. I'm not her conscience and if she wants to risk her life I suppose it's her business. I . . . well, I've got to draw the line somewhere. I make a career of telling people what they can't smoke and can't sniff and can't inject into their veins; I'd better just leave it at that. But she isn't at all well yet, Philip; and she's so damned *intense,* if you know what I mean. You can hardly blame her after what she's been through, but I wouldn't call her exactly a well-balanced young lady at the moment. Didn't her eyes look funny to you?"

That was, he thought, the understatement of the year. He remembered the small shock of recognition that had gone through him when Janet McHugh had turned to look at him directly for the first time. The eyes were a deep violet-blue and the starved thinness of the face had made them appear quite large and luminous. They'd seemed to glow with a cold light he'd seen before and he remembered thinking: *Oh, God, not another one!* Harold Ullman's eyes, although a different color, had looked a little like that; as if a strange heatless fire had been kindled deep inside.

The little blonde Navy wife in Clearwater Beach, Melissa McCulloch, had not displayed the betraying signs; her hurt had not been great enough. She'd lost her parents but she'd still had a husband with whom she was madly in love—but even so she'd had the compulsion to get out there in a boat and find out things for herself and to hell with the incompetent forces of law and order. But Harold Ullman, still walking with a cane due to injuries received and with his marriage broken and his former wife brutally murdered on the eve, it seemed, of a possible reconciliation, had definitely carried the glowing stigmata, the hunting look; and now here was this gaunt, just-widowed young woman only a few days out of the hospital with her violet eyes delivering the clear message that she'd damn well had it with the nonviolent, turn-the-other-cheek routine everybody was supposed to think was so great. Martin found himself wondering if Mr. Meriwether's classification system encompassed doomsday girls; and if Captain Rader acknowledged the existence of lady *lobos*.

"Well," he said judiciously, "I wouldn't call them exactly funny, Elizabeth."

"Well, she's trying to do too much; she's driving herself too hard, too soon. What if she gets sick out on the ocean somewhere, alone on that little boat with those two uglies she's hired?"

"I know," Martin said, "but I don't know how to stop her, do you?"

"That's just the trouble," Elizabeth said. "I'd be surprised if anybody'd ever managed to stop Miss Janet Jaspers as was. She's a fairly impressive girl, don't you think? Which is why I hate to see her get hurt—any more than she's already been hurt, I mean. She hasn't got any reserves left; she's by no means recovered from that harrowing experience; and the big trouble is, she won't admit it, even to herself."

Martin said, "To be perfectly honest, I'm not sure I want to stop her." When Elizabeth looked at him quickly, he went on: "Goddamn it, here I'm sitting helpless, a trained man with a gun and nothing to shoot at. I don't know where the hell Columbus is; none of our investigations has turned up a lead, he's pulled down the curtain completely. I don't know what the hell he's up to. And I'm not a bit sure I'll be able to block it when it comes. He's a very hating man, which was bad enough when he concentrated on hating Castro and just managed to wreck a few innocent lives in a kind of incidental way; but now that we've interfered with his precious Cuba plans he probably hates us all at least as much, and we're a lot bigger and softer target. So if some private citizens with private axes to grind want to do a little private work along the right lines, who am I to tell them no? They may be able to accomplish something I can't, or just stir things up and bring stuff to the surface where I can grab it. I didn't draft them. I didn't even ask them to volunteer—hell, if I wanted to accept a certain amount of hassle, there's a certain redheaded hot-head I could throw in jail for something rather unpleasant he did to one of our people, which he dreamed up strictly on his own as part of *his* private anti-Columbus campaign."

"I see." Elizabeth's voice was carefully neutral. "So Janet McHugh isn't the only one."

"A man who pays as little attention to other people's rights and feelings in pursuit of his private goals, good or bad, as Columbus, can't help making some pretty serious enemies. I know of two who are really working at it; I just hope there are more." When she didn't speak, he went on quickly: "Certainly I could stop them, the ones I know about, at least, but do I want to? I could probably figure a way of keeping this girl from embarking on this search of hers, but can I afford to? She's angry, she's moderately rich, she's smart, she's willing. I'm afraid *not* to let her go. In the end, she or the other person I mentioned may make the difference between success and a rather disastrous failure. At the moment it's the only move I see to make. Or lack of move, if you want to put it that way."

He stopped and looked up, as a shadow fell over the booth.

"Is everything satisfactory, Felipe?"

Martin said, "Elizabeth, this is our host, Mr. Juan Miranda. Juan, Miss Elizabeth Cameron. Everything is quite satisfactory; how goes it with you?" He gestured toward the space beside him. "Why don't you join us? On second thought, I take it all back. I was just telling Miss Cameron your wine isn't fit to drink."

Miranda bowed over Elizabeth's hand and seated himself; a tall middle-aged man with heavy eyebrows in a dark, distinguished face that seemed to be designed around its most prominent feature, the large, bold nose. Miranda was wearing a dark suit. His black hair was gray at the temples.

"Unfortunately, Felipe is quite correct, Miss Cameron," he said. "The table wine is not so good, I admit; it is only inexpensive and plentiful. However, if you will order the specialty of the day, pot roast *Cubano,* I will see if there cannot be produced a suitable little wine to go with it, *Señorita.*"

She laughed. "Sounds like the best offer of the day, Mr. Miranda."

"We are in your hands, Juan," Martin said.

Miranda gave him a searching look. "We are all in God's hands, *amigo.* And, no blasphemy intended, also in the hands of the Internal Revenue Service and other government agencies. And speaking of government agencies . . ." He checked himself, and rose. "But let me first make the arrangements. *Un momentito.*"

When he had gone, Elizabeth glanced at Martin and said, "You said he was a relative? He looks just a little like you."

"Not so much," Martin said. "But I know how it is; it's hard to tell us Chinamen apart."

She said quietly, "You're rather prickly tonight, aren't you, Philip?" Before he could respond, she looked toward the rear of the restaurant, frowning. "You're missing something. There's a girl who'd be truly lovely if she'd dress a little less like a tramp. But how do I know her?"

He'd taken the seat facing the street door; he had to turn his head to look. He knew once more the small pang that wasn't really desire—it felt more like an ancient grief—as he caught a glimpse of the girl Elizabeth was watching as she and her escort slipped out the restaurant's rear door. There were the same ugly skintight jeans; and there was the same cheap flimsy T-shirt and the thick lustrous black hair chopped off brutally short and the breathtaking young face. Then they were gone. Martin cleared his throat.

"You've probably seen a bad picture or two in your Columbus file," he said. "That's the daughter, Francesca. And the handsome goon with the intimate hands is Pedro Orosco, in whom we're very interested. We have reason to believe that he was involved in a rather nasty business last fall, but more important we're beginning to think he's in contact with Columbus now, somehow, with her help. We've been keeping a loose string on them both, hoping they'd lead us to Daddy but they've been smart and careful, or somebody smart and careful is calling the signals for them. And it's a very interesting coincidence, isn't it, that they should try to slip out the back way unseen like that right after Cousin Juan marched past them toward the kitchen to arrange for our orders."

He hesitated, knowing what should be done now but reluctant to do it. He was aware of Elizabeth reaching out to touch his hand lightly.

"What is it, Philip?"

"I have a hunch it's time I had them picked up, at least for questioning. It's time for a little pressure. There's reason enough to think they're concealing evidence in a murder case to justify it legally; I think the police will cooperate if we give them what we have." He grimaced. "If we can't trace the Columbus connection maybe it's better just to break it and see what happens."

Her gray eyes studied him gravely. "But you obviously don't want to."

He laughed, embarrassed. "I'm a susceptible male and as you point out she's a lovely young female. Who wants to see a Madonna in handcuffs? Who wants to put an angel in jail?"

"Pretty much a street angel, I'd say, by the looks of her." Elizabeth's eyes were steady on his face. "Are you . . . acquainted with her?"

"Not really," he said. "I merely shot her brother to death a few months ago, if you'll recall. You read the report of that Coast Guard action." He had not meant to be flippant about it; but at least it was out in the open where it belonged, one of the things about him that, like his racial background, she must remember and come to terms with if the relationship was to endure. "That's one reason I'm reluctant to hurt her further," he went on. "Another is . . . well, that's the track this train didn't take. Do you understand?"

"Not really, Philip."

"It's a might-have-been," he said. "If world history had been slightly different, I'd most likely have married Doña Francesca Elena Maria de los Angeles Colombo y Aguilar or someone very like her. It makes it difficult for me to take any action that may injure her, no matter how things actually turned out." He shook his head quickly. "Difficult but not impossible, as I've already demonstrated once, and must again. Excuse me while I phone."

When he returned to the booth, Miranda was there, and wine was on the table. The restaurant owner rose to let Martin into the booth and sat down once more.

"We will let it breathe a little, first," he said with a gesture toward the bottle. "We were speaking of government agencies."

"Yes," Martin said, "and speaking of government agencies,

that was a mistake you just made with respect to this government agency, Juan."

"No, *amigo*. That was necessary," Miranda said with dignity. "You wish to ask me prying questions once more, *sí*? Questions about one of our people, considered a patriot by some. Well, you cannot reasonably expect me to inform on the father while the daughter eats my food three booths away."

"All right, I'll concede that point," Martin said. "But let's not confuse the issue with big words like patriotism. There are some émigrés around who honestly believe they are still working in the best interests of the country we all fled so many years ago; the country and the people. I respect their feelings even though some of the wilder ones may be responsible for my parents' murder—and even though I think that by now they should start giving some consideration to what they owe this new country that has given us all shelter. But this man is working only in his own best interests, and that of a class that no longer exists." He glanced around the restaurant with approval. "You and I, Juan, in our different ways, have found places here for ourselves, or made them; but Colombo is still trying to regain the hereditary position we've all lost. Well, it was nice while it lasted or so I'm told, and I wouldn't mind being called Don Felipe and having the peasants genuflect as I ride by on my big horse, but I'm not about to kill anybody for the privilege. But Colombo is. That's what he's after, was after, and you know it; not a new deal for the poor downtrodden people of Cuba, at home and abroad."

"*Sí*, I know," Miranda said. "That is why I am prepared now to answer your questions to the best of my ability."

When they reached the apartment house on the quiet side street it was close to eleven at night. Martin was very much aware of the woman beside him, and of all the unanswered questions between them, as he stopped the car on the loading zone in front.

"You're lucky to have found an apartment," he said, carefully casual. "I'm still living out of a suitcase after all these months."

She said, "Why don't you grab that parking space up ahead and come up for a drink?" As he drove a little further and started backing in to the curb he heard her laugh softly, obviously amused by the diplomatic way he'd offered her a chance to terminate the evening if she so desired. "You're really not at all the way I expected, Philip," she said.

"I know," he said. "The romantic Latin; the whirlwind sweep-them-off-their-feet Valentino approach. Kiss the lady's hand and pinch the lady's fanny, right?"

She said a little stiffly, "It wasn't intended as a criticism."

He went around to open the car door for her. "I only pinch unimportant fannies, *Señorita*, when the lady's opinion of me doesn't matter very much."

Her hand pressed lightly on his arm as they entered the building. "Let me think about that. When I get it figured out, I suspect it'll turn out to be a very nice speech." They rode up the elevator in silence, walked down the carpeted hall, and entered the small apartment. "Did you learn anything important from Miranda?" she asked.

He shook his head. "Largely just elaboration on what we already knew. I was interested in learning that young Orosco is more important than we thought at first; he even sat in on their meetings sometimes."

He watched her drawing curtains and turning on lights, liking the way she moved. A man could make taking off a jacket seem like a life-and-death struggle—St. George battling his way out of the clutches of the dragon—but she slipped out of hers without effort and laid it aside and turned, patting her hair into place; and they both knew exactly why they were there but they were adult people and they had all night and they couldn't give it too much importance. The really important things were, after all, all settled and had been for weeks. There was conflict within him tonight, he knew; but between them there was no conflict at all.

"Scotch and a couple of ice cubes, right?" she said. "I'll be right back." When she returned, and they had seated themselves with their drinks, she said, "Ramiro Gonzaga. Who is he and why were you asking all those questions about him?"

"Because he seems to have gone with Columbus," Martin said. "At least he's known to have served Columbus in the past and he's missing now. A professional charter boat captain. Not a very good one as it happens; the word is that Captain Gonzaga is pretty much a nautical stumblebum even though he looks like a salty mustachioed pirate. But maybe that's all Columbus has available after losing his Number One seagoing boy, a gent named Olson. At least Olson seems to have handled the marijuana angle locally, covering the deliveries and collecting the money; we're pretty sure of that much. Columbus must have had somebody else running the hijacking aspect of the operation, and actually making the drug runs south; we haven't spotted that one yet. Apparently Gonzaga has taken over the Olson spot, now that Olson's gone."

"Gone how?"

Martin glanced at her and said, "A young woman involved in the case put five bullets into the guy. He was strangling her to death at the time, after first beating her savagely. Not a nice business at all." He shook his head quickly. "Anyway, if Columbus is planning some seagoing deviltry—and as far as we know he's still got at least a couple of recently hijacked yachts at his disposal—we can hope that his navigators are all as incompetent as Ramiro Gonzaga and run him hard aground. But it's a feeble hope."

"You're still quite certain that he's up to something, aren't you?"

"It would be totally out of character if he were not," Martin said. "And if not, why did he run? You still had no firm evidence against him as far as his drug-smuggling activities were concerned, did you? And we'd all have had a hard time tying him to Ochsner's paramilitary operation if he'd just sat tight. He'd been very careful to conduct all contacts through the *mayordomo*, Jesus Cardenas, and Jesus would happily die before he involved *El Patrón*. No, Columbus broke away because he had something important to do by way of retaliation; and now he's undoubtedly clear out of the country making his arrangements—"

"What makes you think so?"

Martin laughed. "Hell, for all his noble protestations, Cousin Juan would never have told me even the little he did tonight if he hadn't had a hint from somewhere, maybe from Orosco or the daughter, that Columbus was safely out of my reach. The primitive tribal silence taboos must be observed as long as they apply." He drew a long breath. "My father had a pessimistic historical theory. He thought the modern re-emphasis on ancient racial and ethnic and linguistic loyalties would eventually destroy the world after first splitting it up into very small and ridiculous splinters. *I spit upon their crazy self-determination,* he said once, *we will never have a peaceful world until men forget their insignificant differences and remember only their tremendous similarities. . . .*" He checked himself, realizing that he was lecturing again. He glanced at his watch. "May I use the phone?"

"Yes, of course. It's in the bedroom."

He made the call and listened to Masterman's report and hung up after leaving the number where he could be reached for a while. Then he sat on the edge of the big bed trying to bring some order into his thoughts before facing Elizabeth Cameron again—for a man in love, as he knew himself to be, he was certainly giving the lady in question a very hard, or at least a very dull, time. After a little, he became aware that she was standing before him, looking down at him with concern in her eyes.

"Are you all right, Philip? Is something wrong?"

It came out of him harshly: "That stupid little street angel, as you called her, had drugs on her when she was picked up, and she couldn't even stick to plain old marijuana. Orosco, too. It is very satisfactory. Now all I have to do is drown the father and I will have made a clean sweep of that family. I should be very proud of myself, should I not?"

She sat down beside him. "I'm sorry, but it was not really your fault."

He shook his head quickly. "I'm being sentimental. The girl means nothing to me, why should I care if she goes to prison? And why should you be sorry? That's your mission in life, putting wicked people like that away, is it not?"

She winced. After a moment she said quietly, "I know you're fighting something tonight, my dear, but does it have to be me?"

Her words shocked him. He realized that she was quite right. He had been engaged in a struggle with himself and now he was taking it out on her because she was the cause of it—because this was a serious woman who was entitled to his total commitment, a commitment for which he had not, he realized, been quite ready. It did not merely involve Elizabeth Cameron herself but her background and everything she stood for; it meant the final rejection of Felipe Martinez and the total acceptance of Philip Martin. Not that she had demanded the choice of him or ever would. She might even be hurt to think he felt it necessary; she might feel that he suspected her of a lack of tolerance. But it was not that at all. It was simply that he knew he could not be the man she deserved as long as he remained uneasily suspended between two traditions. The decision had been made for him a long time ago, but he knew that he had never quite made it for

395

himself. There had been nobody important enough to necessitate it, until now.

"I'm sorry," he said humbly. "A slight case of schizophrenia, I think."

"I know. But you make too much of it." She hesitated. "And I think we're talking much too much for a man and a woman sitting on a bed."

He looked at her quickly, and her eyes met his steadily enough for a moment; then they wavered and he saw that she was blushing like a very young girl.

"Well, *somebody* had to say it!" she breathed, almost sulkily.

Suddenly she was in his arms, her lips soft, her hands urgent; and her breast was firm and warm under his hand through the thin summery cloth but there was only so much that could be accomplished, only so much contact that could be achieved, by two people sitting side by side fully dressed. Gently disengaging himself he started to unfasten her blouse. He felt his wrists captured and held.

"Please. Not like that, not tonight." When he looked at her questioningly she whispered, "It's not that I'm so innocent, darling; but all this awkward business of the clothes embarrasses hell out of me. It's so damned *undignified*. Just give me a minute. Please?"

For an instant, he was annoyed; then he found himself perversely delighted with her and with the fact that she'd have the courage, and the confidence in his understanding, to make her wishes clear even in this breathless moment.

"You are right, we must proceed with the utmost dignity," he murmured. "I will disrobe in the bathroom. *Con permiso?*"

Afterwards, long afterwards, he awoke in the darkness in the big bed aware that she had stirred in his arms and that he was a very fortunate man to have her there.

"Awake?" she whispered.

"Uh-huh."

"It . . . wasn't very nice of you to laugh at the silly wench just because she's shy."

"I wasn't laughing."

"I'm a terrible phony, aren't I? The so sophisticated goddamn executive lady! Really, I'm just a nice little midwestern girl who was taught very strictly that she must never, never allow a little boy to fool with her clothes—let alone, heaven forbid, see her without them. God, they can sure pound some handicaps into you at that age without half trying." She hesitated. "Philip?"

"Yes?"

"Are you . . . feeling better now? I mean, about everything."

He grinned. "I am feeling very fine about everything, *querida.* I—"

The telephone rang, startling them both. They lay for a moment together listening to it, willing it to stop; then Elizabeth sighed and sat up and snapped on the bedside light.

"Damn, we don't have anything scheduled tonight that I know of; anything that could go wrong enough that they'd call me here." She picked up the noisy instrument, silencing it, and spoke into it. "Cameron . . . I see. Yes, he's here. Just a moment." She covered the mouthpiece with her hand. "For you. Janet McHugh."

He raised his eyebrows, and took the phone. "Philip Martin."

"This is Janet McHugh. Your office gave me the number. I've got a . . . well, kind of a problem."

"Tell me about your problem, Mrs. McHugh."

"Well, I have a man named Montoya here. He says you know him; the assistant dockmaster. He's not in very good shape."

"What's the matter with him?"

"He knew some things I needed to know. I had to get a little rough with him before he'd talk."

Martin drew a long breath, remembering Harold Ullman and his bolt-cutters. *The natives are getting restless,* he thought.

"Perhaps you'd better give me the details, Mrs. McHugh."

"Very well." She cleared her throat, and he knew she'd been about to say something defensive and apologetic by way of introduction; but she thought better of it. She said, "We took him out into the Straits and hung him from the cargo boom in a sort of harness so his feet were dripping into the sea on the downroll. Then we got the chum line going—"

"Chum?"

"Not the British word for palsy-walsy. Chum is chopped-up fish and stuff, kind of a smelly stew, you ladle it over the side as the boat drifts and it makes a spreading trail in the water. The fish find it and start working their way toward the area of greatest concentration, getting all excited about this nice free lunch. You can get some real fishy free-for-alls right at the boat if you work it right; and then you heave your baited hook into the melee and something grabs it without hesitation—but of course we weren't interested in fishing tonight. We were waiting for the sharks to move in as they often

397

do. As Mr. Montoya knows very well. As a matter of fact, it's one of the standard ways of fishing for them, if you like sharks. Well, we didn't get any sharks but we did get a nice friendly porpoise, and it was dark of course and by that time Montoya wasn't making any fine distinctions between fins and fins. He promptly made a thorough mess of his pants and screamed to be hauled in, he'd talk." Janet McHugh paused, and went on: "Is that detailed enough for you, Mr. Martin?"

"But he wasn't really hurt?"

"Not unless you count his manly image of himself, that was very badly hurt." She cleared her throat again, with that faint hint of embarrassment that made her seem more human and likeable. "Afterwards, I let him have a little rum to console himself. Unfortunately, I got distracted by a navigational problem; when I checked back he'd killed the best part of a fifth of Mount Gay, poor guy. So now he's too damn drunk to make it home under his own power. He needs a pair of clean trousers and a place to sober up where he won't attract official attention. I thought you might be interested. He said you've been wanting to get information out of him for a long time; now's your chance. I've got him all softened up for you. And I don't think either of us wants him in the drunk tank, which is where he'll probably wind up if I just dump him ashore. You'd have a hard time questioning him there and he could create problems for me. Sober, I don't think he'll make me any trouble with the police—he can't, not without admitting that he's accessory before the fact to murder and robbery on the high seas—but drunk and dirty like this, God knows what he might say to explain how he got that way."

Martin drew a long breath. To protest that he could not condone such violent and unpleasant behavior would be plain hypocrisy. He'd known that this young woman was going to take some kind of high-handed action from the first moment he saw her eyes; and he'd known he was prepared to take advantage of it. There was no goddamn sense in his trying to soothe his conscience by making self-righteous noises now. His conscience wasn't that stupid, and neither was Mrs. Janet McHugh.

"All right," he said. "I'll get somebody over there to take care of him for you. But first you'd better tell me what you got out of him." As he listened to the calm, matter-of-fact voice at the other end of the line, he was aware that Elizabeth

Cameron had put on a robe and left the bedroom; he could hear her moving in the kitchen. At last he asked, "Do you think you could find the island he mentioned, Mrs. McHugh?"

"Probably. They didn't trust Montoya with the name, but from the conversation he repeated I'd guess it's probably Lucy Cay over in the Bahamas, one of the smaller of the Berry Islands. Private. Owned by a millionaire named DeWinters, but he died some years ago and last I heard they were still fighting each other and the Bahamian government over the estate. Anyway, there's just a caretaker living there now. Either they made a deal with the old guy or just killed him and moved in. But I doubt they're still there; my impression is that by now they're on their way south through the Islands in *Stream Hunter*, skippered by a fat yo-yo named Gonzaga, and if that bastard puts my boat on the coral I'll feed *him* to the sharks—*real* sharks this time."

Martin said, "If I'd known Montoya had so much information, I might have taken stronger measures. . . . And you say the name of the courier, the messenger boy who's been keeping them all, here, in contact with Columbus, is Regan?"

"Yes, Sean Regan. Hardly a boy, I gather. Small, dark, tough, and very Irish; he really makes a career of it according to Montoya. Not local. Montoya had never seen him before he was brought around by a young guy named Orosco accompanied by the top man's daughter, a kid named Francesca—well, you probably know all about that. Mr. Martin?"

"Yes?"

"Montoya may not have seen this Regan before, but I think I have. I think he must be the tough little man who was in charge of the hijackers who boarded *Stream Hunter;* the man who . . . who pretended to shoot Laura Briggs and actually did shoot Babe Gregertsen. The description fits. Montoya says he talked like a competent sailor and asked a lot of intelligent questions—Montoya picks up all the latest navigational information by chatting with people off the cruising yachts that come in. He kind of prides himself on having the latest word available. He says Regan really pumped him."

"About what, exactly? I mean, about what area?"

Janet McHugh hesitated. "I don't think I'll tell you that. You government people have had your crack at doing it your way; now I'm doing it my way and I don't trust you not to interfere. Maybe you can get it out of Montoya, yourself."

"But without your nautical background I won't be able to interpret it so well, will I?"

He heard her laugh. "Good man. You catch on fast."

"At least tell me if Montoya knew *why* Columbus is going where he's going—what he plans to do when he gets there."

"I don't think our dockmaster friend has been given that information, exactly. But he did say Regan was all fired up about it; he seemed to consider it a real challenge. Like a squirrel hunter setting out to shoot elephants, or a seatrout fisherman tackling marlin for the first time. Whatever they're planning it seems to be big and ambitious, Regan did indicate that much." After a moment she spoke in an altered voice to indicate that the interview was at an end. "How soon can you have somebody here to assume responsibility for the warm body?"

"I have some people only a few blocks from the Yacht Club on another assignment. It shouldn't be more than fifteen minutes. Where should they meet you?"

"Nowhere," Janet McHugh said. "I won't be here; I don't have that much faith in you and your busybody colleagues. I'm shoving off right now. And a word of warning: if you send the Coast Guard after me tell them not to bother with any shots across the bow. The only way they can stop me is to blow me out of the water. I'll ram anybody who tries to come alongside and I'll shoot anybody who tries to board. Once is enough; nobody takes *this* boat away from me, I don't care what the hell pretty uniforms they're wearing. They weren't in the Yucatan Straits when I needed them; they haven't accomplished anything useful since. Let them keep right on chasing pot smugglers and stay the hell out of my way while I. . . ." Her voice stopped abruptly. After a moment it returned: "Sorry. I didn't mean to flip like that. I guess I'm a little tired and irritable tonight."

"Where do we find Montoya?" Martin asked.

"His car. A green Chevelle in his parking space near the gate. I don't think he'll sober up enough to try to drive anywhere; but just in case he does I'm taking his keys away and taping them to the first lamppost to the right. And Mr. Martin. . . ."

"Yes?"

"Just in case you had in mind a high moral lecture: remember that this is the man who set us up. He admits he fingered the boat for the hijackers. He admits he put that treacherous little Briggs girl aboard to disable the radio at

400

the right moment and help out in other ways if needed. That's how I got onto him; I remembered that he was the one who recommended her, very highly. He's as responsible for my husband's death as if he'd put a pistol to his head and pulled the trigger—not to mention the Gregertsens who were human beings too, if you want to be technical about it. Granted that Montoya had his reasons, which he explained tearfully and at length, he's not entitled to save his goddamn family at the expense of mine. At least, if he wants to go that route, he's got no kick coming if I then save my boat at his expense. Good-bye, Mr. Martin." He heard her chuckle. "Oh, give my regards to Miss Cameron and my apologies for calling at this ungodly hour."

The line went dead. After a moment, Martin put down the phone and went into the bathroom for his clothes, which he brought out and dumped on the tumbled bed. After dressing hastily and slipping on the gun harness—what the hell good that was doing him these days was hard to say—and covering it decently with his jacket, he picked up the phone again and dialed a number.

"Masterman? Find out what kind of international red tape we've got to go through to investigate a place over in the Bahamas called Lucy Cay. It's supposedly somewhere in the Berry Islands, wherever that may be. We're looking for the people responsible for Tommy Walsh's murder, and a hijacked forty-eight-foot sportfishing boat. And then ... no, you'd better do this first. Whoever's on the Ullman account tonight, down at Dinner Key, have them get right over to the Yacht Club and take care of a guy named Montoya who's supposed to be sitting in a green Chevelle near the parking lot gate dead drunk and kind of messy. I'll be down there as fast as I can, tell them."

When he hung up, Elizabeth was standing in the bedroom doorway with a cup of coffee in each hand. Her robe was blue and rather mannish in style with satin lapels like a tuxedo. Her normally smooth and rather severe hairdo was tousled like a kid's, and she looked younger and more vulnerable than the picture of her he normally carried in his mind, which, he thought, might well be replaced by this one, except that if it made him feel the way he now felt it wouldn't be a safe picture for him to carry around. She came forward and gave him a cup, and sat beside him while he drank it hastily. Then they rose and stood facing each other, both knowing

401

that there were many things that must be said now, that could not wait. But what she said first was:

"I'll make you breakfast if you can wait."

"I'd better not," he said. "Thanks for the coffee."

There was a brief silence; then she reached out deliberately and slipped her hand inside his jacket and touched the weapon holstered there. She drew a long breath and, withdrawing her hand, looked up at him.

"I'm just being wifely," she said. "I'm making sure that hubby doesn't go out in the cold rain without his umbrella. Be careful, darling."

As he kissed her he realized that there had not, after all, been so many things that needed saying; she'd just said them all.

CHAPTER 38

July

Latitude 26°N; Longitude 80°W

As they entered the harbor at Dinner Key, Lavinia Burnett arranged herself gracefully face down on the sex-pad of the rakish sportboat, as they were called nowadays—back when she was a kid spending her summers in Bar Harbor they went a bit slower and were called runabouts. She wondered where the little big-headed freak had picked up this particular souped-up glamor-barge. Well, it was probably legal for a change, cash on the line. Columbus wouldn't be likely to use a stolen boat for regular communication between the U.S.A. and his precious secret cay in another country; there'd be too much risk of trouble.

It had been, she reflected ruefully, a hell of a rough ride across the Stream even slowed to twenty knots—even if the bucket did derive from an ocean-racing hull designed to run at several times that speed in open water. Just like the slightly larger one, not legally acquired, that had been employed for the intercept off Yucatan, to use poor, dead Bucky's elaborate terminology. The big platform aft had originally served the purely practical purpose of covering the oversized racing engines that powered the twin stern-drives, creating a roomy machinery space back there. However, when the boats began to be offered for nonracing use, the manufacturers had quickly realized that it made a very popular area for displaying tanned young ladies in scanty bikinis, and now it was standard industry practice to cushion it accordingly.

Lying back there on the gaudily covered foam-rubber pad, Lavinia Burnett unfastened the top of her white swimsuit to make things look more realistic—not to mention more interesting—to gawkers on the dock. Ogling her there, they'd be less likely to look at her too closely elsewhere.

"Let me know when we're close," she said to Regan. "I don't want to show my face too much. There might be somebody around who remembers me from other boats or other marinas. You never know where these fucking wandering yachtsmen are going to pop up. . . . What's the matter?"

He'd cut the throttles, allowing the boat to drift. He turned and said, frowning, "I do not like putting you ashore like this. How do we know that greasy punk Orosco hasn't spilled his guts in jail? Not to mention his girlfriend with the sweet classy face and the vulgar little arse. You could be walking right into a trap."

She laughed. "Don't let the Don hear you talking like that about his darling juvenile tramp of a daughter. But I think it's safe enough. She may be a tramp, but she's a Colombo and she won't talk; they're very strong on family loyalty. And Orosco's very strong on her so he won't talk, either. Not under the chickenshit kind of questioning the fuzz will give them." She grimaced. "But Jesus I thought the little freak was going to start chewing the rug like Adolf Hitler when he heard they'd been picked up."

Regan shrugged. "At least it forced him to make up his mind to it. To get those others out of jail, Ochsner's group, it was hardly worth a big undertaking like this. Hell, he can pick up another gang of overtrained military supermen just by waving a few dollar bills around; they're not all that special. But with his daughter involved, the decision came easy. And for ten thousand in advance, plus substantial payments conditional upon success, he can have hydrophobia for all I care."

"Regan."

"What is it?"

She sat up, holding the brassiere of her bikini more or less in place. "Don't let's kid ourselves," she said seriously. "You know that getting them out of jail isn't what the little creep is *really* after. Except for the girl; he'll pry her loose if he can. But that vicious little aristocrat bastard doesn't care how many of us peasants die, or languish behind bars. What he *really* wants is to spit in the eyes of the people who've spoiled his sacred home-sweet-home crusade. Maybe even the whole damn country involved in wrecking, or at least delaying, his glorious patriotic plans. The rest is just bullshit to con us all into going along with him until he's ready to take his dramatic revenge no matter who gets hurt. That freak is strictly suicide material. For everybody."

After a moment, the wiry little man at the wheel shrugged his surprisingly muscular shoulders once more. "It's no concern of Regan's, my sweet," he said. "All I've contracted to do is produce the ship, not run it. What he does with the vessel afterwards, whether it's what he says or something else . . ." He stopped and she saw his crooked, reckless smile as he glanced around. "When the client has paid for all the little easy stuff, and paid well, should Regan back out now that it's something big and difficult he wants?" He paused again, and went on: "But I still do not like leaving you like this, not knowing what kind of a deadfall awaits you on shore."

Their early antagonism had vanished, at least temporarily, and as good sailors will they had achieved considerable respect for each other during the rugged crossing from the Bahamas. She'd handled the throttles, racing fashion, while he managed the wheel; and they'd worked well together, synchronizing their efforts to defeat the common enemy, the sea. It wasn't everybody who could bring one of these lousy thunderboats across the Stream in a blow. And of course they still had memories in common of another dangerous enterprise they'd shared, although she did not like to think of that.

She grinned at him. "If they get me, they'll get you. Hell, they've got us now. If there's a trap, they'll know about this boat, and they'll be ready with something fast enough to run her down, even at sixty knots. What's the matter, Regan, are you scared?"

Having said it, she regretted it at once. She had not meant

404

to antagonize him; she had merely intended to tease him a little. She'd forgotten that there were some otherwise reasonable men whose courage must never be questioned; who reacted quite mechanically to such a challenge; and he was one. His eyes grew angry instantly.

He lashed back at her sharply: "Some people, Sean Regan for one, are not crazy in the head and do not like playing unnecessary games with death and imprisonment!"

Vinnie felt the sudden tears coming; the goddamn irrational fucking tears she couldn't seem to control these days; Burnett the human sponge, the leaky faucet, drip, drip, drip.

"Don't say that!" she blurted. "You didn't have to use that word! I'm no crazier than a certain sawed-off jerk who's chasing off on a mad project for a nasty little creep who's got a king-sized hate against the whole human race. The Mona Intercept, for God's sake! That's what another guy who ran errands for Mister Columbus would have called it, and you know something about him? He's dead. Like we're all going to be dead if we follow this big-headed fucking freak much longer!"

The anger had faded from Regan's eyes as she talked; she saw that he regretted his quick retort. He was regarding her closely in a strange appraising way; and she noticed for the first time the color of his eyes, not green, not brown. Hazel?

He spoke deliberately: "And is it your thought, my darling, that we should stop now? That you should forget the larcenous and murderous chores he has set you here? And that I should forget the ambitious piratical project he's hired me for down in the Caribbean off the Mona Passage? That we should take the ketch that's awaiting me for the job—she's been repainted blue since you last saw her and she's called *Pretty Baby* now—and that we should dismiss my ruffian crew and sail off together to the palmy South Seas islands of romance, my sweet?"

His voice was wry and sarcastic, and for a moment she thought he was simply continuing the verbal battle she'd started unintentionally and deliberately poking fun at her by putting into words some stray thoughts that had wandered through her mind during the violent night, when it had occurred to her that the tough little man beside her in the cockpit really wouldn't be a bad guy to have around, to keep around. And it would be nice to get away from the lousy mess she'd made of everything with somebody she could respect and trust, far away. . . . Then she realized, a bit startled, that

Regan was not trying to ridicule her at all; he'd had his night thoughts, too. They were both outlaws, both outcasts; maybe they could work something out together, at least for a while. He was simply laying out the proposition for them both to examine. But in the cold light of day it did not look very plausible or practical; and there was something still to be done. Don't worry, little monster, she thought, it's a nice dream but I know you've got to be fed, and it probably wouldn't work anyway.

She said, "Thanks, Regan. That's the best offer I've had all day, and I appreciate it. But—"

He smiled thinly. "I know. Regan has a romantic soul, but the game has to be played to the end, now."

She nodded. "Put me on the dock over there. We know he usually takes off this time in the morning to have breakfast ashore and do his daily shopping. Those dumb Latin love-birds reported that much before they got themselves picked up with their pockets full of dope. I'll stroll by his boat and have a look, at least."

Regan reached for the throttles. "Well, the word is they're pulling the surveillance off him today. You know what to look for, what I'll need. It's the only home he's got these days; it should be on board somewhere. When you've got it, just show yourself, I'll be waiting. Drop it in the cockpit as I go by. Unless you want to reconsider your decision. It was an honest offer I made, and we might actually get away with it for a while. Think about it. Now you had better fasten that brassiere again before you are arrested for indecent exposure."

She retied her bikini top, pulled on a brief white terrycloth beach coat, slipped her feet into sandals, and picked up the striped beach bag that concealed the little nylon pack with all her worldly goods, and some other materials that had been supplied by Jesus Cardenas, always ready with the forged documents so often required by the *patrón*'s business. She scratched her bare legs irritably. It was really too damn late in the season for the Bahamas. They had sand fleas and things over there that just waited for warm weather to eat you up, and the bites left great itching welts that lasted for weeks. The dock was approaching now, and she moved forward through the cockpit; then she was swinging herself up and the boat was pulling away.

She turned to wave good-bye to Regan, to make it look natural, and he waved back. You couldn't say he made a very convincing yachtsman, but these were democratic days and who was to say a banty little hardcase in jeans and T-shirt couldn't own a fucking speedboat as well as anybody else? And there was another one she could have had, after all, she reflected ruefully; but it would not have worked, not really, if only because Regan knew too much about her. He'd once seen her at her worst, and she knew that he would actually have been adopting her more as a damaged kid sister than as a lover, out of pity—there was a lot of pity in the Irish even if they did keep killing each other—and she didn't really want his goddamn therapeutic affection, or did she?

She walked along the dock swinging the big striped bag jauntily as if she knew exactly where she was going; and there was the little cutter she was looking for. She couldn't read the name from this angle but the description and slip number fit. The *Nancy Lou,* if she had the right boat, was closed up except for a couple of ports in the cabin trunk too small for entry; but as she moved out the finger pier she saw that while the padlock had been dropped into the hasp securing the main hatch, it had not been snapped shut, a common stunt when a boat was being left only briefly.

She could see the name now on the flank of the little vessel—the hailing port would be on the stern—and she stepped aboard, ducking under the awning that protected the cockpit from the sun and, working quite openly as if she belonged there, removed the padlock and laid it aside, shoved the sliding hatch cover back, removed the two top boards of the four blocking the companionway, dropped her beach bag into the cabin, and climbed down after it, turning to replace the hatchboards and slide the cover back into place. There was no way of returning the padlock to the hasp from inside but at least the boat would seem undisturbed and unoccupied to a casual observer if she was careful about the way she moved about below. She didn't weigh much, but it didn't take much to rock a twenty-eight-foot sailboat quite visibly.

In spite of the limited cross-ventilation from the two open ports it was hot and stuffy in the little cabin and she stripped off her beach coat and kicked off her sandals before getting to work. This was a real seagoing vessel and didn't have many fancy lockers and shelves and drawers that might get dumped all over the cabin when the going got rough. Most things seemed to be stored in deep secure bins under the two bunks in the forward cabin and the single settee opposite the galley aft. The stuff forward seemed to be mostly canned goods and staples and boat gear. Returning aft she lifted the settee cushion and found what she was looking for in the middle bin under it, along with a portable typewriter and some typing paper and an old surplus ammunition box full of unexposed film.

But there it was, a heavy plastic bag—most of the stuff on board was carefully bagged in plastic to protect it from moisture in case of leaks or condensation or boarding seas. It was full of the little yellow boxes in which Kodak returned the customer's color slides. Each box had been carefully and conspicuously numbered with a felt-tipped pen. There was even a small spiral notebook marked ASSIGNMENT PETROX PRINCE, and inside were picture data with corresponding numbers, so she wouldn't have to make a special search for that as had been anticipated. You had to hand it to Don Jimmy and his spies, she reflected; they'd done a good job of learning this seagoing photographer's working habits, and they'd also managed to determine that the results of this particular assignment had, for some unknown reason, never been delivered so the films were still available.

Ullman was the guy's name, Harold Ullman. Strangely, they'd almost met once before down in the Keys. Boot Key Marina. He'd brought his boat in just before Thanksgiving, when she was already there staying with those bearded freaks and that big placid, pregnant sow of a girl on board that crazy homemade trimaran called *Freedom Machine*. She hadn't seen him then or even noticed the boat particularly; but she'd heard at the Thanksgiving party on the dock that Ullman and his wife had run into violent trouble when they reached home that night—and now the wife was dead and the guy was still in trouble. Columbus hadn't given her all the details, just enough so she'd know why Ullman had to die and she was just the girl to see to it—as if, just because she'd once shown she could manage to pull a trigger, she was now a professional hit girl or something! Anyway, the guy had to die not only because he'd put the finger on Pete Orosco and by so doing had also got precious little Francesca Columbus jailed, but also because the Ullman family had offended Don Jaime Colombo by being so hard to kill. Hell, even the wife, although she'd eventually been eliminated, had managed to take that big blond gorilla Olson with her; and Columbus had been counting on Olson. There was a funny streak of superstition in Don Jimmy, and he seemed to feel that he'd had nothing but bad luck since he'd almost accidentally got involved with this innocuous-seeming young couple. Now, before starting on his big new project, he wanted to be sure he was rid of both of them for good. Gently now, little monster, she told it softly; we wasted a lot of time over there toward Yucatan, but I think this is the break we've been looking for, the man we've been looking for. He wants Don Jimmy, too; he's got to after everything that's been done to him.

She was perspiring now, all right, in the stuffy cabin, even with hardly any clothes on; and she got a paper towel from the holder behind the stainless-steel sink and dried her hands before opening the plastic bag, and one of the yellow cardboard boxes inside. She drew out a slide and held it to the light; a lovely picture in living color of a fucking rusty steam winch, real camera art. She wondered how much use that would be to Columbus and his new megalomaniac operation—not that there was anything to be surprised at there; you could expect fucking anything from a guy who had seriously planned to conquer a country the size of Cuba practically single-handed. Presumably there was important information he needed elsewhere in this mess of color slides.

She'd been given to understand that the main reason this particular target had been selected was that all the necessary preliminary work had already been done. Not only was a thorough photographic survey of the ship available where it could easily be stolen—and she had to admit that so far, at least, it had been easy enough—but also it seemed that good contacts had already been established for checking on its schedule for some other purpose, unspecified. Now it had been determined that, the vagaries of the oil business permitting, the *Petrox Prince* would soon be coming up from South America by way of the Mona Passage between Hispaniola and Puerto Rico—pretty much its regular route—with a full load of gooey black Bunker C, after first running some other errands around the Caribbean.

Crouching on her heels in the little sailboat's galley or saloon, depending on whether you looked to port or starboard, Lavinia Burnett frowned at the bag of slides. She knew that without the information on these films Regan would not move. He'd made it clear that even with three successful missions under his belt he wasn't going to play his pretty pirate game with a twenty-thousand-ton ship about which he didn't have complete information; this was no crummy little private yacht incapable of holding anything serious in the way of surprises. No films; no intercept. Well, at least not right now.

But if these slides were withheld or destroyed, Columbus would simply take a little additional time to obtain the needed information by other means, perhaps picking a different target; and conditions might not be nearly as favorable as now. Her instinct told her she might not have much time left to horse around. Not that her hostile intentions were suspected; she was fairly sure they weren't. That successful job off Yucatan, which had given her no chance to strike back effectively, dammit, had probably established her loyalty beyond question, which was the only good thing that could be said of the lousy mess—well, that and the fact that the only person involved whom she'd really liked had, according to the newspapers, managed to survive being set adrift as she'd hoped would happen. But loyalty was a one-way street to Don Jimmy; and even if he considered hers beyond question it would mean nothing to him if he decided that, with the changing situation, she'd become superfluous and possibly dangerous for what she knew. He'd simply say a word to Jesus Cardenas, who'd jerk his head at moron Bolo, and out that pretty pair would march to dispose of this diminutive *puta* who'd become a potential nuisance to *El Patrón*.

Anyway, Columbus was definitely taking part in this mission himself, exposing himself to danger at last—and high time, too—but he might change his mind if there were delays. She could not afford to pass up the opportunity; and what difference did it make in the long run? The attempt would be made on some ship, why not this one? Replacing the slide, and the box, she closed the plastic bag carefully with the paper-covered wire tie and made her way back out into the cockpit.

Despite the blazing Florida sun, the air topside seemed pleasantly cool to her damp skin as she emerged into the shade of the cockpit awning. There was a moment of uncertainty; then the sharp-nosed speedster came gliding down the watery lane between the docked boats and cut *Nancy Lou*'s stern close. Lavinia Burnett reached out and dropped the bagged films onto the cockpit sole behind the helmsman's seat. Regan touched reverse briefly and the sportboat hung there while he looked up at her with a question in his eyes. She found the ready stupid tears coming once more as she realized that the tough little mick really liked her, really wanted her to change her mind about carrying out the second of the ugly chores assigned her here by *Señor* Fucking Columbus, and jump back into the speedboat with him and see what they could work out together. It might even be pretty good for a while, she thought; but Regan didn't know that the nicest thing she could do for him was go somewhere and shoot herself. He didn't know what happened to people who liked, or were liked by, Lavinia Jinx Burnett.

Anyway, it wouldn't work for very long, it never did, and she had other things to do. She shook her head minutely and he shrugged those nice strong shoulders and reached for the gear lever; a moment later the boat was disappearing from sight on its way back to the Bahamas where he'd rendezvous with Columbus and hear the final plans for the trap being set off the Mona Passage, the trap she'd have to spring somehow with Columbus in it, but how?

But at the moment she had another trap to worry about, right here, and a different victim—at least he'd been picked for a victim by Columbus, but there were other uses he might serve, if she handled him properly. So to hell with Regan's interesting shoulders and other undoubtedly very interesting attributes; and his strangely, for the kind of man he was, compassionate little hazel eyes.

CHAPTER 39

July

Latitude 26°N; Longitude 80°W

It was odd, Harold Ullman reflected, how you could become almost-friends, marina-friends—even in a rather strained and careful and self-conscious way—with a man who'd helped to shatter your life, a man whom you'd hurt and humiliated rather seriously more or less by way of retaliation. However, it had seemed stupid for them to sit on their separate side-by-side boats pretending not to know each other; stupid and perhaps suspicious to anybody who might be watching. A little normal social contact between neighboring vessels not only looked more convincing but was also more convenient for the task at hand. Unfortunately, the stakeout, as Bill Simonds called it, had turned out to be pretty much a washout.

"Well, thanks for the farewell breakfast," Ullman said, getting out of Simonds' flashy-looking compact car in the marina parking lot. He retrieved his cane and a bag of groceries from the rear, and leaned down to look at the blond man behind the wheel. "If you ever trailer that fishing boat of yours down to Marathon, stop by Boot Key Marina and have a drink."

"That's where you'll be heading now?" Simonds asked.

Ullman shrugged. "Right now I'm heading over to the Bahamas for a short cruise before the hurricane season; but I'll be back in Marathon eventually." He threw a glance around the big, crowded Dinner Kay Marina. "To hell with this big-city living; it gives me claustrophobia."

Simonds hesitated. "You're sure you feel all right about this? I mean, I could stick around a while longer if you're at all worried about . . . You know. If you feel we're pulling away your protection prematurely. God knows none of us wants to pull *that* boner again."

Ullman shook his head. "I'll be all right. Hell, with Orosco in jail awaiting trial for possession, along with the Columbus girl, it doesn't seem likely anybody'll bother me, why should they? I really can't swear to the identification, not in court; and anyway nothing I can say, or not say, about what happened last fall, is going to affect the drug charges against them."

Simonds grinned. "The man actually sounds disappointed that nobody's going to kill him." He winked. "I know somebody who might have taken a crack at it a few weeks back."

It was the closest they'd come to the subject. Now that the first shock of bereavement, and the murderous accompanying anger, had faded, it seemed like an ugly and uncivilized thing to have done.

Ullman said awkwardly, "Look, Bill, I've been wanting to—"

"Skip it." Simonds shook his head quickly. "Folks who play lousy games with other people's lives can expect a little backlash now and then. Particularly when they haven't got sense enough or guts enough to disregard orders they know to be wrong. I haven't ever said how goddamn sorry I am about . . . Ah, hell. See you around."

"Sure."

Ullman watched the rakish little car drive away; then he got a fresh grip on the cane and the groceries and headed for the marina office to pay and check out; after which he hauled his burden out to C-dock where the slip beyond *Nancy Lou* was now vacant. With Ullman's help, Simonds had returned the borrowed sloop *Seabreeze,* on which he'd been living, to its owner's berth, before breakfast this morning. Turning at the finger pier along which his own boat lay, Ullman reflected that it was time to take the old girl out for a run; she was starting to grow weedy whiskers like a catfish lying there. It was time to get the hell away from Miami where they'd been happy and unhappy together, where Nancy had died so terribly. It was time to stop marking time and decide what the hell he was going to do with his lonely, once-again-single, goddamn life. He really had better get in touch with Bartholomew and see if the guy couldn't scrounge him up a nice dirty dangerous job somewhere far away, one that no photographer with any sense would tackle; although after the way he'd backed out of that lousy tanker assignment he'd undoubtedly have to eat a lot of ripe manure before the agent would . . .

The idle run of his thoughts came to an abrupt halt. He'd moved along the finger pier toward *Nancy Lou*'s cockpit, preparing to step aboard; now he'd come to a complete standstill staring at the brass padlock lying on the cabin top beside the closed hatch. Instinctively he glanced toward the parking lot, but Simonds' car was nowhere to be seen by this time.

The sensible thing to do, he told himself, was to stroll off casually to a phone booth—or even run like hell—and call for help; but he'd been sensible and cooperative long enough. He'd have played their game, the government's game, if they'd stuck around but it wasn't his fault they were always wandering off at the wrong time. He realized that his heart was pounding in an accelerated way, partly from apprehension of course—it would have been abnormal not to be a little scared—but partly from savage elation at finding that the enemy, some enemy, seemed to have moved within reach just when they'd all given up hope. He was aware of a return of the bitter, consuming hatred he'd known when he'd first received word of Nancy's murder, and learned the ghastly details.

Somebody had turned his reasonably pleasant world, and hers, into a nightmare place of blood and broken bones and disfigurement and death. Somebody had turned the beasts loose to prowl the earth; well, they could damn well have a few more beasts than they'd counted on. Even gentle intellectual Nancy with her strong nonviolent convictions had finally been goaded, driven, tormented into retaliating violently, even if too late to save herself. Some people didn't need quite that much goading and driving and tormenting. It was about time this was made clear to anybody, whatever his political goals might be, who thought he could safely sacrifice innocent people at random to his lousy private crusades. Don't anger the animals, Mister Columbus. They bite.

Stepping down into the cockpit, Harold Ullman laid down the cane and set the groceries within reach of the main hatch. Then he reached under his left pants leg and brought out the cheap wooden-handled knife he'd liberated from the would-be assassin in Puerto la Cruz, now cleaned up and honed to a fine edge. There was something to be said for his freckled, vulnerable, red-haired complexion after all, he reflected, that forced him to wear long-sleeved shirts as protection from the sun, and concealing long trousers, even in hot weather—particularly in hot weather. Bill Simonds had drawn upon his professional training to give advice about the design of the ankle-sheath Ullman had sewed and riveted out of a piece of scrap canvas; Bill had also given, in return for some pointers on sailboat handling, a quick basic course in the employment of edged weapons to supplement the information Ullman had obtained so long ago from that ill-fated ex-Marine soldier of fortune.

Wearing a hidden knife like that was, of course, strictly illegal. It seemed that anything was illegal these days that enabled you to defend yourself. The police were supposed to do your defending for you—like they'd bravely and efficiently kept him from being beaten and Nancy from being killed, Ullman reflected sourly. In New York you could be mugged and murdered in Central Park while the city's finest were busy elsewhere arresting honest citizens for allowing their dogs to shit on the pavement. So don't let your friendly neighborhood fuzz catch you protecting yourself with five inches of steel in your sock, and whose side is everybody on, anyway? Not yours, that's for certain, there's only one person on that side, and that's you. And isn't it about time for you to open that everlasting hatch and find out what's waiting for you below, Captain Ullman, suh?

He debated the question of a bomb and came up with a

negative answer. The betraying padlock had presumably not been returned to its hasp because it couldn't be, because the person who'd removed it had closed the hatch from inside, not the position from which a bomber would logically choose to view the proceedings. Nevertheless, logic or no logic, it was a relief when he finally had the companionway fully open without having experienced any loud and destructive noises. The first thing he saw, looking down through the hatch, was that the folding table had been set up by the settee to starboard. Casually arranged upon it was a white bikini, top and bottom. Cute.

He recalled that deer hunters sometimes used the bottled scent of a doe as a lure. His mind made note of the fact that if the swimsuit had actually arrived on a girl—if it wasn't merely something brought here in somebody's pocket for purposes of distraction or misdirection—she wasn't a very big girl. Under the two scanty, intriguingly shaped scraps of white material was a large sheet of paper; a nautical chart. He recognized it; he had the same chart on board although he'd never yet managed to cruise the area it covered. There was also a small pile of smaller papers. The top one seemed to be a photostatic copy of a page written in very old-fashioned script. A pair of white sandals peeked out from under the table. A large striped beach bag and a white terrycloth robe lay on the settee. Somebody was selling him hard on the idea of a girl—a girl who wanted him to know she was on board and therefore couldn't be too dangerous—but it could be a fraudulent sale. And girls weren't always completely harmless.

He lowered himself through the narrow hatch and down the steep companionway ladder, holding the knife ready, happy for a change that he owned a small vessel without many hiding places below, none from which he could be jumped in this rather cramped after cabin. There were no lockers or hidden corners big enough. What was here, if it was of human size, you saw; and nobody was here. Whoever was on board just had to be waiting in the little forward stateroom or the tiny head beyond.

Two cautious steps took him to the opening in the main structural bulkhead amidships, just forward of the settee and galley. His boat shoes were quite silent on the laid teak of the cabin sole; but nobody on board could possibly have missed the way the boat had rolled perceptibly in response to his weight as he stepped into the cockpit, or the noise he'd made opening the hatch. Or could they?

The stateroom was closed off, when desired, only by a curtain; it was not drawn. He eased himself through the opening, braced for an assault that did not come. He saw that his own bunk to port, chosen because it was unobstructed and so allowed him to get out of it easily to attend to his nautical duties under way, was empty except for his seabag, which had been moved from the other bunk where he'd left it: Nancy's bunk. This, partly tucked away behind the mast and the small dresser, could not be so readily viewed in its entirety from the doorway, but the object upon it was hard to miss: a rather small human female without any clothes on sound asleep on her right side, her head aft, her back to him. She looked very undangerous snoozing there in her bare skin, and made him feel a bit self-conscious about the knife in his hand; but the feeling was not strong enough to make him put it away.

He moved warily along the narrow passage between the bunks, past the girl, and examined the toilet compartment forward. He found nothing but his good shoregoing clothes in their plastic garment bags hanging to starboard where they belonged, and the seagoing plumbing to port. The little forepeak beyond, way up in the bow, was full of spare lines and anchor gear, too full to hide a human being. Apparently he had Miss Nudie of Dinner Key all to himself, lucky man, and she was still sleeping soundly if you could believe it, but of course he couldn't.

But she was. Returning, he stood over the softly breathing girl, knife still in hand, and came to the reluctant conclusion that her slumber was genuine. Which made her drunk, doped, sick, screwy, or just a very tired little girl. Or any combination of the above. She had a deep all-over tan—apparently misplacing all her clothing was nothing new to her—and brown hair of moderate length, and a neat little naked rump. The stifling heat of the cabin with the forward hatch closed caused her to gleam with a faint sheen of perspiration in a rather interesting way, but Harold Ullman found that he wasn't really interested. At the moment, only the survival circuits were fully operative; the sex connections weren't really functioning. Maybe the fact that the small bare intruder was usurping Nancy's berth and blurring some memories he would have preferred to leave undisturbed had something to do with it.

After a moment, he reached out to touch a leg to arouse her, remaining well back, knife ready; but he had to squeeze the ankle a bit before she responded. He heard her make an odd little whimpering sound before she sat up abruptly, staring wide-eyed at the blade in his hand. He was aware of the small, rather innocent-looking breasts and the intriguing fuzzy dark area, lower, that didn't really intrigue him much at the moment although it did embarrass him slightly—after six years of matrimony he wasn't used to undressed girls he wasn't married to. The face wasn't really pretty but couldn't quite be called plain, either. Certainly it wasn't ugly. It was lightly streaked and smudged with something that didn't seem to be perspiration. He had the uneasy feeling that the kid had cried herself to sleep, if that was supposed to make sense. She drew a deep, shuddering breath, watching the knife.

"It's easier to cut the lousy throat," she said, licking her lips. "They tell me you're apt to hit a rib if you try for the lousy heart. You're Ullman?" When he nodded, she said, "I saw it in a movie. It's supposed to be sure-fire. The good old nekkid-lady-in-the-bed routine, irresistible. Are you going to carve me with that thing? Or would you rather look at a fascinating treasure map, Mr. Ullman? Or just fuck?"

It was, he saw, a perfectly serious question; well, they were all serious questions. He said, "I want to get the groceries out of the cockpit before the milk sours. And what's on the Silver Bank off Hispaniola that hasn't already been found by Jacques Cousteau?"

She grinned boyishly, sitting naked and cross-legged on the bunk. "Oooh, it's a real chart expert, huh? Spots it at a glance, does he? And what did old underwater Jackie-boy ever find down there except the wrong fucking ship in the wrong fucking place? Suppose I could tell you where in that mess of coral heads the *Nuestra Señora de Concepcion* really sank?"

He saw that she was watching him shrewdly; and he realized that she was laying a small trap for him, trying to determine how much he really knew about the subject of lost treasure.

"Who cares about the *Concepcion*, now?" he asked. "A guy named William Phips found her three hundred years ago and grabbed as much of her cargo as he could with the equipment of the time. The loot made him Sir William Phips and governor of Massachusetts. Read all about it in the book

417

written by Jacques Cousteau, who couldn't find her. But last year, or maybe the year before, I don't recall exactly, a guy named Burt Webber did locate her again and got the rest."

"Suppose he didn't get *all* the rest," said the small girl on the bed. She paused, and went on: "Did you ever hear of the *Serenidad?*"

He said, "Treasure-hunting is for nuts." Then he grinned. "But keep talking."

"The *Nuestra Señora de Serenidad.* There were actually two galleons sailing in company, the *Concepcion* and the *Serenidad,* both really loaded. They were both blown onto the Silver Bank by the storm. The *Concepcion* hit first." She leaned forward earnestly. "And the *Serenidad*'s captain, a careful man, noted down in his log the bearing and distance to the wrecked *Concepcion* when his ship struck. So that—"

Ullman laughed. "Let me guess. So that now that Webber has located the *Concepcion* for us, all we have to do is sail down there and measure a few miles and angles and we'll have the *Serenidad,* too. Instant millionaires, that's us. How come nobody ever heard of this *Serenidad* before?"

"It was kept a secret. The authorities didn't want it known what an enormous shipment they were really sending to Spain that year—hell, the fucking *Concepcion* alone carried over two hundred million dollars' worth of treasure. So the second galleon was loaded in secret and joined her consort out of sight of land. And when both ships were wrecked, the captain of the *Serenidad,* aware that his ship and its treasure didn't really exist, officially, got some very larcenous ideas. Unfortunately, while he managed to escape the wreck with his log, fever got him before he could get together a secret salvage expedition and find his way back."

"And now you have the log? That must be quite a story, too, Miss—"

"Vinnie. Lavinia Burnett, if you want to get formal, but you'd better let me get some clothes on before you lay it on me that heavy."

The name was not familiar to him—it had not been mentioned in the general briefing given him by the government man, Martin—but the initials were. A small, rather sexy girl named variously Lucia Barnes, Linda Brown, and Laura Briggs had figured rather prominently in Martin's story. She was wanted very badly. She was supposed to have been involved in at least three yacht hijackings masterminded by Jimmy Columbus, or Don Jaime Colombo, in which more

418

than half a dozen people had died—but what was she doing here? *Nancy Lou* was too small to be good hijacking material. And what was he expected to do about this corny sunken-treasure story, which, while based on well-known fact as they almost always were, had about as much real plausibility as still another yarn about the Lost Dutchman Mine, complete with a dog-eared map perforated with pseudo-bulletholes and sprinkled with chicken blood or catsup?

"Where'd you get my name?" he asked.

"In a marina down in the Keys. A lady said—"

"What lady?"

"Kind of a do-good dame named Ellington, a real busybody. Said you were a hell of a sailor and navigator, and you'd recently been through some lousy experiences and lost your wife so you might be in the mood for something kind of crazy."

Well, the kid had done her homework, at least. She apparently knew a little about Boot Key, and about him. Whether or not the conversation with Myra Ellington had ever taken place was another matter.

Ullman put a sneer into his voice. "So you think you'd like me to sail you down there so you can put on your little mask and fins and pick up a few doubloons off the *Serenidad,* just for kicks?"

"No, just find her," the girl said calmly. "Nobody's going to be suspicious of a little sailboat like this poking around the reefs and swimming and snorkeling and spearfishing. First we find her. Then we worry about getting together a real fucking expedition with a salvage permit and a big boat complete with all the fancy equipment, maybe even one of those underwater vacuum cleaners like Cousteau and Marks and Mel Fisher used, if the water isn't too deep where she's lying."

"What's the point?" Ullman asked, feeling that reluctance was still indicated. "I mean, hell, Fisher went into hock up to his ears to locate the *Nuestra Señora de Atocha* off the Marquesas; and the State of Florida grabbed everything he got off the wreck and last time I heard he was pretty broke and even the U.S. Supreme Court couldn't seem to make them give it back to him. Piracy is not dead in these waters; it's just official piracy now. And those other treasure hunters didn't do so well with the *Maravilla* off those Bahamas reefs; the Bahamian government got into that act with both feet, as I recall. Even if we should find the *Serenidad,* there'll just be

419

another greedy bunch of official robbers breathing down our necks and picking our pockets after we've done all the work. I don't know how Webber made out in the end but I'm sure that if the local authorities carelessly let him keep a reasonable percentage they're making very firm New Year's resolutions never to make that awful mistake again. Hell, I can make more money with my camera with less hassle, and I don't have to worry about getting caught in the middle of that coral trap by a sudden hurricane." The girl said nothing, watching him with rather disconcerting steadiness. Ullman reached around the corner for her bathing suit and dropped it into her lap. "How did you get hold of the *Serenidad*'s log, anyway?"

She grinned and, sitting there, tied on the brassiere; then she stood up and stepped into the bikini bottom and hauled it into place without self-consciousness. She gestured toward the after cabin.

"Let me show you what I've got, so you'll know what I'm talking about."

It was an imaginative and exciting story, of course; and by this time they were both quite aware, not only that it was total nonsense, but that both of them knew it. There had never been a *Serenidad,* she had never had a captain, and that captain had never written any bearings and distances in his nonexistent log. The *Nuestra Señora de Concepcion* had gone to her death alone. But that was not the subject under discussion. The simple fact was that the girl was not selling him, Harold Ullman, on any fucking treasure hunt—to use her own colorful terminology—she was selling him on herself. She'd deliberately given him a good look at the merchandise. Now she was giving him the direct challenge: here was a bright, amusing in a foul-mouthed way, and physically rather attractive little lady who should be fun to sail with; so why the hell should he care if the truth wasn't in her? What could he, now alone in the world, be doing with his time and his boat that would be more entertaining than taking Miss Lavinia Burnett to where she wanted to go and finding out why she wanted to go there badly enough to make up, for his benefit, a wild pieces-of-eight story complete with charts and documents? There was also the intriguing question of who had helped her make it up.

He wondered if he'd betrayed himself and let her know he knew who she was; but that was pretty irrelevant. The fact that she was a wanted criminal, a murderess and associate of murderers, and that she might very well be luring him offshore in his boat simply to shove him overboard some dark night under orders from Columbus—after all, he had put himself here for bait, deliberately; why should he be surprised if a predator had finally arrived?—all that was, of course, only a further challenge, the frosting on the cake. If what he wanted was to strike back at the man whose machinations were largely responsible for everything bad that had happened to him recently, he couldn't let a little thing like that deter him, since the girl might well provide him with a way to do it.

He looked at her for a moment, noting that her gray eyes had a little of the slaty, spacy look kids often displayed these days; the ones who'd subjected their brains to a few too many chemical experiments in the name of kicks. Strangely, he found her small body somewhat more desirable with a bikini than without, or perhaps he'd simply relaxed enough to appreciate it more, but he was going to have to forget about that. A little spice of danger, a little challenge, was all right; but you didn't go to bed with a man-eating tigress or a lady cobra if you liked living. Or even with an obviously screwy little girl who might by schizzy as hell. And it wasn't just that; there was a worse danger here. There was actually something kind of lost and appealing about the kid—he couldn't forget the tear stains he'd seen, although she'd surreptitiously knuckled them away—and he knew that, lonely as he was these days, if he allowed himself to get sexually involved with her he might very well wind up falling in love with her; and he wasn't going to tear himself apart like that ever again. Well, at least not by way of a crazy relationship, doomed from the start, with a probably somewhat unbalanced little fugitive from justice. . . .

"When did you have in mind making this voyage?" he asked.

She smiled slowly. "How about now?" she said.

He regarded her for a moment; and recognized again the mocking challenge in the eyes watching him. He realized that she knew perfectly well that he was aware of her identity. She knew that he understood clearly that whatever they were heading south to the Caribbean for, it sure as hell wasn't the lost treasure of the lost galleon *Nuestra Señora de Serenidad,* which didn't exist and never had. Nancy would have thought it very stupidly *macho* of him to accept the challenge; but Nancy was dead. He moved his shoulders slightly.

"I just stocked up for a Bahamas cruise; we should have enough supplies to get us there if we're careful," he said. "Okay, it's a deal. You cast off the lines while I fire up the mill." He grinned, watching her steadily. "Well, let's go, sailor!"

"Aye, aye, Captain."

Fifteen minutes later they were heading out between the islands. Lavinia Burnett, without being asked, had taken in all the docklines and brought them to the cockpit. As he steered she was making them up neatly for stowage. You could tell a lot about a sailor by the way he, or she, handled a line. A landlubber would wind it proudly around his hand and elbow, figuring he'd discovered a smart, salty way of proceeding, and producing a twisted little coil that would take half an hour to untangle when it was needed; and when he got to the end he'd look at you helplessly wondering how to finish the job. But this girl was expertly laying up each line in nice loose coils, taking a few turns around the finished product, passing the end through and drawing it up tight; and tossing it aside to reach for the next.

"Main halliard to starboard at the aft end of the deckhouse," Ullman said. "Forestaysail halliard to port. On the mast, that reel winch to starboard works the all-wire halliard for the roller-furling jib, which has to be set up very taut. It's a bit slack now; you'd better take up on it before we break out the sail. You know about those reel winches?"

"Sure. They'll take your fucking arm off if you're not careful. I'll watch it. You want me to hank on the staysail?"

"Go for it," Ullman said. "It's in the locker you're sitting on. We'll set everything as soon as we clear the channel. Vinnie."

"Yes?"

"If you can cook, this could turn out to be a hell of a sail."

She grinned. "You'll take fried Spam and canned beans and like it, Captain Ullman, sir. Where do you keep the sheets for the fucking staysail. . . . ?"

It was a hell of a sail. It was the first time Harold Ullman had ever concentrated on getting the most out of his boat; normally he was willing to leave speed to the racers, feeling that cruising should be a leisurely, happy, contemplative occupation. In the past he'd also been reluctant to sail too hard, even when he had the urge, because it would have been uncomfortable for Nancy. But this crazy kid turned out to be a boat-driver in the old, bold, clipper-ship tradition. She couldn't bear to see *Nancy Lou* loafing, not for a minute. It was as if she had a deadline to meet somewhere. When the thought came to him, he realized that the girl probably *was* trying to keep them to some kind of a secret schedule; and it seemed advisable to play along. It was kind of interesting, anyway, to see what the old girl would do if pushed to the limit. For a twenty-eight-footer, she did very well.

They sailed straight through the Bahamas by way of the Northwest and Northeast Providence Channels. That was probably illegal, Ullman thought; they should probably have checked in and out of the country—but were you really *in* a country, for customs and immigration purposes, if you never set foot on land? Anyway, nobody stopped them; and soon they were out in the Atlantic trying to get south as much as possible but forced well out to the east by the prevailing winds. It was a rough wet ride, hammering to windward in the open ocean, and it went on for days before they could tack south at last and hope to hit their destination in the Lesser Antilles, still several hundred miles ahead.

Somewhat to Ullman's surprise, the problem of sex never surfaced at all. He had heard about this phenomenon from other cruising men who'd enlisted female crews for lengthy passages, but he'd never quite believed it. Now he discovered for himself that standing watch and watch on a small boat at sea you were soon just too damn tired for any such nonsense. All you wanted when you came below was a bunk, an unoccupied bunk, in which you promptly died and stayed dead until you were shaken awake and informed that the old bucket was still close-hauled on the port tack, a reef had been taken in the main but the wind was dropping and it could probably come out pretty soon, and now it was your turn to sail her again for four hours, lucky you. Even barefoot in her skimpy halter and her very brief, very ragged cutoffs, hardly clothed at all, the girl quickly ceased to exist as a girl. She wasn't a friend, either, or even a companion, really. She was simply a competent partner in a rugged and demanding enterprise. After a while the thought of making a pass at her actually seemed a little obscene.

It was what he'd needed, he realized; a really absorbing and exhausting project that soon drove everything from his mind but the boat and the sea and the wind, and the sun and the stars by which he navigated. The hurt of seeing somebody else curled up wearily in Nancy's bunk faded as the days passed; after a while it no longer startled and pained him to turn at a sound and see a strange little girl emerging from the hatch instead of the slim familiar figure he'd half-expected. The memories, the guilt, the anger, all became gray and distant. It seemed as if he'd been here forever in the middle of this empty circle of sea and sky with the spray constantly lashing across the decks as *Nancy Lou* drove on to the south on a mad mission that had not even been confided to her skipper. . . .

It was the porpoises that finally changed things. There was a big school of them and they were jumping, not a very common sight. Ullman no longer had the instinctive impulse to call Nancy on deck; and Lavinia Burnett, he knew, would not thank him for awakening her just to look at some fish. She'd seen a fish, even if this fish happened to be a fucking mammal. But his professional instincts told him that a shot of a leaping porpoise was always salable, so he put *Nancy Lou* on autopilot and went below for a camera and a telephoto lens only to find that he'd neglected to reload the box the last time he'd used it—on that long-ago tanker story, he recalled—and there were no films handy in the waterproof case under the chart table. He swore and hastily folded the cabin table, kept set up while cruising, so that he could get at the settee behind it. He lifted the cushion and opened the bin that held his typewriter and the ammunition box in which he stored his main film supply. . . .

He knelt there for a moment, puzzled, steadying himself against the surging, plunging motion of the boat. Something was wrong, something was missing, but what? Then he became aware of the girl in the doorway that led into the sleeping cabin forward. She was holding a shiny revolver in her hand. There was a long silence.

"I've been waiting for that," Ullman said at last, surprising himself with his own calm. "Only I figured you'd jibe and wipe me off the deck with the main boom, or just give me a shove. . . . Why mess it up with guns and bullet holes when boating accidents are so easy?" He shrugged. "Of course, way out here they'll never find the body anyway, so I guess it doesn't really matter, does it?" He looked at her more closely. "What's to cry about, Vinnie? Hell, I'm number four or six or something, aren't I? Do you cry for all your victims?"

"Damn you!" she breathed. "Shut up, damn you! Here, it isn't loaded. I just . . . I just had to see . . . see how it felt, if it really felt like . . . felt the way I remembered. All sick and exciting and . . . Throw it!" she gasped. "Throw it overboard. Please!"

It seemed like a stupid thing to do to a perfectly good firearm, and rather an expensive firearm at that; but people did tend to make them into fearful symbols of something or other. And, come to think about it, he was feeling pretty sick and excited himself, or at least considerably relieved. He rose with the weapon he'd been given and pitched it out the hatch; the sound of the splash was almost covered by the normal sounds of *Nancy Lou*'s headlong progress. He covered the open storage bin, flipped the cushion back into place, and guided the weeping girl to the settee, steadying her as the boat rolled.

After a while he said, "The *Petrox Prince.*" He felt her nod. He said, "You stole that set of slides and gave them to somebody. Who?"

"Regan."

"Who's Regan?"

"The . . . the man who's going to take the *Petrox Prince.*"

"Take? You mean hijack? A big ship like that? That's crazy!"

He felt her shake her head convulsively. "Not if you know Regan. He'll do it, big as she is, just as he did those others. With your slides to show him what she's like inside, how she's laid out, where she's . . . vulnerable."

He drew a long breath, wanting to protest further, but there were other questions needing to be asked. "Where's Regan now?"

"Somewhere ahead of us. Driving hard for the Mona Passage in a thirty-nine-foot ketch with a seasick crew. At least, the last time offshore, half those thugs were puking all over the fucking boat. But maybe they've had time to get their sealegs now."

"So it's Regan we've been trying to catch?"

Vinnie shook her head again. "Not catch. You're a nice little redheaded boy with freckles and you sail a boat real good, but you're no match for Regan and his thugs and all the guns he'll have on board the *Pretty Baby* as she's called nowadays."

"Thanks for the vote of confidence," Ullman said. He caught himself as a violent lurch threatened to throw him across the boat. "If we're not trying to catch him, carrying all this sail, what the hell are we trying to do?"

"Pass him. So we can intercept that fucking tanker and warn her and set a trap for him. . . . Well, not so much for him. I've got nothing against Regan, in fact. . . . Well, never mind *that*. But Columbus himself is heading down there to take over the ship from Regan when all the shooting's finished and it's nice and safe. He's going to use her to get his precious daughter loose, and all those others. He says."

There was something strange in the way she said that, but he didn't have time for it now. Ullman said, "So it isn't just a two-boat race. It's a three-boat race, and that's assuming Columbus has managed to shake off everybody else who's looking for him, and I don't mean just the law. A guy who's got as little consideration for other people's rights and feelings as *Señor* Columbus ought to have a whole lynch mob looking for him with a rope, or at least a bucket of tar and a bag of feathers. But I suppose it's too much to hope for these decadent days." Ullman grimaced. "Which way is he coming?"

"Columbus? He's got a big powerboat, a fast sportfisherman, and he'll be taking the route down through the Bahamas. He's probably somewhere off to the west of us right now, fumbling around in the middle of all those fucking little islands; and if I know his captain, a creep named Gonzaga, fumbling is just the word for it. But I gather Columbus liked the idea of the sheltered inside route; he's not much of a sailor." Vinnie choked on a giggle. "That's kind of funny, isn't it? A guy with a name like that?"

"The Mona Passage," Ullman said. He rose and, steadying himself against the chart table, pulled a small-scale chart from the bin underneath and spread it out. "When's the *Prince* due there?"

"I don't know exactly," Vinnie said. "I wasn't given the date and I didn't dare ask. But Regan knows, and he left Miami the same day we did; and he must be expecting to get there in time, mustn't he? I don't know where he picked up his boat, probably he had her waiting somewhere in the Islands; but she's not very fast, one of those picturesque, beamy, clipper-bowed jobs that go to windward like a bale of hay. I figured, if he could make it, we could."

"That's pretty optimistic," Ullman said. "The speed of a sailboat depends pretty much on the length, dammit. There's not much chance in the winds we've been having that a twenty-eight-footer is ever going to catch a boat eleven feet longer. Let alone pass her." He turned sharply. "Damn it, if

426

you'd let me know all this before we got out of VHF range of the shore, we could have had the whole navy out to help. Now all we can do is hope to meet a ship that'll pass the word for us with its long-range radio; and we sure haven't been bothered with much ship traffic to date."

"I want to be there," Vinnie said softly.

"What?"

"I want to be there," she said. "I don't *want* the fucking navy to . . . I don't want to sit in a jail cell reading about it in a newspaper somebody's kind enough to let me have, damn you! I want to *be* there. I don't insist on pulling the trigger, but I want to *see* the little big-headed bastard brought down. I want him to *know* it's me that helped bring him down, understand?"

He frowned at her. There were more questions to be asked, but he knew instinctively that all the answers would be forthcoming now that the dam had broken. She was going to tell him everything now, and he wasn't sure he wanted to hear it. He'd liked her better as a tough, uncomplaining, uncommunicative little shipmate; but he could understand her feelings perfectly. He would not have done it the way she had, gambling a ship and all its crew for her own vengeful satisfaction; but he also had a strong desire to be there when Columbus was brought down. If he could be brought down by a man and a girl in a twenty-eight-foot sailboat.

He said, "Then we'd better stop wasting time and get topside and start sailing this poor little cutter the way she's never been sailed before, hadn't we?"

When he reached the deck he remembered his original mission, but the porpoises were gone.

CHAPTER 40

July

Latitude 22°N; Longitude 74°W

Janet McHugh took the helm for the approach to Catlin's Island, which was flanked by two great pale sandy shoals between which the channel showed dark and bluish. There were no channel markers of course; this was the remote southern Bahamas where they didn't even pretend to provide such effete aids to navigation—and even when they did put up a light it usually went out. It was all eyeball navigation, mon, and if you didn't know how, too bad about you.

Here at Catlin's you were supposed to run straight at a small wooded cay with mean-looking coral shores until you were almost on the rocks; only then, said the sailing directions, was it safe to turn hard to port and work your way cautiously around the end of the little islet, known as No Name Cay, into the sheltered, invisible harbor beyond. It didn't help the morale a bit to look down through the impossibly clear water and see, on the bottom, keel tracks of boats before you that had made it just barely or not at all. Well, they were probably deep-keel sailboats trying it on the wrong tide, Janet McHugh reassured herself. With a three-foot draft, *Searcher* should be able to get herself into anything dignified by the name of harbor, even in these shallow waters; and Catlin's Island was a well-recognized rest stop—one of the standard stepping-stones, so to speak—for southbound yachts island-hopping their way down from Nassau toward the cruising grounds of the Caribbean. That was why *Searcher* was there.

Cutting them off at the pass, Janet thought wryly, *well, let's hope it works.* The trouble was, she no longer really trusted her own judgment. She was very tired, impossibly tired, with a sick, bone-deep weariness that she had never known. Along with the weariness was anger at her own stupid weakness because it hadn't been that bad a run. The plan she'd formulated had been very simple. Under duress—well, what did he expect when he fingered people's boats for a bunch of pirates?—Reuben Montoya had indicated that, with a doubtfully competent captain and landlubber crew, Don Jaime Colombo intended to do it the easy way, taking *Stream Hunter* down the sheltered route through the Islands. Unaware that he was in a race, perhaps even unaware that Montoya had talked, he was throwing away his speed advantage. The *Hunter* was, of course, by far the faster boat but nobody navigated those shallow banks at night. You had to be able to see the unmarked and uncharted sandbars and coral heads to avoid them. So Columbus' doubtful Captain Gonzaga would have to find them an anchorage almost every evening while *Searcher,* pounding through the deep, safe water of the Old Bahama Channel, could keep going night and day, and had done so. Surprisingly, they'd aroused no Cuban interest whatever; no patrol craft had appeared to check up on them.

That was the bright side. The dark side was that it had been pretty rough, trying to make speed against those head seas and that lousy current but, dammit, anybody—any seaman at least—ought to be able to take a few days of hard windward going. Actually, the boat had stood up well; she was really a fine, faithful little ship, driving steadily into that lousy chop day after day, pitching heavily to be sure and sometimes even taking a green one over the bow, but losing nothing, breaking nothing, and with never a murmur of complaint from the hard-working diesel. Everything had kept right on functioning well despite the strenuous conditions; everything except the feeble lady skipper whom the violent motion had, after a while, almost reduced to tears.

And now that they were here at last there was, of course, a very good chance that it had all been in vain. If Captain Ramiro Gonzaga, urged on by his aristocratic employer, had really pushed the *Hunter* hard, he could well have reached Catlin's ahead of them and be long gone to the south and east by now. Or, if he was as incompetent as he was supposed to be, he might never appear here at all because he'd hung them up on a reef or shoal somewhere to the north and west. And if that dark, hawk-faced government gent, who'd obviously never been born to the good old Anglo-Saxon name of Martin, had got cooperation from the Bahamian authorities, the boat could be impounded by now and the crew in jail. But all these newly independent little nations were very jealous of their sovereign prerogatives; there was only a slight chance that Mr. Martin had been able to get quick official action out of Nassau, or quick official permission to take action of his own—and then he'd still have to find the boat to take action against. In any case, all Captain Jaspers' little girl Janet could do now was anchor in the quiet harbor up ahead and wait for her stolen dreamboat to appear, or not to appear, as the case might be. If nothing happened, she'd have to figure out her next move. At least she'd be able to think more clearly after she'd had a little rest in a boat that wasn't forever standing on its head, or tail. . . .

"Oh, Jesus!" she breathed.

"What's the matter?"

That was Brodie Kotoski, standing beside her on *Searcher*'s flying bridge, but she didn't answer him. Steering carefully, staring over the bow to determine the best and deepest water ahead, she hadn't really examined the little cay they were approaching. Now, glancing up, she saw something above the jungly low trees and brush, something moving deliberately toward the rocky point to port. It was the tall tuna tower of a sportfisherman in the hidden harbor beyond, obviously about to leave by the same channel by which they were entering; and there was a sickening familiarity about it—sickening because she realized that she'd made no plan at all to deal with this contingency, although it should have occurred to anybody with half a functioning brain that two vessels heading for the same place might just possibly meet. Perhaps she'd never really expected her strategy to work; certainly she'd never expected it to work so soon. Not before she'd recovered from the hard passage and had a little time to think. . . .

She heard her own voice, commendably calm: "I should have taken you up on that bet you wanted to make, Brodie. There she is." Before he could speak, she said: "Take over, I'm ducking below. They don't know this boat and there may not be anybody on board *Hunter* who'd recognize me, although I met a few of the gang a long way from here when they took her; but even so I don't want to start them thinking about a strange trawler yacht with a blonde lady helmsman. Wave to them happily as they go by and count the heads. I want to know how many we've got to deal with." She grimaced. "Or maybe you'd better count the legs and divide by two; there's no telling how many heads one of those murderous freaks is apt to have."

The ladder from the bridge was still a cruel obstacle to her, even descending—when was she going to stop being so goddamn *weak*? Anybody'd think she'd really been sick, for God's sake, instead of just a little hungry and thirsty. Safely down the ladder she rested against it for a moment; but she saw Billy France's mean little eyes watching her from inside the deckhouse, and she pulled herself together and went inside, taking the seat at the lower controls where she could watch through the windshield. The view wasn't as good down here. From this lower elevation the channel ahead was not clearly visible, the reflections on the water interfered; and there was no depthsounder at this station to tell her how much water was under the keel. It was all up to Brodie, topside, and she didn't have much faith in his judgment although, to be fair, this kind of piloting was well within his capabilities; he knew most of the tricks of shoal-water boat-handling and he was a pretty good seaman when he worked at it.

"Let me have a beer, please, Billy," she said without taking her eyes from the island ahead and the point to port. "Thanks," she said when the can was put into her hand.

She sipped the beer without pleasure. For one thing, it was warm; their last ice had melted several days ago. For another she didn't really like beer very much. She drank it because she needed the moisture and because she had an idea the stuff would help her gain back some of the weight she'd lost; ironical, she thought wryly, when for years her problem had been the other way. Brodie was making his turn now, right up against the rocks as the directions required; and it was an awkward place to meet another boat but there was *Stream Hunter* coming around the point toward them, so familiar, so beautiful, but oh so uncared-for-looking.

She was riding low in the water as if Columbus had her heavily loaded with stores. Her topsides were streaked and scarred as if she'd been allowed to lie unprotected against rough docks and tarry pilings, and other boats had been allowed to bump her heedlessly. There was other evidence of careless handling and slovenly maintenance—the anchor hadn't even been hosed clean or properly secured—and as she came abreast in the narrow channel Janet could hear the uneven pulse of one of the big Detroit diesels that indicated a damaged propeller or a bent shaft. Apparently that lubberly

431

yo-yo Gonzaga *had* got them too close to the coral somewhere up the line. There would be endless work getting her ship-shape again, Janet thought bitterly; but that thought was, she warned herself, slightly premature. But what kind of people would treat a lovely vessel like that? Even if you had to steal a boat you didn't have to abuse her! Then all emotion died abruptly as she realized that the passing boat, her boat, was crowded with men like a Barbary pirate.

There were four on the flying bridge. She recognized them all from Montoya's descriptions: fat Gonzaga at the wheel with his buccaneer mustache, small, wiry Cardenas, hulking Bolo, and Columbus himself, seated beside the helmsman so that his inadequate body was not visible, only his handsome wicked face. Those had been expected, those she'd been prepared to cope with somehow, but not the three in the cockpit and the half-dozen others she thought she could count through the deckhouse windows—no wonder the poor *Hunter* was buried to her boot-top, carrying that many men and all their gear. She saw Gonzaga raise his hand in salute as they glided past and she knew that Brodie, above her, must have waved a friendly greeting as instructed. She wanted to bury her face in her hands and let the hopeless tears come. The task she'd set herself, crazy enough to start with, had in a moment become obviously impossible.

Even if she could talk Brodie and Billy into making the attempt, and they had very high regards for their own skins, there was clearly no way she could tackle a gang like that with any hope of success. With such a crowd there would always be a substantial watch left on board no matter where they anchored. She'd had a romantic vision of staging a cutting-out expedition in the fine fashion of Captain Horatio Hornblower, sneaking alongside silently, intimidating or overpowering one man perhaps, and taking off with a splendid roar, thumbing her nose at Columbus and his remaining henchmen standing helpless on the beach, but that was just dreaming. This was the way it was: impossible. No way.

"Better get out there and give Brodie a hand with the anchor," she heard herself say dully, and Billy moved off in his usual silent and reluctant fashion.

When he had gone, she turned to look after the receding sportfisherman. The name on the transom had been changed, she saw, to *Lolita*. She couldn't feel anything about it. She drained the last of her warm, nasty beer like medicine and stumbled aft and down into the big stern cabin, closing the hatch behind her. She caught a glimpse of herself in the previous owner's dainty vanity mirror; that damn mirror that persisted in showing her things she'd have preferred not to see. What she saw now was a stringy-haired female cadaver—well, it was upright and ambulatory, but that was about all you could say for it—in grimy dungarees. She looked as bad as *Stream Hunter,* she realized, neglected and dirty. She wanted to weep for the way they'd once been and the way they now were. It had been a pretty nice world for a while, but it wasn't any longer.

She drew a long breath, more annoyed by the whiny weak thing she'd become than by her unprepossessing appearance. Looks didn't count here, she told herself firmly; and actually she didn't look must worse than after any long cruise. Hell, showers and shampoos were always rationed on a small yacht and the owner, in particular, always had to set an example of water conservation or everybody on board would let the damn stuff run as if there were a direct connection to the city mains. She reminded herself that she looked unattractive largely because she'd made a deliberate attempt to look unattractive; it was part of the calculated non-sex program she'd inflicted upon herself in self-defense. Spending days and weeks in such cramped quarters with a guy like Brodie, you wanted to be very careful not to stimulate those goddamn glands between his legs by looking pretty and feminine. Hence the baggy dungarees; and the meticulous care she'd taken never to leave her cabin incompletely dressed even if it meant sleeping in her clothes if there was any chance she'd be called in a hurry, and there was practically always that chance.

And all that, she admitted to herself, was just brave talk to hide from herself the fact that recently she'd got just too damn exhausted to comb her hair or even wash her face. It was all backing up on her suddenly, she realized: the lack of sleep, the endless efforts to fight the boat's violent antics with her limited strength, the strain of keeping her cutthroat crew under some kind of control by not letting her weakness show too much, and the dragging suspense of the whole idiot project that had just revealed itself to her in its utter idiocy. She swayed, caught herself, and moved uncertainly to the big double bed in the center of the cabin, and fell upon it too tired and numb to even remove her shoes.

Vaguely, she heard the anchor go down. She found herself waiting; then the diesel rumbled as Brodie backed down to

set the hook, at least he had that much sense. With a great
effort she raised herself to look out the nearest cabin window.
The small island to starboard remained at a constant angle
despite the straining motor; obviously the anchor was well
dug in and holding. Off to port was Catlin's Island itself with
its small settlement. The diesel stopped. All secure. She could
let go now and, glorying in the strangely motionless mattress
on which she lay, she let sleep carry her away.

When she awoke in the dark it was with the sudden feeling
that something was wrong; that she was not alone in the
cabin. However, when she managed to open her eyes and sit
up, nobody was there. She looked out the window again and
saw that the island to starboard, now a black shadow on the
calm water, had exactly the same bearing as before. The tide
hadn't changed yet and the anchor wasn't dragging. Maybe it
was only the wonderful stillness after all the days of pounding
that had awakened her—and wasn't that a hell of an attitude
for a girl brought up on the wave-lashed coast of Maine? But
she'd at least caught up with a little of her lost sleep,
although she still had a long way to go. Give her another few
hours, she reflected wryly, and she might even find the
strength to kick off her shoes.

Lying down once more, she realized that, now that she'd
had a little rest, the answer to her problem was obvious. She
was not, after all, a total failure; in fact if she hadn't been so
damned exhausted she could have treated herself to a few
moments of triumph because, after all, she had guessed right.
She'd found the trail; now all she had to do was follow it.
Shadow them, at a safe distance of course; a day or two
behind. There were only so many places they could go from
here. They couldn't lose her now. And when they finally
lighted somewhere, with some indication of permanence, she
could get on the horn and get discreet word to that handsome
hidalgo type back in the U.S. that his chickens were here for
the plucking . . . and just what did he see in that skinny
Cameron woman, anyway?

Janet McHugh decided that she must be feeling better; at
least she could laugh at herself for her automatic and quite
irrelevant feminine jealousy. She told herself firmly that
they made a handsome couple, and that Cameron was really
quite an intelligent and attractive person, and that she,
Janet McHugh, while she rather admired the ruthless, sexy-
looking Martin, wouldn't have him on a bet even if he were
available, which he was obviously not. In fact, she reflected,

her phone call had apparently caught them in bed together and more power to them. It was nice to know that there were a few people in this world who didn't have to fight their battles alone.

She found herself wondering idly, sleepily, lying there on the lovely, motionless bed, how it had been and if Elizabeth Cameron had wanted it or had just done it because she knew she'd lose him otherwise. It was difficult to think of that cool and smartly dressed lady really *wanting* it; but then, there had been that rather lovely, intimate smile she'd given him that could hardly have meant anything else. But, wanting it, had she got it the way she wanted it when she wanted it, or had it come as a rude surprise to her to discover what hair-trigger people men really were? Well, maybe her tall dark man was stronger than most, and maybe he loved her enough to indulge her fancies even though it strained his will to the utmost; but you always had to remember that they could be controlled, they could control themselves, only up to a point. You never really knew what was going to set one off or when; which was why she, Janet McHugh, was being so very careful with Brodie Kotoski. It wasn't fair to expect real self-control from a man like that; you simply had to avoid triggering those ancient reactions that had been designed strictly for the perpetuation of the human race, not for the convenience of romantic ladies with fastidious notions about love.

She'd been one of those ladies once, she remembered, until Chuck had opened the forbidden door for her on that sexy champagne picnic they'd perpetrated on a lonely Bahamian beach. Even then, with her fine New England inhibitions in wild disorder, she'd been rather startled when, later, her supposedly very civilized husband had taken her one step farther toward real understanding by indicating at the damnedest times, for no apparent reason, that he wanted her badly and he knew it was crazy and inconvenient but it really meant a great deal to him and he'd be very grateful if she'd humor him, right now. She remembered clearly how, the first time this happened, it had really shocked her deeply to realize that right now did not mean five minutes from now decently undressed and in bed. Right now had meant right now in her good clothes on the living-room sofa. . . .

"Chuck," she protested. "No, Chuck, please, you'll ruin my . . ."

The sound of her own voice caused her to wake with a start;

435

and it wasn't Chuck whose hands were holding her down, and it wasn't a party dress that was tangled untidily about her. This time there would be no sudden laughter at the ridiculousness of this irresponsible wrestling match between two respectable married people, no quick wanton yielding and to hell with her pretty clothes because he was a nice guy and she didn't really love him quite as much—or at least as uncritically—as she should, so if he wanted it like that, wanted her like that, it was the least she could do for him since she could not help shortchanging him a little in other respects. But Chuck was dead, dead, dead.

She checked her struggles and lay perfectly still, bitterly angry at herself for letting herself be caught like this in the middle of her nostalgic erotic dreaming. She was aware of the sour unwashed smell of the man above her, and tonight she wasn't so damned dainty herself, and this was no friendly, sexy, after-party horseplay between man and wife that could be stopped by a word.

"That's better," Brodie's voice said. "Easy now. . . . Okay, I've got her."

The cabin light went on. It took her a moment to understand that she was not to be raped; that she did not have to prepare her mind for that ultimate indignity, at least not yet. Brodie would hardly have brought an audience if that had been his purpose. There were strangers in the deckhouse looking down at them through the cabin hatch, only they weren't really strangers. She'd seen them before, only a few hours ago. There was the wiry little one called Cardenas and the big moronic-looking one who was named after a bolo knife or maybe a bolo tie; and she sensed the presence of others behind them. Glancing up she saw the loom of a boat through the cabin window and she knew that *Stream Hunter,* now *Lolita,* lay alongside to port. She reminded herself that she was the girl who'd proclaimed so loudly and proudly that nobody would ever again take a boat away from her. . . .

She licked her lips. "I hope you got a good price, Brodie," she whispered. "I wouldn't want to think you sold me cheap. How . . . ?"

But the question was superfluous. In her weariness she'd forgotten that Captain Ramiro Gonzaga and Captain Broderick Kotoski had been engaged in the same line of work in just about the same geographical area; and that the Florida charter fishing business was fiercely competitive in some respects but quite cooperative in others. She remembered

436

hat Captain Jim Easley, a mild-mannered man normally, had had a special innocuous-looking hand signal he'd give to neighboring boats when he was fed up with a particular client. It meant, *Don't follow me, I'm just taking this loud-mouthed cheapskate for a fishless boat ride.* There were other signs, asking the other boat to stand by you inconspicuously in case of anticipated engine trouble, or inviting the other boat to follow along because there was enough for two where you were heading and of course you expected the favor to be returned some time. All stuff you didn't care to put on the air or have the client overhear; some of them wanted a whole ocean to themselves and none of them needed to know that the boat they'd hired was, maybe, not quite perfect. Or maybe Brodie had simply got on the VHF and put his proposition in plain English; she wouldn't have heard him down in the deckhouse with the motor running.

"Sorry, ma'am," Brodie said. "But Billy and I didn't hire out to get ourselves killed bucking a stacked deck for a crazy lady. When I saw the crowd on that boat you want back so bad, I knew it was time to stop this fool project of yours, right now."

"But I wasn't going to . . ."

But it was too late for explanations that should have been made hours ago. Now the betrayal was an accomplished fact. But he was easing off, releasing her, standing up; and it seemed that Brodie was also tired after the long rough passage because he'd forgotten something too. She hadn't undressed and was there ever a sailor who didn't carry a knife somewhere in his clothes? It came smoothly out of the deep narrow pocket along her pants leg that had probably been intended for carrying a folding rule or maybe a wrench or screwdriver. She did not try for anything vital; she just slashed at his face so that he recoiled sharply with a yell of surprise; then she was off the bed reaching for the shotgun that might still give her a fighting chance—and it wasn't here.

Belatedly, she remembered how she'd awakened thinking that somebody was in the cabin. She remembered Billy France and his sneaky, silent way of moving; and who could see a black man in the dark? She turned helplessly, knowing that the knife was not enough, knowing that she was lost; and she sensed the billy club, Brodie's fish-killing priest, slashing down. The world exploded in a sheet of white flame.

Distantly a voice spoke: "No, please do not kill her, *Señor*. We may have need of her. Can she navigate?"

Brodie's voice said, "Hell, this blonde bitch can squint at the sun through a soda straw and tell you where you are within half a mile."

The funny thing was, he'd sold her out, he'd struck her down, and still he sounded quite proud of her. She carried the strange thought with her into unconsciousness.

CHAPTER 41

July

Latitude 22°N; Longitude 69°W

Sean Regan didn't even bother to duck as spray flew high off the bow of *Pretty Baby* (ex-*Spindrift*) and was blown slantingly aft across the decks and into the midships cockpit where he sat at the steering wheel only partly sheltered by the spray hood, or dodger, over the main companionway. Day after day of driving the clumsy tub to windward, a direction that did not please her at all, had got them all used to—well, resigned to—being constantly wet and forever hanging on to keep from being thrown across the boat, or off it, by the crazy motion; all except the kid, Joey Barbera, who was still retching weakly below, even though he'd long since thrown up everything he had to throw except his blood, guts, and gonads; and it wouldn't be long before those made their appearance. People had, after all, died of seasickness. So let that be a lesson to the boy not to claim salty experience and endurance he did not have.

Pretty Baby drove into another sea and tossed it aft, almost burying her bowsprit in the process, the wet old bitch. The one thing to be said in her favor was that she remained in one piece after all the pounding. Those Taiwan craftsmen had done a pretty good job for a bunch of gooks; but the designer who'd drawn that pretty clipper bow with its submarine propensities should have been shot—or at least condemned to live with his creation for a week or two or three hard on the wind, and the wind a steady Force Six, and the seas with a fetch clear from Africa and nothing to stop them growing as they pleased to the full height to which the wind entitled them. And the idiot ketch rig with the sails forward forever backwinding the sails aft when you were close-hauled like this.

Regan glanced aft at the empty sunlit sea-horizon and thought: it's gaining, they are back there, I can feel them, but who? A powerboat of any size would have caught us long since or at least, if shadowing was the object, have shown herself once or twice astern. And that little cutter from Dinner Key could not possibly have kept up, let alone cut the distance between us, or could she? It's a fine tall rig she had and a lean slippery shape compared to this undercanvased fat sow of a boat, but twenty-eight feet against thirty-nine? The physics of the thing are against it, a simple question of wave mechanics. Big waves run faster than small ones and so do the boats that make them.

And who'd be driving her so hard after us? All the girl was supposed to do was take him offshore and lose him; but then she's a secretive little thing and damaged and dangerous and a fine sailor, and who knows what's in her strange, bright, warped mind today? And perhaps it would have been foolish to get involved with that, but the sentimental side of Regan would have liked to try. There was something worth saving here and you have saved little enough in your life . . . and maybe it's a different boat entirely and different people, but *somebody's* back there over the horizon following along steadily, and gaining. After a lifetime of looking over the shoulder one always knows. But they haven't much more time; we're soon there. They'll have to show their intentions shortly.

Regan spun the wheel hard in an attempt to avoid the steeper breaking portion of an oncoming sea, but *Pretty Baby* stuck her nose into it anyway, this time diving deep enough that the flat plank of the bowsprit smacked the water with a crash that jarred the whole ship. He hunched down a bit this time to let the spray slash past. He dismissed the problem astern and recalled other problems long past: the killing he'd left behind and the red killing ground on which he'd been born. Well, a man was a violent animal and on matters he considered of true importance there could never be a final

439

decision except by force. Strong political and religious and racial convictions could never be overcome by mere rational persuasion; but after a while one got tired of killing for a line on a map or a cross on a book or the same language spoken with a slightly different accent by boyos who did not look so very different from oneself. So one went elsewhere and left them all to their bloody slaughter and did the thing one had learned for the money it would bring, a simple and comprehensible reason at last.

Harry Bernard, a big dark man who looked fat and soft but wasn't—his slob appearance had fooled some people who thought they were tough—stuck his head out the main hatch and winced as more spray rattled against the vinyl and plastic of the dodger.

"Some people do this for fun," he said. "What the fuck are we doing it for?"

"It's green and rectangular and has pretty numbers on it," Regan said. "We get the second and final payment when we make delivery."

"I'll be happy when we're finished with that misshapen little creep," Harry said. "He makes me nervous. What the hell does he want with it, anyway? How the hell is it going to get him back his fancy estates in Cuba?"

"You know, I didn't ask. Maybe he merely desires a large toy to sail in his bathtub." Regan grinned. "It's a fine piratical system we've developed here, Harry. Are you not curious to see how it works on something big?"

"Not that curious, pal." Harry grimaced, and indicated the forward cabin with a jerk of his head. "Not with that dumb little prick still plugging for the long-distance Atlantic puking championship, junior division. Goddamn it, what with him and those other jerks who can't piss straight in a seaway standing up at the pot and won't take the trouble to sit down, it's like sailing a public shithouse on a drunken Saturday night." He made a face. "You'll be interested to know that Joey's whining to be put ashore. I told him the closest shore we've got is about three thousand fathoms straight down and any time he wants to pay it a visit I'll be happy to help him over the side. I'll even find him some nice pigs of lead ballast he can put in his pockets for a faster ride."

Regan grinned. "Harry, you're all heart. Go kick Lou awake and tell him he's on deck. Then we'd better review the situation, you and I, before we get on the radio and let *Stream Hunter*—excuse me, *Lolita*—know we'll be coming on station

440

soon. Let's hope our big pigeon isn't ahead of schedule. It's distressed I'd be to see her appear over the horizon before we're ready for her. Chopping down the masts under the eyes of their bridge watch wouldn't look very convincing, would it now?"

Harry said uneasily, "It's a screwy deal, Regan. I mean, goddamn it, for a cargo of gold bars or diamonds and a chance to be rich, okay; but it's a hell of a thing to do for a hundred and forty thousand barrels of stinking bunker fuel we aren't even going to cash in on; and the Don isn't paying us enough for the risk, not really." He spat to leeward. "Ah, hell! I'll get Lou."

Alone in the cockpit, Regan shook his head ruefully. It had been a long, rough sail and it had taken a lot out of everybody—and as Harry had said, it wasn't as if they were doing it for diamonds and rubies. The glamor was lacking. Regan glanced astern. The pursuit was still there, he knew, although he could not see it; but a more immediate worry was an odd-looking haze now appearing along the horizon. There was weather making to the north. Actually it might be good in a way, it would make the trap more plausible when set; but poor visibility could queer the whole operation. But fog was never seen in these low latitudes—although never was not a good word to stake your life on.

Lou Ansteiner, a sandy, freckled, blocky man who was a rather ham-handed helmsman with a compass fixation—he'd never dream of steering around a wave if the course led through it—took over the cockpit, and Regan went below. With six men on board, one chronically seasick, and none with any sense of responsibility for their hijacked boat, the handsome teak-paneled cabin was a pigsty by this time and, with hatches and ports battened down against the endless spray, just as foul as Harry had indicated. Up in the wedge-shaped stateroom in the bow, Joey Barbera could be seen on his bed of pain—at least his feet were visible through the door at the end of the short passageway. In the larger stateroom aft, invisible from the main cabin, the other two crew members, Hank Motta and Jake Turner, off watch, were presumably catching up on their sleep. Regan picked up an empty beer can that kept traversing the cabin sole in a nervous, noisy manner, and threw it out the hatch before sitting down to leeward at the cabin table, beside Harry Bernard who already had the battery-powered slide viewer set up.

"Lucky for us that photographer jerk used film like it was going out of style," Harry said. "Okay, here's the engine room again, my job. I don't know that Fiat diesel but I can figure it out; I worked on plenty of those big babies in my time. But the way it is, if everything works I won't have to since the Don is bringing his own personal engineering expert; all I've got to do is secure the machinery space and get back on deck in case Lou needs me, right?"

He was working slides through the viewer as he spoke. Regan nodded, and asked, "How many do you think you're likely to have to deal with down there?"

"Not more than two or three," Bernard said. "I mean, there'll be an engineer officer on watch with maybe an assistant, but they'll be in the control room, here." He stopped a slide and pointed. "You see how it's sealed off, glassed in like a fucking observation booth, and air-conditioned; so I won't have to worry about anybody in there if you get your job done fast. All I'll have to do is make sure of any motormen working around the engine."

"Well, try not to put a bullet through anything important," Regan said. "Mechanically important, I mean. Now let's consider my route again. It's lucky we are that the sick bay and air-conditioning room are on the same deck. . . ."

"Hey, Regan." That was Lou Ansteiner, topside. "Better get your ass up here. We've got some weather coming, fast."

Regan said to Bernard: "Put it away, we'll have to do it later." He squirmed out from behind the table and climbed the companionway ladder far enough to put his head out the hatch. The helmsman's gesture wasn't needed to show him that the horizon-haze astern had, during his brief absence from deck, hardened into a gray-black wall of cloud that was bearing down on them rapidly. The wind had gone slack, but that wouldn't last, he knew. There'd be plenty of wind behind that menacing cloud front. "All hands," Regan shouted, scrambling into the cockpit. "All hands on deck. . . ."

By morning they were racing southeastwards under a gray sky with nothing up but the small triangular forestaysail. The damned old hard-mouthed bitch was trying her best to slew around in a wild broach with each steep wave that rolled up from astern, and it seemed incredible that the steering would survive the strains involved in keeping her straight before it; but at least they had a favorable wind at last and the misbegotten tub was reeling off the miles in a very commendable fashion even though she was making the helmsman sweat blood in the process.

By evening, the disturbance had passed on, leaving an uncomfortable lumpy sea and a moderate breeze, still favorable. The sky cleared enough that Regan managed a round of star sights using the fine Plath sextant he'd found on board, on the handsome wooden case on which was an engraved brass plaque: TO HOBIE FROM MARTHA, CHRISTMAS 1974. The date indicated that the vessel's previous owner must have received the gift well before his retirement from military service, not to mention his purchase of the boat. Perhaps it had been a deliberate gesture on the part of the wife, to indicate her approval, or at least acceptance, of her husband's nautical retirement plans, and you had to hand it to her, many wives weren't all that agreeable. But it did no good to speculate about the dead, particularly those for whose deaths you were responsible.

Bent over the navigation table, Regan frowned at the spot on the chart where the three star-lines of position crossed, forming a triangle that was respectably small considering the motion of the boat. He made a pencil-mark in the exact center of the triangle, and stood up to call to Harry Bernard at the wheel.

"Let's get in the jib and main and heave to right here. Mizzen sheeted in hard, staysail backed to windward, and see how she rides." He switched on the SSB radio over the nav table and found the prearranged frequency. "*Lolita, Lolita, Lolita,* this is *Pretty Baby.* Come in *Lolita.*"

He'd expected some nerve-racking delay, perhaps no answer at all to this first call; but Ramiro Gonzaga on the big, fast sportfisherman, which should already be in position well to the south and west, actually on the other side of the rugged Caribbean islands still invisible over the horizon, must have been waiting nervously by his set, the fat incompetent. He knew damn well the Don would skin him alive if anything went wrong.

"*Lolita* calling *Pretty Baby.* So you make it hokay, *amigo.*"

"We're close," Regan said. "The wind wasn't exactly cooperative, but we're here. What kind of a passage did you have?"

"Hokay, but there was . . . was a small interference problem. Is solved now."

Ramiro was apparently reading some careful English words written out for him by somebody else on board. Interference.

443

That was a warning. Apparently *Lolita*, too, had found herself not quite alone on the ocean. . . . Solved. The difficulty had been attended to, somehow. Of course there was still no solid proof that there had been somebody astern of *Pretty Baby* the whole way down; but it was not for Sean Regan to disown his instincts ungratefully after all the years they had kept him alive. He wanted to ask questions, but the matter could obviously not be discussed further on the air.

"What do you hear from Pete?" he asked.

"Pete says he join you day after tomorrow, perhaps very early. He say you should have a bottle of Mount Gay open and waiting for him."

"Nuts to Pete. What's he been doing, towing a sea anchor? The drinks should be on the last man in, but okay, maybe he needs cheering up. Well, see you soon. Keep in touch. *Pretty Baby* out."

Shoving the microphone back into its clip, he drew a long breath. The first contact had gone off without a hitch after all the days of hard sailing. It was a good sign. When he looked up, he saw that the whole crew had gathered around to listen. Even Joey Barbera was sitting up feebly on his soiled bunk and peering aft.

"So far so good," Regan told them. He showed the chart and pointed. "We're out here on the Atlantic side of the Mona Passage. *Lolita* is down here on the inside, the Caribbean side, probably fishing or pretending to. Who pays attention to a sportfishing boat with outriggers in position and lines in the water? And it's through this gap between the islands, here, that our pigeon has to steam. The Don has contacts in South America to give the time of departure. Apparently, coming up from Venezuela full of oil, she'll hit their position late in the evening because *Lolita* just said to expect Pete—that's her—to reach our position in the early morning. *Lolita* will give us a call when she passes them. Knowing her speed—she cruises at fourteen knots—we can then fix more closely the time she'll arrive here and be ready for her." He grinned. "It would not do for us to make our preparations early and be gloriously rescued by the wrong ship, would it now?"

There was laughter in response. There was suddenly a good feeling of suspense and expectation on board; and it no longer mattered that there was no cargo of solid gold bars, or pieces of eight, awaiting them. The feat they were about to attempt was enough in itself. They were all dead men in their different ways, and they only came alive at moments like this.

"Interference?" Harry Bernard said, but he said it a little apologetically, as if reluctant to introduce a disturbing thought.

Regan shrugged. "I don't know. Maybe just a local gunboat snooping around; and they had to grease a few official palms to be left alone. You can be sure the Don has figured all the legal angles. But we'll keep a good watch just in case."

It was no use saying more. If he told them there was somebody astern, felt but unseen, they would think he was slightly unsettled upstairs and lose confidence in him. Some people were blind and some were deaf. Others were simply insensitive and one could pity them for that as for any other handicap. Just as an experienced hunting dog could probably never, even if he could talk, tell someone with an inferior sense of smell exactly how it was he scented game at a distance, so a mad Irishman, seasoned in conflict, was better off not trying to explain how he sensed danger behind.

It was a long night that followed, and a longer day. The ocean remained empty around them which was just as well, even though it made Regan check his position twice; there should have been some ship traffic using the well-traveled passage between Puerto Rico and Hispaniola and heading up toward the U.S., this way. The lack of it was unsettling. But it was often that way at sea, the ocean was a big place, and at least they were not troubled by concerned vessels changing course to inquire if all was well on board the small yacht hove to there out of sight of land. In the evening, the message came.

"Pretty Baby, Pretty Baby, Pete's on his way. Acknowledge."

"This is *Pretty Baby.* We've got the rum but he'll have to bring his own ice, we just ran out."

"Lolita clear."

Just a bunch of crazy Yankee yachtsmen kidding around, if anyone was listening on that frequency. By three in the morning all preparations had been made except for taking the last step, the one that would commit them fully. Regan's head sported a dramatic bloody bandage—it was odd, he reflected, how it was easier to expose oneself to deadly injury than to deliberately inflict upon oneself a small bleeding cut to drip on a piece of cloth. Harry Bernard's arm was in a dirty sling. Other crew members were patched up to a lesser degree, except Joey, whose pallid face and obvious weakness needed no embellishment. Already unshaved and unbathed, they made, he thought, he hoped, a convincing band of shipwrecked yachtsmen.

"Leave the seabags below until I give the word," Regan said. "It's well we should not seem too eager to abandon our darling boat. And Harry, don't forget to bring your captain the ship's papers and his precious sextant when the time comes."

"Check."

"I wish we had a girl on board. I'd have her fall between the boats, first. Nothing like a well-soaked young lady climbing a ladder in her wet clothes with everything showing through to keep sailors' minds pleasantly occupied." Regan grinned and glanced at his watch. "All right, take the bolt-cutters and hacksaw topside. But remember, after it's done, I will shoot the man who tries to start the engine before everything is cleared away. If it should not work, if they should fail to see us, for instance, we will need that to get away, and I do not want the propeller tangled in masses of trailing rigging. Understood?"

He collected their nods of agreement. Their faces were sober now after the hours of waiting. In some respects it wasn't well, before an action, to speak of the possibility of failure; on the other hand it might make some minds easier to be reminded that, should the attempt prove a total fiasco, they would not be hopelessly stranded out here. Of course, *Lolita* should be coming eventually, but Captain Ramiro Gonzaga could not be trusted to find a female orifice with his penis—or, to be fair, that was perhaps the one thing in the world the lecherous Latin clown could be trusted to find. A boat drifting on an empty ocean might elude him forever.

"So let's be at it now," Regan said. "Mainmast first. . . ."

The old girl was stubborn to the last. Even with all starboard main shrouds cut away she refused to let her big mast fall for the longest while; but when it went at last, in response to a sudden gust of wind, it took everything with it. It would seem obvious that on a two-masted boat each spar should be supported independently as far as possible so that one would be left standing for a jury rig if the other were lost; but here there was a high triatic stay joining main to mizzen, and when the forward mast went the one aft bent like a fishing rod, first, and then as the upper mizzen shroud gave way, folded over at the spreaders leaving only a stump from which everything seemed to hang, a mass of torn sails and tangled wire and twisted aluminum spars that banged heavily against the boat's side as she rolled.

Glancing at Harry Bernard's heavy face, illuminated by the glow from the cabin, Regan surprised a look of guilt that mirrored what was in his own mind. To be sure, they had all detested the awkward tub, but she'd brought them a long way safely and this did not seem quite the proper way to treat her. Regan cleared his throat.

"Start cutting away the rigging now, but slowly, slowly. Let's not be too shipshape when help arrives. And those assigned to the bucket brigade get below and carry out instructions but for God's sake don't sink us, at least not yet. I will let you know when to start flinging water out the companionway, fighting bravely to save the ship even after the pumps have become hopelessly clogged. It's proud I am to have you for shipmates, you indomitable salty heroes. . . ."

"Ah, stuff a rag in it, Irish," said Harry Bernard, but he was grinning. It never hurt to give them a little bright chatter to pass the time while waiting.

Without the damping pendulum effect of the masts the boat's motion had become more jerky and violent, but it eased as the crew below let water into the hull through a seacock in the head from which the hose had been detached, stopping before she became too sluggish and endangered. Then there was only to wait for the dawn. With it came the ship. She still had her running lights burning and this was the first sight they had of her; the low white star on the horizon suddenly appearing where there had been no star before. Presently the second white range light appeared, lower and farther forward, and the green sidelight—since she was leaving them well to starboard on her present course she would show no red. By now the tall white superstructure aft had become visible in the growing light, and the long, low black hull.

"My God, she's big!" whispered Lou Ansteiner softly.

"Flare," said Regan.

Harry Bernard pulled the firing strip of the waxy red cylinder he held aloft. With the crack, the flare shot high and ignited well and hung there from its parachute, burning red in the dawn sky. Regan watched the distant ship carefully.

"Another," he said, and then quickly: "No, belay that. She sees us; she's turning. It's a good watch they keep considering the number of rustbuckets plowing the oceans these days on autopilot with everyone on the bridge asleep or reading comic books."

447

They watched the two white range lights swing into line, one above the other. The red sidelight appeared opposite the green, as the ship turned directly toward them.

"Bail," said Regan. "They'll have the binoculars on us now; so bail, me hearties! When she comes up, of course, we will all wave our arms and cheer for our narrow escape from a watery grave."

It did not seem quite real and he knew what was missing. The eager hatred was missing. It had been a fine feeling always, back then, that burning conviction that you were ambushing and fighting and destroying men—and sometimes women, too—who deserved nothing better than death for their foul beliefs and miserable ancestry and tyrannical behavior; for the beastly injuries they'd inflicted on you and yours in the past. He could remember the times it had seemed he could not wait to be at their throats once more; but there was, of course, none of that here, and it was a cold damned business without it.

"Get your arm back in that sling," Regan said sharply to Harry Bernard. "Keep them bailing, keep that water coming out the hatch. Make it look well now, make it look truly desperate. Lou, get some long lines ready and take one forward. She'll stop to windward to give us a lee, but we're going to have to warp the old tub around to come alongside with all that wreckage out to port. They handle that big thing prettily, do they not? It's seamen they are, and more's the pity. Now, the cheers. . . ."

Pretty Baby's motion eased as the great bulk of the tanker moved in to weather to block the wind and smooth the seas. Lines flew and a rope ladder dropped. Regan saw two officers looking down from the open wing of the high bridge aft; at least he presumed they were officers, although nautical uniforms and caps were notable for their absence. Apparently this was not a dressy ship. Still, they'd spotted the first flare fired, and they'd laid their vessel into position with casual expertise—but it was never well to think too much about the boyos on the other side, particularly now that there was no ancient hate involved.

"Haul her around there," Regan snapped. "Hank, get below and bring the kid on deck, and any gear that's to be saved. Pass Harry my sextant and the ship's papers; loop a sail stop through the handle of the sextant case so he can sling it around his neck. . . . Heave, now! To hell with the bowsprit, just swing her around and get her starboard side up to that ladder before she sinks beneath us. . . . Joey first. Then Harry with his arm and Jake to help him; then pass the gear up. . . ."

He was acting now, of course, conscious of the men watching from the bridge and from the ship's rail not too high above; those tankers rode low when loaded. It was broad daylight by this time. He hesitated, knowing that there was a gesture that should be made here and discovering that he wanted to make it, after all. He stood by the shiny, varnished steering wheel for a moment, and caressed it briefly, with regret. After all, he thought, she'd done her best, she could not help her clumsy ways. She deserved better than this.

"It's sorry I am, old girl," he said softly. "Sorry, indeed."

He found himself running a sleeve across his face quite convincingly—was there ever a sentimental Irishman who could not produce wet eyes on demand, not to mention a wet nose like a spaniel?—and turning away sharply to scramble up the rope ladder after the rest. Now came the real acting, starting with a display of dizzy weakness at the top, and hearing Harry Bernard explain what a bad crack on the head he—Regan—had received when the rig went over the side, and how his—Harry's—arm was nothing, nothing at all, he'd stay there if they didn't mind and look after the salvaging of their belongings, just get the skipper to the infirmary fast, and, no, he didn't think the ketch could be saved, the wreckage had punched a hole in her side you could swim a porpoise through, it had been all they could do to keep her afloat this long. Harry was no beauty, but he was a good reliable man; and brighter than he looked.

"Sextant?" Regan mumbled. "Papers?"

"I've got them right here, pal," Harry said. "I'll take care of them for you; you just go along with . . ."

"I want . . . given me by my wife, God rest her soul. Let me have . . ."

"Sure, pal. Here you are. Carry it yourself if it'll make you feel better. Boat documents, too, I'll tuck them inside your shirt, okay? Now run along with the man and don't worry about a thing."

Acting his part, Regan was aware of the growing warmth of the sun and the strange, solid feel of the steel deck under his feet as, clutching the wooden sextant case, he was led aft into the air-conditioned superstructure and up several flights of stairs to the ship's sick bay; and it was hard to believe it was all working so well, just as planned. The blood was
449

singing inside him now, as it always did when the moment approached; there was no coldness now and hatred was no longer required, now that the job was here to be done.

He was aware of the young man in slacks and sports shirt—one of the ship's officers trained in first aid, apparently—opening the door for him and letting him pass and turning to push it closed behind them. He was not a very large young man and he was totally unsuspecting so no weapon was required here, although weapons had been provided in case of need. Setting the varnished box aside, Regan turned and struck. The young man—he had black hair that needed trimming, Regan noted—went to his knees, and Regan was on him in an instant, applying the lock that broke the neck.

Then back to the sextant case; and the gas mask and the ugly, deadly little canisters and a few tools were quickly distributed in various pockets, bulging them awkwardly, and the blackjack up the sleeve, and the pistol under the belt with the shirt loose over it, and extra clips stowed away. Regan, a different man now, breathing in another way, moving with a changed, catlike stride, stepped over the body that lay with its head oddly askew and after a quick look slipped out into the passageway and turned left, remembering the posted accommodation diagram for this deck so carefully copied by the conscientious photographer who'd doubtless never dreamed of the use to which his work would be put. Apparently, everyone on board not absolutely required elsewhere was watching the drama of the rescue; he met no one at all. The air-conditioning room was plainly marked, and unlocked. He stepped inside and let the door close behind him, and drew a long breath, listening to the rumble of the fans and wondering how Harry was doing out on deck, stalling ingeniously, no doubt, to give him time in here.

Regan put on the respirator and found the inspection plates the photographs had shown him and removed them. He set off the canisters inside as the Don's tame engineer had instructed, and screwed the plates back into place. He glanced at his watch and wished he could have a cigarette for company while death traveled through the ducts and distributed itself around the ship; and he wondered again how Harry was doing. He decided that a soaked wench with a good figure would indeed have been a great help to Harry at this moment, holding everybody's attention out there as she wrung herself out and tucked herself in and tidied herself up in a casually provocative manner. Next time, perhaps. He wondered what the girl called Vinnie was doing.

Time up. He pocketed the blackjack he'd been holding just in case somebody should stumble in, and took out the bulky Browning Hi-Power with its thirteen-shot clip. It was not the most potent firearm in the world despite its name—the 9mm Luger cartridge was no real powerhouse—but it did have just about the largest magazine capacity available, which might count here. Leaving the air-conditioning room, he met no one in the passage outside, but there was a man sprawled at the foot of the stairs when he reached them; a man who'd apparently been overcome part way up and had rolled back down. At the head of the stairs were the cabins and offices of the captain, empty, and of the chief engineer who was sitting at his desk with his head on the papers he'd been studying, unmoving, unbreathing.

One more flight, the stairs narrower and steeper now, put Regan between the navigation room to starboard, empty, and the radio room to port where a man lay on the floor surrounded by impressive electronic equipment. So far so good. These were closed areas in which the poison could do its work well. The bridge itself, while it was also air-conditioned and could be closed in inclement weather—except for the outer wings—was generally, according to the color slides he'd studied, left open port and starboard allowing cross-ventilation that might make the effectiveness of the gas more questionable there.

Opening the door cautiously, Regan found himself looking straight into the eyes of a reasonably healthy man who'd been bending over one not so healthy. The second man had apparently been heading inside, perhaps to the radio room with an urgent emergency message and, almost overcome, had managed to stagger back out here, collapsing just beyond the door. Regan shot, and shot again, dropping the first man on top of his already-dead colleague. He stepped over the pair and whirled as an unsteady figure rose up by the bulky radars to starboard raising a red fire-axe to throw. Regan's bullets sent him staggering back against the equipment, smashing glass—there was the dull, thudding sound of imploding vacuum tubes—in his swaying attempt to master the growing weight of the axe that finally became too heavy for him to hold. He dropped it and fell on top of it. Why, feeling himself sickening mysteriously, the man had gone for the axe before even seeing an enemy, was a question that would

451

never be answered; perhaps his had been the instinctive human fear of facing the unknown unarmed.

That was the lot, up here, but Regan's shots had been the signal for which Harry Bernard and the lads out on deck had been waiting. Regan could hear several guns chattering; that would be the pistol snatched from Harry Bernard's convenient sling, reinforced by the ugly submachine guns hauled out of the seabags and disentangled from the clothes in which they'd been wrapped. When Regan stepped out on the starboard wing of the bridge the task had already been completed; the enemy was annihilated and the deck was theirs. Harry Bernard had thrust his Browning under his belt, put on a gas mask, taken one of the Uzis, and was now loping aft to attend to his business in the engine room. He raised a hand in salute to the bridge before he disappeared from sight.

Regan looked around and found a loud-hailer—bullhorn, in Yankee terminology. Out on the open bridge wing again, he removed the respirator so he could use it.

"Bring up the rest of the gear from the ketch and cast her adrift," he called. "Then you can heave those bodies over the side. Unless you want to die, don't enter the superstructure. Don't enter any enclosed space until we've aired her out. Stay out in the open. Keep your guns handy until we've got them all accounted for. Understood?"

Lou Ansteiner waved acknowledgment. Replacing the mask, Regan went back inside and stood there a moment peering through the goggles at the dead men and the smashed radars—one of his bullets, getting full penetration, had taken the one not demolished by the axe. Too bloody bad about that. He felt the old sickness of reaction take hold of him. It was always that way immediately afterwards; the sense of triumph and accomplishment came later. But they'd bloody well taken the bloody ship, had they not? Like clockwork, and not a man in the boarding party hurt if Harry was being careful in the engine room; and he was a careful man.

But this optimistic appraisal was, Regan discovered, not quite true. Working his way back down to the main deck, checking cabins along the way, he discovered two crumpled figures inside one of the heavy sea doors: one of the ship's seamen and Joey Barbera, both dead. Presumably advised to join his skipper in the infirmary, the ailing youth had accompanied his solicitous helper inside, apparently without protest, although the plan of operation had been made clear to everyone. Regan wondered what had been in the boy's mind, why he had let himself be led to a known death without balking and screaming out the truth and wrecking the entire enterprise. Perhaps he had felt himself an object of scorn because of the embarrassing weakness he had displayed so long; perhaps he had felt a grim need to prove himself at last, even if it killed him. . . .

Shaking his head, Regan opened the steel door cautiously and stepped outside. What was there did not register immediately. There was a body on the steel deck near an open door leading back inside; but he had seen too many bodies already for another to concern him greatly, and his mind first dismissed it as just a member of the crew who'd managed to achieve the open air before the poison took effect. Then he realized that there was something familiar about the heavy sprawled figure and that it had not died from gas; the head was shattered and a heavy wrench lay beside it. It was Harry Bernard, apparently surprised as he emerged after settling matters in the engine room, and his Uzi was missing. . . .

Regan threw himself aside too late. The bullets hit him solidly, driving him back against the white-painted steel superstructure. He saw the man step out of the dark doorway—the pump room, he remembered, not air-conditioned—where he'd obviously lain in wait for Harry with the wrench, and now for Regan with the gun. He was a large man in greasy work trousers and a filthy T-shirt; a large dark middle-aged man with a large belly and enormous greasy hands that handled the submachine gun with a kind of loving nostalgic tenderness—a man remembering a war in which he'd once fought, and fought well, and found an importance he'd always remembered even as he tended this tanker's ailing pumps.

Regan had slid down to a sitting position now, unable to move. He saw the man bend over Harry's body and possess himself of the gas mask and a couple of extra magazines, after which he moved quickly to the ladder that would take him to the platform above, from which he could command the whole deck of the ship. He vanished from sight. Presently, Regan heard the Uzi begin to fire up there, in a ruthless, businesslike, professional manner that spoke more clearly than words of the deadly work it was doing.

Not even a real military officer this time, Regan thought bitterly, just a bloody grease monkey; and the whole plan

ruined and everyone killed. Why must there always be someone to throw a spanner in the works by fighting back?

Then he thought: but would it not be a dreadful world if
there was not?

CHAPTER 42

July

Latitude 22°N; Longitude 69°W

Nancy Lou's sails lost their wind as the little cutter came into
the lee of the drifting tanker's tall superstructure.

"Down staysail," Harold Ullman said, starting the motor.
"Down main."

"No, leave them up! Bear off and let's get the fuck out of
here!" Vinnie Burnett protested. "I tell you, we're too late, it's
that Regan I told you about. He's got her and he's just lying
low up there, letting us sail up fat and sassy to where he can
grab us or shoot us. . . ."

"If he wants us, he's got us," Ullman pointed out. "All he
has to do is fire up that great big thing and run us down.
With fourteen-fifteen knots on tap against our five or six, he's
bound to catch us; we can dodge him for a while, perhaps, but
not forever. If it is your friend Regan. So we might as well
climb aboard and say hello. Get that staysail halliard, will
you?"

He had to admit that it was eerie, almost six hundred feet
of ship lying motionless on the sunny, empty ocean—well,
there was land somewhere to the south, Hispaniola on one
side of the Mona Passage and Puerto Rico on the other, but it
wasn't visible from here. It had been a pretty good run, if he
did say so himself, and a pretty fair piece of navigation. To be
sure, the course of the *Petrox Prince* was quite predictable;
she seldom strayed more than a mile or two from the direct
line up from the Caribbean; but for a small sailboat navi-

gated simply by sextant and dead reckoning to stay within sighting distance of that line had involved some pretty fancy chart work. Anyway, they'd found her; but the dismasted blue yacht lashed alongside indicated that they'd found her too late. But if she had been hijacked, where the hell were the hijackers? There was no movement on deck.

Vinnie Burnett, a slight barefoot brown figure in her frayed cutoffs and faded bandana halter, had gone forward reluctantly to haul down and secure the forestaysail. Ullman, in the long-sleeved shirt and long pants forced upon him by his vulnerable complexion, stepped up to the cabin top to furl the mainsail. There was still no sign of life on the drifting ship to windward except for a mechanical murmur indicating that, while her main propulsion machinery was idle, her auxiliary equipment was still functioning.

When they had finished, Ullman said: "Okay, I'll lay us alongside that ketch, what's left of her. She'll keep us from banging against the ship. You stay down here. Leave the motor running. If anything happens when I climb up, cut the lines and blast off. In the meantime, why don't you get some fenders ready?"

"Aye, aye, Captain Bligh, sir."

She seemed to have recovered her good humor, now that they were committed. He reminded himself that she was hardly a sheltered-flower type girl; by her own rather shocking accounts, given him piecemeal the past few days, she was by this time fairly well acquainted with hijacked vessels and violent death. He found a clear spot near the bow of the damaged ketch where he could lay the smaller boat alongside without too much risk of fouling the propeller on the trailing wreckage. As he swung himself aboard, after making *Nancy Lou* fast with Vinnie's help, he could feel the sluggish roll of the derelict indicating large quantities of water inside the hull. He concentrated on that, trying to estimate how much longer the ketch would float; he'd have to get the cutter clear before the wreck went down. Assuming that she was leaking at all, he reminded himself; they might just have flooded her a bit, deliberately, as part of the vessel-in-distress routine Vinnie had described to him. It was easier to think about this than about what might be awaiting him at the top of the rope ladder. Well, if you spent your life worrying about reefs and hurricanes and being run down by big ships in the night, you'd never go sailing. And if you spent your life brooding about what might be lying in wait for you at the top of this and around the corner of that, you'd never go anywhere. And it wasn't, he reflected a bit grimly, as if it had been such a hell of a wonderful life lately, anyway.

He made his way across the deck to the side of the ship and started up the dangling ladder, pleased that his leg was now well enough not to cause him more than a few twinges. As he neared the top he felt the ladder jerk, and looked down. Vinnie had turned off *Nancy Lou*'s motor and was scrambling up after him. He started to speak and thought better of it. Whatever he told her to do, she probably wouldn't do it; and she was really no safer down than up; and her safety was, strictly speaking, not his responsibility. He hadn't invited her along; she'd invited herself. The gate in the ship's rail had been swung back and lashed out of the way. He hesitated, but there was nothing to be gained by being tricky. If they were there with guns, they were there with guns, and that was all there was to it.

He heaved himself up onto the tanker's familiar deck and stopped abruptly. After a little he was aware of Vinnie pulling herself up beside him. He heard her gasp. After a moment she started retching violently. He was interested to note, vaguely, that she was sailor enough to hold it until she could put it over the ship's side; not that a little vomit would make much difference to the gory mess before them. There seemed to be dead bodies everywhere. . . .

Later, having worked his way aft to the platform over the pumproom, he straightened up from the crewman named Lorenzo who'd once complained to him about the ship's pumps, now sitting dead with an Uzi in his lap and endless bright little fired cartridge cases littering the steel deck around him. Lorenzo had done an efficient and thorough job, but one of the hijackers had apparently managed to get off a burst before the searching fire cut him down.

"But they can't *all* be dead!" Vinnie protested wildly. "Jeez, everybody couldn't have fucking killed *everybody*, it doesn't make sense!"

The slow ponderous roll of the deeply laden tanker was, Ullman thought, a pleasant relief after the frantic motion of the little boat off which they'd come. Otherwise, well, the tropical sun was hot and getting hotter and the stench was already quite perceptible. Yesterday, Ullman decided, applying his photojournalistic experience to the problem; maybe the day before but I think yesterday. They spoil fast in this climate. Say yesterday morning. We didn't miss by very much. If Vinnie had just opened up sooner. If we'd just met a ship that could have relayed a warning. If. . . . But all the ifs in the world never changed the way things were. Ullman grabbed the girl's arm as she started past him toward the nearest door in the superstructure.

"Easy, Vinnie," he said. "I don't think we'd better go in there. At least not without that on." He pointed to the gas mask lying on the deck beside Lorenzo. "Not until we're sure the air conditioning has cleared it out, whatever it was they used."

"Oh, my God! Is that how they did it? I didn't know; they didn't tell me their plans." She glanced around uneasily. "What are we going to do?"

He said, "You stay here. I'll put that mask on and see what it's like up in the radio room. Maybe I can get a message out, if the air is breathable and I can figure out how to work all that complicated electronics gear. I wish to God I had a canary."

Vinnie looked at him aghast, obviously thinking he had suddenly gone crazy. "Canary? What the hell do you want a fucking canary for?"

"They use them in mines, or used to. If your canary keels over you know the air isn't fit to breathe and it's time to get the hell out."

"You'd do that to a poor little bird?" Then she looked around, startled, at the deck full of dead men. A snort of hysterical laughter escaped her and she swayed against him. As she fought desperately for control, he held her one-handed, keeping the submachine gun he'd picked up on the deck below—it had seemed stupid to go wandering around this charnel ship unarmed—pointed in a safe direction. "Oh, Jesus!" she breathed at last. "Oh, God! All these fucking bodies just staring! Why the hell can't they die with their eyes closed?"

"I'll tell them next time," Ullman said. "Please shut your eyes as you go, fellows. Miss Burnett doesn't care to have you looking at her after you're dead."

"You bastard."

"Vinnie."

"Yes?" When he didn't speak at once, she asked, "What is it?"

He cleared his throat. "There's a boat coming. I hope it isn't the one you told me about."

She stepped away from him quickly and turned to look.

They stood staring at the small white dot on the horizon that seemed to fluctuate oddly in size as the sheets of spray hurled aside by its bow flashed out widely and subsided again.

"Sorry, Mister." The hysterical note was gone from Vinnie's voice. "That's the one. *Stream Hunter*. They call her something else now, but they didn't tell me what and I didn't dare make a point of asking. The big sportfisherman we took off the Yucatan Straits." She glanced at him. "Now what?"

"How many on board, would you say?"

"Well, the little freak's bound to have his gofers with him, Cardenas and that scary moron Bolo. And then he'll have a skeleton crew to take over this ship from Regan and his gang of hijack specialists—all Regan contracted to do was deliver the ship; he wanted no part of running it. At least half a dozen, maybe more. And, if it matters, all the weapons and explosives from the second shipment, the one that never got to that Florida key where his junior-grade invasion army was training, because the government moved in on Major Nazi Ochsner too soon. What the hell can we do?"

"Here, take this. Do you know how to use it?"

Vinnie looked down at the Uzi that had been placed in her hands. "I've shot a pistol a little; I guess I can figure it out. But we can't possibly . . ."

"We can hold the bridge while we get a radio message off. I might even be able to get this bucket moving so they'll have a hard time getting aboard. There's a way of setting the engine room telegraph on automatic so you can work her from the bridge like a runabout; it depends on how things are rigged below. The boys showed me when I was taking all those pictures on board." As he talked he was taking the submachine gun from dead Lorenzo's lap and fitting a fresh magazine into place. He straightened up and frowned at the approaching vessel. "I thought you said that gold-plated fishing machine was good for thirty knots in a pinch."

"That's what Janet—Mrs. McHugh, the owner's wife—told me once; although I don't think I ever cruised at much over twenty-three or -four."

"Well, she's not doing anything like that now," Ullman said. "She's not even crowding twenty, although you'd think they'd be in a hurry to . . . well, to hell with that, the slower the better. Let's get topside and do our talking there." He picked up the gas mask. "We'll go up by the outside ladders since there's only one of these. . . . What's the matter?"

"Regan!" Vinnie said, searching the deck with her eyes. "I

just remembered, I didn't see Regan himself anywhere among all those . . ." Her voice stopped.

Ullman turned to look where she was looking. The man who was leaning heavily against the corner of the deckhouse was not very big, but he had strong-looking shoulders for his size. He had matted dark hair and a wry monkey-face that normally, no doubt, had a cheerful and disrespectful look; now it was a greenish-gray color and looked more like death than the faces of many of the men around who were not on their feet and would never be again. There was blood on his clothes but not in tremendous quantities; where he'd been hit, low, the bleeding would be mostly internal. He had a large automatic pistol in his hand. It was quite steady.

"It's distressed I am that you should forget Sean Regan so soon." The voice sounded rusty from disuse but like the gun it was quite steady. "Gently now, my darlings. We do not drop, we do not throw, this is not the telly. We lay down very tenderly and rise with the hands empty, so." He gestured with the gun barrel as they straightened up obediently. "And now we move a decent distance away, so." He frowned at the girl. "Why are you here, love?" When she merely shrugged her shoulders slightly, he spoke to Ullman: "She was to kill you and take your boat and disappear, her work complete."

"I know, she told me. That would have been nice for your friend Columbus," Ullman said. "He'd have been rid of both of us. We talked it over and decided it would be more fun this way."

"I know your motive. I don't know hers."

Ullman shrugged. "Atonement? Or maybe he just pushed her around a little at the wrong time. People like your friend are always pushing people around. It never seems to occur to them that anybody could possibly get mad and start pushing back."

Vinnie Burnett licked her lips. "And now, Regan?"

"Now we wait for that idiot Gonzaga who has taken twenty-four hours to locate a ship of twenty thousand tons lying in the exact position he was told to look, barring a little drift." He showed her a ghastly smile and shook his head. "No, darling, it cannot be. There was a moment but it is past. To this Irishman a turncoat means little, we've had so many of them, but to Mister Columbus over there, getting closer by the minute, it is a different matter. . . . I regret it deeply, but it was a good operation until that grease monkey took a hand; a good clean operation and I would not spoil it by

459

letting you go to raise the alarm even if there were a practical way of doing it. The client's interests come first. I agreed to deliver this ship in a satisfactory manner, free and clear, and deliver it I will." The death's-head smile came again as he looked at Ullman. "It was a fine sail you made in that little boat. I wondered who was pressing so hard astern. But do not watch me so; Regan will not die until this business is completed."

It was a nightmare wait in the steadily increasing heat with the sick-sweet smell of death all around. Then the big sportfisherman was close aboard at last; and a couple of men came scrambling over the tanker's side to cast off the two boats lying there and make room at the boarding ladder. No attempt was made to secure the sailing vessels elsewhere; they were simply set adrift together. Ullman started to call out, but checked himself. He watched *Nancy Lou*'s mast—all he could see of her—move slowly away downwind. If they'd only cut her loose from that hulk before the two boats beat each other to pieces, he thought; she'd have a chance then. Somebody might find her drifting crewless before she shattered herself on a beach or reef; but instinct told him there was nothing to be gained, and perhaps something to be lost, by pleading for favors that would not be granted. But the debt was mounting. Don't anger the animals, Mister Columbus. Some of them have teeth—one tooth, at least.

Columbus came aboard annoyed because he'd had to be helped up the swaying rope ladder; because he'd obviously wanted to board this giant prize with the dignity of a conqueror and instead he'd wound up on hands and knees at the rail. He struck away the helping hand of the dark-faced, jockey-sized man who'd come over the side with him, and rose, and slapped irritably at his clothes, waiting for the second member of his guard of honor before he moved—he was playing a part, Ullman saw, and the role was easy enough to identify. Other men had done the Bonaparte routine before him. He was really a beautiful specimen, Ullman thought, from the neck up. He had never seen a more photogenic face, refined and aristocratic and totally evil. The enemy.

Only eight months, Ullman thought. Eight months ago, returning with his wife from a pleasant cruise of the Bahamas, he'd been a reasonably happy man with a reasonably happy life ahead of him—in fact, as he recalled, things had actually been looking pretty great. Then this arrogant individual now approaching, who hadn't even known the Ullman family existed, had given a casual order and nothing had been or would ever be the same again. . . . He forced himself not to think at all about the liberated knife he still wore in its homemade sheath. If it did not exist for him, it might not exist for others. There was no weapon, he told himself firmly; no weapon and no hope. Look scared, he told himself, and admit to yourself it isn't hard to do.

Columbus paused at the head of the metal stairs. Other men were now disembarking from the sportfisherman; and a stout dark man with a great sweeping mustache—Captain Ramiro Gonzaga, from Vinnie's description—was supervising the unloading of a cargo consisting partly of impressive-looking weapons, partly of mysterious-looking crates and boxes without any identifying marks whatever. Columbus paid no attention to this activity behind and below him. He glanced at the dead man, the two guns on the deck, and the two prisoners standing together unarmed; then he looked to Regan for an explanation. Regan licked his gray lips, but his voice was clear enough when he spoke, if pitched a little low.

"That's Ullman, the man she was supposed to take offshore and drown," Regan said softly. "They seem to have come to an agreement of sorts. He's the man whose wife cost you Olson; the man who fingered Orosco and is therefore, one could say, responsible for Miss Columbus languishing in jail at this moment. The young fellow you've been trying to kill in a casual way for better than half a year, or have killed. About time the two of you made each other's acquaintance, don't you think? He doesn't look so very durable, but these stringy redheads are deceiving. And now that you are in full possession of this ship, as agreed, I must ask you to excuse Regan. . . ."

The voice stopped. The little Irishman pitched forward onto the steel platform. Vinnie made a small sound and released Ullman's arm as if preparing to run to the fallen man's side; but the heavy, swarthy man known as Bolo had instantly stepped in front of them with a ready knife that seemed to have come from nowhere. The smaller man, Cardenas, stepped over cautiously and freed the pistol from Regan's hand, before making a quick inspection.

"Dead, *Señor*," he said to Columbus, rising. "It is unfortunate, under the circumstances."

He was looking down at the open deck where Ramiro Gonzaga was bellowing orders in Spanish and heavily accented

English; and Columbus followed his glance, and spoke grimly:

"Yes, we needed Regan. What do you suggest now?"

Cardenas glanced at the prisoners in an appraising way. "The girl is acquainted with boats, we know, but it is also established that she does not know navigation. But the man has apparently just brought his own little sailboat directly to this spot, crossing a thousand miles of ocean to do so. A considerably better performance than some we've seen, eh, *patrón?*" His glance touched Gonzaga again, and returned to Ullman. "I suggest that this one should be preserved in case our other, er, precaution should fail. The girl, too; her treachery can be dealt with later. At the moment she may prove useful if persuasion should become necessary."

"It is in your hands, Jesus. Find a place to keep them under guard. I could not spare the time to deal with them properly now, in any case."

"*Sí, patrón.*"

Shortly, they were being shepherded into the deckhouse structure by Bolo, after pausing at the door for two men to emerge carrying a dead man between them—one of the ship's officers, Ullman saw. It seemed unfriendly and disrespectful of him not to remember the name, considering that he'd got to know them all moderately well in the weeks he'd spent on board.

"Inside," Bolo said. "Upstairs."

Aware of the girl's hand on his arm, Ullman moved forward into the air-conditioned coolness wondering—and he knew that Vinnie was also wondering—just how thoroughly the atmosphere inside had been tested, and how anybody could be sure some pockets of lethal gas didn't remain. Bolo apparently suffered from no such problems of imagination. Jesus Cardenas had told him it was safe and Jesus was never wrong. He herded them briskly up two flights of stairs and shoved them into an empty cabin—by coincidence, it was the same cabin that Harold Ullman had occupied on his earlier voyage: the pilot's cabin. On second thought, Ullman decided, it wasn't much of a coincidence. Most of the other staterooms were assigned to the ship's permanent personnel.

This was a seagoing guest room of sorts maintained for the convenience of pilots and others attached to the ship temporarily. Currently unoccupied, it did not have to be cleared of dead bodies, and personal belongings that might contain potential weapons. Having the same cabin again wasn't much of an advantage, Ullman thought wryly; he hadn't thought to conceal any useful objects on the premises last time he was here. But nobody had searched him. Cardenas must have assumed that Regan, a pro, had frisked them routinely when he'd first captured them, not quite realizing, perhaps, that the Irishman had been dying on his feet the whole time, just holding himself together by sheer willpower.

As the door closed behind them, Vinnie Burnett turned toward Ullman and threw her arms around his neck.

"Hey, what—"

"Play up, you stupid bastard!" she hissed, sniffing loudly. "Hold me, stroke my hair, console me, tell me I shouldn't cry because everything's going to be all right. . . . Go *on!*" Clinging to him, she managed a sob that shook her very convincingly, and whimpered loudly, "We're going to die, we're going to die, they're going to kill us both, I know it!"

"Easy, Vinnie," he said mechanically, stroking her hair as instructed. "Take it easy. We'll figure something out. Everything's going to be all right. . . ."

The door opened abruptly, and Jesus Cardenas's dark face looked in at them, as they moved apart self-consciously. Cardenas nodded as if he had learned something and was pleased by it.

"My apologies," he said. "Unfortunately, there seems to be no way of locking you in securely, so I thought I should inform you that there will be a guard outside the door at all times with a submachine gun and orders to shoot to kill if you make any trouble whatever." His eyes were cold as he looked at Vinnie Burnett. "I hope you are happy with your choice, *Señorita*. The *patrón* is generous toward those who serve him; but he is ruthless toward those who betray him. You would be one of the bodies being thrown overboard at this moment if he did not think there was a way in which you might still prove useful." He let his eyes move from one to the other of them, and smiled thinly. "So make the most of your reprieve."

When the door closed again, Vinnie said, "Okay, he's had his look, the creep. Now: step two."

There was an odd, crooked little smile on her face. She stepped forward and put her arms around his neck once more and drew herself up to kiss him on the mouth, now letting her body make deliberate, suggestive contact with his. Instinctively, he reached up to grasp her arms and free himself—not that the idea she seemed to be proposing didn't have consid-

463

erable merit, after the weeks of self-control, but it was crazy at this time and place.

"Vinnie, for God's sake!" he protested. "Don't go all nympho now, we can't—"

"What are you using for brains?" she breathed, refusing to let him disengage himself. "We're probably going to die, aren't we? Hell, the man said to make the most of the reprieve, didn't he? You heard him. And if we don't die it'll be because we're shot with luck—and because we put on a hell of a good act to fool them. Even if you find me totally repulsive—"

"Cut it out," he snapped. There was nothing more ridiculous than a healthy, unattached male fighting for his virtue, but he couldn't help glancing toward the big, forward-facing cabin windows. "You're desirable, you're practically irresistible, consider yourself raped, okay? But I want to see what the hell's going on out there so I'll know—"

"I can tell you what's going on," she said. "All that's going on out there is one bunch of fellas throwing another bunch of fellas to the sharks, who're all going crazy because they haven't had such a swell meal in months. And after they've got that taken care of, Columbus will put them to work rigging this ship like a floating bomb with all that nasty stuff he brought aboard, so nobody'll dare interfere with him because the little freak will have his finger on the bang-button, all ready to cover the ocean with a few million gallons of black goo—he'll have it fixed, he says, to give himself and the crew just enough time to scramble aboard that sport-fisherman escort vessel before it blows. That's what he says. And then, after they've got all that done, maybe they'll get the ship under way at last and it'll help to take a peek and see which way they're heading but it'll take hours." She smiled wickedly and touched her lips to his again, repeatedly, lightly, making small kissing noises, still holding him tightly. "So what the hell else is there for us to do in here? I'm sorry as hell but I forgot to bring my fucking chess set and I can never remember the way all those crazy pieces move, anyway."

He drew a long breath. "Romance in the public morgue! Just tell me what the hell we're trying to prove."

"You look very funny, Mr. Ullman, all stubborn and pure like that. And we're trying to prove that you're mad about me, what else? That after our long intimate voyage together you can't keep your lousy hands off me. That I've got you going so bad that even on this death ship with your life in

464

anger you can't bear to let us pass up a single lousy bed
without—"

"And how's that going to help us?"

"If you can't figure it out, I'll tell you later." There was a
sudden darkness in the gray eyes so close to his. "But right
now. . . . Ah, that's better! I thought maybe I'd wound up in
his floating prison cell with one of those day-old corpses for
company."

Angered by his own involuntary reaction he pulled her
arms away roughly and turned and strode to the window and
looked out on the deck below, to see exactly what she'd told
him he'd see. Some men were still performing the gruesome
task of mass burial, if their casual method of human disposal
could be dignified by the name; others were working at the
hatches to the cargo tanks—which had been opened—with
wire and explosives, if that was what was in the mysterious
boxes and cartons that were now distributed around the deck.
He looked for *Nancy Lou,* but she was nowhere in sight;
apparently she'd drifted astern out of his range of vision. He
knew a painful sense of loss, almost as strong as if the boat
had been human. She'd been a damn good loyal little ship.

When he turned, Vinnie was still standing by the cabin
door. He had spent several weeks with this girl in a space no
more than twenty-eight feet long and nine feet wide; and now
there were no more sails to trim and watches to stand. He
hadn't realized the magnitude of the forces that had been
generated by her constant nearness. He saw that she was
smiling a little, aware that she was witnessing a simple
masculine protest, a brief assertion of independence—who
was running this damn seduction, anyway?—a *macho* gesture, Nancy would have called it, but this was no time to be
thinking of Nancy, and there was one more thing to be done.

He saw Vinnie's eyes narrow, puzzled, as he bent down;
and then widen with quick approval as he straightened up
with the crude Venezuelan knife in its homemade sheath. It
made him feel better to know that she wasn't completely in
charge of the situation; here was one thing she'd overlooked.
She'd seen the weapon when they'd first met and in the
intimacy of *Nancy Lou*'s cabin it was impossible that she
shouldn't have learned where he wore it and guessed why.
But apparently she'd forgotten about it until this moment.
He glanced around for a suitable hiding place. Vinnie jerked
her head toward the sofa, and he slipped the weapon under

the cushion there, making sure that none of the trailing straps of the sheath were left exposed.

Then he straightened up, turned, grinned, and strode swiftly to where the girl awaited him; and he heard her laugh softly as he picked her up and carried her to the bed and dropped her onto it so hard that she bounced. Even in that moment he was pleased to note that his weak leg didn't protest very much against the effort he'd asked of it. Of course she wasn't a very big girl. He bent over her as she lay unresisting on the covers, deliberately passive now, leaving it all to him, laughing up at him. The halter and cutoffs were no problem at all; and he'd long since learned—again, there were no intimate secrets on a small boat at sea—that as far as Miss Burnett was concerned, the man who'd invented underwear had been wasting his cottonpicking time.

It was, he noted, a very nice little body that was now revealed to him fully for the second time. Undressing hastily, he let her draw him down to her, discarding the passive role that had amused her briefly. He quickly discovered that, while she'd been an obedient crew on the boat, in bed she was a managing young woman with very definite, and quite interesting, ideas about how this act should be performed. But he'd made his gesture of independence; and he was too good a seaman to argue with a pilot who was obviously navigating very familiar waters. Then the storm burst over them and the rushing winds swept their laboring ship, totally out of control, out onto a wild and wonderful sea where there were no memories, where there was no bereavement or grief or guilt. . . .

He became slowly aware once more of the vibration of the auxiliary machinery in the tanker's engine room far below, still doing its duty steadily in spite of the strange antics of the tiny humans infesting its giant hull. The girl lay close to him, warm and damp, her arms around him.

"Welcome back," she murmured.

"Oh, Jesus!" he breathed. "Are you all right?"

She laughed at his concern. "I don't break so easily, don't worry about me. Don't ever worry about me."

It was quite mad, but very pleasant, to be lying there in broad daylight feeling a great peace inside him and, for the moment, no concern at all for those who had died on this ship and those, including himself, who might still die and probably would. Vinnie's small face on the pillow beside him was serene and lovely, half-smiling; and he kissed it lightly.

"Vinnie, I—"

She shook her head quickly, her smile fading. "No. Not like that."

"What did I say wrong?"

She drew a long breath. "Don't . . . don't go all mushy on me now. It isn't like that at all and you know it isn't. The gentle, grateful, loving peck and the tender voice, and what else? The offer to make an honest woman of the little girl now that you've got around to laying her at last?"

"Damn it, Vinnie, don't—"

"Stop it!" Her voice was sharp. "Look, baby, it's been great. It was a swell sail and you were a lovely guy to do it with and what we just did was good, too; and that's it. The End. Curtain. Understand?"

"No," he said. "I don't understand. Unless you're saying that it's no use for us to talk about anything because we haven't got a chance in the world of getting out of this alive."

"I'm not talking about *this!*"

"Then what—"

"For God's sake, this is Vinnie, Mister Ullman!" she said harshly. "Remember Vinnie? Remember Lavinia Burnett, Lucia Barnes, Linda Brown, Laura Briggs? Remember that catamaran I told you about, with a couple of bearded creeps who kind of drifted off and died? Remember that busted-up ketch we found here just now that wasn't busted when I sailed on her with some . . . some nice folks who got suddenly dead? Remember the hijacked sportfisherman that's lying alongside right now? Remember that only one of her crew survived? Only one besides Vinnie, that is. Sure, you remember Vinnie, baby! And even if you don't there are lots who do."

He started to speak and stopped himself. Her laughter was soft and bitter.

"Now you remember Vinnie," she murmured. "I laid it all out for you in spades and you'd heard it all before—well, most of it—from that government guy, remember? You know what I'm trying to say. You know why you didn't make a move toward me, lay a hand on me, all the way down; because you didn't want to get stuck with any lost causes and, baby, is this one lost! You didn't want to get involved in the mess, my mess, so you played eunuch like you wouldn't know an erection if you met it on the street. And why the hell should you get involved? So don't do it now!"

"Vinnie, I—"

"I'm not blaming you for anything, damn it! Don't apologize. It was the smart thing to do. Just keep right on doing it. You don't owe me a damn thing, nothing's changed. We just . . . just did something kind of nice we both wanted to do and it made a lot of sense because of the lousy trap we're in, so why should you figure it obligates you in any way? Just fuck and run, baby. Because where do I go from here, assuming that we live long enough for me to worry about it? You know where. And you don't want to have to stand by me nobly in the fucking courtroom or visit me faithfully in that lousy place they'll send me because they haven't got the guts to kill off somebody decently when they're tired of having them around. That's called humanitarianism or something. So they'll call me crazy and ship me back to that . . . that gray hellhole with bars on the windows, or another just like it, where they'll tinker with my goddamn brain some more as if they hadn't done enough to it already. That's called rehabilitation. And do you really want to waste the rest of your life fighting loyally—you'd be just that kind of a dope, wouldn't you?—to get them to turn me loose when you and I both know I don't belong loose?"

"I don't know—"

"Then you haven't been listening to what anybody's been telling you, including me! And now get the hell over to that window and see how they're coming out there; and then get back in bed with me so when they come in they'll see us all cozy together; and while we wait for an audience we can talk about things that make some sense for a change." When he hesitated, she pushed at him irritably. "Go *on!*"

He stood up and moved to the window. Not much had changed below. There were still dead bodies going over the side. The deck was clear but they seemed to be getting them out of the engine room now. The explosives crew had barely got going on its job, way up forward; it would take them hours, as Vinnie had said, if they planned to work their way clear aft. He'd felt as if he'd been away a long time, but apparently Vinnie and he, in the bed, had been operating on a different kind of time. . . .

As he watched, there was a sudden flurry of movement down there; several men were running toward the sport-fisherman lying alongside, but they were too late. A change in the attitude of the ship with respect to the wind, or a change in the period of the seas, had started the powerboat rolling violently and, as might have been expected when you

ecured a vessel with a tall superstructure against a high-
ided ship—he'd used the ketch as a landing stage for *Nancy
Lou* for just that reason—the gyrating tuna tower with its
igh control station and its radar and radio antennas was
now smashing repeatedly into the tanker's rail. Before they
could get the boat pushed off, considerable damage had been
done. You had to hand it to them, Ullman thought sourly,
remembering the wrecked condition of the ketch; for being
rough on boats they could hardly be beat. But of course they'd
had a lot of practice being rough on people.

Ullman went back to the girl, who'd pulled back the covers
and, belatedly, got into the bed the way it was supposed to be
got into.

"They're still fixing to blow us all to hell," he reported. He
started to sit down beside her, but she lifted the covers and
moved over invitingly, and he got in beside her and, after
she'd made her desires obvious, drew her close. "Frankly, I
think this is kind of ridiculous," he said. "We're supposed to
be making clubs out of the furniture and ropes out of the
sheets and blankets, aren't we? John Wayne and Clint
Eastwood would disown us if they saw us. What the hell are
you doing now?"

"Don't you like it?" she asked.

"I thought it was the man who was supposed to think about
nothing but sex, sex, sex."

"I'm just reminding you that you're crazy about me," she
said. When he glanced at her, she went on quickly, "That's
the way you've got to play it; I'm just trying to make it easy
for you. You're nuts about little Vinnie and her cute little
tricks. . . . Oh, my. Now he's embarrassed. Didn't his
wife ever. . . . Sorry, I didn't mean that. Please delete that.
But you're gaga about me, understand? You'll do anything,
but anything, to keep the nasty men from hurting a hair on
my sweet innocent head. Oh, you'll be brave and stoical as
long as they're just pushing *you* around; but the minute they
go to work on *me,* you're mush. Okay?"

"All right, but I don't see—"

"Jesus, what kind of oatmeal are you using for brains
today?" Her voice was scornful. "You saw it, didn't you? The
way they looked at fat Ramiro. And you noticed how slowly
that boat was running, coming in here; and if you were
looking at all as they maneuvered alongside you saw the
vibration it had. There's at least one damaged prop, maybe
even a bent shaft. That great navigator Captain Ramiro

Gonzaga must have bounced them off some coral on the way down. And then it took him a whole fucking day to find this ship, although how the hell he could get that far off the course is hard to understand. They're fed up with his incompetence; but with Olson and Regan both dead, who else have they got? Three guesses and the first two don't count. They've got you."

It had been at the back of his mind; even so it startled him to hear it said. "Hell, if that's what they're thinking, they're crazy," he protested. "I've never handled a ship this big. Dammit, I've never handled a real *ship*."

"Big or little, what's the difference?" She grinned briefly. "And was there ever a sailor who got on board somebody else's boat, no matter how enormous, and didn't ask himself, now how the fuck would I manage this monster if I really had to? Are you going to tell me you never gave it a thought, all those weeks you were on board? Anyway, you don't have to run it; they'll run it. All they want is for somebody to tell them *where* to run it; and is there much difference between navigating one boat and another except that this bucket probably draws at least twenty feet?"

"Thirty-three, fully loaded like this," he said mechanically.

She shrugged her small naked shoulders. "So if you can find five feet of water to sail your boat in, you can find thirty-five or fifty for this brute, it's just a matter of looking at the chart, isn't it? Anyway, that's obviously what they've got in mind for you; that's what they're saving you for even though you were kind of responsible for getting the *patrón*'s sacred daughter thrown in the slammer, and a few other things. Of course you'll be brave and noble and refuse to help in any way with their evil plans, whatever they may be; and they won't be able to pound on you too hard because you can't navigate for them if you're dead. But they'll haul little Vinnie up there to the bridge—that's what they're saving me for—and turn me over to Bolo; and of course, mad with love, you'll go through all the good old loud-mouthed TV routines about how you'll rip the guts out of the dastardly bastards if they dare to lay a finger on me. So Bolo will crack me one in the eye and you'll fold right up and run their boat like a good little boy. Naturally, they'll have Bolo standing by with his mean old slicer, ready to slit my throat if you pull any tricks whatever. And then—" She stopped.

"And then," he said, "what?"

She was silent for a moment; then her small body turned

against him strongly, her nails digging into his bare back as she drew them together once more.

"And then," she breathed in his ear, "then if you see any chance to louse them up, any opportunity whatever, you'll take it, okay? You won't hesitate, you won't think any mushy-slushy thoughts, you won't consult your tender conscience, you'll just *do* it and to hell with that lost cause known as Lavinia Burnett." Her breath brushed his ear, quick and uneven, and he thought he could feel the heavy beating of her heart as he held her, listening to her fierce whisper: "No, you're not supposed to talk, damn you! There's nothing to talk about. You've got nothing to say! Just *do* it when it's time, understand? That's what this is all about, stupid, to convince them it's the last thing in the world you'd ever do so they won't be expecting.... And now we'll just forget all about it." She laughed softly, with a sudden, startling change of mood. "What's the matter, don't you think I can make you forget a little thing like that? Silly boy...."

CHAPTER 43

July

Latitude 26°N; Longitude 80°W

The courtroom wasn't crowded and Martin sensed that Francesca Columbus had recognized him among the scattered spectators. She had, of course, seen him at Miranda's the evening of her arrest; but she'd undoubtedly also had him described to her long before as the killer of her brother. The ancient clannish attitudes still prevailed in that family and anybody responsible for the death of one would carefully be made known to all. She probably also knew that he had ordered her arrest and was therefore the cause of her being here today. It was quite possible, he reflected, that she thought of the whole business as a kind of family feud complicated by old tribal allegiances and thought he had simply come to gloat at his latest victory over the clan Columbus and those patriotic Cubans whom he, Felipe Aurelio Martinez, had betrayed.

She was wearing a plain black dress, dark stockings, and black pumps with very high heels—he wondered why, the minute they got out of their jeans and sneakers, they had to climb into, or onto, those spikelike heels. Her slim figure was very straight; and she listened to the sentence without flinching but showed some impatience at the lecture that accompanied it. As she was led away she turned and looked directly at Martin. There was hatred and contempt in her eyes and he knew that, despite her aristocratic antecedents, she would have spat at him like a street trollop if he had been within range. There was, he saw, already a kind of hardness in the face, a shadow on the beauty he had seen. They would teach her more hardness, and less beauty, where she was going now.

When she was gone, he got up and walked blindly out of the building. He was not really aware of reclaiming his car and driving to the apartment, but he did experience a twinge of conscience as he took out the key he'd been given and let himself in, and wondered at himself a little. He had moved in with other women when it was convenient, or had them move in with him—it was a common enough arrangement these free-wheeling days—and it had never occurred to him to feel guilty because, in old-fashioned terms, he was damaging, or allowing them to damage, their reputations. But he was forever discovering how very old-fashioned his feelings were with respect to this one. After disposing of his coat and gun, he made himself a drink and sat down with it; but he did not drink it. That was too easy an escape, he decided, from the thoughts that pursued him; he had to meet them sober and put them to flight. But he was very glad when he heard Elizabeth's key in the lock, and her footsteps crossing the rug, and felt her hand on his shoulder.

"That bad, Philip?"

"It is not pleasant to shoot down the last trumpeter swan," he said. "Particularly when the pretty bird is distantly related to you by blood. That place will destroy her."

"She would have destroyed herself eventually, Philip. As you pointed out once, your cousin Miranda has made it here, his way, and you have made it here, yours; but she could never have made it, not the way she's been taught to think.

472

She's been trained to look back, not forward. And there's really nothing she can go back to, nothing." Elizabeth hesitated. "Shall I make you a fresh drink? The ice is melted in this one."

"Please."

When she returned she had removed her jacket and run a comb through her hair and she looked quite fresh and attractive but, knowing her so well now, he realized when she came closer that she was quite tired and, he thought, worried about something connected with her work. And you, he told himself grimly, you think only of your own stupid identity problems—who is this Philip Martin?—and feel that she is obliged to help you with them, too. He took the glass she gave him, and watched her sit down to sip her own drink.

"I am grateful," he said after a little.

"That is not a good word," she said with a faint smile. "I don't want your gratitude, darling; and I don't know what in the world I've done to deserve it."

"No jealousy," he said.

"Oh, that." She grinned at him boyishly. "Little does he know. The lady is seething inside, naturally, at the gentleman's sentimental concern for another, younger, woman, but it just doesn't seem diplomatic to show it." She stopped smiling. "Can you put it to rest now, Philip?"

"I can try." After a moment, he said, "You look tired. Are they giving you a hard time?"

"Yes," she said, "but let's not talk about it. You know how dull government politics are. . . . Philip."

"Yes?"

"I can't . . . I mean, we can't, tonight. Or now if you had a quickie in mind. I'm sorry."

He was disappointed, of course, but he grinned to hide it. "I didn't know I was so obvious," he said. "And you're blushing."

She looked at him and laughed. "It's funny, I can talk about the biological functions of cows and horses and dogs and chickens, using all the correct barnyard terms, but when it comes to people . . . I was brought up to think that was very dirty. Isn't it awful?" She was still a little pink. She said hastily, "I'd better do something about feeding us lunch. I've got to get back and I suppose you do, too."

"It seems unlikely that the government can survive much longer without Martinez," he said. "Can I help you?"

She laughed, rising. "You're a nice man, I can . . . think of lots of places where you're a wonderful man, but not in a kitchen." But she stood looking down at him for a moment longer. Suddenly she went to her knees by his chair and said, "To hell with lunch. I want to talk. Do you mind?"

"Of course not."

She rested her elbows on his knees looking up at him. "Don't be scared," she said. "It's not so serious."

"Now you have me really frightened."

"Well," she said, "well, it's . . . I know you love me for my money, of course; so naturally I can't expect you to do anything but walk out on me if I quit my job. Can I?"

After a moment, he said very carefully: "But of course! A woman with no dowry and no employment? It is not to be thought of!" He reached out and tucked back a wisp of hair that had fallen across her forehead. He said, "I have not asked that, *querida*." When she did not speak, he went on: "What do you wish me to say? That it would make me very happy? I am an old-fashioned male chauvinist pig, Latin variety, the very worst kind. Woman's place is in the kitchen. Knock them up and take their shoes away. Naturally I want you for myself, not for those people down in that madhouse office of yours. But I will gladly take you on any terms, because I do not care to be without you."

She drew a long breath and smiled. "You are a very satisfactory man, my dear. You not only have the right answers, you deliver them so eloquently."

He grinned. "Now you're making fun of me." After a moment, he asked, "There's trouble?"

"Nothing I can't handle," she said. "Of course, that business, that dreadful business at the Manatee Keys, didn't help my position any, but . . . I can handle it, but do I want to handle it?" Abruptly she found his hand and gripped it hard. "Philip, it's terrible, I'm just not *sure* any longer. I was so sure, so positive, but I'm not any longer. That girl today. Do I . . . do I have the right to destroy her with prison just to keep her from destroying herself with something else? It's an evil thing, I've never doubted that and I never will; but are we perhaps building a greater evil fighting it? You have to be *certain;* and after being part of the awful bureaucratic octopus that's grown up to combat it—a very expensive octopus, I might add—I'm not that certain any longer." She drew a long, ragged breath. "And I'm tired, Philip, very tired. Do you know what worried me most when I went on that crazy nautical expedition? I'd never been on a boat before and I didn't know what to wear! I've never played in my life, my adult life, do you realize that? I've never really relaxed, not once. It's all been a long grim fight to get away from Des Moines, Iowa; there's never been time for anything else. And it seemed so simple and straightforward all this time, but now I seem to have lost my way. I'd like to stop and . . . and kind of catch up with myself, if I may leave my options open. I mean, if you start boring me stiff—*when* you start boring me stiff—naturally I'll have to find something else to do to get me out of the lousy house."

"Naturally," he said gravely. "You will probably be looking for a new job within the month, but in the meantime I will be a very happy chauvinist pig. However, under the circumstances I do think we should regularize this unseemly and illicit relationship as soon as possible."

"Regularize," she murmured. "I like that. Let us by all means regularize." She allowed him, rising, to help her to her feet, and stood facing him, smiling. "And now that we are formally engaged, if that's what it is, may I kiss you, or will that arouse all kinds of unruly passions I'm not at the moment in a position to satisfy?" But their lips had barely touched when the telephone rang. Elizabeth drew back and said, "One day I'm going to drown that thing in the john." He watched her disappear into the bedroom; a moment later she was back in the doorway holding the phone at the end of its long spiral cord. "It's for you," she said, and there was concern in her eyes. "Washington," she said.

He nodded, coming forward to take the instrument. "Martin here," he said.

"Meriwether," said the familiar voice at the other end, and continued without further preliminaries: "P.P. has misplaced a twenty-thousand-ton tanker loaded with bunker fuel. Estimated position somewhere north of the Mona Passage, which leads, I am informed, from the Caribbean out into the Atlantic Ocean between the islands of Puerto Rico and Hispaniola. When last heard from she was a day out of Puerto la Cruz, Venezuela, bound for New York."

Martin asked, "P.P.?"

"Petrox Petroleum."

He was annoyed with himself; he should have remembered that. "Misplaced how?" he asked.

"They were having some instrument problems," Meriwether said, a thousand miles away. "Loran, if that means anything to you. It comes in two sizes, apparently, A and C. They'd been having chronic trouble with A. It was repaired on their last visit to New York, but it died again on their way to South America. That wasn't considered serious; Loran A seems to be practically obsolete. But apparently the disease was contagious; the Loran C went out right after they left South America; and that is their main navigational instrument, although the company representative assures me that they do have excellent radar and a good radio direction finder and that the officers are skilled at celestial navigation. However, the radio operator arranged to talk with a technician from the factory, hoping he might be able to suggest a temporary repair. When the man was ready and the call placed, however, the *Petrox Prince* didn't answer; and nothing has been heard from her since."

"And you say she should have negotiated this passage and be out in the Atlantic by this time?"

"Unless they got lost without this Loran gadget and ran on the rocks somewhere; but in that case you'd think they'd have got off a distress call, at least." There was a short pause. Meriwether went on: "It may not be of any significance, of course. Maybe their radio just went the way of their Loran and they're right on course, steaming up the Atlantic at fourteen knots. But since certain people we know seem to have been heading in that general direction, and since the tanker just happens to be the one on which our young friend, Harold Ullman, the photographer, spent a month quite recently, well, it just seemed like a coincidence of which you should be aware. Not that I can see, at the moment, how Ullman's boat ride could possibly be connected with—" Meriwether fell silent abruptly.

Martin said, "Yes, sir. If anybody wanted to take over a tanker, and needed all the information about the ship he could get, what better source than a photographer who just spent weeks on board recording every detail on film? The photographer or his pictures, maybe both. And I've already reported that Ullman and his sailboat are missing and that a small, sexy girl in a very, very scanty bikini was seen to go aboard just before he sailed away."

"And Mrs. McHugh hasn't been heard from either. We seem to be losing subjects right and left. . . . Wait a minute, I have another call."

Sitting there holding the phone, Martin looked up to see Elizabeth enter the bedroom, where he'd seated himself on the bed, with a cup of coffee. She smiled as she handed it to him.

"We'll have to set up a permanent disaster center one of these days," she murmured. "Coffee and doughnuts around the clock."

But Meriwether was back. "Confirmed," he said. "The U.S. Coast Guard is receiving a transmission from the Patriotic Front Liberation Party, or something like that, as represented by Don Jaime Colombo—well, he transmitted all his names and titles but I won't bother. He wants us to understand the situation clearly. He has two hostages, Ullman and McHugh, so that answers our questions concerning their whereabouts. How they fell into his hands has not yet been established. He has a tanker loaded with roughly five and a half million gallons of heavy oil—called Bunker C if it matters—and this ship has been carefully booby-trapped to sink and discharge its whole cargo if he pushes the button, which he will do without hesitation if anybody interferes with him in any way. He is headed for a point off the Florida Keys where the oil, if discharged, will travel up the Gulf Stream and, driven by the prevailing winds, distribute itself along the whole southeast coast of Florida, maybe farther—I have somebody checking to see just how much of a menace that is, but I suspect I know the answer and it isn't good."

Martin said, "So we have the threat. What is the demand?"

"Just a minute. Let me read some of these. . . ." After a moment, Meriwether resumed: "All right. He wants release of his daughter and her boyfriend Orosco. Release of the thirty-four men who were captured on Big Manatee Key. Return of all confiscated weapons and munitions. He suggests transfer arrangements as follows . . . well, that's still coming in. I have already made the suggestion that the ship should be found immediately and sunk in its present position. The answer to that was just put on my desk. State refuses to consider it because of the international complications."

"Yes, I can see that some of those island nations might object to having our oil dumped in their laps. Wherever you put it, it's going to smear somebody." Martin cleared his throat. The question had to be asked, although he was fairly sure he knew the answer. "You're not giving any consideration to the hostages, I gather?"

"My dear boy, they went of their own free will. We owe them nothing."

Martin drew a long breath. It was probably the way this war should be fought, but you didn't have to like it.

He said, "To get to Florida by the most direct route, if he's down there off the Antilles, he'll have to come up the channel between the Bahamas reefs and the Cuban coast. What can Castro's people be expected to do about it?"

"Nothing at all," Meriwether said dryly. "Unless they decide to give him a guard of honor, even though he's officially *persona non grata* to the present regime. Anything to get him through to where he can mess up our coastline rather than theirs. And the Bahamians undoubtedly feel the same way."

"Have you got an estimate of the possible damage?"

"Wait a minute. . . . Ah, there it is. Thank you, my dear." Meriwether's voice had dimmed; it became clear again. "Damage estimate. Heavy, according to one source. Irreparable, according to another, but these ecologists tend to exaggerate. It seems rather unlikely that the whole southeastern United States will melt away, or even become uninhabitable, under the influence of a little petroleum. I think we can say that it is not the end of the world, a holocaust, if I may retrieve that world from some people who seem to have appropriated it for their own use. It is, however, potentially a fairly serious disaster which we are obliged to prevent if at all possible, since it was the inefficiency of one of our people that turned this man loose, and the repercussions could be damaging."

Martin grimaced. Obviously Meriwether was really more concerned with the possible damage to the reputation of the agency he represented than to the state of Florida and neighboring areas. Well, that was the way things were and would probably always be.

He said, "Of course it's a bluff."

"What do you mean?"

"Hell, remember Ochsner," Martin said. "You invented the term yourself: the doomsday men. Don Jaime is making his death run, just as the Major did. Naturally, he'll do what he can for his daughter, while he can, and pry loose Orosco and those others just to spite us; but when the time comes Don Jaime Colombo is going to blow that ship regardless. And then he'll laugh and laugh, as he goes to hell, at the thought of all those fat, perfidious *Americanos* wading knee-deep in oil on all their expensive beaches. All the rest is really just razzle-dazzle to make sure we don't take some kind of drastic action before he gets that ship into position."

Meriwether was silent for a little; then he said, "Yes, the

thought had occurred to me. Do you think he could get his crew to go along with that suicidal program?"

"He's the Don. He doesn't ask them and he doesn't tell them. At least he doesn't tell them much, just enough to keep them quiet and docile as long as he needs them."

Meriwether said, "Then you do not feel it will help in any way to yield to his demands? He will simply take what we give him and fire his explosives anyway."

"That's my feeling," Martin said. "Of course I could be wrong."

"Let us hope you are not, my boy," Meriwether said, "because there is a final demand. . . . You understand, you are still in charge. I have no intention of telling you what to do. The decision is entirely yours."

"What is the final demand?"

But as he asked the question, he knew the answer; there was one more thing Don Jaime Colombo would obviously want. He listened to the voice from Washington, hearing it only distantly, bitterly aware that his hands had suddenly been tied. You could not gamble with disaster, even if that disaster was not of holocaust proportions, if the gamble conveniently saved your life. He was aware of Elizabeth watching him steadily as he laid the phone back into its cradle, drained his coffee and put the cup aside, and got up. She did not speak until he had finished putting on his coat.

Then she said, "Tell me, please."

He said, "It is too complicated, *querida*. Columbus has got himself a ship and is making certain threats and certain demands. I have to go see to it now."

"No," she said. Her voice was very soft. "You must not treat me like that." She took a step forward. She said, still quite softly, "Damn you, Philip, don't you dare to shelter me from what I ought to know! What do you think I am, a child? What does that man want? Tell me!"

He regarded her for a moment. "You know what he wants, Elizabeth."

She drew a long ragged breath. "Yes, of course. The Aristocratic Restoration Front, or the Fine Families Preservation Movement, or whatever that blue-blooded jerk calls it, requires delivery of the traitor Martinez, that hireling of the *Americanos,* to stand trial for the murder of . . ."

"Yes," he said. "I did kill the boy, remember?"

"But you're not *really* going to . . ." She stopped.

He said, "This is the lady who took a disastrous boat ride
479

for a sense of obligation after being thoroughly warned to stay home."

She licked her lips. "That's not fair. It's not the same—"

"As it turns out, it is exactly the same." He grimaced. "I am in charge. The decision is entirely mine, says my chief. A great *hombre*, my chief, and a very clever man. He knows, if he puts it like that, that I must do it. If he ordered me, I could refuse to be sacrificed by him; but if he leaves it to me I am obliged to sacrifice myself on the chance that it will help. But sacrifice is too big a word. The ship is still far down in the Atlantic; many things can happen—"

"Please let's dispense with the soothing syrup!" Elizabeth's voice was sharp. Then she sighed. "Philip."

"Yes?"

"I'm sorry. I always thought those whiny wives were for the birds. You know the ones I mean, on TV. They marry a cop or a soldier or an airplane pilot, and then spend the whole show bitching every damn time he goes out copping or soldiering or piloting. And now you've got me doing it, even before we're married, but I'm stopping right now. I'd just like you to do something for me, darling. Two things. Maybe three things."

"Tell me, *querida*."

"Well, I'm sick and tired of living in this man's shadow." Her voice was even. "You've got a gun, go out and shoot the sonofabitch so we can live in peace—at least until the next one comes along. That doesn't seem very much to ask, Philip. Just one little bullet, just for me?"

He watched her with understanding and appreciation. She was not, of course, really ordering him to commit homicide. What she was doing was letting him know that any action he found necessary to solve this problem would be accepted here without question; that he need not worry about her opinion of him because it was already formed and would not change.

He said very carefully: "Request noted. One Columbus, to be disposed of suitably. And then?"

Her breasts stirred the thin material of her blouse strongly; she had control of her voice but not of her breathing. She said, "I'm taking the day off. More if necessary. You did say the ship still has quite a ways to come, didn't you? I'll be out for a little while, there's some shopping I must do; otherwise I'll be right here. As long as it takes. It's not very far, Philip, and the phone works. If you need to eat, rest, or just talk, while it's going on, please come . . . home. That's what it's for, you know." After a moment, she said, "Sacrifices are spectacular, but they're not often essential. I would be very much upset, *really* upset if . . . if I thought I'd fallen in love with a man dumb enough to let himself get killed unnecessarily."

He started to speak and checked himself; the time for clever, careful words was past. Suddenly she was in his arms, clinging to him desperately, her mouth fiercely possessive as they kissed. At last she released him and stepped back. He left her without looking back. Outside the building it was cool for the season and the palms along the street rustled in the wind.

CHAPTER 44

July

Latitude 22°N; Longitude 69°W

Harold Ullman awoke with a start, shocked at himself for sleeping under these uncertain circumstances; but standing watch and watch on a small boat at sea you got in the habit of dropping off whenever the opportunity presented itself. He was aware of the small girl in his arms and he reflected wryly that she certainly knew how to get the most, if not the best, out of a man; he'd never considered himself a sexual prodigy, but maybe the imminence of death had helped. When you might have very little time left, there were things to be said for utilizing it in the most interesting manner possible.

But it had changed his feelings for her slightly. It was hard to feel real tenderness toward a girl who was so damned proficient at it; you couldn't help wondering how the kid had learned these things. But that was unfair, he'd been willing enough to take advantage of her experience, and being cooped up in this cabin with an immaculate virgin wouldn't have been much fun. . . . Suddenly he realized what had awakened him: there were people in the passageway outside. Hastily,

481

he slipped out of the bed and hauled on his shorts and jeans; he was just sitting down to put on his socks and shoes when the door opened.

"What is it, baby?" Vinnie murmured sleepily.

Then he felt her clutch his arm; he heard her gasp. He found himself staring in shocked—almost superstitious—horror as two men carried a barely conscious figure into the room between them: a woman whose face was a fright-mask of dried blood. For a moment it seemed to Harold Ullman that the dreadful photograph he'd left on board *Nancy Lou* had come to life; that the broken figure it represented had clawed its way out of its distant grave to catch him sitting guiltily half-dressed on a bed with a naked girl beside him. But it was not Nancy, of course. This young woman was silver-blonde where her hair was not darkly matted; and there was, he realized with relief, no real disfigurement except for an ugly little scalp wound, the source of all the gore.

"You will clean her up and bring her to her senses."

Columbus was standing in the doorway, watching his henchmen lead the hurt woman to the sofa. Then he looked toward the bed. He smiled thinly at the clothes strewn about the floor, the nudity of the girl, and the shirtless, shoeless, sockless condition of the man. Ullman knew a sudden respect for Vinnie's judgment. They could have done nothing more effective to disarm suspicion. Nobody was going to worry about dangerous schemes cooked up by a couple of prisoners who couldn't think of anything more sinister to do than climb into bed together.

Columbus said, "Take care of her. I may have need of her."

They sat there a moment after the door had closed. Abruptly, Vinnie giggled; there was a touch of hysteria in the sound.

"Jeez," she said, "that's Janet McHugh, the one I told you about. God knows what she's doing here, but don't you see what the crazy little freak is doing? He's making a collection of amateur navigators because the professional he's got is no damn good." After a moment she wrinkled her nose distastefully. "Jeez, she's not in very good shape, is she?"

Ullman got up reluctantly. It was obviously going to be an unpleasant and rather embarrassing task and he did not look forward to it. As Vinnie had said, the girl on the sofa was not in very good shape. She'd obviously lain helpless and untended for several days; her clothes were stained with vomit and badly soiled. It was certainly not a day for weak stomachs,

Ullman reflected irritably. They messed themselves in every conceivable way when they died violently; he'd already seen enough today to last him for a while. But at least this one wasn't quite dead.

The girl on the couch made a small moaning sound and stirred uneasily. Her eyes opened and looked straight at him. They were an odd blue-violet color, wide and distressed in her streaked face, apologizing for her disgusting condition, asking him to make allowances because she'd been hurt and unable to help herself: reminding him—although she could not know this—that he'd been an ocean away when another girl needed his help. Shocked at his own callousness, he stepped forward quickly and knelt beside her, followed by the big blue-violet eyes, which closed again wearily after he reached her as if reassured and comforted by his presence. It was just as well. He could make a better appraisal of the situation without those disturbing eyes watching him.

There was nothing he could do for the scalp wound, he decided. It should really have some stitches taken or a butterfly bandage applied to draw the edges together or it would leave a scar—that is, if the girl lived long enough for the cut to heal which, under the circumstances, seemed doubtful. Anyway, he had nothing with which to work and the injury seemed to be several days old already and taking care of itself pretty well, as far as he could tell through the matted hair. If a small scar did result, it would be hidden by the hair anyway. He was more worried about the rather extensive bruising and swelling of the area. She must have taken quite a heavy blow. The fact that she was still conscious only intermittently, and that she had been violently ill, judging by the state of her clothes, suggested that there could be a concussion or even a skull fracture. But there was nothing he could do about that, either. She'd have to make it on her own.

What he could do was get her cleaned up a little and wash off the dried blood that made her look like a ghastly clown; but there were some other matters to be taken care of first. He slipped the sheathed knife out from under the cushions on which she lay and strapped it above his ankle once more, put on his socks and shoes, also his shirt, and made sure his jeans hung well down to cover the weapon. Again it was like going to sea for the first time and working entirely from theory since he'd had no practice. He remembered something Bill

Simonds had said, instructing him, that had seemed odd at the time.

"You've got one advantage, pal, just one. You're an amateur. Amateurs are supposed to be softhearted. They won't expect you to be playing for keeps, not really. Even though you don't know what you're doing with that sharp thing—watch out you don't cut yourself—and we probably won't have time to teach you much, if you go in all the way right away, if you go in to *kill,* you may take them by surprise. If you try to be nice and humanitarian and sportsmanlike about it, you're dead."

It had made him feel a little funny to hear Bill say that, because it had never occurred to him that he wouldn't kill, this time, if he got the chance. Maybe there was something wrong with him by civilized standards, but after all, he'd had the point hammered home hard. That ragged creep in Puerto la Cruz would have had him when he hesitated, if the man had had any guts at all. And that grim night last fall when he'd had Uncle Hal's old shotgun in his hands, if he'd been allowed to shoot then—and maybe he had been a little slow pulling the trigger, at that—he might have gone to jail, and he'd probably still have wound up with a broken marriage since Nancy would have been horrified; but horrified or not she'd still be alive and he wouldn't be walking with a cane and seeing a slightly unfamiliar face in the mirror. No, you didn't have to tell Mister Ullman to ram it all the way home and turn it around twice, he thought grimly, as he made sure the knife was well concealed; just give him target and opportunity and he'd be on his bloody way. It was time to look at some of *their* gore for a change, preferably the blue stuff that presumably ran through Don Jaime Colombo's aristocratic veins. And speaking of gore. . . .

He glanced at the girl on the sofa; but there was still one more thing to be settled before he embarked on the cleanup campaign, and he said:

"Mrs. McHugh, can you hear me?"

The eyes opened again; and the head moved a little in a positive direction.

He said, "There are three of us in this cabin. If we all work together, pool our information and our resources, there may be a chance—not much of a chance, but a chance—that we can make it. If we waste time on a lot of accusations and recriminations we might as well cut our throats right now. Do you understand?"

She licked her lips. "Laura?"

"Oh, you recognized her." Ullman nodded. "Yes, Laura, but at the moment she's Lavinia Burnett and we call her Vinnie. It may even be her real name, if it matters. And when this is all over what you want to do about her is between the two of you, assuming you both survive. In the meantime, we're all in the same boat, if you'll excuse it, and who did what to whom in the past is the least of our worries. Agreed?"

"Are you sure—"

"Sure of her?" He grinned abruptly. "Am I sure of you, Mrs. McHugh? Maybe they just poured ketchup over you and put you in here to spy on us. I'm as sure of Vinnie as I need to be; let's call it a working hypothesis. Incidentally, my name is Ullman, Harold Ullman."

"Chub Cay," she whispered, her big eyes still intent on his face. For a moment he thought her mind was wandering, but she went on quickly: "Last November. Just before Thanksgiving. Chub Cay, in the Bahamas. A little sailboat called *Nancy Lou*. Right?"

She was watching him with painful eagerness now, and he realized that her head was hurting badly and that she was dreadfully afraid that there had been some damage inside. She was trying to prove to herself that she could still think and remember clearly despite the pain. For a moment he could not make the connection, but she had the name right, and *Nancy Lou* had certainly been in Chub Cay in November. Suddenly the picture came to him: a big sportfisherman expertly handled by a competent-looking young woman whose husband thanked him and called him "fella" when he helped with the dock lines. He should of course have recognized the boat, now lying alongside, but as a sailing man he always had some difficulty in telling all those cookie-cutter power craft apart.

"Chub Cay, right," he said. "You came in after we were docked. You took the last slip down by the sea wall."

He was trying to keep the shock out of his face and voice, now remembering clearly that tanned and healthy figure in shorts and jersey—maybe a little too sturdy and healthy by some standards. The wraithlike girl on the sofa gave a grim little laugh, obviously reading his thoughts.

"Seems like . . . every week is beat-up-on-Janet week anymore," she breathed. "Can't seem to go for a boat ride without . . . coming back an awful mess."

"How did you get here?" Ullman asked. "I mean, how did

you get back aboard. . . . That's your boat down there, isn't it? The one that was stolen from you? How did you wind up on her again?"

"Looking for her," Janet McHugh whispered. "Bought a . . . a little trawler to go . . . hunting. Nobody else would move a finger, damn them, all those bureaucrats shuffling papers. . . . Never mind. We cut them off at the pass. Catlin's Island. Only, too many on board and I . . . sick. Too weak to. . . . Stupid. Crew sold me out." Her eyes shifted to where Vinnie had come to stand nearby, casually zipping up her cutoffs as she listened. "I really pick them, don't I?" Janet McHugh said, softly and bitterly. "Mr. Ullman?"

"Yes."

"Favor?"

"Name it."

She made a distasteful gesture toward herself. "You . . . do it. Please. Don't let her . . . touch me." Her hand moved quickly in a gesture to forestall what he was about to say. "I know. I'll be good, I promise. Just this. I just . . . don't want her to touch me." The violet eyes were steady on his face. "Don't you see? I . . . I hate to be so corny, but I thought she was my friend."

He was aware of Vinnie turning sharply away and moving to the windows to look out. He said, "All right, Mrs. McHugh. Now, which way did you come in that trawler of yours?"

"Along the Cuban coast, that channel."

"Any problems?"

She shook her head minutely. "Not really. If I hadn't been so damn feeble. . . . Wind and current both against us, of course. They always are, coming this way. No problems with the Cubans, if that's what you mean. Why?"

"It looks as if I may have to navigate this tub; and I'm just guessing, but it seems likely that Columbus will be taking it back toward the U.S. Is there anything I ought to know?"

She said, "That's why they kept me around instead of drowning me; that Gonzaga can't find his ass with the toilet paper, pardon me. Beat up my boat on a simple run like that. But I guess it will be you, since you're in slightly better . . . navigating condition. Are you any good, Mr. Ullman?"

"I manage."

The big violet eyes studied him carefully out of the stained face. "All right," she whispered. "Remember. Cap Moreno light out. Cay Rojo light rescheduled, three flashes, fifteen-second period. And I've been thinking . . . if you've got the sneaky kind of mind I've got, Mr. Ullman, you should take a good look at Las Arenas Blancas on the chart and see if it doesn't give you ideas, six fathoms over the reef and shelving sand beyond." She drew a long breath. "Now, please. I don't know how you can stand me. I can't stand myself any longer. If you help me, I think I can manage to get out of these stinking rags and into a shower. Please?"

It took all her strength, but afterwards she insisted on waiting until a subdued Vinnie had finished washing out her undergarments and had wrung them out hard inside a dry towel, so she could put them on once more, saying that even if they were damp she preferred not to meet the end of the world—or even Mr. Jimmy Columbus—stark naked. Then she swayed and would have fallen if Ullman hadn't caught her. He carried her to the bed, laid her down gently, and covered her with the bedclothes, reflecting that he seemed to be getting into the habit of lugging young ladies around this cabin, destination bed, but there had been nothing very erotic about this latest chore—or perhaps it was just that, after Vinnie, he didn't have much left, for the moment, to be erotic with.

He stood over Janet McHugh, looking down, discovering that his real emotion had nothing whatever to do with sex; he'd simply found a strange and bitter satisfaction in being allowed to help this unknown young woman in a small way. It had been a little like being given a second chance after fumbling the first one. The eyes were closed and the face was very thin and fragile-looking, but clean now; and the fine hair clung damply to the nicely shaped head, although it was still clotted over the wound he'd been afraid to touch lest he start the bleeding again. It had been a very awkward experience to start with, of course, until he had caught a glimpse of her expression when she thought he wasn't looking, and had realized that she was by no means as painfully humiliated by the situation as he'd feared. Instead, she'd seemed to be wryly amused by her own ridiculously soiled and bloody condition and comical unsteadiness, and at the clumsy embarrassment of the man assisting her. All right. So the girl had a rather special sense of humor and could laugh at herself even under these outrageous circumstances. And he was an old married man and he'd seen a lady taking a shower before and perhaps even helped a little, just for fun. . . . He was aware that Vinnie had come to stand beside him.

"Her clothes ought to dry pretty fast, I wrung them out as

well as I could," Vinnie said. "Oh, damn it! I do the lousiest things to people, don't I?" She was looking down at the girl in the bed, and he saw that her eyes were wet.

"Don't take all the credit," he said. "You had a little help."

She turned to him with startling fierceness. "If a girl wants to indulge her fucking guilt complexes, what the hell is it to you? Just leave me alone, I . . ."

She stopped abruptly as the door opened without warning. Jesus Cardenas entered, with Bolo one step behind. The smaller man came forward and looked at Janet McHugh.

"*Qué pasa?*"

Ullman shook his head. "Not too good. We got her fixed up a bit, as you can see, but I'm afraid somebody just got too damned strong with a blackjack or something; she isn't really focusing yet."

Cardenas nodded. "We will leave her for the moment. Bring the little girl. Come."

Moments later, emerging from the narrow stairs into the passage between the navigation room and the radio room, Ullman heard the radio crackling. Columbus was standing in the doorway speaking to someone inside.

"It is obvious that they merely want it repeated so they can use their radio direction finders," he was saying. "As if it matters if they find us now; we are ready for them now! So give them the list again if it pleases them." He turned and saw the prisoners and escort. "Take them into the navigation room first, Jesus."

"*Sí, patrón.*"

It seemed strange to Harold Ullman to enter the familiar cubicle in which he'd spent considerable time on his previous voyage on this ship watching the officers at work. The stout mustached man in dirty khakis and a greasy fishing cap, whom he'd identified as Captain Ramiro Gonzaga, was inside, studying a chart without enthusiasm. Although the room itself was relatively small, the chart table was huge by yachting standards, taking up one whole wall. At Columbus' gesture, Ullman stepped forward and, disregarding Gonzaga, looked at the chart lying there, labeled "Straits of Florida and Approaches." It showed Cuba, most of the Bahamas, and southern Florida.

It took him only a glance to spot the names Janet McHugh had whispered. They were all located where the open water between the shallow Bahamas bank to the north and the solid Cuban land mass to the south tapered, like an irregular funnel, into the channel that ran along the Cuban coast for roughly a hundred miles: the Old Bahama Channel. At the entrance to this slot, the light on Cap Moreno on the Cuban side faced the light on Cay Rojo in Bahamas waters. North of Rojo, which seemed to be little more than a lump of coral, a barely dry part of the barrier reef, was the extensive shoal area known as Las Arenas Blancas, the White Sands. Ullman wondered idly how many other White Sands there were in the world. You could start counting with the well-known testing ground in New Mexico.

He could hear the radio operator across the way speaking distinctly but with a pronounced accent: "The following prisoners of Yankee oppression to be liberated and permitted to proceed to the specified rendezvous in good health in a suitable vessel as specified with equipment as specified, without surveillance. The names follow: Columbus Francesca, Orosco Pedro, Carstairs Peter, Mondragon William, Deutsch Hans, Jaramillo Eugenio . . ." Ullman lost some of it, studying the chart before him, but the final sentence caught his attention: "Also to be delivered up to counterrevolutionary justice: the traitor-murderer Martinez Felipe, who hides under the Yankee alias Philip Martin."

It was an interesting sidelight, and it indicated that the tall man he knew might be in a tough spot, but then, who wasn't? Ullman was aware that Columbus had moved up beside him.

"Here is the rendezvous." The well-manicured tip of a long finger indicated a heavily circled dot in the Straits of Florida south of Key West. After pausing a minute there, the finger moved to the east. "Our position is here, off the edge of this chart, but we should be able to reach the desired spot in two days by the use of this passage." The slender fingertip caressed the Old Bahama Channel. "However, our brave captain claims that under the present circumstances—he has just permitted the boat for which he was made responsible to roll itself against the ship hard enough to damage its radar antenna—he claims that without radar it is impossible for him to bring the ship safely into American waters by this route."

He glanced sharply at Gonzaga, who licked his lips weakly under the fierce black mustache. "I tell you, *Señor*, I cannot do it, not that narrow channel, not this big ship. Not in the dark with all our radars broken; and by the time we reach there tomorrow it will be dark."

489

"There are lighthouses to show the way," Columbus said, pointing once more. "Here and here. And here. At least you told me once those colored marks indicate lights. You can navigate by those, can you not?"

"Bah!" Gonzaga said with sudden strength. "Bahamas navigation lights function sometimes and sometimes not, *quién sabe?* Cuban lights they turn off as they please so they will not be invaded. Look what it says right on the chart: 'CAUTION, many lights along the Cuban coast have been reported to be irregular or extinguished.' I spit upon their lights, *Señor!* I will not do it. You will kill me if I fail and I will fail, so kill me now!"

Ullman could not help feeling some sympathy for the stout charter-boat captain, obviously a fearful and uncertain man who was being asked to perform beyond his courage and skill. Then Columbus inclined his head slightly, and Bolo stepped forward and struck. Gonzaga staggered back and went down, and sat helplessly, running a hand across his mouth and looking at the blood smeared across his palm by a split lip, quickly swelling.

Columbus turned his back on the fallen man. "Jesus. Throw this incompetent pig aboard the fishing boat. Put a reliable man with him and tell that man to make certain Gonzaga follows close and comes in fast to take us off this ship when we call." Columbus turned to Ullman. "You will navigate here."

Ullman put a look of consternation on his face. "Me? You've got rocks in the head, man! I never navigated anything bigger than a—"

Columbus took a threatening step forward. "You will address me with respect, *Señor.* And you will not play games with me. We know you spent considerable time on this ship quite recently. We know you are a sailor. We know you brought your own little boat straight here from the north; there is no doubt that you can find your way across the water if you wish. Must I threaten you?" Casually, he reached out and backhanded Vinnie Burnett across the face. "You like this little girl, *sí?* To me she is dirt, treacherous dirt. Shall I let the men have her; let them pass her from one to the next—by lot, perhaps? They have been many days at sea; they will be happy to share her. When she is worn out and ceases to give satisfaction, by that time I should have thought of an interesting way of disposing of their leavings. . . . Bolo!"

Ullman said quickly, "Never mind. I get the point." Perhaps he should have resisted a little longer to carry conviction; but he was getting very tired of looking at the damaged faces and cracked heads and worse this arrogant man kept leaving in his wake. "Leave her alone! What do you want me to do?"

Columbus studied him suspiciously. "You understand, Bolo will be with her every minute. He will have his knife. If the slightest thing goes wrong, he will use it. Any tricks, *Señor*, and her death will be your doing."

Ullman said, "I've got the picture, Mister; I've got it sharp and clear. Now if you'll just have one of your boys hand me the sextant the chief mate used to keep in that cabinet behind you—that big wooden box, right—and have somebody stand by to take time off that chronometer, preferably somebody who understands a little English, I'll make a start at finding out where we really are."

He didn't look directly at Vinnie Burnett, who was rubbing her bruised cheek with a convincing appearance of distress, but he saw one eyelid flutter faintly as he turned away. The crazy kid was, he realized, reminding him that she had anticipated this scene in practically every detail, although he had not put on quite as dramatic a performance as she'd advised.

He remembered what she'd asked him to do if the opportunity presented itself; but dismissed the thought, or tried to. Maybe it wouldn't come to that. Maybe the authorities—some authorities—would take a hand, or the problem would solve itself some other way. He hoped to God it would. But it was, he reflected, a good thing that navigation was like marksmanship, simple to those who knew it but incomprehensible to those who didn't. Of course, navigators had been making a deliberate mystery of it since the dawn of seamanship. Back in the old tough square-rigger days, many a potential mutiny never materialized simply because the aggrieved seamen had been carefully indoctrinated to believe that they were totally dependent on the officers to get them home; and of course he was going through exactly the same mystification act here. He knew perfectly well where they were. They couldn't have drifted very far from the last position he'd established on *Nancy Lou*. There was no need for any sextant mumbo-jumbo; if they headed south and a little west the coast of Hispaniola should show up shortly and after that there would be nothing much to do but follow it.

However, the sextant was an impressive instrument and the business of timing the sights properly made a fairly awe-inspiring ceremony, followed by the ritual of consulting those large religious tomes, the *Nautical Almanac* and the Sight Reduction Tables. By the time he got through, and had his line of position, he thought he had convinced everybody, even Columbus, that he was a high priest of a sacred and essential mystery, a man they couldn't possibly do without. When he then set the course and, after they were under way at last, gambled on predicting the time the lookout would sight the coast ahead, and hit it within ten minutes, he knew his indispensability was confirmed. Later, having set a new and more westerly course to parallel the distant shore, he pointed out that he'd need some food and rest if he was to navigate through the night ahead; and he was escorted, with Vinnie, back to the stateroom two decks below. A few minutes later the guard at the door admitted a man carrying a tray, which he placed on the low table by the sofa. Apparently, the ship's galley was back in commission.

On the bridge, it had seemed like a rather intriguing and entertaining contest. Strangely, it seemed more real and serious down in this cabin with the hurt girl's presence as a reminder of the stakes involved. Janet McHugh, aroused by their return, sat up and reached for the bowl of soup Ullman brought her, but he shook his head.

"Not like that, Mrs. McHugh. You're a very sick girl; practically helpless. You can hardly swallow the stuff even if I feed it to you slowly."

"But I'm really feeling much better. . . . Oh."

"Right. Let's hope they come popping in the way they do and see me spooning it into you tenderly; we can't have anybody thinking you're getting well, can we?" He grinned. "I think I've got the situation pretty well under control up there, but if you start looking too damn strong and healthy they may figure a way of playing one of us great navigators against the other."

It made him feel a little odd, sitting on the side of the bed spoon-feeding a young woman in her underwear; he couldn't help noticing that her shoulders, though thin, were strongly formed and nicely shaped. Maybe the Vinnie treatment was wearing off, he reflected; and the thought made him glance toward the smaller girl, seated on the sofa and eating hungrily; but there was a sharpness in the look she threw him that indicated that she wasn't entirely happy with the situation.

She'd had a man all to herself in here and now she had to share him with a not altogether unattractive invalid. But the darkness in her eyes represented something deeper than this mechanical jealousy, reminding him—most of the time she made it easy to forget—that this was still a girl who had no future, no matter what happened here; a girl with a terminal case of guilt more deadly than cancer and quite aware of it.

Hunger satisfied, they discussed their plans briefly, but there wasn't much to discuss.

"Did you get a good look at the firing gadget?" Ullman asked Vinnie. "You were closer, where Bolo had you sitting. I didn't dare show any interest. I don't want to get them suspicious of me."

"You mean that black box on the ledge just back of the windshield or whatever you call it? Starboard side? With all the wires?" She shrugged. "What can I tell you? It's just a black plastic box. There's some kind of a sliding cover. I suppose it protects the switch or button or whatever makes things go bang, but I wasn't about to investigate, either. That creep would have cut my hand off."

That was about the extent of the conference. There was actually very little to talk about. There was nothing to do but play it by ear; objective, the destruction of the enemy and the frustration of his plans, but if you talked about it like that—three unarmed prisoners, one injured—the ultimate hopelessness of it became discouragingly apparent, so it was really better not to talk. Ullman appropriated the sofa for a nap, pointing out that the bed was already spoken for, and that Vinnie was a better size for the cabin's one large upholstered chair. It occurred to him, as he settled himself to rest, that he'd picked his company well. It did not seem to occur to either girl to launch into the standard, shrill, movie-ingenue routine: *how-can-you-sleep-at-a-time-like-this?* Both knew, apparently, that the best thing a man could do at a time like this was sleep, so that he would be fresh and ready to take advantage of any break that presented itself.

Surprisingly, he did fall asleep again; when he awoke he thought for a moment that he was back on *Nancy Lou* with Vinnie shaking him awake for his watch on deck. It was Vinnie all right but this was a different ship and Jesus Cardenas stood behind her.

"It will be dark soon, *Señor*," the little Cuban said. "The *patrón* wants you on the bridge. You, too, *Señorita*."

Vinnie made a face at him. "Sure, I'm the insurance policy,

aren't I?" Her eyes found Ullman's face. "I hope you've got that clearly in mind, baby. No fucking tricks, damn you. Have you seen the size of the shiv that moron carries, and sharp, my God!"

The second act of the Great Navigator drama went off, Ullman thought, even better than the first. He tested them all by performing a round of star sights for them as dusk came. They passed the test; they did not question why a man would, ridiculously, be shooting the stars within sight of land. It did not matter tonight but it set the scene, so to speak; and he prayed for a clear sky and a good horizon the following evening. There followed a whole night of flashy piloting with a multitude of impressive lines and circled dots drawn on the chart to show their hour-by-hour progress along the Hispaniola coast and finally, after a great deal of spectacular and unnecessary work with the bridge pelorus— big-ship navigators really had it easy with their steady vessels and elaborate equipment—he gave them another prediction: at daybreak they would be looking into the open Windward Passage, the next one west from Mona, and of course they were.

With full daylight, Cuba appeared, a low gray mass off the port bow. Ullman was aware of an odd sense of satisfaction as he watched the landfall from the high bridge of the big ship for which he was now responsible in this peculiar way. It was, he supposed, kind of like playing pro ball after making a reasonable record on the college team. As Vinnie had said, no real sailor ever got on board any craft without asking himself if he could handle it. Well, he had his answer, at least so far; but personal satisfaction wasn't exactly what he was there for.

There had been planes overhead from time to time. He'd wondered if they were U.S. or Cuban; but there was no doubt about the gray-green gunboat that came racing out from the shore that was now rising out of the sea to port, extending endlessly toward the horizon. The craft was an odd combination of speedboat and battleship. There were domed gun-turrets fore and aft on a fat sixty-foot hull with a broad stern sporting enormous exhausts for the big diesels that threw black clouds of smoke when somebody got gay with the throttles. There was something about the Latin temperament, Ullman reflected, that just couldn't resist jazzing any motor no matter how big. Columbus, who'd gone below for a while, could now be heard in the radio room speaking rapid Spanish. After a little, the junior-grade dreadnought sheered away and roared back toward the coast at a good thirty knots, leaving a white curling wake astern. Ullman's crippled Spanish had made nothing of what little of the one-sided conversation he'd managed to hear, and nobody offered to translate for him.

Columbus went back below. It was a long day, even with an occasional rest, and now there was always one of the Cuban patrol craft in sight, shadowing them, but they were paid no more official visits. Astern, the sportfisherman, looking battered and disheveled with its damaged tuna tower—thank God for that negligence—followed docilely in their wake. The evening turned out to be beautiful from every point of view including the navigational one. As the sky darkened and the stars appeared, Ullman went to the sextant again and performed his witch-doctor routine again, and scratched his head and frowned over the results. He repeated his calculations with a worried look on his face, aware that Columbus had returned to watch him.

"What is the difficulty, Señor?"

"Current," Ullman said gravely. He tried to make it sound as if they had contracted a dangerous disease.

"Current?"

"Yes, it's a big problem around these banks and reefs, always. The old Spanish galleons were forever being swept onto the coral by unexpected currents. Of course, they were slow and clumsy and dependent on the wind, and we've got ten thousand horsepower, but still. . . . We're supposed to be here," he said, pointing to the line he'd drawn on the chart representing the desired course into the channel ahead. "Actually, we've been set to port quite a bit, shorewards, to here. We're getting too damn close and we'd better head out a little. . . . Course two-eighty. Pass it along to the helmsman, you're closer."

He hadn't really expected it to work. It had seemed pretty childish, but worth a try. Actually it worked beautifully: Columbus instinctively opened his mouth, turning to obey. Then he realized what he was doing, swung back angrily, and lashed out with his open hand.

"You do not give me orders! I give the orders here!"

Ullman drew the back of his hand across his bruised lips, stepping forward. "Listen, you arrogant sonofabitch, I'll run your fucking ship for you, under duress, but I'll be damned if I'll take your aristocratic crap—" A gun barrel touched him in the back.

"You will take whatever *Señor* Columbus wishes you to take," said the voice of Jesus Cardenas behind him.

"Well, instruct the *Señor*, with the utmost respect of course, that while he worries about his goddamn status or whatever the hell it is he's worrying about, this ship is getting closer to the rocks by the minute! Now, shall we navigate or shall we be polite? It's all the same to me."

"What was the number?"

"Course two eight oh, two hundred and eighty, and take that goddamn cannon out of my back before I make you shoot it!" Ullman snorted angrily. "Hell, what's the use of trying to be sensible and cooperative if I'm going to get punched and poked anyway. . . ."

He saw Vinnie watching him, pokerfaced, but he thought there was a glint of approval in her eyes. By the time everything had settled down, and the course had been changed, nobody bothered to check on the rather peculiar calculations that had led to the alteration, although the discrepancy could have been spotted by anyone who could add and subtract. Later, after entering the erroneous position in the ship's log, Ullman casually wadded up the work sheet involved and dropped it into the wastebasket, relieved to have it out of sight. He knew that he had gained by the exchange. They'd been getting a little suspicious of his helpful attitude; the flash of anger had reassured them. If he'd really been trying to trick them, he'd have controlled it.

"Cardenas," he said.

"Señor."

"I don't want to get socked again so I'm not going to ask *him*, but will you please tell the lookout to let me know as soon as he spots this light here, Cap Moreno. He should pick it up some time in the next two-three hours. Three flashes every fifteen seconds."

Columbus was back beside them. "That is not what it says on the chart!"

"That's what it says two decks down," Ullman retorted. "That blonde woman with the damaged head. She's just been through that way in her own boat—"

"She would not answer our questions."

"You didn't give her a bath and feed her soup with a spoon.

She thinks I'm nice. The Cubans are always switching the signals; they've apparently changed this one recently."

"And this lighthouse on the north side of the channel entrance, Cay Rojo?"

"Oh, that's out, like half the lights in the Bahamas." Ullman hoped his voice sounded sufficiently casual. "So unless there are any objections, or anybody wants to punch anybody in the mouth just for fun, I'll figure on clearing Cap Moreno right about here, leaving it roughly two miles to port. Satisfactory?"

Columbus was looking at him sharply. "For the sake of the little girl sitting over there, we all hope it is satisfactory, Señor Ullman."

It was full dark now and the *Petrox Prince* rumbled on through the night with her outsize diesel turning her sixteen-foot propeller at a hundred revolutions per minute for a cruising speed of fourteen knots. Technically, she was operating illegally since nobody had bothered to turn on the running lights, but under the circumstances it seemed a small illegality not worth mentioning. He was, Ullman reflected, committed now. There was a kind of scary fascination to it, all that navigational razzle-dazzle and the plausible lies told with a straight face and lining up in his head what he'd have to do when the time came; but it was too bad in a way. She was a fine ship and it seemed unlikely anybody would ever give him another one this big to play with. Sorry, old lady, he thought, it can't be helped and if it works right you shouldn't be hurt too badly. And then, of course, there was Vinnie, but he did not want to think of that.

The lookout picked up the light shortly after eleven o'clock, written twenty-three-hundred in the log. Going out onto the wing of the bridge to study it, Ullman glanced astern. *Stream Hunter* alias *Lolita* was still following obediently in their wake. And what do you bet, he thought, that the fat slob is doing just that and nothing else, no piloting of his own—and how many destroyers was it they put ashore near Cape Arguello following the leader blindly like that? Well, what are you complaining about? Do you want Gonzaga to wake up and get on the horn and ask if we're absolutely sure we have the right lighthouse in the right place?

It was time to plan the next step, as far as it could be planned. He went back inside, leaving the lookout alone out there. One, he thought. And the helmsman, two. And Columbus, Bolo, and Cardenas. . . . Totally impossible. It was a job for Superman with an assist from Wonder Woman. Not a hundred and-sixty-pound amateur with a weak leg and a cheap South American knife. If he could just get hold of one of the Uzis in the confusion and figure out how to use it, fast, he might stand a chance; but Cardenas had the only one on the bridge and Cardenas was the toughest and most competent of the lot. Okay. So you're not going to make it, none of us is going to make it; all you can do is start whittling and keep at it as long as you last. But at least you can console yourself with the fact that neither is Columbus going to make it if nothing happens in the next half-hour. The next twenty minutes. The next ten minutes. . . .

Ullman placed himself casually behind the helmsman. Five minutes left to the point of no return. He was aware of Vinnie watching him but he did not let himself be seen looking her way; there could be no betraying signals yet. . . . Zero, he thought. Unless I've miscalculated badly, it should be done now, for all practical purposes. She takes three nautical miles to stop at fourteen knots. Even backing hard they can't halt her now. And if they try to turn her, with the radius she needs, they'll rip her wide open on the coral on either hand.

"Señor, señor!"

That was the lookout, waking up at last. Columbus and Cardenas rushed out onto the port wing of the bridge to look ahead where he was pointing. Ullman saw Vinnie's face, pale in the dusk of the darkened bridge; and he gave her a definite nod to let her know he'd taken her at her word and it was really coming; and her eyes were very bright and not frightened at all.

"Back!" That was Cardenas in the bridge doorway. "Your Lovato! The engine control! Back! Reverse!"

Then the little *mayordomo* was yanked out of the doorway by Columbus, who spun him aside heedlessly; and there was no doubt at all in Ullman's mind where Don Jaime was heading with such determination, ruthlessly brushing aside all obstacles in his path without apology. Ullman remembered a warning phrase used by the agent, Martin, that had seemed childishly melodramatic at the time. The doomsday men. It seemed neither childish nor melodramatic now. Columbus' purpose was clear. Faced with disaster to his plans, whatever they really were, he was about to blow up the *Petrox Prince*, now. Perhaps they were not quite in the right position, the one that had been so carefully calculated, from which the most damage could be done, but the ship could still be blasted apart with its cargo released. The resulting slick would drift across the Bahamas banks and might still reach the Florida Straits and the Gulf Stream, and the U.S. coast: millions of gallons of oil leaving an endless trail of destruction. After all, the stuff from that blown-out well in the Gulf of Campeche, off Yucatan, had managed to drift clear across the Gulf of Mexico to Texas.

But first things first, Ullman reminded himself sharply; the engine-room telegraph must not be touched until the thing was certain. As the helmsman started to obey Cardenas' order, Ullman drove the Venzuelan knife in hard, clear to the hilt. Then he saw that the sea ahead was eerily pale less than a mile ahead of the onrushing ship. Okay. The White Sands. Nobody could stop or turn her now. But the knife had jammed in a rib or something and would not come free—even in that moment, Ullman was rather surprised at the cold inhumanity of his thoughts; his first reaction was that the dying man before him was being damned inconsiderate, refusing to release the weapon that had killed him.

But too much time had gone by. Columbus was getting too close to the black box at the starboard side of the bridge. As Ullman released the bloody handle of the knife and started that way, a small figure eluded the hulking shape of Bolo and made the tackle, bringing Columbus down. Ullman heard Bolo give an outraged bellow of protest against the indignity inflicted upon the person of his Don; and Vinnie was snatched away, struggling helplessly in the moron's grasp. Columbus regained his feet, but the delay had been enough. Ullman charged across the intervening space and crashed into him and carried him past the firing mechanism, through the door beyond, and out onto the starboard wing of the bridge.

There was amazing power in Don Jaime's misproportioned body as he tried to fight his way back to the firing switch. For a moment it was all Ullman could do to hang on, taking considerable punishment. Then a glance showed him that the pale water of the shoals was almost under the ship's bow. A small part of his brain was working coldly and efficiently in the midst of all the confusion; and he knew exactly what was coming and how to take advantage of it. He went to his knees, clutching the straining, struggling, fanatic figure below the hips, riding out the storm of unskilled blows—it was probably the only time in his life that Don Jaime Fernando Colombo y Menendez had ever had to do his own fighting, Ullman reflected grimly. Then the *Petrox Prince* drove onto *Las Arenas Blancas* at fourteen knots.

Already braced against the bridge railing, Ullman felt himself pressed against it violently by the impact. Inside the enclosed bridge and on the far wing, he was aware, everyone was being thrown about helplessly. Now was the time and, still braced against the low, white-painted wall of steel, Ullman tightened his grip about his enemy and straightened up, lifting Columbus off his feet, hearing him scream with sudden understanding, feeling him claw for a handhold somewhere, anywhere, as he was raised into the air. The ship lurched, twenty thousand deadweight tons of steel and oil protesting angrily against being brought to a halt in this sudden and unseemly fashion. Ullman made a final effort, heaving his burden higher. He felt it snatched away from him by the tremendous forces of deceleration. His shirt ripped away in Columbus' grasp; he heard a thin wailing cry as the man's own momentum carried him over the bridge railing to fall to his death on the ship's steel deck far below.

There was a great deal of violent, earthquake motion and an endless roaring rumbling sound. Then came a sudden stillness broken only by the steady distant pounding of the big diesel, now turning without effect. Ullman turned toward the bridge door feeling slack and drained. He was panting from his efforts, but he knew it was not the loss of breath that had hit him so hard, but the loss of hate. The job he'd come here for was done and there seemed to be nothing left to live for. Columbus was gone, and in going he had taken Nancy away for good. There was nothing more, Ullman reflected grimly, that he could do for her and, to be honest, she probably would not have appreciated greatly what he had just done, although, perhaps, after what she'd been driven to do, herself, she might have understood. . . .

"Baby, watch out!"

Bolo, he thought dully, I can't handle Bolo without a weapon, hell, I probably can't handle him with one. And where the hell is Cardenas? And the lookout, what about the lookout? It seemed as if an age had passed since the man had first cried out in warning; and Ullman's thoughts were slow and sluggish as he moved through the doorway, because the thing had to be finished now even though there could be only one ending. Bolo was there, coming toward him; and behind the hulking, advancing figure Ullman saw Vinnie hunched over and hugging herself tightly as if she were terribly cold, but he knew it was not a chill. Bolo was grinning happily, and the knife in his hand was no longer bright but dark and wet.

"Tome el cuchillo, Gringo," he said, pointing down.

It was crazy, it was ridiculous, but it was true. The moron was waiting chivalrously, childishly, wanting a fair fight in which to display his skill; and there at Ullman's feet was the body of the helmsman where it had been flung in the moment of grounding. From the back still protruded the hilt of the cheap Venezuelan knife. Feeling like a man in a dream, Ullman reached down and wrenched the weapon free. He heard himself speak with similar idiotic courtesy.

"Ready when you are, *amigo.*"

"Bueno."

There were some moments of wary shuffling as they maneuvered on the cluttered bridge. Ullman remembered again the advice of the doomed ex-Marine mercenary named O'Brien; but this was not a timid gutter-rat like the one in Puerto la Cruz. He knew he could not possibly survive even the first contact unless . . .

"Remember," Bill Simonds had said, "in a real pinch it's your right arm and the knife you save, you need them. Your left arm, to hell with it. Wrap something around it if you can, but to hell with it. Better that than your throat or guts, okay?"

There were cases on record of that deliberate sacrifice play; and he watched Bolo poise himself for the attack and move in fast. Ullman clenched his teeth against the pain to come and carefully intercepted the bloody knife as it drove toward him, and then flung out his left arm, now transfixed by the blade, as he stepped forward and, avoiding Bolo's defending hand, lunged low with his own knife, edge up, and ripped upward. It wasn't much of a weapon, soft stuff that would take an edge fast and lose it faster, and it had already encountered bone once tonight, but it was still sharp enough. It went in with surprising ease and slashed like a razor or a surgeon's scalpel. Ullman threw himself back and saw Bolo, shocked, look down and let out an animal-like moan at what he saw. Holding himself together with both hands, or trying to, he staggered back against one of the radar cabinets and sat down heavily while his life ran out on the deck all around him.

It wasn't pretty, but it took one more out of action. Three down, Ullman thought, you're just a little one-man massacre tonight, aren't you, Buster? But the bridge was reeling around him and he leaned dizzily against the engine-room telegraph, sick with the pain of his left arm, which still held Bolo's knife. He didn't know if he had the courage to pull it out, and there was still Cardenas, wherever he'd got to, and the lookout; but then he saw the lookout crumpled on the far port wing of the bridge. Apparently, he'd got thrown against something violently enough to render him unconscious. Vinnie was down, too, and he should do something about that, Ullman thought vaguely; but he was a sailor and his ship was suffering. He reached out and slammed the telegraph lever to STOP. Apparently, somebody was still functioning below; the ugly useless vibration ceased.

Then Cardenas was in the doorway with blood on his face and the automatic weapon steady in his hands and he, Harold Ullman, was about to die, but it did not seem tremendously important since he'd expected nothing else. He heard the gun start to speak and waited for the shock of the bullets and nothing happened. After a little, Cardenas dropped the gun. After a little longer, he fell on top of it.

Ullman waited, uncomprehending. A voice spoke, telling him not to shoot. This was nonsense; he had nothing to shoot with. A woman in dungarees appeared in the doorway carrying a weapon identical to the one Cardenas had dropped. She looked a bit like a tough female revolutionary or a female Israeli soldier, except that they were seldom so blonde.

Janet McHugh said calmly, "You know, I never fired one of these things before, Mr. Ullman."

Then she fainted.

CHAPTER 45

August

Latitude 24°N; Longitude 82°W

Usually, early-season hurricanes were spawned in the distant reaches of the Gulf of Mexico and did not make news in Key West. This one, however, was a maverick roaming farther east than customary at this time of year; it had done some damage in Puerto Rico and had briefly threatened to come roaring up the line toward the Keys, before turning out to sea, so it got a little publicity. Mentioned also in the newspaper story was the fact that the salvage job on the tanker *Petrox Prince,* recently grounded under rather dramatic circumstances on the Great Bahama Bank north of Cuba, had been completed before the edge of the storm brushed the area; the cargo had been lightered off and the ship refloated successfully.

Okay, old lady, Harold Ullman thought, sipping his after-lunch coffee alone, I promised you wouldn't be hurt too badly. Be good.

But *Nancy Lou* was gone. She had not been found before the storm and there was no chance in the world that, drifting untended with ports and hatches open, helplessly lashed to a larger craft half full of water, she could have survived it. A clean sweep, Harold Ullman thought; and maybe it was just as well. The boat had borne Nancy's name and Nancy had been a part of her almost from the beginning, strange for a girl who hadn't liked boats very much. Now they no longer existed, girl or boat. . . .

"Ullman." He didn't recognize the voice. "Harold Ullman?"

He could not help an instinctive start; or the instinctive movement of his hand toward the knife that no longer lived against his ankle; but this was a peaceful Key West restaurant and the two people coming toward him were no threat. The girl was large but well-proportioned in her neat slacks and boyish shirt. She had soft brown hair and, strangely for such a big girl, a rather sweet face, particularly when she smiled. Ullman did not think he had ever seen her before. He would, he thought, have remembered the smile even if he forgot the girl.

The man was not much taller. He was moderately good-looking in a lean and suntanned way that might be attractive to women but was not offensive to men; he was wearing jeans and a blue jersey. Ullman recognized him but had trouble, for a moment, in remembering the name. Fenwick. Paul Fenwick. Dr. Paul Fenwick of the catamaran *Haleakala,* which had been hijacked. . . . Dr. Paul Fenwick, who had sailed away from Boot Key Marina with a small girl who'd called herself, at that time, Lucia Barnes, and come back with a big girl named Procter, Wilhelmina Procter. They were all public figures now, Ullman thought wryly; and everybody knew everything about everybody. The shook hands, and Ullman was introduced to Mrs. Fenwick, and the Fenwicks said thanks they couldn't join him, they'd just stepped out to get some lunch because the galley stove had gone on strike, but they'd finished eating and now they had to get back to the baby. Hiring sitters, even just the kid from the neighboring boat, was awfully expensive these days.

"I guess you had a pretty rough time," Fenwick said with a glance at the sling that supported Ullman's left arm. "We read about it in the papers."

"You two had quite a boat ride yourselves, I understand," Ullman said.

"Well, we're staying over at the marina," Fenwick said. *"Faraway,* Valiant 40. We'll be heading down into the Caribbean as soon as the hurricanes go away this fall; then maybe west to Panama. But we'll be here for a while yet; come by and see us."

"I'll do that."

But they all knew that he wouldn't; and that he wasn't really wanted. He had been part of it, as they had; and they all wanted to get away from it now. Fenwick had merely stopped because they'd once had boats in the same marina and it would have seemed too unfriendly to walk by without speaking.

"It's nice to have met you, Mr. Ullman," Billie Fenwick said politely.

He watched them leave, and remembered the quite lovely Mrs. Fenwick who had died of cancer; then he saw Fenwick speak as he held the door for the girl accompanying him. He saw Billie Fenwick smile at her husband in that special way she had; and Ullman decided that Dr. Fenwick was really a very fortunate man. But he was certainly not going to visit them on their boat, the *Faraway,* and look at the man and wonder just what he remembered about a small strange girl who had died, knowing that the man was wondering exactly the same thing about him.

Ullman finished his coffee and paid for his meal and went out to the rental car parked in front. Soon he'd have to grab a bus to Marathon and retrieve his own vehicle, still waiting at the marina there; but first there was something he had to get settled here in Key West. Talking them into letting him hire a car, with his injured arm, had been a little difficult; but paying for it wasn't going to be as hard as he'd expected. Bartholomew, whom he'd summoned in haste from the hospital where he'd been taken after being brought ashore, had done noble work, retrieving the whole set of tanker slides from the authorities—they'd been found, actually, in the seabag of the man called Regan—and getting them to the proper publications while the story was still hot and good pictures of the *Petrox Prince* were otherwise unavailable. So he wasn't in too bad shape financially, and the agent had forgiven him and hinted that, with the current interest, there'd be more work for him as soon as he could replace his lost equipment and get his arm into shape. There was also the insurance for *Nancy Lou,* and the cameras that had been on board, although the companies—there were two different policies involved—were still being sticky about proof of loss.

He sat behind the steering wheel for a little, working the fingers of his left hand without thinking about it, knowing that he was a fortunate man also: they all worked. The damage had been painful but, according to the doctors, it would not be permanent. But getting Bolo's knife out of there had been one of the least fun chores of his life.

There had been one worse, of course. He remembered again kneeling beside the small figure in the halter and cutoffs, which designed for play and pleasure, looked totally out of place there on that blood-splashed and bullet-torn bridge; kneeling beside her and seeing her eyes open to look at him and taking her hand and feeling the small reassuring pressure of the fingers intended to let him know that it was okay,

505

what he had done, she'd meant what she'd said, she wanted it this way. He had crouched there with Cardenas' Uzi beside him but it had not been needed. Nobody had come to the bridge. They had all—all who were left—been too busy five decks down helping Captain Gonzaga get the sportfisherman alongside to take them off.

He had knelt there until the eyes watching him dulled and the fingers relaxed their grip on his hand; then he had gone to the radio room and sent the Mayday. Tanker *Petrox Prince* aground on *Las Arenas Blancas*. Latitude. Longitude. No visible cargo leakage. Ship abandoned by hijack crew, hostages still on board, medical assistance required. Repeat: tanker *Petrox Prince* aground. . . .

It had been strange to stand there afterwards, like a mere spectator in an observation booth, watching through the glass of the bridge as they carried Columbus' body aboard *Lolita* (ex-*Stream Hunter*), an unexpected gesture of respect for the dead that was, he thought, rather touching. Presumably he could have been enterprising and gone out on the bridge wing with the Uzi and tried to hold them for the authorities, but he knew that if he did he would be forced to shoot, and there had been just too damn much blood and death already. He didn't think they'd be going very far anyway, and he was right. As the sportfisherman pulled away, two Cuban gunboats had closed in like hungry sharks, searchlights glaring.

Then at last he'd gone to the blonde girl lying by the doorway still unconscious; but it was an unconsciousness he knew he could do nothing about. He'd simply found somebody's coat with which to cover her against the ship's air conditioning that was still operating faithfully as if nothing had happened. He'd sat by her until the choppers started clattering overhead.

Now Ullman started the rental car and, driving mostly one-handed—the left could be used in a pinch but it hurt— headed through the city and out the Overseas Highway in the direction of Miami; but after a little he made the left turn that brought him to the hospital. He parked in the lot and went inside. He'd been there recently for treatment, himself, of course, and he'd come back as a visitor but had been turned away because it was too soon after the operation and he was not a member of the patient's family. This time he was permitted to make the journey upstairs to the room that was not very far from the one in which they'd had him while they were repairing his arm. As he approached the door with the right number, a tall, quite slender woman came out and started past him, but stopped.

"Mr. Ullman?"

He waited for her to come back to him. He had never seen her before; a handsome dark-haired lady in pale blue slacks and a shirt of the same color, open at the throat.

"I'm Elizabeth Cameron," she said. "I've seen your picture in . . . certain files. I'd like to kiss you, Mr. Ullman."

He did not recognize the name; but it did not seem like a good time to be stuffy. "Be my guest," he said.

She took his face in both hands and pressed her lips to his lightly and stepped back. "Thank you," she said, and smiled. "I'm marrying Philip Martin next week. I much prefer him as a husband than a hero, perhaps a dead hero. Does that explain my unladylike behavior?"

"I hope you'll be very happy," Ullman said.

She glanced at the door through which she'd just come. "She's asked about you. Be gentle with her, Mr. Ullman. She's had a very bad time." Elizabeth Cameron studied him for a moment longer, and nodded as if satisfied. "Well, so have you, haven't you?" she said.

He watched her walk away and was a little annoyed at her. It was none of her damned business; and she seemed to be assuming a relationship between him and the young woman beyond the door that did not exist because it had never had a chance to get started, and might never exist even if it did get a chance. And with a good Scots name like that, she seemed like a strange choice for Phil Martin, born Martinez. . . . Ullman checked the thought immediately, asking himself irritably if he, Ullman, Uehlmann, had gone out and carefully selected a healthy female from good Aryan stock when the time for matrimony approached. What the hell did he think this was, Nazi Germany or something?

He realized that he was stalling because he was afraid. He knew that something very important could be awaiting him inside the room. He did not know whether he was afraid it was or afraid it wasn't. The girl inside, he knew, had shown considerable courage and resourcefulness. Weak as she was, she'd managed to dress herself; then she'd waited patiently until she'd seen the gleam of the shoals through the water ahead. She'd got the guard to open the door and held his attention until the ship struck, when she'd stepped aside and simply let him go hurtling the length of the cabin and knock

507

himself out, while she braced herself against the impact.
She'd calmly picked up his fallen submachine gun and
proceeded up the outside stairs, or ladders, to the bridge, to
see if she could help. She was, in other words, quite a
formidable young lady, a real heroine. It took all the courage
he had to knock on the door.

"Come in."

The voice was familiar, and not too weak. He opened the
door and stepped inside, letting it close behind him. Janet
McHugh had a neat white cap of bandages on her head. Her
face looked small and pinched and very pale, and the violet
eyes were enormous. She did not look like a very formidable
heroine. She licked her lips.

"Why, Mr. Ullman," she said. "How nice."

It didn't seem like quite the right note for a reunion
between two people who had shared danger and death; two
people who, not knowing each other at all, had worked well
together to save the world from destruction. Well, a small
part of the world, at least, and a limited kind of destruction.
His fear deepened, and he reminded himself of the embarrassing and humiliating, for her, circumstances under which
they'd met. A proud woman might not be altogether happy to
greet a man who'd once seen her like that; a man who, a
complete stranger, had undressed and bathed her, even fed
her, like a helpless baby. And on the other hand there was
the awkward fact that when she'd first seen him on the ship
he'd been sitting half undressed on a bed containing a nude
girl to whom he'd obviously just made love. It was really a
pretty hopeless beginning, he told himself; and then he saw
the glint of perverse humor in her eyes that he'd seen once
before. He knew that she was also remembering the laughably
unfavorable and unromantic conditions of their previous
encounter. He saw that she was quite aware of the inadequacy of her greeting and asking him silently just what greeting could be adequate under the circumstances. Those words
did not exist. She found a push-button control and let the
electric bed raise her up to a sitting position. She gestured
toward a chair.

"They've been drilling holes in my head," she said. "Subdural
hematoma. Isn't that impressive? Every girl should have a
subdural hematoma so people can have the fun of drilling
holes in her to let it out." She licked her lips once more. "It
was . . . pressing on the brain. That was why I kept blacking
out. I'm supposed to be all right now. How's your arm?"

"Everything works," he said. "Not too well at the moment, but it works. They say it'll be okay eventually."

"Columbus?" she said. "He died, didn't he? I was told, but that was while I still had my subdural hematoma and it didn't all stick."

"Yes, he died."

"And Laura?" she asked. "I mean Vinnie?"

Ullman said, "It was a sacrifice play and she was the major sacrifice. She asked me to do it that way."

After he'd said it, he wondered if it sounded too much as if he were trying to justify his own actions, but Janet McHugh nodded minutely.

"Winter people," she said, and smiled. "You don't know what that means. Some day I'll tell you. Don't worry, it's complimentary." There was a silence; then she said, "I was hoping you'd come."

"I tried a few days ago but they wouldn't let me in," Ullman said. "I wasn't family."

"I don't have any family," she said. "Just a lot of money, now. . . . Well, not a lot by Rockefeller standards, but a certain amount."

"That is a handicap," he said gravely. "I haven't had much practice talking to rich girls."

He could not quite see where the conversation was leading them, but she seemed to have something in mind, and he found that he was comfortable with her, willing to let her guide them wherever she wanted them to go.

"I even had two yachts for a while," she said. "Ostentatious. But I don't suppose the Cubans will ever give *Stream Hunter* back. But the trawler is down in San Juan, Puerto Rico. The Coast Guard caught Brodie and Billy, my mutinous crew, when they had to come in for fuel. I was worried about her, in this recent hurricane, but she seems to have made it all right; I just called. They didn't get hit very badly." There was another little pause. "When . . . when we both get well enough, and the hurricane season is over, we could fly down there and bring *Searcher* back."

The violet eyes were steady on his face. There was no humor in them now. In their depths he saw a terrible fear and a terrible need, and he realized that it had been very close for her and was still close; she was still by no means certain that she could ever make it back to the girl she'd been, after everything that had happened to her. He'd heard enough of her story to know that she'd been brought to the ragged edge of existence not just once, but twice; it wasn't surprising that she had no reserves left to fight with, that she needed help. She was trying to let him know that she didn't really think she could make it alone. Again it was like being given a second chance. He'd failed one girl who needed him.

But it was not primarily a question of atonement. Something of great value was being offered him here, he knew; he merely had to earn it. This one you cherish, he told himself. This one you don't throw back like an undersized fish because she doesn't measure up to your high standards of matrimonial perfection. This one you take not at all, or forever.

"Not only rich," he said, "but bossy."

She grinned, and suddenly the darkness was gone from her eyes. "You'd never have suggested it, so why shouldn't I? But I don't think we'll come back by way of the Old Bahama Channel."

He said, "Who's navigating this damn bucket, anyway?"

She was still smiling, as she reached out to take his hand. "We'll have to work that out, won't we?" she said.

GREAT ADVENTURES IN READING

THE MONA INTERCEPT   14374 $2.75
by Donald Hamilton
A story of the fight for power, life, and love on the treacherous seas.

JEMMA   14375 $2.75
by Beverly Byrne
A glittering Cinderella story set against the background of Lincoln's America, Victoria's England, and Napoleon's France.

DEATH FIRES   14376 $1.95
by Ron Faust
The questions of art and life become a matter of life and death on a desolate stretch of Mexican coast.

PAWN OF THE OMPHALOS   14377 $1.95
by E. C. Tubb
A lone man agrees to gamble his life to obtain the scientific data that might save a planet from destruction.

DADDY'S LITTLE HELPERS   14384 $1.50
by Bil Keane
More laughs with The Family Circus crew.

This offer expires 1 September 81   8106

THRILLS * CHILLS * MYSTERY
from FAWCETT BOOKS